MW01247811

BEYOND EMBER AND HOPE

First Paperback Edition, September 2024
First Hardback Edition, September 2024
First eBook Edition, September 2024

ISBN: 978-3-9505180-8-5 (Paperback)
ISBN: 978-3-9505180-9-2 (Hardback)
ISBN: 978-3-9505180-7-8 (eBook)

www.authorsjbandak.com

BEYOND EMBER AND HOPE

JENNIFER BECKER, ALICE KARPIEL

SAPHAROS

ALLAMYS

AMRYNE

LAKE OF NUBILAE

LAZULI

PARAE

KENSYN

CHRYSA

THE BORDER

EMERLANE

CINNITE

JAZDEL

RUBIEN

LIRAEN

THE FAE LAND

THE CLEAR SEA

OPALIA

THE STRAIT OF TENAE

QUARNIAN

THE SILVER SEA

OBLIVERYN

SARNYX

TUROSIAN

THE CURSED WOODS

PYRIA

CARNYLEN

LIRAEN – THE FAE WORLD
The Seven Kingdoms

Kingdom of Turosian
Capital: Parae
Ruler: King Karwyn Adelway
Royal Stone: Turquoise
Patron: Falea, Goddess of Fortune

Kingdom of Allamyst
Capital: Amryne
Ruler: King Wryen Rosston
Royal Stone: Amethyst
Patron: Bellrasae, God of Beauty

Kingdom of Carnylen
Capital: Pyria
Ruler: King Tarnan Ellevarn
Royal Stone: Carnelian
Patron: Hamadrae, God of Wisdom

Kingdom of Sapharos
Capital: Lazuli
Ruler: Queen Kaede Garrock
Royal Stone: Sapphire
Patron: Saenrytas, God of Strategy

Kingdom of Obliveryn
Capital: Sarnyx
Ruler: King Quintin Nylwood
Royal Stone: Obsidian
Patron: Kalvaeros, God of Courage

Kingdom of Quarnian
Capital: Opalia
Ruler: Queen Kaylanthea Zhengassi
Royal Stone: Rose Quartz
Patron: Shinlea, Goddess of Loyalty

Kingdom of Emerlane
Capital: Jazdel
Ruler: King Mayrick Palendro
Royal Stone: Emerald
Patron: Vilvosmae, Goddess of Vitality

The Abandoned (Eighth) Kingdom
Kingdom of Rubien
Capital: Cinnite
Ruler: Variel Sartoya, deceased
Royal Stone: Ruby
Former Patron: Adeartas, God of Justice

Pronunciation Guide

Characters

Eyden: Ai-den
Karwyn: Kar-win
Wryen: Ry-an
Sahalie: Sa-ha-lee
Cirny: Sir-nee
Kaylanthea: Kay-lan-thea
Damir: Dae-mir
Kaede: Kay-dee
Farren: Fah-ren

Gods

Caelo: Ca-eh-lo
Falea: Fah-lea
Bellrasae: Bell-ras-ey
Hamadrae: Ha-madra-ey
Shinlea: Shin-lay-ah

Places

Liraen: Lee-ren
Chrysa: Cry-sa
Parae: Pah-ray
Allamyst: Allah-mist
Amryne: Em-rin
Cinnite: See-neet

BEYOND EMBER & HOPE

To you, the reader—
Hope burns brighter than any pain.
Don't let anyone force you to ashes.

CHAPTER 1

LORA

The sound of crashing waves rising with the furious wind disoriented Lora as the blinding light of the portal subsided. She forced her eyes open, taking in her surroundings—so familiar, yet completely different. The icy wind bit into her bones, and she shivered in her ruined satin dress.

"Look at their eyes!" A foreign voice Lora couldn't locate rose above the noise of the riptide.

Turning right, then left, Lora tried to get a grip on her surroundings, overstimulated by numerous voices shouting close by. The street lamps on the beach lit up the dark area in front of her. Visible through the snow-covered wire fence which blocked off the portal, they were like spots of floating light. The electricity of the portal behind her heated her skin, so at odds with the familiarity of the cold sand beneath her boots. Her eyes travelled down to the wet sand mixing with the torn hem of her bloodied dress.

"Lora," a familiar voice whisper-yelled beside her, forcing her gaze up to striking pale blue. She could see a faint reflection of her hometown in Eyden's eyes. It was utterly startling. "We have to go before more humans notice us," Eyden warned.

That snapped her out of her daze. Lora pushed back the growing anxiety, the rising, overwhelming sadness. She was back on Earth, her home. But it would never be the same. Not without—

"Call the police!" someone shouted, and Lora finally realised a small group had formed on the other side of the fence, up the snow-covered beach.

"They're on their way. Stand back," a middle-aged man said, meeting Lora's gaze across the beach. With nightfall throwing the beach into shadows and the circumstances of her return, the familiar setting of Bournchester made Lora's skin prickle as a light layer of snow fell on her skin. She had escaped Tarnan and his guards, barely. What awaited her now?

A sharp slashing noise drew her attention to her left. Elyssa had cut open the fence. "We don't have time for this. The goddamn guards could follow us," the redhead said, her wild curls coming out of her high ponytail.

The police would give them trouble too. They were all weakened. The cut on Elyssa's throat made Lora's pulse speed up. She glanced at Ilario and Damir—who she'd once known as the Turosian guard Layken—close by, both worse for wear. Damir barely held on, swaying on his feet. He groaned as he attempted to straighten himself, fresh blood staining his shirt where the almandine sword had gone through his chest, almost killing him. She didn't know what to make of the shapeshifter and Karwyn's former spy now, but that was low on her list of priorities.

Her gaze swung to Rhay. Still lost. Still hurt beyond repair. He had taken the chance to act and she knew he regretted it all—most of all Karwyn's death. A death that promised irrevocable consequences for Lora, too. She knew Rhay would blame her for it, and he had reason to. Rhay had thrown the almandine sword to save Amira's life, but it was Lora's fire that had deflected the blade, redirecting it right into Karwyn's heart.

Lora's eyes drifted back to Eyden, who was helping his sister cut a big enough hole in the fence for them to get through, all while ignoring the shouts of the humans. Once upon a time, Lora might have stood with them, appalled at the sight of fae in her world. Now she was the enemy. After the ritual which merged her powers with Karwyn, was she even human at all anymore?

The thought was too immense to contemplate. All she needed to focus on was getting away from the beach and to her family before Tarnan could capture them and use them against her.

They needed to get somewhere safe. Then they could figure out how to get the human-fae agreement before Tarnan could break the one thing that made it impossible for him to force humans into fae blood contracts, enslaving them as they had been seventy-five years ago before the treaty agreement. If he found a way to break it, he could coerce any human to do his bidding even without his dark power of compulsion, which had no effect on humans. Lora had vowed revenge, and she would have it. She was done letting other people collect their winning cards and shock her with the hand they played. She would win this one. She would not let Tarnan ruin her world or the fae's. Amira and Farren had sacrificed much by staying behind, buying them time to get away.

Eyden's hand brushed against hers, and Lora shut her emotions down and let what was left of her ignite, burning her sorrow away.

"Ready?" Eyden tilted his head to the hole in the fence. Elyssa was already ducking through the cut wire, a throwing star in her hand. Her bow was strapped to her back, but she had no arrows left.

Breathing in sharply, Lora followed after Elyssa. When she crossed the last barrier separating her from her hometown, Lora took in the group of humans more clearly. They seemed shell-shocked, yet most reached for their phones anyway, their cameras pointed towards Lora and her friends. *Not good.*

Yet, a phone could be useful. She'd had to leave hers behind in Liraen.

Lora headed towards the spectators, up the beach to civilisation. Each step was heavy, her legs numb, but adrenaline pushed the pain away. As she walked towards the humans, the group kicked up sand and sprinted away. Some still had their phones in their hands as if they were afraid to die, yet more afraid of missing out on recording this spectacle.

"They're coming for us!"

"Fae scum!"

"Where are the bloody cops when you need them?"

Lora glanced down at herself. She wanted to yell that this was her home, that they had nothing to fear, but they wouldn't believe her. With their blood-drenched clothes and fae eyes, they must look dangerous.

Sirens echoed through the chaos. Red and blue flashing lights appeared in the distance.

"Come on!" Lora yelled over her shoulder as she headed the same direction the humans had fled towards, away from the open beach. Eyden was next to her, helping Ilario drag Damir forward. The shifter had lost his strength once more. Rhay's eyes glossed over. Elyssa's stare was determined, yet the corners of her mouth dropped as she looked at the portal behind her.

"What's the plan?" Eyden asked, panting next to her. Damir hissed as they pushed him onwards, the blood stain on his shirt growing.

"We need to get to my family and then regroup," Lora replied, her eyes locking on her mum's diner not far from them. The lights were off. "I need to call them."

The humans picked up their pace as a shrill yell tore through the night.

"For fuck's sake, they followed us," Elyssa muttered, her fist clenched. Lora spotted them right away—fae guards behind the wire fence, going up to the hole they'd ripped.

Car doors slammed in the distance. Police officers ran down the beach. If they didn't hurry, they'd be surrounded. But would the fae guards attack others if they didn't stay and fight them?

"I know what you're thinking," Eyden said, eyeing her, "but if we all die, it won't help anyone."

Lora bit her lip as she fought back angry tears. "Let's go!" she shrieked, upping her tempo as panic settled in her heart. They ran on pure adrenaline, leaving the sand behind and reaching the closest street filled with shops and restaurants. Her feet stung from the hard pavement, different from the sand they had left behind. Thankfully it was late enough that the shops were closed, their window lights providing a guide in the dark. A few people stumbled out of a bar, too intoxicated to notice her friends. Loud, cheery music broke through the icy night. Behind her, she knew the police and the fae guards were fast on their heels.

They needed to get the hell away and avoid the city centre, which was only a few streets over. And she needed a bloody phone. Her eyes fixated on a woman running backwards with her phone in her outstretched hand. On instinct, Lora pulled on her life source, opened her palm, and tugged on her power. The phone flew into her waiting hand with such force it was sure to leave a bruise. The woman screamed bloody murder.

Eyden stared at her with wide eyes, but Lora had no time to dwell on what this meant. She dialed her father's number, knowing it by heart. He didn't pick up.

She called her brother next. Still no reply. All the while, they kept running.

Sweat coated every inch of her even though tiny snowflakes covered her dress. Her chest heaved with each step, reopening her stab wound. Why did no one pick up?

She dialed Maja next.

One ring—the guards clashed with the police behind them. Lora flinched.

Two rings—another police car arrived, followed by reporters from a news station. Was any of this real? She felt she was trapped in a nightmare, drowning.

Three rings—a voice cut through the speaker. "Hello?"

Lora gripped the phone tighter. "Maja, listen, I—"

"Lora?"

Lora swallowed the lump in her throat. "Yes, it's me. Listen, you're in danger. So is my family. We need to meet. Where are they?"

"Whoa, hold on! You sent me a video basically announcing your death and now—"

"There's no time. I—" A gunshot tore through the night. Lora almost stumbled, her foot missing the sidewalk, but Eyden steadied her. *Guns.* This was going to get ugly. She forced her legs to move faster.

"What was that?" Maja shrieked.

Lora pushed her dirty dark-blonde hair from her face. "We're being hunted. I can't explain. Meet me wherever my family is and then we all need to *run*."

"*Run?* What the fuck is happening?"

"Maja! My family, where are they?" Lora all but screamed into the phone as more gunshots sounded behind them.

"The hospital," Maja replied in a strained tone. "Lora, your mum—"

"I know," Lora rushed to say. She couldn't hear it. Not yet. "Meet us in the parking lot. Get your family too."

"*Us?*"

"Just hurry." Lora hung up and searched for a place to pocket her phone, but there was none. Eyden took the phone from her, putting it in his blood-stained jacket.

"Thanks," she breathed.

"Where are we heading?" Eyden replied as if he'd follow her anywhere.

"How much longer?" Ilario's eyes were focused on the barely conscious Damir.

The hospital was just a short walk away, the path there a quiet suburban street. Glancing behind her, police cars flashed in the dim light. A few guards headed their way up the beach, but most were distracted by the gunfire. They wouldn't be killed; the police had no almandine weapons to kill fae. Why would they when they had been protected by a spell to keep all fae out? Tarnan had taken that away too. He had doomed them all.

"We're almost there," Lora replied. She took a sharp right, a quick detour to lose the guards. They ran into a dimly lit street. The houses lining either side had their lights turned off. She hoped the people there could go on sleeping peacefully and would never feel as she did now. Her body felt utterly hollow, but she pushed on. One more stop, then they needed to get out of Bournchester before the adrenaline keeping them upright fizzled out and they were left defenceless.

Stepping into the Bournchester hospital, Lora knew she looked like she'd escaped a murder scene. Eyden was with her, but everyone else was hiding in the parking lot. Curious eyes met hers as the receptionist looked her over in the too bright, white room before her gaze settled on Eyden, his head tilted down to shield his fae eyes.

Lora should have done the same, but she wasn't used to any of this. The few people in the waiting area gave her suspicious glances.

Lora took a deep breath as she walked up to the receptionist. "Excuse me, I'm looking for my father, Isaac Whitner. I think my mother Karla has been brought in. She's—" *Dead.* The word chilled her bones. She had tried so hard not to say the word, not to *think* it.

"Are you all right, miss?" the receptionist asked, staring at the blood on her.

Lora felt Eyden move closer, still not raising his gaze. "We're fine, it's not real blood. Just a costume. Can you tell us if anyone by the name of Whitner came in?"

Lora forced a smile on her face, and the receptionist turned to her screen, typing.

Pressing her lips together to force back tears, Lora craned her head to the right. Her hands twitched. Her legs shook as if her knees were about to buckle. The room spun—until her gaze caught on a figure heading out of one of the rooms at the end of the hall.

Lora's gaze sharpened, her eyes burning from unshed tears. Her breathing stuttered and her heart stopped as she spotted him. He wasn't looking her way yet. As he ran his hand through his dark hair, longer than when Lora had left, his shoulders were hunched. Still, she'd recognise her brother anywhere, in any world.

Oscar's head turned as if he could feel Lora's gaze. His hand froze on his head. An endless second stretched between them. The receptionist's voice was nothing more than a faint mutter in her ear. Lora needed to move, but her feet wouldn't work. All she could do was stare from across the hall.

Then Oscar lifted one hand, and she ran.

Lora hiked up her dress to go faster. Oscar took a slow step forward, then he was running too. They collided with force, a sting of pain radiating through her, but she didn't give a damn. She threw her arms around him, pulling her little brother close to her, holding onto him as she wished she could have done through all of this. She barely felt the tears on her cheeks.

"You came back," Oscar whispered against her hair. He was taller than her, but Lora still saw him as a little kid she wanted to protect.

Pulling back, she cupped his cheek. The shadows under his eyes and the faint stubble on his jaw made him look older than seventeen.

"Your *eyes*," he said, and her gaze swung up. His eyes flashed a rainbow of colours: confusion, anger, sorrow, *betrayal*. It didn't come as a surprise, yet it still stole her breath, needles pricking her heart.

"I—" Her voice broke off as her step-father walked out of the room next to them. His eyes widened as he took her in. She started towards him, but Eyden's voice stopped her. "Lora, someone called the police."

She looked between Oscar, her father, and the fae she'd come to care so much about. Her family stared at him as if he was the enemy. Lora had imagined this moment many times and it had never played out like this.

Forcing a deep breath, she said, "We have to go. Maja is meeting us outside. I'll explain once we're safe."

For a second no one moved. Lora turned, hoping her family would follow, but her father grabbed her arm. "I can't leave without your mother."

Lora saw his lips move, but the words didn't make sense. She felt her blood freeze, yet her skin burned.

Her body. That's what he meant.

"I can't leave her in this condition. And if we're not safe, then she isn't either," her father added. The ground was swallowing her whole.

What was he talking about? She didn't dare hope.

"Your wife, is she all right?" Eyden asked for her.

Her father held her gaze. "She's in a coma, Lora. I'm so sorry."

"She's...she's alive?" Lora's voice was nothing but a faint whisper. It was as if she was standing on a cliff, waiting to be pushed off.

"Yes." Her father frowned. Lora pushed past him on unsteady legs into the room she now realised must be her mother's.

And there she was: her skin pale, her long dark hair dull, but it was unmistakably her mother. *Alive.* Breathing. Fast asleep on a hospital bed, hooked up to a bunch of machines that showed her heart was still beating against all odds. She wasn't on a ventilator, so she must be able to breathe on her own. There were no visible traces of the virus, the veins on her arms no longer purple and bruised. Had Lora managed to save her after all, even with Karwyn's death dooming them?

Her father appeared next to her. "Are you all right, honey? The police—"

"I'm fine," she cut him off. *Keep it together.* They were all alive, but not for long if they didn't get away. "The police won't understand. And neither will the fae guards who followed us here." Her father's mouth dropped open. She could hear Oscar's sharp inhale behind her, but she was focused on the wheels on her mum's hospital bed. "Mum's coming with us. We're all going. *Now.*"

"Lora, honey, let's take a breather. You're hurt and—" He moved forward, but Lora stepped back.

"You need to trust me on this. If we stay, we *all* die. The border has fallen and people are after me, after *all* of you."

Eyden stepped into the room then, the phone in his hand. "Maja's here."

Lora frantically looked between her brother and father. "*Please,* trust me."

Her father nodded, and the pressure on her chest lightened as he went to the bed and unhooked the machines from her mum.

"How are we getting Mum out of here?" Oscar asked, a frown on his face.

"We're stealing an ambulance," Lora announced. To her surprise, her father merely nodded, quickly grabbed a bag from the closet, and filled it with medical equipment. As he pushed her mother's bed through the door, he gestured at the IV drip, and Oscar picked it up and any extra bags lying on the shelf behind it.

As they walked into the glaringly white hallway, people stared and a doctor yelled at them, but they only moved faster.

Soon enough they were outside, rounding the building. She vaguely heard someone call for security. Noticing a paramedic leaving an ambulance, Lora spotted car keys peeking out of his pocket. Eyden followed her line of sight and gave her a subtle tilt of his head.

The ambulance was parked at the back entrance. She started towards it, but a car sped forward, its lights blinding her in the dark, wheels screeching as it stopped next to her.

Her best friend rolled down her window. "What in the fucked-up world is going on here?" Maja's eyes landed on Lora's family and then on Eyden.

"Where's your family?" Lora hit back, feeling time slip away.

"They went to visit my grandparents."

"Good, tell them to get somewhere safe. Does your aunt still have that cabin?" Lora asked.

"Yes, why? Will you tell me what the hell is going on now?"

Lora met her father's gaze. "Get Mum into the ambulance. I'll be right there."

"Isn't it locked?" Oscar asked.

Lora glanced at Eyden, who took the stolen keys out of his pocket and threw them into Oscar's startled hands.

"I'll never make fun of your pickpocketing skills again," Lora said, looking at Eyden, almost forgetting that her family was watching as they headed to the ambulance.

A small smirk played on Eyden's lips. "I doubt that."

Maja cleared her throat. "I have about a dozen more questions, but I'm getting the sense that we need to get on the road, so please give me the cliff notes."

"The cliff notes?" She huffed. "The border has fallen, anyone can cross. The Turosian king, *my cousin*, is dead. There's an evil king trying to kill us all. Guards and the police are chasing us, and I feel like I might pass out any second, but I won't until we're all safe." Lora pulled up her brows. "Got all that?"

Maja blinked at her. "Yeah, I got all that and a million more questions, but let's go."

Spotting Elyssa's auburn hair at the other end of the parking lot, Lora gestured for them to come closer. To their right, her father and Oscar lifted her mother's bed into the ambulance.

"I'm going with my family. Can you take the others?" Lora asked Maja.

"Others? You mean Mister Broody here?" Maja inclined her head to Eyden, who crossed his arms.

"It's Eyden," he said.

"Oh, I figured," Maja said, her gaze drifting over him. "Would've been a shame if I had to make good on my threats, but I see you two seem to be getting along."

A smile played on his lips, but his eyes surveyed the area.

"Eyden's coming with me. Your car will be full." Maja looked confused until she spotted Elyssa, Rhay, Ilario, and Damir rushing towards them.

She was about to reply when sirens cut her off. The paramedic they'd pickpocketed and a security guard hurried out the back door of the hospital at the same time.

"Get in the car!" Lora yelled at her friends before running to the ambulance. The security guard put a hand on her father's shoulder as he tried to step into the back of the ambulance, her mother on the bed in the middle of it. Oscar was seated on the bench next to her.

Lora tore at the guard's shoulder, pulling him back. "Let go of him!"

The guard turned to her, cocking his head. "Miss, I can't let you steal an ambulance with a patient." Red and blue flashing lights pulled up behind them. They didn't have time for this. Lora kneed him in the groin, hard.

"Lora!" her father shouted, appalled.

"Get in!" Lora yelled back. Her father, breathing heavily, stepped inside, and Lora rushed to shut the door, gesturing for Eyden to get to the passenger seat. She jumped into the driver's seat, and before she could ask, Oscar threw the keys through the tiny open window between the back and the front of the vehicle. Eyden leaned out the window, checking on the others, who were closing their car doors. Waving her arm out the rolled-down window, Lora signalled for Maja to speed away.

Just as Lora pulled the ambulance out of its spot, a loud voice announced over a speaker, "Stop the car and step out of the vehicle." In the side mirror, multiple police cars drew closer.

Her foot smashed the gas pedal but at the same instant, the ambulance's back door opened and the guard jumped into the vehicle. The left door flapped behind them, the metallic sound mixing with the chilly night air infiltrating the space.

"Stop the car!" The guard pushed her father against the wall, knocking his head back. Medical equipment fell down from the shelves on the wall.

Shifting next to her, Eyden turned to the window separating them from her family. "Give me that small knife," he shouted at Oscar, eyeing a scalpel. Her brother didn't move.

Her father tried to push the guard off, but he wasn't strong enough. Lora whirled the steering wheel sharply to the left, forcing the guard to stumble. But while steadying himself, he leaned against her mum's bed. It slid towards the open door.

Oscar grabbed the metal frame as the right side of the double doors in the back flew open too. Holding onto the bed with one hand and to the seatbelt on the bench with his other hand, Oscar cursed. As the guard stumbled closer to the door, he grabbed the bed frame again, taking it with him.

"Let go!" Oscar yelled desperately.

The bed inched closer to the doors. Lora could already imagine her mum flying out the car and crushing all her bones.

Glass shattered. The noise splintered the tension-filled car.

Eyden launched himself over the window bank separating him and Lora from the back, glass splinters falling around him. The scalpel was in his hand before Lora could even track his movement in the rear-view mirror. And just as quick, it punctured the guard's hand, forcing him to let go of the bed.

As Eyden secured the bed, Lora stepped on the gas and steered to the left. The guard was thrown through the open door onto the street. Hair covered Oscar's terror-stricken face as icy wind barreled into the car. Lora blinked away tears, guilt tearing at her. Eyden pulled the back door shut.

Lora exhaled, and a flash of relief washed through her until red and blue lights blinked in her peripheral view. The police must have tracked them from the hospital or the beach. Hitting the gas with force, Lora turned to the side mirror to spot police cars pulling closer on either side of them just as a gunshot splintered the glass into shards of crumbling hope.

CHAPTER 2

❦

ELYSSA

"They're gonna get them," Elyssa said, turning from Lora's vehicle surrounded by flashing lights to Lora's friend. She sat at the front while Rhay was squished in the back between Ilario and Damir. The silence between them was heavy. Ilario spied over Rhay's shoulder to the still-bleeding shifter while Rhay, a sour look on his face, angled his body as far away from both of them as possible in the small space. His face was ashen as if not used to the speed they were travelling at. Elyssa wished they could go faster in this carriage without horses. The road they were taking was broader and much more well-maintained than the small pathways leading through Turosian.

As Lora's friend spun the wheel, the strange vehicle zigzagged on the road, trying to avoid the flashy pieces fired at them from behind. The wind outside mixed with the shrill sound of the weapons made it hard for Elyssa to pick up anything else with her impaired hearing.

"They're shooting at us!" Lora's friend yelled, her frantic gaze locked on the tiny mirror above her. "Jesus, it's like they think we're terrorists. They must know you came from Liraen."

The humans had to be scared out of their minds with the border having fallen. Shoot first, ask questions later had to be reserved for big danger like fae invading. "Do you have any weapons?" Elyssa turned in her seat to look around, her last throwing star in her hand.

"No," Lora's friend said, her voice rising. She couldn't be used to any of this. But Elyssa was. This crisis was the only thing keeping her going, keeping her thoughts from circling to Amira and Farren. Where were they now? Had Tarnan taken them back to Carnylen? They should have never fucking trusted him.

"I have a knife," Damir croaked from the back. As he moved his hand to grab it, he hissed, his violet eyes almost turning black. He pulled a small knife from his blood-soaked Turosian guard's jacket.

Scoffing, Rhay readjusted himself, his elbow poking Damir. The king's shadow glared at him. "You better watch out, Messler."

"What's your name?" Elyssa asked as she turned back to Lora's friend, this mission the only thing allowed in her head.

"Maja." Sweat lined her forehead.

"I have an idea, Maja." Elyssa turned to the street ahead of them. They had left the city and were now surrounded by trees on either side, the path narrowing. "We swerve, block part of the road, let Lora and the others pass, aim at the wheels of those *things*—"

"Cars," Maja threw in. "And that's madness."

"Is that a no?"

"Just a fact. It won't work. You'd need a lot of strength to puncture those wheels."

"I can block the car with my power," Ilario said, a hand in front of his mouth, his face green. "If we stop. I can't focus like this."

"Sure, that sounds not cryptic and totally smart." Maja chuckled, as if not believing her own words. She glanced over her shoulder. "Brace yourself, boys."

Elyssa didn't get a chance to chime in before Maja slammed her foot down and turned the wheel. The car swerved as it went diagonal to the road, forcing Elyssa to hold on to her seat. She had a clear view of the cars coming at them with frightening speed, highlighted in the night by dim lamps lining the street. The trees surrounding the path cast shadows on the paved road.

Ilario grabbed the knife from Damir's weak grip, avoiding his pointed gaze. Elyssa had no idea what Ilario and Damir—a guard and spy of their now dead enemy—had in common, but she sensed they had a past. Twirling the knife, Ilario smashed the handle into the window at his side.

"What the fuck? You could've rolled it down!" Maja screamed at him before her eyes widened in terror at the incoming vehicles, their lights bright in the dark.

The cars flashing red and blue came closer. Lora's car was surrounded by one on either side. Elyssa's head spun as dots of colour took over her field of vision. They didn't slow down. Elyssa rolled down her window, leaning half her body outside. Ilario did the same in the back. Loud noise filled the air as more metal pieces were fired. One hit Maja's car in the back, and she shrieked, ducking. Another hit the car inches from Elyssa's arm, but she refused to flinch.

"Now, Ilario!" Elyssa screamed.

Ilario curled his hand into a fist, sweat dripping down his forehead. He must be pushing through absolute exhaustion. But the pavement in front of the police car split open, small cracks lining up the path to Maja's car, enough to force them to slam to a halt.

Ducking back into the car and closing the window, Elyssa would have grinned if Amira and Farren's absence wasn't lingering in her mind. Lora's car passed them. "Hit it," she told Maja.

Maja turned the car to get away, but they weren't fast enough. Two humans got out of their car and fired. Ducking, Elyssa covered her head as her window exploded.

"Faster!" Elyssa shouted. She couldn't hear anything but glass breaking and loud bangs filling the air. She turned back to her broken window nonetheless, leaning outside. They just needed a bit more time.

"Get back in!" Maja screamed, clutching the wheel with white knuckles. "Did I mention I failed my driving test three times? And that was without bullets hitting my car!" Her voice was barely distinguishable to Elyssa's ears. A bullet zipped over her head, and Maja pulled at the wheel, making them zigzag as she sped up. Elyssa's shoulder hit the window frame, glass splinters scratching her skin.

She gripped her last throwing star, looking straight at one of the officers. Her body trembled from the speed, wind whipping at her harshly, but she aimed true. The throwing star hit the officer's arm, and the gun dropped to the ground. As it fell, it fired.

Shards of glass flew from the back to the front. Elyssa ducked back into the car, shielding her eyes. The rear window was shattered. Rhay touched his neck, where a streak of red ran down his throat. The bullet or glass must have grazed him—either way, it wasn't almandine; it would heal fast enough.

Maja and her, on the other hand...

"Move!" someone shouted. Elyssa turned right then left, disoriented. A hand appeared in front of her before a yell of pain assaulted her ears.

Ilario lowered the hand he'd used to catch the bullet aimed at Elyssa's head.

"Fuck, that would have hurt," Elyssa said. "Thanks." Pulling his bleeding hand to his chest, Ilario nodded, dark hair falling into his tired emerald eyes.

"We're in the clear," Damir said, his voice weak as he turned in his seat to look through the broken window. Cold wind filled the car through the shattered glass. Elyssa spied over his shoulder. The officer who had just shot at them was now treating the officer she'd hit in the arm. They were mere shadows with the distance between them. Elyssa couldn't detail how bad the injury was, but she was sure he'd survive and not entirely sure he goddamn deserved to.

Rhay drew a crumpled handkerchief from his pocket. It had the Turosian emblem on it. His gaze lingered on it as if he was looking at a past that no longer existed. Handing it to Ilario, he turned away with a stoic expression.

Maja turned right onto a narrow street, deeper into the woods. "Everyone okay?" Pieces of glass covered Maja's dark hair, and a thin line of blood ran across her cheek.

"Everyone's alive." Elyssa's heart slowed, the adrenaline wearing off. Her mind drifted back to Liraen. Back to Amira and Farren. Were *they* all right? Were those who survived from the rebel camp okay?

"Where are we going, anyway?" Elyssa asked, bouncing her leg.

"A cabin. It should be safe from whatever or *whoever* we're hiding from. It's not just the police, is it?"

"No. We were followed. Some of us didn't make it here. We have to make a plan to get Amira back," Elyssa said, more to herself, brushing tiny pieces of glass off her seat.

"Who's that?" Maja pushed back her glasses.

"Karwyn's fiancée," Rhay replied at the same time as Elyssa said, "My girlfriend."

Maja raised her brows as she glanced at the mirror. Elyssa followed her line of sight to Rhay, whose eyes widened for a split second. Then he tilted his head down, his face showing nothing at all.

Elyssa didn't know how close Rhay and Amira had been, but she did know Rhay had saved her from Karwyn's attack. For that she was grateful, even if Rhay seemed to regret it now. But with or without Rhay's help, she *would* free Amira and Farren.

They had to hold on until then. Knowing Tarnan, he had some sort of twisted plan for them. *Tarnan*—the name alone made her blood boil and her heart beat faster. He would goddamn pay. If he touched Amira, if he did anything to harm either one of them, he would fucking regret it.

CHAPTER 3

AMIRA

Amira's heart immediately sped up as she opened her eyes. She was in the dark, in a moving carriage as indicated by the sound of the wheels rolling on the bumpy road. Cold wood dug into her back. Her whole body was sore, as if she had been crushed under a boulder.

"Nice of you to join us again," a distant voice echoed in her ears.

As her sight slowly adjusted to the darkness, Amira straightened herself and realised that her hands were shackled in front of her, iron cutting into her skin.

A wave of memories came crashing in. Karwyn was dead. So was Varsha—the image of her lifeless body plaguing Amira's mind. She had almost died too, at Karwyn's hand. Rhay had saved her life. All because of Tarnan. The Carnylen King and secret heir to the Rubien throne had turned on them, on her. *Elyssa...* Had she managed to escape the guards?

Shimmying, Amira sat up on the wooden bench. The position forced her face to face with Tarnan, who emerged from the shadows. A burning sensation seared through her body, pure hatred—a feeling that had usually been reserved for Wryen and then Karwyn. Her hands twitched, straining against the shackles, her skin reddening. She desired nothing more than to let her magic out—*her gift*—but she was depleted.

"I was beginning to worry," Tarnan said in an even tone, like he hadn't betrayed them. Like he was still the same person who Amira had seen as a father figure.

"Where are you taking me?" Amira spat, fighting back burning tears.

"Home." Tarnan's voice was barely a whisper, almost giving out. A drop of blood ran down his neck from where Eyden had thrown the dagger to silence him in order to keep him from using his dark power of compulsion.

"Where is Farren?" She dreaded the answer. Surely, Tarnan would have kept him alive. He was a witch after all, making him *useful*.

"The witch is in another carriage." A wince wrinkled up his face as he took out a silver flask engraved with vines. "Water?"

Amira shook her head. Did he really think that her trust was going to be won *ever* again? Tarnan couldn't help where he came from and who his blood relatives were, but he had chosen to play into the legacy of the Dark King. He'd chosen to *use* her.

Tarnan screwed the lid back on. "You can at least trust that I don't want you dead. I have been fighting for you since the beginning, Amira. Now you're free from Karwyn. A thank you would be appreciated."

"But I'm not free from your contract," Amira said between gritted teeth. "Or your shackles." She moved her arms, letting the cuffs around her wrists clang together.

His eyes turned kind, which only enraged Amira further. How dare he pretend to care about her still? "The shackles hurt me too. You're focusing on details instead of the big picture."

"The big picture is that you're a killer. You would've killed all my friends if they hadn't fled. Why should I trust you when you have me bound in a carriage?" A thin veil of sweat lined her forehead as she tried to call on her power to no avail.

"I will remove them once we arrive in Pyria." Sizing her up, Tarnan let out a sigh. Her dress clung to her, the blood, dirt, and sweat creating a very unpleasant second skin. "I shall provide you with some new dresses once we're home."

Home. A few days ago, she had wished for Pyria to be her home. It was a place far away from Wryen and Karwyn. The place where she had fallen for Elyssa. The place she'd thought was under the protection of a righteous king. After Tarnan's betrayal, Pyria could never be her home. She couldn't believe that for *months*, she had trusted a *Sartoya*.

Tarnan moved the curtain away from the window, and the first rays of the morning sun almost blinded her. They had reached the gates of Pyria. The carriage stopped, and Amira saw an opportunity. She jumped at Tarnan, headbutting him before scrambling to open the door.

"There's no need for that," Tarnan croaked. He tried to grab her, but she kicked at him with the last of her strength. With a satisfying thump, his back hit the bench.

Turning, Amira threw herself out of the carriage. With her hands bound, she fell flat on her face, knocking the breath out of her.

"*Amira, stop.*" Tarnan's ice-cold voice halted her as he peeked out the door. His power crept into her head to take control, but his hold was fragile. Tarnan must have exhausted his energy. Amira wasn't in much better shape.

"Think of your witch friend," Tarnan added. "He needs you here." It wasn't a threat, yet at the same time it was.

"You should have kept Cirny alive if you needed a witch."

"That was my plan at first. I promised her I would compel Lora to break Cirny's contract with the Adelways. But I decided against it. She didn't share the bond you and I have."

Amira scoffed. "We share nothing except that contract you talked me into."

A guard jumped down from the front of the carriage and took Amira's arm, forcing her back into the carriage. After Tarnan pulled the door shut, the carriage moved again, tiny rocks hitting the wheels.

Tarnan leaned back across from her. "Glad you got that out of your system. You'll realise soon enough that you're right where you belong."

The carriage came to a stop inside the gates of the Pyrian palace. The sun was rising, tinting the clouds pink. The palace that had once seemed like the symbol of a new hope now looked like a golden cage, wrapped in vines as binding as her contract.

Tarnan offered his hand, but she brushed past him out of the carriage and missed her step. He steadied her, his hand tight on her arm. Feeling the warmth of his grip on her made her want to throw up. "Welcome home," Tarnan whispered in her ear, sending cold chills over her skin. Amira squeezed her fists so hard her nails left bloody imprints on her palms.

Coming out of another carriage, Farren looked beaten down, but still managed to give her a warm smile. Amira wasn't completely alone, she had an ally—a friend, even. When she had lived in Amryne under her brother's hold, she had been all alone. With Farren by her side, she would end Tarnan before he could do any more irremediable damage. Amira was done giving up.

And she knew Elyssa would be thinking the same, wherever she was. They would meet again, one way or another. She would get out of here, reunite with Elyssa, and save her mother from Wryen's wrath. The thought of being too late echoed through her mind, but Amira shut it out.

As more guards exited the carriages, Amira was surprised there was no sign of Saydren. The royal healer could only be up to something twisted. Had he always been Tarnan's spy in the Turosian palace, whispering in Karwyn's ear to manipulate him?

Her feet moved in Farren's direction, but Tarnan's hand stayed on her arm. "I'm afraid your reunion will have to wait. I am taking you to your room."

Amira felt too drained to fight back. She exchanged a desperate glance with Farren. Trying to reassure herself of her friend's fate, Amira let herself be led inside.

Every servant they crossed paths with lowered their gaze when they saw Amira's bound hands, her skin under the shackles red and sensitive. How long had they known they were working for a monster?

Stepping into her quarters without Elyssa, Amira's heart twisted, causing bile to burn her throat.

"I trust you'll find your rooms to your convenience. Of course, I've had to brick up the windows; I wouldn't want you to fall during a futile attempt at escaping. I've also assigned three guards to you, for safety reasons. And I will have a *chat* with Farren to make sure he knows his place is right here." Tarnan spoke with a sickening warm tone as if he'd truly meant her no harm.

Taking out a rustic key, he removed her shackles. As she lifted her arms, ready to strike him with all her might, Tarnan grabbed her hands surprisingly gently. "Let's not waste your time or mine. I'm sure you remember that if I die, you die. I know you need time to let all of this sink in, to see that my vision of Liraen is the right way."

Amira bared her teeth, staring him down. "I won't let you use me."

Tarnan caressed her head. "That was never my intention, Amira. I want you to work *with* me. I've never lied to you." At her mocking gaze, he added, "I *withheld*, yes. I am guilty of that. I knew you wouldn't see my vision right away, but everything I said was true. I'm still the same person who simply wishes for you to realise your potential." A crazy light sparked in his dark red eyes.

"I won't help you." She braced her hand against the wall as she swayed on her feet, her whole body slowly shutting down. "Let me see Farren," she demanded, her voice wavering too much for her liking.

"All in good time. I need to be sure I can trust you first."

Trust. That cursed word. But maybe Tarnan had given her the key to defeating him and breaking her contract. He was so insistent on Amira working *with* him. If she managed to make him believe she would fight for him, maybe she could use his trust against him. Had Cirny tricked them into thinking they could break a contract without both parties agreeing, or was there really a chance?

"You talk about trust, but what about your broken promises? You said you would protect my mother." Amira knew she couldn't pretend to trust him straight away, Tarnan was too cunning. The game she intended to play required finesse. For once, instead of being a hand to be played, Amira wanted to have all the cards to herself.

"I will take care of your mother's situation soon. With the fallen border, I have a lot to accomplish in a short time. I'm going to remind the humans what their purpose is, as the gods and goddesses intended. They have no power like we do."

This time, Amira forced herself to hide her revulsion. She lowered her gaze, her fists balled behind her back. "We do."

His smile grew. It would've looked calming if Amira didn't know better.

When Tarnan finally left her room, Amira uncurled her hands, her wrists stinging. She let herself fall to the ground, the exhaustion rendering it impossible for her to stand. Grounding herself against the hard wooden floor, she refused to let herself be sucked back into hopelessness. She knew she was stronger than everyone had thought possible. Everyone except Elyssa, who had always seen something in Amira that she herself had almost given up on.

Tarnan might be gloating now, but Amira would make sure she had the last laugh.

CHAPTER 4

RHAY

Maja's machine—a "car," she'd called it—finally slowed down as they neared a rustic cabin deep in the woods. It was a mere speck compared to the palace Rhay had lived in. Stopping the car, Maja looked over her shoulder, meeting Rhay's gaze first before she glanced to either side of him. Rio and Damir were squished to his left and right, making this a very uncomfortable ride. As much as Rhay had tried to block out everything, Rio and Damir's emotions were anything but hidden.

Rhay had a sneaking suspicion Damir was the past love Rio had thought he'd lost, even though he couldn't imagine what Rio could have seen in Karwyn's shadow. Rio was kind and gentle. All Rhay knew about Damir was that he was someone who hadn't wasted a second following Karwyn's orders.

Yet, hadn't Rhay done the same? And when he'd finally acted, he'd damned Karwyn. He could still picture Karwyn's dead eyes. They haunted him every second, trapping him in a nightmare that Rhay had created himself by following Lora and Amira's plan. Had this always been their goal?

"Get out before you get even more blood on my seats," Maja commanded as she exited the car, glancing at the phone in her shaking hand.

Rhay dreamed of finding something strong to drink, but he was stuck in between the two moody...*ex-lovers?*

"By Caelo, can you get a move on?" Rhay asked Damir, who had made no effort to exit the vehicle as he slumped against the closed door. Rhay looked at Elyssa with envy when she got out.

"I'll help him." Rio opened the door on his side, glass splinters raining on the ground from the broken window, and stepped out. His hand dripped blood through the handkerchief he'd wrapped around it. Rhay's empathy evaporated as the blood filling his vision morphed into Karwyn's.

Struggling to shake the image, Rhay followed Rio. He dimly heard Damir grunt in pain as Rio helped him out of the car.

Feeling the cold air on his skin, Rhay realised how suffocating the whole night had been. Between Karwyn's death, Tarnan's betrayal, and crossing to the human world, Rhay had hardly been able to catch his breath. Inhaling deeply, he tuned out Maja anxiously trying to reach Lora on her phone. They had lost track of her vehicle along the way.

Once upon a time, crossing over would have been an exciting adventure. But now all Rhay wanted was to disappear into a hole as dark as the night sky. The trees were too green, the air too fresh, the stars too bright. Who was he to deserve any of it?

The burn of his betrayal, the blood on his hands, came at him like a crushing wave, taking over his conscience. The fae who had imagined seeking an adventure on Earth, the one who would joke about their current predicament, *that* fae had died with Karwyn. Rhay didn't know who he was anymore.

Or did he? He *was* a king slayer, a backstabber.

"Oh, thank God," Maja said.

Reluctantly, Rhay turned his head and spied a car appearing at the edge of the dark woods. Unfazed, Rhay sat down on the icy ground. No one paid him any attention as Lora stopped her big vehicle in front of the cabin. Lora and Eyden exited quickly, rushing to open the back door. An elderly man pushed out a bed on wheels, a woman fast asleep on top of it.

"Is she still breathing?" Lora asked, her voice high and strained as she looked at the human man. Who in Caelo's name were they? They were all strangers to him, even Lora.

"She's stable," the man replied as a younger man jumped out behind him, his gaze skeptical.

Lora looked up then, taking in Maja, Elyssa, Rio, Damir, and then Rhay. He turned his head, not wanting to see her pity. He didn't want anything from her anymore. If it wasn't for Lora, Rhay would still be playing his game of pretence. It had torn at him every day, but it had never destroyed him. Not like now.

"Is everyone all right?" Lora asked.

Elyssa huffed. "All right might be aiming a bit too high."

"Lora, honey, I'm going to take your mum inside. Take care of your...*friends* and then let me have a look at your wounds, please," the human man said.

Mum? Rhay thought Lora's mother had died in Liraen? How did Lora have family on Earth? And why did he care? He already knew Lora had been using him just like Amira had. He had been right all along; he had no real friends. He had never been able to have any friends with Karwyn around, and now that Karwyn was gone, he was utterly alone. The thought almost made him laugh.

Lora seemed torn as she looked between her family members and her friends—not him. "I'll be right in," she finally said. The younger man shook his head as he helped lift the bed up the porch steps and inside the house.

Damir coughed loudly next to him, leaning against Rio's shoulder. Droplets of blood landed on Rhay's baby-blue jacket. It was already drenched in so much blood that the difference was barely noticeable.

"What do we do with the traitor?" Elyssa asked, red curls flying in the wind as she pointed at Damir. Rhay wouldn't have been surprised if she had pointed at him.

"We have to lock him up somewhere," Eyden said, clutching at his bleeding arm. "Is there—"

Rio cut him off, "He's injured; we can't lock him up somewhere and leave him to bleed to death."

"He won't die." Eyden's eyes held a grudge.

"We hardly have a choice." Lora put a gentle hand on Rio's arm. "We can't risk him running off and giving away our location." She looked at Maja. "I told Oscar and my dad to turn off their phones in case anyone's trying to track us."

Maja pushed the lenses framing her eyes up her nose as she took out her phone.

It dawned on Rhay then. Lora didn't just know people here, she *belonged* here. Belonged to this strange place he had only seen through his television back home. The beach with its Ferris wheel, the typical hospital, even the little getaway cabin they were at now... Rhay wasn't unfamiliar with them, yet it still felt like he was watching through a screen.

"I vote we lock him up now and get moving," Elyssa said, clearly pressed for time.

"Moving?" Maja's dark brows pinched together.

Eyden shifted his feet. "You know we can't move now. We have to rest and work out a plan. For Amira's sake, we have to figure this out carefully."

Amira. There was her name again. How had she become part of this circle of...rebels? Had she chosen them over him? A whisper in his mind told him he had turned on her first, but he blocked it out.

Elyssa shot daggers at Eyden but then she nodded, her fist unclenching.

"What should we do with Layk—Damir, Rhay?" Lora asked softly, avoiding his eyes. He saw the exhaustion in the circles under her eyes, in her uncertain stance. Eyden must have noticed too; he reached out, steadying her.

Everyone weirdly had a place here, didn't they? They had a part in this revolution. They had people who cared about them. Damir might not, but he played the part of the enemy-turned-prisoner to a tee. Where did that leave Rhay? He was *no one*.

Rhay stood up, dusting off his trousers that were as stained as his soul. "I don't fucking care." His gaze reluctantly met Rio's. His emerald eyes were soft, pitiful. "Lock him up or put him out of his misery."

Rio's gaze turned scornful.

Rhay could handle that look; he knew he deserved it. He pressed his lips shut as he walked to the door with one thing in mind: Drown his mistakes in booze before they took him down completely.

"So how is it?" a voice Rhay shouldn't want to hear asked. He had ducked into the farthest corner he could find after raiding the alcohol stash in the small kitchen. Everyone had been running around, helping out, cleaning their wounds. But not Rhay. His wounds were impossible to heal, anyway.

Rhay looked up after taking another swig of the unfamiliar brand of vodka. He sat on the floor, leaning against a wooden cabinet that had a TV on top of it. Leaning over him was Rio. He shouldn't seek Rhay out. Not now, not ever.

"I wouldn't even call this alcohol," Rhay replied drily. He had drunk half the bottle and barely felt a thing. The more he drank, the angrier he got that it wasn't saving him from his thoughts.

Rio lowered himself next to him. His right hand was wrapped in a bandage covering the bullet wound, but he was still wearing his blood-stained, ripped shirt. It revealed another bandage on his chest and one on his upper arm. Even so, he looked peaceful. As if all the violence couldn't touch him, couldn't twist his insides and crumble the good in him to dust.

Rio tilted his head, and Rhay realised he'd been staring. His gaze settled on Rhay's torn sleeve and the cuts marking his arms. "Lora's father can wrap that for you."

"I'm good."

"We both know you're not, and no one expects you to be. But don't turn away from us. You know Lora didn't want it to go down that way."

Rhay gulped down more vodka so fast he had to cough. "*That* way?" The laugh coming out of him was like razor blades running down his throat. "Do tell, what wasn't supposed to happen? Karwyn dying or me being the one to deal the killing blow?"

Rio cringed. "I'm sorry, I really am. But this is a chance to start over. I know it won't happen in a day, but I saw how torn you were over your life at the palace. Now you can—"

"Can what? Move on from the blood on my hands?" Rhay gestured at the stiff blood drenching his shirt. "I'm not like you. I've never done the right thing. Even when I thought I did, all it did was backfire. I can't *move on*."

"Nix..."

"You should go back to your boyfriend."

Rio went stiff. "Damir hasn't been my *anything* for years," he ground out, his voice deeper than usual. He moved his head closer, his eyes too trusting, too kind.

Rhay couldn't take it. "I don't give a damn; go bother someone else and stop trying to convince yourself we're *anything* either." He looked away before he could see the hurt flash in Rio's eyes. The sound of footsteps was the only indicator that Rio had left.

Rhay tilted the bottle in his hand, watching the liquid swirl at the bottom—so clear, pure, nothing like his rotten soul. It wasn't just that he didn't know who he was anymore. The fact was, Rhay had never known who he was. He had always played a role. Karwyn's best friend. The pretend advisor. The party boy. The distraction.

How could Rhay move on, start over, when he didn't even know if he had ever been himself?

CHAPTER 5

LORA

Letting her head fall against the cold wooden door in the hallway, Lora tried her hardest to not let her thoughts run wild. Too much had happened in a single night. She was sure it was technically already the next day, but she still hadn't been able to sit down or scrub the dirt and blood from her skin. Judging by the moon high up in the sky and the utter darkness outside, the sun wouldn't rise for a few more hours.

Visible down the hall, her father was treating the gruesome cut on Elyssa's throat in the kitchen. Oscar was focused on helping him as best as he could. Maja was running around somewhere, trying to gather fresh clothes, and Ilario had offered to help. Rhay, on the other hand, had not shown his face since they had arrived. For once, she couldn't even blame him for his inaction.

"You should go talk to your family." Eyden crossed his arms next to her, his voice quiet. "I'll stand guard." His gaze flicked to the ebony door behind Lora. They hadn't found a better place for Damir than the storage room in the hallway. Her father had patched him up before they had locked him in. She still couldn't wrap her head around the fact that Layken, the guard who had taken innumerable fae to Karwyn to experiment on, was Ilario's Damir—his ex who he'd thought had been taken and killed by Karwyn.

"Are you sure this is going to hold him?" She took a step forward to detail the door. Her legs gave out, and she would have landed on the floor if it weren't for Eyden's quick reflexes.

"You really need to sit down, special one. I don't know how you're still standing."

"The same way you are. Don't underestimate me."

"*I* wasn't part of a magical ritual meant to kill me." The power merge with Karwyn felt like it had happened another lifetime ago. Eyden's dark brows pulled up, his ice-blue eyes challenging her. With his arm around her shoulder, he pulled her closer. "How are you *really* feeling?"

Lora bit her lip, tasting her own blood. "I can't even begin to answer that." Her gaze drifted to her family and beyond to the corridor where her mother was laying in a coma. Because of *her.* Lora had lost all hope when Karwyn had taken his last breath, but now a new wave of hope was blossoming in her exhausted heart. It scared her. Hope was fickle at best.

"I don't even understand how my mum is still alive," Lora added, turning to Eyden. "Is it a glitch, is it magical? Is it...temporary?" Shivers ran down her back. *Temporary.*

"I wish I had the answer. My best guess is that because Rhay killed Karwyn but the ritual was concluded it messed with the rules of your blood contract." Eyden's hand moved from her shoulder to grasp her hand. "Once we save Amira and Farren, they can figure out how to break whatever magic is holding your mother captive. Until then, we have to assume the contract isn't broken, so you can't speak about it."

He squeezed her hand, but the reassurance didn't erase the ice on her skin. Was it because of the contract or her situation? She was too tired to tell.

"Lora, it's your turn," her father called from the kitchen. She had insisted everyone else should go before her. She didn't want them to *see* what had happened to her.

"It'll be all right. I can see how much they love you." Eyden squeezed her hand once more. Her eyes flickered over his burnt forearm, the knife wound on his other arm, and the bruise above his left eye.

"You should go first."

Eyden chuckled quietly. "Don't worry about me." He dropped her hand hesitantly. "I'll be waiting. Whatever you need, I'll be here."

Lora felt her knees would give out again, but this time for another reason altogether. Too many emotions were running through her, but she forced her legs to move.

Elyssa passed her, joining Eyden by Damir's door as Lora entered the small kitchen.

Lora's gaze wandered over the flickering warm light above the table to the open beige curtains and the bright green fake plants in front of the narrow window that Maja had once insisted made the room complete. The dining table was littered with bandages, disinfectant, and other medical equipment Lora had no mind to name. Stealing an ambulance had its perks.

Her father was throwing away bloody compresses when she finally joined him, one hand braced against the large ebony table. Oscar stared at her for a few seconds, standing across from her. His dark brown eyes were so much like their mother's—it was both reassuring and damning.

Her father pulled back a chair, and Lora gratefully sat down, running her hand through her tangled dark-blonde hair that was matted with blood. What did they see when they looked at her? Someone else entirely, no longer the Lora they knew?

"Where's the worst of it?" Leaning closer, her father took in the state of her. She knew she couldn't hide her exhaustion from him, a doctor. His expression said as much as his brows pinched together.

"I suppose the knife wound." She pointed at the hole in her dress where Karwyn's knife had gone in between her lower ribs. His sullen eyes flashed through her mind—how the light had left them as Rhay knelt beside him, willing his former best friend to stay while everyone else would have jumped with joy if it weren't for Lora's contract.

Her father picked up the scissors lying on the table and knelt before her. Carefully, he widened the tear in the satin fabric.

"Hand me some antiseptic wipes, please," her father said to Oscar, who immediately acted. "You might need stitches."

"No, I'll heal." Her father met her fae eyes. They both knew what it meant.

As Oscar handed everything to their father, he asked, "How did it happen? And don't lie."

"Oscar, this isn't the time for an interrogation." Her father gave him a stern look as he brushed over her wound with the antiseptic wipe. She bit back a grunt of pain.

"It's okay," Lora replied. "It was never my intention to lie."

Oscar's eyes narrowed. "It doesn't change the fact that you did."

Lora swallowed, fighting back exhausted tears.

"We can talk about this in the morning," her father intervened. "Oscar, take a look at your sister. Clearly, she's been through a lot. She was stabbed. She's had to rely on these *fae* to help her get here—"

"*These fae* aren't the issue, Dad. I know you must both be in shock, but these fae, they've helped me—*us*," Lora cut in.

"Are *they* the reason it took you so long?" Oscar's hand turned white as his grip on the table tightened.

"No, that's because..." How could she explain? Even now, she was bound to her word.

Oscar tapped his finger on the wooden surface. "Why did you stop replying to us?"

"I..." She sucked in a breath as the disinfectant set her skin on fire.

"And who the hell stabbed you?" Oscar asked, his voice rising. Lora's eyes travelled to the corridor, where she glimpsed Eyden's eyes on her. She couldn't explain it all, but someone else could.

"Stop looking at them!" Oscar yelled. "*We're* right here. Jesus, if we're not worth your time, why did you even come back?"

She sucked in a pained breath as an invisible knife twisted her heart.

"Oscar, that is enough!" her father replied, standing up as he reached for a bandage. "There's no need to interrogate your sister when she's hurt so badly she shouldn't even be able to sit upright! You know what she's risked for our family."

"Why do you think she's doing so well? She's *fae* now. She's—"

"*She* is your sister," Eyden bit out as he appeared by her side. "And she's been through hell to make sure *you* would be all right. She's taken risk after risk, fought as hard as she could, so *your* family would live." Eyden's eyes flashed as he stared at her brother. "You think she *chose* not to talk to you? She was, quite possibly still *is*, bound to Karwyn to not speak about their agreement. An agreement she was forced to make to get that cure you all desperately needed. She—"

Lora cut him a glance. "It's okay, Eyden." Her gaze shifted to Oscar. "I get why you're angry, but I did what I had to. I promi—" No, she couldn't use that word again. "I'll *try* to answer any of your questions as best as I can." Her father bent to put a bandage over her clean wound before addressing her less serious cuts and bruises.

Oscar crossed his arms over his chest. "You still haven't told us who stabbed you. Elyssa said you were running from King Tarnan. Did he do this to you?"

"No, it was Karwyn."

"Karwyn Adelway of Turosian? The one you're bound to?"

"He is—*was*—my cousin."

Oscar's eyes widened. She knew what thoughts were running through his head, so she braced herself against the creaky wooden chair to get up. Her bones felt heavy, her skin glistened with sweat, but she pushed on. She put her hand on Oscar's arm. "He was...a bad king and needed to be stopped. I...had to help."

Oscar's eyes lingered on her hand. "Why did it have to be *you?*" When he looked up again, he looked younger. Besides the faint stubble, he was still a child deep down. A child let down by the world, by his older sibling who was supposed to always be there.

Footsteps echoed through the hall, and Oscar tore his gaze from her face just as Maja and Ilario entered the dining hall with clothes stacked in their arms.

"I've set up the rooms and picked out some clothes that will hopefully fit you all," Maja announced before she took in the group gathered around the table. "And I'm clearly interrupting something." She put the clothes on the edge of the table that wasn't covered in gauze and bloody compresses. Ilario followed her move.

"We can pick this up later. Lora should rest," her father decided. His brown-green eyes looked over everyone present. "And so should you all."

Maja clapped her hands. The movement caused her glasses to slip down her nose. "Good. Ilario can show you to your rooms." She took Lora's clammy hand. "You're coming with me, roomie." Lora threw Eyden a glance, and he nodded as if to tell her to go.

"Wait, can you give Rhay some fresh clothes?" Ilario asked, picking up a sweater and a pair of sweatpants from the pile of clothes.

Maja fixed him with a calculating gaze. "Drunk guy, you mean? Sure thing."

Lora forced herself to get going as Maja pulled at her arm. Somehow, Maja knew exactly where to find Rhay. He sat on the floor in the living room, clutching a half-empty bottle of vodka as if it was his saving grace. With the remaining glitter smeared under his eyes and his blood-streaked blue hair, Rhay looked as if he had come from a Halloween party.

"Hey, you, got some clothes for you," Maja told him. Rhay stared blankly into his bottle. "Your clothes may have once been fancy, but your blood kinda ruins the look."

Rhay looked up then, his ocean eyes like pits of utter darkness. "It's not my blood." Maja stiffened beside her. "Lora knows all about that."

Lora took an unsteady step forward. "Rhay..."

Shaking his head, Rhay pulled the bottle to his lips. "Don't bother, little Adelway."

Lora stood rooted in place, unsure if another apology would do any good and feeling as if the slightest wind could knock her over.

"I'll drop these here," Maja said as she put the clothes on the cabinet behind Rhay. "You'd be doing everyone a favour if you changed and took a shower. Self-pity doesn't smell good."

Before Rhay could react, Maja pulled Lora into the next corridor. Lora had been at the cabin once, years ago when she went with Maja's family for a weekend trip. She remembered that this corridor only held an office. All the bedrooms were on the other side, near the kitchen.

Maja pulled open the door to the small, cosy office. The warm beige curtains, pulled-out chocolate-brown sofa, and old ebony desk made the room feel warm and inviting.

Her whole body feeling heavy, Lora let herself fall onto one side of the sofa bed. Only now did she let herself fully feel the exhaustion. The fire in her veins was more silent than it had ever been since she'd first used her power back in Rubien. To some extent she craved it, and earlier today, she wouldn't have felt guilty about it. But now Oscar's eyes stared back at her disapprovingly, reminding her that her mother would resent her too.

The cushion dipped as Maja laid down next to her. With difficulty, Lora turned her head to look at her best friend who had come when she'd called. Maja's dark brown fringe hung over the top of her glasses. Her wavy hair was longer now, falling beyond her chin. She wondered what Maja was noticing about her. Probably her eyes, no longer just aquamarine but a striking turquoise.

"I'll let you sleep tonight," Maja started. "But tomorrow, I want to hear every last detail about your time in Liraen. I couldn't do much to help you when you were away, but I'm here now."

"It's not the happiest story." Her finger ran over the bandage on her stomach, then moved to the cut on her arm, barely visible in the dim light.

Maja scooted closer, taking her free hand. "But you made it out." An encouraging grin spread on her friend's face. "You're truly the smartest cookie I know."

Lora couldn't help but laugh even as tears slid down her cheek. Had she really made it? The border had fallen. Tarnan had two of their friends and was planning on taking over both her worlds. And her mother wouldn't wake up.

But she hadn't lost yet either. She had to cling to that.

"And I *know* there's a story between you and Mister Broody," Maja added, her smile widening even as her eyes radiated concern. "You once promised me all the details, and you can bet I'll be collecting."

Lora opened her mouth to reply, but a knock on the door startled her. Before she could force herself to move, Maja got up and opened the door, revealing Oscar.

"Can I talk to my sister for a minute?" He shifted on his feet.

Lora scrambled up, all her bones feeling paper-thin. She gave Maja a nod, and her friend retreated into the adjoining guest bathroom. Lora had to hold on to the doorframe to keep upright.

"I know I should let you sleep, and I will," Oscar started, "but I just needed to ask you one thing."

"You can ask me anything." A part of her hoped he'd come to tell her he understood.

Oscar looked anywhere but at her. "Why did you think Mum wasn't alive?"

Lora's grip on the door tightened. "I...I thought I failed you."

"She..." Oscar stuttered as he wiped away a tear. "She did die for a moment. She stopped breathing. I thought she was gone forever."

Lora's knees buckled. The room spun. She wished she could tell him their mum would be all right, but she had no idea what it all meant. How could she ever explain how much she had tried to keep her promise? How could she ever convey how much she had wished she could go back and be with them? Meeting Oscar's gaze, Lora knew she couldn't.

"I guess I did fail you," she said.

Oscar didn't answer, and the silence broke her more than any words could.

CHAPTER 6

EYDEN

"We need weapons," Elyssa said, leaning back on the rustic chair in the kitchen, her arms crossed over the faded grey shirt Maja had given her. Seeing his sister dressed in what Eyden understood to be casual human clothes, without weapons strapped to her, was a strange sight.

Through the window Eyden glimpsed the first rays of the morning sun. The small lamp above the table gave the room an orange glow. If Eyden listened closely he could hear the lightbulb flickering, the refrigerator buzzing—everything was hooked up to electricity here, whereas back at home, it was all magical and peacefully quiet.

It had been two days since their arrival. They had all needed the rest. Lora was still sleeping, according to Maja.

The cold wood of the table digging into his elbows, Eyden pushed his empty plate back and forth. Bread, cheese, and ham as well as a jug of water were laid out in front of him. Maja sat next to Elyssa, across from Eyden. Ilario was on Eyden's other side, his gaze flicking to the storage room door every so often.

"Weapons are a good first step," Eyden agreed. "We need to find out where the humans keep the agreement with the fae." His eyes met Elyssa's hazel ones. Shadows marked her eyes, and a bruise covered her left cheek. The cut on her brow bone had closed thanks to Lora's father, but it was still as red as her hair. The wound on her neck was wrapped with a bandage.

Elyssa absently ran a finger over the bandage on her arm where Amira's brother had burned her. Eyden's own burn from the force field had almost healed but was itching underneath the bandage.

"We can't leave Amira and Farren with Tarnan for long." Her voice was eager and impatient for good reason.

"Do you think he'll hurt them?" Ilario asked, his tone caring even though he barely knew them.

"I think, in a twisted way, Tarnan wants Amira on his side, so I don't think he would hurt her. And Farren is his leverage to make sure Amira complies." Elyssa's gaze connected with Ilario. "But the more time passes, the greater the risk that he goddamn snaps."

"Let's go over what we *do* know," Ilario said, straightening in his chair. "Tarnan wants to remake Liraen, which includes enslaving humans again and taking the high king title in the contest. As long as he doesn't break the agreement between humans and fae, he can only compel fae and not force humans into slave contracts." His hand fumbled with the sleeve of his white sweater. "Lora can't be compelled, and she apparently has Karwyn's air power now as well as her fire; she could possibly win against Tarnan if she were to take part in the contest instead of Karwyn." Ilario's eyes set on Eyden.

Eyden knew he had a point, but the thought of Lora being put in the middle of another one-on-one battle made the air leave his lungs. She'd already been forced to go up against Karwyn, and it had cost her. As much as Eyden was glad to have Karwyn gone, it hadn't brought him the kind of relief he had been hoping for. His thoughts often drifted to his late father, who had been experimented on and killed in the Turosian palace. Even though Karwyn was gone, Eyden's father was still dead and nothing would change that.

"Amira is currently bound to Tarnan," Elyssa added, her fist clenching. "If he dies, so does she. Lora may be able to win the contest if Tarnan doesn't have something else up his sleeve, but we can't take Tarnan out for good. We need to keep the human-fae agreement alive *and* break Amira's contract."

"And Lora's contract to Karwyn," Eyden commented.

Elyssa nodded. "Which we can't do without a witch."

"Bringing us back to freeing Amira and Farren." Ilario let out a long breath.

Eyden's hand moved to the pocket of his trousers, his fingers brushing against the cold amulet, the ancient artefact that Amira had thrown over to him before she'd told him to go. He hoped Tarnan couldn't do much damage with the other artefact. Did he have other witches on his side, or was he counting on compelling Amira and Farren to fight his battles?

"Well," Maja threw in, chewing her bottom lip, "this conversation sounds straight out of a fantasy novel, but I'm gonna go with it." A nervous laugh tumbled out of her. "I don't know where the human-fae agreement is, but if I had to guess, it's probably at some protected government building. What I *do* know is that we have some hunting guns here and I think an old bow. Any takers?"

Elyssa almost jumped out of her chair. "Lead the way."

Maja rose to her feet. "It's Elyssa, right?"

"Call me El. Anyone giving me weapons is a goddamn friend of mine." An excited grin softened Elyssa's features. And with that the two left the room. Eyden was glad to see her smile. He didn't know much about Maja, but he was aware that she had been there for Lora when she'd needed advice back in Liraen, before Karwyn had taken away her phone.

Eyden turned his head to the only other person in the room, but Ilario's gaze was set on Damir's door. Eyden and Ilario had taken shifts standing guard. Lora's father had blown up a strange mattress and given Damir a blanket and a pillow, mumbling something about having made a vow to treat all patients equally.

"Have you talked to him?" Eyden asked.

Ilario lowered his gaze to his hands, twisting the fabric of his sleeve. "If he had a good reason, wouldn't he have already defended himself? I don't even know who he is anymore. Damir, Layken...how many personas did he have? I'm scared I never knew him. I'm scared that if I ask, I'll never be able to unhear the answer."

When Eyden had met Ilario the night Damir had gotten captured by guards, he had felt bad for both of them. As Ilario had told him afterwards, that night Damir had used his shapeshifting powers to take the identity of a royal to fetch a free meal. Unfortunately, his cover had been blown when a guard had noticed him. Just like Ilario, Eyden had assumed Damir had met the same fate as Eyden's father along with a long list of other innocent fae: killed by Karwyn and Saydren's experiments. How had Damir become the one doing the capturing? Eyden had never known Damir. Now that he knew that Layken, who had practically been Karwyn's lackey—delivering fae to be experimented on— was the same person, Eyden had no intention of ever knowing Damir.

"What about Rhay?" Eyden added. The fae had been sulking around the living room.

Ilario sighed. "I don't know who he is either."

Eyden was about to reply when a voice he'd been craving to hear drifted to him.

"Hey," Lora said, her voice raspy from sleep. She had changed out of her ruined dress. Dressed in loose grey trousers, bright orange socks, and an oversized ivory sweater, she looked different. If it weren't for her bright *fae* eyes, she could have easily passed as fully human. But no matter if she was half-fae, human, or fae, she was incredible to him. And so damn beautiful.

Walking towards her, he leaned into the doorframe next to her. "How are you feeling?"

"Better." Her gaze drifted over his shoulder to Ilario, who had gotten to his feet. "How are you two?"

"I think it's safe to say we're doing better than Rhay. Or Damir," Ilario said. "Speaking of, I better get back to keeping watch. See you later, just Lora." He gave Lora a quick smile before disappearing down the hall.

Lora's eyes followed him until Eyden reached for her hand, his finger brushing over the back of it. Her skin was soft but colder than usual. "Okay, let's try this again." Lora tilted her head up at him. "How are you *really* feeling? I can tell when you're lying."

The corner of Lora's mouth turned up a notch. "Or you *think* you can."

"Another lie." His smile faded as Lora's expression sobered.

"I knew it would be hard coming back here, but with my mum in a coma and the border gone..." She bit her lip, a tear forming in her eye. Eyden squeezed her hand. "I can't help but think I've failed them. My family. The whole world, actually." She laughed without joy, wiping at her eyes.

"The whole world is not on your shoulders alone." He drew a circle on her hand. "No one was able to stop Tarnan; and as for your family, you didn't fail them. Without your sacrifice, they would have all succumbed to the virus. I know your brother is in shock, but he should've never said those things to you."

"He looked at me like he didn't even recognise me," Lora whispered, her lips trembling. "And how can I blame him when I can barely recognise myself? I can feel this new power coursing through me and I can't help but wonder, am I still human at all?"

Eyden tugged at her hand, pulling her closer. "You're *Lora*. That's all that matters."

She opened her mouth when someone cleared their throat behind them.

"Morning," Oscar said, his tone sharp. Lora's father walked in after him.

Oscar's eyes moved from Lora's face to their joined hands, and Lora pulled her hand back quickly. Eyden tried hard not to let it affect him. They were in a difficult situation, but he couldn't help but worry Lora would change her mind. Would she keep pulling back for the sake of her family?

"Morning. How is Mum?"

Oscar dropped his head. "No changes."

Lora nodded silently, but her eyes spoke volumes. He wished he could comfort her, but she obviously didn't want him close.

"Can I see her?"

"Of course, honey," Lora's father replied, taking a slice of bread from the table. "I'll come with you." He inclined his head, and Lora followed after him, giving Eyden a faint smile. A sullen Oscar walked up to a machine that Lora's father had called the "coffee maker." The hot drink tasted like caftee that had gone bad. After pouring a cup, Oscar left to follow Lora.

Eyden heard Maja's footsteps before he heard her voice. "Jesus, you got it bad, don't you?"

Eyden tilted his head at her. "It's that obvious, huh?"

Maja crossed her arms over her colourful cropped sweater. "Blindingly so. You know, you're not how I pictured."

"Did Lora not mention my incredible looks?"

Maja laughed, tucking her dark hair behind her ear. "She didn't have time to talk much about you. Until I saw you two together I didn't know how...real it was. I think you're good for her."

"Not everyone sees it that way."

Maja stepped closer, her eyes warm. "Give it time." A dangerous light gathered in her gaze. "That said, if you hurt her in any way, I wasn't lying when I said we have guns in this house. Even if bullets can't kill fae, they sure hurt like a motherfucker. Got it?"

Eyden raised his hands, holding back a chuckle. "Got it. I'm glad Lora has you. She needs you right now."

"She needs you too." Maja's eyes flickered to the hallway leading to the bedroom she was sharing with Lora. A smirk brightened her eyes. "Actually, I think I know exactly what you *both* need."

CHAPTER 7

◊

AMIRA

At twelve bells precisely, Tarnan knocked on her door. The past two days, Amira had come to expect her captor's visit for lunch. Forcing herself to hide the hatred in her eyes, Amira stood up from her bed, smoothed down her long dark brown locks, and pinched her hand three times.

Opening the door, Amira didn't go as far as to fake a smile, but she avoided frowning. Tarnan wore a new crown; the dark red rubies mixed with carnelian crystals glistened in the midday sun like droplets of fresh blood. In his hands was a tray full of delicious food that Amira's stomach was too knotted to digest properly. Without a word, she let him in and took a seat.

Tarnan arranged the plates on the polished oak table. "I've brought you some roasted turkey. I remember how much you enjoyed it during your first visit."

"Thank you." She folded her napkin on her lap, almost tearing the edges.

Taking out a book from his golden jacket pocket, Tarnan reached across the small table. "For your reading of the day."

Tarnan had decided to "further her education" by handing her books about the Sartoya line and the gruesome death of the Dark King and his family. Finding it the perfect way to earn his trust, Amira had read them all.

Tarnan sat opposite her and delicately placed some meat and roasted vegetables on his plate. "I'm curious to hear your thoughts on the last book I gave you."

Keeping her tone soft, Amira recounted what she had rehearsed in her head. "I knew the Adelway bloodline was twisted, but not to this extent. I can't believe that it was Karwyn's grandfather who suggested the use of dark magic to the Dark King to rip a tear in the universe to reach Earth." She was careful not to say too much. After what Karwyn had put her through, blaming the Adelways wasn't a far stretch.

Tarnan put his fork down and anchored his blood-red irises on Amira's face. "I wish for you to stop calling him the Dark King. It is an insulting nickname. My father was no saint, but he was misunderstood. I'm sure you can relate as a witch."

Misunderstood—as if he hadn't left a legacy of murder and slavery behind. Twisting her mouth into an apologetic frown, Amira sat up straight. "I will do better."

Tarnan watched her closely as if expecting her to say more. With Tarnan, fewer words were sometimes smarter. Less chance to mess up. "My father has done great things for Liraen. He ended famine and raging wars between kingdoms. Under his reign, Liraen grew richer and safer. He's made mistakes, but *I've* learned from them. Dark magic was his downfall, twisting his mind, making him mad before he could figure out how to control it. I won't fall down the same path."

Yet he'd broken the curse on his family line to set his power of compulsion free. A power his father, Variel Sartoya, had acquired through dark magic.

She couldn't resist the question burning on her tongue. "How will you avoid it? Dark magic always comes at a price." She let the corners of her mouth drop as if worry plagued her.

The Dark King, mad with power, had turned to syphoning the life source out of fae to keep his magic up. She didn't know how such a thing was possible, but if Tarnan wanted to keep from turning mad, would he need more energy to sustain himself and his cursed power?

"I appreciate your worry, but I'll handle it," Tarnan said, laying a hand on top of hers. Amira gripped her fork tighter. Tarnan narrowed his eyes at her. Was he buying into her act? Tarnan was no fool; two days was not enough time to earn her trust.

Removing her hand from his grip, Amira put down her fork. "You won't tell me how you'll handle it? How am I supposed to trust you won't repeat the same mistakes?"

Tarnan pulled his hand back to his lap. "Trust means not always having all the answers."

Huffing, Amira bit back the anger bubbling up her throat. "Sometimes it means giving all the answers without even having to ask. I understand why you've kept things from me, but I wish for us to have a different relationship moving forward. Don't you want us to be equals?" Tarnan detailed her face, and she rushed on to not give him too much time to over-analyse her every word. "Who wrote the book you gave me? Even if the Adelways were corrupt, your father was the one who lost his way. Yet the books don't mention him feeding on fae life sources, turning on his own people. I find it awfully convenient."

Tarnan wiped his mouth with his napkin, a small smile gracing his lips as if not at all displeased at Amira's questioning. "I told you, Amira, history books are always written by the victors. Yet history is more nuanced than that. My father was the only one willing to risk his own life to find a solution to the famine and misery on Liraen before we had humans working for us. Everyone was grateful for his sacrifice back then, when it brought prosperity to all fae. A ruler always has to favor the greater good, even if it means sacrificing a few people on the way."

Amira took a sip of water to prevent the bile from rising up. "How can you be so sure that was your father's only goal? You were just an infant when your father was killed."

A glint of sadness washed over Tarnan's face, but he quickly erased it, returning to his deceptively welcoming features. "I had just turned twenty when Saydren informed me of my heritage. He told me everything I needed to know about my father and what a good man he had been until the dark magic ate his mind. He also told me about the loophole to my bloodline's curse. I needed the blood of a half-fae turned full fae. Half-fae are such a rarity, almost impossible to produce, so inconvenient to find. We didn't think it would take us that long to find two compatible half-fae who could merge. There was a lot of trial and error before my faithful Saydren found Karwyn."

He waved his hand, as if his retelling was some light banter and not a horrifying reveal. Tarnan had been planning this for decades. Lora and Karwyn had been pawns in his game all along. Saydren had never been Karwyn's loyal royal healer. He had always been guiding Karwyn for Tarnan's sake.

"The looming contest finally made Karwyn act." He paused, his eyes lost in the memory. Amira dragged her fork over her plate, loud enough for him to come back to himself. "You and I have a lot in common. We both had to keep a part of ourselves hidden for fear we'd be punished. Even to this day, I cannot share everything. But one day, I want both of us to be free."

But not humans.

Amira hid her gag in a coughing fit. How dare he compare himself to her? She knew she should play along more, but she blurted, "You remind me more of Wryen, keeping me locked away."

Tarnan took a deep breath. "Your brother is a pathetic excuse for a king. Always scheming to get more power for himself with no care for the state of Liraen. He's never been taken seriously by anyone. *I* will be taken seriously." His tone was calm, yet Amira could hear the tremble of barely contained rage. "I won't abuse you. I won't ask you to keep your witch power hidden. *I'm* not a monster, but I will be a great high king, and that title comes with sacrifice. I simply want you to be yourself and stand by my side—help me turn Liraen into what it should've always been. I want witches to be free and accepted by fae, working together to improve Liraen. And I want Rubien to rise again. Harten claimed Adeartas abandoned the kingdom because of my father's dark magic. But where is his proof?"

Tarnan paused to catch his breath. "Do you know what the Void is, Amira?"

She shook her head.

"It's a dreadful place, full of twisted, illegal deals. Like fortae. Fae buy humans for their blood. I will shut down the market and rebuild Rubien. For too long, it has been a place of darkness, a place for Harten and then Karwyn to banish fae to." He squeezed Amira's hand. "I know how much damage this cursed drug has caused."

Amira closed her eyes. She could almost taste fortae on her lips. It had been over a month since she had last taken a pill, yet there was still a part of her that ached for one last taste of it. No matter how right he was to eradicate it, that didn't erase the fact he wanted to enslave humans.

He stood up abruptly. "I'll prove my good intentions to you."

Amira's heartbeat sped up, her hands anxiously pulling at the hem of her sleeves.

Tarnan opened the door to her room. The three fae standing guard immediately straightened themselves. "Follow me," Tarnan said.

"You're letting me walk around freely?" Amira dared ask, her knees weak.

Freedom. The word had felt foreign for the better part of the last eight years.

Tarnan's smile dropped, almost regretful, as he straightened his jacket. "I'm taking you to see Farren."

The walk to the underground was surprisingly short. Knowing Farren had been this close to her for the last three days made her heart ache and sing at the same time. Amira made sure to take a mental note of the way to his room, remembering the different corridors thanks to their various paintings of the Carnylen kingdom and its royal line.

The door opened on Farren's surprised face, and Amira rushed to hug him. They hadn't had much time to bond before their capture, but Amira was in such desperate need of affection that she didn't overthink it. Farren welcomed her in a tight embrace. He wore fresh clothes, and his wounds had been cleaned and bandaged. Yet he winced when she held him.

"Are you okay?" Farren whispered in her ear while her face was buried in his neck.

"I'm fine. Are you?"

Tarnan cleared his throat behind them, and Amira forced herself to break away. Over Farren's shoulder, Amira caught sight of his room. Even though it was located in the dark and cold underground, the bedroom was not a cell. It was comfortably furnished, with a large bed framed in dark chestnut, a desk, and a peach-coloured lounging chair.

"You see, Amira, I do keep my promises," Tarnan said, a satisfied grin on his face.

"Thank you; you have at least kept this one promise," Amira said as fast as possible, to avoid the bitterness burning her tongue. Farren stared at her, his dark brows wrinkled.

"I didn't solely bring you here for this touching reunion. I require your assistance with something of the utmost importance. I wish for you two to help me rebuild Rubien, purge the darkness."

The shock didn't even have time to settle in before a guard came running down the stairs. Out of breath, he furiously whispered in Tarnan's ear. Amira tensed. Had they caught Elyssa and the others? Farren grabbed her hand, keeping her arm from shaking.

Tarnan's grin grew as the guard finished his report. "I'm afraid we'll have to cut this short. Your brother has decided to pay us a visit."

Amira froze in place, Farren's hand the only thing keeping her grounded. Had her brother come to announce he had executed her mother? A few days ago, she had believed Tarnan when he had assured her that her mother would be safe. With Tarnan's betrayal, her mother's situation seemed hopeless.

A deep line creased Tarnan's forehead. His voice turned as sweet as syrup, yet it froze her skin. *"Farren, you will stay here. If anyone other than myself or Saydren tries to take you out of this room, you will kill yourself."* Farren's eyes went blank, as if he had lost control of his own soul.

Amira's face fell. Tarnan hadn't compelled her to do anything yet, so she had held on to the secret hope that they could find a way to escape together. But she would never leave without Farren.

Heading back inside his room, Farren wordlessly said goodbye. Before Amira could even wave, Tarnan pulled her with him down the corridor. "I think we should let Wryen know he is no longer welcome in our palace."

Our. As if Amira truly belonged here, with him. Her skin crawled with disgust, and it took everything in her to not rip her arm out of Tarnan's grip. She'd never belonged to Wryen or Karwyn, and by Caelo, she didn't belong to Tarnan either.

CHAPTER 8

ELYSSA

The gunshot echoed in Elyssa's ears. Even with her bad hearing, the noise was obnoxiously loud. Maja had warned her about the kickback, but she still felt it in her bones, the force almost pushing her back. It was a powerful feeling, a sense of control she'd longed for. A few days ago the police had been shooting at them and now she was the one to fire a bullet.

The rifle felt smooth against Elyssa's skin as she lowered it to see if she had hit her target. Maja had drawn a generous red circle on one of the snow-covered trees at the back of the cabin.

Icy snow melted beneath Elyssa's boots in the afternoon sun. The woods reminded her of the rebel camp but the weather was colder than it had ever been back at her old home. Not for the first time, she wondered how everyone was faring after the battle. She knew they had chosen to fight, but it still made her skin itch with fury knowing not everyone had made it out. She'd wanted to give them something to fight for. Had she really delivered or brought them to a slaughter? Would Jaspen whisper lies into their ears, turning everyone against her while she was gone?

"Are you sure you've never fired a gun?" Maja asked, a rifle slung over her shoulder.

Elyssa smirked. The bullet had hit dead centre. Of freaking course she'd be good at this. "What can I say, I've got good aim." Elyssa aimed her rifle again. "You should teach the others too."

Maja cocked her head. "I'll go ask them."

As Maja left to go inside, Elyssa switched out the rifle for her bow. Although she'd lost all her almandine weapons except for her brass knuckles, at least she still had her bow. The arrows Maja had found weren't as sharp as Elyssa would like them to be, but the weight of them in her hand felt familiar and comforting.

Elyssa aimed an arrow, pictured Tarnan's red eyes, and fired. It struck true. When she closed her eyes, flashes of blood drifted through her mind. Amira's when Karwyn's blade had struck her. The humans' as Tarnan's guards attacked them from all sides. Lora's as she fought off Karwyn. Breathing in sharply, Elyssa forced it all away and aimed. Before she could fire again, movement to her left made her whirl around.

Lora's brother took a quick step back, kicking up dirt mixed with snow. Elyssa lowered her weapon. "Don't sneak up on people."

"I wanted to get some fresh air." Oscar lowered his arms. He had a lost look about him. Elyssa hadn't heard everything he'd said to Lora, but she'd gotten the impression from Eyden that Oscar hadn't been as understanding as he goddamn should be.

"How's your sister? I haven't seen her today."

Oscar put his hands in his pockets. "She's all right."

"All right?" Elyssa huffed. "No one here is freaking all right."

"You sound like that guy, Eyden. I don't need another lecture about *my* sister."

"First of all, *that guy* is my brother, and he's done a lot to help Lora, so watch your tone. Secondly, have you tried putting yourself in her shoes?"

Oscar ran a hand through his wavy dark hair. "Eyden is your brother?"

Elyssa tilted her head up at him, gripping her bow. "Yeah, got a problem with that?"

His eyes widened. "No, no. I...uhm...didn't see the resemblance." His eyes travelled over her fair, freckled skin. Compared to Eyden's brown skin and dark hair, Elyssa didn't look anything like him.

"Listen, Lora's your sister—you owe it to her to let her tell you the full story." Oscar's gaze lowered to the ground, his feet shifting on the wet ground. Sighing, Elyssa asked, "Do you want to try shooting an arrow?"

A hint of a smile appeared on his face, and after a moment's hesitation, he walked towards her across the snow. Moving forward was the only way not to lose one's mind. She goddamn knew that better than most.

Just as Oscar pulled back another arrow, Elyssa saw the back door open from her peripheral vision. Maja, Lora, Ilario, and Lora's father walked outside. Lora's expression brightened as her gaze locked on her brother.

"Be careful, Oscar," Lora's father, Isaac, shouted, taking a seat on the swing by the back door. He pulled his winter coat tight around him. Oscar looked over his shoulder and gave him a thumbs up.

"Keep going," Elyssa told him before walking up to the group. "So who's up for firing some guns?"

"I suppose learning to use these metal things would be a good idea." Ilario took in the unfamiliar weapon.

"Come on, then, I'll show you," Maja offered, and they walked to the table next to Oscar, picking up a rifle.

"What about you, Lora?" Elyssa pulled Lora's focus to her.

"Back at the palace, Rhay started teaching me some basic fighting techniques." Lora bit her lip. "I don't think he'll continue our training."

Elyssa snorted. "Not unless you want to train for a drinking contest."

Lora's lip twitched, but the smile didn't break free.

"How about you try your luck against me? I won't go easy on you, though."

This time, the smile lifted the corners of Lora's mouth. "I wouldn't expect anything less." Lora's uneasy gaze drifted to her brother, then to her father. "Let's do it."

Moving farther away from the door, Elyssa corrected Lora's stance before stepping back and raising her fists. "Show me what you got." She rushed towards Lora.

Lora whirled back in time to avoid Elyssa's fist connecting with her face. She tried to grip Elyssa's arm, but Elyssa spun around quickly, kicking out and catching Lora's hip. Lora grunted, but she wasn't deterred. Her friend blocked her next kick and almost landed her own blow, but Lora's fist merely grazed Elyssa's shoulder.

Strands of auburn hair came out of Elyssa's ponytail, but she didn't pay it any mind. When Lora raised her foot, aiming to kick, Elyssa gripped her ankle and pulled. Lora landed on the ground, her breath visible in the cold. Snow covered her clothes and face, mixing with her wavy blonde hair.

Elyssa took a step forward, meaning to help her up, but Lora rolled to the side and stood up on her own. She stormed forward, fist aimed at Lora, but she blocked her strike. As Elyssa raised her other arm to block Lora's next attack, something pushed Elyssa back with such force she was knocked on her ass.

Catching herself as she threw her arms behind her, Elyssa met Lora's shocked expression. Lora's hand had never connected with her. Yet Elyssa had been thrown back as if by magic.

Elyssa got up, dusting off the snow. Lora's eyes were set on her brother, who stared at her as if she had struck *him*. It was hard to imagine that he had grown up in a world where displays of magic were foreign. But it was precisely that magic and damn bravery that would save them.

"Hey, it's all good," Elyssa said, willing Lora to look at her. Lora had come such a long way with using her powers, Elyssa would hate to see her reject this new badass one. It was only fair that the dead king's power would now be used for good.

Lora swallowed. "I...I'm going back inside." She brushed a wet leaf out of her hair. "I need a shower." Oscar watched her as she rushed back inside. Elyssa wished she could knock some sense into him, but the humans might frown upon that.

She thought about her own sibling. Since arriving here, she hadn't had a proper conversation with Eyden. Taking a rifle from the table, she headed inside. She always felt better with a weapon strapped to her; it was like a safety net she could rely on.

Eyden sat on the floor by Damir's door, twirling a kitchen knife in his hand.

"I doubt that'll do much damage," Elyssa said. Eyden's gaze snapped to hers. She took the rifle off her shoulder and lowered herself next to him.

"Do you know how to use that?" His chin tilted at the rifle leaning against the wooden wall.

Elyssa grinned. "Please, I got the hang of it in five minutes." Her smile faltered. "But we need more." Her gaze dropped to the bandage on her arm, but she didn't need the wound to be reminded of Amira. The princess was a constant presence in her mind. Her amethyst eyes were in front of her every time Elyssa closed her eyes.

Eyden's shoulder knocked against hers. "Tomorrow we'll get more weapons. But you do know that it's not your fault Amira and Farren stayed behind?"

Elyssa leaned her head against the wall. "I just wish people wouldn't be forced into situations where they feel the need to make that kind of sacrifice. I wish..."

"That you could have made that sacrifice yourself?"

She would have—for Amira, for her friends, for the rebel camp—in a heartbeat. "I guess I'm a goddamn hypocrite, aren't I?" She could still hear Amira's voice telling her she deserved to be saved. Elyssa believed her, but she owed it to everyone who had made sacrifices for her to see this through. To create a new Liraen—a home to fae, humans, and witches alike. She dreamed of a future where everyone, especially the human camp, was free—never to be hunted again.

Eyden ducked his head. "If you are, then so am I."

"This isn't how you pictured it, is it?"

"What is?"

"Being in the human land, crossing over." Elyssa had never given it much thought. Her parents had thought Earth would be safe, but Elyssa had never wanted *safe* if it meant leaving others to fight their battle. Liraen had always been her home. She'd die before giving up fighting for her rightful place.

Being on Earth with their strange clothes, magical electricity, and overly processed foods, Elyssa felt more out of place than ever. Except for the part where they were hunted. That she had been used to for as long as she could remember.

Eyden laughed under his breath. "I pictured safety."

"What do you think our parents would think if they could see us?" Would they have lived in a house like this one? In the woods, hiding from civilization to hide Eyden's faeness?

Eyden's voice turned quiet, but loud enough for her to catch every word. "I think they would be proud of you for stepping over the border." *Even though that was what had killed them.*

She pictured her mother's smile. It had gotten harder to conjure up, as if her memory was fading even though the sadness pushing against Elyssa's chest was ever present. "They would be so grateful to you for always looking after me."

"They might not agree with my ways."

Elyssa let out a curt laugh. "*You* don't always agree with your ways. I know they wouldn't judge you for it as harshly as I did. I'm sorry I did. If only they hadn't risked their lives for us."

"They wouldn't have if the camp had never been discovered. If they had never kicked me out."

"Why do you say that like it's your fault?" It wasn't. They had never found out how fae guards had discovered the camp, but she knew Eyden hadn't given away their location and the password to the camp.

"I was never supposed to live there, was I?" His shoulders sagged.

She could almost hear his thoughts. If his father hadn't been taken to the palace, never to be heard from again, Eyden wouldn't have been at the camp. Elyssa's parents would have had no reason to take Eyden in as their own.

Turning, she met his stubborn eyes. "Listen to me, Eyden." She'd always thought she was the only one carrying the guilt over her parents' death. But of course her brother was just as goddamn stubborn as she was. "My parents loved you. They saw you as one of us, as a son. The camp turning on you is in no way your fault. I've never thought that for a second and neither did they."

Eyden exhaled loudly. She knew this kind of guilt wouldn't go away in a day. "Life has never been easy for us, has it?"

"No, but I'm glad that I can always count on you." Elyssa took his hand. She remembered the times when she was still a child and Eyden would take her hand whenever she'd been scared but too stubborn to ask for comfort. She'd always wanted to appear strong, but Eyden knew her too well to be fooled.

"I know if our parents could see us now, that's all that would matter to them," Elyssa said, and she full-heartedly believed that. She'd always thought she had something to prove. Why had she survived? As much as she wanted this revolution to work—to beat Tarnan and make a future for themselves—she now realised her parents wouldn't be looking for anything but their children sticking together, supporting each other.

Elyssa tugged on his arm. He looked lost in the past, remembering every loss. "Both of your parents," Elyssa added, and Eyden squeezed her hand as if banishing the guilt they both carried.

CHAPTER 9

LORA

Eyden was waiting in the hallway in front of the office space Lora was sharing with Maja. As she opened the door after hearing a knock, his gaze set on her. She didn't think she would ever get used to him looking at her with so much care.

Swinging her towel-dry hair over her shoulder, Lora tried to get a grip. Yet a part of her wanted this distraction. After Oscar's pained reaction when he'd witnessed her use her powers and checking in on her mum again, Eyden's reassuring presence was most welcome. Eyden's eyes travelled over her oversized emerald T-shirt and black leggings. Not exactly her best outfit, but he didn't seem to mind, judging from the sparks in his blazing eyes.

"Can I come in?" Eyden asked, peeking inside Lora and Maja's room. "Maja sort of suggested she could stay in Elyssa's room." Meaning he could stay here. With her. *Alone.*

Lora tilted her head up at him. "Did she, now?"

"She did." His voice turned husky. "She seemed pretty sure you'd appreciate it."

Lora took a step forward, falling deep into his gaze. She felt it go straight through her, fire awakening her senses. "Who am I to disagree?" She grabbed his grey shirt with both hands, surprising him as she pulled him into the room.

Her lips met his, and it felt like forever and no time had passed since

59

their lips had last touched. She heard Eyden lock the door behind him with one hand as the other drifted to her face, cupping her cheek as he deepened the kiss, his tongue running along her bottom lip. She sighed into his mouth, wanting so much more.

Stepping back, she dragged him with her until the back of her legs hit the sofa bed. Eyden sighed appreciatively as she lowered herself on the bed, gripping his shirt. He rested one hand next to her head, keeping his full weight off her while his other hand played with the hem of her long shirt.

His lips left hers to travel to her ear, then to her throat, his breath tickling her as his tongue branded the side of her neck, turning all her thoughts into mush.

Lora hooked one leg around his waist, wanting—*needing*—him closer, and Eyden seemed to follow her desperation as his hand went under her shirt, touching her bare skin and setting her aflame. She shuddered as Eyden's hand travelled up her stomach, over her ribs and then grazed her bandage.

"*She's hurt, again, every damn time,*" Eyden whispered.

Lora pulled back. "I'm keeping the tradition alive," she joked. At Eyden's blank stare, she frowned. "You, me, a bed—we can only find the time when the fight's over and all that remains is a bandage on my skin. You said I'm hurt again, but I'm fine enough." Her hand went to the back of his head, playing with the ends of his dark curls.

Now Eyden was the one frowning. "I get what you mean, but I didn't say anything."

"Yes, you did. You said I'm hurt every time."

Eyden's eyes widened. "I think you just got even more special." Lora's hand stilled in his hair as dread spread through her body like cold water. "You read my thoughts."

Lora scrambled back, sitting up. Her heart raced for an entirely different reason. She pulled her knees up to her chest, swallowing the knot in her throat. Eyden moved his hand to stroke her back, but Lora leaned away.

"I wish I could read *your* thoughts now." His voice was careful, like he thought she was about to break. She supposed she was.

Hugging her legs, Lora shook her head. "No, you don't. Trust me, it's a mess up there."

"Remember when I said I would take any part of you?"

Lora turned her head, almost losing her breath at Eyden's expression —the honesty there struck her every single time.

"The messy parts too. Talk to me, special one."

"I..." She tried to find the words, but there was so much noise in her head, so many worries that dragged her into the abyss. "I shouldn't have this power. It's not mine to have. It's not...*me*."

"Maybe you're meant to have them. I know it's an adjustment, but it took time for you to accept your fire too."

"That's because I realised my fire has always been part of me. I always had it. It was passed down to me by my...father." *Lozlan.* Her fae father who had broken off all communication with her mother once she'd told him about her pregnancy in a letter. Lora had never voiced her recent discovery aloud. "Karwyn showed me a drawing of him once. To taunt me."

"Your biological father?" Eyden moved closer until their knees touched. Lora waited to hear his thoughts, but thankfully nothing came. It felt as if a part of Karwyn was now hers when she wanted no such thing. Yet she *was* an Adelway; she could never change that.

Lora tugged a wet strand of hair behind her ear, letting the coolness refresh her mind. "I recognised him. Remember that fae who told us where to find Farren and the others in Rubien?"

Eyden's lips parted. "Your father has been banished to Rubien by his brother and he's still there."

Lora nodded. Karwyn had told her Lozlan had tried to kill his own brother, the late king. "I wonder if he recognised me, his own blood. He looked so...lost."

"Do you want to look for him once we've rescued Amira and Farren?"

"I should, shouldn't I?" Part of her wished she wouldn't have to deal with this. It was yet another thing tearing at her heart. She didn't know how much more she could take until the flood drowned her completely.

"It's your choice," Eyden replied.

"What if he could help us?" Lozlan had to be powerful, and he was an Adelway—someone who could have intel they didn't even know they needed. "The rumours say he tried to overthrow Harten Adelway. Given everything we know, that doesn't make him the villain. Don't we need every resource we can get to fight Tarnan?"

"He's not any resource, he's your father."

He was right, but with everything going on, did she have a right to act on her emotions rather than practicality? "He is. So I should want to talk to him, rescue him from his banishment. Shouldn't I?" She pressed her mouth shut tight as if to take back her words.

"I'd understand if you didn't, but I think in the long run, you'd want to hear what he has to say. I would want to know."

"Did it help?" Lora asked, remembering when Eyden had found his father's name on the list of Karwyn's victims.

"I thought it would, but no." He sighed, and she wished she could erase his sadness. "But I wouldn't want to keep wondering."

"What if he rejects me?" Her voice was barely a broken whisper. "Again." Lozlan had never wanted to know anything about her.

Eyden put a hand on her arm. "Then he'd be a fool, but at least you would know. We both know you'd never be able to let it go."

Lora felt a smile sneak up on her even as a tear ran down her cheek. "Are you sure *you* can't read my thoughts?"

Eyden's smirk was pure arrogance. "I'm just highly intelligent."

A laugh flew from her lips, but she sobered quickly. "Why aren't *you* freaking out? I could be reading your thoughts right now."

Eyden tilted his head, his forehead almost touching hers. "I trust you. And I have nothing to hide." *No more lies.* "That said, I'd rather you didn't. I do have some...insecurities."

"You—the one who never loses—insecure? Why?"

"You." Eyden drew closer, one finger drawing a circle on her bare arm. "You're my weakness."

"I am?" she breathed, drunk on his fiery gaze.

"I'm afraid you'll pull back. Change your mind. I know you don't want your family to see us...*together.*"

Lora half turned, putting her knees on the mattress and scooting closer on the sofa. In all the chaos, she hadn't considered where his own worries were taking him. Her family had barely had any time to adjust to any of this. She didn't want to give them more to disapprove of, to adjust to. "It's not because I don't..." She swallowed back the words that seemed to drift in her mind endlessly but she didn't dare think yet. The words neither one of them had said. "...want you. Because I do. I do so much that sometimes it bloody scares me. It's just a lot to handle all at once for my family."

Eyden's hand clasped hers. "Are you scared now?" he asked, his tone somehow both caring and laced with wicked ideas.

"Terrified," Lora rasped, her gaze wandering to his full lips.

She felt his breath on her lips. "Maybe we can be terrified together." His mouth brushed hers before he finished the last word. She savoured the heat between them as the kiss deepened, their tongues intertwining in a way that was all too familiar to her now. She wanted to kiss him until all her thoughts were about him—his touch, his kiss, the care in his eyes.

Eyden pulled back barely. "Is this okay? We can always talk more." The question made her want him all the more.

Lora pushed against his chest, and he gave in easily, his back meeting the sofa mattress. "I think we've done enough talking," she said, straddling him. He strained against his sweatpants beneath her and groaned when she rolled her hips slowly. A teasing smirk graced her lips.

"You're killing me." Eyden's voice had dropped low, making her stomach flutter as every inch of her turned scorching hot.

Instead of answering, Lora pulled her shirt over her head and tossed it to the side. She wasn't wearing anything underneath. He reached out to touch her, but she pulled at his shirt instead, evening the score.

His eyes wandered over her bare chest before his fingers clasped around the necklace he'd given her, pulling her in to steal another kiss, drawing a shaky breath from her lips. His free hand moved to the swell of her breast, sending goosebumps over her skin.

He didn't waste any time before his thumb brushed over her nipple, and she bit his lip as she moaned. He drank it in greedily, his tongue running along her bottom lip as his hand splayed over her breast and a flutter went straight to her core.

His grip on her necklace loosened, and she felt him try to switch their positions as his hand landed on her waist, but she pushed back against his bare chest, feeling his hard muscles ripple under her touch. "Stay," she said, and his eyes seemed to flash at her command.

"As you wish," Eyden replied, his voice thick and smoky. He leaned back, his eyes daring her to do her best—or worst.

His heated gaze made her feel unstoppable. Letting her hand wander down his chest, she planted a kiss on his bare skin. His hooded eyes watched her as she moved down his body, kissing a path to the bands of his trousers before hooking her fingers under the elastic and pulling both his sweatpants and underwear down.

Heat shot between her legs as she freed him from his trousers, her hand running down his length. His breaths came in short gasps as she worked him, all the while watching him watch her. She quickened her tempo, and Eyden grabbed her wrist as a rumble left his chest. His eyes screamed pure desire.

His gaze caught on her leggings. "Off," he said, groaning as her hold on him tightened before she let go. His voice made her tremble from head to toe. Lora shuffled out of her leggings and underwear, aware of Eyden watching her every move. He wasn't even touching her, but he might as well have as his gaze burned through every layer of her—saw everything, every part of her soul.

She straddled him, feeling him against her thigh as Eyden's hands gripped her waist almost desperately, seeking the same friction she craved. Leaning down, Lora captured his lips, sighing against his mouth, letting him know how much she wanted this—*him*. With one hand, she gripped the back of the sofa over Eyden's head while the other ran over the length of him. The hiss of pleasure leaving his lips was everything.

She pulled upright as she guided him to her. Eyden's heated eyes were set on her face as she lowered herself onto him inch by inch, connecting them—body and soul. Like two flames meeting, intertwining.

She tightened her grip on the back of the sofa as her other hand went to his chest. Starting a rhythm, she rolled her hips. Eyden's hand scorched her waist as he watched her take her pleasure and encouraged her on, increasing their tempo.

"*Faster*." His voice echoed through her head. She was too far gone to overthink it.

Lora bit her lip to keep silent, still aware there were other people in the cabin even as the voices in her head quieted and nothing but Eyden and her remained. Eyden's scorching gaze moved from her face down to where they were joined, and a growl of approval filled the room.

When Eyden's hand moved between her legs, touching just the right spot, she couldn't help the shattered cry leaving her lips as her back arched. Her eyes fell shut and she moved her hips faster, desperately, hearing Eyden's own sighs of pleasure.

His hand was unrelenting. Sparks skittered over her skin, light exploded beneath her eyes as she tightened around him before falling forward, catching herself on his chest as he followed her into utter bliss.

Her body felt boneless as she rolled off him, pushing a sweaty strand of hair from her face. Eyden's arm went around her hips, pulling her closer.

"You're wicked," Eyden whispered, his low voice curling her toes.

She put a hand on his bare chest, feeling his heartbeat. She was sure her own was running marathons. "You love it," she answered without thinking, and his eyes seemed to spark a million colours.

"Maybe." His hand ran down her thigh as one corner of his mouth pulled upwards.

The words she couldn't think out loud were getting louder in her head as she stared at him. Amidst everything, lying here with Eyden made her feel as if she could trust hope after all.

"Lora? Are you up?" a familiar voice said, drifting into her sub-consciousness as Lora blinked her eyes open. For a moment, she felt disoriented, expecting the walls of her room in the Turosian palace, but instead she glimpsed Eyden's face—his brown skin highlighted by the sunlight streaming in through the closed curtains.

"Lora?" Oscar said, his voice muffled by the wall separating them. Lora sat up fast, alerting Eyden, who shot up, his eyes scanning the room for danger. She tilted her head to the door, and Eyden reached for his clothes.

"Yes, I'm up," Lora called back to her brother. "I'll be right out." Her hands searched for her shirt and Eyden threw it to her, one brow raised suggestively. She bit back her grin as she dragged the shirt over her bare skin. She hastily pulled on her leggings, then took in Eyden standing next to the sofa bed, his trousers hanging low, revealing a stretch of bare skin that her lips had touched not long ago.

Her thoughts got hung up on last night until she remembered who was waiting for her. It would be better if Oscar didn't see Eyden here.

Lora cringed at her own thoughts, but Eyden seemed to catch her drift. He scolded his expression into a small smile before vanishing in an instant. Relieved, Lora smoothed down her tangled hair and went to the door.

"Morning," she said, taking in Oscar's expression, trying to read him, which she'd failed to do more than once.

"I made breakfast. Your favourite."

Lora smiled. "Mum's pancakes?" She could picture it. All of them sitting around the kitchen table back home before the pandemic had happened, before their lives had changed forever. Back when eating breakfast together was so utterly normal and not a rarity she never realised she would miss so much.

"Yes," Oscar replied, one hand in his pocket. His mouth formed a straight line. "I know it's not much, but I realised I never thanked you...for everything and I wanted to do something."

An invisible weight lifted off her shoulders. Fresh air filled her lungs as if she was back at the beach, back home. "You don't have to do anything but be here," Lora said, pulling him into a hug before he could change his mind. Oscar returned the hug hesitantly at first, then his arms tightened around her. For a second, they were younger again—unplagued by dark troubles.

When she pulled back, Oscar's eyes had turned glassy with unshed tears. "I'm sorry. I know I've been horrible. I just...don't really know who you are anymore." He wiped at his eyes with the sleeve of his sweater, his dark eyes hollow. "When I first saw you, I thought you made it back *for us*."

"I did." Lora's fingers curled into the soft material of his sweater as if to reassure him she was really here.

"Not entirely, though. Were you running to us or running *from* people?" The question knocked the breath out of her. Lora couldn't disagree even as she opened her mouth to reply. "It's like you started a whole new life and only came back because you were forced to. I know it's not fair of me to say that when you risked so much to save Mum—all of us—and I *am* thankful." He blinked away tears.

"These past months," Oscar continued, "they've been the hardest of my life, and I found myself picking up the phone and trying to reach you more than once. And there was just...nothing."

"I would have talked to you if I could." Her voice wavered as she pictured her brother, his phone clutched to his chest as he imagined his sister far away, unresponsive.

"I know that now. But when Mum almost died and suddenly there you were—I thought to myself that you heard me. You *knew* I needed you." Oscar turned his head, his lips quivering. "But you didn't hear me."

Something inside her broke with every word. "I would have come to you," Lora whispered furiously.

Oscar nodded, his dark hair falling into his teary eyes. "I wish we could go back. Back to before all of this started." A sob got caught in his throat. "I...I just want Mum. And you. Together. At home."

Lora pulled him towards her as tears escaped her eyes. "I know. Me too. I know there's been changes, but I'm still myself. Fae eyes or not. Powers or not. It doesn't change me."

She wasn't sure if she believed it herself, but a smile broke on Oscar's face, and that was all that mattered. No matter what, she'd always protect him. Even from the truth about herself.

CHAPTER 10

AMIRA

Tarnan scoffed as he spotted Wryen lounging on the Carnylen throne. Amira's heart raced in her chest, a veil of cold sweat coating her back. Following Tarnan and Amira, four guards spread out in silence inside the golden throne room.

"I see my dear sister never respects my wishes." Wryen twirled his extravagant dark gold crown sprinkled with amethysts in his lap, not moving from Tarnan's spot.

Approaching her brother with slow steps, Tarnan squinted at him. "You are no longer welcome here, Wryen."

"What are you going to do? Make me disappear like Karwyn? Rumours are starting to spread, Tarnan. Of course no one can find the body, but I'm sure you've gotten rid of all evidence of your betrayal. Karwyn had shared his suspicion about the Quarnian attack with me. You seem to have this strange fondness for my sister, but I never thought you would go as far as to kill another king. That will surely be grounds enough for you to be thrown out of the contest."

"*I* didn't kill Karwyn. And don't fool yourself into thinking you'd ever be picked by the advisors if I was thrown out," Tarnan snarled.

Wryen sprung up from the throne, his crown in his hands, trying but failing to hide his displeasure. "You admit it, then? He has been killed? By whom, if not you?" Wryen's gaze zeroed in on Amira, who stood back, fearing her mother's fate. "In any case, Amira will come back with me to Allamyst."

As he made a move towards her, Tarnan slapped the crown out of Wryen's hands. It crashed to the ground, the metallic clatter echoing through the throne room. "Amira is staying with me."

"I'm her brother, she will do as I say," Wryen growled. He pushed Tarnan back, flames sparking from his fingertips.

Tarnan barely reacted, his gaze never leaving Wryen's stormy lilac eyes—a colour that haunted Amira to this day. "If those rumours were true, it would be unwise for you to go against my wishes."

Hissing between his teeth, Wryen's fire decreased before he could singe Tarnan's jacket. His gaze travelled to Amira. "If you want your mother to survive, you'll come with me." Turning back to Tarnan, he added, "If you even entertain the thought of getting rid of me, if anyone touches so much as a hair on my head, Amira will never see her mother again—only her ashes."

Tarnan glared at him, calm, yet Amira could glimpse beyond the facade. This kind of calm meant he was furious underneath. "*You will let Amira decide for herself if she will join you.*"

Wryen's spine straightened as his eyes widened. *Compulsion.* It always stung like sharp ice against her skin.

Tugging on Tarnan's jacket, she got his attention. "Make him release my mother." Tarnan's eyes gleamed. She was taking advantage of the situation, but Tarnan understood it to be a sign of trust.

As Tarnan opened his mouth to reply, fire blasted him. As much as Amira despised him, Wryen wasn't as weak as she'd hoped. He held Tarnan behind a wall of flames as menacing as the fiery memories of her past. If she squinted she could almost picture her mother going up in flames, exactly like her first love had.

"I swear to you, Tarnan, if you try to pull dark magic on me again— or whatever it is you've stooped so low to use—I will find a way to end her mother's life even if it kills me too," Wryen screamed as guards rushed at him, but they were stopped by the flames. Dropping his fire wall, a victorious light swirled in Wryen's twisted eyes.

Tarnan stood very still, his blood-red eyes chillingly serious. Then he gave a slight nod, and Amira thought that would be the end of it. Instead, the guards charged forward again, drawing their almandine swords. The nearest guard got a fireball to the chest, but the second guard slashed at Wryen's arms. His furious gaze met Amira's across the room. She saw the promise in his eyes—her mother's death.

"Stop this," she begged Tarnan. "I don't want my mother to get hurt. *Please*. Let him go."

Tarnan snapped his fingers. "*Enough*," he yelled with his dark, cavernous voice. Everyone except Amira and Tarnan froze in place.

A faint smile appeared on Tarnan's lips. "I suppose we're at a stalemate, then." He gazed at Wryen, who clutched his injured arm, blood staining his dark purple satin sleeve. "I won't hurt you as long as you keep Amira's mother safe. But Amira decides for herself if she wants to stay."

Amira wondered why Tarnan didn't compel Wryen to bring her mother back. Were his powers limited by distance? Or maybe he had taken a page out of Wryen's book, aware that Amira would be more willing to do as Tarnan said with her mother's fate in his hands. He pretended Amira had a choice when, once again, it had been made for her.

Wryen's lips twisted into a cruel frown. He hated being outplayed, but Amira could tell he didn't see a way out of this one. He only had so many cards to play when he didn't have Amira as the ace up his sleeve.

Tarnan put his hand on Amira's shoulder, and she eyed his movement. Clenching the fabric of her dress, she restrained herself from knocking his hand off her. For a second, she thought about telling Wryen the truth about Tarnan, about Karwyn's death. She thought about going with her brother and letting him torture her until he would allow her to see her mother again—if he ever would. But Amira knew this was much bigger than herself. All of Liraen was in danger if Tarnan got his way.

Meeting her brother's insistent stare, she forced air into her lungs even as dread stole her breath. "I want to stay with Tarnan."

The lie burned her throat, but she forced herself to smile. Somehow, it seemed as if she'd prepared her whole life for this—silently plotting Tarnan's ruin while plastering a grin on her face. She had thought years of hiding her pain and faking happiness had trained her for a life as Karwyn's wife, but now she knew this was her true purpose.

CHAPTER 11

EYDEN

"Jesus Christ," Maja cursed as Eyden appeared in the kitchen, having drifted in from Lora's bedroom. "Can you give a girl a warning before you show up out of nowhere?"

Walking to the small kitchen table, Ilario held a plate of something sweet-smelling in his hand. "I'm fae and *I'm* not even used to that." He gave Eyden a pointed look, taking a seat next to Elyssa, who had her feet up on the table. Ilario's gaze met hers before moving to her legs, and she rolled her eyes as she put her feet on the floor.

Seeing Ilario and Elyssa interact—two important people in his life who he had kept from crossing paths—made Eyden smile. "Noted," Eyden replied.

"Get yourself a plate of pancakes," Maja told him as she picked up some sort of syrup and applied a generous amount to her plate. "Oscar made them."

Lora's brother wasn't Eyden's favourite person, but he knew he should try to keep out of it unless Lora asked him to intervene. He tried not to let it get to him, but this thing—this connection—between Lora and him, it was still new, fragile. He couldn't help but fear it might break and his heart along with it.

He could still hear Halie's voice in his ear telling him to get his shit together, to voice his feelings out loud. He hadn't. Not precisely, at least. But he hoped Lora knew, hoped that she saw right through to his burning heart.

Running a hand through his bedhead hair, Eyden followed Maja's suggestion and took a seat across from her with a plate of pancakes.

"Sleep well?" Maja asked after swallowing a bite, her grin teasing.

Eyden cleared his throat. "Very well."

"Very well?" Maja continued, tapping a finger on her chin. "Would you say it was *satisfying?*"

Elyssa almost choked on her glass of water.

Ilario glanced between everyone. "I feel like I'm missing something."

Maja grinned at Eyden. "I think Lora and Eyden got *exactly* what they were missing." Elyssa snorted, and Eyden threw her a dark glance, but he couldn't keep his own laugh contained. He was glad Elyssa could still laugh at all.

"What's so funny?" Oscar asked, entering the kitchen with Lora. Eyden's gaze met hers, and there was a new lightness behind her eyes that made his heart swell.

"Nothing," Maja quickly said.

Oscar, a small smile playing on his lips, got both him and Lora a plate. Taking a seat next to Eyden, Lora accepted the food.

"So where are we going for weapons?" Elyssa asked, gripping her fork as if she wasn't against going in with nothing but cutlery as protection.

"I was thinking I should go with you," Lora interjected before Maja could answer.

"I don't think you should unless you absolutely have to," Maja replied. "The police might not recognise Eyden and El, but someone might identify you. You were all over social media. I switched my data off when we met up, but I saw you guys all over the internet before then. You went viral in under half an hour. Every one of you could be recognised, but most of all you, Lora. I don't know how they identified you so quickly."

Lora's eyes widened.

Eyden tried to catch her gaze as he searched for an explanation, but

Ilario was quicker. "I'm not the only one who has no clue what Maja's saying, right?"

Lora quickly explained.

Oscar sat up straighter and the chair creaked loudly, catching everyone's attention. "I was in the hospital at the time. I haven't looked at my phone. Can...can I see these videos?"

"I don't think we should go online," Lora replied, speaking in her foreign slang. Eyden had noticed her British accent had returned too. He still remembered how quickly Lora had copied their Turosian accent.

"I do have one video," Maja threw in. "The first one I saw, I saved it to my phone." Maja threw Lora a quick look before removing her phone from her pocket. Her fingers flew over the screen, then she handed it to Oscar. He got up, taking his plate with him to the sink. His eyes were glued to the screen.

"So to sum up, I'm public enemy number one?" Lora said, her voice thin.

Maja leaned forward. "It'll be cleared up once all of this is over. In the meantime, I can go."

"Are you sure?"

Maja glanced at Eyden. "What the heck? I'm up for a little teleporting. We should go soon."

"Couldn't agree more." Elyssa shot up from her seat.

"Going where?" a deeper voice Eyden recognised as Rhay's said. Lora tried to catch his attention while Ilario shrunk back in his chair.

"You're up." Lora's eyes travelled over his wrinkled, mundane clothes. His trousers were a light grey and his pink sweater had words written on it. It said: "I care." But there was a round chocolate thing in the middle of the words. Judging by his hair sticking in all directions and the shadows under his eyes, he was hungover. No crystal would save him now.

"Smart observation, little Adelway," Rhay bit out. "I'm out of alcohol. So, where are you going and is there booze?"

"We're getting weapons, not booze," Maja replied, sternly. "We'll need to do a food run at some point and hit up the gas station nearby. Wait until then."

"Maja is right," Lora said. "We can't take the risk to get alcohol, and besides, it would be better if you'd—"

Rhay marched forward and slammed his hands on the table in front of Lora. "You know what would be *better*? Not being tricked into killing my best friend."

Lora flinched, biting her lip so hard Eyden thought she'd draw blood. "I told you, that was never my intention."

"I'm having a hard time believing someone who isn't even honest with themself," Rhay said, his voice vicious. Ilario dug his fingers into his arm.

"You're out of line." Eyden rose next to Rhay.

Elyssa crossed her arms. "Like, *way*."

Lora stood up too. When she took a step forward, Rhay moved back, his eyes punishing. "Can we talk about this? Alone?" Lora pleaded. Rhay froze, and for a second it seemed he might agree, but then another voice cut through the room.

It took Eyden less than a second to recognise Lora's voice even though it sounded strangely far away. "I needed to break out of this shell, this *lie* I've lived in. It's like...my whole life, I was only half alive. I *am* half-fae."

Lora's lips hadn't moved. Panic flashed in her eyes as she whirled around, her gaze catching on Maja's phone in Oscar's hand.

Lora's voice coming from the device cracked. "And I don't regret it. I don't regret feeling the fire swirl inside my veins. I don't regret meeting the friends I've made here, the revolution I've joined."

In the present, Lora stopped in front of Oscar, whose eyes were fixed on the screen with a look of betrayal. "Turn it off." Lora reached for the device, but Oscar held tight.

Her voice from the past continued, "I don't regret falling... I don't regret any of it. So please, please, see this as a positive in all the darkness. I would do it all over again in a heartbeat—" The sound cut as Maja snatched her phone from Oscar's hands.

"You weren't meant to watch that," Maja said. Lora's eyes were locked on Oscar, her lips trembling.

Oscar seemed eerily calm for once. "Who was this meant for?" Lora opened and closed her mouth. "What? You have no more lies for me now?" His voice was rising, his calmness evaporating quickly.

"Oscar—" Lora started, but her brother pushed himself off the counter and rushed to the door.

He halted in the doorway. "I don't know what's worse, that you don't regret leaving us or that you lied to my face when you said you were still the same." He looked over his shoulder, his gaze lit with blinding sorrow. When Lora stepped forward, Oscar raised his hand. "Don't." He left.

The room was utterly quiet. Eyden stepped next to Lora, pulling her stoic body against his.

Elyssa cleared her throat. "I think this is our sign to get ready. Sorry, Lora." Her hand brushed Lora's shoulder as she left the room. Ilario and Maja followed after her.

Eyden's hand reached for Lora's and she intertwined their fingers. "You should go. Get those weapons," she said. "I'll try to reason with Rhay. At least one person should forgive me today. Just be careful and take care of Maja, okay?"

Eyden nodded. She let him hold her for a minute. It was a minute well spent, a minute his heart was content even as he wished he could take all the weight off her shoulders.

Maja had been gone longer than expected. Eyden could tell Elyssa was getting impatient as she paced up and down the alley behind the store. He had drifted them a few towns over to make sure no one would track them back to the cabin. The brick walls in the empty alley-way reminded him of Chrysa. Yet the roofs here weren't flat. The shop's sign above the door was strikingly bright instead of merely painted on. The huge advertisement on the wall next to the door showed a young woman with weapons stacked in her arms, the prices all displayed in pounds instead of silver. He definitely wasn't home anymore. He had never really been anywhere, and he strangely found himself missing the familiar streets of Chrysa. Back there, he knew what would await him around every corner, even if it was often danger.

As Maja was the only one not *online*, as Lora had said, she was the best option to go in, and so she had entered the store alone a while ago. The midday sun was out, but it was colder than in Turosian. Even bundled up in jackets, the air was icy. Maja had suggested they wear thick winter coats, but both Eyden and Elyssa had refused, hating the restriction of movement. Instead, they froze as they waited for Maja to buy as many weapons as she could carry. She had told them that stores like this one weren't too popular, but since fae had invaded Earth seventy-five years ago, they weren't illegal either.

"I should've gone in," Elyssa muttered, straightening her hat that hid her face.

Eyden was about to reply when a blaring alarm caught his attention. Elyssa followed his line of sight to a police car pulling up at the front of the alley.

An officer, as Lora had called them, got out of what he now knew was a car. "No loitering, move along." He waved his hand past the car to the open street. A second officer was waiting in the passenger seat, her mouth set in a straight line.

Eyden's eyes were partly shielded by a hat that Maja had given him.

"We're waiting for our friend." Elyssa tilted her hat back just enough to show him an innocent smile.

The officer glanced at the sign on the building displaying "Weapons & More."

"What's your business here?" he asked.

Eyden's hand twitched as he thought of the pocket knife in his jacket. Usually he had more weapons on him.

"You there." The officer stared at him. "Take off your hat."

"I don't see how that's necessary," Elyssa threw in, not hiding the annoyance in her tone. She grabbed the officer's arm as he headed towards Eyden.

The officer stilled, his hand firmly on his gun. "Miss, take your hands off me. Now."

Eyden could see in his sister's eyes that this wasn't going to end well.

Elyssa pulled closer to the officer, her eyes innocent, her small smile anything but. "Or what?" *Damn you, Elyssa.*

The officer shrugged off her grip, his hand clasping his gun, but before he could pull it out of its sheath, Elyssa's boot connected with his knee, throwing him off balance. She was a vision of blurry red hair as she kneed him between his legs and reached for the gun, kicking at his shin.

Aiming the gun, Elyssa glared at the officer. "Get back in your car and go."

One hand on his stomach, the officer tried to catch his breath. Eyden barely heard the metallic click of the gun of the second officer before she pulled the trigger. In a flash, Eyden drifted in front of Elyssa and the bullet hit his shoulder. His hat fell off as the force of it made him spin ninety degrees. It wasn't almandine, but he could feel the little metal piece tearing through layers of skin, forcing its way out. The burn made his breath hitch, the sensation of getting shot unfamiliar. He didn't care to repeat it.

"Eyden!" Elyssa shouted as he clutched at the blood pooling from the bullet wound.

"He's fae!" the first officer yelled as the second one ran forward, her gun in her hands.

"Raise your hands!" the female officer screamed, and Eyden reluctantly followed her command. Elyssa remained stubborn until Eyden tilted his head at her. She dropped the gun.

The officer pointed her gun at them. "I told you they can't hold the border! Look how far one has gotten already. Jesus, I think he's part of the wanted group who crossed first. It's the bloody apocalypse. We should kill them now. Line the border with fae corpses like the old times."

Eyden gritted his teeth. Was this how Elyssa had felt every day in Liraen?

"Fuck you," Elyssa spat out. "I don't need to listen to this."

"El—" Eyden started, but she wasn't listening. She rushed forward, and a gun was fired as Elyssa twisted the human's hand. The bullet hit the wall behind them. The other officer ran forward, but Eyden drifted in front of him and punched him in the face so hard he slumped to the ground.

When Eyden turned his head, he spotted the female officer on the ground, Elyssa above her—hitting her again and again. Elyssa's eyes were glazed over in rage. Her fists were hard and unrelenting.

Eyden stopped next to her, gripping her fist before she could strike again. She struggled against his hold. "No, I have to keep going," Elyssa muttered, trying desperately to throw another punch even as her body trembled. Her knuckles were raw and bloody. "They could have hurt us. She could be hurt..."

"*She?*" Eyden said, and Elyssa's struggles ceased as she turned to him.

"I...I can't do anything to save her," she said, her voice desperate. "I can only do this." She stared at the unconscious officer as if coming back to herself. Her brows creased as she glanced at the blood on her hands. "Fuck." Elyssa scrambled to her feet.

Maja chose that moment to reappear, a metal cart on wheels filled with weapons in front of her. "Jesus, what happened?" she shouted, halting on the other side of the alley.

"Funny story," Elyssa started, laughing without joy. Alarms blared through the air so loud even Elyssa seemed to hear it as her gaze swung to the street. Another police car was approaching fast. They were trapped in this alley. It was time to go.

"Can you drift us with the cart?" Elyssa screamed at him over the noise.

"I can try." Eyden had a deep fear of showcasing his powers, but he had already been forced to use them before. And who here would put him on a list to be experimented on? Karwyn was gone. It was over, wasn't it?

Car doors slammed open behind them. He went to reach for Elyssa's hand at the same time as Maja put one foot on the bottom of the metal cart and kicked off the ground with the other, rolling towards them fast.

A voice behind them shouted, "Freeze!"

"Get on the cart," Eyden yelled at Elyssa, knowing it moved too fast to drift to without them colliding and possibly falling over.

Eyden distantly heard footsteps approaching and guns being drawn. Everything seemed to slow as they ran forward. Elyssa ducked, catching the gun of the unconscious police officer a split second before she jumped onto one side of the moving cart, almost tipping it over before Eyden stepped on the other side.

Gripping the moving cart with one arm, Elyssa half spun, firing a shot at the approaching car and shattering the front window to gain them another second.

A bullet sliced the air nonetheless, hurtling towards them so fast it was nothing but a blur to Eyden. He followed its path right to Elyssa's chest just as the cart tipped over and he threw them into nothingness.

CHAPTER 12

RHAY

No one had noticed him sneaking away. Why would they? He was *no one*.

After walking along the empty icy road for what seemed like an eternity, Rhay spotted the shop Maja had spoken of. Two cars were parked by the entrance. Someone was holding a pump attached to their vehicle. Rhay recognised this sort of place from his extensive knowledge of reality TV. Here, people bought cheap alcohol to get *absolutely pissed*, as they liked to say. Just what he needed.

A woman hurrying out of the shop gave him a strange look as Rhay walked by, tilting his head down on his way to the entrance. She wore a thick coat, and Rhay was reminded of the cold seeping into his veins, his sweater providing little protection. The human world was too cold for his liking, but maybe frostbite was exactly what he deserved.

Pushing the sunglasses he had stolen from the cabin up his nose, Rhay stepped inside the shop. The cashier barely glanced at him. Rhay was thankful for it as he wore the worst clothes he had ever seen.

Browsing the shelves, he found nothing from Liraen. He picked up a basket and filled it with random items that appealed to him. The humans seemed to have a passion for flashy packaging and every possible flavour of crisps.

Looking around, Rhay couldn't find any hard liquor. However, he did find something intriguing—a box of what looked like hair dye. Rhay caught sight of his reflection on the strange round mirror above his head. His pastel blue hair sticking out of his hood looked washed out and miserable. But it was still too joyful for how he felt. Rhay picked up a box of hair dye and put it in his basket.

On his way to the cashier, Rhay noticed the hard liquor locked in the cabinet behind him. Putting on a large fake smile, Rhay approached the visibly bored cashier. The young man had curly red hair and multiple piercings in his ears. His gaze was fixed on a small TV playing behind the counter.

"Hey there, my friend." Rhay flashed him a smile.

"How can I help you?" His tone made it clear he hated his job. It was such a movie reaction. The old Rhay would have been amused.

"Three bottles of vodka," Rhay said as if it was a regular order. He enjoyed his misery with a side of vodka.

The cashier eyed him up and down. He took note of Rhay's wrinkled clothes, his bright pink sunglasses, and his basket filled with crisps and candy. "Planning a big party, mate? You look like you haven't come down from the last one."

Rhay forced himself to talk in a seductive tone, each word hurting him more. "You wanna come?" He lowered his sunglasses and added a wink for good measure.

The cashier stilled for a second, Rhay's power subtly changing his mood. Rhay had always tried to refrain from using his powers for his own benefit—and, frankly, he had never needed to, charming as he was. Now, he only cared about getting his hands on booze. But two days of non-stop drinking had weakened him.

"Whatever, mate. Can I see some ID?"

What in Liraen was an ID? "I don't think that's necessary. *Mate.*"

"It's the law. I can ring your other products, though." The cashier gestured to Rhay's basket.

Gathering his strength and keeping the hangover at bay, Rhay let a sickly sweet smile spread across his lips. "Mate, you know what would really stick it to your boss? If you'd let me leave without paying. And if you added three...no, four bottles of vodka." Rhay tapped into the human's emotions and twisted them to his needs, fighting against the headache plaguing his mind.

Transfixed, the cashier turned around and opened the cabinet behind him. Smiling briefly, Rhay turned his head, catching sight of the TV. He gasped as he recognised himself on the screen. A video of the group's arrival on the beach was playing. The headline on the bottom of the screen read: 'The border has fallen—Fae sighting in Bournchester.'

Rhay had always dreamed of appearing in one of the humans' little films. But he had hoped he would look devastatingly handsome, not a bloody mess.

"Oh yeah, that's crazy, mate. It's all they talk about on the news. The army's here now trying to secure the border." The cashier had followed his gaze. "They're blasting anyone coming through, as they should. Those freaks should be sent back where they came from. The shop's been pretty much deserted. Everyone's getting as far away from the border as possible." Rhay might have cared about the cashier's insulting tone, but he had stopped caring the moment his best friend had died in his arms.

The screen switched to a picture of Lora. A younger Lora, looking incredibly human. The headline said she was suspected of conspiring against humans and should be brought in for questioning. Fearing his own identity could be compromised any minute, Rhay grabbed the bags the cashier had filled and left.

As he exited the shop, Rhay was violently pulled to the side, the bottles in his bags clinking against each other.

"Are you out of your bloody mind? You've put us all at risk for booze?" Lora pushed him behind the building, away from the road, a storm brewing in her eyes.

Rhay knew he should feel shame, but instead, he let a dark laugh escape his lips. "Is there a better reason to put someone's life at risk?"

Lora stormed forward, forcing Rhay's back to the wall behind him. He set his bags on the ground. "This isn't a joke, Rhay! You could have been discovered."

"Don't pretend you care. Your only concern is your precious human family. How about I do you all a favor and get out of your hair?" He turned, but Lora pushed against his chest. His back almost hit the cement wall.

"Don't you dare run away. I—"

"Don't want anyone to trail my steps back to you? It would suck if anyone found you, wouldn't it? I've seen your picture on TV. Apparently, you didn't just betray me, but all of humankind."

Lora reached out so fast Rhay barely tracked her movement as she pushed against his shoulders until he hit the cold wall behind him, stealing his breath.

He kicked off the wall. "Did it feel good? Violence comes naturally to you now it seems."

Lora stepped back half a step, a sigh on her lips. "It doesn't. You know me, Rhay. Do you really think I wanted things to go down this way?"

Rhay laughed again, the broken sound echoing through his bones. "I *know* you? That might be the worst lie you've told yet. I have *no idea* who you are." He threw up his arms, gesturing around them. "You never told me shit, nothing *real*, at least. *I* told you plenty, all the intel you needed."

"I couldn't tell you everything, but that doesn't mean I wasn't your friend. I still *am*," Lora said. Rhay shook his head, his hood falling back from the vicious breeze. "You once told me you *see* me. Remember that? I'm still that person."

"I don't know anything anymore." His skin was ice cold, but not because of the weather.

Lora walked closer, trapping him in her gaze. "Well, I *see* you, Rhay. I *care*."

"What do you see?"

"I see someone in pain who cares deeply but doesn't want to confront his own emotions. I see someone falling into darkness when he could shine so bright. I see the person I once told he needed to choose who he wanted to be." Her eyes shined bright, the warmth infuriating when all he wanted to feel was pain. "You still have that choice, Blue. Don't waste it."

"How can I care about any of it when I've betrayed everyone and everything I've ever known?" Rhay dropped his gaze, his heart pulling him down into a pit of guilt. "Why should I get a choice?" A strand of blue hair fell into his eye. Rhay couldn't muster the effort to push it back. "I'm nothing now, just...*blue*."

To his surprise, Lora embraced him, her arms pulling him towards her. Rhay's arms went limp at his sides. For a second, Rhay thought about letting go. He imagined himself burying his face in Lora's neck, letting tears stain her coat. Then the shock wore off and he pushed against her, not wanting—not *deserving*—any of her kindness.

"You can wipe away that smile, little Adelway. I'll never forgive you for how it all ended." *And I'll never forgive myself for killing my best friend.*

Not looking back, Rhay grabbed his bags from the ground and walked away. He knew what he had to do: drown his sorrows until he forgot that he hated everyone—especially *himself.*

Lora trailed him the whole way back. Glancing behind him, he caught her with her arms crossed, her fingernails digging into her soft coat. Rhay looked ahead and with relief noticed the cabin a short distance away.

Rio sat on the front steps, his foot bouncing against the snow-covered ground. He was wrapped in a moss green coat that couldn't top his striking emerald eyes. Rhay's last words to Rio haunted him, but he needed a distraction.

"Come with me, I need your help." Rhay crossed over the threshold, Rio on his heels as Rhay knew he would be. In silence, he led him to one of the bathrooms. Rhay closed the door behind them. In the tiny space, their chests were almost touching. Confusion and anger mixed with intrigue in Rio's eyes, making them sparkle.

Taking a step back, Rhay put his bags on the tiled floor.

"What are we doing here?" Rio whispered, his breathing shaky.

Rhay took out the black hair dye. "I need your help dyeing my hair."

Rio's eyes widened. "I've never done...I mean sure, I can help."

"Great; you better read the instructions." Rhay shoved the box into Rio's hands.

While Rio tried to decipher the instructions, Rhay took off his horrendous sweatshirt, exposing his bronze skin. He noticed Rio's not-so-discreet glance. Maybe Rhay needed more than alcohol to forget.

"I think I got it. You should sit." Rio avoided looking at Rhay's exposed chest. He was so easily flustered it almost made Rhay smile. Almost.

Looking around the tiny space, Rhay grabbed the small stool by the shower. He sat down, the back of his head above the sink.

They stayed silent while Rio finished preparing the coal black mix. Rio took a strand of Rhay's hair in his hand. The washed-out pastel blue looked dreary. It reminded Rhay of the last time his hair had been dyed. By Varsha, another person lost to him. Her smile had brightened every room she entered. She'd never failed to cheer him up and now she'd never smile again.

"Are you sure you want to do this?" Rio asked.

Rhay sighed, pushing the memory back into the abyss. "Paint it black, love."

The first stroke of the brush against Rhay's scalp felt incredibly cold. Rhay tried to hide his shiver, but Rio noticed. "Are you sure you're fine?"

"Let's get this over with." Rhay closed his eyes, trying to focus on nothing but Rio's touch. Slowly, Rhay's hair was coated in ash black dye. His hair hadn't been black, his natural hair colour, in almost fifteen years. Against his will, Rhay let out a pained sigh.

Rio's hand stilled. "We don't have to talk about what you said last time." Rhay's eyes were closed, but he felt Rio's presence everywhere. His voice was strained as if he was unsure of Rhay's reaction. "When did you first dye your hair?"

"I was a teenager." Rhay tried to picture himself with bright yellow hair—he'd done it himself before he'd met Varsha. "My father hated it."

"Why did you dye it?" Rio asked, his fingers running through Rhay's wet hair.

"I..." The past caught up to him as his chest tightened. He could see his father's eyes when he'd first seen his dyed hair. It hadn't been the reaction he'd craved. "I wanted my father to see me."

"In what way?" Rio massaged his head to get the dye on every strand. Rhay forced himself not to enjoy it.

"Any way," Rhay whispered, squeezing his eyes shut tight. "He tried his best to ignore me. All he saw when he looked at me was my mother. I thought I could change that. Him. *Myself.*"

Rio's movements slowed but his fingers were still curled in Rhay's hair. "I'm sorry," Rio said, his voice loud in the small space. "I—"

"Rio..." Rhay opened his eyes. Rio's breath caressed Rhay's forehead, sending a tingling spark down his back. His eyes were much too kind for his own good. He was expecting so much of him, things that Rhay could never live up to. "You're done here, I'll manage the rest." Rhay stood up hastily, forcing Rio back.

"But the dye is still in your hair." Rio raised his stained hands.

"I'll rinse it off. Just go."

"What if I don't want to go?" His eyes tracked Rhay's lips, and Rhay bit back a gasp. Rio reached out, pushing back a strand covering Rhay's forehead. The gesture was so simple, yet Rhay's knees went weak.

Rio's hand went to his cheek, staining it black. The acidic smell of the dye burned Rhay's nose, but he was only focused on Rio. "If you let me, I'll be there for you. You're not alone, Nix. Don't push me away."

Rhay swallowed, losing himself in emerald green—the colour radiating comfort, yet a simmer of heat too. His head inched closer to Rio by its own command. Rio's hand warmed his face as electricity covered every inch of him. How easy it would be to cross the distance between them. To capture Rio's full lips and discover what drove him wild. The thought went right to his lower belly.

But he couldn't pull Rio in just to ruin his kind soul.

Rhay stepped back fast, Rio's hand dropping from his face as his brows drew together.

"I told you to go," Rhay forced himself to say even as he felt a tear pricking his eye. Opening the door, he waited for Rio to take the hint.

Lowering his head, Rio walked out. He stopped in the hallway, throwing a glance over his shoulder. "I meant what I said. I'm here if you want to talk. But you can only push me away so many times before I stop coming back."

CHAPTER 13

☾

LORA

A mix of anger and regret filled Lora as Rhay headed into the cabin with Ilario. She couldn't blame him for feeling betrayed. Lora had known Karwyn would most likely not walk away from that night, but she'd never imagined it would be Rhay dealing the killing blow.

Heading down the hall, Lora entered her mother's room as she'd done many times these last days to reassure herself that her mum was still breathing. Oscar slept in a sand-coloured armchair next to the stolen hospital bed. His head fell forward, his dark hair almost covering his closed eyes.

"He barely leaves her side." Lora's gaze snapped to the corner of the room where her father lounged on one of the beds. Both him and her brother had been staying in this room. They didn't have all the equipment a hospital would have to track her mum's heartbeat, but her father kept close watch. Lora wondered if her mum was alive because she was in some sort of magical coma. She tracked the IV bag that was hooked to her arm. Would she be alive at all if magic wasn't involved? If something was holding Lora to her contract even with Karwyn gone, they had to break that connection to free her mother.

"No change?" Lora took a seat next to her father. The old wood of the single bed creaked loudly, but her brother remained peacefully asleep.

"No. Do you really think your friends, the witches, will be able to break..." He trailed off, probably remembering what Eyden had said about Lora not being able to talk about Karwyn's agreement. "...to save your mother?"

Lora took a deep breath, her hand running over the soft sheets. "I have to believe there's a chance. I almost lost all hope, but I didn't give up. Even if I had to..." Her fingers clasped the cool crystal around her neck. In her memory she saw the heart-shaped almandine pendant her mother had given her—the one Lora had worn for the better part of her life to block her powers.

"Why haven't you freaked out?" Lora asked. "I know you must have noticed that I'm not...the same."

A small smile lifted the corners of his lips. "I'm just happy you're alive. Nothing else matters. I can't begin to imagine what you've gone through. Your mother—whatever magic is keeping her alive, it's thanks to you. Remember that, Lora. Whatever happens, you did save her from the virus. *All* of us."

Lora's throat tightened as she let the honesty of his words wander to her bruised heart. She hadn't realised how much she needed to hear him say that.

Her gaze wandered from her mother's closed eyes to the medical equipment spread out on the bedside table. "Do you have enough supplies here to keep her alive?"

"For now, yes. But we can't stay here forever. Do you remember my uni friend Bradley? He works at a hospital a few hours from here. Maybe we could convince him to get us more supplies."

Lora twisted her hands. "You should." Her father's gaze met hers, and his startled breath told her he got her meaning. Her family would have to relocate, hide somewhere else. But not Lora. She had an enemy to defeat and friends waiting for her.

Her father's eyes drifted to the crystal on the chain around her neck, still in her hand. "When your mum gave you that almandine necklace as a child, I knew the day would come when you would take it off."

Lora blinked back tears, clutching the crystal almost painfully. "I had to. To survive. But I don't regret it. It was inevitable."

"I want you to know I'm proud of how strong you are, Lora. Oscar, he's scared. He needs more time."

A sob echoed through her as she wrapped her arms around her father. She buried her head on his shoulder, feeling like a child again—utterly safe. For a split second, she wondered if she'd ever feel even a sliver of peace with her birth father. It seemed unfathomable.

A crash coming from the front door struck through her train of thoughts. The others must be back. She pulled out of their embrace.

"Go," her father said. "We'll be fine."

A smile pulled at her lips as her heart lightened. Lora glanced at her sleeping brother one last time, wishing—hoping—he would come to accept her. Then she headed to the front door, her feet quick as worry drove her on.

"Jesus, that stings," Lora heard Maja curse. A tipped-over shopping cart lay on the porch, weapons sprawled across the wooden floor. Maja knelt next to it, her hand pressed to her upper arm over her thick winter coat.

Elyssa cringed as she lowered herself next to Maja, tugging at Maja's coat. "Let me see."

Eyden was with them. His hand pressed into his shoulder; his sweater was drenched with blood.

Lora rushed towards them, her gaze swinging from Eyden back to Maja. "What the hell happened?"

Eyden turned to her, smiling faintly as if the wound wasn't bothering him all that much.

"The freaking police fired at us," Elyssa answered for him, helping Maja out of her jacket. Eyden shot her a look. "Okay, fine, I may have provoked them a tiny bit—but they had it coming."

"Fuck," Maja ground out between clenched teeth. Her arm slipped free from the torn jacket and Lora spotted the blood on her upper arm. Falling to her knees, Lora gently turned Maja's arm towards her. The wound looked deep, blood gushing. She grabbed Maja's jacket and pressed it to her skin. Maja let out a pained scream. "Motherfucker. Remind me not to get shot ever again."

"I tried to get us away as quickly as possible," Eyden said, his face ashen, pressing on his own bullet wound.

Footsteps came from inside the house. Her father's gaze landed on Lora's hand on Maja's bleeding arm. "Get her into the kitchen and keep pressing on it," he said. Lora and Elyssa steadied Maja as they headed into the house.

In the kitchen, her father took over, cleaning Maja's wound with a grim expression. "It's a scrape, thankfully; it could have been much worse." He eyed Eyden's blood-drenched sweater. "You're next."

"Everyone okay?" Ilario asked as he entered the kitchen.

"We got weapons and we got away," Elyssa said as if that was enough, arms crossed while leaning against the kitchen counter.

Biting her lip, Lora wasn't so sure. Sending Maja had been a mistake. Eyden walked up to her, his finger subtly brushing the back of her hand.

Sitting on the kitchen table, Maja brushed her fringe out of her face with her free arm. The smile on her face was too big. "I feel like this is the part of the movie where a montage shows everyone training for the big battle."

"We don't have time to train," Elyssa said, her red curls coming out of her ponytail as she pushed herself off the counter. "The question is, how do we get that goddamn agreement? *Soon.*"

"And how do we know Tarnan doesn't already have it?" Maja threw in, watching Lora's father bandage her arm.

"If he did get his hands on it, it would have been a big attack on the government. So big they wouldn't have been able to hide it," Lora replied. After Rhay had mentioned seeing her on TV, Lora had gotten curious. "I found a radio here and I've been listening to what they're saying about us. Some fae have crossed the border, but besides the guards, I don't think Tarnan sent them. He can't enslave humans if his guards kill them all."

"Tarnan is waiting for something," Eyden said.

Ilario nodded next to him. "He's been planning his revenge for decades. He must know something about the location of the human agreement."

Lora's lips parted as an idea sparked in her mind. "We need to get one of Tarnan's guards." She glanced at Eyden. "If I can read their mind, I can get intel."

"Whoa, did you just say you can read minds?" Maja asked, her mouth gaping open. Her father's hand stilled on her arm for a few seconds before he continued. "Jesus, what *can't* you do?"

"I don't actually know how it works yet. I've only done it accidently." She had to look away from Eyden's piercing gaze before her skin set on fire at the memory.

Elyssa paced back and forth. "We can't keep waiting. Once we have the agreement, we storm the fucking palace."

"No holding back." Eyden tilted his chin. Elyssa's hazel eyes brightened, her smile true.

Lora didn't know if it would work, but she did know that they would try. They would fight while keeping her family safe. Giving up wasn't in anyone's cards.

It was Lora's turn to keep watch at Damir's door. Eyden had offered to take her shift, but she had reasoned with him that he needed rest just as much as everyone else. A bullet wound might not be a big deal for him, but he still exerted himself. It was past midnight when Lora silently sneaked through the hall.

Stepping around the corner, she glimpsed Ilario sitting by Damir's door, his head turned away from her. Her feet stilled as Ilario swung the door open, his hand visibly unsteady.

"I was wondering when you'd open the door," Damir said. She couldn't see him from her position, only the back of Ilario's head. Damir's voice was deeper than Layken's had been, but she could hear the similarity of their tone—unbothered as if nothing could catch him off guard.

Ilario's shoulders sank. "So you knew I was out here."

"Of course I knew." The arrogance in Damir's tone made Lora's skin prickle.

"Is that all you have to say?" Ilario asked.

"You didn't ask me anything."

"You know the question. Give me a reason, an excuse, *anything*. Why did you make me believe you were taken, *dead*, for the past three years?" Ilario's voice rose, but his tone was as if he'd been beaten down.

She wished she could see Damir's expression as he said, "I don't have anything to say that you would want to hear, Marsyn."

"You care so little that you don't even think I deserve an explanation?" Ilario sighed. It was a pained, betrayed sound. "Why did you save me at all, then?"

"Call it gut instinct."

Ilario shook his head, his black hair shining in the low light. Lora shifted her weight and a floorboard creaked beneath her foot. Ilario turned, stepping out of the storage room.

Lora moved forward. "Sorry. I was going to take over. If you want me to."

"He's all yours. You better lock the door." Ilario brushed past her fast, his face drained of colour. He rounded the corner without looking back.

"Cosy space you got here," Lora commented as she took a seat on the carpeted floor in the doorway. Damir sat on an air mattress which took up almost the entire space. Behind him were shelves filled with food and bottles of water. Bloody bandages covered the top of the bin in the corner.

Damir's dark violet eyes watched her every move. They were so different than Layken's lazuli eyes, yet she could see the Layken she'd known in Damir's face. His hair was now shorter and lighter, a few shades darker than Lora's. She remembered seeing a scar running through his left brow, but it was gone now. He wasn't wearing a shirt, but the majority of his chest was covered in bandages, dried blood visible over the spot where the sword had gone through.

"What do you want, Adelway?" Damir snapped, leaning his arms on his knees as he sat up straighter.

"What's your deal?"

"Currently? I'm a wounded prisoner." He gestured at his chest. "Thought that was obvious."

"You know what I mean. Why did you keep Ilario in the dark and start working for Karwyn?"

"I don't see how that's any of your business."

Lora leaned her head against the doorframe as she crossed her legs. "Fine. Then tell me this, why did you rat me out to Saydren yet didn't tell Karwyn about me sneaking out?"

Damir watched her. She wished she could tell what he was thinking. She tried to focus her energy, tried to break through his façade, but she got nothing.

"Why do you think it was me who told Saydren?" Damir asked.

Lora huffed. "Because you're Karwyn's spy."

He was silent for another beat. "It wasn't me."

"Then who was it?" Lora leaned forward, trying to read him again, but he was like a block of ice, reflecting her own thoughts back at her. "Why should I believe you?"

"Frankly, I don't give a shit."

"If you don't care then why didn't you tell Karwyn about Eyden visiting me? Because of Ilario?" The name softened his gaze the tiniest bit. "You *do* still care about him."

"Not in the way it matters."

Lora laughed. "You're so good at pretending you even fool yourself. Do you even know how not to pretend?"

"Do you?" he shot back. "The kitchen is so close, I can hear most of your conversations."

"What's your point?"

"I heard you talk to your brother. I wonder, are you only pretending for his sake or are you pretending for yourself too?" She gave him her best cold stare, but the corner of his mouth pulled up. "Do you pretend the ritual never happened? That you're not more fae, more powerful than ever?"

Lora's blood pumped faster, yet her heart seemed to slow. "You don't know what you're talking about."

His grin widened dangerously. "No, *you* don't know what you're talking about, Adelway. You don't know shit about me."

"I know Ilario was with you once, so you can't be all bad."

"Wrong. It makes me the worst kind of person of all."

"Which is?"

Damir's gaze chilled the air. "The kind that would hurt someone as pure as him and not think twice about it."

"I can't imagine Karwyn gave you a choice. What was the alternative to spying for him? Death?"

Damir let out a dark chuckle that went right under her skin. "He did give me an ultimatum." The look he gave her almost made her flinch. His gaze was as piercing as the sharp edge of a blade. "But I never signed a blood contract."

Lora inhaled sharply. She'd been trapped by Karwyn, forced to abide by his commands. If Damir had never entered such an agreement, why had he stayed in the place Lora had wished nothing more than to escape?

Damir shifted on the air mattress, laying on his back, his eyes trained on the ceiling as if the conversation was over. Yet he spoke one last time. "I may play pretend, but I've never claimed to be good."

CHAPTER 14

AMIRA

Amira remembered the way to Farren's room. After sending Wryen away a few days ago, Tarnan had allowed her a bit more freedom. He had forced her and Farren to cast a spell over the palace, preventing them from leaving, but she was able to walk around the courtyard without a guard once a day. She had taken advantage of this newfound trust to sneak out to see Farren.

Walking fast in the winding corridor, Amira thought back on the spell they had cast to secure the palace. She had studied it closely, aware of how to break it. Tarnan had been using his compulsion power daily on Farren to prevent him from leaving, which told her Tarnan's power wasn't limitless. Escaping wasn't impossible if Farren's compulsion was lifted. She had to bide her time, figure out how to use Tarnan to their advantage while they were stuck here.

A guard entered the hallway, and Amira flattened herself around a corner just in time. She was supposed to have lunch with Tarnan soon, but she wanted to see Farren. They had been training for two days straight under Saydren's watchful eye. From dawn till dusk, with only a short break for Amira to have lunch with Tarnan, they practiced their magic.

She was growing stronger, her powers responding to her like never before. Saydren thought she showed great promise. Under different circumstances, she would have felt proud. She longed to see Elyssa and the others again. She wondered how Rhay was dealing with Karwyn's death, if the guilt was tearing him apart. Knowing him, his coping mechanisms would only hurt him further. At least he had Lora there to console him.

Once she reached the underground unseen, her one concern was the guards standing in front of Farren's room. Amira tried to gather all the energy she had left. Using her powers, she smashed the two guards against the wall. Running up to them before they could scramble back to their feet, she pressed a moonstone against their skulls to make them fall asleep. Amira had managed to swipe the crystal during a training session when Saydren hadn't been looking.

She grabbed the key to Farren's room from one of the guards' pockets and opened the door.

"Amira? How did you get here?" Farren rose from the bed.

Amira closed the door behind her silently. "Tarnan's intent on showing me his trust by letting me walk around the courtyard freely."

Farren raised an eyebrow. "This isn't the courtyard."

Amira let out a laugh. "What he doesn't know can't hurt me."

Farren hugged her tightly. "I'm glad to see you without Saydren and Tarnan breathing down our necks."

Amira broke away but held onto Farren's hands. "I'm still trying to gain Tarnan's trust, to find a weakness and possibly some hint as to how to break my contract."

Farren sighed. "I wish I knew more about that. I really believed Cirny, but I think we'll need the physical contract, and even then, I don't know how we would gather enough power to break a blood contract. I wish we could look at her spellbooks."

"I've had no luck so far. And I'm worried about the others. I wish we could join them."

"So do I, but with Tarnan's compulsion..."

Amira pressed Farren's hands. "I promise I won't leave without you. I'm starting to gain Tarnan's trust. I'll convince him to stop compelling you when the time's right. But I have no idea where the others are."

"We could wait at the rebel camp. El—"

Yelps of pain outside the room halted their conversation.

"I have to go. I'll see you later for our training session." Amira snuck out of the room before the guards fully woke up. Hurrying down the corridor, she missed her turn and found herself in a long, badly lit hallway that reminded her of the underground in the Turosian palace. It shared the same eerie silence. The walls were lined with carved black stones.

The sense of deja-vu was as strong as a tidal wave. Memories of the underground back in Turosian gripped her, forcing her feet forward. She knew she shouldn't risk upsetting Tarnan, but she couldn't turn back to her room as Nalani's dead face flashed through her mind, Cirny standing next to her.

Unable to shake the memories of Karwyn's experimentation room, Amira walked along the corridor, reliving her past. She noticed what appeared to be a walled-in door and studied its shape. One of the darker stones forming the old archway had a small hole. Drawing closer, she spotted a tiny ruby inside it. Carefully, Amira pressed the ruby, and the old arch door moved back to reveal a dark staircase.

The slow descent into darkness made her hyperconscious of her heavy breathing. Keeping her hand on the wall to steady herself, Amira counted her steps. The light at the end of the short tunnel seemed weirdly reassuring. She walked towards the light as fast as she could.

Her breath got stuck in her throat as she entered the sparsely lit room. If the experimentation room in Karwyn's palace was terrifying, this one was hard to even stand in. Her blood curdled in her veins.

In the centre of the room stood a large table covered in dried blood. Body parts floated in a strange yellow liquid on the high shelves. Spells had been scribbled on the walls like a burst of madness, alongside frightening drawings of fae and human anatomy.

Against her own will, Amira walked to the door at the back of the room. She retched at the sight of iron cages big enough to fit an adult.

"You shouldn't be here," a dark voice said behind her.

Amira turned so fast pain shot down her neck. Saydren was looking at her with obvious pleasure as he took in her tear-filled eyes.

"What has Tarnan done here?" Amira suppressed a gag, the musty iron smell seeping into her.

"The king rarely comes here; it is my domain," Saydren said with an even tone.

Who had he tortured here? It must have had something to do with Tarnan's desire to unlock his powers. Amira couldn't help but wonder if Saydren hadn't whispered in Karwyn's ear, would he have fallen quite so far?

Amira felt sick to her stomach. "You were the one who created the room in the Turosian underground."

A cool grin stretched across Saydren's face. "I did. But this place here, it's my masterpiece. Karwyn's experimentation room was nothing more than a pale imitation." He grabbed her arm, his fingernails digging into her soft skin. "Now come with me; Tarnan is expecting you for lunch and then we're going right back to training."

Tarnan didn't say anything when Saydren dragged Amira inside her quarters, taking in her teary eyes. A cold plate of mashed potatoes and grilled meat was waiting for her. She didn't think she could eat after what she'd seen.

"I found her in the underground." She could still feel his cold touch lingering even after Saydren let go of her.

"I see," Tarnan replied evenly. "Leave us, Saydren. I will take her back to training after lunch."

Saydren bowed his head and exited the room.

Tarnan gestured for Amira to take a seat at the table. Would he punish her? Had she lost his trust completely now? "I'm afraid your food is cold. I will ring the servant to warm it up."

Crossing her arms against her chest, Amira let her disgust shine through her eyes. It was too late now. He already knew what she thought of her discovery. "I'm no longer hungry."

Tarnan took a sip of water before slowly drying his lips with his napkin. "Great things don't happen without a few sacrifices. As I've told you, it took me years to discover how to break my curse and even more years to succeed. Death was inevitable. Eat, Amira."

Amira pushed her plate away, scratching the table, the noise hurting her ears. Breathing in deeply, she tried to clear the cobwebs in her mind, to focus on her task. "I want to trust you," she forced out despite the bile in her throat. "You keep repeating you're not a monster, but all the evidence says otherwise."

Tarnan's nostrils flared. "I don't lie, Amira. My end goal wasn't to kill anyone; some unfortunate circumstances caused their deaths. Noble sacrifices for the greater good of Liraen. I needed to break my curse. Not for myself, but for Liraen. Don't you see how far Liraen has fallen under Harten and Karwyn's rule? Missing fae. Humans used for their blood when they should serve us, not die. Witches enslaved." Tarnan extended his hand to grab Amira's. "I know I still have to earn your trust, and I'm grateful you're training hard with Farren. I even allowed your visit today."

Amira's breathing stopped.

Tarnan gave her an even smile. "You are free to walk around the palace. That doesn't mean I don't know *everything* that goes on here."

Chills ran down her back. As always, the threat was hidden yet obvious. Amira stared him down. "If you want my trust, stop withholding information. What were those sacrifices you mentioned?"

Tarnan's brows rose as if trying to read whether a confession would benefit him. "I'm not proud of my experiments, Amira. It wasn't my goal to cause pain. Whatever I could do to limit the damage, I did. And not all outcomes were deadly. I tried to make up for the pain I've caused as best as I could." He lowered his head as if he was expecting her to praise him for his goodness. No matter how hard she tried she couldn't fight off her unease. He hadn't given her any real answers and they both knew it. They were both losing the game they played. Tarnan sighed, then straightened. "I shall introduce you to someone very dear to me. You'll see, I'm telling the truth."

As Tarnan rang a small silver bell, a guard immediately entered the room. Bending, Tarnan whispered something in his ear. The guard quickly left and Tarnan stood up, extending his hand to Amira. "Shall we take a stroll in the courtyard? I suppose you didn't have time to do so with your detour."

Stunned, Amira got to her feet but didn't take his hand. A part of her was curious. How could he possibly make up for whatever experiments he'd let Saydren conduct under his roof?

They walked down the stairs very slowly as if Tarnan was giving the guard time to accomplish his task. Tarnan's silence unsettled her, and Amira felt her stomach rumble. She should have eaten something when she had the chance. But she only had to think back on Saydren's experimentation room and her stomach stopped screaming.

A cold breeze welcomed them into the courtyard. The large oak tree in the centre had lost all its leaves, its long branches reaching for the sky. Behind the tree, on the small bench Amira usually sat on during her outings, she noticed a young fae, her back turned to Tarnan and Amira, revealing a long strawberry-blonde braid.

As they got closer, Amira could see her profile. She seemed to be in her late teens, barely eighteen or maybe even younger.

"Saige," Tarnan called out to her.

The fae, Saige, turned her head and sprung up, almost losing her balance in her haste when she noticed Tarnan and Amira. Amira took note of her pale skin and honey-coloured eyes that had a red tint to them.

"My...king," Saige said in a strangled voice, bowing her head.

Tarnan's smile was warm. "Let me introduce you to Princess Amira Rosston, a dear friend of mine. I'm sure she will be a good friend to you as well." He patted Amira's shoulder, sending shivers down to her bones.

"A friend?" Saige's tone made it seem like she had no idea what a friend was. She clasped her hands together, her eyes wide yet her gaze lost. "I shall be a great *friend* to you, Princess, if that is the king's wish."

Amira forced a smile. The girl's behaviour was peculiar, as she acted younger than her age. Was she one of the fae Tarnan had experimented on? Was he trying to prove he was treating this...survivor well?

"I'll arrange another meeting between the two of you where you can get to know each other better. But for now, Amira has to return to her training." Walking up to Saige, Tarnan gently caressed her cheek. "I shall visit you later, Saige. I expect you to tell me all about your studies."

As Saige beamed at Tarnan's words, Amira's fingernails dug into her palm. She didn't like the power Tarnan seemed to hold over Saige, it reminded her too much of her own relationship with him.

As they made their way out of the courtyard Amira gave Saige one last look. The girl seemed completely lost in her own world, singing to herself softly. Was she oblivious or truly happy?

Tarnan looked at Saige with a fondness in his eyes. "I told you some light has come out of the darkness. Saige is the living proof, and I'll protect her at all cost. I don't introduce my daughter to just anyone. She would be hunted if fae knew about her heritage. I hope you see now how much I'm willing to trust you, Amira."

Amira's throat closed up. Did that mean Saige was half-fae, an experiment of Tarnan to break his curse? If so, was she his victim, stuck here, or a wolf in sheep's clothing like her father?

Turning, Amira stared at the girl who was now inspecting a rose bush. Saige seemed so innocent. Had Tarnan been willing to experiment on his own flesh and blood to access power? If Tarnan really thought introducing Amira to Saige would help earn her trust, he was dead wrong. Saige wasn't a sign of trust, she was proof Tarnan was willing to stop at nothing to get what he desired most. He craved the same thing Karwyn had been after. *Power.*

CHAPTER 15

EYDEN

The air was cold enough to refresh his mind as Eyden stepped out the back door onto the porch. To his surprise, Oscar was sitting on the swing, a cup of coffee in his hand. It was still early, yet judging from the dull grey sky and the rain drizzling down on the roof over their heads, it could have been any time of day.

"Where's Lora?" Oscar looked over at him. His bright yellow cup steamed between his tightly gripped fingers. A thick coat was wrapped around him.

"Still asleep, I think."

"You think?" Oscar rolled his eyes. "You think I don't know that you're sharing a room with my sister?"

Eyden kept his expression blank. Denial lay on his tongue, but he sensed Oscar wouldn't believe him. Pulling the back door closed, Eyden took a seat next to him on the wooden swing. Oscar lowered his cup from his lips, watching him with a suspicion Eyden wanted to put to rest.

"I'm assuming you wouldn't be happy about that," Eyden said, keeping his tone neutral.

"I'm surprised you're not denying it."

"I didn't confirm anything either." Eyden was aware Lora should be the one telling him.

Oscar nodded. His gaze turned misty as he looked towards the sky.

"It doesn't matter what I think anyway. Lora is doing her own thing." *Without us.* Eyden could almost hear the words written on Oscar's face.

"It wasn't easy for her," Eyden started, waiting for Oscar to turn to him again. "Embracing her fae side—I could sense it always felt like a betrayal to her. The guilt weighs heavily on her and a big part of that is because of you. Give her a chance. It's not right to judge her for being *herself.*"

Oscar shook his head. "I'm not mad at her for being herself. It's what it means. She's going to keep leaving us. I understand she has a role in this and it's not necessarily her call, but why *her?* Why can't she choose us?"

Eyden's chest tightened at the confession. The feeling pushed him back to a time he had felt similar. He leaned forward, resting his elbows on his knees. "Years ago, when Elyssa was living with me, I used to think we were all we needed. But El, she was meant for bigger things than staying hidden in my apartment. She had a purpose on her mind and it led her to join a camp of human rebels. For a time, I blamed myself for not giving her everything she needed. At the same time I felt anger towards her for leaving."

"How did you get over it?" Oscar's voice skimmed the edge of breaking.

"I realised she didn't leave because of me. *I* was the reason she'd stayed for as long as she did. She may have left, but she was never fully gone. And Lora won't be either."

"Do you love her?"

Eyden dragged his feet over the wooden porch. No one had point-blank asked him that before. Yet he knew how he felt. He'd known for a long time, if he was honest with himself.

Eyden met Oscar's expectant gaze. "I do."

Oscar nodded as if he'd assumed as much. "Is Lora in love with you?"

"You'll have to ask her yourself." She had never said the words. But neither had he. It was the last barrier still between them. They'd played around it, skirted close to the edge, but he'd always drawn back.

The back door opened, and Eyden's eyes set on Elyssa and Lora.

"What are you two talking about?" Lora asked, glancing at the two of them on the swing.

"Nothing." Oscar finished his drink in haste. "Can you show me how to shoot arrows again?" Oscar asked Elyssa, his smile excited.

"Sure, kid." Tilting her chin to the shed holding their weapons, Elyssa stalked off. Oscar's face soured at her use of "kid." He offered Lora a half-smile as he passed her.

Stepping closer to the swing, Lora whispered, "What did you say to him?"

Eyden's fae ears picked up movement inside. The kitchen was just behind them. Ilario and Maja were comparing typical English breakfasts with the ones served in Turosian. "Do you want to take a walk?"

Lora caught his drift and zipped her jacket closed. Zippers were a strange invention to Eyden, too complicated.

She walked down the porch steps and Eyden followed. As they stepped out from under the roof, a drizzle coated the top of his hair. When they walked deeper into the woods, Eyden remembered the time they'd gone looking for firewood in Rubien. It had felt like a dream then, getting to kiss her, touch her. He wished he hadn't walked away from her a day later.

Tilting her head up at the grey sky, Lora took a deep breath. "Is it weird that I missed this?"

"The woods?"

"No, the rainy English weather that used to frustrate me. Now it feels strangely reassuring."

He stepped closer to her, his eyes tracking a raindrop sliding down her straight dark blonde hair. "It's not strange." He glanced up at the moody sky. "Okay, maybe a little. Maybe you don't have an eye for beauty like fae from Allamyst do."

"Oh, I see," Lora replied, a sly grin on her lips. "That's probably why I keep looking at you."

He smirked. "Are you calling me pretty?"

"Quite the opposite, actually." Lora took a step forward. Eyden felt the air around them charge with electricity. "But I can see why comments like that would go right over your head."

"I know you just called me stupid," Eyden said, his skin heating, "but dammit, all I want to do is kiss you."

"No comeback?" Her cheeks blushed the faintest pink.

He cupped her cheek as he leaned forward, capturing her lips— soft at first before his tongue slid in, and she sighed as her arms went around his neck. It was a gentle kiss. The kind of kiss shared between people who would give their all to each other.

Lora pulled back much too soon. "You still owe me an answer. What did Oscar say to you?"

He dropped his hand to give them space to think. "He figured out we're sharing a room."

Lora's eyes widened, her breathing sharp. "He shouldn't know yet."

"He already guessed."

"It's my choice to decide when he's ready to find out yet another thing he'll disapprove of. What exactly did you tell him?" Her tone turned accusing and a bit of his heart cracked.

"Nothing." *Only that I love you.*

She wasn't looking at him, couldn't see how much it was killing him. "Don't talk around it, Eyden. I need to know what Oscar knows so I can do damage control."

"Damage control?" Eyden's sigh turned into a broken laugh.

Lora's shoulders sagged. "I didn't mean it like that. I just, I can't add anything else to the list of things he hates about me."

He leaned back against a tree, suddenly feeling unsteady, his heart dragging him down. "You don't think we're worth risking his judgment?"

Her gaze snapped to him, and for a moment she was silent. "I didn't say that."

"You sort of did, Lora. If you really feel that way, you better tell me now because I..."

"You what?"

"I think you're worth everything."

Her breath caught, her gaze warming. "I'm sorry." She stepped forward, her hands moving to his shoulders. "You *are* worth it. It's just...I don't know who I am anymore. If I can't even explain myself to Oscar, how can I explain this...connection between us?" He brushed a strand of hair behind her ear as he tracked her honest gaze, the hidden sadness behind her confusion. Then her eyes cleared, fire extinguishing everything else. "But even within the chaos that is my mind lately, I am sure about one thing. *You.*"

A smile pulled at his lips as everything in him sparked alive. "I meant what I said a few days ago," he said. "You're still *you.* And I'll remind you of who you are every day if I have to." A slight grin stretched her lips. "You're a flame that refuses to be extinguished. You're an ever-lasting ember, shining brighter than the most brilliant fire. You're fae, you're human—you're a special mix of both."

His hand went to her cheek, his finger stroking her face. He finally let go of the last bit of fear holding him back. "And I love you."

Her lips parted, her eyes glassy. "I..." she breathed, blinking up at him. "You don't have to say anything—"

"I love you too." A smile so bright graced her lips, it would have stolen his heart if it wasn't already hers. "I love you for always honouring your promises. I love you for seeing me when I can't even see myself. And most of all, I love you for never giving up on me even when I pushed you away."

The words hit his heart in a wave of pure warmth as if it was touched by golden light. In the past, he would have been scared to let someone in like this. To let someone own his heart, giving them the power to betray him, to rip his heart to shreds. But with Lora, the risk had been inevitable. He would have taken anything she'd given him. But now that she'd given him her all, now that he could name the emotion in her eyes—the love shining through—Eyden could never settle for less.

"I thought the day would never come," Lora teased, laughing. The sound vibrated through him. "Eyden Kellen/Kelstrel is speechless."

Eyden grinned at her remembering both his given name and the one he'd chosen as his trader alias. "I think we're beyond words now."

He didn't give her a warning as his hand grabbed the front of her coat, pulling her towards him. His lips met hers with a newfound fire, a deep love echoing through them, binding them together.

As he ran his tongue along her bottom lip, she shuddered, pulling him closer. The kiss turned desperate as she lightly bit his lip, drawing a groan from him that he felt in his whole body.

He pushed her back until she hit a tree. His hand went to the zipper on her coat as her hands tangled in his wet hair. He'd barely noticed the rain turning heavy, seeping into their clothes. As he unzipped her coat, sliding it off her shoulders, Eyden changed his mind. Zippers were a great invention.

Eyden's gaze wandered over her chest, the thin sweater wet from the rain, revealing her peaked nipples through the fabric. Drops of water ran down her cheek, her chin, but Lora didn't seem to mind. She pulled his head towards her again, her lips dancing with his.

Her hand went to his chest, his own sweater drenched from the rain now, sticking to him as if it was a second layer of skin. Lora's hand travelled down his abs. The groan on her lips mixed with the rushing of the rain around them was the sweetest sound.

His hand drifted from her cheek down her chest, his thumb brushing over her nipple, making her back arch. Eyden let his hand stray further down as his mouth gently bit her lip before moving to her jaw, then her neck. The rain on her skin made everything hotter.

Reaching the button on her trousers, he popped it open before pulling the zipper down. Lora's hand in his hair tightened as his finger slipped underneath her underwear. It would never not make his heart skip, feeling her need firsthand.

His tongue branded her neck as his finger entered her, and the moan leaving her lips drowned out the rain pouring down on them. She moved her hips with his strokes, and desire shot through him with each sigh of pleasure. He wished there was nothing between them.

Lora's hand on his chest wandered to his belt. Her mouth was right at his ear as she rasped, "*More.*"

Eyden's hand pulled back and Lora rocked her hips forward as if to chase just one more touch. Both his hands set on her hips as his fingers dug into the wet fabric that was in his way. Catching her gaze, he waited for her permission. A distant part of him remembered they were out in the open. But as she gave a subtle nod, he realised she was as desperate for this as he was.

He tugged at her jeans and underwear, pulling the wet fabric down to her ankles. As soon as he straightened himself, Lora pulled him to her chest again, her hand diving into his trousers and freeing him.

Eyden's hand went to her thigh, sliding over wet skin, hot to the touch, before hooking under her knee and pulling her leg up to his hip. He lined himself up with her and she squirmed under his touch, arching her back to get closer.

Her breath danced over his lips as she whispered, "I'm yours, Eyden. Just in case I wasn't clear enough before. My heart, my soul, it feels right at home with you. No matter what anyone thinks of us, I'm yours." Her eyes pierced his heart, filling it with so much love Eyden almost forgot to breathe. "I promise."

Promise. She once told him she hated the word—was plagued by all the promises she'd never been able to keep. But now she'd promised him her heart and he would make sure to honour it.

He kissed her harder, feverish, the water on her skin almost evaporating as passion fuelled every fibre of them. He edged closer, a groan rumbling through his chest.

Eyden broke the kiss to meet her heated gaze once more. "You have all of me, special one. I promise whatever you need, whatever you have to overcome, I'll be there for you."

Keeping eye contact, he tried to convey how much he loved her as he pushed into her and there was no barrier between them at all anymore. It was almost as if he could see their connection, the love binding them together with invisible fire.

In drenched clothes, Lora and Eyden broke away from the trees surrounding the cabin and neared the back porch. Elyssa and Oscar stood under the roof in the backyard. Their bows were trained on the target on the tree in front of them.

With the rain, it added another layer to the challenge as the water must blur their vision. He was sure Elyssa must hate the loud sound of the rain hitting the roof above her and the way it affected her bad hearing. Yet she didn't let any of that on as she let her arrow fly, hitting dead centre. Oscar's arrow missed the tree by quite the distance.

Lora's father, sitting on the porch, cheered anyway.

Eyden felt Lora's hand clasp his and he tilted his head at her, unsure if she wanted everyone to see. She gave him a brilliant smile.

Elyssa spotted them first, her lips curling into a grin as she noticed their joined hands. Oscar followed her gaze. His expression remained reserved as he watched them. Lora's father gave her a small smile, and he could feel the anxiety leaving her body as her hand squeezed his.

"Ready to train with us?" Elyssa asked when they'd gotten closer.

"I think it's time I try my powers again," Lora threw in, and Oscar raised his brows. Her eyes set on a hunting knife by the shed where weapons were sprawled on the ground.

Lora extended her arm, her forehead creasing with concentration. Her eyes gleamed bright and he was reminded again that he should show her how to dim the fae light in them before they headed out into civilization.

With a flick of her hand, the knife rose from the ground, lifted by magic air. A grin formed on Lora's lips as the blade shot towards her. The knife flipped around but not fast enough. The blade nicked her skin as the knife landed in her hand. It caught on fire as Lora had shown him once before. Her smile widened as she moved the blade in front of her face, ignoring the cut on the palm of her hand. Fire illuminated her face, the flames dancing in front of her absolutely brilliant.

Elyssa laughed, pride shining in her eyes.

Lora took in her brother's expression. He seemed uncertain yet unfrightened, and Eyden could tell that was more than she'd expected.

Meeting Eyden's gaze, Lora tilted her chin at the weapons on the ground. It was the only invitation Eyden needed.

CHAPTER 16

RHAY

They had left Maja in charge of watching Damir, not trusting Rhay with the task. It was fine by him. Now that he had more vodka, he was happy to retreat back to his corner of misery. But Maja had asked him to stand in for her for just a few minutes, forcing him to move down the hall. She had some pressing *business* to attend to. Rhay would have said no but she hadn't left him much of a choice, scolding him with her raised finger. *Fine.* With Rio, Lora, Lora's boy toy, and Elyssa—the boy toy's violence-prone little sister—gone to capture one of Tarnan's guards, Rhay sought a distraction.

Leaning against the wooden door to Damir's so-called prison, Rhay took a swig of alcohol as he stretched his legs on the floor. He pried open the door and stared at Damir, sitting on his sad-looking mattress. Raising the bottle, Rhay teased, "Care for a drink, prisoner?"

Damir leaned his elbows on his legs. "You haven't changed one bit, Messler. Your best friend dies in front of you and you're still downing bottles as if nothing's changed."

Pulling the bottle to his chest, Rhay's teasing grin disappeared. "What would you have me do? Take on another persona altogether and live someone else's life? That's what you would do, right?" Rhay took another swig, the alcohol burning his inflamed throat. "I always thought I was the master of pretence, but you have me beat."

Damir's face was stoic, reminding Rhay of Layken's stern expression.

"There is a difference between pretending to avoid seeing what's really going on and pretending for a purpose because you *do* see everything." Damir's stare was haunting, diving straight at Rhay's guilty heart. All he had done was avoid. Until he hadn't and it had ruined him just the same.

"At least I'm not wallowing in self-pity," Damir continued. "You don't deserve the affection the others seem to have for you, least of all Ilario's." A hint of emotion carried his voice. What had Rio seen in Damir? Someone lost? Someone to save? Is that what he saw in Rhay too?

A dark chuckle escaped Rhay's lips. "You think *you* deserve it?"

"None of us deserve him."

"For once, we agree. Why did you let Karwyn rule over you?"

Damir stayed silent for too long, and when he replied, Rhay wished he hadn't asked. "Who said I did? You're the only one who let himself be blinded by Karwyn's friendship. I always knew what I was getting myself into; you were too busy thinking about your next drink."

Rhay winced, clenching his jaw. Damir knew where to hit, both with his sword and his words. His reply was cut short by Maja's appearance in the hallway.

Her fringe fell into her chocolate brown eyes as she stopped short. "What the hell are you doing? I leave you for five fucking minutes for a bathroom break and you're fraternising with the enemy!"

Rhay raised his almost empty bottle. "You should drink too, love, that'll numb your fear."

Maja crossed her arms against her chest, a deadly glint in her eye. "Oh please, don't flatter yourself. I'm not scared of your drunken mess. Or the injured prisoner." She eyed Damir, who fought a smirk, but it was gone so quickly Rhay could have imagined it.

Standing up, Damir crept closer to the door, his gaze set on Maja, who managed to hold her ground. "I can do a lot of damage while injured, little girl. Rhay's got nothing on me and neither do you."

Maja's face didn't betray her move as she gripped the gun jammed into the back of her trousers quicker than Rhay had expected from a human. Aiming at Damir, Maja's lips pulled into a threatening grin. "Call me little girl again and you'll get a bullet between your eyes. Let's see what you got then."

The air seemed to grow warmer as Damir stared at her. Then he laughed and Maja's façade crumbled. She slammed the door in his face. Rhay raised his brows at her and Maja clenched her jaw, glaring daggers at him.

She put the gun back, then spun to lock Damir's door. "I could use a drink." Before Rhay could offer his last sips of vodka, she strode into the kitchen.

Throwing a glance at the closed door, Rhay grabbed his bottle and followed her. When he entered the kitchen, Maja was sitting on the cool tile floor with a bowl and spoon in hand. Without saying a word, she started eating spoonfuls of a light brown substance.

"I thought you wanted a drink. What are you eating?" Rhay lowered himself to the ground next to her. They could still see Damir's door from their position.

"You're kidding, right?" Her spoon clinked against her white bowl, her anger replaced by curiosity. "Cookie dough ice cream."

Now that she said it, Rhay did remember seeing humans eat this kind of thing on TV. "Never had it."

Maja reached behind her, opening a drawer and taking out another spoon. "Here, it's the cure for heartbreak, trust me." She handed him the spoon with an inviting smile.

Bewildered, Rhay took a spoonful of ice cream. The flavours were more muted than the foods in Liraen, but the sweetness of it mixed with the lingering alcohol taste in his mouth was a pleasant combination.

"You said it's good for heartbreak," Rhay observed. "Who broke your heart? Boy? Girl? Both?" Rhay started, longing to see some of Maja's fire again to distract himself from his own heartbreak. Ice cream and booze weren't enough.

Maja snorted. "It's for *your* heartbreak. I don't get my heart broken."

"How come?"

"Don't get me wrong, fancying people is fun." She licked her spoon clean and Rhay couldn't help but watch. "But beyond fun...I'm not interested." Her gaze met his and a shadow passed in her dark irises. "You can read emotions, right?" Rhay nodded. "Is that why you said I was scared before?"

"The border has fallen and you're hiding out in a cabin from guards who wouldn't hesitate to kill you. By Caelo, you've even been shot, I've heard. I don't need to read your emotions to take a guess."

Maja swallowed, setting the bowl of ice cream on the floor. Her hand went to her shoulder. Under the short sleeve, a thick bandage peeked out. Not looking at him, she whispered, "I don't want to be afraid. I don't do *scared*."

Noticing a spot of ice cream on her face, Rhay reached out and gently erased the mark on Maja's chin. He picked up on her heartbeat increasing as her mouth opened slightly.

To his surprise, she inched closer, her lips dangerously close to his. "What are you reading now?"

He opened his senses to desire mixed with fear. Tilting his head, he whispered in her ear, "I think you're seeking more than ice cream to let go of your fear."

Her hands grabbed his shirt and then Maja's lips shushed him as she pulled him to her. Rhay hadn't expected her to make the first move but he more than welcomed it. Maja tasted like lilies mixed with ice cream, different than—

No, he wasn't going to think about anyone else.

He deepened the kiss, and a sigh escaped her lips that inflamed his own desire. Losing himself in the kiss, Rhay's hand grabbed Maja's waist, the fabric of her shirt a barrier he wanted to erase. Playfully, she bit his lower lip, and Rhay was done being gentle.

Breaking the kiss, he pulled her up to kiss her again, roughly pushing her against the kitchen counter, seeking any kind of friction. The moan escaping his lips seemed to spur her into action and Maja pushed him away only to drag him down the hall and into the bedroom she shared with Elyssa.

Rhay couldn't think of anything but the building pleasure in his core. The alcohol turned his thoughts blurry. There was only Maja and him and the single bed Maja pulled him towards. Tearing at his sweater, Maja removed it. Her sharp nails dragged down his torso. She gave him a push and Rhay fell back on the bed, his eyes drinking her in as she removed her shirt before straddling him. Now, he could fully see the bandage where she had been shot.

His hand grabbed her waist to guide her just right, pushing against her through their clothes until moans filled the small room. This, *this* was exactly what Rhay needed. And *more*.

He gently pushed against her shoulder to switch their position, but she held on. Grinning, Rhay hooked a finger under the band of her trousers. "Love, if you don't move, I can't go down on you. And trust me, we'll both be missing out."

Hands trailing his lower abs, Maja bit her lip as if in thought. Huffing, she moved off him. "Prove it."

In a flash, he was above her, capturing her lips as his hand trailed from her neck over her breast. She was still wearing a bra, but Rhay had another goal right now. With a devilish grin, Rhay kissed a path down her body until he reached her trousers. She writhed underneath him, not so unsure about what she wanted now, and a satisfied rumble left his chest.

Unbuttoning her trousers, Rhay laughed when he saw tiny little stars printed all over her underwear.

"A starry night indeed," he said as Maja lifted her hips.

Lowering her underwear, he gave her no warning before his tongue flicked over the centre of her. Her hips lifted off the mattress as she cried out. Pushing her back against the bed, Rhay went deeper, tasting her fully, letting this feeling erase anything else. The sweetest distraction he could have asked for.

CHAPTER 17

&

ELYSSA

The gun tucked into the band of her jeans kept Elyssa grounded as her thoughts returned to Amira and Farren. As she curled her hand into a fist, her cold brass knuckles rubbed against her skin. She had to fight the itch to run to the border every day. But she knew Amira wouldn't want her to be rash and go on a suicide mission.

Having decided Lora's house was a safe bet to find Tarnan's guards, Eyden had drifted them close by after Lora had pointed it out on a map. As his powers were limited, he had taken Elyssa first and then Lora and Ilario had joined her. Not spotting anything off in the deserted street with all the house lights turned off, they drifted into Lora's house.

Drifting in would limit their chances of being spotted.

The cold wind vanished as Elyssa's boots almost slipped on the wooden floor and Lora steadied her. Before she could even take in her surroundings, Eyden disappeared again to get Ilario.

The cosy living room was decorated in warm tones. It seemed as if the house was merely waiting for Lora's family to return. The flowers placed next to the TV were still in bloom. A thin layer of dust had settled over the colourful carpet and bookshelves. Elyssa spied family pictures on a wooden shelf. Lora stared at them as if imagining another lifetime.

As Eyden reappeared with Ilario, Elyssa carefully moved to the window, drawing the curtain back the tiniest bit. There was still no movement on the empty street outside.

"I don't hear anything," Eyden stated, his back to the wall next to the door leading into a hallway. Elyssa glimpsed a staircase going up.

It didn't take long to check every room and soon Eyden and Lora, who had taken the upstairs, joined them downstairs again.

"I guess we'll have to wander closer to the beach to get one of Tarnan's guards," Ilario said. That had been their back-up plan if there were no guards around Lora's house.

"I need to check one more thing before we leave," Lora said, walking around the sofa on the soft carpet. She pressed a button on the TV. The screen lit up.

The TV at the cabin had no signal and only showed a grainy picture. On this one, a human woman appeared on-screen, arms crossed on the shiny table in front of her. Her voice sounded as if she spoke through a runia but more sharp. "...the military is hard at work containing the border in what has now been deemed the beginning of the Second Dark War."

The screen behind the woman filled with images of the border. Large cars and humans dressed in green clothes raising big guns were stationed around the perimeter as fae appeared through the portal. They were immediately gunned down—only to get up again. Smoke rose above the beach where the border was located. Without almandine, the humans wouldn't be able to contain the border if Tarnan were to send a whole fae army through. The fact that he hadn't yet meant he had a bigger plan.

"The government has urged people to evacuate in an orderly fashion," the woman on-screen continued, her voice strained as if she was seconds from running off too. "Take only necessities—" She stopped as her hand drifted to something in her ear. "I'm just getting a message that the fae have sent a statement." The woman's gaze turned off screen as her voice lowered. "I'm not sure we should be broadcasting..."

Elyssa didn't hear a reply. Her hand fisted at her side as she waited for the woman to continue. Glancing at Lora, Elyssa could tell she was nervous too, her hand twisting around her necklace.

Clearing her throat, the woman turned back. "Take a look at the first contact we've had from Liraen since they provided us with a cure for the virus."

The screen faded to black before Tarnan's face appeared before them. A golden crown rested on his short dark hair. The Carnylen crown, not Rubien's. His eyes looked more amber than red now; he must have dimmed the fae light in them. *Hypocrite,* Elyssa thought, but then the air left her lungs as Amira appeared next to him, her hands locked in front of her.

Elyssa moved closer to the screen as if she could reach out and take Amira's hand and pull her to her side where she belonged.

Amira's gaze was impenetrable. She looked healthy, her golden dress flattering her olive skin tone. Yet Elyssa knew there was pain behind the princess' façade, a pain she wanted to erase even more so than her own.

Tarnan's voice was calm and neutral. "People of Liraen and Earth, as you might know, my name is Tarnan Ellevarn. I'm the King of Carnylen, and if I dare say so myself, the future High King of Liraen."

He paused for dramatic effect. "It has sadly come to my attention that our interim High King, Karwyn Adelway, has been murdered in cold blood after breaking the border spell that provided peace between fae and humans. Though I seek to establish a new rule between humans and fae without constricting the border, I must proclaim my distress over the current mayhem that has been unleashed on both our worlds. Karwyn Adelway has ruled over Turosian with the grace of a child, yet he didn't deserve to be taken to the Sky so early. Whoever is responsible should be brought forward. Although it pains me to voice my suspicion, we should note that the Turosian throne has remained empty since Karwyn's disappearance. Loraine Adelway hasn't shown her face since, and I have good reason to believe she is involved in her cousin's murder."

Eyden cursed under his breath while Lora clenched her jaw. *That fucker.* Tarnan was putting the blame on Lora; with no proof otherwise, would the other kingdoms all turn against her? It would be hard enough to fight Tarnan, they couldn't fight against all the royals.

Tarnan's stoic but warm voice continued. "Her absence is reason enough to doubt. I will leave you with this thought. My message to Earth is the following: A new dawn is coming. Don't fight it and you will find your rightful place amongst us."

The video cut abruptly and the screen switched back to the stunned woman whose neck had gone red as if anxiety was consuming her. "Well, that was...informative. We have reason to believe that the mentioned suspect, Loraine Adelway, is in fact Loraine Whitner, who is wanted for questioning—"

Lora switched off the TV, a frown on her face. Letting out a slow breath, she sank onto the couch. "He's trying to force my hand. I have to go back to clear my name and claim my...throne, don't I?"

Claim the throne... It did feel as if Tarnan wanted Lora in the contest. Three rulers had been chosen by the royals and their advisors. With Karwyn out of the picture, Lora had to be next in line. Tarnan wanted to beat her. He wanted her back in his grasp.

Eyden knelt next to Lora. "He wants you to go back to Turosian and give up on finding the agreement. But that also means he hasn't been able to get his hands on the agreement himself. We can still win this round."

Elyssa blew out a long breath as she chased away the image of Amira next to Tarnan. Eyden was right, Tarnan hadn't won yet. And if they had any chance she would take it and give it all the fire she had left in her until nothing but ashes was left of Tarnan and his new dawn. Looking up at her, Lora seemed to mimic her thoughts, a fire swirling in her eyes that Elyssa knew could be their salvation.

The corner of Elyssa's mouth tipped upwards. "You might be the most wanted person in any world right now, Lora, but when we're done with him, we'll be known as the ones who went head to head with the Dark King's son and *won*."

Lora smiled back, yet her eyes were dim.

A loud crash assaulted Elyssa's ears. Instantly, the gun was in her hands, the metal reassuringly cold as she flicked off the safety. Eyden drew his knife. Her eyes flickered around, her ears unable to pick up where the sound had come from. A face peeked into the living room from the kitchen—probably having broken in through the back door—and Elyssa fired, hitting the intruder's left shoulder.

Grunting in pain, the fae leaned against the doorframe. He wasn't wearing the sunset-orange Carnylen uniform Elyssa had expected. He was dressed in black from head to toe. Maybe Tarnan didn't want any attacks linked to him?

Four more fae rushed in. Elyssa felt the presence behind her before she spied the fae approaching her. Dropping down, she swung her leg as she turned in a half circle, one hand on the ground for balance. The fae stumbled to the ground, a surprised gasp leaving her lips. Elyssa fired, and the bullet went through the fae's hand. She had to hand it to Earth, guns were fast.

Just as the thought left her, a knife struck her arm and the gun fell from her grip. It skittered across the floor, under the sofa. Out of the corner of her eye she spotted the other fae lifting a sword, blood drenching his uniform where the bullet had gone into his shoulder. He swung his sword at Eyden just as her brother hit another guard's shoulder with his knife.

Elyssa yelled a warning as the sword inched towards Eyden, dangerously close to his neck. Spinning, Eyden ducked in time. Ilario, seemingly having lost his knife, dropped a vase on top of the guard's head. A flower got stuck in the guard's hair and Elyssa almost laughed as Ilario punched his face, adding blood to the dirt sticking to the guard's cheeks.

Meanwhile, fire spread across the living room as Lora trapped another fae in a circle. He threw himself through the flames and pushed against Lora's chest. Her back hit the bookshelf, wood splintering. Picture frames fell to the ground. As Lora stepped to the side to avoid a punch to the throat, her boot crushed glass.

The fae behind Elyssa had gotten back up and she dove for the sofa, her knees burning as she hit the ground. This fight was exactly what she needed. Before she could reach the gun, someone grabbed her legs and pulled. Her chin hit the carpeted floor and she tasted blood as she bit her tongue. Kicking out, she flipped onto her back, catching the fae's nose with her boot. The female fae stumbled, the back of her knees hitting the glass table. With a yell, Elyssa kicked again. The fae fell, her back shattering the table. The shrill sound of breaking glass echoed through her ears. Besides the heat on her skin from Lora's fire close by, Elyssa had blocked out everything else.

Elyssa took note of the remaining enemies and finally got hold of the gun. Eyden was locked into a fight, his knife against an almandine sword—not a fair fight, but Eyden could handle it. Ilario threw more punches at the fae with dirt in his hair. But the fae had fire at his disposal, catching Ilario off guard, singeing his sleeve. Lora didn't waste a second to throw her own fire at him as Ilario split the ground open, roots tangling the fae's legs. The fire swallowed the female fae on the broken table.

Almost stumbling from the shaking ground, Elyssa's gaze locked on the last fae across the living room. She fired. The guard sidestepped and the bullet hit the window, more glass littering the ground. She fired again but no bullet came. She was all out. Dropping the gun, she readied her brass knuckles.

Elyssa jumped onto the sofa, her hand on the back of it as she leapt over the cushions. The fae barely had time to react as she came at him, fists raised. He stumbled back into the broken window and snatched a glass shard from the frame, holding it out like a knife.

He swung at her, the sharp edge coming dangerously close to her face, but Elyssa grabbed his arm and kicked him in the groin. The glass tore into the fae's hand as he tried to hold onto it. Grunting in pain, he let go. With his bloody hand, he hit her cheek faster than she expected, and a metallic taste filled her mouth. For a moment Elyssa went still, and the fae grinned as if he had her beat. *Think again.*

But then a sword ripped through him from back to front. As the fae dropped, Eyden winked at Elyssa.

"Watch out!" Ilario shouted, and Elyssa dropped, pulling Eyden to the side with her before the sword of another fae could impale either of them.

A streak of fire made its path through the living room, clawing at the fae in front of them.

Elyssa got back to her feet, taking in the destroyed room. "I have to give it to us, we're damn good."

Out of breath, Ilario stared at her incredulously, rolling up his burned sleeve. His skin had barely reddened. Lora wiped soot off her jacket.

"Three out of five are dead," Eyden said, surveying the damage. The fae's sword was still in his hand, dripping blood.

Elyssa followed his line of sight. The fae Eyden had impaled through the shoulder was knocked out but still breathing. The one Elyssa had hit with multiple bullets was scrambling out of the room, leaving a trail of glass behind as he ran to the kitchen. Before he could turn the corner, a strong wind dragged him back to the living room.

Landing at Lora's feet, the fae spit up blood. "Kill me if you want, our true king Tarnan Sartoya will get you soon enough. You can't stop him," he hissed, writhing in pain.

Lora tilted her head down. "We'll see about that." She kicked him in the head and the guard lost consciousness. "I say we keep this one," Lora suggested, and Elyssa had no arguments.

Taking a fallen sword, Elyssa finished off the other guard.

Ilario drew back the curtain to glance outside. "I don't see anyone else, but I bet there are more guards close by."

"Let's head back," Eyden said, his voice gentle as he watched Lora. Her expression had changed as her eyes took in her home which now bore the casualties of their fight. The shelf decorated with family pictures was broken, the frames cracked. The ground had been split open, a jagged line ruining the wooden floor. The sofa was badly singed, as was the carpet beneath it. Smoke filled the air, replacing the pleasant flowery scent that had been drifting through the air on their arrival.

Lora met Eyden's protective gaze. "Take the guard first. I need a minute."

"I'll stay with her, take Ilario too," Elyssa said at Eyden's worried glance.

Eyden squeezed Lora's shoulder, then scooted down to touch the guard's shoulder. Ilario put his hand on Eyden's arm and in a second they were gone.

Scanning the room, Elyssa's gaze drifted back to the broken frames. She knelt down and picked up a picture of young Lora with her brother and mother, brushing off pieces of glass. They looked genuinely happy, laughing together. The photo was ripped on one edge but otherwise in one piece. Turning to Lora, Elyssa handed it to her.

"You should take it with you." Elyssa wished she had anything to remember her own parents by. Their faces were getting harder and harder to remember, but she would never forget their sacrifices.

Hesitantly, Lora took the photo, sliding it into her back pocket. "Do you ever wonder if your parents had been able to cross, would they have stayed here in Bournchester?"

Elyssa swallowed the constant sadness tearing her up from the inside that was only pushed back by her anger at the world. "There's no point in wondering. All we have is the future. That's what we *can* control. And I'll make the most of it."

Lora looked up, a tired smile on her face. "For them?"

Nodding, Elyssa pointed at the picture in Lora's hands. "I can never get them back, but I *can* try my goddamn hardest to make sure every-one else is safe."

"All this loss..." Lora shook her head. "We *will* get Amira and Farren back."

Before she could reply, Eyden reappeared. His eyes travelled between them. Lora put two fingers behind her ear, a gesture Eyden and Elyssa had come up with when they were children to reassure each other they were all right without words. Elyssa returned the gesture with a smile, realising in the midst of everything, Lora had become her family.

Reaching out, Eyden grasped Lora's hand, and a saddened smile tugged at her lips.

Elyssa took a step forward, intending to take Eyden's free hand when an explosion assaulted her ears. Raising her arms to cover her face, she could barely catch sight of the living room wall crumbling when the sudden blast threw her backwards violently.

CHAPTER 18

AMIRA

"You're not trying!" Saydren yelled at Farren. His wounds had healed, but Farren had to be as exhausted as she was. They exchanged a quick smile through the glass separating them before Saydren turned his attention to Amira.

"Go with him," Saydren ordered her with no ounce of empathy.

They had been training for eight hours straight and Amira's back was covered in cold sweat. She had channelled her powers into a wave of water, drenching the walls of the training box Farren was standing in. The glass square was placed in the middle of a huge empty room that seemed to have been used for events in the past. Tables and chairs covered by tarps had been pushed to the side and the "square of doom" —as Amira and Farren referred to it—stood in their place.

Amira entered the box, joining Farren. "How are you feeling?" she whispered in his ear.

"I'm okay." His smile was always wide despite their circumstances. "Saydren's knowledge is vast, more than I could have ever taught myself. I just wish we could use our powers in a different context."

Sharing his sentiment, Amira wanted to say so, but Saydren cut her off. "Take out your crystals. I have a test for you." He put a small wooden chest inside the glass square before quickly exiting and closing the narrow door behind him. "Open the chest."

With a trembling hand, Amira followed his order. Immediately, dark smoke filled the room, blurring the glass walls. "This chest has been cursed. Use the spells I've taught you and remove the curse." Saydren's voice was muffled by the buzzing sound of the cursed smoke. It lingered in the air, clouding them in shadows. Yet it didn't harm anything other than her sight.

To Amira's surprise, Farren sat on the ground. "What are you doing?"

Farren let out a warm laugh, his face shadowed. "Taking a well-deserved break. We'll solve this curse eventually."

Enjoying his perspective, Amira sat next to him. Saydren couldn't see them through the dense smoke cloud.

"Can I ask you a question?" Amira started.

"Sure."

"What triggered your powers? Elyssa told me that it's usually something traumatic and I wonder if that's true for all witches."

Staring into the dark smoke, Farren replied in a low voice, "I watched my parents die in front of me. There was an attack on our camp when I was thirteen. I'm not sure if El has mentioned it to you. She lost people too."

Amira's heart constricted in her chest when she remembered Elyssa's confession about her uncle's death. She had so badly wanted to be able to remove Elyssa's pain. Nudging Farren's shoulder, she whispered, "I'm sorry."

Farren gave her a sad smile. "I'm guessing you've had your fair share of trauma."

"What is taking so long?" Saydren screamed at them.

"We're trying our best!" Farren yelled. Standing up, he extended his hand to Amira. "Let's show him we're stronger than this lame curse."

Amira accepted his hand and jumped back to her feet. They both grabbed their black jasper stones to ward off dark magic and joined hands over the open chest. Closing her eyes, Amira's power slithered through her veins, fuelling her with strength. The curse fought back, sending an icy burn to Amira's heart, but she held on as Saydren had taught them this past week. When she opened her eyes, the smoke around them seemed to quiver from their attack. In her hand, the crystal heated, burning her skin. Amira pushed back against the curse, Farren's power in sync with her own.

The smoke ran back to the chest as it closed with a loud crack. Someone clapped behind Amira. Tarnan had joined Saydren outside the glass square. "Impressive! I see Saydren's training has done wonders. Just in time for our trip to Rubien."

Amira pressed her nails into her palms, suppressing the urge to throttle him. The last time she had been with Tarnan was this morning, when they had taped his message to the human world. Amira had to stand by his side, pretending she didn't despise him. Once she had been sent back to her room, Amira had thrown up her breakfast.

She longed for a way out of here, but there were still things she could accomplish by Tarnan's side. She needed more time for him to trust her. But would Tarnan ever agree to break their contract? To stop compelling Farren? Would Elyssa have broken out by now if she was in Amira's place? But she wouldn't have left Farren behind either.

"I will let you go back to it. I have much to plan for our upcoming departure. *Farren—*" Tarnan started.

Amira interrupted him, smiling innocently. "I don't think that's necessary; we both enjoy our time here harnessing our powers. Let both of us prove it to you."

Tarnan responded to her smile with his own. "I'm sure you are, Amira. But I still have some doubts about your friend. *Farren, if you leave this palace, kill yourself.*"

Farren went limp for a second, the compulsion taking hold of him. Amira forced the disappointment off her face.

Satisfied, Tarnan walked out of the room.

Saydren clapped his hands. "We're going to take a small break." He left the room, following Tarnan.

Farren grabbed a jar of water and poured two glasses while Amira went to sit on the one bench that wasn't covered up. Brushing over the faint marks on her palms, Amira thought of her strange encounter with Tarnan's daughter the day before. "I met Tarnan's daughter."

"He has a daughter?" Farren handed her a glass. She welcomed the fresh water with a smile. "What is she like?"

"She's...odd. I don't think she has interacted with many people. She acts like a child but she must be around seventeen. I think she was one of Saydren's experiments, a half-fae used in an attempt to break Tarnan's family curse. And now he's acting like he's father of the year." She shuddered. "What he must have done to her mother... Do you think he cares about her to some extent? Is he even capable of caring for anyone?" Not long ago, Amira had thought he truly cared about her well-being. She'd been naive. She wouldn't underestimate him ever again.

Farren sat next to her, a crease forming on his forehead. "Maybe he has grown fond of her over time. Maybe he cares for her in his own twisted way and that could be used against him. But what if she's different from her father? Could we truly use her? It doesn't feel right."

"I don't like it either. I could at least try to question her about Tarnan's plan, maybe she knows something." Amira took a deep breath. "I think Tarnan is starting to trust me. I'll try again to convince him to stop compelling you. And maybe after we've shown we're trustworthy by rebuilding Rubien he'll agree to break my contract."

She had thought about searching for it, but she had no way of breaking it even if she could find the contract. But if she could escape with the physical contract, she could search for a way to break it. As long as she was bound to Tarnan she couldn't take him out. Could they fight him, lock him up, if she couldn't break their connection? Would it be enough to stop him?

"If you can't convince Tarnan to break the contract, we should run away before I've outlived my purpose. Elyssa and the others need you."

"They need *us*."

Farren's smile calmed her nerves. "You know I've been to Rubien before," Farren added, tipping his glass of water.

"How come?"

"I was captured by blood traffickers along with a few other members of our camp. It was actually El, Eyden, and Lora who came to free us." Farren closed his eyes.

The Void, as Tarnan had mentioned. Amira lowered her eyes, ashamed of the indirect part she had played in this. "I used to take fortae. It wasn't for fun, it was to keep my power at bay." Farren opened his eyes and she stumbled over her next words. "Not that it's any excuse. But I didn't know how it was made. If it wasn't for Elyssa, I don't think I would have survived."

Farren pressed her hand and gave her a sad smile. "El told me; I knew it was our way in. You're not the one who invented that cursed drug or the one chasing humans for their blood."

Amira bit her lip. "I wish it wasn't how I met Elyssa."

"But we wouldn't be here today if it wasn't for that."

Amira raised an eyebrow, looking around the training room.

Farren laughed. The sound warmed Amira's heart. "Not that *here* here is ideal. But you know what I mean. You wouldn't have met El. Discovering your power is life changing; everyone reacts differently. Without support, it can drown you in fear."

"I miss her so much." She missed them all.

Farren's bright smile chased away the dark cloud threatening Amira. "I know. We will be reunited again. I have faith in them—and in us."

As expected, Tarnan joined Amira for a late dinner. The servants brought them a hearty stew made with potatoes and white meat. Her stomach rumbling, Amira started eating immediately with no care for manners. The rest of their training today had been successful but exhausting.

Tarnan carefully placed his napkin on his lap. "I will ask Saydren to give you a day off tomorrow. You look exhausted." His tone was warm but she didn't fall for his concern.

Amira stopped mid-bite. "We're not leaving tomorrow?"

"We'll leave the day after tomorrow; I still have a few details to iron out." Tarnan put his hand on hers, his smile making her shiver. "I've only been to Rubien once. Saydren took me there to show me the ruins of what my parents had built. My whole family died in the palace, their home. Rubien was once the most promising kingdom in all of Liraen. I regret that my father's mistakes have outshined my mother's deep kindness. Saydren told me how generous she was with the people of Liraen, always willing to help out any lost soul. Their legacy was ruined, but I'll repair it."

He seemed to believe the stories Saydren must have told him about his family. How truthful were they? Sensing Tarnan's sorrow, Amira didn't pull back her hand as she said, "I understand your pain. I'm afraid my brother is ruining our father's legacy with his cruelty. I'm sorry I ever compared you."

To Amira's joy, Tarnan smiled, squeezing her hand. "Once I'm high king I'll help you reclaim your throne. You would make a much better ruler than him."

Amira lowered her eyes. The thought seemed daunting, impossible. Would the people of Allamyst ever accept her if they knew who she truly was? "I don't think I'm fit to be a queen."

"Have some faith in yourself, Amira. I do." His smile sent shivers through her body, yet she forced a grin on her lips. "I have something, *someone*, I want you to see. I think you're ready."

What in Caelo's name was he talking about? So far none of Tarnan's surprises had been good. But then a glimmer of hope ignited her heart. What if Tarnan had managed to free her mother?

"If it is my mother, tell me." She bit back her anxiety and gave him a small smile. "I can't handle the suspense."

His smile dropped a bit. "It isn't your mother, I'm afraid."

Amira's chest tightened, but she forced her tone to be gentle. "Why not? I'm spending my days training to rebuild your kingdom. I'm by your side, envisioning the future you want for Liraen. But I will never be able to fully support you if you're unwilling to see what I need." Tarnan watched her closely, but Amira held her ground. He wouldn't expect her to forget her family, her friends. She could only earn his trust if she was still herself. The lies had to be wrapped up in truth. "You can't expect me to agree with everything you do and abandon everyone

I love. If you truly care about me and not just my powers, then when are you freeing my mother? When can I see my friends?"

Tarnan sighed. "All in due time, Amira. I want you to see your friends, to be happy. But they have chosen the other side. You must understand why I can't welcome them here unless they side with me."

Amira glanced at her almost empty plate, letting her fork drop against it.

Flinching at the high-pitched sound, Tarnan put down his spoon and got up. "You'll see I have your best interest in mind. Come with me."

Following him into the winding corridor, Amira's heart sped up. They reached a room in an unfamiliar, dull hallway. The guards bowed to Tarnan before opening the door.

"I'll leave you to it," Tarnan said. "I think you two have a lot of catching up to do." His smile was too kind—never a good sign.

Amira held her breath, readying herself to face another one of Tarnan's tricks. But nothing could have prepared her for what waited inside.

Her eyes settled on the small bed in the room. On it lay Karwyn's corpse, his eyes closed. Amira couldn't understand why Tarnan had decided to keep Karwyn's body instead of burning it. To punish him in death, not letting him join Caelo in the Sky? Inflicting on him the same fate Karwyn had bestowed upon others?

Moving closer, Amira leaned over the bed, taking in Karwyn's pale face. He wore the same clothes, the satin drenched in dried blood. The image of a tear-streaked Rhay flashed through her mind. She wished she could see him again, thank him for choosing a side. *Her* side. Would Rhay have chosen differently if he could see Karwyn now?

Just before Amira could hazard a guess, Karwyn's eyes snapped open. Amira jumped back, a scream dying in her throat. For a second she thought she was seeing things, but then Karwyn's cold stare met hers and her whole world turned as though the floor had dropped out from beneath her feet.

CHAPTER 19

LORA

Hitting the living room floor, the force of the blast knocked the breath out of her. Smoke clung to Lora's lungs, restricting her breathing further. There was a ringing in her ear and her head pounded as if a hammer hit her skull. She tried to pry her eyes open but the smoke was too dense to see anything clearly. The glint of an almandine blade was all she could spot before it swung at her.

As she rolled to the side, the blade splintered the wooden floor mere inches from her face. The fae above her pulled at her sword, but it was stuck in between the floorboards. Coughing up smoke, Lora scrambled to her feet, her head as foggy as the room. The ringing in her ear made it hard for her to stay balanced. She searched for something to lean against but there was just so much smoke. What the hell happened? Had Tarnan's guards managed to call for back-up before they'd taken them out?

She rubbed at her stinging eyes, trying to find Elyssa and Eyden in the chaos.

"Lora!" Craning her neck, she tried to follow Eyden's panicked voice. At that moment, the fae freed her sword and rushed at Lora. She ducked, but the blade sliced her arm. Swaying on her feet, Lora pulled up her arms, throwing the fae back a few steps. In her disoriented state, Lora couldn't quite reach her powers.

Just as the fae seemed to come to the same realisation, Eyden emerged from the smoke and ashes drifting through the room. He held a figure in his arms. With the soot coating the red curls, Lora almost didn't recognise Elyssa. She didn't think she'd ever seen Elyssa passed out, vulnerable. Her blood ran cold even with the fire heating up the space.

As the fae turned to Eyden, who clutched Elyssa tighter, Lora didn't think, just acted. She threw herself at the fae from behind, forcing her to the ground. The fae dropped the sword as Lora landed on top of her. Eyden bent to pick up the sword, holding Elyssa up with one arm. Lora got an elbow to the nose. Cursing, Lora was thrown off the fae, her bruised back hitting the floor. The fae got on top of her, trapping Lora's arms. She gritted her teeth as her fresh wound on her arm burned. Everything felt heavy: her body, the air, the mere act of breathing.

The fae raised her fist and Lora turned her face just as Eyden impaled the fae from behind. With her remaining strength, Lora pushed the fae off her and scrambled to her feet.

"We have to go. The building is going down," Eyden said, his tone warm yet frightened. He held out his hand but Lora froze, his words forcing her to fully realise what was happening.

Dread spread through every inch of her, shivers dancing on her skin. The ringing in her ear turned to white noise. Slowly, she turned her head. One wall of the living room was almost completely torn down, flames clawing at every inch. The ceiling and floor were scorched, the once clean white walls marked by misfortune. The sofa she'd sat on more times than she could name was covered in ashes, one corner going up in flames. The TV had been knocked over, lying broken on the floor next to the splintered table. The faces in the pictures on the walls turned indistinguishable, most of them either scorched or going up in flames—burning the memories away. Burning her past, her childhood, her home. Glancing at the ceiling, she spied the fire taking the first floor, spreading fast.

"Lora, take my hand," Eyden pleaded next to her, but she felt unable to move. Was this really happening?

Through the dense smoke she glimpsed the sun coming in from

the torn-down wall. And more fae. Two of them had their arms outstretched, directing the flames. Anger set her skin on fire. They had done this. They had...she couldn't form the thought, the reality too harsh to face.

"Lora, please," Eyden asked again, Elyssa still in his arms.

A fae with a sword stepped into the room. A cracking noise made the three of them glance up. The ceiling split open and dust forced her to blink. Then it cracked open completely and Lora watched in horror as it came crashing down at them just before she felt Eyden's hand on her arm. And then she was gone, the image of her house going up in flames vanishing from her sight. Gone like her house, her family home, her anchor to her past self. With it, a part of her turned to ashes too.

As soon as her feet landed on solid ground, Lora bent over, coughing up a storm. The harsh kitchen light revealed the dirt, blood, and soot on her skin as she turned over her arm.

"Are you okay? What happened?" Ilario asked. Lora's gaze fell on the unconscious guard tied to a chair in the kitchen.

Gently, Eyden set Elyssa's feet on the ground as she blinked her eyes open. "Hey, welcome back." Swaying on her feet, Elyssa touched the back of her head where her hair was matted with blood.

"Goddamn, that was one hell of a blast," Elyssa said, forcing a fake smile through the hiss of pain.

Keeping Elyssa steady, Eyden turned to Ilario. "It was an ambush. They..." His gaze met Lora's and she shook her head. Not now. She didn't want to hear the words. They'd captured a guard. That was what she had to focus on instead of the needles puncturing her heart and the smoke lingering in her throat.

Elyssa's eyes travelled to Damir's unattended door in the hall. Lora frowned. Breaking away from Eyden and leaning against the kitchen table, Elyssa asked, "Where is everyone?"

"I'm not sure," Ilario said as he stood up, throwing a quick glance at Damir's door. "I checked on Damir quickly but I couldn't leave the guard by himself."

Before Lora could panic, her father walked into the hall. His eyes radiated relief before his brows drew together as his gaze caught on her state, the blood and grime, and then the knocked-out guard. Raising her hand, Lora gestured for him to stay back. She couldn't tell him now. Just thinking about what happened...now wasn't the time.

Seeming to understand, her father walked back to his room.

Turning her head, Lora found Eyden pulling at the rope, dissatisfied. "This won't hold."

"I'll get more chains." Elyssa turned to the back door on unsteady legs. They stored all their weapons in the shed outside. Lora's father had to take a close look at Elyssa soon.

"I'll find out which corner Rhay has crawled into," Lora huffed. "And what the hell happened to Maja."

It wasn't like Maja to go against her word. What had made her abandon her watch over Damir? After this day, Lora couldn't handle losing anything or anyone else.

Lost in thought, Lora didn't bother to knock as she pushed open the door to Maja's room. For a long second her brain didn't catch on to the image before her: Maja sitting on the edge of her bed, pulling her shirt over her head. A shirtless Rhay standing before her, his back to Lora as he pulled his sweatpants up.

Rhay whirled around but Lora was focused on Maja, whose lips parted as she hastily sprang up, straightening her shirt.

"You're back early," Maja stated, her eyes travelling over Lora, concern flashing in her gaze.

Lora's gaze drifted back to a smirking Rhay. His sweatpants hung low but he seemed in no hurry to fix it.

"Anyone ever tell you it's rude to stare, love?"

Lora's eyes snapped back to his face.

"You might want to lock the door next time if you don't want anyone to see," Ilario snarled, his tone strangled. He stood frozen in place behind Lora with a clear view of the room and who had been sharing it.

At Ilario's words Rhay's easy smile crumbled. Without another word, Ilario pivoted and strode off. Lora's heart squeezed. She'd seen the way Ilario looked at Rhay. But Rhay...she had no idea if he was serious about anyone that way.

Hissing under his breath, Rhay tied his sweatpants, grabbed his sweater, and headed after Ilario before he even pulled the fabric over his head.

Maja remained, her hand running through her tangled short hair. She went to retrieve her glasses from the bedside table. "Are they together?" Maja's arms crossed over her chest. "Because I didn't know...I thought Ilario and Damir had history."

"They did, years ago. Ilario and Rhay...they're *something*. I think."

Letting out a long breath, Maja straightened her shirt. "Jesus. And I here thought Rhay was the less complicated hook-up option compared to Damir."

Lora's skin prickled as she let her words sink in. "I'm sorry, but *what the hell* were you thinking?"

Maja pinched her dark brows together as she stared at her. "It's just sex, Lora. Relax."

"You can sleep with whoever you want—but Rhay, really?—but you were supposed to watch over Damir, not decide who to hook up with!"

"Damir's all locked up, and what's wrong with Rhay besides the obvious? He's a drunk who clearly isn't looking for more than fun. Works for me." Maja shrugged, but there was irritation in her high tone.

"He's in a bad place right now," Lora snapped. Rhay didn't need another distraction. He needed to face his demons.

Maja huffed. "Well, so am I!" She laughed, but it wasn't cheerful as Lora was used to. This was another laugh, one Lora had only heard a few times. "In case you haven't noticed, I'm not used to being on the run, hunted by fae who would literally slice me in half if given the chance!" Maja shouted, catching Lora off guard as her voice drove straight to her heart. "I got shot at by officers! I *was* shot. And let's not forget that less than a bloody week ago I thought I would have to tell my best friend's parents that their daughter died."

Dragging her fingers through her matted hair, Maja clenched her jaw. "You put it all on me, Lora. And I've been trying to be there for you because I *know* you've had it so much harder than me. But I'm not fine. I'm *so* beyond fine. I'm on a whole other level—"

Lora pulled Maja into an embrace as she felt tears well in her eyes. In all the chaos and madness of their situation, Lora had never even asked Maja how she was doing.

"I'm sorry, I should have realised," Lora whispered, pulling back to look into Maja's pained eyes. "I hate that I pulled you into this."

Maja shrugged. "It was my choice to get pulled into this mess. And you've had a lot on your mind. Like saving the whole world."

Lora buried her face in her hands. "Let's not phrase it that way or we'll both go crazy." Pulling her hands back, Lora got stuck on the soot and blood beneath her fingernails. A deep hollowness took a hold of her, an emptiness that she could never fill. It really hit her, flashes of the fire invading her mind. It wasn't a bad dream, it was her reality. Lips trembling, she couldn't help the tears from falling.

Maja took her hands, forcing Lora's gaze up. "Hey, we'll both be okay. I want to help you, Lora. I couldn't turn my back on you and your family when you've been by my side for all these years, listening to me complain about my fucked-up mum."

Her shoulders shook as Lora cried harder, her body weightless. "It's all gone." The words were barely audible through the sobs. "My house...they burned it."

Maja breathed in sharply, then her arms went around Lora, holding her tight. She whispered, "I'm so sorry, Lora. They'll pay. I know they will. You still have me and your family. I won't leave you to deal with this by yourself."

For a minute, Lora savoured Maja's embrace, throwing her back to her childhood. Although her heart felt like ashes trying to stick themselves back together, Lora forced herself to back away. She wiped at her eyes, breathing out deeply. This was all Tarnan's fault. He'd regret forcing her to return to Liraen. He'd regret sending guards after her, her family, her home. Lora would return to Liraen, she'd even claim the

Turosian throne just to get close to Tarnan, to take part in the contest. And then she would make him understand how it feels to have one's world ripped to shreds.

With a worried look, Maja brushed back a strand of hair sticking to Lora's cheek. "So you think I went crazy?"

Lora snorted, but it turned into a cough. She welcomed the distraction. "Well…"

Maja laughed, a joyous note to it this time. "We can't all have our own Mister Broody."

A grin stretched Lora's lips. "He's special."

"Damn, you're even more gone than I thought."

Lora bit her lip. "I've never…loved anyone this way."

"Love? Never heard you say that either. I'm happy for you. I know you must feel awful right now, but focus on that. You're not alone."

Reaching out, Lora took Maja's hand. She swallowed another sob caught in her throat. "And I'm sorry, I really am. If you need to talk, I'll be here. And if you want to hook up with Rhay, I won't judge." Maja squinted. "*Much*."

"It's not about Rhay. It was nothing more than a distraction. Which might have cost me a potential friendship with Ilario. Of course I happen to insert myself into a love triangle. I'm such a moron. You know me, I'm no strings, no drama."

A yell pulled Lora's attention to the door. Focusing her hearing, she could make out the guard cursing them all.

"Duty calls, huh?" Maja observed, tilting her head to the door. "Let's go."

Lora followed Maja out into the kitchen. No one was guarding Damir's door, but they could see it from the kitchen.

The guard was now bound to the chair with multiple thick chains. Eyden leaned down to meet his angry stare. Elyssa stood close by, the guard's sword in hand, ready to intervene. Ilario and Rhay weren't present.

"How is Tarnan planning on getting his hands on the agreement?"

Eyden asked, his face stern. His sleeves were rolled up, muscles straining as he put one hand on the armchair.

"Just kill me. I won't tell you anything," the guard spit out, trying to move his arms, but they were locked down tight.

Eyden tilted his head, catching Lora's gaze, and she understood his plan. Eyes set on the guard, Lora tried to imagine reaching out to him silently, catching his thoughts.

"Do you really want to die for your king?" Eyden kept the guard focused on him as Lora pulled on her energy.

Clenching her teeth, she imagined a bolt hitting the guard's head, letting her inside. She hit an invisible wall, the façade as hard as stone. Sweat built on her forehead.

The guard's head abruptly turned to Lora. "What the fuck are you doing?" Lora's focus snapped and she would have tripped if Maja didn't steady her.

"Fuck this," Elyssa exclaimed. She pushed Eyden to the side and before anyone could say a word, Elyssa punched the guard's face with her brass knuckles. His nose dripped blood as Elyssa swung another time, then another. Eyden grabbed her arm.

Sighing, Elyssa shook him off. "Let's try this again." She leaned down, getting right in the guard's face. "Where's the goddamn agreement? Does Tarnan know?" At the guard's silence, Elyssa raised her almandine sword, the sharp edge pointed at his chest. With the soot sticking to her skin she looked like someone no one would dare mess with. "If you don't give us something, death will be too good for you."

Closing her eyes this time, Lora tried to reach for the power that wasn't supposed to be hers.

The guard laughed, and Lora's eyes snapped open. His teeth were stained red. "Your attempt is pathetic."

Elyssa pulled her arm back and struck the guard across his face with the hilt of her sword. The fae spat blood, yet he was still laughing.

"You better speak now or my sister will lose all her patience," Eyden ground out, now twirling a knife in his hand. "And so will I."

Shaking his head, the guard's grin looked half insane. "I can't, you fools. Tarnan made me sign a blood contract to keep quiet."

The room grew tense as Lora met Eyden's frown and Elyssa's crestfallen face. Of course Tarnan would take precautions. But if Lora could read his mind, he wouldn't be telling anyone, would he?

The question in her head was interrupted by a loud noise as if something heavy hit the ground. Lora whirled around, spotting Damir in the hall, his door on the ground—knocked off its hinges. Damir's eyes flickered over their group as if searching for something and not finding it. Or *him*.

Eyden tensed beside her, having stepped closer to Lora. But to her surprise, Damir didn't run; instead he walked up to them in slow steps, his violet eyes hard and unrelenting—a guard's stare.

Watching his every step, Lora was unsure what to do, but her decision was made for her as Damir sped up. Before anyone could intervene, he gripped Elyssa's sword as he kicked at the chair, knocking the guard to the hard tile floor. The guard grunted as Damir lowered himself, digging the blade into the guard's neck. Blood swelled from the cut.

"I think you'll find that talking is not in your cards anymore," Damir sneered, pressing the blade into the guard's skin.

"Don't kill him, goddammit!" Elyssa yelled.

Gripping his shoulder, Eyden tried to pull Damir back. Damir's gaze met Lora's over his shoulder, the darkness in his eyes taking her breath for a second. She had been wrong before, this wasn't the look of a guard. It was the one of an assassin.

"If you want to read him, now's the time, Adelway. But you'll have to get real close."

Voice strangled, the guard cursed, blood dripping from his mouth as his body twitched, trying to escape the cold blade.

"You better let her in, or heads will roll," Damir snapped.

Her stomach turning, Lora knelt down to put her hand on the guard. Up close, the blade digging into the guard's throat looked even more brutal. Shutting her eyes against the violence, Lora tried to read him for a third time. This time the wall felt thinner, and as she pushed against it, she felt it give in.

The guard's thoughts were a strangled mess of pain and anger, but in the middle of it all one thought rose above the chaos: *I don't even know where the fucking agreement is. Tarnan will never get the human ruler to talk.*

Eyes snapping open, Lora met the guard's hazy gaze. "Which human ruler?"

The guard grunted as Damir increased the pressure of the blade. So much blood was drenching the guard's black uniform, gathering on the once-clean tiles.

I don't know, some minister or whatever the human term is, the guard thought.

"Tarnan captured him? So he doesn't know where the agreement is yet either?" Lora asked.

You think he'd wait if he did? As he struggled to stay conscious and his breathing slowed, the guard's eyes turned pleading. *Please let me go. I don't know anything else.*

Tarnan wouldn't trust any guard with sensitive information. He was too smart. But Lora couldn't help but think they were missing something. Something this guard couldn't give them.

Rising to her feet, Lora said, "He doesn't know—"

Damir pulled back his blade and then swung it down before she could stop him, decapitating the guard in one strike. Maja gasped. Blood seeped from the guard's detached head. Bile rose in Lora's throat.

"Was that necessary?" Maja asked, a hand on her lips.

Damir wiped at the blood on his face with his sleeve as he dropped the sword. "Told you I could do some damage." His gaze set on Maja before his eyes turned to Lora. "I just did you a favour, Adelway."

"What do you want, a thank you?" she shot back.

"I don't need a thank you." He walked closer and Eyden stepped into his path, pointing a sword at his chest. "Easy, Kellen."

"What's your plan here?" Eyden asked. "If you try to run"—his eyes drifted to the dead guard—"I'll return the favour."

"I could leave if I wanted to. You won't kill me, Kellen. Don't kid yourself. I watched you just as much as you watched me."

Eyden's face hardened, the vein on his forehead pulsing.

Damir's face remained stoic, a perfect mask. "But it won't be in my best interest." That was all he knew, wasn't it? *Pretence.* Right now, Lora wanted to pretend too. Pretend her house still stood intact, that she wasn't scared about what Tarnan would plan next. But unlike Damir, Lora didn't have the luxury to sit by idly.

Yet Lora wouldn't have expected his next words. Turning his head to Lora, Damir said calmly, "I happen to be in the market for a new position."

CHAPTER 20

RHAY

Rushing after Rio, Rhay almost fell as he put his shoes on, holding the front door open with his elbow. Rio didn't slow down, disappearing between the trees. Wishing he had his flask with him, Rhay shivered against the cold and followed after Rio, snow crunching beneath his feet. When Rhay entered the small clearing where Rio had stopped, Rio didn't turn around.

"Bit cold for a stroll, isn't it?" Rhay started, attempting to diffuse the tension.

"Walk away, Rhay."

Rhay breathed in sharply, his chest caving in. *Rhay.* He didn't think Rio had ever called him by his real name.

Even a non-empath could guess Rio was pissed off. But Rhay didn't know if he wanted to truly consider why. A few minutes ago, nothing had mattered. Now, real-life consequences had once again caught up to him.

"Come on, let's go back inside. It's freezing and you didn't take your coat." Rio sat on a tree trunk and crossed his arms against his chest. "Don't be a child, Rio. I never promised you anything."

Rio scoffed before springing up, dusting off snow. As he spoke, he walked closer, finally meeting his gaze. "You know what I don't get?" The emerald in his eyes had darkened, tearing at Rhay's heart—if he still had one. "You'll kiss her—you'll kiss every random fae who flirts with you—but every time I get close to you, you pull away. What's wrong with me?"

"You're not wrong, *I* am. You're...perfect." Couldn't Rio understand that love was not in the cards for Rhay? That the one time he had tried, he had ruined everything?

"Why does everyone always run?" Rio's voice broke. Was he talking about Rhay or still caught up on Damir? The thought troubled Rhay more than he'd like to admit.

"You're not *wrong* either, Nix." Rio tilted his head at him, a sad chuckle on his lips, the anger still present underneath. "Do you remember the first time we met? I'd had the worst day, my healing herbs had grown all wrong. No one wanted to buy them. And then you strolled in, wearing that extravagant pink satin shirt."

Was Rio trying to prove that Rhay was not *wrong*? The thought was laughable, Rhay knew he was *nothing*. All Rhay kept doing was hurt Rio, and yet Rio was insistent on making Rhay feel better. And a part of him enjoyed it. A part of him wanted Rio to keep coming back even though he didn't deserve it.

Rio cleared his throat. "I thought you'd be the sort of customer who would throw a tantrum if you didn't get your way. But you just laughed. You saw right through my anxiety and made a grand spectacle of buying my herbs, making sure everyone was listening to your praises, spouting the funniest lies I've ever heard. No one had looked at me that way in a very long time." The words lingered between them like heady smoke. "But I guess it didn't mean anything to you."

He hadn't thought Rio would remember that day so clearly, and now he couldn't think of anything else but Rio's relieved smile from back then. Would it really be so bad if Rhay just gave in once? Rhay leaned in, ready to kiss Rio, to finally cross the line he had sworn he wouldn't breach. His breathing turned heavy, the anticipation burning a dark hole in his chest.

Maybe it wouldn't blow up in his face. Maybe it could erase the emptiness in him.

But Rio moved away and Rhay's lips brushed his cheek in a disappointing finale.

"I don't want to be one of your distractions," Rio whispered, stepping back.

"It's not like that," Rhay defended himself in a pathetic attempt to save face. It *was* like that.

"Only kiss me," Rio started, and Rhay almost leaned in again, "if you truly mean it."

Rhay clenched his jaw. He knew why Rio rejected him, but it still stung more than it should—more than it ever had, not that he had gotten many rejections in life. "There's no reason to be so serious. Why complicate things?"

"You know why, you're an empath." Rio's tone was daring with a hint of desperation.

Rhay turned his back to Rio, unable to admit what they both knew. He couldn't handle Rio's serious tone. He couldn't let himself see all of Rio when Rhay had no grip on his own feelings. Forcing a laugh, Rhay shrugged. "You're so dramatic."

Rio scoffed. "Every time things get a little bit too real you run away. Have recent events not shown you that life is too fleeting to hide behind deflection? Talk to me when you're ready to live."

Without letting him reply, Rio passed by Rhay, bumping his shoulder as he hurried out of the clearing. Left alone, surrounded by large pine trees covered in freshly fallen snow, Rhay's shoulders caved in. Opening his mouth, Rhay let out a silent cry before crumpling to his knees. As he lay on the ground, the massive trees towering above him, Rhay felt like his heart had been ripped out of his chest.

Rio was right, he kept running away. But couldn't he see Rhay wasn't made for the kind of blissful love Rio deserved? He had no heart to give. In its place was just an empty hole that Rhay would never be able to fill no matter how hard he tried.

After spending much longer than he cared to admit lying in the forest clearing, Rhay knocked on Lora's door. On his way, he had spotted Elyssa and Damir dragging a decapitated corpse out of the kitchen. If he wasn't feeling so low, Rhay would have questioned Damir's new role in their team—if he could call it that. But who was he to ask that question? He didn't feel like he was part of it.

The door opened on a clearly pissed-off Eyden. "What do you want, Rhay?"

Great, another fae ready to chew him out.

Dragging his fingers through his damp hair, Rhay put on a fake smile, fighting against the cold lingering on his skin. "I want to talk to Lora."

Eyden turned around to Lora sitting on the sofa bed, her shirt half untucked from her trousers. Lora stood up, her legs shaking a bit. "I'm in no mood to be yelled at." She had clearly exhausted herself. Her eyes were puffy. But Rhay couldn't turn back now or he might lose his nerve.

"You owe me, little Adelway." They both cringed at the nickname, and Eyden's hand tensed on the doorframe, the wood creaking. "You said I could talk to you whenever I want," Rhay finished as he let his sadness shine through his eyes. With his clothes wet from the snow, his dark hair dreary, he must have looked as much of a mess as he felt.

Lora sighed. "Fine." She gave Eyden a light kiss. "I'll be with you in a minute." On his way out, Eyden elbowed Rhay in the ribs.

"You have a good guard dog." Rhay stalked into the room, closing the door behind him while Lora sat back on her bed.

"If you're not planning on having a serious conversation, you should go. I'm in no state to entertain your ever-changing moods." Lora's face was stern, her arms crossed over her chest. In her eyes, he saw the exhaustion of the looming battle ahead. But there was something more, an overbearing sadness.

"Are you okay?"

She squinted at him. "You don't want to hear it. You made that clear."

Rhay sat on the bed beside her. "I wouldn't have asked if I didn't care."

Lora paused, then took a deep breath, but a sob got caught in her throat. "It's my home. It got...destroyed during the fight today."

A wave of icy water splashed against him, grounding him back to reality. "I'm...sorry." Rhay scooted closer to her and put a hand on her shoulder hesitantly, afraid she would reject him. "I still dream about my childhood home. We left it in such a hurry after my mother's death. I have no idea what has become of it."

To his surprise, Lora leaned into his touch. "I feel like I lost a part of myself. I'm so tired of Tarnan taking and *taking* from me."

Tarnan couldn't keep getting away with this, couldn't keep hurting the people he cared about. And he *did* care. He realised that now. Lora hadn't been completely honest with him, but he hadn't been forthcoming either. He could see Lora cared about him in a way Karwyn's twisted heart could never.

Rhay pointed at Lora's chest, right at her heart. "Your memories are still here. Tarnan can't take that away from you."

Lora smiled through her teary eyes. "What happened to you? Did you finally sober up enough?"

Rhay suppressed a sad laugh, remembering his fight with Rio. "Do you think I messed up?"

Lora raised an eyebrow. "You'll have to be more precise. I have a long list of times you've fucked up."

Rhay put his head in his cold hands. "With Rio. I didn't mean to hurt him. But I seem to always hurt the people who stupidly care about me." He raised his head to meet Lora's hard gaze. "Did you know that I was the one who triggered Amira's powers? All because I stupidly kissed her."

"You kissed Amira?" In shock, Lora sat up straight on the bed. "I think you'd better never mention it to Elyssa if you want to live."

"I knew her first!" Rhay moved the hair sticking to his forehead away from his face. "It doesn't matter anyway, she never cared about me that way. But Rio...Rio cares so much, too much. I'll mess everything up, like I always do." Rhay sprung off the bed and paced the room.

"After what we've been through, it's hard to envision letting love into your life," Lora said. "But what about after? What will you do when we're back in Turosian?"

Will you help us? He could hear the underlying question.

Lora walked up to him, forcing him to stop his pacing. "I'm not going to talk you into anything this time. It's your decision; you can keep deflecting here or you can go make a difference. That's all I'll say."

Opening the door, she gave him one last look before leaving him with much to think about. He heard Eyden's voice down the hall as Lora joined the others. How had Lora been able to let love in with everything that had happened?

Because she deserves it, a voice in his head haunted him, threatening to drag him even further into despair.

But Lora's voice was louder. *It's your decision.* Rhay had friends right here and another one under Tarnan's grasp. He had to help. For Amira, for Lora, for Rio. He couldn't stay here, drinking until he became a shadow of himself. He had to go through the door he had already opened and fight until the end. For his friends but also for himself—for the better version of him that he would like to see one day.

CHAPTER 21

AMIRA

Karwyn's eyes had changed, no longer looking merely fae. The striking turquoise had dimmed and a strange layer of silver framed his irises. Amira had never seen anything like it.

"How are you still alive?" were the only words Amira was capable of uttering when Karwyn looked her over. His face was sickly pale and his golden blond hair had lost its shine. It contrasted the white walls of the small space. A single beam of light came in from the tiny round window close to his single bed. The room reeked of death, the air stale with a mix of sweat and vomit. With no decor in sight, it looked like the person it belonged to was long gone. Yet Karwyn's chest was rising and falling with every living breath.

Karwyn erupted into a coughing fit. "I am wondering that myself."

"I saw you die." Amira held on to the wall as her vision started closing in. She wanted to put as much distance as possible between her and Karwyn, but the room was so small. If she extended her hand, Amira could touch the dark wooden frame of Karwyn's bed.

Karwyn tried to rise on his forearms, but his body shook and he was unable to hold the position. He gripped his once-white bed sheets that showed multiple bloodstains. "My dear fiancée, always so clever. I was the one who got a sword through the heart, I am well aware of how impossible my existence is. I would have rather stayed dead than be Tarnan's prisoner—and I suppose yours too. Bravo, you played your cards well."

"You're not *my* prisoner. But you tortured me for weeks when I was living in Turosian, making life hell for me, and let's not forget your attempt to kill me. So, no, I'm not going to pretend to be unhappy about your current situation." Maybe this was his punishment, his doom.

Karwyn let out a dark laugh. "Always complaining about inconsequential details. You think I was mean to you? Poor little girl. You have no idea the pressure I have been under since birth. My father took great pleasure in reminding me every day. I have been nicer to you than he ever was to me."

Amira scoffed. "You mocked me at every turn. You threatened me repeatedly, almost pushing me off the balcony. You gave Wryen every reason to torture me and you enjoyed watching me squirm. You killed Nalani." Karwyn furrowed his brows. "Do you deny it?"

Karwyn clenched the sheets, the rustling sound irritating Amira's ears. "I did what I had to since you were unable to behave."

Amira's mouth dropped open. "You're saying it's my fault? You tried to *kill* me!"

"You turned my best friend against me!" Karwyn yelled, rising up before falling back again, a pained sigh on his lips.

Amira balled her hands into fists, forcing herself to stay still. "No. You did that all by yourself. All I did was help Rhay see. *What* he saw is all *your* doing."

Karwyn flinched, turning away from her. Yet there was nowhere to escape.

Amira managed to calm her voice. "Why do you hate me so much? We share a similar upbringing. Your father, my brother, they never played their part as they should have, handing us pain instead of love. We could have related to one another. You could have seen another lost soul in me and shown me kindness instead of lashing out at me. You decided to follow in your father's footsteps. I chose to fight back."

Karwyn squinted at her, the purple shadows underneath his eyes prominent. "Yet here we are, both prisoners of Tarnan." She saw the question in his eyes, and the hesitation cost her. "I thought as much. I suppose our choices did not make that much of a difference in the end. You want to know why I despise you?"

Amira sighed. "We're both stuck here, so what's the point in lying anymore?"

Karwyn's disenchanted laugh ended in another coughing fit. When he removed his hand from his mouth, there was blood, the metallic scent infiltrating Amira's nose. "My health seems to be worsening rapidly, another thing my father would be disappointed about. His son slowly dying as his enemy's prisoner..." He cleared his throat. "You say our upbringing was similar, maybe that is why I have always despised you—since the first time Rhay gave you a carefree smile that he had not given me in years. He was the *one* good thing about my childhood. Perhaps that is what drew you to him too. We both know it was not his flirting that pulled you in."

Amira narrowed her eyes at him.

"Do you deny it?" Karwyn raised a brow. "I thought there was no point in playing games any longer. He might have been interested in you, but I knew you were not interested in him since that day I read your mind when Varsha was painting our engagement portrait. You were more *fascinated* by her." The name made Amira's heart ache. "For a brief instant, I imagined we might be able to live with each other after all, platonically, but you had a knack for causing me trouble and I could not let it go on."

"And you thought threatening me, forcing me to watch the execution, would teach me a lesson?"

"It should have frightened you straight." Karwyn's gaze drifted from her face. Amira pondered what Karwyn's end goal had been. Frighten her into pretending to be straight when they both wanted different things? Force her to ignore her true feelings as Karwyn seemed to have done his whole life?

Karwyn's strained voice pulled her attention back to the present. "It was Saydren who suggested fortae might help with your behaviour, but it only made you reckless." His sickly pale skin and hollow cheeks made Amira shiver. He did look like he was dying.

"He offered me fortae once, but I didn't take it back then." Even now, the taste of fortae lingered on Amira's tongue.

Karwyn's chapped lips turned into a mocking smile. "Dear Amira, do you not see the bigger picture?"

A knot formed in her throat when she realised what he was getting at. "The fortae dealer, the one who disappeared, you sent him, didn't you?" At Karwyn's insistent stare, Amira's heart sank. "Saydren did. And Saydren works for Tarnan."

The air left her lungs. The betrayal cut deeper than she had expected. The bright walls turned blurry, shrouding her in a cloud of dark thoughts. All this time, had Tarnan been waiting for the chance to whisk Amira away? And to think he had her believe he would close down the Void—as if he hadn't played a part in it.

She turned her head as the door opened behind her. Tarnan entered the room, and Amira curled her hand into a fist behind her back, drawing blood. He looked almost disappointed, as if he had expected to find Amira strangling Karwyn.

"I'm assuming you've had time to catch up. Let's go, Amira. Karwyn needs to rest. Begone in fortune." He let out a short laugh.

Amira gave Karwyn one last look. He tilted his chin as if to say 'I told you so.' They had both been played. She turned and walked out.

"Did you like my surprise?" Tarnan asked once she joined him in the spacious hallway, much bigger than Karwyn's room. Sunlight streamed in through the large windows lining the hall, throwing warm light to the orange-coloured walls. Tarnan seemed in an awfully good mood, the kind of mood Amira was wary of.

She fell into step beside him. "What did you do to him? He shouldn't be alive."

"Saydren is very gifted," Tarnan offered as an explanation while they passed by paintings of the Carnylen kingdom. One of them showed the Pyrian library that Amira had glimpsed on the stroll she had taken with

Tarnan and Elyssa not long ago. She had marvelled at it back then; now the memory only left a sour taste in her mouth.

Amira shook her head. "He was *dead*. No one can bring back the dead."

"When there's magic involved, there are endless possibilities. Perhaps I'll share more with you once I've fully gained your trust back."

Furrowing her brows, Amira tried to make sense of it all, pushing past the sting of betrayal heating her veins. "What do you plan to do with him?"

Tarnan opened the door to her quarters and she followed him in. Amira hated being confined to these rooms. Everywhere she looked—from the bookshelves stacked with ancient knowledge gifted by Tarnan to the wardrobe filled with clothes he had picked out for her—everything reminded her of his attempt to mold her to his will.

Tarnan patted Amira's cheek. "For Karwyn, being powerless—basically human—is worse than being dead. Keeping him alive in this state is my gift to you and myself. I wish Harten could see me now, but his death was a necessary sacrifice."

Treading lightly, Amira pushed away her disgust at Tarnan's action and let the darkness in her heart speak. "Thank you. He deserves it."

Tarnan grabbed Amira by the shoulders, his smile growing. "It was never part of my plan for you to endure any of Karwyn's abuse. You must realise that. I'll do anything for you if you stand by my side. I've been thinking about what you told me at dinner. You're right, I haven't given you enough. I promise you I will get your mother once we're back from Rubien, you'll only have to say the word. And I promise I won't hurt Elyssa—unless she attacks me, of course."

Amira couldn't help but smile. "Thank you."

As sickening as his words were, they made it clear she was on the right track. Tarnan was buying into her act. She could win this—free herself and doom Tarnan in her place.

Letting go of Amira's shoulder, Tarnan took out a scroll from his jacket's pocket. "To assure you of my intention, let's put it in writing."

Amira's eyes widened as her heart slowed down. Her skin turned ice cold. Her head emptied. This couldn't be real. Amira hid her hands behind her back to stop herself from snatching the contract from his hands. "What is this?"

"Just a little addendum to our current blood contract. I've added my promises about your mother and Elyssa so you know I mean it." He placed the scroll on her desk. "It also says that any substantial injuries or life-threatening conditions, both magical or non-magical, I might sustain, you will sustain as well. To make sure that your friends understand which side you're truly on. And this way, if you wish so, I'm willing to let Elyssa live with us."

A shiver ran down her spine. "If we trust each other, why do we need a contract at all?"

Tarnan smiled at her but it wasn't kind. It was telling her they were playing a dangerous game and she was about to lose again. "It's a proof of our trust, Amira. Have I misread you?"

All this time, she had thought she was playing him perfectly. But she should have known Tarnan would always be two steps ahead. Her heart felt as if it was constricted by a razor-sharp fence, stealing her breath. She had to concede her defeat. If she refused to sign she would be back to square one, and who knew what Tarnan would do to her and her mother then? What would he do to Elyssa and her other friends if he caught them? All Amira wanted was to be free, to be reunited with her friends.

Tarnan would compel her to sign if she didn't agree willingly, Amira was sure of it. There was no sense in fighting when she would lose either way. It was heart-shattering to have the contract this close but be unable to break it.

Amira forced a breath, her chest hurting. "I'll sign if you promise to stop compelling Farren. Give him a chance to prove himself. After all, he wouldn't dare harm you once he knows about our link."

Tarnan smiled at her as if he'd won and they both knew it. "All right. But at the first sign of betrayal, I'll have to resort to alternative measures."

Swallowing hard, Amira took the pen Tarnan had produced from his pocket. The sharp nib pricked the delicate skin of her finger, drawing her blood. In scarlet letters, Amira signed her name at the bottom of the scroll, feeling her freedom escape her once more.

CHAPTER 22

🔥

ELYSSA

The cold morning wind drifted through Elyssa's thin coat as she headed to the entrance of the London Police Headquarters—the centre of the police force according to Lora. The others were waiting around the corner for Elyssa's signal. Elyssa and Maja were the only ones who could enter the police station without immediately turning heads, and Lora had refused to put her friend in harm's way again. So Maja had been tasked with guarding Damir again who they haven't yet decided what to do with.

Maja had given Elyssa a platinum blonde wig as a disguise in case anyone did recognise her from one of the videos taken at the beach. The wig itched, and Elyssa had to stop herself from ripping it off. Approaching the building alone, she couldn't help but think back on the camp. Would her friends back home help if they were here now? Or would they never listen to Elyssa again after what happened with Tarnan?

Shaking her head, Elyssa curled her hand into a fist in her pocket. When she reached the glass door at the front of the huge building, it opened automatically as if by magic. If she could find the answers they needed without a fight, she'd try for Lora's sake. But they were all braced for a fight.

The room was filled with people, desperate voices blending together, making it impossible for Elyssa to understand anything. Surveying the big open space, she craned her neck. She spotted several desks in the back, humans in uniforms rushing about—clearly distressed—and a smaller desk with a 'reception' sign close to her. A group of people had gathered by the entrance and around that desk.

The floor was a dull grey, but the high ceiling was made of sparkling glass. *Think, then act,* Elyssa reminded herself, even though her hand craved the handle of her knife and her feet wanted to rush forward.

Elyssa pushed her way through the mob of people to the restricted area. The burner phone in her pocket weighed down her jacket. With no runia or fire messages, they had to settle for the human way of communication.

As she turned her head, a policeman stepped into her path before Elyssa could reach the area filled with desks and other officers. They were closed off by glass walls.

"Can I help you, miss?" the officer asked, his face stern and suspicious as his gaze lingered on her neck. The cut was barely visible but not gone.

"I've come across some intel about the fae. Who can I talk to?"

The officer laughed in her face. "You and everyone here, honey. Go to the receptionist."

He was about to turn, but Elyssa's next words stopped him in his tracks. "You don't want my information about the prime minister's kidnapping?"

Slowly, the officer looked her over, and she stared right back. "I think you're mistaken."

"I guess you don't want to know who has him, then?"

The officer's gaze travelled over her head to the glass offices. She could see his mind going over his options. His hand absently drifted to the gun strapped to his side. "Come with me."

Elyssa followed him to one of the offices, keeping track of the number of officers and weapons on their bodies. If she couldn't get the intel they needed, this would get tricky, but not impossible. Lora's father had warned her not to overdo it. If there was one thing Elyssa didn't excel at, it was taking it easy.

The officer gestured for her to take a seat across from his desk as he sat behind it. "Go on, then."

"Quid pro quo," Elyssa said, crossing her arms. "I'll tell you who has him if you tell me what you're doing to keep the humans safe."

The officer leaned back in his chair. "We're doing our best to keep the border contained—"

"No." Elyssa straightened her back. "I'm talking about the agreement. How are you keeping that secure?"

"That's confidential."

Elyssa leaned forward, never breaking her stare. "You know something. I can tell."

"Are you wasting my time or do you actually know something?" the officer asked. "Because withholding information is illegal."

"Really?" Her hand went to her pocket inconspicuously, pressing a button on her burner phone. "Well, you'll have to forgive me, I'm not exactly from around here."

The man's eyes widened as he shifted in his seat. "You're not fae."

"Nope, but as you all might have forgotten, you left some humans behind when the border spell was created."

The officer tensed, his gaze flicking to his colleagues close by. In that precise moment, all hell broke loose.

Beyond the glass office, people panicked, running in all directions as officers stormed out of their offices, guns drawn. Elyssa couldn't see what had set them off, but she knew. She couldn't keep the grin off her face as the officer's lips parted in surprise at the scene playing out on the other side of the glass.

Springing to her feet, she tilted her head to the door. "Let's go."

The officer got up, his hand drifting to the gun strapped to his side, but Elyssa was faster, a small knife slipping out of her sleeve and into the man's shoulder. He grunted as his hand went to his wound, his gun forgotten. Her gaze travelled to the closest officers, their guns moving to point at Elyssa behind the glass wall, but she was quick.

A shot was fired, spraying glass everywhere just as Elyssa rolled on the ground, hands covering her face. She dove behind the desk, then sprang up, moving behind the officer. She pulled the knife out of his skin, keeping it close to his throat from behind. The other officers held their fire.

Moving backwards with the guard, Elyssa kept her back to the wall. She was aware that with every second, more guns were pointed at her. But she didn't have to wait long. Through the chaos and panicked screams, Elyssa couldn't pick up the words, but she was sure the mob recognised Lora.

She spotted her friends as the crowd rushed away. Officers were pushed to the side, Ilario and Rhay keeping them busy, their almandine swords deflecting bullets. The humans closest to Rhay seemed to calm down as they headed to the exit.

In front of them, Lora and Eyden strode through the crowd with purpose, Eyden with his sword and Lora with her hands raised as she walked towards Elyssa.

"I don't mean any harm," Lora announced.

"Then drop the swords and tell your friend to lower the knife," the female officer at the front commanded, gun pointed at Lora. Eyden tensed next to her. Subtly moving her head, Elyssa tried to tell her that the officer she held at knifepoint might have the information they needed.

Getting her signal, Lora took a step forward—she needed to touch him to read his mind as Rhay had taught her since his recent change of heart—but all guns turned to her. The sound of the safeties clicking off echoed through the room.

"Don't shoot to kill!" the female officer shouted. "We need to keep her alive for questioning."

Lora met Elyssa's eyes and they seemed to silently agree: This fight was damn well happening.

Gunshots rang in Elyssa's ears. Yet no bullets connected as Lora raised her hand and the air around her seemed to pulsate, creating a shield to deflect the bullets, halting their momentum and forcing them to the ground. Training had paid off.

The officers, on the other hand, were appalled, shock twisting their features. The female one raised one hand. "If you cease now, we'll give you a chance to explain yourself."

Lora's hand remained raised. "I need to have a chat with your officer first." She pointed her chin at the officer in Elyssa's grip.

"All right, but the men with swords stay put," the female officer said. Ilario and Rhay stood behind them now. Eyes surveying the room, Eyden shifted his feet ever so slightly.

Lora nodded, but the second she strode forward Eyden gripped her arm, pushing her to the side just as a bullet from above tore through the air. Elyssa's gaze snapped to the narrow indoor balcony. An officer pointed a gun at them. He fired again, but this time Lora had noticed him, and with a stroke of air, the officer was pushed against the wall, slumping to the ground above them.

Lora whirled around, and Elyssa followed her gaze to Eyden's chest. A circle of blood soaked his sweater. He'd taken that bullet for Lora. He swayed on his feet, his eyes losing focus. It wasn't almandine, but he must still be weakened. The fury in Lora's eyes spoke volumes, and it must have unsettled the female officer as she moved her hand above her head, pointing forward. Instantly, officers stormed at them. Lora lifted her arms, throwing air at them more aggressively. Rhay ran forward, sword raised, and Ilario commanded the closest plants to grow, tangling the humans' legs.

The officer in Elyssa's grip took advantage of her distraction and elbowed her in the ribs. A grunt of pain forced its way out of her. He tore away, heading for his gun that was only a few paces away. Elyssa swiped his legs from under him with a strategic slide to the ground.

The officer knocked his head against the edge of the table as he fell and lost consciousness. Goddamn, the one time she hadn't meant to knock someone out, she had. *Brilliant.*

A bullet zipped past her, barely missing her shoulder. More officers came in through the back entrance, visible through the glass wall. Elyssa found Eyden's gaze. He gripped his sword in his bloodied hands. They needed to retreat. If they stayed longer, they might win, but it would be a bloodbath, and these humans weren't their enemies.

As she rushed to join the gang, Elyssa felt a grip on her arm. She whirled around, knife pointed at the face of an officer she hadn't seen before.

"Don't!" he screamed, freezing. "I can help. I heard what you said before. You're from Liraen, right?"

Elyssa cocked her head. "How did you hear that?" It had been only her and the other officer in the glass room.

The officer swallowed, seemingly trying to gather his words. His dark brown hair hung in his eyes. Elyssa almost moved back but then the officer's eyes lightened the tiniest bit, turning from a moss green to a brighter emerald.

"You're fae?" she asked, perplexed, pulling the knife back.

"Mate, did you think it only went one way? That only humans got trapped on the *wrong* side?" She hadn't thought much about it, if she was being honest. "Look, I like it here. This is my home now and almost everyone I care about is human. So I don't want anyone breaking that bloody agreement and enslaving humans again any more than you do."

Elyssa narrowed her gaze at him. "Spit it out, then."

Before he could reply, the officer pushed her to the side as a bullet zipped past them. Elyssa grabbed his arm and pulled him down behind the desk.

Breathing heavily, the fae whisper-yelled, "There's a secret facility on Holdenstern Road. It's locked up tight. Mostly made from almandine, but also heavily decked out with cyber security." The sounds of bullets rattled the desk. "You better get out of here now. Do you have a car?"

Elyssa shook her head. Not close by. Eyden had drifted them part of the way. But he was now wounded, limiting his power.

The fae reached into his pocket and put a set of keys in her hand. "My police car is parked out front. Get out of here before the bloody military shows up."

Elyssa didn't have to be told twice. Nodding her thanks, she peeked over the desk, then dove out of their hiding spot. Her gaze instantly connected with Eyden—his eyes telling her to hurry up. Beside him, bleeding from her leg, Lora stumbled. She was trying to hold off as many officers and bullets as possible. What they needed was a bit of a distraction.

Rushing forward, Elyssa barely dodged a bullet before she punched the nearest officer in the face. She threw a nasty kick at the same time as she swiped his gun. Wasting no time, Elyssa aimed at the transparent ceiling and fired three times. Glass exploded, raining down on them. Everyone ducked, and Elyssa ran to Eyden and Lora. Eyden took her hand and then the air lifted her. Seconds later, cold wind brushed her skin as Eyden drifted them out.

Turning her head to the entrance, Elyssa spotted Ilario and Rhay rushing to join them. With a hand gesture from Ilario, the trees close by stretched their roots, blocking the entrance.

"I don't think I can drift all the way back to the car," Eyden said, sweat curling his dark hair.

Elyssa fumbled for the keys in her pocket and pressed the button. "Let's ride, then."

Eyden pointed to a police car close to them, its lights flashing. He kept an arm around Lora, whose leg was bleeding badly, and they rushed to the car. Eyden's bullet wound had drenched the front of his sweater with blood.

"I'll drive," Lora said as the front doors were thrown back open. A bullet flew through the air towards them. Lora turned her head. She lifted her arm to block it, but the blood loss must have slowed her down. Eyden yanked her back and the bullet grazed her arm.

The back door of the car was closest, so Eyden yanked it open and Lora crawled in, a hiss of pain leaving her lips that Elyssa couldn't hear but felt nonetheless. Elyssa jumped into the front seat. Rhay ended up in the passenger seat beside her as Ilario got in behind Eyden.

Remembering how Maja had driven her car, Elyssa pushed the button that read "Start" until the engine roared to life. "What do I do?" she yelled. Lora leaned forward, pulling at a little handle that was blinking red as she winced. She'd used too much of her power at once.

A bullet shattered the window in the back and the group ducked as glass sprayed them from behind. "Select 'D' in the middle, then hit the right pedal on the floor," Lora gritted out as she sank back in her seat.

Slamming her foot down, the car lurched forward at Elyssa's command. Tires squealed as Elyssa wrenched the steering wheel, throwing everyone to the side. The street was much too narrow for her liking, the road lined by trees. People strolled along the sidewalk peacefully until they spotted their car and the officers firing at them from the front steps of the London Police Headquarters.

An elderly woman stepped onto the street, and Elyssa tore at the steering wheel in a panic. The woman threw up her hands, shouting something indistinguishable. Elyssa swerved dangerously close to a car—the driver honking aggressively. Bullets zipped past them, almost scratching the small side mirror. As blonde hair drifted into her face, Elyssa ripped her wig off and tossed it into Rhay's lap.

"Faster!" Rhay shouted next to her, pushing the wig to the floor.

The car squealed, but she stomped on the pedal anyway, pulling at the wheel and driving in zig-zag. How did Maja drive straight? She came so close to the incoming traffic that her side mirror snapped off. Her heart beat so fast she could rival the speed of the car.

Lora screamed as a traffic light came up in front of them. "Shit, it's turning red. Smash the break. Left pedal!"

She hit the right pedal instead. The light turned red, and the car coming from their left almost hit them as Elyssa pulled the wheel abruptly to the right. They barely missed the brick wall lining the street, yet the street lamp came out of nowhere. The car door on Rhay's side dented as it hit the lamp post. Glancing over her shoulder, Elyssa could spot red and blue flashing lights. She stepped on the pedal, lurching forward once again.

Hand on the seat in front of him, Eyden said, "Remind me to never let you drive again."

"As if you could do better," Elyssa shot back. The adrenaline in her veins gave her a thrill until the flashing lights came closer behind them. *Freaking police.* "Take Lora and Ilario out of here."

Eyden met her gaze in the rear-view window. "I can't drift back into a moving vehicle."

"If you go now it will take you like, what, a minute?" She took in the street in front of her. "See that green building up ahead? I'll jump out there."

"El—"

"I know you'll get me. *Go.*"

"Good to know I'm part of this conversation," Rhay said, sarcasm dripping from his tongue. "Seeing as I will also have to jump out of a fucking car."

Eyden's gaze hardened to ice, then he disappeared with Lora and Ilario.

"This feels like deja-vu," Rhay huffed.

"Can't argue—" Elyssa's words were cut off as another police car appeared from a side street, nearly knocking into them. "Fuck." She tried to hit the pedal harder, but it was at its limit. Bullets hit their car. People on the sidewalk ducked, running the opposite direction of their car.

Rhay reached over, and Elyssa was about to yell at him when his hand gripped the gun jammed into her jeans. "Well, guess I'll give this bad boy a try." Pulling down the window, he leaned outside, firing round after round. The car behind them slowed the tiniest bit.

The green building was right ahead of them to their right. "Time to jump."

Twisting, Rhay pulled back inside.

"Three, two, one!" Elyssa slammed on the breaks. The car jerked to a halt in the middle of the road, and she threw her car door open. She curled her body to protect her head as she rolled on the hard asphalt. The breath was knocked out of her. Her body screamed at her and her lungs felt like they were on fire.

A hand touched her shoulder just as she raised her head to see the lights of an oncoming police car. Seconds before it could smash into her, Eyden threw them into the wind. Elyssa barely found her footing as they reached Rhay on the other side of the street. A mix of gunshots and the stormy wind rushed in her ears, throwing Elyssa off balance as Eyden tore them away from the scene. Lost in nothingness, Elyssa's head emptied and her vision turned dark even as she yelled at herself not to slip away.

"How often do I need to break out until you get it, Adelway?" a loud voice brought Elyssa back to consciousness.

Her head hurt like hell, as if hammers were thrown against her skull. Passing out was on the top of Elyssa's most-hated list. It meant being out of control, vulnerable. Two times in one week was way too much for her.

Blinking, Elyssa found herself in the living room at the cabin, lying on the sofa. How had she gotten here? Eyden couldn't have drifted that far. They must have gotten back to the first car they'd initially taken to London.

Damir leaned against the doorframe; Lora was in front of him, a bandage on her arm and leg. Elyssa wasn't sure if she was actually awake. Before they had left, they had chained Damir up and fixed the door, adding an extra lock.

"You're not doing yourself any favors by breaking out," Lora shot back. "We can't even trust you to stay put. How can I trust you with anything else? Why should I?"

The silence was unsettling, but then Damir's gaze snapped to Elyssa on the sofa. "She's awake." Lora followed his gaze, her eyes softening. Damir's hand landed on her uninjured arm. "I'll leave you two, but, Adelway, you and I need to have a chat later. I'll be in my *room*."

Sighing, Lora waited for him to leave, then hobbled towards Elyssa. "Where's everyone?" Elyssa asked.

"My dad is treating Eyden right now." Lora sat on the edge of the sofa and Elyssa pushed herself into a sitting position. She noticed her right arm was in a sling. Her bones felt badly bruised, her right shoulder burned. Pulling back the corner of her shirt, Elyssa took in her scraped-up skin.

"You're lucky you didn't break your arm, but it's badly sprained," Lora said.

Huffing, Elyssa let the fabric fall back into place. "Who knew jumping out of a moving car came with downsides?"

Lora laughed, pointing at her own bandages. "So does walking into a police station as the country's most-wanted criminal."

"That's a pretty badass title, though."

Her smile widened. "Funny how life goes." The corner of her mouth pulled downwards. Was she remembering her family home? Earlier, Lora had told her brother and father what had happened. Oscar had stormed off while Lora's father had insisted all that mattered was that his children were safe. Even though Elyssa didn't know him well, she could tell he only said it for Lora's sake, sensing his sadness. "I didn't get *anything*. I tried so hard to read every officer close to me, but..."

Elyssa scooted closer. "It wasn't for nothing. Quite the opposite."

Lora's brows drew together, but her eyes lightened, her faith in Elyssa clear. A grin stretched Elyssa's lips as the adrenaline rushed back to her. They hadn't lost. No, this round, they'd fucking won.

CHAPTER 23

LORA

Although Lora had known she was wanted by the police, seeing them look at her like she was the enemy had hurt. That thought lingered in her head as Lora left her bathroom. Her wet hair brushed her shoulders. She'd added fresh bandages to her bullet wounds. The one on her thigh still hurt, but she found putting weight on it didn't make it much worse.

As Lora entered her make-shift room, Eyden sat up on the sofa-bed. His eyes took her in, settling on her bare legs, barely covered by her oversized shirt.

"Except for the bandages, I must say, I'm a fan of this look." Eyden's smirk lifted the weight of tomorrow a tiny bit. Would they be able to get the agreement from the building Elyssa had told them about? They *had to.* She wondered if Tarnan had been glad to hear about Lora's house burning down. He was probably still gloating. As hard as Lora tried to move past it, she couldn't help but linger on all the items she'd lost. They had held memories of her childhood, of Oscar's, of a time unplagued by viruses and life-threatening battles. Biting her lip, Lora hobbled to the bed, still unsteady.

"You okay?" Eyden scooted to the edge of the bed.

"All things considered, I'm fine." Her gaze went to his chest, but his own wound was covered by clothes. Eyden had taken that bullet for her. It hadn't been almandine, but she couldn't help but worry that one day it might be. "How about you?"

"Don't worry, special one," Eyden replied, reaching out to take her hand. "I've had worse."

Her fingers wrapped around the fabric of his black shirt as she leaned closer, now standing between his legs. "Do you think we'll make it tomorrow?"

Eyden's fingers stroked the back of her hand in a comforting gesture. "We'll go when it's dark. Take them by surprise."

"And afterwards..."

Eyden squeezed her hand. "If you want to claim the Turosian throne, I'll stand with you."

Sighing, Lora put her free hand on his shoulder. "It's our best shot, isn't it?" Yet the mere thought made her shiver all over. Who was she to claim the throne? She had no idea about the Turosian kingdom or their politics. She didn't want the responsibility, but if not her, who would take over?

Running a finger over her thumb, Eyden tried to catch her gaze. "I wish you didn't have to make this decision. I wish you could feel...*free*."

Pulling her hand free, Lora cupped his cheek. "One thing at a time. I think we need to take Damir with us tomorrow."

Eyden startled. "We can't trust him."

"I know. But if we want to go all in, he could be an asset. And because we can't trust him, I don't want him alone with my family and Maja anymore."

Eyden dropped his head, defeated by her reasoning. "Ilario won't be happy."

"Ilario can handle it. I'm honestly shocked how well he worked with Rhay today." She'd been pleasantly surprised when Rhay had announced he would go with them. Yet, she couldn't be certain it was an honest step in the right direction instead of seeking another kind of distraction.

"Damir, Rhay...I wish he'd find someone better. And Maja, too."

A small smile broke across her face. "Maja isn't attached. I appreciate your concern, though." Before he could reply, Lora crossed the distance between them, her lips capturing his, savouring their connection more than ever now that their feelings were out in the open.

Eyden's hands went to her hips, then lower, toying with the hem of her shirt. Her heart fluttered in anticipation. On instinct, she moved forward, her legs planted on either side of him, but her wounded leg strained in protest. She failed to hide her hiss of pain.

Eyden pushed her back gently, standing up with her. "Let's take it easy." He pushed a strand of her hair from her face. "You know what I want to do right now?"

Lora's stomach flipped as she bit the corner of her mouth. "I have a guess." Groaning, she took a step back. "But I have to talk to Damir first. I have a feeling if we start this, we'll be busy for a while."

A dangerous grin tugged at Eyden's lips. "You can bet on it."

Heat blossomed in her core, but she forced herself to pull a pair of sweatpants from the closet, quickly slipping them on.

"Let's go, then," Eyden said, his hand on the door knob.

"Actually, I think I should talk to him on my own."

He stared at her for a second before opening the door for her. "Be careful. I'll be with El if you need me."

Nodding, Lora headed towards Damir's door, where a tired Ilario stood guard.

Ilario's gaze found hers. "If you're about to make a deal with him, I want to be there."

Lora didn't argue with him as she unlocked the door and found herself staring at Damir's back. He took his time turning around, his arms crossed as his gaze flickered to her, then to Ilario behind her.

"Come to take me up on my offer, Adelway?" Damir asked.

The name infuriated her every time. "First of all, it's *Whitner*."

Damir cocked his head to the side. "Feels like pretence to me, princess."

Ilario snorted next to her. Damir's eyes hardened, but something Lora couldn't quite name flickered in his dark violet eyes. "Anyway, shall we talk payment?"

"Payment?" Lora leaned against the doorframe to keep the weight off her injured leg.

"I'm not going to help you out of the goodness of my heart. Karwyn paid a handsome amount, and with him gone, the Turosian crown is all yours."

"So that's it?" Ilario asked, his emerald eyes not hiding his pain. "Your loyalty can be bought?"

"Careful, Marsyn. Don't ask what's better left unsaid."

The air seemed to glow with silent tension. "I changed my mind," Ilario said. With one last glance, he strode away.

"You really are an ass," Lora said once Ilario was out of sight.

"Maybe," Damir replied, stone-faced. "But I'm useful and you know it."

Huffing, she let her head fall back against the cool door frame. "Fine. Here's the deal—if you help us tomorrow and don't screw us over in *any* way, I'll match whatever silver Karwyn has promised you on a trial basis once we're back in Turosian."

Damir paused as if to consider her offer, but this time, Lora could tell it was all for show. "You got yourself a deal, *Adelway*."

Turning her back, Lora reached for the door, yet her hand halted on the knob. "I can't help but feel I'm paying you to keep up pretence." When she looked over her shoulder, Damir's gaze was unsettling as if his eyes were working overtime to keep whatever was inside hidden. "I meant what I said before. It must be lonely." Damir didn't reply, but his eyes flashed.

Heading down the hall, Lora couldn't wait to go to bed. Her head was heavy with important decisions. She had almost reached her room when Oscar's voice pulled her attention back to the hallway. "Can we talk for a second?"

Her skin flushed, nerves eating at her. She never knew if he was going to blow up again. They had barely said more than a few words to each other since the house burned down. She had tried to be there for him, but he'd refused her attempts. "Are you...what do you want to talk about?"

His gaze shifted, landing everywhere but her face. "I want to go with you tomorrow."

That she hadn't expected. She took a calming breath. "I don't—"

"Before you say no, hear me out." Oscar's gaze snapped to hers, and she could see some of her own determination reflected back at her. "Elyssa mentioned the place is locked down tight, and I might be able to help. No one else here can code."

"This isn't like coding a video game, Oscar. It's too dangerous."

Playing with his grey sleeve, he whispered, "I've had some spare time when the whole world shut down." His tone tore at her heart. She'd been through hell, but so had Oscar. "I've made some coding friends online and we're good."

"You should stay here with Mum and Dad."

"That's all I've done, Lora! And things just keep getting worse." He bit his lip as if frustrated with himself for raising his voice.

She thought of reaching out, her arm lifting, but then she dropped it. "I'm sorry about the house, Oscar. You know that, right? I would've done anything to save it. To keep the memories alive."

"We'll make new memories," Oscar added, his tone lighter than Lora had imagined. "Let me come with you, please. I'm trying really hard to understand, to see who *you* are and not just a fae I don't recognise. I'll never be able to fully get it unless I'm with you, unless you stop pretending. You risked it all. Let me return the favour."

His words hit her like icy waves, waking up her senses. She had kept him at arm's length, trying to be the sister he knew instead of letting him see who she really was. "I was trying to protect you, but instead I should have tried to help you understand."

A half-smile graced his lips. "I want to help. Please let me."

How could she refuse when she would ask the same thing if the roles were reversed? Putting her hand on his arm, she said, "Okay, on two conditions. If things go to hell, Eyden will get you out of there. And you have to ask Dad first."

"All right." The smile on his face brightened. "But I will get a weapon, right?"

The address Elyssa had gotten from the fae police officer led them to the outskirts of London in the middle of nowhere. The streets were deserted and barely lit by the street lights highlighting the cold night. There were no homes in sight, just factories with a few trees in between. An electric fence surrounded the one-storey building, but Eyden had teleported them inside the fence. He hadn't teleported them directly into the building because they had no idea of the layout or how many officers awaited them inside.

The group was hiding behind the dumpsters, taking cover from the officer keeping watch outside the back entrance. Snow covered the top of the dumpsters, water dripping down. Elyssa's jacket was drenched on one spot as she kept her back to the dumpster while spying around it to see the officer.

Among them was Oscar. Before leaving the cabin, Lora had made Eyden promise to take Oscar out of there if there was any sign of trouble. It was quite a distance back to the cabin—which meant it required quite a lot of Eyden's energy—but even a few streets over would be safer. Oscar looked lost as he clutched a small knife she'd agreed to give him. His backpack must be weighing him down but he didn't let it on, as hidden as the fear Lora knew he had to feel. She'd hoped their father would talk him out of it, but Oscar had joined them, telling her Dad had agreed.

Giving Elyssa, Eyden, Rhay, Ilario, and her brother one last glance, Lora joined Damir. He had shapeshifted into the police officer at the back of the building. Her friends would wait for her signal. Their plan was to attract as little attention as possible.

As Lora and Damir neared the front of the secret government facility, he pushed the gun to her back, cold metal digging through her thin coat. It wasn't lost on her that he could very well shoot her now and make a run for it. Whatever his motive was, somehow Lora didn't think Damir would betray them. It had been her idea to use Damir's ability to their advantage. Eyden and Elyssa hadn't been happy about her plan but could see her reasoning. Damir could have told on Lora multiple times when she'd been in the palace. And as much as he liked to pretend to be above it all, he had saved Ilario the day of the ritual.

Lora turned her head to the dumpsters hiding her friends and the high electric fence they were leaving behind. A coldness settled in her bones, but it wasn't from the weather. What if they went in only to find out Tarnan had gotten there before them?

As they neared the entrance, the security guard there removed his gun. "What's going on here, Harry?"

Damir, disguised as Harry, pushed Lora forward aggressively. "Caught this one lurking around. Figured we should question her. *Quietly.*"

The guard seemed suspicious, but only for a moment. He turned to the door, unlocking it. He held it open as Damir pushed Lora forward, the gun digging into her back. She did her best to look distressed. It really wasn't much of a stretch.

The entrance they found themselves in had two more officers stationed in front of a big steel door. Before they could even speak, Lora felt the pressure of Damir's gun leave her back and she took it as her signal, throwing up her arms. The two guards rose from the ground and hit the steel wall behind them, slumping to the ground.

A bullet almost grazed her before Damir plunged his knife into the officer's hand. He screamed in pain. The man dropped his gun. Damir wasted no time, hitting the guard in the face with his fist more than once before pulling him to the steel door in front of Lora.

"Open it," Damir commanded.

In that moment, the front door burst open behind them and Eyden walked in—Elyssa, Oscar, Rhay, and Ilario right behind him.

"*Now,*" Damir hissed at the terrified officer, pulling the knife from the guard's hand. A yelp of pain escaped the officer's lips. "Unlock the door, or the knife won't just go through your hand—it'll take it right off." His tone was chilling, and Lora was almost tempted to tell him to knock it off, but the officer fumbled with his pocket and took out a key card.

His voice was shrill as he unlocked the door. "This is all I can do. None of us have the code for the vault."

Smiling, Damir nodded as if he understood, then knocked the officer's head against the steel door. The sound echoed through the otherwise sparse room. He slumped to the ground.

Damir's eyes travelled to Eyden. "Why don't you hate me a little louder, Kellen?"

"Don't provoke me," Eyden bit out.

Damir inclined his head. "Let's go."

"Rhay, Ilario, can you stand guard?" Lora asked. Ilario nodded while Rhay huffed, but turned to the entrance nonetheless. Ushering Oscar closer, Lora stepped through the door into a darkly lit cold grey corridor. Eyden and Elyssa followed close behind them, weapons raised.

It didn't take them long to spot the vault at the end of the corridor. It was massive, made out of thick almandine. Eyden wouldn't be able to drift in like they'd hoped. Just standing in front of the vault made Lora's skin crawl, bringing back memories of her time in that almandine cell back at the palace.

"Lora?" Oscar asked, concern radiating off him.

Swallowing her memories, Lora turned her gaze to the panel next to the vault where a code was needed to open the door. Focusing, Lora pulled at the cover on the panel with her magic, and it broke off, revealing the mechanics behind it. The simple gesture cost her more energy than it should.

"Can you crack it?" Lora asked her brother. He was already removing his backpack and taking out the laptop they'd gotten on the way here. He connected it to the panel, then opened a group chat, linking up with his coding buddies who would help him override the security system. Oscar had been right. They did need him. With this much almandine involved, they couldn't break the door open with their powers.

"Hopefully," Oscar replied, sinking deep into focus as he worked on writing a code with his friends. Everyone else seemed even more confused by the numbers flashing on the screen than Lora was.

The silence was unnerving. The only audible sound was Oscar's typing. Elyssa spun a small knife in her hand, gaze locked on the door they'd come through.

It seemed like forever and no time at all when a clicking noise echoed through the empty corridor and Oscar jumped up in joy. "Yes!" he shouted as the door to the vault opened automatically, sliding to the left.

Elyssa turned to him, her smile bright. "Brilliant!"

Oscar blushed. He was about to speak when a blaring alarm assaulted their ears. Lora covered her ears as she spotted the door at the end of the hall closing. Then a weird, sharp sound came from the ceiling. Lora followed Eyden's gaze to where the ceiling opened and some sort of gas streamed out.

"What the fuck is that?" Elyssa yelled as the air started to grow foggy.

Lora covered her mouth, the smell vile. It could be sleeping gas or it could be something more potent. They couldn't afford to stick around and find out.

At that moment the vault door seemed to short-circuit; it started to close on its own. Oscar turned to the screen, trying to override it. "Bloody hell, the system is rebooting." His eyes were panicked.

Taking in the gas filling the room, Damir jumped into the vault that was still clear of gas.

Lora tugged on Eyden's arm. "Take Oscar out of here."

Oscar shook his head, gaze set on the vault door. "You'll be locked in!" His fingers flew over his keyboard.

"Go!" Lora shouted, her eyes pleading with Eyden, and he kept his promise, taking Oscar's arm. And then they were gone.

Lora felt a hand on her shoulder and Elyssa gestured at her, coughing as she used her sleeve to cover her mouth. "We have to get in!" Lora had no time to argue as the vault door was almost shut. They dove for the door just before it shut completely.

Coughing into her elbow, Lora tried to free her lungs from the gas as her blurry eyes took in the almandine-decked-out room. The walls glinted red in the light coming from the ceiling. She felt the effects of the almandine deep in her bones as if someone was squeezing her heart.

Glancing at Damir, who had shifted back into his real appearance, she knew he must feel it too, even though he didn't show it.

Elyssa, being fully human, didn't have any issues with the almandine, yet her eyes appeared teary from the gas. Knife still in hand, she walked forward. Lora tracked her steps to a glass-covered podium in the center that showcased an ancient scroll. The human-fae agreement.

Walking up to it, Elyssa swung at the glass with the hilt of her knife. The glass cover shattered, and she brushed the shards aside. Damir and Lora moved next to her, transfixed by the contract.

"So this is it," Lora whispered, taking in the scroll. It felt strange to be so close to what they'd been working towards for over a week now.

Damir reached out, but before his fingertips touched the scroll, he was thrown backwards. His head hit the steel wall with a loud thump. Grunting, he straightened himself. It was true, then; only a human could take it from its hiding spot.

Elyssa gently touched the scroll. Nothing happened.

"Well, we might be trapped," Elyssa said, taking the scroll with a wide grin, "but we have what we came for." She unzipped her jacket and tucked the agreement inside.

Footsteps drew Lora's attention back to the closed vault door. Elyssa followed her line of sight, catching her drift even though she probably couldn't hear anything.

Standing in a row, the three of them waited before the door. With the alarm having gone off, Lora was sure they wouldn't stay trapped for long. But as soon as the door opened, the officers would open fire and the almandine took away her powers. Reaching into her boot, Lora removed a knife, letting the weight of it calm her fears. She didn't only have her powers to fall back on.

The door creaked open. Damir, standing to Lora's left, was the closest one to the opening. Before Lora could even see the officers on the other side, Damir aimed the gun he'd stolen earlier and fired.

The sounds of bullets hitting metal mixed with screams of pain rattled her, and Lora was momentarily shocked as the door opened fully and her gaze landed on three dead officers—bullets through their skulls. Damir wasn't supposed to kill them. They were simply following orders. They had been innocent in all of this.

Distracted by the dead officers, Lora almost got hit by one who was still alive. The air was thick with fog and she couldn't see how many there were. But Elyssa pushed her to the side and they barely avoided another round of bullets.

Eyden yelled at them from somewhere near the exit. He must have teleported back. Through the fog, Lora thought she spotted Ilario and Rhay taking down guards left and right, knocking them unconscious. It was impossible to count the officers.

An officer rushed her, and Lora dropped down and slashed at his leg with her knife. Next to her, Elyssa kicked out until he fell, and her heel connected with his head. The corridor was a mess, fog draping everything in a veil of uncertainty. Officers bled on the floor. Shouts came from all directions.

Elyssa pulled at Lora's arm and they ran through the chaos until Elyssa slowed down considerably. Confused, Lora stopped. Elyssa coughed into her elbow, her legs wobbly. "I feel funny," she said, her eyes rimmed red. It had to be the gas. Lora wasn't affected, but Elyssa was human.

Putting an arm around her, Lora pulled Elyssa with her, glancing every which way to make sure no one was firing at them. Lora's gaze connected with Eyden, who was trying to make a path for them. They all rushed through the door and towards the exit of the building. Her eyes found Rhay clutching his bloodied arm. Ilario protected his back, sword lifting to deflect a bullet from a guard who was trying to rise from the ground. As Damir walked by, he kicked the gun out of the officer's grip and stepped on his hand, crushing his bones. The yell of pain mixed with the rushing in Lora's ears, adrenaline pumping through her veins.

They were so close to the exit. They would make it. She rushed to join Eyden, Elyssa leaning heavily on her, and the two of them pulled open the front door. Lora savoured the fresh, cold air outside for a split second before an almandine sword appeared in her field of vision—in the hands of a fae guard. And he wasn't alone.

CHAPTER 24

AMIRA

Two days had passed since Amira signed that damning contract, yet she could still feel the pen pricking her finger, sealing her fate with a drop of blood.

Karwyn's survival kept nagging at her mind. Tarnan had refused to go into more detail even after she had signed the addendum. The only silver lining was that since Karwyn was somehow still alive, Lora's mother may have survived as well. And Rhay would be relieved to hear about Karwyn, wouldn't he?

A maid entered her quarters, halting her thoughts. Were they leaving already? Tarnan had told her that their departure was delayed until this afternoon. Last night, Amira had heard guards leaving the palace. A good number of them, judging by the loud stomping of their feet.

"Lady Saige has requested your visit," the maid said.

Saige. What did she want with Amira? Was it a trap set by Tarnan? The girl seemed blissfully unaware of her father's evil nature, but it could also be merely an act. Should she refuse Saige's request?

But at the same time, Saige was probably the closest person to Tarnan, except for Saydren. This visit could be a way to gain some intel on Tarnan.

Rising from her chair, Amira went to her door. To her surprise, the maid led them to a familiar corridor. She had been here once before with Elyssa. Filled with paintings of the royal Ellevarn family, this was the corridor where they had seen a servant disappear. The irony wasn't lost on Amira that she had once found Elyssa's spying inconsiderate of their host.

The maid stopped in front of a painting representing the late King and Queen of Carnylen holding an infant. *Tarnan*. They shared very few physical similarities with him. Their skin was more tanned, their hair a lighter shade of brown. Amira wondered how they had explained their son's lack of resemblance. Or maybe they had said nothing, letting rumours swirl until fae got bored. Amira herself had never doubted his ancestry. As far as she knew, Tarnan was supposed to have earth magic like his adoptive mother. Now she figured that was all a lie.

Carefully, the maid moved her lips closer to baby Tarnan's head as if to kiss it. Instead, she whispered words Amira was unable to catch.

The painting moved to the side, revealing a set of stairs. The maid stepped away, letting Amira enter the passage alone. The painting closed behind her with a sharp clicking sound.

Amira had barely made it to the top of the narrow, winding stone staircase when Saige's excited face greeted her. "Princess Amira, I'm so happy you're here." She gestured for Amira to enter her room. Amira was surprised to find no guards present.

The bedroom contrasted with the bare and badly lit staircase. Multiple lights were strung across the ceiling, brightening every corner. It was a decent sized room yet crammed with furniture and little knick knacks. In a little nook, a bed was partially hidden by an ornamented screen. On the far wall, a small window overlooked the nearby forest. The rest of the walls were covered in bookshelves filled to the brim, the sunset orange wall barely peeking through.

"I've never had a princess in my room." Saige nervously fidgeted with her dress in a gesture that reminded Amira of herself. "Do you like it?" Before Amira could reply, Saige rushed towards one of her shelves. "I could show you my favourite book?" Saige started to pull one book out before putting it back and picking another one. "Mmh, it's too difficult; I think I love them all. They've been the best of friends."

Taken aback, Amira *really* looked at the room. There had to be over two thousand books here, as well as an easel with various drawings tucked away next to it. The room was clean, but there was a lingering stuffy odour, as if it had been a long time since anyone opened the window.

Amira stepped closer to her. "Saige, do you ever leave this room?"

"I did when I met you," Saige replied with a large smile while carefully piling up books in her arms. A strand of long strawberry-blonde hair fell in her face, but she had no free hand to push it back. "I'm trying to pick the *very* best book."

"Do you go outside every day?"

Saige halted in place. "Father says it's very dangerous outside. Evil fae would try to hurt me. And I have everything I need right here." She pulled the books towards her chest. "But I do have one friend, Zastan, the fae who stands guard every night in front of my door. Sometimes he lets me go on the roof to watch the stars. But you can't tell Father, he'd be worried."

Amira wondered if Saige shared her father's compulsion powers now that the curse on the Sartoya bloodline had been lifted. And if so, would she use them for good, or would she follow in her father's footsteps? Would she turn mad like her grandfather, the Dark King? Tarnan said he had found a way to prevent it, but Amira doubted it.

Even through the fear plaguing her mind, Amira still felt for Saige.

"Does your father ever talk to you about the future?"

A smile spread Saige's lips. "Yes! It will be wonderful, won't it? He will make the world so safe we will be able to go anywhere. You are from Allamyst, are you not? One day, will you show me your kingdom?"

"It's not my kingdom," Amira said out of habit. It hadn't felt like her home in a long time. It was hard to imagine that it ever would be again. She forced herself to smile. "But of course I can. Has Tarnan mentioned how he will make it *safe?*"

"He tells me it's very complicated but I shouldn't worry." When Amira's smile slipped, Saige said, "He'll keep us *both* safe." Amira nodded, sensing Saige was more oblivious about Tarnan than Rhay had ever been about Karwyn. Her chances of learning anything useful from Saige dwindled the more the girl spoke.

"I think I have decided on the best one." Saige dropped the books on the floor before picking a new one from the shelf. She went to sit on her bed, her smile so proud that Amira couldn't refuse to follow her. She reminded Amira so much of herself; daughter to an abusive family figure and confined to a miniscule world.

Saige opened the book, her eyes wide in wonder. It looked to be a children's book with bright beautifully drawn pictures on the left pages.

As Amira put her hand on Saige's, the young fae looked up at her with hopeful eyes. "Do you also like this book, Princess Amira?"

"It looks lovely." Amira squeezed Saige's hand.

"Father gifted it to me. In this one, the princess lives a wonderful life in her palace, safe from any danger. No one is allowed in, but she has her family with her always, so it's all wonderful. Then one day, an evil king tries to steal her away, claiming to save her. But thanks to her magic, the princess defeats the evil king and lives happily ever after in her palace."

Amira saw the irony in Tarnan giving Saige that book, but she felt the girl wasn't ready to face the truth. "It sounds like an interesting story."

Saige beamed. "I knew you'd love it. We'll be great friends, won't we?" Saige opened her arms to hug Amira but then immediately pulled back as if she wasn't sure what she was doing. "I am so glad my father introduced me to you!"

"And so am I," Tarnan's deep voice said. Amira jerked her head up. Tarnan stood in the doorway of Saige's room. His clothes were too light for the cold and damp Carnylen weather.

It was time for them to go to Rubien, to rebuild the city that had once been destroyed. At least afterwards Tarnan would free her mother from Wryen. And then Amira would escape with her mother and Farren, contract or not. She would need to find a way to steal it back later in order to break it—if she could find a spell with Farren's help—but at least she wouldn't be under Tarnan's roof anymore. Their bond would still stand, she wouldn't be free and would feel every wound inflicted on Tarnan, but there had to be a way out.

Amira gave Saige one last look. No matter who the girl's father was, Amira felt a strong urge to save her. She wouldn't let history repeat itself.

For once, the journey went faster than Amira expected. Maybe because she was dreading reaching her destination. Tarnan sat next to her in the carriage for the whole journey, while Farren rode in another carriage with Saydren. Tarnan had kept his promise and hadn't compelled Farren. Instead, he had shackled his hands.

As they had crossed the Cursed Woods, the burned trees were a sad omen for what lay ahead. A few months ago, crossing those woods with Elyssa had seemed like an opportunity to run away from her cursed destiny. Now, Amira was more doomed than ever.

They left the eerily silent woods behind and their carriage approached Cinnite, the capital city of Rubien. Amira felt like it was now or never to ask the question that had been plaguing her mind since her visit with Saige.

Amira bunched up the fabric of her dress in her lap. "Who is Saige's mother and where is she?"

Tarnan turned his head away from the window and sighed. "She passed away giving birth to Saige. You know how difficult pregnancies can be." His tone was dry and flat, like he was recalling his meals of the day.

Had Tarnan ever cared about Saige's mother, or was she merely a human Tarnan had experimented on?

Amira needed to know more, to hear him confirm her worst fear: that Saige was half-fae, a result of Tarnan's attempt at breaking his curse. "Especially half-fae pregnancies," she carefully added.

Tarnan avoided her gaze. "You should remain focused. I'm counting on you, Amira." His lack of denial seemed proof enough.

Soon, the carriage stopped in front of the impressive ruins of an arch. It must have once been the majestic entrance to the city. Now, the limestones had been carved by the unrelenting wind and sand. Tarnan stepped out of the carriage, offering his hand to Amira. She was left speechless at the ruins of what must have been one of the grandest cities in Liraen. She exchanged a worried glance with Farren, who joined them with Saydren.

"My father's city..." Tarnan touched the stone arch, then gripped the rubble with clawed hands.

"You will return it to its former glory, Your Majesty," Saydren said and squeezed Tarnan's shoulder.

Tarnan straightened himself, placing his hand on Amira's back. Shivering at the touch, she had no choice but to let herself be led inside the ghost city, the hot wind whipping her hair. Sweat lined the back of her long flowy red dress. Tarnan had made her wear a ruby tiara as well as a heavy gold and ruby choker. Proudly, he had explained that they used to belong to his late mother. He had spent years trying to find pieces of the Sartoya legacy.

The hair rose on Amira's arms, a dark chill spreading in her heart. The city was too silent, hauntingly so. Her mouth went dry. She could sense the terrible things that had happened here.

Tarnan led her to the ruins of what must have been the royal palace. Only a few walls were still standing. They entered what was left of a long hallway. Her feet sank in the sand as they moved along. Broken items and pieces of old furniture littered the open space, the ceiling long gone.

Stopping in a room that was only rubble and stones, Tarnan turned to her. "This used to be the throne room. This is where my father was killed. Can you feel it?"

A layer of ice coated Amira's heart. Strangely, she could feel it; it was as if the whole room was coated in death. The heaviness of it stuck to her, infiltrating her pores and filling her with a chill that stole her breath. She could almost hear the screams of agony, the clashing of the swords, the smell of the blood that had drenched the sand seventy-five years ago.

The dark magic used by Tarnan's father lingered in the room as if it had never been purged after Variel Sartoya's death. It was suffocating. Exchanging a glance with Farren, she noticed his breathing stuttering as if ice coated his entire being too, the dark magic blocking his lungs. Tarnan closed his eyes, his hands pressed against his heart. Saydren stood by his side, a dark cloud in his gaze. He was the only one who had seen the fall of the Dark King.

"Let's get to work, then," Farren said with his eternally optimistic smile.

Saydren took out a multitude of crystals they had used in their training sessions and the ancient amulet with a turquoise crystal Cirny had used—along with the other artefact Amira had given to Eyden before Tarnan could get it—to make the border fall. Carefully, Amira put the amulet around her neck while Saydren placed black jasper stones around Farren and her. The shiny black surface of the stones gleamed in the sunlight.

Joining hands, Farren and Amira released their powers in unison, draining the stones' protective magic and fighting against the dark magic lingering around them. The task was daunting—purging the palace of its darkness and rebuilding it. Holding on to Farren's hands, Amira felt her feet being swallowed by the burning sand. The hairs on her arms stood up as an electrifying chill coursed through her blood. Her breathing quickened. The lingering dark magic brushed against her skin, scraping like claws trying to get a hold of her. Tarnan's yell of encouragement was lost in the raging wind whipping her hair in her face. Her energy left her, her body so light she could have blown away.

But she thought of Elyssa's warm smile, of her fiery attitude. Elyssa wouldn't give up; she wouldn't let herself disappear into the darkness. With an aching heart, Amira held on. The amulet around her neck grew hot, almost burning through her dress.

Opening her eyes, Amira tracked the sand rising from the ground, twisting into shapes, slowly rebuilding the room. Soon, dark red walls surrounded them. Under her feet, she felt smooth black marble instead of sand. Paintings appeared on the walls, lit up by the biggest chandelier she had ever seen. And then the throne appeared on a stone pedestal, decked in blood-red velvet with rubies adorning the copper frame.

The wind stopped howling all at once. The dark energy surrounding them disappeared with the ice coating her skin.

Tarnan climbed up the steps to the throne, each step replacing Amira's exhaustion with anger flowing under her flushed skin. Seeing him so triumphant made her want to burn this whole place down.

Turning his blood-red eyes to her, he smiled as if he'd already won. "Continue," he ordered as he sat on his throne, gesturing to the palace.

CHAPTER 25

❦

EYDEN

Eyden wasn't thrilled about their odds. Ten fae guards barred the way in front of them, and at least five officers were still alive behind them, with who knew how many on their way for backup. Lora and Damir weren't in the best shape thanks to their exposure to almandine, and Rhay and Ilario looked worse for wear, too. Elyssa was barely awake, her eyes fluttering as she leaned on Lora.

But there was only one way out of this, and that was through the guards. Had Tarnan told his guards to wait for them to get the agreement? As his gaze connected with Elyssa's, she tilted her head, her eyes fiery but dazed.

Eyden moved fast, striking the guard who had his sword pointed at Lora and Elyssa. The guard lost his grip enough for Lora to sweep in and take the sword from him. Just in time, too, as another guard lifted his blade, and Lora spun to deflect the blow. Elyssa moved back, her stance too unstable for Eyden's liking.

Turning, Eyden ducked as another guard swung at him. He drew closer to Elyssa, protecting her. Rhay and Ilario—their backs on either side of the door to avoid the bullets being fired through the open door —tried to subdue the human officers who rushed out of the building.

Eyden kicked at a guard's stomach and the fae fell to the ground as another ran at them. But a sword pierced the fae's chest from behind before Eyden could even lift a hand. The guard dropped dead to reveal Damir standing behind him with a bloodied blade.

Guards stormed at them from both sides, and Eyden's feet moved on instinct. He found himself back to back with Damir as they took on their opponents, keeping them away from Elyssa, who leaned against the wall. Her eyes appeared to slowly clear, her posture straightening. Aiming his fist at the guard's throat, Eyden knocked the breath out of him.

"Left!" Damir shouted, and Eyden sensed his intention, leaning to the left as Damir pushed the sharp edge of his sword behind him, hitting the guard and not Eyden. Catching sight of a knife looped through Damir's belt, Eyden snatched it and threw it at the guard approaching Damir.

Avoiding Damir's gaze, Eyden didn't want to think about the fact that he was fighting alongside him. *Layken.*

He searched for Lora and their eyes met as a guard snuck up behind her. Eyden was about to drift to her when the butt of a gun hit the back of the fae's head. Swirling around, Eyden didn't see Lora's reaction as she turned to her brother. Oscar had come back. Eyden had drifted him a few streets away. Yet, there he was. Oscar had swung at that fae.

The guard nearest to Oscar lifted his sword to strike, and Eyden yelled another warning. But Lora must not have heard him correctly. She turned towards Eyden instead of her brother.

The world slowed. The blade swung towards Oscar's back and Eyden didn't think, only acted. His thoughts filled with Lora as he drifted between Oscar and the guard, intending to deflect the weapon. But the second he reappeared, the blade struck his chest.

A scream filled Eyden's ears and then fire clawed at the guard who had struck him. Breathing hard, Eyden touched his bleeding chest, the diagonal cut across it deep. The pain forced him to his knees as the almandine of the blade stole his breath. Oscar knelt next to him, his eyes wide with panic.

"He...he came out of nowhere," Oscar mumbled. Eyden's gaze lifted to Lora, who had somehow found the strength to use her fire. She balled her hands into fists, increasing the blaze. With her hair trailing in the wind and her breath visible in the chilly night air, her blazing flames were a stark contrast against the sky.

He searched for Elyssa and found her with a sword in hand, fighting off a guard with new-found energy, but her movements were slower than usual. They had to get out of here.

Lora gestured for Rhay and Ilario to move away from the door and then lit the area on fire, forcing the officers back with a fire wall. There were still Carnylen guards around them, Elyssa and Damir busy in their own battles. Eyden coughed and shuddered, gasping through the pain. His heart hadn't been punctured but the blade had struck deep, the almandine slowing the healing process. His eyes felt leaden as he fought to stay conscious.

He had thought about drifting but he couldn't take all of them at once, and the remaining ones would be overrun by the guards. And now he couldn't do fucking anything. They had a car waiting a few streets over, but they were trapped here.

A sharp cry made Eyden turn his head to Elyssa, who was fighting off a fae holding her by her jacket. The front of it ripped, revealing the scroll in her inner pocket. Elyssa tried to kick out but the fae grabbed her throat, picking her up. Her legs dangled in the air, her hands scratching at the fae.

"El!" he screamed. Eyden's chest tightened painfully and he tried to rise, but it felt like razor blades digging into his skin. The fae took the scroll with one hand, the other still wrapped around Elyssa's throat. Her face lost all colour.

Fire hit the back of the fae and Lora stormed forward as the fae let go of Elyssa, who slumped to the ground. She coughed, her hands on her reddened throat.

"Don't let him get away," Elyssa croaked. Lora stormed off, but two guards blocked her path. She raised her arms, her fire attacking them, but it dwindled fast. Oscar, next to Eyden, whimpered at the sound of blades clashing against each other.

They were fucked. Everyone was locked in a battle, and the fae with the scroll rushed towards the fence.

Falea must have been on their side tonight. A big car appeared on the dimly lit street, breaking through the chain-link fence surrounding the facility and crashing into the fae with the scroll. The fae flipped over on the hood of the car before hitting the ground hard. Reversing, the van headed towards them, hitting more fae guards.

Halting, the driver cracked open a window. "Get in!"

Who in Liraen was that? Elyssa's gaze connected with the driver and a smile appeared on her tired face, so at odds with the bloody cut on her forehead that matted her hair and the red fingerprints on her throat.

"Let's move!" Elyssa said, already running, the van having made a path for her. She took the scroll from the unconscious fae.

"Get in the van, I'll hold them off!" Lora yelled.

Elyssa rushed to help Eyden to his feet, then secured the scroll with the band of her trousers. Oscar seemed out of his depth but followed after them. Slowly walking backwards, Lora created a line of fire, cutting the guards off from them as they filed into the van.

Eyden grunted as he pulled himself into the vehicle after Oscar. Elyssa went to the front of the car. Ilario, Rhay, and Damir rushed in, and Lora pulled the door shut behind her just as a guard jumped through the fire, rushing at them.

The driver, who looked somewhat familiar now, drove off, wheels screeching. Eyden sat up straighter on the bench in the row of seats behind the driver, hissing through his teeth as the cut on his chest started bleeding again. He turned his gaze to Elyssa, who sat in the passenger seat. Everyone else was squeezed into the back two rows. Lora and Oscar were next to Eyden. Reaching over, Lora took off her jacket and applied pressure to Eyden's wound. He bit back a yelp, his mind fuzzy from the blood loss. At the sight of his blood soaking Lora's jacket, Oscar turned his face away.

"Who the fuck is that?" Eyden mouthed to his sister.

"He's the fae officer who told me about this place," Elyssa replied aloud. Turning her head, she asked the guy, "How did you know we were here?"

"I was keeping track of one of the street cameras," the officer admitted. "I thought you might need help and...I guess it was kind of crazy of me to show up, huh?"

"I approve of crazy." Elyssa leaned back in her seat. Her hand clutched the scroll, shaking—a sign even she had thought they might lose.

"I felt like I wasn't doing enough," the officer replied.

"We appreciate it." Lora leaned forward, her hand still pressed on Eyden's chest. Her brows drew together, the corner of her mouth pulling down at the sight of his blood.

"Do you think it will ever get back to normal again?" The officer looked at the tiny mirror in the front of the car.

Lora's eyes turned haunted as she glanced at her brother, who had turned to look out the window, his hand bloody and shaking badly. Ilario leaned forward from the row at the back, his face weary. "I don't think things should be as they were before." Damir glanced at him and Eyden could tell Ilario sensed it, but he stared straight ahead. "I think our worlds have been broken for a long time. It's time for a change."

Eyden could only agree, but his eyes were so heavy and his lips wouldn't open to say so. He tried to clear the fog in his mind but it seemed to drape his whole body and he couldn't hold on any longer.

"You should've known better!" Lora's father yelled, pulling Eyden back to the land of the living. He blinked, a bright light forcing his eyes to water. A hard surface dug into his back. Disoriented, Eyden turned his head. He recognised the kitchen at the cabin and the wooden table he laid on.

"He said you agreed!" Lora argued. She stood opposite her father, multiple bandages covering her skin. Two on her arms. One around her leg. The wound must have re-opened.

Isaac's breathing came in fast. "He's just a kid, Lora. He shouldn't be mixed up in this any more than he has to."

Lora's lips trembled. "No one should." Isaac hung his head, his mouth opening and then closing.

As Eyden rose on his elbows, Lora's gaze swung to him. "Hey, how are you feeling?" Eyden glanced at his chest; the cut hadn't closed yet, but it was covered in some sort of salve. Whatever medicine humans used, it stung. He wished they had fae healing items instead.

"I'll live. Where is everyone?" Eyden replied, biting back a sigh as his chest wound strained.

"My father treated everyone, so they've all gone to rest." Her voice was off, her arms crossed as she looked at her father. Their conversation from earlier drifted back to him. Had Oscar not asked his father for permission before joining them?

"You should rest too, Lora. We can continue our conversation to-morrow," Isaac said in a clear dismissal. Lora avoided his eyes. "I'll check on Eyden's wound again."

Eyden gave her a slow tilt of his head and Lora nodded, brushing his hand on her way out of the kitchen.

Moonlight streamed through the kitchen window as Isaac tried to fix Eyden up as best as he could, applying a fresh layer of salve to his clean wound. Just yesterday it had been a bullet wound and now this. Yet he didn't regret it one bit.

Another dab to his pierced flesh and Eyden bit back a yelp.

"Apologies," Lora's father said, reaching for a bandage. "I'm sure fae healers could do this much better."

Eyden sat up straight as he took the bandage from Isaac and gingerly placed it on his skin. "You're doing fine, Mr. Whitner."

"You can call me Isaac."

Eyden nodded, slowly rising to his feet.

Isaac took off his rubber gloves. "As Lora's father, under normal circumstances, I would feel the need to tell you to treat my daughter right. But seeing as you already took a bullet and a sword for my kids, I'll just say I'm glad Lora had you in Liraen."

Eyden didn't miss a beat. "She'll always have me."

Isaac paused for a long second. "Always is a long time." Isaac eyed the bloody tissues he'd used to clean his wound. "Your always isn't necessarily *her* always. You do know that, right? No one knows how long half-fae might live."

The thought had never crossed his mind. He'd been too caught up in his feelings that nothing else had mattered. But it didn't change anything.

"Hey, Eyden?" Oscar's uncertain voice pulled Eyden from this revelation. Lora's brother entered the kitchen, his eyes not fully open.

"Lora's in her room," Eyden replied.

"Actually," Oscar said as his eyes flicked from Isaac to him, "I wanted to talk to you."

Gathering his equipment, Isaac excused himself and headed towards his room.

Eyden leaned against the edge of the table and raised his brow at Oscar.

"I..." Oscar rubbed his eyes, but it seemed more out of frustration than sleep. "I wanted to thank you. For, you know, saving my life."

"Any time," Eyden replied.

"I know it was stupid." His lips trembled slightly. "I never...I knew Lora had to fight before. I saw her wounds. I saw her bloody clothes. But being there...I feel awful for ever making her feel bad for taking all of that on. Again and *again*." His voice broke off as a sob left his throat.

Eyden moved forward, putting an arm on his shoulder. "All that matters is that you're there for her now. Don't be too proud to tell her you were wrong."

Oscar bit his lip and then he took Eyden by surprise as he pulled him into a hug. Stunned, he returned the embrace even as his wound screamed at him not to. This boy Eyden had judged quite harshly since arriving on Earth was just a kid who wanted his sister by his side. His pain had overshadowed everything else. That was something Eyden understood all too well.

CHAPTER 26

RHAY

Deep in his thoughts, Rhay bumped into Elyssa in the sunlit hallway on his way to late breakfast. She seemed to bite back a wince, her frail human body probably not made to endure so many battles. Her right arm was back in a sling.

"Watch it," she growled, massaging her shoulder.

"Sorry, love. Forgot how fragile you humans are."

Her fists rolled up tight, ready to throw a punch. "I don't know who ever told you calling anyone *love* was endearing, but they were wrong." She rushed forward faster than he expected, pushing him back with her good arm. His back hit the wall. The picture frame next to him clattered against the wood.

"I'm tired of your goddamn act, Rhay." She pulled her arm back, glowering at him. "For some reason Amira seems to care about you. Even Lora, and I guess Ilario, even if he tries to hide it. You should be glad Karwyn is dead." Rhay flinched. Elyssa's tone didn't lighten. "It's done, it's over. There's nothing you can do to change that. And even if you could, would you have let Amira die?"

Rhay swallowed hard. He hadn't considered what the alternative outcome would have been. It was too difficult a question to answer. Rhay forced a laugh. "What, are you jealous it wasn't you who saved her?"

Elyssa pulled back, shaking her head. "Jokes only get you so far. Are you going to let all of this be for goddamn nothing? Because so far the only thing you've got to show for it is a mountain of empty bottles."

Elyssa had good aim with her weapons and her words. But she was wrong; Rhay had helped. "I was there yesterday, wasn't I? And at the police station."

She scoffed, eyeing him up and down with a deadly glare. "And you think that's enough after all the shit you pulled? You've been playing it safe. Lora lost her home. Maja was shot. Eyden got hurt multiple times. My arm is in a fucking sling. Where are your wounds?"

His heart sank as he realised how little he had contributed so far, too busy sinking into the ground with each drop of alcohol. "You're right." He had already taken the leap. He'd better make sure Karwyn's fall would leave an impact. He gently grabbed her by the arm. Elyssa stared at him, her anger still present. "I'm famished, let's go get breakfast."

Elyssa shrugged him off but followed Rhay into the kitchen. Lora and Eyden were already there, setting the table as Isaac finished up cooking while Oscar and Maja watched. On the opposite side of the room, Rio and Damir avoided looking at each other. Damir absently flipped through a human magazine. They all sported scars from the night before, but sleeping in had done them some good.

As Lora sat down, her gaze swung to the doorway, her brows raised as Rhay and Elyssa walked in together. Elyssa grabbed the plates from Eyden's hands and went to the table.

A delightful smell filled the room, and Rhay turned to see Isaac opening the oven and removing a large steaming dish. "I hope everyone is hungry; I made veggie lasagne," Lora's father proudly said.

Curious of this strange concoction, Rhay sat at the table while Isaac set the dish in the centre. Everyone sat around the table. Rio made sure to avoid sitting next to Damir or Rhay. Lora and Eyden sat next to each other, and, strangely, Oscar sat between Eyden and Elyssa. Which left Rhay sitting between Elyssa and Damir. Perfect, two of his biggest fans right by his side. Maja shrugged at him when he smiled at her across the table. They hadn't talked about what happened between them. Rhay found Maja endearing but he knew their hookup had stemmed only from the trauma they had gone through. He didn't think either one of them cared about pushing their fling further.

Isaac served everyone a large portion of the steaming food. Rhay was so hungry, he ate a spoonful with no care for burning his throat.

"Now that we have the agreement, we need to do everything in our power to keep it safe. Tarnan can't get his hands on it. We have to assume the prime minister is in his grasp already, so he's probably after me and the agreement," Lora announced after taking a bite of her food. Rhay was there when the group had taken a good look at the agreement. It seemed legit, the signatures of the human ruler and Karwyn's father on the bottom of the page in blood red. With Karwyn dead, Tarnan must need Lora in his place to break the agreement.

"So the agreement stays far away from Tarnan at all times. We can lock it up and have Amira spell it shut. When are we storming Tarnan's palace?" Elyssa asked, clearly eager for another fight if it meant freeing Amira. "I say today."

"We can't risk another fight so soon, especially when Tarnan is clearly expecting us," Rio reasoned, his plate remaining untouched.

"Maybe we should regroup in Turosian first? Hide the agreement there and then stake out the situation in Carnylen?" Lora suggested.

"And keep risking Amira and Farren?" Elyssa's raised voice made everyone turn quiet as her grip tightened on her fork. Rhay had gathered that Farren was their witch friend who he had seen during Caelo Night.

"Tarnan needs both of them alive," Eyden tried to reassure his sister.

"What if Farren has outlived his purpose?" She took a deep breath, the grip on her fork loosening.

"Can I say something?" All faces turned to Rhay.

"Do you have a better plan?" Eyden scoffed.

"I have *a* plan." He kept his tone playful, charm oozing out of his words.

Lora rolled her eyes, yet smiled. "I can't wait to hear your master plan."

"I will take Elyssa to Tarnan as my hostage."

Eyden hit the table with his fist, the plates clinking against the wooden table. "I'm sure you don't fucking care if she dies, but I, *we* do."

Lora's father moved closer to Oscar, who had recoiled.

Rhay remained perfectly calm. "I can trick Tarnan into thinking I'm on his side."

Eyden didn't drop his deadly glare.

"Imagine this: I arrive in Pyria with Elyssa, requesting a meeting with Tarnan. I tell him how much I despise all of you for tricking me into killing my best friend." His gaze sought Lora's and he gave her a half-smile to make sure she knew he didn't mean it any longer. "As proof of my good faith, I'll bring Amira's lover as my prisoner. We'll be the distraction while you ambush the palace. Then I'll stay to spy on Tarnan. I'm willing to risk myself to get answers." To make sure he'd do something right, finally. He could take risks too.

"I don't trust a word you say," Eyden replied, a suspicious glint in his eyes.

"It's not a bad plan," Rio interjected, much to Rhay's surprise. "The one way to earn Tarnan's trust is to pretend to offer up the human-fae agreement as a trade. And Rhay is the only one Tarnan might believe. As an empath, he could probably resist Tarnan's mind control, like Lora and Elyssa can."

Rio had a point. Rhay had known how to block Karwyn's mind-reading power. They had trained each other to resist mental powers. Maybe he could manage to block Tarnan too.

"No way in hell are you bringing the real agreement." Elyssa flipped her fork in her hand. "You meant a fake one, right?"

Rio nodded. Everyone was silent. Rhay could feel their mixed emotions, but no one disagreed.

"Then we need to make a copy. A damn good one," Rhay added.

"We don't have anything to lose if we use a fake one," Lora admitted, biting her lip. "Even if it fails, at least it'll be a distraction." Lora anchored her gaze in Rhay's. "But there is no reason for you to stay there."

No reason except to make a difference for once.

Isaac glanced at his daughter, forehead creasing with worry. Lora avoided his gaze. Were they still fighting?

Eyden leaned back in his chair. "I agree with sending Rhay in first. He's the most disposable if all fails." The look Eyden gave him seemed to amuse Maja, who let out a curt laugh. "But sending El in with you is too risky. He could kill her on the spot for all we know," Eyden finished through gritted teeth.

Elyssa pointed her fork at him. "It's my life to risk. You know I have to do it."

"I say let's go with Messler's plan." Damir's mischievous smile grew wider as he saw Eyden's pissed-off face. "I'm curious to see how long he'll last. If he even gets through the gate."

"I'll be fine," Rhay hissed. "I *so* appreciate your concern." Damir's grin only widened.

"As much as I hate agreeing with..." Rio didn't finish his thought. Agreeing with Damir or Rhay? Both? "I don't think we have a better plan as of now, and time is running out. But Rhay shouldn't stay behind with Tarnan. He might be able to resist his compulsion but probably not forever. We don't know how powerful Tarnan is."

"It's too risky," Lora agreed, concern in her eyes. "Tarnan would only use you against us."

Rhay rolled his eyes, knowing what he needed to risk. Clapping his hands, he said, "Who here has the best handwriting for forging an agreement?"

CHAPTER 27

◊

LORA

Their plan decided, everyone was busy packing up to leave the cabin. Lora was loading things into the ambulance—still parked outside the cabin—which her family was going to take to meet up with Marcel, Maja's father who used to work at the black market and who had helped Lora cross to Liraen. Together, they would pay Lora's father's doctor friend a visit to get more medical supplies. They had to be careful, but they would be safer here than in Liraen.

Since their argument last night, Lora had had a pit in her stomach. Her father had been the most understanding, yet even he had his limits. Lora should've known he wouldn't have let Oscar go with them. Her brother had wanted to go so badly that he'd lied to Lora about their father's approval. She couldn't even blame Oscar when she would've done the same.

Two more stolen cars were parked out front to get them to Bournchester, where they would cross over to Turosian. Although Lora had known this day would come, she didn't feel at all ready to take on whatever waited for her back in Liraen.

As Lora set a bag full of medical equipment into the back of the ambulance, Maja came out the front door, a bag thrown over her shoulder. Maja loaded the bag into the ambulance.

"Are you sure you don't want to head out with my family to meet up with your dad?" Lora asked. The cold dug into her bones, and Lora crossed her arms over her thick coat. A thin layer of snow covered the driveway in the late afternoon gloom.

Maja's breath turned cold as she pushed her glasses up her nose. "I talked to him briefly on the phone. He knows he won't convince me otherwise."

"I bet he wasn't happy about it."

"I don't think anyone's happy about what's going on right now," Maja said, her tone more serious than usual. "But I don't want to be waiting on the other side again. Waiting fucking sucks. So I'm afraid you're stuck with me."

Lora uncrossed her arms, a smile spilling free. "I could never be stuck with you."

Turning towards the front steps, a crushing weight seemed to drop on her. This really was happening. She was about to say goodbye to her family. *Again.*

Maja studied her. "It'll be different this time." Bumping her shoulder into Lora's, she eased the tension building in Lora's heart. "Come on. Let's head back inside before we freeze to death."

Lora was about to follow her in when she spotted Rhay on the side of the house, leaning over the railing on the porch. Walking closer, she noticed a cigarette in Rhay's hand, smoke drifting through the chilly air.

"Where did you get that?" She leaned her arms on the railing next to him. The smoke made her crinkle her nose.

"Found it in the kitchen." Taking a puff, Rhay tried to play off his cough.

"Right. Are you—"

"Let's not rehash the past again." Flakes of snow covered his black hair. It still startled her to see his hair dark instead of a bright colour. "Tell me your favourite reality show."

"Why?"

His ocean eyes were clouded in darkness as if torn by his desire to go back to denial or anger. "Because I'm in need of a distraction and I'm trying to pull back on my bad...habits."

"This isn't the best habit either." The smoke of his cigarette blew in her face as the wind changed, and Lora waved her hand to disperse it. She'd never liked smoking, but she had a suspicion the cigarettes Rhay had found were Maja's. There had been a phase.

Rhay leaned back against the railing, still waiting for an answer to his absolutely irrelevant question.

"I guess I'd have to go with 90 Day Fiancé," she said.

He pushed his cigarette down on the snow-covered railing, killing its flame. "Wrong."

"Enlighten me."

Leaning closer, he was smiling as he said, "It's obviously Naked Attraction." Lora couldn't help the laugh bubbling out of her. "Never seen anything more bizarre in my life."

"It definitely wins the most bizarre award," Lora agreed, though after living at the Turosian palace, a silly reality show didn't seem that strange in comparison. The thought made her smile drop, and Rhay must have noticed as his own grin slipped. She took a breath, bracing herself. "I'm sorry, but I have to say this before we head out."

"Go on then, love. Lay it on me. You don't like my plan? Or has Eyden gotten to you and you don't trust me to execute it?"

She laid a gentle hand on his arm. "I do trust you." She was still unsure if she might regret it, but she knew the person Rhay was deep down.

His mouth opened, then closed. "As you should." A smirk graced his lips. "I rocked your best friend's world, after all."

Lora hit his arm. "You had to ruin it." She tried to sound serious, but there was laughter in her voice. "I trust you because you're choosing to be someone who steps up when the world is falling apart. But you can't go back now. I'm putting my faith in you."

His gaze dropped. "I'm not sure that I am that person. I haven't figured out who I want to be yet. I just know I want to be different. I want to make it all worth it. It *has to* be worth it."

Lora nodded. "I don't know who I am yet, either." She'd been using her powers more frequently and it felt freeing in a sense, yet at the same time it made her feel like an outsider in her own world.

"But you know who you want to be, don't you? You once told me it's a choice, and I think you know what you want. Don't waste your time denying it. As the king of denial, I'm telling you, it'll bite you in the ass."

He wasn't wrong. What she wanted was to be both human and fae. And she didn't want to keep apologising or be criticised for either side of her—least of all by herself.

Her mum looked so still lying on the hospital bed. Closing the door, Lora went to sit in the chair next to her. She'd come here with a purpose, yet now all words seemed lost to her. If only her mum would wake up, take her hand, and tell her everything was going to be all right. She'd give anything to have that, but there was nothing on Earth that could help.

Lora reached out and took her mum's unresponsive hand. Her tan skin was paler than Lora remembered as she'd been stuck in this room, unconscious, for over a week now. Breathing in deeply, Lora tried to reach her mum's mind, but she came up empty. Was she unable to use her newfound power or was her mother no longer there?

Just hold on a little longer. Lora tried to project the thought into her mum's head, but she had no way of knowing if it worked.

Clearing her throat, Lora whispered, "I know you probably can't hear me..." Watching her mum's face, she foolishly waited for any sign. "I just wanted to say that I'll try everything I can to bring you back. When all of this is over, I'll come back." Tears threatened to spill. "I...I promise I'll try."

Pulling her hand to her lap, Lora's gaze lingered on her mum's closed eyes. Hands shaking, Lora pushed a strand of hair out of her face. "I hope that once I come back you'll see that, even with everything bad that has happened, I'm the way I am—human and fae—for a reason. This is who I'm meant to be and I...I don't hate it. I don't hate who I am. Not anymore. And I don't want you to hate me for it either."

The room was eerily quiet, yet Lora's thoughts were loud in her head. Would she be able to say all of this when her mum was awake—*if* her mum ever woke up?

Footsteps in the hallway forced Lora into action, and she wiped the tear that had escaped her with her sleeve before getting up and pulling the door open. Her dad came down the hall.

Stopping before her, her father seemed at a loss for words.

"I'm sorry," Lora blurted, hating this rift between them, especially since they were about to part ways yet again. "I should've known better. I was just relieved Oscar wanted to see me as I really am. But I never wanted him to go. I'm glad you will both be safe, away from this madness."

Her father squeezed her arm. "I know, and I wish I could take both of my kids with me. I want you to know that. I'm worried about you just as much, but I know there's nothing I can do to change your mind. You have to go."

Nodding, Lora felt another tear slipping down her cheek. "Take care of each other. Of Mum."

Oscar barged into the room, a backpack swung over his shoulder. "I'm ready to go."

Her father took her in, his green eyes telling her a million things. The first time Lora had left she hadn't been able to get herself to say goodbye, and she felt similar now. As if the word *goodbye* might swallow her whole if she uttered the syllables.

Her father seemed to understand as a sad yet encouraging smile turned the corners of his mouth. "Stay safe." The words sounded strangled.

Biting her lip, Lora nodded forcefully, and her dad walked past her towards her mum's bed. He unlocked the safety on the wheels and gently pushed it into the hallway. Everything seemed to crumble down around her, ready to bury her alive with every step he took.

Turning her head, she met Oscar's gaze as he leaned against the wall in the hallway. Further down, she could pick up chatter coming from the kitchen.

"This feels oddly like deja-vu, doesn't it?" His eyes were misty, and Lora wished she could promise him it was all going to be okay.

But there was one thing she could say. "You know I'll come back if I can, right?"

His eyes turned sadder. "I know that now," he finally replied.

A loud noise from the kitchen made both of them turn their heads, and Lora instinctively ran forward. Turning the corner, her heart dropped in her chest. Fae stormed through the back door. They were dressed in all black again, but she knew Tarnan had to be behind it.

Elyssa, Eyden, Ilario, and Damir were already locked in fights. Maja gripped a pan and swung it at a guard's head. How the hell had they found them? They'd been so close to leaving.

Panic chilled every fiber of her being as Oscar appeared next to her, and Lora's gaze snapped to the other hall leading to the front door where her dad had disappeared through to transport her mum to the ambulance.

As he raised his sword to block one of the guards, Eyden's eyes met hers across the room. Behind him, a guard threw Elyssa on the table, and she kicked out as Ilario came up from behind the guard, a kitchen knife in his hand. Damir was engaging three guards at once, no sign of fear on his face.

"Get Oscar out of here!" Eyden yelled as he sliced at his opponent, spilling blood. His movements were stiff, his injury hindering him.

Heart in her throat, Lora grabbed Oscar's hand and dragged him through the mess, using her air magic to make a path for them. The cold air outside helped clear the fog in her mind as she steered Oscar towards the ambulance outside.

Frantically, her gaze travelled to her dad, who sat inside the ambulance, pulling open the driver's door as if to get out again. In that precise moment an arrow shot down, blocking their path. She diverted her course, pushing Oscar behind the nearest car. Her dad closed the car door and the arrow hit metal instead.

Looking up from behind the car, Lora spotted more fae stationed on the roof. Lora pushed her air towards them, but she spotted one of the guards lifting his hand, deflecting her move with his own air magic.

Footsteps behind her made her whirl around, and she barely avoided the sharp edge of a blade. Pulling a knife from her boot, she slashed at the guard's forearm and drew blood.

"Get to Dad!" she screamed at Oscar, who was still ducking behind the car. But as her gaze briefly left her opponent, she spotted more arrows raining down on them. Oscar wouldn't make it to the ambulance.

More guards rushed out of the woods towards them. Lost in dread, Lora felt the blade of the guard's sword graze her shoulder. She bit her lip as she kicked out, putting more distance between them. Pulling on her magic, she snapped the sword from the guard's hand. Stunned, the guard didn't see her kick coming and fell backwards onto the icy gravel.

Her gaze flickered from the guards having almost reached the back of the ambulance where her helpless mother lay to the arrows raining down from the roof and then to her brother hiding next to her.

"He needs to go!" Oscar yelled. If their dad didn't move now, the guards would be upon them.

She was torn. Risk Oscar staying behind or risk the guards reaching the ambulance?

Oscar was shaking as he gestured to their dad. "I'll be fine, now tell him to go!"

The frantic look in his eyes pushed her to act. Out of the corner of her eye, she saw the guard she'd fought get up. She half-heartedly threw him backwards again with her air just as she yelled at her father, "Go!" She gestured with her arm, and her father's face fell as he glanced at the side mirror, at the guards approaching.

Her father seemed just as torn, his gaze flickering around wildly as if searching for another way. As one guard reached for the back door of the ambulance, Lora pulled on her life source and pushed the vehicle forward with her air. Her dad finally hit the gas.

She barely had a second to process him driving away before Rhay's voice pulled her back. "Watch out!" he warned as he came running from the side of the building.

Lora ducked as a guard attacked, and in that moment the rest of the gang stormed out of the cabin.

"We need to get out of here!" Ilario yelled as he pushed a guard back. Maja flinched behind him, a gun in her hand. The group tried to get off the front porch, but the arrows coming from the roof kept them from joining her and Oscar in the driveway.

Seeking Eyden's gaze, Lora tilted her head to the roof. Getting her signal, Eyden appeared next to her. Lora threw Oscar a quick glance, telling him to stay put, and then Eyden teleported her to the roof.

The guards didn't see them coming. Before the one with air magic could react, Eyden threw a knife at his chest and Lora lifted her arms, pushing the rest of the guards off the roof. She grabbed Eyden's hand and he threw them back into the air until their feet hit the ground again. Almost stumbling, Lora hurried with the others to the cars.

Maja yelled something before lifting her arm and throwing a shiny key her way. Catching it, Lora turned it in her hand. Maja dove into the front seat of one of the cars, and Lora sprung into action and unlocked the car Oscar hid behind. Oscar hurried in and so did Lora. Eyden was fighting a guard trying to reach their car. Lora tracked Elyssa as she picked up a bow and arrow from one of the guards and fired, all while heading her way. Ilario, Rhay, and Damir piled into Maja's car, and Lora gestured for her to get going.

Lora put the car in drive and stepped on the gas, the car roaring, and Eyden turned to face her. As if sensing her intention, he spun so the guard was in front of her vehicle. She hit the gas pedal hard and knocked the guard over. A split second later, Eyden reached the back door of her car at the same time as Elyssa.

Lora didn't even wait for the doors to close before she drove off. The guards couldn't keep up with them. An arrow struck the back of the car but glanced off. Soon, they were in the clear.

Finally able to breathe again, she glanced at Oscar next to her, his lips pressed together tightly. He wasn't supposed to be here, but now that he was, what other choice did she have than to bring him with her?

When they arrived in Bournchester hours later, Lora pulled into a familiar parking lot. She'd been here once with Marcel, back at the start of what felt like another life entirely.

On uneasy feet, she stepped out of the car. The sun had set on their drive here and now it was dark around them, the sparse street lights providing little light. Eyden appeared next to her, his hand brushing hers, and a little bit of peace washed over her until her gaze met her brother's as he shut the car door.

She had told her father Oscar would be safe and now he was heading into danger once again.

They regrouped with Maja, Damir, Ilario, and Rhay at the little corner shop where the secret entrance to the black market was hidden. Lora knew crossing at the beach wouldn't be possible with the military there. And most likely Tarnan's guards.

The shop looked ransacked and empty, much like the rest of Bournchester. The door leading to the underground market was wide open. Eyden raised his sword and Elyssa drew an arrow. Stepping to the side, Lora let them take the lead as they entered the grey corridor leading downstairs. The door at the bottom was made of steel and just as massive as Lora remembered, but strangely, it was also open.

With a queasy feeling, they kept going. Lora kept close to Oscar. Maja's expression was almost as blank as Damir's, which meant she had to be freaking out. Although she had made deliveries for Marcel, Maja had never been to the black market with her father as it was too dangerous.

As the market came into view, a foul smell drifted through the air and Lora pulled her sleeve up to cover her nose. She didn't understand why it was so quiet until they rounded the last corner and she nearly retched at the sight.

Corpses littered the floor. Some obviously human, others seemingly fae, their striking eyes wide open with no life left in them. Blood painted the floor red and broken items cluttered the space. It was the scene after a battle with no happy ending.

The border shimmered behind the trading spaces. A fight must have broken out when the fae had come through, leading to a bloodbath. And now they stood in the middle of it, Lora's feet sticking to the floor as blood painted the soles of her boots red.

A heaving sound caught Lora's attention and she turned to find Oscar hunched over, throwing up his lunch. She wished she could erase the image from his mind and save him from the horrors she had witnessed these past months.

When Oscar pulled himself up again, Lora put her arm around him. She turned back to the grey shimmer of the border, showing a glimpse of the other side. As they walked into the trading space, a blurry image of the market in Chrysa appeared before her and it seemed to mirror the mess here.

As the electricity of the portal called to her, an anxious feeling crawled over her skin. Standing before the border, it felt much like it had when they'd fled from Tarnan—terrifying, yet unavoidable.

But now they had a plan. Lora took Oscar's hand and pulled him through the portal, readying herself for what was to come.

CHAPTER 28

AMIRA

Amira woke up in the carriage to the sound of Tarnan boasting about his late father's darling city. His voice was like nails scratching inside her head. Amira and Farren had spent the last two days rebuilding most of the palace, exhausting themselves.

Looking out the window, Amira spied the first rays of sun gleaming through the dark clouds. She recognised the outer walls of the palace in Pyria. Her heart squeezed in her chest. She would be seeing her mother soon. And with Farren no longer compelled by Tarnan, they would be out of the palace as soon as her mother was free. And then she would finally reunite with Elyssa. She missed her fierce grin, her wild curls, her pine scent.

When they reached the palace's gate, the carriage clattered to a stop at the circular paved entrance. Tarnan opened the door and held out his hand to help her out. Amira was too exhausted to refuse his help. Her bones felt like they were made out of stone as Amira stepped outside, the morning sun momentarily blinding her.

Amira noticed Tarnan furrowing his brows, his gaze anchored on the servants waiting by the entrance. Weariness spread through her veins like ice scraping at her skin. Squinting, Amira took a closer look, and the air left her lungs. Now that her tired eyes had adjusted to the bright sun, Amira realised they weren't servants.

Amira's heart stilled in her chest. Held by two guards each, Rhay and Elyssa stood in front of the gate.

Elyssa had a purple bruise on her cheek and her clothes hung loose around her. Rhay was bleeding through the torn sleeve of his sweater. His hair was strangely dark and matted, a far cry from his usual bright colours. Were the others here too—Lora, Eyden, and Ilario? The question quickly left her mind as her eyes met Elyssa's. Her heart shattered and rebuilt itself in one motion. Her breath caught as she took in Elyssa's face, her eyes strangely void of any emotion. Had Elyssa and Rhay tried to break into the palace? Would they become prisoners now too?

Taking a step forward, Amira was ready to run into Elyssa's arms with no care for the two guards fiercely holding her, a sword pointed at Elyssa's throat. But Tarnan stopped her.

"Stay," he told her as if she was his dog.

Three guards placed themselves next to Tarnan as he stalked forward. A vein pulsing on her forehead, Amira followed Tarnan, refusing to obey her *master's* command.

Tarnan folded his hands behind his back. "Well, where's the rest of your group?"

Rhay tried to shake off the guard holding his bleeding arm. "As I've tried to explain to your idiot guards, I've come here to join you. As proof of my good faith, I've brought you Amira's lover."

Elyssa struggled against the guards' hold to no avail. Amira's hand twitched. Rhay had betrayed them? After finally making a step in the right direction, he had decided to take a hundred back? It couldn't be true. Confused, Amira stepped forward, ready to intervene, but Tarnan held her back.

"I know how happy you must be to see your friends, Amira. But I'm afraid I will have to throw them in the dungeon for now." An apologetic smile spread across Tarnan's lips. "If Elyssa can contain her rage, I'm willing to let her live with you for your sake."

Rhay glared daggers at Elyssa and Amira. "Did you really think I would stay on their side? After they betrayed me and forced me to kill my best friend?"

"We didn't force you to kill Karwyn!" Elyssa croaked out. Amira was surprised her voice sounded so...broken. A shiver ran down her back.

"You might as well have!"

"Enough with the bickering. Put them in separate cells." Tarnan turned his back to them, still holding Amira's arm.

"Let me speak to her," Amira begged Tarnan, trying to remove herself from his grip.

"Later, Amira," Tarnan said in a low voice, as if he was her father, admonishing her.

The door to the other carriage opened and Saydren appeared. "Young Messler and the human girl. I thought the guards on Earth would have already dealt with them. How disappointing." Burning bile travelled up Amira's throat.

"If you had let me finish"—a smug smile played on Rhay's lips—"I could've told you that, compared to your sad excuse for guards, I took them by surprise and snatched the agreement from Lora."

Amira tried to catch his gaze, but Rhay hadn't looked at her once. What was going on in his head? Did he blame them for his part in Karwyn's death?

Thrashing against the guards holding her, Elyssa yelled, "You fucking traitor! Do you realise what you've done?"

"That's an interesting turn of events." Tarnan's voice was thicker than poison. He let go of Amira's arm and moved forward, patting Rhay's cheek. "Smart move. *Now give it to me.*"

Moved by Tarnan's compulsion, Rhay tried to shake off the two guards. Tarnan gestured for the guards to ease up. Amira prayed for Rhay to use this opportunity to attack, to fight back. But Rhay didn't even try to strike Tarnan. Instead, he removed a scroll from his jacket and handed it over. A scream died in Amira's throat.

Footsteps sounded from behind her. Farren had left the carriage, catching up to what was happening. In a desperate move, he threw some air at Tarnan, but the king held on to the scroll.

"You shouldn't drain your life force, witch, not after using so much energy rebuilding my city." Tarnan gestured for a guard to take a hold of Farren, and they pinned his hands behind his back.

"You can't destroy the agreement, it would be madness," Farren screamed at Tarnan.

"It wouldn't be madness, it would be *balance*."

Shaking her head, Amira furiously thought of a solution. Maybe she could use her magic to hide it somewhere safe?

"I don't think I can break such a powerful agreement," she argued, trying to stall. She willed Rhay to turn her way, but his face remained stoic.

"Don't worry about the details." Tarnan gave her a smile that Amira wanted to smack off his face. "I thought we shared an understanding, Amira. I have done so much for you already. Go inside with Elyssa, let the guards take her for now. Think of your mother."

Amira couldn't argue. She was trapped. But she couldn't let Tarnan take Elyssa either. Even if Tarnan kept his word and didn't kill her, he would use Elyssa against her at every turn.

She sought Elyssa's gaze, wordlessly telling her to run. To her surprise, Elyssa twisted the guard's arm with a strength Amira had never seen and turned his own blade on him, catching him in the heart. Relief washed through her, but only for a second—another guard drew his sword.

A knife plunged into the chest of the guard holding Farren back. Out of thin air, Lora, Eyden and—Amira's mouth dropped open—*Elyssa* appeared before them, all decked out in weapons and slashing at the guards. There were two Elyssas. One who had come with Rhay and now a second one, with knives strapped to her from head to toe.

How were there two? What in Liraen was going on?

The first Elyssa, close to Rhay, took advantage of the confusion to stab the closest guard with his own sword and then her face shifted, morphing into the features of Karwyn's shadow. They had tricked Tarnan into thinking *Elyssa* had been brought here by Rhay.

Rhay gasped. "I can't believe you used me again." Had they also tricked Rhay?

Taking a guard's sword, Rhay launched himself at Damir, and everything around them erupted into chaos. Eyden and the real Elyssa attacked the nearby guards. Lora threw fire at Saydren, the healer barely moving out of reach as his arm caught on fire. He dropped down and rolled in the dust to smother the growing flames.

Amira used whatever magic she had left in her to throw a gust of wind at a guard coming dangerously close to Elyssa's—the *real* Elyssa's—back. Light-headed, Amira swayed on her feet.

"Thanks, sunshine." Elyssa winked. Amira was dying to kiss her, but this was definitely not the time.

"*Don't let them leave alive.*" Tarnan's voice turned dark and cavernous. "*Damir, kill Eyden,*" Tarnan ordered. Before he could say anything else, Lora threw a barrier of fire around Eyden, protecting him from Damir's reach. Like a puppet, Damir headed for Eyden anyway, his sword raised high. He jumped over the fiery barrier. Clashing together, Eyden drifted away with Damir.

Using the distraction, Elyssa threw a knife at Tarnan. Tarnan and Amira yelped in unison as the blade sank into his shoulder, yet his grip on the agreement remained fierce.

Eyes widening, Elyssa took in the bloodstain spreading on Amira's blouse. Tarnan let out a victorious laugh. "I would think twice about throwing that." He tilted his chin at the new knife Elyssa had drawn. "Whatever injury I sustain, Amira will as well. I would consider your next move very carefully."

CHAPTER 29

ELYSSA

Fuck. That was all Elyssa could think as her eyes travelled from the blood on Amira's shoulder to Tarnan's injury in the exact same spot. Their plan had gone well enough until now. As they'd hoped, with only Rhay and Damir—disguised as herself—at the gate, Tarnan hadn't called for more guards. They'd taken him by surprise. But goddamn, so had he.

When she looked at Amira, a deep fear gripped her. Even with her skin paler than usual, her eyes exhausted, and long hair tangled from the wind, the princess remained breathtaking. Yet she was bound to Tarnan. How would they goddamn get out of that one?

Farren stepped closer to them and the slight twitch of his lips told her how relieved he was to see her again.

Behind her, Lora's flames warmed Elyssa's back. Elyssa focused on Tarnan's blood-red eyes. Her body yearned to storm forward, but she couldn't when it would hurt Amira too.

Rhay appeared next to Tarnan, and Elyssa was about to warn him not to hurt the king, but Rhay spoke first. "I want to clarify that I had no idea Damir was pretending to be Elyssa. I brought you the human-fae agreement. I have no place in Turosian anymore and I'm willing to put in the work and join your court if you promise not to lie to me as"—his eyes shifted from Amira to Lora—"they have."

Dammit, Rhay. They'd told him a distraction was enough. Why was he still playing this role?

Tarnan's calculating eyes lingered on Rhay. Subtly eyeing their surroundings, Elyssa took in the empty carriages. They needed to wait for the right moment to flee.

"You can't be serious," Amira hissed. "What has gotten into you? He killed Varsha, your *friend.*"

Rhay flinched, his features darkening, but then his eyes turned cruel. "She was collateral damage. This is war, Amira. People die. That list of names we always talk about? What's the point of fighting against it when I'll end up at the end of it?"

Amira leaned back as if Rhay had hit her with more than words. What the fuck was Rhay doing?

A path of fire lit up next to Elyssa and she turned her head to see Lora stalking forward, her arm raised at Tarnan as guards rushed after her.

"Stop! You can't hurt him!" Elyssa yelled. Lora pinched her brows but dropped the flames.

"Glad to see you're learning," Tarnan said, his satisfied grin twisting Elyssa's insides. "Guards, halt your forces."

As Lora joined them, Elyssa tried to find Eyden, but he was nowhere to be found. And neither was Damir. At her questioning gaze, Lora quickly put two fingers behind her ear.

Lora looked like she was about to address Tarnan, but he spoke first. "Pleasure to see you again, Princess. Or is it queen now? My sources say you haven't claimed your title."

"Did your sources tell you that your guards didn't stand a chance against us on Earth? Where's the prime minister?"

If Tarnan was surprised, he didn't show it. Hands balled into fists, Lora glared at him. "I wouldn't step any closer. As I've already shared with Elyssa, every wound you inflict on me, Amira will feel as well." Lora's gaze snapped to Elyssa, and she tilted her head. "I have to say, I had hoped you learned your lesson. Amira will stay with me. For her sake, I will let you all leave now before I'm forced to make sacrifices." His cold eyes turned to Rhay. He curled his fingers around the scroll of paper. "I appreciate your gesture."

"But you don't trust me, do you?" Rhay asked, walking towards Tarnan. "You don't believe I didn't know it was Damir. And you're right. I did know." Tarnan lifted his dark brows and Elyssa's skin prickled. Something was off. Was he distracting Tarnan so they could run? They were surrounded by guards. "They told me to pretend to capture Elyssa and offer you a fake copy of the agreement." Before he even said his next words, Elyssa's heart dropped in her chest. "But I took the real one."

Tarnan was quiet for a moment. Elyssa followed his gaze to Lora, who shook her head silently as if trying to piece together a puzzle that wouldn't fit. Tarnan turned back to him. *Tell me the truth, Rhay. Is this the real human-fae agreement?*

"Yes," Rhay rushed to answer. Elyssa sensed the truth even though she was unsure whether Tarnan could truly compel Rhay.

"Why?" Lora's voice was strangled, torn.

"You know why," Rhay replied, his tone hard.

Lora lifted her arm and the agreement flew from Tarnan's grip, but Saydren stepped into Lora's path, catching the agreement and pushing it into the pocket of his coat. Before Lora could charge forward guards were upon her, surrounding her. She threw fire but there were too many to strike all at once.

Elyssa let go of a throwing star, stunning Saydren but not for long. Charging at him, Elyssa tried to get the agreement, but a loud yell drew her attention.

Knife at his throat, Tarnan had Farren in a death grip. "Stop or your friend will die." A gust of wind from Amira tripped Tarnan enough that he let go of Farren.

"I suppose it was foolish of me to hope you would take my side over your friend's." Tarnan's gaze turned murderous, and Elyssa turned to Farren, thinking Tarnan would target him. "You've forced my hand."

Another throwing star aimed at them, Elyssa didn't hear Saydren until he was upon her. A sharp blade dug into her shoulder from behind.

Falling to her knees, Elyssa tried to catch her breath. Fire burned her left shoulder where the blade had entered. The air vanished from her lungs. Her throwing star clattered to the ground.

"El!" Amira screamed her name.

Elyssa gritted her teeth, prepared to fight back, when the knife twisted in her back and Saydren pulled it out. The pain rendered her immobile. She pressed her lips together to keep her grunt of pain inside. Her whole body shuddered. She felt blood gushing out, making her light-headed. Before she could regain her senses, Saydren stepped closer, pulling at her hair to reveal her throat and putting the bloody blade to her skin. A dreadful sense of deja-vu overtook her.

Amira's eyes welled up. "Stop it, Tarnan. *Please.* You wanted me to trust you, this isn't the way."

Tarnan had his grip on Farren again while Rhay stood there, emotionless. "I gave you every chance, Amira. I now see that you'll never learn if I coddle you. *Don't move.*"

Amira's gaze turned depleted. Tarnan gave Saydren a nod, and the healer twisted Elyssa's head back further. She couldn't help the hiss of pain. Amira leaned her body in her direction but her feet wouldn't move. Trying to tell her to run, Elyssa glanced from the princess to the carriage. She had to get out of here. Elyssa wouldn't fail at saving her or Farren, who tried to shake Tarnan off to no avail.

"You backed me into a corner, Amira. It hurts me too," Tarnan argued, his gaze almost sad as if he wished he could act differently.

Amira turned to Rhay, pleading with him.

Fucking traitor, Elyssa thought as the edge of Saydren's blade nicked her skin.

Eyden appeared out of nowhere, right behind Tarnan, a knife in his hand. Elyssa screamed, "Eyden, don't!" The strangled words came out just before his blade could strike. Eyden threw himself at Tarnan, pushing Farren to the side and removing Tarnan from the scene completely.

Freed, Farren lifted his arm, and Elyssa felt the blade leave her throat. The sudden freedom forced her forward. She caught herself on the hard ground, the earth dry and cold beneath her numb fingers. Her back tingled as she strained her muscles, pain rendering her breathless.

The guards seemed at a loss without a new command coming their way. Lora had kept them at bay with her fire, but she looked exhausted.

Elyssa bit back the sharp sting flashing down her back and swept the knife on the ground out of Saydren's reach as he stared at the spot where Tarnan had been. She raised herself onto one knee, her shoulder screaming in pain, and pounded her fist into Saydren's stomach. A blast of wind lifted the curls that had escaped her ponytail as Farren pushed back the guards, Lora helping him.

Amira ran towards Elyssa and with a flick of her hand, Saydren fell backwards. Judging by the sweat lining her face, Amira was at the end of her strength. The princess raised her arm again, gaze set on Saydren's pocket that held the agreement, but nothing happened. Elyssa was about to make a grab for it, her legs unsteady as Amira helped her up, when guards approached her, swords drawn.

Lora shouted behind them, "Let's go! The carriage!" More guards flanked Saydren.

Trying to keep the guards off them, Lora and Farren moved backwards, and Amira swung an arm around her as they hurried forward. The princess almost tripped, a drop of blood running from her nose as they both stumbled. Yet Amira kept Elyssa upright.

"I've got you," Amira whispered, looking at her as if she was dreaming.

Amira threw open the carriage door and Elyssa gestured for her to get in first. Reluctantly, Amira stepped inside, offering her hand to Elyssa. Glancing over her shoulder, Elyssa signalled for Lora and Farren to hurry the hell up. Elyssa followed Lora's gaze to Rhay who still stood by the gate.

Shaking her head, Lora gained speed and rushed into the carriage. Eyden reappeared and when he spotted them, he drifted to the carriage and jumped onto the driver's seat. "Let's go before Tarnan finds his way back!" he yelled.

Farren threw one last gust of wind behind him as he reached the carriage. Turning to Elyssa, his back to the guards, a small smile graced his lips even as exhaustion darkened his eyes. He gripped the door to enter the carriage on shaking legs, swiping at the blood dripping from his nose.

Elyssa grinned back at him before an arrow shot at them, impaling itself in Farren's side. Time seemed to slow as he looked to Elyssa, then to the blood seeping through his shirt. The air froze in Elyssa's lungs.

Fuck.

Another arrow zipped through the air, and she pushed Farren to the side as he raised his hand, a guttural scream leaving him. A strong wave of air came flooding towards the reinforcements arriving at the gate. Their bows and arrows dropped at the intensity of Farren's magic. Their eyes were wide as they stood there, weaponless.

Lora pulled Farren into the carriage and Elyssa hurriedly closed the door, slumping against it. The carriage started moving immediately. Twisting around, Elyssa pushed her hair out of her face. Her hand went to her back, pressing on the wound to try and stop the bleeding. It hurt like hell, but they'd gotten away.

"That was badass," she joked, impressed by Farren's magic, but her grin died as she took him in.

His eyes were half-closed, blood dripping from the corner of his mouth and smeared across his nose. His veins stood out on his face, his dark skin strangely ashen. Lora knelt in front of him, her forehead wrinkled. The arrow was still stuck in his side. Pushing her hand into her pocket, Lora took out a bottle of healing paste she'd taken from Eyden's place. She applied some around the wound, glancing at Elyssa, a question in her eyes. Elyssa shook her head. She'd be all right as long as Farren was. He made no sound as Lora applied her whole supply to his skin, as if he could no longer feel the pain.

"I don't know what to do," Lora said, her voice distraught. Farren's breathing stuttered. A drop of blood spilled from the corner of his lips. "It's not working. And if I pull out the arrow, he'll bleed to death."

"*No.*" Elyssa knelt next to Farren, desperation setting her skin on fire. "You're *not* dying." Farren blinked, but no words escaped him. Amira watched on with shock, tears gathering in her eyes.

"I..." Farren croaked, coughing up blood, his body too still, depleted of all energy. His eyes had lost their spark, their light. That was when she understood. Farren looked up at her with half-hooded eyes and she *knew*. Knew that he had drawn on his own energy to hold off the guards despite his own life source already dwindling from the arrow piercing his skin. He had known. And he had done it anyway.

"*No*," Elyssa said again. It was as if no other words existed. Furious, she knocked her fist against the wall. She barely felt it, a different pain overtaking every part of her. "Stop looking at me like you're dying. You're *not*. I won't allow it." She angled her body to the window. "Eyden can drift—"

"It's too late," Farren whispered, barely loud enough for her to catch. He tried to lift his hand but failed. "It's all right. The pain...it's gone."

Elyssa shook her head, her gaze drifting between Farren and the carriage door. Maybe it wasn't too late. Maybe they could find a healer—

"Don't..." Farren's broken voice stopped her stream of thoughts. Elyssa squeezed her eyes shut. Death after death flashed through her mind. Her uncle. People at the camp. Her parents. Iris. She hadn't been able to say goodbye to any of them and she refused to do so now.

Yet she forced herself to move, leaning down, knowing she wouldn't understand Farren otherwise. He had a faraway look in his eyes as if he was half there, half somewhere else. Somewhere Elyssa couldn't follow.

Tears ran down Lora's cheeks. Elyssa could feel her own eyes turning glassy, but she fought against it. She had to be strong.

Reaching for his hand, Elyssa turned to Farren's face. His lips parted, stained red. "Don't..." he said, his eyes barely open, "blame yourself." His gaze drifted to Amira kneeling beside him, tears flowing freely.

"I promised we'd get out of there together," Amira whispered.

A bloodstained smile graced his lips. "We did."

Amira shook her head, her lips trembling. "I promised I wouldn't leave you behind. Please don't leave me either," Amira begged, her voice shaken by tears.

He swallowed with effort. His voice was paper-thin. "I'll...be with you always." His gaze met Elyssa's again, but his eyes seemed unable to focus. "My sacrifice..."

Elyssa opened her mouth to reply, but what could she say? How could she possibly say goodbye to her oldest friend?

Farren's chest stopped moving and her window of opportunity died with him as well as a part of her heart. A crushing weight settled on her chest and she knew she'd never be the same.

"Farren?" Amira's voice drifted through the carriage, her voice thick with tears.

Elyssa squeezed his hand but Farren didn't react. He was gone. *Forever.* He'd died much too soon, and for fucking what?

Her insides cracked open, unleashing a well of red-hot anger stronger than she'd ever felt. Her heart felt utterly hollow, but she let her fury fill it to the brim. Instead of letting her tears fall, she yelled, her fist connecting with the wooden wall. She barely felt the sting as her skin split open.

If she couldn't blame herself, she knew who she could blame. And he would not go down gently.

CHAPTER 30

ᘒ

LORA

Travelling with the dead body of one's friend was a cruel fate. The carriage ride had been the longest one of Lora's life. Elyssa had been uncharacteristically quiet after her initial outburst. Head leaning against the cold glass of the window, Elyssa stayed awake, watching Amira sleep as if the princess could slip away any moment.

The sun had set when Lora finally spied Chrysa through the foggy windows. Not long after, the carriage slowed in a familiar street by Eyden's flat. She didn't wait to open the door. As soon as her feet hit the ground, Eyden was there, pulling her into a hug. Lora bit back a sob. Farren should be here. Rhay...should be here.

Glancing over Eyden's shoulder, Lora spotted Damir jumping from the driver's seat. They'd picked him up on the way, Tarnan's compulsion having released him, probably because of the distance. Reluctantly, Lora pulled back, seeking out Elyssa. She stepped out of the carriage with a stoic expression, blood staining the back of her shoulder. They'd stopped the bleeding, but it had to hurt nonetheless.

Unsteady, Amira made her way out too. Eyden's gaze drifted inside the carriage, finding Farren's body which they'd covered with a cloak. Lips pressed into a firm line, Eyden reached out, embracing Elyssa, and she seemed to let herself feel her grief—but only for a second. Then she stepped back, nodded determinedly, and walked up the steps to Eyden's flat, Amira's hand in hers.

Lora followed Elyssa up the steps. As soon as she entered Eyden's flat, Oscar rushed towards her, looking her over with concern. Ilario had stayed with him and Maja in case anything happened.

"Are you okay?" Oscar asked. Maja walked up to her, her eyes holding the same question. Lora was sure the tears in her eyes were still visible. Her eyes darted to Elyssa sitting on the midnight black sofa, her face in her hands. Amira took a seat next to her, her eyes blank.

"I'm fine but..." Lora started just as Damir and Eyden entered the flat, carrying Farren's body wrapped in a cloak. They set the body on the ground before locking the door.

"Who...who is that?" Oscar asked, his voice sounding small and child-like.

Lora's lips trembled as she tried to answer. Eyden stepped up next to her. "Farren. He was a friend of ours."

Ilario's eyes turned sympathetic as he glanced at Elyssa and Amira before his head turned every which way, lingering on Damir. "Where's Rhay?"

Rhay. Lora had tried her best to not think about his potential betrayal.

"Messler had his own agenda," Damir said, impassive. Ilario turned to Lora, dismissing Damir.

Lora swallowed her anger. "He chose to stay. He gave Tarnan the real agreement—at least that's what he said. Maja, can I see the agreement?" They had left what should have been the real agreement here for safe keeping.

Maja removed the paper from her pocket, unfolding it. "It does look like the copy we made, but I'm not sure."

Amira rose on shaky legs. "Let me see." At Lora's nod, Maja handed the agreement to Amira. Fingers moving across the paper, Amira closed her eyes. A deep sigh left her lips. "I don't feel any magic." Her eyes snapped open. "He must have given Tarnan the real one." Swaying on her feet, from the betrayal or exhaustion, Amira sat back on the couch next to Elyssa.

"No, that can't be true." Ilario pressed his lips shut tightly.

How could Rhay have stolen the real agreement from her and handed it to Tarnan? What the fuck had been going through his mind? It had seemed as if they'd finally found common ground, yet he had stabbed her in the back ten times worse than what she had done to him. Was he so fixated on making Karwyn's death worth it that he felt the need to spy on Tarnan?

"It is," Eyden threw in. "He's a selfish prick." Ilario's face fell and Eyden's furious expression eased. "I'm sorry."

"I think he thought he was taking action," Lora added, her gaze meeting Amira's tired eyes who seemed to agree with her. "We went through so much to get that agreement. We have to get it back before Tarnan breaks it." Flames clawing at her living room overtook her mind. Rhay knew what Lora had lost to keep Tarnan from finding the agreement. He knew and yet he had chosen to follow his own plan. A bitterness ran across her tongue. Now they had to get the agreement all over again. It was time for Lora to claim the throne and get reinforcements. It was the only way to make sure Tarnan wouldn't turn every kingdom against her.

"I'm honestly not surprised." Damir shrugged.

"No one asked you," Ilario hissed at him. "You don't get to throw in any comments! You're not entitled to this conversation."

Damir's eye twitched as if he was about to hit back verbally, but the sound of a body hitting the floor made them all whirl around. Elyssa had fallen off the sofa, her face a smudge of white, the stab wound on her shoulder bleeding again. Panicked, Amira knelt next to her. Elyssa had held it together, but her wound was worse than she had let on.

"Get Halie," Ilario said, catching Eyden's gaze.

Lora rushed towards Elyssa as Eyden disappeared. "Oscar, get me a towel and some water."

Maja grabbed a knife and cut open Elyssa's shirt. Seeing the bleeding wound up close, Amira bit back a strangled cry, her face draining of colour.

As Lora took the wet towel from Oscar, pressing on Elyssa's wound,

Eyden reappeared with Sahalie. Elyssa yelped in pain, her eyes squeezing shut as she passed out.

Sahalie rushed towards them but then her gaze halted at the body by the door. Her supplies, a mix of crystals and herbs, fell out of her hand, the thumping sound loud in their silence.

"Who..." The indifference Lora had loathed about Sahalie when they'd first met was gone as dread shone through her eyes. "Where's Farren?"

The silver gates of the Turosian palace stood in front of her, sending a wave of anxiety through her body. Lora had tried to prepare herself for her return, but she realised now that nothing could.

It was just her and Eyden, the rest of their group waiting close by for their signal. Everyone except Elyssa and Amira, who Eyden had suggested should rest up at his place. Sahalie had promised to check in on them before she hurriedly left Eyden's place, looking everywhere but at Farren's body.

Lora pushed aside the grief digging into her own heart. Taking a deep breath, she straightened the dark cloak around her shoulders and walked up to the gate. Two guards stood watch in front of it, their eyes widening.

Keeping her expression even, Lora lifted her chin. "You know who I am, don't you?"

"We have orders from Nouis Messler to not let anyone in."

"Tell him I'm waiting for him, then," Lora said.

Lifting his runia to his lips, the guard turned away. A minute later, he returned. "He's on his way."

The cold wind lifted the ends of Lora's hair. It felt surreal to be here again. Not as a prisoner trying to escape but as someone choosing to be here, choosing to take charge in order to go up against Tarnan. Every minute increased her anxiety until, finally, Nouis walked up to the gates, two guards trailing him.

"Princess Loraine." Nouis took her in before his gaze landed on Eyden. "And your friend. What brings you here?" Lora wondered how much he had known about Karwyn's plan.

Straightening her back, Lora drew on her confidence. "I'm sure you've heard that Karwyn has passed."

"We have no proof of that rumor." Nouis squinted at her. "But I did hear you were involved."

"I saw him fall," she said, and Nouis tensed. "It was Tarnan's fault," Lora hastily added.

"By Caelo, that is most unfortunate. I will have to discuss within the Turosian court how to handle—"

"*I* will have to discuss with *my* court," Lora threw in, the words casual but her tone deadly serious. She thought she saw Eyden grin out of the corner of her eye. "As the last Adelway, I'm in charge now."

Nouis laughed. "Princess, you have no experience—"

Fire lit her hand up. She aimed it at the sky, lighting up the starry night. Before Nouis could act, Lora threw out her arms, pulling on her last energy but hiding the effort it took her. The gate flew open.

"As you can see, I have more than enough power to take Karwyn's place in the contest. I was hoping, as the court's head advisor, you'd be glad to show me the ropes." When Nouis remained stubborn, Lora added, "You have no right to turn me away, Nouis. And no reason to, either. From what I've heard, you're loyal to the Adelway line. That's me now."

Nouis reluctantly stepped to the side as he gestured for them to enter. "Of course, Princess. We have much to discuss."

"In the morning. We've travelled far and we have guests."

"Guests?" Nouis looked behind her and Eyden took his cue, speaking into his runia. Oscar, Maja, Ilario, and Damir stepped out of the surrounding woods.

"I take it you will ensure everyone treats my guests with respect?" Lora asked. Nouis couldn't keep the shock off his face.

"Are they human?" His gaze turned to Damir. "And here I thought

Karwyn's shadow died with him." Craning his neck, Nouis looked behind them. "Where is my son?"

"He chose to abandon the Adelway line." It wasn't really a lie. Even if Rhay was playing double agent, he had chosen to go against Lora's plan. He had chosen to betray her trust and hand Tarnan what he needed to doom Earth.

Nouis gestured towards the palace, avoiding eye contact. As Lora walked forward, her friends following after her, Nouis asked, "Will you return to your previous quarters?"

Her room had been a prison, a place to keep her contained, to remind her of her doom. She would never go back. When she walked into the palace, she would do so as the future Queen of Turosian with her head held high.

Meeting Nouis' gaze, Lora hoped her turquoise eyes sparked bright. "I require new ones fit for a queen."

As they entered the cold stone walls of the palace, Lora felt as if she'd been taken back in time. Everything looked the same, yet it felt different. When they headed up the stairs, she saw the ghost of Varsha rushing down, laughing, her golden eyes sparkling as they never would again.

With a heavy heart, Lora headed into the corridor where Karwyn's room used to be, but they walked past it to the rooms at the far end. Lora had insisted they all stay close together. The servants and guards had given her a mix of glances on their way up. Surprise, suspicion, sometimes even a hint of relief. Tomorrow, she would have to address them. But tonight, Lora needed to get her act together. She felt seconds away from breaking down as Nouis gestured to the silver double doors in front of them.

"You may stay here and your...friends in the rooms down the corridor. Begone in fortune." Nouis bowed before moving away. A few guards stayed at the front of the corridor. Because of them or for their sake, Lora couldn't be sure.

Lora was too tired to ask more, yet she didn't move as her gaze flickered to Oscar and Maja. Ilario seemed to catch her concern. He said, "I'll look after them. Get some rest."

Oscar's eyes were wide as he took in the high ceiling and then her. "I'll be fine, Lora. Go lie down, you look terrible."

"I second that," Maja said.

Damir remained quiet. He turned his back to them and crossed his arms, watching the guards.

"I'll keep watch too," Eyden said, but Ilario shook his head.

"You've been up the whole day. I got this."

His pale blue eyes meeting Lora's, Eyden waited for her to decide. He would stand guard day and night if she asked.

"If anything happens, wake us," Lora told Ilario before her gaze shifted to Damir's back. "That goes for you too if you want your payment."

"Sure thing, Adelway," Damir grunted.

Ilario rolled his eyes. Wearily, Lora moved forward and laid a hand on Oscar's arm. "Try to get some sleep too." She swayed on her feet, and Oscar grasped both her arms to steady her.

Oscar let go of her as Eyden swung an arm around her.

They headed into the bedroom. The room was spacious and decked out in sparkling silver and turquoise. It reminded her of Karwyn's room, but the furniture appeared older, the style old-fashioned. She glanced at the bedpost carved out of dark wood and the tiny writing desk in the corner. The dark wood of the walls had patterns of silver and turquoise vines drawn on them. Drapes of shiny turquoise hid the windows.

Exhausted, Lora sat down on the edge of the giant bed.

"Hey," Eyden said, sitting down next to her. "Talk to me, special one."

"I...I'm so exhausted by everything." She tilted her head at him. "It's not going to stop, is it? The risks, the danger...death." She fought back fresh tears. "If I become queen, then even after we take down Tarnan—if we can—I'll never be free. It'll never stop. Am I selfish for not wanting that?" Her gaze drifted over the room she was in, the silver and turquoise blinding her even in the low light. Blinding her like the future she never wanted.

Eyden's hand landed on her chin, gently turning her head back to him. "It doesn't make you selfish, it makes you smart." A broken laugh left her lips. "You see the truth of the situation, and I don't blame you for not wanting this fate. You are committed to taking on this position. That's the least selfish thing you could do."

As Eyden dropped his hand, Lora leaned against his shoulder, her safe haven. Eyden let himself fall back on the mattress and Lora went with him, turning her head on his chest.

Eyden's voice was quiet, yearnful. "People tend to leave or die"—his voice shook—"or turn out to be something different. But you've always been this intense fire, this selfless flame. Deep down, I've always known it. It just took me some time to see it."

"Because you're stubborn as hell," Lora joked. She pulled back enough to look into his warm, icy eyes. "I won't leave. And I'm not planning on dying if I can help it."

"I've lost so many people in my life. It's partly why I didn't want to trust anyone until I met you." Shifting on the mattress, he put an arm around her. "Every minute I spend with you is worth everything."

Her hollow heart warmed. Something flickering in his gaze that told her there was more to it. "There's something you're not saying."

"It's something your father brought up. He reminded me that we don't know *how* fae you are."

Her lips parted. "You're talking about my lifespan. Does it bother you?" Her lifespan was the least of her worries. She wanted to survive this. She wanted everyone else to survive too. As long as fate let her, she wanted to stay with Eyden.

"No. I'll take any time with you I can get."

Her thoughts travelled to the ones they'd lost. Varsha. Farren. The image of her mum in a coma made her skin turn cold. "For the record, you're not allowed to die, Eyden."

"Wasn't planning on it either." His arm tightened around her as his forehead brushed hers.

"I love you. I mean it," Lora whispered. "It's actually scary how much."

"Is it scary?"

She drew back, and his striking eyes made her breath hitch, the emotion there running so deep she felt it touch her soul. "It used to be. Right now, I'm just grateful."

A sly grin spread Eyden's lips. "I'm the gift that keeps on giving."

Lora lightly tapped his chest before letting her head fall back into the crook of his arm. "And you're back to being insufferable." Her voice was heavy with sleep as her eyes drifted shut, exhaustion pulling her under.

"You love my insufferableness." Eyden's free arm curled around her protectively, and she felt sleep take her as she relaxed into his arms. "And I love you, special one."

CHAPTER 31

AMIRA

Lying on the bed in Eyden's apartment next to Elyssa, Amira was overcome by sadness, darkness shrouding every inch of her. She had dreamt of the moment they'd reunite. Yet, with Farren's death and Rhay going rogue, what should have been the best feeling in the world was now tainted.

Elyssa stirred, slowly waking up after sleeping off her injury for almost ten hours. "Hey there, sunshine." Elyssa's voice was barely a whisper. She moved closer, lying on her stomach to keep her weight off her wound.

Amira's lips brushed Elyssa's, the kiss tame but warm. She had the instinct to pull back, her heart twisting at the thought of enjoying even a second with Farren gone. She had doomed yet another person.

But Elyssa deepened the kiss, her hands tangling in Amira's matted locks.

Kissing Elyssa's forehead, Amira tried to shake the darkness overtaking her spirit. "I can't believe I'm finally holding you."

"All I could think about was saving you. You and...." Elyssa's eyes wandered to the place Farren's body used to be. "Guess I couldn't save everyone."

Amira's heart tightened in her chest. Taking Elyssa's chin in her hand, Amira guided her gaze up. "You've done everything you could." But Amira knew she herself could have done more. Farren had used his life source to protect them while Amira had only thought of getting away. She should have stayed by Farren's side as she'd promised him. He'd said to not blame herself, but how could she not? They should have tried to escape sooner.

Tears burned her eyes. Letting go of Elyssa, Amira fell on her back, staring at the ceiling. "Without me, Farren would've never ended up there. *I* was the one who decided to trust Tarnan. *I* got him involved." *It's my fault.*

"I didn't question Tarnan either," Elyssa said into the heavy silence filling the apartment. "He played us all. But we're not going to let him win. I won't let him hurt anyone else." Elyssa's voice was stern. "I can't believe Farren is gone. And I didn't even say goodbye. I fucking lost all my words when I still had the chance to tell him how much I loved him."

Amira was trying so hard to keep herself together for Elyssa's sake, but tears flooded her cheeks anyway. Elyssa had lost so much already. It wasn't fair that she'd lost her best friend too. Everywhere Amira went, everyone she met, she only brought them doom.

If she had been stronger during Caelo Night, she could have helped Eyden drift Farren away. If she had tried harder yesterday...

A dark light ignited Elyssa's eyes as she set her jaw. "He's not the one that should be dead. It will not be for nothing." Her voice was quiet, but the anger in Elyssa's tone was loud. "I have to focus on that. I can't handle saying goodbye."

"What can I do?"

Elyssa opened her eyes, sadness mixed with anger. "Can you just hold me?"

Amira drew Elyssa to her. Resting her head against Elyssa's red curls, she inhaled her pine scent that she had dreamt of when she had been locked up in Tarnan's palace.

"I've missed you so much," Amira confessed in Elyssa's ear, holding her tight against her chest. A little voice in her head told her she didn't deserve this. She didn't deserve comfort when all she did was fail. She wanted to give Elyssa everything she ever wanted, to live freely, to give the human rebels a real home. Instead, yet again, there was only pain.

"I was going crazy thinking about what Tarnan was doing to you. I can't believe he forced you into another goddamn contract."

Amira lowered her gaze, her cheeks burning red. She had been so stupid to think she could outsmart Tarnan when he had clearly spent over fifty years planning his revenge. "I wanted so badly for him to trust me. But I played right into his hands."

"He would have forced you into it no matter what. We all failed. But I won't let it happen again."

Amira repressed her tears. "Who knows what he will do now that I have betrayed him?" Her hands fidgeted with the hem of her wool sweater. "El, I think I need to go to Allamyst to save my mother. Tarnan could make an alliance with my brother just to spite me. I know we've just found each other again, but I have to." She couldn't be responsible for another death.

And maybe Elyssa is better off without me, a poisonous voice whispered in her mind.

Elyssa shook her head against her chest. "Sunshine, you're crazy if you think I won't go with you. Tarnan won't win this one."

Walking through the gate of the Turosian palace, the afternoon sun casting shadows over the entrance, Amira couldn't shake the weird feeling creeping under her skin. The first time she had crossed this gate, she had been a naïve young princess hoping her upcoming wedding would save her from her brother. After her stay in Pyria, she had returned to the palace with newfound hope that her fate was about to change for the better.

Now she was more careful about hope, knowing doom always lurked close by. Not wanting to make any plans for the future, Amira only wished no one else had to suffer through more deaths. For her young life, she had already witnessed multiple murders: Quynn, Mylner,

Sydna, Nalani, Varsha, and now Farren. Farren, whose everlasting smile was still ingrained in her head. Farren who, just like the others, had died because she had failed to save him.

Her feet led her back to her former quarters. Looking at her clothes perfectly folded in her dresser, Amira felt like she had left for Caelo Night yesterday. Unscrewing the pillar at the top of her bed, Amira noticed that the little comb she had hidden on her first day was still there. She removed it from its hiding spot and put it in her pocket. Its presence was strangely reassuring, as if her father, who had gifted her the comb, was with her.

A knock on the door tore her away from her thoughts. Lora stood at the entrance to the bedroom. "A guard told me you were here. How's El?"

"She's resting, but her wound looks better. Sahalie's with her now, so I thought I would grab a few things. It's so strange to be back here after everything that happened."

"I get it. We were both prisoners before and now I'm...something else and you're no longer Karwyn's fiancée."

"Speaking of Karwyn, there's something you should know." Amira took a deep breath. "He's alive. I saw him. Tarnan is keeping him prisoner."

Lora's mouth dropped open. "*How?* I saw him die. I have his powers."

"Tarnan wouldn't tell me how he did it. But he's...different. His eyes...they were so strange, so unlike him. He told me he was dying, so whatever Saydren did to him must not be permanent."

"That would explain my mum's state. If Karwyn's not dead..." She broke off, the look in her eyes heartbreaking. "Tarnan has Karwyn and the human prime minister. There's nothing stopping him from breaking the contract between Earth and Liraen. We'll have to come up with a plan."

"I should warn Rhay with a fire message. He deserves to know. Maybe he can delay Tarnan somehow?" Whatever was going on with Rhay, Amira still believed in the good in him even though he was making it very difficult.

"Are you not afraid it might break him? He has to keep a cool head if he wants to act like he's on Tarnan's side." Lora shook her head, clearly biting back her frustration with him. "If Tarnan manages to break that agreement, I don't think I can ever forgive Rhay."

"Would you lie to him again?" Amira asked, her guilt expanding.

Lora sighed angrily. Elyssa had filled Amira in on how Rhay had gone off book. "No, it won't do anyone any good."

"There's something else." Amira had thought a lot about her next steps. Besides saving her mother, there was one thing she knew she could do right away. "Lora, now that you're almost the queen, I have a favour to ask. Do you know about the underground?"

Gravely, Lora nodded. "I've been there. I can still see the experimentation room, feel it."

A cold shiver ran along Amira's spine. "I keep having dreams about it. My maid, Nalani, Karwyn had her executed, and I found her body there while searching for you."

Lora's brows drew together. "Searching for me?"

Amira laughed softly. "We never really had the opportunity to talk about that day. I saw Saydren capture you. I was following him. I actually met Elyssa for the first time while trying to hide from the guards. I knew of the underground and the experiments Karwyn had Cirny do on high-level fae. I thought I'd find you there. But instead, I found Nalani's body." The image came back to haunt her. Amira closed her eyes, gasping for air. So much death that she hadn't been able to prevent. Would she ever truly win when she had already lost so much?

A gentle hand landed on her shoulder. "Let's shut it down."

Amira opened her eyes and was met with an unrelenting fire in Lora's gaze.

"For good," the future queen of Turosian said.

CHAPTER 32

EYDEN

Putting a fresh bandage on the slash on his chest—which was healing nicely—Eyden walked out of the blindingly silver bathroom to find Lora returning to their room, her face tense.

"It didn't go well?" Eyden leaned against the doorframe.

Even though he could see Lora was irritated there was a spark in her eyes as her gaze landed on his bare chest. He had taken a much-needed shower and left the bathroom in his underwear.

"I told Nouis to order the guards to watch the border and keep anyone from crossing. He said it'll be difficult but he'll make sure they'll do it."

Eyden kicked off the wall to cross the distance between them. Their quarters were bigger than any room Eyden had ever stayed in. Being in the palace was more than strange to him. They were in the belly of the beast, trying to turn it all around. A few floors beneath him, his father had died. He'd never known the details about his father's death. Had they buried him?

He wished he could take Lora far away from here. He wanted to take her hand and drift them to somewhere no one could find them, somewhere with no responsibilities, no battles to fight. He would never do it. But for a second, he let himself envision a future where they were safe.

Lora sighed, running her hand over her face. "Nouis said that as long as Lozlan is out there, people—guards, *everyone*—will most likely protest my...*reign*." Her tone soured. "They know he's out there, banished. That he could still be alive."

"So Nouis suggested seeking him out and you don't want to go there?"

"I...don't know."

Reaching out, Eyden took her hand. "I know your situation is entirely different from mine, but if my father was still alive, I'd give anything to talk to him one more time. You might not get the answer you crave, but at least you'll be able to stop wondering. And with Harten and Karwyn involved, you can't trust them to tell the true narrative."

"I don't even know if it matters whether I find Lozlan or not. I talked to Amira on my way back." A dark laugh left her lips. "Karwyn isn't dead. She saw him in Carnylen."

His heart dropped in his chest. His skin prickled, a familiar anger bubbling up. "By Caelo, he was dead. It could only be..."

"Be what?"

"Dark magic." Eyden had never heard of any fae coming back from the dead, but what other explanation could there be? He drew Lora closer. "I'm sorry."

She hooked her arms around his neck, her head against his chest. "Can I even be upset? If he was dead, *stayed* dead, my mum would be too, right? Do you think she has a chance to recover?"

That could explain it. In a twisted way, whatever had brought Karwyn back might have saved Lora's mother too. "Possibly. But..."

She turned her face up to him. "I shouldn't get my hopes up. I'm afraid of what Tarnan will do next."

He tightened his hold on her. They were all worried Tarnan could break the human-fae agreement Rhay had handed over, and it was even more likely now with Karwyn in Tarnan's grasp. "Even if Tarnan breaks the agreement, we'll protect Earth however we can." Lora sighed, worry tearing at them both. "And Karwyn can't reclaim the throne. He can try, but you have his powers. He has nothing to show for anymore. In a way, that must be the cruelest fate to him."

Pulling back, Lora bit her lip. "You're right. And Amira seems to think Karwyn is dying. Does it make me a bad person that I kind of...enjoy it?"

"If it does, then I'm the worst of them all because I say he deserves all the fucking suffering in the world." For his father, for all the fae Karwyn had taken and experimented on.

"I just worry that if Karwyn really is dying..." Lora swallowed, her breathing shallow. He could almost hear her thoughts. *What does that mean for her mother?*

Lora hung her head. "Amira tried to..."

"Break your contract?"

Lora didn't reply, and that let him know the agreement was still intact. He hoped that with the merge completed and whatever Tarnan did to Karwyn, Lora's mother wouldn't die with Karwyn. He didn't want her to experience that kind of loss. It was crippling.

"We'll find a way." He tugged at her hand, and her eyes drifted to his bare chest and then lower. Heat spread across his bare skin.

"My eyes are up here," he joked.

Lora rolled her eyes. "You're distracting." The blush on her cheeks shot fire down his body. They hadn't had the time or energy to do more than kiss in some time, and he couldn't help but think of throwing her on the bed and having his way with her. His hand curled around the hem of her sweater.

Lora bit her lip again and *that* was utterly distracting. "I told the others we're holding a meeting in an hour." There was a mischievous spark in her eyes.

"An hour?" The corner of his mouth tipped up. Eyden pulled her closer by her sweater and her breath hitched. "Whatever will we do with all that time?"

Lora put her hands on his chest and if he wasn't on fire already, he was now. "You're pretty smart, I'm sure you have ideas." A thought struck him, and the fire in his eyes must have dimmed because she asked, "What is it?"

"The birth control tonic, I need to get more."

Realisation dawned on her, and, by Caelo, if her disappointment didn't turn him on even more.

"I do have other ideas." Leaning in, Eyden let his breath scatter on her cheek. He could hear her heart beating faster.

"Go on," Lora whispered, excitement in her voice.

One hand drifted to her cheek as he looked her straight in the eyes. "I was thinking you take off all of your clothes, lie on the bed..." He trailed off as he moved his lips to her ear. "And I'll kiss a path down your body until you can't think of anything but me." He flicked his tongue, nibbling at her earlobe, and the sharp inhale of breath leaving her lips almost sounded like a moan.

She pulled back enough to reveal a smirk on her lips. "I have ideas too, and I think you'll find them brilliant." Before he could respond, her hand reached the band of his underwear and went under the fabric. He grunted in surprise.

His eyes half closed as Lora moved her hand up and down. "I do like this idea..."

When she pulled her hand back, Eyden's eyes snapped open again.

"I thought you might, but my next one is even better." The confidence in her voice went straight between his legs.

Lora gently pushing him, he walked backwards until his legs hit the bed. "Pull them off," Lora said, her voice sure. He didn't need to be told twice. He took off his underwear, and that fiery look in her eyes made his breath hitch in anticipation.

"Sit," she ordered, still confident, but the blush in her cheeks revealed her nerves. Following her command, Eyden sat on the edge of her bed. Lora knelt on the ground, and that was when he finally caught on. Her hand slid down the base of him. Her eyes were big and full of want, desire with a hint of anxiety. Yet she didn't drop eye contact as she moved her head closer to him.

Her tongue flicked over the head of him and he shuddered, hissing through his teeth at how good it felt. The sound must have given her confidence; her lips stretched into a sinful smile just before she pulled him into her mouth and fuck if it didn't feel amazing.

Eyden's eyes closed as he let her set a rhythm. "You're right, I fucking love this idea." His tone was raspy as pleasure rang through him.

She hummed around him in agreement, drawing a moan from him. His hand went to her hair, guiding her softly. The rumble coming from his chest sounded almost foreign to his ears. She seemed to enjoy it. Lips still around him, she sighed, and that sound paired with her tongue circling him as her hand went up and down, was too much. It was too fucking good.

He tried to pull back to give her a signal, but she held on, increasing her speed until fire lit him up from the inside. He would be lying if he said he wouldn't have that image of Lora in front of him in his mind for a long time.

Lora pulled back, wiping her mouth, a smile on her face. "Told you you'd love it."

Eyden grinned. "Cocky, I like it."

Her cheeks heated. "I might have picked up on a few thoughts to give me direction. Not on purpose."

Laughing, Eyden kissed her quickly. "That's handy. Your turn."

He pulled at her sweater, and she lifted it over head with no hesitation. Eyden lifted her onto the mattress as he pulled off her trousers and underwear until she was in her bra. Her hair was wild as she gazed at him, leaning back on her elbows on the mattress.

"Open your legs, special one," Eyden said, voice raspy. The command darkened her gaze with arousal as she leaned back further, letting her knees fall apart. He grunted in approval, tracing a finger down her centre until she shuddered.

Stilling for a second, Eyden pulled back, catching her impatience. And then he smirked, not warning her as he pulled one leg over his shoulder. She squealed in surprise before his tongue was on her and she was writhing beneath him, eyes falling closed.

"Eyden..." she whispered as he worked her, knowing what her body needed. "God—" Her voice cut off as he moved one hand up her thigh before sliding a finger into her. She cried out. Her hands fisted the

244 JENNIFER BECKER, ALICE KARPIEL

sheets, her hips moving desperately until her whole body shuddered and her head fell backwards onto the mattress.

Eyden pulled back. "Brilliant, wasn't it?"

She sat up, leaning closer to kiss him. "I'll give you that compliment if you're still counting."

An hour later, dressed and showered again, Eyden and Lora entered the council room. An oval oak table took up most of the room. Ilario, Maja, Amira, and Oscar were already sitting around it. Ilario sat up straight but his forehead was wrinkled. Maja leaned back in her chair, her eyes wide as if eager yet also worried. Amira's gaze quickly connected with Eyden before moving to the door.

Oscar didn't seem to know where to look or what to do with his hands as he put his elbows on the table before pulling them to his chest. Slowing down, Lora's eyes narrowed at the head of the table. Her spot.

After patting Oscar's shoulder, Lora took a seat in her chair. Eyden took the spot on her right.

Lora's hands shook as she clasped them in front of her on the table. "This is weirdly official." She turned to Amira. "I assume you filled everyone in on our Karwyn-is-alive problem?"

"Son of a bitch," Maja cursed.

Ilario's eyes went wide while he exclaimed, "By Caelo."

Amira cleared her throat. "I was getting to that."

Eyden shifted in his seat, his gaze wandering over their self-established court. "It goes without saying that anything we discuss here can't leave this room. No one can know Karwyn is alive."

Lora subtly elbowed him under the table. She had more trust to give than he did. Rhay had already betrayed them.

Just as Lora opened her mouth to reply, the door swung open on Elyssa, a bloody throwing star in her hand.

"You should be resting," Amira said, but her tone suggested she'd expected her to show up.

"Resting is for the dead. And dead we are not." Elyssa strode forward, taking the empty seat next to Oscar. The door fell shut behind her. She slammed the bloody star onto the table.

"Do I even want to know?" Eyden teased, trying to get her to smile. Her expression was much too serious, Farren's death hanging heavy in the room.

"The guards wouldn't let me in and I got impatient," Elyssa huffed, leaning forward. Eyden didn't miss her slight grimace at the movement. Her stab wound must still hurt. Catching her gaze, he put two fingers behind his ear. Instead of returning the gesture, Elyssa shook her head. "This Nouis guy eventually gave in."

"Rhay's father," Lora replied. "We can't trust him, but we do need him. The guards listen to him. But if he knew Karwyn was alive, he might take his side."

"You're right." Amira sighed. "The Carnylen contest dinner is in two days. I don't know what Tarnan has planned, but it can't be good. I don't think he would involve Karwyn, but we shouldn't attend."

"If I don't go Tarnan will poison all the kingdoms against me," Lora said. "We have to assume Tarnan has most likely broken the agreement by now. I can scope out the place and try to get some intel, at the very least confirm if the agreement has been broken or not. We have to do something and we can't count on Rhay."

"I'll go with you," Eyden added, but he already suspected Lora's answer.

"I have to go on my own. Tarnan can't compel me and I don't think he wants to kill me if I am to take part in the contest to replace Karwyn."

Amira nodded. "He wants to win *fairly*." She grimaced. They all knew there was nothing fair about Tarnan's dark powers.

Eyden reached out and took Lora's hand. The thought of Lora going on her own froze the blood in his veins. His thumb drew a circle on her skin in an attempt to soothe her.

"You shouldn't reveal your cards," Ilario added, "unless you can't help it."

Eyden crossed his arms. "I'll stay close by. One fire message and I'll get you out of there." He turned to Amira. "Is the palace warded?"

"Tarnan made us ward it." Amira dropped her chin. "But I know how to get past it."

Lora squeezed Eyden's hand as she smiled at Amira. "Good. Can you place some sort of ward here over the wing with everyone's bedrooms? I don't trust all the guards. You should move to that floor too."

"I'll try. I wish..." She broke off as she glanced at Elyssa, who gripped the bloody throwing star.

She probably wished Farren was here to show her. Seeing Elyssa like this, overcome with grief and putting it all into anger, seemed to worry Amira as much as it did Eyden.

"The question is, how can I convince Tarnan to stay away from Earth?" Lora asked.

"The only thing I can think of is bringing up Tarnan's daughter," Amira said. The room turned quiet as everyone turned to the princess. *The evil king had offspring?* "I just found out myself. Tarnan doesn't want anyone to know about her existence."

Lora leaned forward, catching Amira's gaze. "Okay, let's go over everything you know about Tarnan later. No detail is too small. Next topic, who can we ally with? We can't win this alone." The air grew thicker as everyone let that sink in. Eyden had never been good at gathering allies, and it hadn't gotten any easier after recent betrayals. "I've talked to Queen Kaede and Queen Kaylanthea before. They don't like Karwyn. They see right through him." Lora focused on Amira again. "Do you know any of the other kings?"

Amira glanced at Elyssa. "Besides my brother, no. I've met them, but I couldn't give you a proper assessment."

"Your brother?" Lora asked.

"Is not to be trusted," Elyssa finished. Amira picked at the fabric of her lavender dress. "But Amira and I have an axe to grind with him."

Amira had already informed Lora that they would be heading to Al-lamyst to free Amira's mother. Eyden wasn't thrilled about it as Elyssa was still recovering, but he knew she could make up her own mind. If he had been separated from Lora for as long as Elyssa had been from Amira, Eyden wouldn't want Lora to go by herself either.

"Even if Wryen can't be trusted, it would be better if he wasn't on Tarnan's side," Ilario said. "He has fire magic, doesn't he?"

Eyden agreed with him. The more power Tarnan had at his disposal, the worse their odds.

Amira shuddered. "He does. But he won't listen to me."

Elyssa twirled her bloody throwing star. "We'll goddamn make him listen."

"That leaves the other kings and...Rhay." Ilario's shoulders sank.

"Rhay is a lost cause," Eyden hissed.

"We don't know what he was thinking—" Amira started.

"He did sort of stab us in the back," Maja threw in.

Lora rubbed her eyes, her tiredness surely not only from physical exhaustion. "We can't influence what Rhay is doing. We can't count on him to help us."

Ilario leaned back in his chair, avoiding Maja's gaze. "Let's table Ni—Rhay." He ran a hand over his face. "What if we intercept the two queens before they make it to Carnylen? Explain what's happening before Tarnan can feed them lies at the dinner?"

"It's worth a shot." Lora tilted her head to Amira. "Do you think you can wait one more day to help me talk to them? They must know you've stayed in Carnylen."

"Yes." Amira's amethyst eyes locked on Elyssa. "Then we'll head to Allamyst."

"There's one more thing I need your help with," Lora said, taking a deep breath. "Lozlan Adelway is in Rubien. As long as he's out there my...it might threaten the hold I have over the Turosian court."

"He was banished, wasn't he?" Amira asked.

"Yes, and Nouis believes my blood can lift the banishment. With your help and Cirny's spellbooks."

"Adelway," Oscar muttered. His lips parted. "Is he...is he your father?"

"No, our dad is my father." Lora swallowed hard. "But yes, Lozlan is my biological father. I need to see which side he's on. Either way, he's a risk. We'll have to find him without alerting all of Turosian."

"I can—" Amira's reply was cut off as the door opened once again.

Nouis strode through the door, followed by a servant. "You're holding a court meeting without members of the court?"

"They *are* members of *my* court." Lora held her chin high. Eyden fought back a grin as Nouis observed their group with disdain.

"It's not your court until there's been a coronation, Princess," Nouis pointed out, and Eyden clutched the arm of his chair to stay seated. The man was even more infuriating than Rhay. "You need me in your court if you want this." He gestured for the servant and the young man hurried forward, a scroll in his hand. Grabbing it, Nouis walked around the table towards Lora. Eyden tensed. He didn't trust Nouis, had seen very little reason so far to sway his opinion on the royal advisor.

"What is it?" Lora asked.

Nouis unrolled the paper but didn't offer it to her. "Lozlan's banishment." Lora reached out to grab it, but Nouis pulled back. "Only the crown can alter it with magic. You're not it, Princess."

Lora's lips formed a straight line. "Fine. Let's do the coronation."

Nouis smiled. "Very well. Perhaps in a few weeks."

"Tomorrow morning."

Nouis blinked at her. "Tomorrow? That is much too soon."

Lora's gaze was as hard as steel. "We don't have any time to spare. Tarnan is a threat to us all."

Hands tightening on the paper, Nouis replied, "I will make it happen and give you Lozlan's contract if you promise to keep me as head advisor."

The silence in the room was deafening.

"You will keep your title if you keep to your promise and protect the border."

Eyden heard Lora's careful words for what they were. A title wasn't a promise he could act as such.

"I can't promise we'll be able to catch everyone crossing," he said.

"I might have an idea about that," Oscar said. At Nouis' gaze, he shrunk back in his chair. "If there's any tech around, maybe I can put something together to alert the guards."

Lora smiled at him gratefully. "Rhay might have something in his room." Turning to Nouis, she added, "I also want you to let go of all the guards who captured fae for Karwyn's experiments."

"I don't know the details about Karwyn's...hobby."

Lora didn't reply, but the way she stared at Nouis made Eyden think she was trying to read his mind and failing. "Damir does. We'll handle it and you won't stand in the way. Deal?"

The advisor handed over the scroll. "I shall get started, then." He turned towards the door but halted. "Oh, and as head advisor, I will of course accompany you to the contest dinner."

Lora's smile was a sign of barely contained impatience. "Of course."

The doors swung shut, and Maja let out a long breath. "I do not like that guy. I mean, Jesus Christ, he's Rhay's Dad? The apple fell *far* from the tree."

"They don't get along," Lora and Amira replied simultaneously.

Giving Amira a smile, Lora straightened herself. "We should divide and conquer. Amira and I should discuss what to tell the queens to-morrow. Eyden, can you handle the guards?"

He knew what she meant. *Can you handle Damir?* Better him than Ilario, who was sinking into his chair.

"I'll find out where to intercept the queens." Elyssa pocketed her throwing star.

"I can help," Ilario offered, sounding relieved to have something to do. "Fae might be more willing to talk to me."

"I wasn't planning on asking. But sure, *Eyden's imaginary friend,* let's go." Elyssa got up so fast that Ilario almost tripped as he pushed his chair back to follow her.

"El," Eyden started. He'd wanted to talk to her. She turned as she reached the door, but her expression told him she didn't want to talk. She wanted to *act.* Tilting his chin up, he let her go, Ilario hurrying after her.

As Lora turned to Amira, Eyden headed for the exit. He expected to find Damir in the hallway, but he was nowhere to be seen. Footsteps made him whirl around.

"He's close by but never within sight," Maja said, appearing next to him. "Do you know what his deal is?"

"He only cares about himself. He's an opportunist." He wanted the crown's, Lora's, silver. For what reason, Eyden didn't care. He saw nothing that could possibly excuse Damir's past.

Maja's brow wrinkled. "I think it's more than that."

"Whatever he tells you, don't believe him."

Maja laughed. "Don't worry, I won't. Boys like him are only good for one thing."

Crossing his arms, Eyden stared at her.

"Oh, no, that's not...I wasn't saying that *I* would," Maja explained in a rush. "I was just stating a fact." Eyden kept staring at her. "Okay, this is my cue. I'm going."

He bit back a laugh as Maja hurried off. His smile quickly died as he rounded the corner of the stone hallway and found the person he'd been looking for. Damir looked healthier than before, no doubt the work of fae healing items that they hadn't had access to in the human world.

"Am I summoned or do you just like staring at me?" Damir asked, and Eyden's blood boiled.

"I need you to give me a list of all the guards involved in capturing and torturing fae."

Damir assessed him, his dark purple eyes flashing. "All right. I'll take care of it."

"We're not *taking care* of it. We're letting them go. Some of them might not have had a choice." He knew a thing or two about doing the wrong thing out of desperation. Some of the guards might not have even known what they were doing for their king.

"Whatever you say," Damir replied, his tone saying the opposite. "But just so you know, some of them knew *exactly* what they were doing. And they enjoyed it."

The half-smile on Damir's face made Eyden think he had enjoyed it too. And like those guards, Eyden couldn't wait to get rid of him.

CHAPTER 33

RHAY

Drying his inky hair with a towel, Rhay stared at himself in the golden mirror of the room Tarnan had provided for him. It hadn't been much longer than a day since his move to the Carnylen palace. He hadn't realised how tired he had been until the guards had left him in this spacious room with a bed that was like a pillowy heaven. Part of him had wanted to ask for all the alcohol in the palace, but he knew his attempt at gathering intel wouldn't work unless he was of sound mind. This was his chance to be useful. The others would understand once they'd beaten Tarnan.

Rhay wasn't a prisoner, Tarnan had assured him of that. Handing over the agreement had worked. But Tarnan still wasn't fully convinced Rhay was on his side. He would have to be careful.

His door opened to reveal a guard. "His Majesty has requested your presence in the throne room."

"Can't get enough of me already," Rhay joked. The guard merely gestured for Rhay to follow him.

Trying to brace himself for whatever challenge would await him, Rhay walked after the guard. They stopped in front of an open pair of golden doors leading to the throne room, which was decked in the Carnylen colours, bright orange and golden yellow. But Rhay noticed that Saydren, reading a scroll alone in the room, wore a ruby-red jacket, representing Rubien.

Saydren raised his head, a scheming light in his eyes. "Young Messler, what are you doing here?"

"Do you mean in this room or in Carnylen? Because to answer the second one, I thought I made myself pretty clear by handing over the agreement." Rhay flipped his dark hair from his eye.

"I don't buy this new act of yours. I've told Tarnan to be wary of you." Saydren stood up and slowly stalked towards Rhay. Rhay eyed him up and down, refusing to step back.

"And I've told Saydren that I believe you've chosen the winning side," Tarnan remarked as he entered the room. "He has reason to doubt. But I think you and I both know what you did; Lora will never forgive you for it. It wouldn't be smart of you to try and trick me when you have no one else left."

Rhay kept his expression blank even as his blood started pumping faster. She'd forgive him. This was the right move, wasn't it? He wasn't playing it safe this time and it would pay off, wouldn't it? "Well, what is the point of summoning me here if you don't trust me?"

"I want to trust your intentions are good." Tarnan put his hand on Rhay's shoulder. "For your sake and mine. But I don't have time to waste, so let's get to business. *Rhay, tell me, what is Lora's plan for the contest?*"

Rhay felt Tarnan's compulsion digging into his mind, prying for the truth. It took all his strength to resist. It was his first real attempt at dodging Tarnan's power. He kept his emotions balanced, fighting the urge to spill the truth as he pulled up a glass wall in his mind. "They haven't decided yet. They were focused on getting the agreement before you could take it. Elyssa was very insistent on freeing Amira and Farren."

Tarnan frowned. "How disappointing. I thought welcoming you into my palace would be more mutually beneficial." Tarnan gestured for one of the guards standing in the throne room to come closer. He whispered something in the guard's ear, and the fae left in a hurry. Rhay's hands started sweating.

Tarnan turned to Saydren. "How long until we can relocate half of the court to Rubien?"

"Without the two witches, it will take longer than expected. Servants are hard at work to rebuild the palace. But now that we have the human-fae agreement, we will soon be able to enslave humans to replace our fae workers."

Rhay forced himself to still his pounding heart at the mention of the agreement. Tarnan wouldn't be able to break it. It was a powerful one, woven between the rulers of Earth and Liraen. Rhay wouldn't have handed it over if he wasn't sure it would be useless to Tarnan without Lora, who was the last remaining Adelway. Karwyn's uncle, Lozlan, had been rumoured to be dead for years now. It had been Harten Adelway who had signed on behalf of Liraen seventy-five years ago. Maybe there was a way to break it with powerful witchcraft, but Tarnan had lost both Amira and Farren.

Tarnan readjusted the ruby and carnelian crown on his head. "We won't have to wait much longer."

Rhay froze, dread freezing his skin. "What do you mean?"

"This is why I summoned you, Rhay. To thank you. I thought you'd want to witness this moment in history."

The guard from earlier came back, but he wasn't alone. With the help of another guard, they dragged in a passed-out fae, his head down, dark hair shielding his face.

"The agreement is already broken." Tarnan's smile iced Rhay's heart.

"That's great news," Rhay forced out evenly. Tarnan had to be lying. "But are you certain? I thought you might need my assistance to gather everything, *everyone*, to break it."

Walking up to the passed-out fae, Tarnan grabbed his knotted hair, pulling his head back. The fae opened his eyes and Rhay realised that he wasn't fae at all. He was *human*. Rhay had a sinking suspicion he knew exactly who he was looking at.

Tarnan stared straight at Rhay. "To prove my theory, I want you to influence this human, a ruler from Earth, into signing a life contract with me, stating he'll follow my every command." Tarnan gestured to Saydren, who brought him a scroll. The desperate human thrashed against the guards.

Rhay was trapped. He couldn't go against Tarnan or he'd risk blowing his cover. And it couldn't be true, could it? He didn't have Lora here to break the agreement.

Staring into the poor human's eyes, Rhay lowered his fear and heightened his sense of trust. Tarnan pricked his finger and signed the contract before extending the pen to the human. The human accepted the pen with shaking hands and signed with his own blood.

The contract glowed brightly, binding the human's life to Tarnan's. Rhay felt like he was choking, his breaths shallow and his fingers tingling as his mind went numb. *What the fuck have I done?*

"I knew I could trust you." Tarnan patted Rhay's shoulder with a proud smile Rhay had never even seen on his own father.

The human's eyes turned dull when the guards let go of him.

"Now, kill yourself," Tarnan ordered the human. Rhay's hand twitched, ready to grab a sword from the nearest guard to protect the human. A million paths went through his head when a sickening noise filled the room.

Void of any emotion, the human hit his head repeatedly against the stone wall, the sound of his skull cracking making Rhay sick to his stomach. He should intervene, do *something*. Tarnan watched the human with a pleased smile.

"Guards, put him out of his misery," Tarnan ordered. One of the guards took his sword and plunged it into the human's back. His lifeless body slumped to the floor. Spots filled Rhay's vision and he blinked to regain control.

"Didn't you want to keep him enslaved? You said he was a ruler on Earth," Rhay asked, his voice calm. Yet inside, he was shaking from head to toe.

Tarnan tilted his head, the crown's jewels reflecting in the light of the chandelier above them. He looked possessed by the devil. "This one has outlived his purpose. I hope you'll prove to be more useful."

How could Rhay have been so stupid to think his plan would work? Tarnan had been right, Lora and the others wouldn't forgive him. He had thought he was taking the right risk, but he had no idea about fucking anything.

The only upside of today was that Tarnan had called off the guards trailing him. Walking aimlessly around the palace to find a quiet spot to think, Rhay noticed a balcony overlooking the nearby forest. Closing the glass door behind him, he took a deep breath, inhaling the fresh night air. He couldn't stay here any longer. Tarnan was too cunning, Rhay would never be able to spy on him. How long could he resist Tarnan's compulsions?

A voice coming from above halted him. "Who are you?"

Rhay turned his head to the roof and noticed a young fae sitting on the tiles by a window. Her strawberry-blonde hair was tied in a long braid and she wore loose pale blue trousers and a knitted white sweater. Her wide honey-coloured eyes were looking at Rhay with a mix of fear and wonder.

"Hey there, love. I'm Rhay. Who are you?"

"I'm Saige. I'm not supposed to be here, so please don't say anything to the king. He's always worried about me. But I wanted to see the stars and my friend lets me watch them once a week." She had said it all in a single breath, each word colliding with the previous one. Twisting her hands in her sweater, she pulled her knees up.

Was she a prisoner of Tarnan? But then she wouldn't be out here and Tarnan wouldn't worry about her. Rhay really looked at her, noticing the shape of her round face, her eyes tinged with red. Could she be Tarnan's daughter?

"Can I join you? I love watching the stars," Rhay asked, wanting to prove his theory.

Saige nodded excitedly, and Rhay used the vines wrapped on the wall to climb onto the roof. He sat next to Saige, leaving some space between them to avoid scaring her off.

"Are you a friend of the king?" Saige asked with bright eyes.

"Yes." *Never.*

Saige clapped her hands. "Can you be my friend as well? I had another friend, Princess Amira. But the king said she left." Her face fell. "Maybe she is waiting for us in Rubien? Will you also go there?"

"I think the king wants me to come with him." Rhay felt compelled to be nice to the young fae. Had Amira trusted her? She was endearing in her almost childish way. Or maybe she was another broken doll Rhay wanted to fix. That was what Karwyn had told him once, that he was always drawn to the broken ones. Thinking of Karwyn made Rhay's heart freeze in his chest.

Sitting with her knees pressed against her chest, Saige seemed to pick up on his mood. "What's wrong? Do you not like Rubien? I know it has been destroyed, but the king has told me they are rebuilding it better than before. It will be like something out of a storybook. I love stories."

Rhay stretched his legs on the roof tiles. "It's not that. I was reminded of a loss."

Saige peered at him. "Who did you lose?"

"A friend. Or maybe more. It's my fault he died." Rhay pressed his head against his hands.

"I...know loss. I've never known my mother. Father said I killed her when I was born," Saige blurted out. Rhay turned to her, sensing her sadness behind the harsh words Tarnan had told her. Who was her mother? To Rhay's knowledge, Tarnan had never been married.

"I lost my mother too," he said. "Not in childbirth. But I was very young."

"You must be very close to your father, then, as I am with mine." Saige's smile was true and Rhay couldn't help but feel bad for her.

With the contest dinner drawing near, would his father come to Pyria? Or had he resigned after Karwyn's disappearance? Rhay didn't know if seeing him after everything that had happened would be beneficial to either of them.

A burning sensation in his palm made him curse under his breath.

He pulled his hand to his side, out of Saige's sight, just before a paper appeared in his fist. In the darkness, Saige didn't seem to have noticed. Rhay covertly opened the paper.

I have to tell you. Karwyn isn't dead. Tarnan holds him captive in the palace. He's going to try and break the agreement. Be careful. –Amira

The breath in his lungs iced over, his heart almost stopping. It couldn't be. As if he had imagined it, the paper disappeared in a burst of smoke. Rhay thought back on the moment he had seen the light leave his best friend's eyes. He had seen the pool of blood around his unmoving body. He had felt his pain.

But if Karwyn was alive, it would explain how Tarnan had been able to break the agreement—he had both the human ruler as well as an Adelway under his roof. Rhay cursed again.

Saige lifted her brows. "My tutor tells me curses are insults against Caelo."

Rhay scrambled up. "Sorry, love, I have to go. I don't think the sky will clear tonight."

"Wait, don't leave," Saige cried out. But Rhay had already climbed down the roof and disappeared inside.

The way back to his room was a blur, the walls moving in front of him. Every portrait he encountered turned into Karwyn's face.

In his room, Rhay flung open the drawer of his nightstand, revealing his trusted flask. Tarnan had seen to it that Rhay was provided with it even though Rhay had refused to ask for it. It was hard to believe just how fucking badly Rhay had messed up this time. It was impossible to believe that Karwyn was still alive. But Amira wouldn't lie about such a thing.

Inside this palace, hidden somewhere Rhay hadn't found yet, Karwyn was alive. As soon as hope rose in his chest it was crushed by a suffocating tightness. Rhay knew he would have to face his friend. He would have to face the fact that he might have doomed all of humanity.

But tonight, he wasn't ready to face his mistakes. He tipped the flask back and drank deep.

CHAPTER 34

&

LORA

The turquoise dress with its voluminous skirt made Lora feel as if she was staring at someone else in the mirror. Someone about to be crowned. Someone she never envisioned she would become. Maja had braided part of her hair half-up with a few strands framing her face. The dark silver eyeshadow made her eyes appear brighter. Her hands shook, and she squeezed them into fists to try and lighten the scorching anxiety in her veins.

The click of the door made Lora turn on her heels. Oscar stood in the doorway. She'd expected Eyden. She was aware she should be out there by now. Nouis was probably growing impatient, but it was like she'd forgotten how to breathe, how to move.

"Eyden sent me to come and get you." Oscar walked closer to stand next to her as she turned back to her reflection. In the mirror, she glimpsed his silver shirt paired with a pale blue jacket. He almost looked like he belonged at court and not back home where he should be.

Oscar met her gaze in the mirror. "I thought you never looked more foreign than when you showed up at the hospital with all that blood on you. But this—*this* is different."

She smoothed the satin fabric of her dress. "You should be with Mum and Dad."

He stepped in front of the mirror, blocking her view of herself. "I think they'd want me to be here for you. I realise you don't want this, but it's selfless of you to do it anyway. And I want to help. Maja and I have been raiding Rhay's room, and I think I can put something together to alert the guards of anyone getting too close to the border."

Lora gave him a smile. "Thank you." Tears filled her eyes as she looked back in the mirror. "I think Mum would tell me I'm crazy."

Oscar laughed. It had been too long since she'd heard that sound. "Probably. But it's temporary, right?"

She'd never pictured her future like this. It was partly why she wanted to find Lozlan. A part of her hoped he was decent enough to take over. He might be a shit father, but that didn't mean he couldn't be a good ruler.

"That's the plan," Lora replied, hearing the hesitation in her tone.

"Lora." His tone had turned more serious.

She turned back to him.

"She will be okay, right?"

Mum. The question strangled her heart.

"I will do everything I can." She took a deep breath, straightening her back. "Starting with becoming the bloody Queen of Turosian. *Temporarily.*"

Oscar offered his arm and Lora gratefully took it, letting him lead her out of her room and downstairs to the throne room. When two guards pulled the heavy silver doors open, Lora overlooked the crowd gathered in the vast space. Besides familiar faces, the members of the Turosian court as well as guards stared back at her bleakly from rows of seats. Her friends sat up front, heads craned to glance her way.

The big throne room looked the same as always, no decorations in sight. She had insisted she didn't need anything, but now the dark stone benches and grey walls made her feel like she was walking into a funeral. Nouis waited at the end of the central aisle leading to the silver throne, a crown on a small pillow in his hands. He handed it to a servant and took a scroll out of his pocket.

Lora caught Eyden's stare as she walked up to the throne, his small smile giving her a sense of peace. He could have easily gotten her himself, but he must have known she needed Oscar's support today. Her brother squeezed her arm before stepping away to stand next to Eyden. Everyone rose to their feet.

In front of the throne, Lora turned to Nouis, her breathing too fast.

Nouis addressed everyone. "As we grieve King Karwyn Adelway's death, we are here to assure his legacy lives on with the next Adelway in line. Turosian stands proudly as the most powerful kingdom in all of Liraen, our blessed Falea providing us with luck for centuries. And so she shall bless our future queen and her reign."

Nouis unrolled the scroll and moved closer to Lora. "Princess Loraine Adelway, do you hereby swear to reign with care, protect our people as you lead them into victory, oblige Caelo's will, and praise our Goddess Falea as long as you shall uphold the queen's title?"

Nouis handed her a sharp pen. He had informed her about this before and she had read through it thoroughly, yet signing another blood contract still made the hairs on her arms stand up. She was really doing this. Last night, when she couldn't sleep, she'd had the overwhelming urge to run. Unless they found another ruler, she was shackling herself to Liraen, to this palace that so far had brought her nothing but pain.

Turning her head, she found Eyden's gaze. She could see in his light eyes that he'd run away with her in a second. But she couldn't. She would go through with this. Reaching for the pen, she willed her hand to stay still as she pricked her finger and signed her name in blood. Nouis took the scroll, then gestured for the servant to come forward. He removed the silver crown decorated with intricate turquoise stars from the pillow. Lora had never seen Karwyn wear it. Gesturing towards the throne, Nouis urged her forward. Lora lifted the hem of her long dress and stepped forward. As she took a seat, the cold of the iron mixed with silver seeped through her clothes. Nouis lifted the crown above her head.

An image of Karwyn flashed through her mind. Had he sat there like she was now? Had he made the same promises and then found loopholes to break them?

"Princess Loraine Adelway," Nouis stated, his voice echoing loudly through the room and chilling her blood, "in Caelo's name and with the fortune of our Goddess Falea, may you reign for as long as you shall live and lead our people into good fortune. With the gods' and goddesses' blessings and the ancient blood of the Adelways running through your veins, you shall hereby be crowned Queen Loraine Adelway of Turosian."

She tilted her head forward and Nouis placed the delicate crown on her head. It was heavier than she expected, pulling at her as much as the worry in her heart. She had tuned out the applause around her until now, but as she raised her head to face the crowd, the sound filled her ears like a torrent of rain. They were all counting on her. Her friends. Her court. Her people. She would do anything to protect them. She would rise where Karwyn had failed.

Rumor had it Queen Kaede and Queen Kaylanthea planned to meet up at the edge of the Cursed Woods. Ilario and Elyssa had come through with gathering information, so it was time for Lora and Amira to have a conversation with the other queens. It was strange to think about her title now. *Queen.* It felt utterly foreign on her tongue. Who was she to be queen? To rule over a kingdom she barely knew? Nouis had wanted Lora to stay and learn about Turosian politics, but they had more pressing issues than taxes and trading agreements. Though Nouis had insisted Lora was to bring guards with her everywhere, she had left with Amira and Eyden before Nouis could even attempt to stop her. He would soon learn his title was in name only.

A dark hood pulled over her head, Lora staked out the tavern where Kaylanthea and Kaede were supposedly staying until the morning. Eyden had drifted Lora and Amira here soon after the coronation, as it wasn't far from Chrysa.

Pulling her hood back to not raise suspicion, Lora walked out of the woods with Amira by her side. Eyden stayed behind to keep watch. The guards gave them curious looks but didn't stop them.

As they walked in, loud chatter reached them. It was early afternoon, yet the tavern was already full. Lora craned her neck to spot the queens. She almost skipped over them as she hadn't envisioned them dressed quite so casually, blending in with the crowd. Kaede and Kaylanthea sat at a table in the corner, glasses of ale in their hands. No crowns or fancy jewelry made them stand out.

Amira followed Lora's gaze and headed in their direction. Kaylanthea spotted them first, her eyes narrowing, gleaming with suspicion.

"Princess Loraine, Princess Amira," Kaede said, having looked up too, "to what do we owe this surprise? Are you staying here too?"

Lora glanced between the two queens. "It's queen now, actually." She had to force the words out. It was the first time she said it out loud, and it sounded like a bad joke. "We'd like to have a word."

Kaede stared at her for a second too long before pulling two empty chairs from the table. Kaylanthea's gaze went over their heads, no doubt making sure guards were within reach. Lora couldn't blame her. They must be wondering what had happened to Karwyn.

Amira and Lora both took a seat.

"So the rumors are true, then," Kaylanthea said. "Karwyn is dead?"

Lora shifted in her seat. "Not by my hands." *Technically.*

"Are you taking Karwyn's spot in the contest?"

"It's not my goal to win the high queen title."

"But you are taking his spot?"

Lora sighed. "I don't have much of a choice."

Amira leaned forward. "As Karwyn's former fiancée, you should take my word that we are all far better off with Lora on the Turosian throne. I was there when Karwyn was attacked. It was all part of King Tarnan's devious plan. That's why we're seeking you out. To warn you."

"Warn us of King Tarnan?" Kaede exchanged a look with Kaylanthea, gripping her cup of ale tightly.

"I've never seen him behave in any way to suggest misdeeds," Kaylanthea shot back.

Amira clasped her hands in front of her. "I hadn't either until recently. Until he revealed his true self."

"He's the Dark King's heir," Lora finished, "and he's after revenge."

It was quiet for a moment, then Kaylanthea laughed, almost spilling her ale. "If you're trying to sell us a lie, you might want to go with something less far-fetched." Lora opened her mouth, but Kaylanthea raised her hand. "I like you, Loraine. Or I *liked* you. I'm in your debt for fighting against the attackers at my dinner, but you must see that we have no reason to believe anything you're saying. *Are* you here to warn us? Or are you trying to scare me off the contest dinner as a plan to take me out of the running?"

Lora swallowed hard, unsure how she could convince them of her intentions. "I understand your doubts. I do. But if I'm right, which I *am,* imagine what that means. Tarnan is a Sartoya. He has the power of compulsion. He can tell you to do *anything.* So yes, I am here to scare you, but not for my own gain."

"He's killed people," Amira said quietly, her hand scratching her arm under the long sleeve of her blouse. "Friends of ours. You know I've spent time in Carnylen. I trusted him more than anyone, and I was completely blindsided. This dinner...it will be deadly. You shouldn't attend for your own sake. We don't want you to end up dead. We want to ally with you."

Lora crossed her arms on the table. "We need to work together to stop Tarnan before he takes out every last one of us and dooms all of Liraen. And we can't do that if you're dead. *You* can't win the contest if you're dead."

Kaede's finger drummed a nervous rhythm on the table, but it was Kaylanthea who spoke again. "Even if what you're saying is true, I can't skip the contest dinner. It won't reflect well on me."

Lora leaned back in her chair as cold realization spread through her. She didn't want to rule Liraen. Tarnan couldn't—*wouldn't*—as long as Lora lived to fight another day. There was only one other option: Kaylanthea, since she was the third and last one selected for the contest. If she was dead, there was no one left. "I hope for the both of us that you'll make it through."

CHAPTER 35

ELYSSA

Elyssa kept herself busy. That was all she could do. Amira, Eyden, and Lora were off doing their part and Elyssa was left with no task. Wandering around, she tried to map out the palace, but Farren's dying words echoing in her head kept distracting her. The thought of never hearing his voice again made her breath hitch.

Her steps quickened as an image of Farren flashed through her mind.

Farren when he was merely a child, running after her as they played in the woods. The two of them as teenagers, whispering in the dark and joking about Jaspen's stubbornness. Elyssa leaning in to kiss him for the first time. Farren hugging her tightly when they decided they were better off as friends. Farren's hand on her shoulder to pull her back from doing something reckless—over and over again.

Elyssa glanced at her shoulder now, but there was no one there. Farren would *never* be there again. He'd never smile at her, laugh at her jokes, pull her back from the brink of utter fury. She sprinted down the hall, trying to tire her mind, and stopped short in front of what looked like a training room.

Curious, Elyssa entered the room and took in the targets on the wall before she locked on the open chest in the corner overflowing with weapons. There were daggers, swords, a bow, and arrows—everything her heart desired. Yet she couldn't grasp the happiness she usually felt at the sight, as if her heart could no longer feel joy.

Taking out a dagger, she planted her feet and aimed for the furthest target. Bull's eye. Instead of victory, hollowness filled every part of her. She hated the emotion, hated how utterly useless it was when she could change nothing of the past. She threw another dagger, and another—a dozen holes in the target just like her heart. It wasn't goddamn enough.

Her gaze locked on a dummy in one of the corners. Moving it into the middle of the room, she put her brass knuckles on. Her stab wound strained, but she didn't care. The pain was merely a reminder that she couldn't fail again. She put all her weight into the blow as she aimed at the dummy's head. Picturing Tarnan's easy smile, Elyssa gritted her teeth and kept hitting, one punch after another. Nothing existed except Tarnan and her fists.

She kept going, drowning in rage. It was better than the alternative—better than accepting the deep sadness that had nestled into her heart. With each hit, she sank further. Sweat stuck her hair to her forehead as she spun around and kicked with enough momentum to detach the dummy's head from its body. Only then did she slow. She stared at the broken dummy, the image morphing into Farren's lifeless body.

She stopped moving altogether. She thought she might have stopped breathing, too. Farren's dull eyes swam in front of her face as the training room around her blurred and she fell to her knees. A faint pain flashed through her as she hit the ground. Her shoulders shook. Each breath slashed at her throat, her heart, everywhere all at once.

A pain so deep she couldn't keep it inside any longer flooded through her, and she hit the ground in front of her with her fists. She could barely feel the sting over the rushing in her ears and the overwhelming sense of floating in nothingness. Without Farren, the world had lost its light.

A hand landed on her good shoulder and Elyssa tensed, intending to attack, but the familiar scent of lavender stopped her. Amira lowered herself to the ground in front of her.

"He's gone," Elyssa breathed, tears stinging her eyes. She fought them as hard as she'd beaten the dummy. A tear ran down Amira's face as she nodded. She took Elyssa's hands in hers, and Elysa realised she'd beaten her knuckles bloody. Blood stained the ground where her fists had struck.

Gently, Amira pulled the brass knuckles from her reddened skin.

"I'm so sorry," Amira whispered. "I should have..." Her last words got lost in the white noise filling Elyssa's ears.

The princess pulled her into a hug so tight she might bruise, but it was worth it. Elyssa's hands stung as much as her beaten heart. Winding her arms around Amira's neck, she squeezed her eyes shut, letting the tears finally fall until her eyes felt drained. A dull ache pounded in her head.

They stayed locked in their embrace for quite some time. Finally pulling back, Elyssa wiped her tears with the sleeve of her sweater. She straightened, trying to leave the pain behind, trying to compose herself and be strong once more. "How did it go with the queens?"

Amira sighed. "Not good. They're going to the contest dinner."

"But you aren't."

Amira shook her head. "This might be the perfect chance to get my mother, since Wryen won't miss out on it."

"We'll go tomorrow, then. I'll have to stop by the rebel camp first." She hadn't been there yet and she had to make sure they were all right. Would they send her away? Would they blame her for how the ritual had gone down? They had wanted to fight, but Elyssa hadn't expected it to turn into a bloodbath once Tarnan betrayed them. She didn't even know how many of her friends at the rebel camp hadn't returned. How many were gone just as Farren was now?

Amira dropped Elyssa's bruised hand. "I was thinking maybe it's better if you stay here."

Elyssa studied her, taken aback. "Why?"

"You might be needed here, and I don't know what will await me."

"Exactly, you don't know if you'll have to fight your way to your mother." Elyssa's voice rose. "Why would you want to go alone?"

"I..." Amira twisted her dress in her hands.

Hands on Amira's shoulders, Elyssa pulled her closer. "Where you go, I go—to hell or any other goddamn place. Promise me you won't leave without me."

Amira bit her lip but nodded. Drawing closer as if to jump over whatever distance was between them, Elyssa captured Amira's lips— first softly, then more deeply as she thought of the path ahead of them. She nibbled at Amira's bottom lip, drawing a sigh from her. Elyssa moved her hand from Amira's neck to her heart, feeling her heart beat. She didn't know what awaited them, but as long as they were together, she could regain the strength to face it.

Amira broke the kiss, looking breathless but beautiful. "There's something else. I was talking to Eyden..."

"And he doesn't want me to go either?"

"No, nothing like that." Amira's thumb stroked a pattern over the back of her hand where her skin was unmarked. "If we're leaving to- morrow, that means tonight is the last time we could hold a funeral for Farren." They couldn't wait until after they returned. Farren deserved peace.

Elyssa's breath hitched, but she refused to fall apart again. Once was enough. Swallowing the lump in her throat, she said, "We should."

The fear in Amira's eyes strangled Elyssa's heart. They had both attended too many funerals in their life. She hadn't been able to save Farren, but she would keep Amira safe from her psychotic brother. Wryen still had a place on her revenge list.

Elyssa tilted her head, planting a kiss on the princess' cheek. "We've both been through hell, haven't we?"

Amira's hand drifted to her shirt, pulling her closer. "We have. But I would do it all over again for you."

Farren's funeral was brief. They all gathered in the palace's courtyard garden, Amira's favourite place. Surrounded by blooming flowers, the scent of lavender drifting through the night air, Elyssa and her friends stood around a pyre. Farren's body, covered by a white sheet, burned brightly, lighting up the night as if telling her the world hadn't lost all its light yet. Not if Elyssa could still make an impact, change the future in the name of those lost.

Elyssa met Eyden's gaze across the fire, and when he put two fingers behind his ear, she returned the gesture this time. She owed it to Farren to push on, to avenge his death and keep the fight up. She would re-make this world in Farren's name.

Amira held her hand the whole way through. Tuning out every sound, Elyssa felt Amira shaking next to her, letting her tears fall. Elyssa had no more tears left to cry. The only thing left were the promises she whispered in her mind to her memory of Farren as she finally said goodbye.

The fire in front of them stretched higher, reaching for the stars, and Elyssa vowed to her friend that she would avenge him. Ashes drifted through the air, embers catching on the dry ground beneath her feet. She would not be extinguished. She refused to give up, refused to let anyone take someone from her ever again. Anyone who tried would pay a deadly price.

CHAPTER 36

RHAY

One sip had led to another, and a pounding headache awaited Rhay in the morning. Flipping onto his back, Rhay squinted at the yellow ceiling, too bright for his eyes. He pulled a pillow over his head. A strange taste lingered on his tongue, turning his stomach.

Everything was so messed up. How could Karwyn be alive? Should Rhay search for him? Tarnan must have hidden him somewhere in this huge palace. Maybe he could ask Saige about it, using his power to render her more...trusting.

Throwing out his arm, Rhay searched for the flask on his bedside table. He had ordered a servant to refill it during the night. Rhay brought the cold metal to his lips, then froze. What was he thinking? Alcohol wouldn't save him. It had only ever doomed him.

A knock on the door had Rhay pushing the flask under his pillow. Rising to his feet, he straightened his clothes from the day before. The door opened on Tarnan, the picture of royalty. The crown on his head sat perfectly straight.

"Rhay, I hope you slept well." Tarnan strode into the room.

"Very well, Your Majesty." Pushing a hand through his messy hair, Rhay closed the door. The king regarded him closely from the middle of the sunset-orange carpet and Rhay was sure he saw right through him. Leaning against the chestnut wardrobe by the entrance, Rhay attempted to gather his thoughts before Tarnan's first strike.

"I'm sure you're aware that the contest dinner is tomorrow." Tarnan stepped closer, his gaze piercing. "I was hoping you would join me. Show the other royals that choosing my side is in everyone's favour."

Lora would be there. And he imagined his father would be as well. The looming reunion made his stomach turn, but Rhay pushed a smile onto his lips. "It would be an honour." He had no idea how he could help now, but he had to try; otherwise they would truly never forgive him.

"I'm glad. What is your prediction for Lora's plan tomorrow? Do you think she will bring any of her friends?"

Rhay didn't falter with his words. "I imagine my father might accompany her. As for the others, I doubt she would want to risk them, seeing as your power is superior."

"*Do you think Lora stands a chance against me?*" Tarnan asked, his tone cutting into Rhay's head. The pounding increased, and Rhay fought to not show his distress.

"Lora is stronger than before now that she has Karwyn's powers, but she's still untested." Rhay curled his sweaty palms into fists behind his back, fighting the compulsion.

"What about Elyssa? I can't compel her and it would be difficult to force her into a blood contract. *Would she come with Lora?*" Tarnan's voice was like honey, sticking to everything in its path, pulling at Rhay's words. He felt unable to push back.

"I can't imagine she would leave Amira's side, and she might be busy with the camp." Rhay stopped himself. He was talking too fast, influenced by Tarnan. Tasting alcohol on his tongue, Rhay dug his fingernails into his palms, forcing himself to focus.

"I've heard little of this camp. *Where is it located?*"

"I've never seen it myself." Tarnan stared at him as if waiting for more. Rhay feared Tarnan's next question, not wanting to tell him anything about Lora's friends. He was barely holding on as it was, the bitter taste of alcohol still in his throat. "I met Saige yesterday," Rhay blurted.

Tarnan's stare was unrelenting. "I'm aware."

"I wonder what brought her to the palace." Rhay didn't break their stare.

Tarnan smiled at him warmly, yet it chilled his heart. "You may visit her again if you wish, but make no mistake, her life is worth more than yours."

Rhay nodded, feeling the threat slither under his skin. Before Tarnan excused himself, Rhay called after him. "Can you promise me my father will be safe tomorrow?"

No matter how terrible his relationship with his father was, Rhay couldn't risk losing him.

"As long as you stay on my side, your father will be off limits." Tarnan turned and walked out. Rhay had no other choice but to trust Tarnan's word.

To get his mind off the contest dinner, Rhay decided a visit with Saige was just what he needed. She was his way of finding out where Karwyn was hidden. He asked the closest guard to take him and was only half surprised when his request wasn't denied.

Saige was busy painting the night sky on a blank canvas when Rhay entered her tight quarters. The floorboards creaked under Rhay's feet, startling her.

"Oh, it's you." She had paint on her left cheek. Her smile was bright and hopeful. Rhay wondered how long she could keep on being so sheltered. "What do you think of my painting? Do you think His Majesty will like it?"

Rhay sighed. "I don't think Tarnan really cares about art right now."

"Why not?"

Rhay felt like he needed to open the young girl's eyes. Maybe that was how he could help. "Don't you see what is going on in this palace? Don't you realise what will happen at the contest?"

Saige furrowed her brows. "Yes, the king will win the contest and become high king. And then it'll be safe for me to walk outside." Hope bloomed in her eyes, but Rhay's was dwindling fast. Tarnan must have kept her hidden for fear she would be killed and the Dark King's lineage would end. But would it ever be safe for her? Would *she* be safe to be around?

"Yes, he will," Rhay conceded, his heart heavy. She was Tarnan's daughter. It would be unwise to push her further, to show his true colours.

Saige jumped to her feet and grabbed Rhay's hands. "And you will be his advisor and we will all live together in the Rubien palace. We can even be friends! Wouldn't that be wonderful?"

She giggled with excitement. *Friends?* Rhay had a bad track record with his friendships. Would he end up betraying Saige like he had betrayed Karwyn? He had already befriended her under false pretences.

Yet, he had no other choice. "Of course, that sounds lovely." He let his power coat his words, like a carnivorous plant luring its prey closer. A twinge of guilt pulled at him. "You say this palace is safe, but I wonder if there are some places I should avoid."

Saige furrowed her brows. He placed a hand on her shoulder, pushing through the walls in her mind to instill a sense of trust. He was surprised he didn't have to push much, Saige's wall crumbling down as if she had been waiting to trust him all along.

"There is a room in the left wing, tucked away in an endless corridor. The king has told me I should avoid it at all cost." Her eyes widened in terror. "He said there are bad people. But they won't bother us." Her gaze warmed, a small smile breaking free.

Rhay gently caressed her head, her long strawberry blonde hair soft. In a flash, he saw his sword piercing through Karwyn as Lora's fire tore at him. He could feel Karwyn's pain when he had asked Rhay to break his promise. Rhay dropped his arm, giving her a small smile, yet inside his heart squeezed so tight it stole his breath. Whatever would await Rhay, their relationship had changed forever and he would not let himself get pulled back into Karwyn's web.

"Rhay." Karwyn's dim, silver-lined eyes met Rhay's.

Rhay had been surprised how easy it was to break into Karwyn's room until he spotted Karwyn on the bed. By the looks of it, he could barely sit upright, let alone flee. His cheeks were hollow. His eyes were lined with shadows. If Karwyn hadn't spoken, Rhay would have thought he was imagining him.

Raising his head, Karwyn gritted his teeth. "Have you come to finish me off?"

Rhay swallowed hard, the sound of Karwyn's dying breath lingering in his mind. "How are you still alive?"

"Are you disappointed you were unable to kill me on your first try? Are your little friends mad at you because I am still alive?"

Rhay's chest tightened painfully. He reached Karwyn's bedside in three quick strides, the room tiny, and grabbed his hand. It was so cold. Karwyn yanked his hand back.

"You're not an illusion," Rhay wondered aloud.

"Did you expect me to haunt you? I would not bother to come back for you. What are *you* doing here?"

"I...I've joined Tarnan," Rhay admitted with a knot in his throat, refusing to tell Karwyn the whole truth, fearing Tarnan would learn of it. Would Karwyn think Rhay had made a terrible mistake, betraying him further?

Karwyn let out a laugh that turned into a coughing fit. "Of course, you always have to side with my biggest enemy. First Loraine and now Tarnan."

Rhay stood back, Karwyn's words digging into his heart. "It's not like that; you were losing it, turning on your own people, on your own family. I wanted to stop you, to *save* you. I thought they were going to force you to abdicate."

"I did not think you were that naive." Karwyn tilted his head closer. "Tell me, if you had known they were planning to kill me, would you have chosen me or *them?*"

He averted his eyes from Karwyn's unrelenting gaze. Rhay still couldn't answer that question. Or maybe he didn't want to admit he could.

"Why are you here, Rhay? To gloat? Then go ahead and put me out of my misery. You seemed eager to do so on Caelo Night," Karwyn taunted, his raspy voice sending chills down Rhay's spine.

"I never wanted it to end that way and you know it. I tried all I could to not see the real you, to stand by your side. You made it impossible!"

"You were *my* friend, the one I trusted the most." Karwyn gritted his teeth, his tone as sharp as the blade that should have killed him. "I gave you *everything*—silver, a title, freedom to do anything you wanted even if it was drunkenly strolling through Chrysa's night clubs. And what did you do? *You* betrayed me."

"*You* betrayed me first!" Rhay snapped, remembering all he had to give up because of Karwyn. "We said we would never hurt each other, yet you trapped me in your twisted web. The one thing I could have was your *friendship*. Everything else, *everyone else*, was taken from me. You wanted me only for yourself."

"You had all the freedom that a king never has, and you took advantage of it. I never saw you complain when I gave you endless funds for your tasteless parties. When you drowned yourself in booze and lost yourself in some fae's arms." Karwyn glared daggers at him, but Rhay refused to avert his gaze.

"I was *never* free!" He leaned over Karwyn, the past spilling free inside his mind like a tsunami that couldn't be stopped. "I drowned myself because of *you*. I drank to push away what I knew in my heart was true —that you were a monster." Karwyn flinched. "I lost myself in meaningless sex because I knew if I entertained anything more you would find a way to take them from me. Do you deny it?" His first love at fifteen had been a young stable boy. Rhay had been so happy, so overjoyed to tell Karwyn all about his crush. It hadn't ended well. It never did.

Karwyn stayed silent, his hands balled into tight fists.

Rhay took a deep breath, finally willing to lay it all out. "You were my best friend. I trusted you. I cared for you. I *believed* in you. And you failed me on every possible level."

"I am your king," Karwyn snarled. "You were my advisor. It is *you* who failed *me*."

"You *were* my king." The words dropped from Rhay's tongue like hot coals. Once upon a time, Rhay would have come here seeking forgiveness. But now all Rhay wanted was to be honest with him for once.

Karwyn's strange eyes dimmed. Rhay kept going, unable to stop himself. "And you were a sorry excuse for one. You were cruel. You were heartless. You never learned from your father's mistakes. Instead, you carried on with them, didn't you? All the sick experiments in the underground, the twisted agreements you forced people into, the violence you've shown to those who should've been your allies. The way you manipulated me at every turn."

Karwyn averted his gaze, focusing on the small window next to his bed as if he could run away from this conversation when they both knew the time for avoiding questions had long passed. Rhay took in the blood-stained covers on the bed, the handkerchiefs on the tiny bedside table, and the odour of death in the room. Taking a deep breath, Rhay's heart pounded as if it also dreamt of escaping the suffocating room.

Karwyn turned his gaze back to him and broke the deafening silence lingering between them. "It is easy for you to recount the errors of my ways, but you have never been in my shoes, Rhay. You have never been king. It is not a fate full of glory, parties, and glitter. It is not merely power, it is a burden too. You would have crumbled under it in seconds." Karwyn's eyes warmed a smidge. "It is futile to argue about the past when I will not be here for much longer. Let me give you one final piece of advice. Do not go down this path. Run away as you had once suggested. Start over somewhere new. You will not have me there to cramp your *freedom*. If you stay and betray Tarnan... One of us will be dead soon, but it does not have to be both of us."

Rhay shook his head as he stepped back, Karwyn's words twisting his heart. "You still don't get it. Running away was never the right call. You and I...we've never known what the right call was. But I'm trying to learn."

Rhay had made so many mistakes, when would it end? It had to end *now*. As he looked at Karwyn, he knew arguing was fruitless. He couldn't change Karwyn, but he could better himself.

"Karwyn, I—"

"Such a touching reunion. The king and the king slayer."

Karwyn's gaze snapped to the door and Rhay whirled around. Saydren stood at the door, a wicked grin on his face.

Karwyn scooted back on the bed.

Rhay left Karwyn's side to march up to Saydren. "What have you done to him, Saydren? If I'm part of your court, I have a right to know."

"If you wish," Saydren replied with a strange rictus. "Karwyn, you remember the pill I gave you to increase your powers before the merge?"

"Clearly a pathetic attempt," Karwyn bit out.

"I lied."

"You made me lose against Loraine, did you not?" Karwyn spat, fury swirling in his eyes. "I am certain I would have gotten the upper hand if it was not for your meddling."

"The pill had nothing to do with that, you're just weak." Saydren had clearly chosen his words carefully. He knew how Karwyn's father had treated his son his whole life. "No, this pill I've been working on turns humans into fae. When you lost against Loraine, you lost your fae side, turning fully human, and then you died. The pill kicked in and here you are. You're lucky I reanimated your heart. You'd be dead without my experiment."

"If I am fae again, why did I lose my powers? And why am I dying?" Anger underlined Karwyn's words.

"Because dark magic comes at a cost. You weren't human to begin with, that must have messed with the magic of the pill." Saydren laughed. "You should really thank me. If it wasn't for my pill, you would have never been able to get this last reunion with Rhay. Isn't it nice to look into the eyes of your killer?"

Karwyn looked Saydren straight in the eyes, chilling Rhay's bones. "Yes, it is nice, is it not?"

Saydren grinned, clearly not phased by Karwyn. "Follow me, Rhay. Tarnan has requested to speak with you."

Rhay gave Karwyn one last look, unable to find real closure with him. Instead of coming to peace with one another, Rhay and Karwyn had proved once more why their friendship had always been nothing but ruin.

He turned his back on the fallen king and followed Saydren out the door.

CHAPTER 37

LORA

The warm brown colours and the vines cascading from the Carnylen palace walls didn't fool Lora as she and Nouis, accompanied by four Turosian guards, walked through the gates. She didn't know what to expect from this dinner, but she'd had a pit in her stomach ever since the carriage had left Turosian.

Her hand went to her necklace, the beautiful purple-blue crystal reminding her that Eyden could find her anywhere. A spelled paper was hidden in her pocket. With one flicker of a flame, she could send word. Amira had used the supercharge spell on him earlier today, so he could drift all the way to Carnylen at a moment's notice.

Amira had also helped Lora lift Lozlan's banishment. She had been filled with both relief and dread when the spell had broken. Amira and Elyssa would be heading to Allamyst while Wryen was still in Carnylen, so today had been her last chance to do so. But even with the banishment annulled, Lora couldn't think about her biological father now. Today, she had the contest dinner to get through. The crown on her head reminded her of the weight of her fate.

Servants greeted them as they were ushered into the palace, into a grand, golden-painted ballroom, a large table placed in the centre. Lora tilted her head, eyeing the murals of gods and goddesses staring down at her.

Lora spied Kaede and Kaylanthea already sitting at the table as well as Wryen and the other kings before her eyes met Tarnan's across the room. His eyes appeared honey-coloured, no trace of the blood-red they had been the last time Lora had seen him. He offered her a falsely friendly smile.

As she took her seat, Nouis went rigid next to her. Anxiety rose in her throat in anticipation of some new threat until she spotted Rhay sitting across from them, next to Saydren. By Tarnan's side. He wouldn't meet her gaze. Did he realise how wrong he'd been to take the agreement from her without her permission? What had possessed him to be so reckless? He reached for his wine glass but dropped his hand before he could pick it up.

A shrill clinking sound echoed through the room as Tarnan tapped his spoon against his glass. "Welcome to the last contest dinner." He rose from his sunflower-yellow velvet chair. "It is an honor to host everyone in my palace. As such, I want to take this opportunity to make an important announcement that might come as a shock to you all. But I want to assure you, it doesn't change the contest. Just the stakes."

Everyone glanced at him, confused. Kaede met Lora's gaze briefly. The queen tensed as she exchanged a look with Kaylanthea. Under the table, Lora's hand drifted to the dagger hidden under her dress.

"I'm not merely the heir to the Carnylen crown," Tarnan said, causing whispers around the table. "I'm also the rightful heir to the Rubien crown, Variel Sartoya's only living son."

"Is this some sort of joke?" King Quintin Nylwood from Obliveryn asked, his tone careful.

Tarnan's smile was easy, as if the king had given him a compliment. "Quite the opposite. Please see my honesty as a sign of my goodwill. I want to enter the contest as my true self, uniting both my kingdoms. We have much to discuss, but be assured, it won't affect the contest."

"Why should we believe you?" Kaede asked, glancing from Tarnan to Lora. Lora averted her gaze, not wanting Tarnan to suspect she had talked to the queens beforehand.

Tarnan turned to one of the royal advisors at the table, wearing a pale pink uniform, the colours of Kaylanthea's kingdom. "*Dump your water over your head."* First, Kaede seemed irritated, her gaze connecting with Kaylanthea as she raised a brow. But then the advisor picked up his water glass and poured it over his head.

Shocked gasps drifted through the air. Lora took in everyone's expressions. Some surprised but unsure, some hateful. Mostly disgust and confusion. They had all thought the power of compulsion had died with the Sartoya line.

Wryen sprang up from his chair. "This is ludicrous! The Dark King's son can't be part of the contest. I will take his spot."

Tarnan rolled his shoulders. "Sit down, Wryen. No one is taking my spot."

"Don't speak as if you're above me, Tarnan. You're not. You're an *imposter* who—"

Lora saw the second the light shifted in Tarnan's eyes, turning red. *"Sit down,"* he commanded.

Wryen was forced to obey. The colour drained from his face, the vein on his forehead pulsing visibly as he sat down. Everyone at the table went quiet. The confusion in the room turned to panic.

"You can't expect us to take this...*news* as if it doesn't change everything." Kaylanthea tilted her chin up. "You were selected as an Ellevarn, not a *Sartoya.*"

Tarnan put his hands on the table as he leaned forward, turning his head to the queen. "One does not cancel out the other. I'm as much an Ellevarn as I am a Sartoya."

"Nonsense," Wryen whispered angrily.

"Wryen, I'm getting tired of your remarks. You would never be in the contest even if a spot opened up. You can't even keep your sister under control. Where is she? Do you have any idea what she's up to? I tried to help her, but it seems she's lost her mind."

"Amira is in Turosian grieving her fiancé's disappearance," Lora replied before Wryen could throw insults Amira's way.

"Yes, how fortunate for us that another Adelway could take his spot." Tarnan turned from her to the group. "This is a delicate matter. Crowns have been exchanged, a king is gone. Yet our law, *the gods,* say the contest goes on. And so it shall. Let's let Caelo decide who shall carry the burden of ruling over Liraen."

Wryen huffed. "Bullshit." He snapped his fingers. "Guards." The Allamyst guards walked forward.

Tarnan sighed. "So be it." He looked at the royals at the table, ignoring their advisors. *"Grab your knife and point it at your throat."* Guards stormed forward but Tarnan said, "If any of your guards come charging, I will compel you to slit your throats." The guards halted, unsure how to act as they watched their rulers raise sharp knives to their own skin one by one. Everyone had followed his command, except Kaede, who was a powerful empath like Rhay. The advisors watched, distraught.

Lora didn't feel the effect of Tarnan's compulsion but she grabbed her knife anyway, to keep up appearances. Rhay leaned back in his chair with a perfect poker face. Did he really think he had made the right choice?

Tarnan turned to Kaede, his smile wavering. *"Follow my command."* Locked in a staring match, Kaede's hand shook as the compulsion slowly took hold. Just like Rhay, she had an easier time deflecting mental powers because of her own high-level mental power. But Tarnan was stronger and Kaede lost the fight.

Kaylanthea turned her way, her brows raised. Her fingers tensed around the knife. Next to her, her husband watched her closely with pinched brows.

Tarnan sat down. "Look what you made me do, Wryen. For your sake, I would recommend choosing to side *with* me instead of against me." He stared at each ruler. "I'm not my father, I don't intend to recklessly extinguish lives, but I'm just as powerful and I will do what must be done for a better Liraen. The contest will go on as planned, and *when* I win, with Caelo's blessing, I will combine both my kingdoms, Rubien and Carnylen. You want to stand with me when I do so. I suggest we hold the contest in Rubien this year to honor its return." He paused as if waiting for a response when he knew everyone was too afraid to disagree, then clapped his hands. Usually the advisors would choose the location and handle preparations. "Glad we all agree."

The compulsion lifted and everyone dropped their knives. Lora hastily dropped hers too. Sighs of relief flooded through the room. Nouis was breathing heavily next to her.

"I'm not doing this," Wryen muttered, shifting in his chair as he grabbed the arms to stand up.

"*Put the knife through your leg,*" Tarnan said, picking up his own cutlery and taking a bite of the roast in front of him.

Wryen slumped in his chair and stabbed himself in his left thigh. A strangled cry left his lips. Kaede put a hand over her heart.

Tarnan didn't look up from his food. "Anyone else have something to complain about?"

Lora observed everyone at the table. Kaylanthea and Kaede were intensely locked in what seemed to be a silent conversation. Rhay was watching them too; he gave a barely noticeable shake of his head that the queens failed to notice.

Afraid the queens would get themselves killed and wanting to leave here with some sort of intel that could help them, Lora asked, "Tarnan, may I speak to you in private?"

Tarnan slowly put down his fork before wiping his mouth with a napkin. "After dinner."

She fixed him with a glare. "It's about Amira. I can discuss it here, but I think you'd prefer we talked in private."

Throwing the napkin on the table, Tarnan rose to his feet. "*No one moves from this table.*"

Gesturing to the hall, he waited for Lora to get up. She kept still, narrowing her eyes at him. Tarnan watched her intently, his eyes appearing redder every second. Was his command a trap? Did he suspect she could resist his compulsion and was waiting for her to reveal that to everyone? She hadn't fallen for it after the merge, but that could be explained since Tarnan had just unlocked his power then. Now he was more in control. Maybe Rhay had revealed Lora's power to him and Tarnan was trying to trick her into showcasing it.

"All right," Tarnan finally said. "*If any royal except Lora moves*"—he turned to address the royals' guards—"*attack all of them.*"

Whispers filled the ballroom. Getting to her feet, Lora followed Tarnan outside before she could lose her nerve.

In the hall, Tarnan leaned closer to Lora, his eyes flickering to the ballroom. "What is it that you think gives you the right to call me out of my own dinner?"

Lora forced her breathing to remain even. An image of Farren's hands covered in blood flashed through her mind. She cleared her throat, trying to cast her panic aside. "I know Karwyn is alive. What are you planning?" She knew he wouldn't give her a straight answer, but any insight into his plans could help.

Tarnan's sigh was almost a laugh. "Don't worry, Lora, he won't give you any trouble. Is that all?"

Lora's hand drifted into the pocket of her dress, fingers brushing the spelled paper. "That's not the only thing Amira has told me." Tarnan's gaze narrowed. "I know you have a daughter."

Tarnan moved closer, yet his facial expression didn't change one bit. "It's irrelevant."

"Is it?" Lora tilted her chin up at him. "Something tells me you'd care if people found out." Amira thought so, at least.

Tarnan's lips stretched into a smile, but a hint of distaste spilled through. "What do you want? You and your friends safe? You know you can never kill me unless you're willing to sacrifice Amira. If you stop standing in my way, I can be convinced to let you and your friends live. I'm not a monster."

Lora clenched her teeth. "Right. So you're not planning on killing everyone at the contest? You do want it to be fair, right? I hope you know taking out any competition today would make you a hypocrite."

Tarnan detailed her face, his own expression completely neutral. "This is a civil dinner, Lora. I have no intention of taking anyone out unless they force my hand. You are aware no one taking part in the contest has to die? The most powerful fae wins, but it's not a duel to the death."

"Unless you choose to make it one," Lora said, reading between the lines. Sighing, she sensed she wouldn't get anywhere. But there was something she was hoping she could achieve. "I'll make you an offer—I'll keep my mouth shut about your daughter if you stay away from Earth."

"And why would I do that now that I've broken the human-fae agreement?" He watched her closely.

The fire in her veins scorched her skin, but she didn't act on it. That was what he wanted, for her to act out and lose her head. Her anger at Rhay rose the more time she spent with Tarnan, seeing exactly who he had betrayed her for. But she pushed that aside too.

"My silence," Lora offered, "in exchange for you staying away from Earth. Neither you nor any of your lackeys can cross over."

Oscar had almost finished building his device—an alarm system of sorts, to alert them if anyone crossed the border into the human world —but even so, Tarnan could wreck her world if he chose to.

Tarnan crossed his arms. "I can agree to that. Until the contest. Then it's time for a new dawn."

Lora mulled it over. After the contest, Tarnan would either be dead or they had lost and then Tarnan would go back on his word anyway. "Fine." At least it gave her time to come up with a plan, and it gave the humans time to run as far away from the border as possible. She turned to head back to the dinner, but Tarnan grabbed her shoulder.

"There's another matter to discuss. I believe you're in possession of one of the amulets. If you hand it over, I can give you something you want."

Eyden still had the amulet Amira had thrown to him after the ritual. It was a powerful amplifier that Amira had used more than once. Cirny had tricked her into breaking the border spell with it.

Lora shrugged Tarnan off. "And what is it you think that I want?"

"I can break your contract with Karwyn. I can save your mother. All you have to do is give me the amulet."

Lora sucked in a breath. After everything, Tarnan was offering her what she had set out to do from the start: save her mum. A way out was within reach. Yet she knew she couldn't take it, even as her heart broke at the thought of letting her mother down. If Tarnan wanted the amulet, it could only mean something bad. He would use it against them. Amira would need it to fight against Tarnan and to amplify her power in order to break her bond with Tarnan—they had to find a way to unlink them.

"You should be grateful I'm offering you a deal instead of compelling you," Tarnan added, holding her gaze.

Her head pounded. She was walking a fine line here. He couldn't compel her, yet he shouldn't find that out. "You shouldn't have taken Amira with you that night. She knows your power is not limitless." Tarnan's stoic expression faltered. "If you compel me now, it will wear off the further away I am. You don't have enough power yet to control me long enough."

"I can force you to sign a blood contract."

Lora couldn't help her flinch. She wouldn't sign anything, but then she'd be forced to reveal her power.

"Consider your answer carefully," he said. "I'll ask nicely once. Hand me that amulet or you'll pay the price."

Lora swallowed the lump in her throat. This conversation wasn't going at all the way she'd hoped. "Why do you want it?"

"Collector's value." His tone didn't give anything away, but Lora suspected that was far from the only reason he wanted it. "Do we have a deal?" Lora considered saying yes to stall and backtrack later. But then he said, "If you lie to me, I can kill Karwyn and your mother anytime I see fit."

Lora opened her mouth to counter his threat with one of her own —his daughter—when a pained cry cut through the air, followed by multiple voices yelling. On instinct, Lora turned and ran back into the ballroom. This time, Tarnan didn't stop her. Somehow, where danger waited, she was always headed right into it. As she hurried inside the dining room, she caught sight of a guard slashing out at his own ruler. All hell had broken loose.

CHAPTER 38

ELYSSA

Nearing the familiar clearing in the woods, Elyssa whispered the password to her old home, and through the trees, the rebel camp appeared. The chilly wind made a curl escape Elyssa's ponytail. She wondered how everyone would react to her. Would they turn her away? Would they ask about Farren?

She could tell Eyden was tense next to her, his hand flexing and relaxing as if that would make Lora's fire message appear any faster. Eyden was saving his strength to be ready in case Lora called from the contest dinner.

Amira was packing up and would be waiting in a carriage by the woods soon so they could leave for Allamyst. The upside of Lora being the freaking Queen of Turosian was easy access to carriages.

For a second, Elyssa felt a deep familiarity as she glanced at the camp, like coming home after a long time away. In some ways, it was still her home. But the feeling didn't last. As Elyssa looked closer, she found the tents in the distance destroyed, torn apart. The camp was in ruins.

A shockwave zapping through her, Elyssa lurched forward, but Eyden pulled her back, a finger pressed to his lips. Carefully, Elyssa removed the bow from her back and drew an arrow. She glanced around their surroundings, the quiet rustling of the leaves of the trees the only distinguishable sound to her, before silently walking forward. Her blood boiled at the sight before her.

Tents were ripped to shreds, blood staining some of them. The ground was cluttered by broken items. She kept glancing at the dry earth beneath her to avoid making any noise.

Eyden halted next to her. She spun around, following Eyden's line of sight to the broken glass under a bird's claw. It fluttered its wings and disappeared into the bright sky. Elyssa hadn't heard it, but someone else might have.

Where was everyone? Had they gotten away from whatever—*who-ever*—attacked the camp? Her skin heated at the thought of what they must have gone through and that she hadn't goddamn been there for them.

She tilted her chin towards her old tent. Maybe some of her things had survived.

Eyden drew closer. "I'll check the other side." Putting two fingers behind her ear, Elyssa went ahead.

She swung open the flap to her tent, an arrow aimed forward. The inside appeared mostly untouched. Whoever had found their camp must have seen no one was in here and left it alone. But if someone had found the camp, why was the spell to hide it still working? Had someone revealed the password? It had happened before.

The first camp she grew up in, someone had betrayed them then too. They'd blamed Eyden, but it hadn't been him. Elyssa had been ten years old at the time. Her memories of that day were a mix of blood and pain. She remembered losing sight of her parents and then her uncle had come running her way. He had told her to hide, but there had been nowhere to go. Fae guards had them surrounded. Tents had been turned over. Her uncle had pointed towards two bodies stacked over each other. She hadn't wanted to move but he told her to take cover behind the dead, putting a dagger into her shaking hand.

She'd stayed there, the dagger clutched to her chest, watching the guards attack through the space between the dead men's heads. One after another, they'd fallen. Her friends. Her home. It had all been stained by death. Blood had dripped from one of the bodies she was hiding behind onto her arm. She remembered the smell of metal and dirt. She had willed herself to stay still as a guard slashed at her uncle's stomach until he was almost split in two. Dust had settled in the air as he'd dropped to the ground, and Elyssa had cursed herself for hiding, had felt a sense of guilt she'd never known until that day.

When she had spotted her mother on the battlefield, Elyssa had clutched her dagger tighter and sprinted through the field. A guard had her mother pinned to the ground when Elyssa had made her way over. With fury burning in her heart, Elyssa had grabbed the guard's shoulder and when he had turned, she stabbed her dagger straight into his eye. And then his heart. Her first kill. She had barely heard his screams over the blood rushing in her ears. She had saved her mother, but a part of Elyssa had changed forever that night. She'd no longer felt safe, had lost her childish naivete.

Shaking off her past and current dread, Elyssa removed a duffle bag from under her bed and started throwing clothes and her few remaining belongings into it. She wouldn't be coming back here ever again—the thought struck her like an arrow aimed at her heart. They would have to rebuild once she found out where everyone had gone. Elyssa's skin itched at the fact that she hadn't been there to help them. Her eyes burned, but she swallowed the lump in her throat.

Swinging the duffle bag over her shoulder, Elyssa headed outside to Farren's tent close by. She breathed in deeply, not letting herself fall apart at the familiar smells and the sight of his things. Quickly, she stuffed Farren's spellbooks into her bag. Amira could use them.

As she walked out, Eyden appeared by her side, shaking his head.

"Who do you think is behind this?" Elyssa asked.

"It could have been anyone. Tarnan, Rahmur Piers, anyone who dislikes humans." Eyden shifted his feet. "If it was Rahmur, I'll find them." He and Lora would be heading to the Void to find Lozlan. If it was Rahmur, the humans were most likely there.

Elyssa felt an itch under her skin, a fury waiting to be avenged. Rahmur Piers, the leader of human blood traffic, was someone she'd vowed to take down after she and Amira had run into him in Carnylen what felt like ages ago.

But Wryen had to be dealt with first.

"Let's go," she said. There was no time for falling apart about the past when the future was waiting for her to kick its ass.

"Wait." Eyden's head turned right, then left. "I hear something."

"Want to fill me in?" Elyssa asked, knocking back another arrow.

"I think it's coming from the woods. Other side of the camp."

He led the way, and as they drew closer, Elyssa picked up the sound, but she couldn't determine where it was coming from until she spotted him. Ian—a teen from the camp and Jaspen's trusted sidekick—bound to a tree, his foot pushing a stone against the tree opposite him.

Elyssa stepped in front of him and the boy shrunk back, his leg halting. She kept her arrow pointed at him. "What in Liraen happened here?" she asked. Drawing closer, she noticed the tears streaking his face.

"I...they were taken," Ian sobbed. His hands were tied behind his back to a tree. "I don't know why he did it. Nothing makes sense anymore."

Elyssa's throat tightened, her fears becoming reality. "Who did this to you and why?"

Ian dropped the back of his head against the tree, his shoulders shaking as fresh tears streamed down his cheeks. "Jaspen."

Fury as red as fire spread in Elyssa's veins. She leaned forward. Ian's gaze was locked on the arrow pointed at his chest, his eyes wide with terror. Lowering her weapon, Elyssa knelt next to him.

"I tried to warn them. I really tried, Elyssa. He wouldn't let me."

Elyssa tilted her head at Eyden and he walked around the tree to free Ian's hands.

Elyssa put a hand on Ian's shoulder. "Tell me everything you know."

"Jaspen...he gave up the camp. I don't know why. I overheard him making some sort of deal. I confronted him but he got the upper hand and then he just left me here." The rope binding his hands snapped, and Ian hissed as he pulled his hands to his chest. Red marks stained his skin. "I think he left me to die."

"So he handed everyone except you over to Rahmur Piers, is that it? Why leave you alive? And what did he get in return? Silver?" Eyden asked. It made no sense. Jaspen loved being the leader of the camp. What kind of a leader was he without anyone to follow him?

Ian shook his hand. "I don't know, I guess he took mercy on me. Maybe he wanted to give me a chance to survive—a small one, at least. But it wasn't Rahmur. It was some other fae. Jaspen called him Saydren."

"Fucking hell," Elyssa muttered, her fist clenching so hard she thought she might break her bones. If Saydren was involved, that meant Tarnan was too. How had he managed to take from her *again?* How had she been so fucking dumb to think he wouldn't go after the camp when they'd been involved in their plan to take down Karwyn? And Rhay had handed him the one thing that could be their doom, a fate worse than death. If Rhay hadn't gone against their plan, maybe Farren would still be alive. "What did he want in return?"

"I don't know. I couldn't hear. I swear. But there's something else." Ian turned to Eyden, his blond hair falling into his face. "Jaspen reminded Saydren that he helped him once before. He said he told Saydren about Lora?"

Elyssa's attention snapped to Eyden. His eyes blazed. "Are you sure that's what you heard?" he asked.

"Yes."

Eyden planted his dagger in the ground between him and Ian. "And there's nothing else you're keeping from us?"

Ian pulled his legs to his chest. "I have no reason to lie. I have nothing..." His lips trembled. He looked younger than seventeen with his blond hair dirty, his shirt full of grass stains and his grey eyes glassy.

Eyden picked up his dagger before getting to his feet. "We should go. If Tarnan has them, then we're already too late. We have to regroup."

Elyssa felt like screaming, but she clenched her teeth instead—hard enough to hurt her jaw. Tarnan was one step ahead of them every fucking time. Every fibre of her being was lit with rage. Here she was, outplayed by Tarnan yet again, and she couldn't do anything to hurt him. She couldn't lay a fucking finger on him as long as he was bound to Amira.

But there was one person she could make pay.

"Do you know where he is?" Elyssa asked through gritted teeth.

Ian dropped his head into his hands. "Jaspen? No."

Elyssa rose to her feet. Knowing how close Ian had been to Jaspen, they couldn't fully trust him. Jaspen had proven himself to be even more of an asshole than Elyssa had imagined. All this talk about not trusting fae and then he went ahead and sold them all out. For what? What was his goddamn goal? Was he a fucking idiot? *A dead fucking idiot.*

"If you want shelter," Elyssa said, meeting Ian's gaze, "tell me where Jaspen would most likely have run off to. You know him. Don't bullshit me. He sold everyone out, you don't fucking owe him anything."

"El—" Eyden started, but she held up her hand. "Okay then," Eyden said, gesturing for Ian to get up. "You talk, you can come with us. Don't do anything stupid." His tone was sharp, a veiled threat carrying his voice.

Ian braced himself against the tree as he rose from the ground. "I won't. There's an inn Jaspen sometimes visits. It's called Raven's Nest. But I can't promise he'll be there."

She'd heard of the place on the outskirts of Chrysa. Good enough for her. They were even close by. "Let's go."

Eyden grabbed her arm to halt her. "Now?" He squinted at her. "Isn't Amira waiting for you?"

She was. But this might be Elyssa's only chance to pay Jaspen back for everything he'd done. She had to do something. *Someone has to pay.* It wouldn't take her long to take Jaspen out once and for all.

"Let's not be reckless," Eyden reasoned. The runia strapped to his hip went off. He pulled it to his ear, pressing a button. Elyssa couldn't catch the words coming through the spelled device.

As Eyden's attention turned elsewhere, Elyssa ran. He called it reckless, but to Elyssa this was her lifeboat. She *had to* do this. She had to take Jaspen down. She had to do something right in this fucked-up world.

Eyden might have called after her but Elyssa ducked behind the trees, making sure he couldn't see her and drift to her. She felt her lungs constrict as she ran faster. Her wound ached, but it only reminded her why she had to do this. Someone had to bleed. Someone had to feel her vengeance or she might combust.

She ran all the way to Raven's Nest; it was only half an hour away. Stopping short, Elyssa leaned a hand against a tree, ducking out of sight. The inn was deep in the woods, no other buildings in sight. Her breathing was laboured. Her legs felt like jelly, but she was alive, so she had no right to complain, to back out.

The front door was old and rustic, almost falling off its hinges. It seemed abandoned, but then the door opened and two fae headed out as a carriage arrived from the dirt road. As it stopped, two fae men and a fae woman got out, dragging out two girls, gags over their mouths. Even from her position, Elyssa could tell they were human. The driver jumped off the carriage and the girls were ushered towards the house.

Goddamn blood traffickers.

Were there more inside? Was Jaspen here? After what he'd done, Elyssa wouldn't put it past him. Either way, she had to save them. She couldn't let anyone else die.

Drawing an arrow, Elyssa didn't let herself think—she fired. One after another, she hit the fae surrounding the girls and they dropped their grips on them.

"Run!" Elyssa yelled at them as she ducked behind the tree again but the fae had spotted her.

As the girls fled, the five fae headed straight to Elyssa. Five against one, not quite a fair fight. She could run. She could turn, fire more arrows and sprint off. She could lose them.

But her heart wouldn't let her. Her heart that had been broken, crushed, emptied, and then refilled with nothing but scorching ashes. It wanted violence. It *needed* vengeance. It craved an outlet for all her anger, the satisfaction of winning instead of losing. She had had too much of the latter, and now there truly was nothing too reckless for her liking.

Staring at the five fae approaching her, Elyssa swung her bow over her shoulder and curled her fists. This one would hurt, but damn her if she didn't make them pay.

CHAPTER 39

EYDEN

"Keep up," Eyden told Ian as they neared the palace gates. He didn't want to use his power until Lora called for him, so they were running. He'd been worried about Lora all day, but now he had more than one reason to be distressed. Fearing Elyssa would get herself in trouble, he had wanted to go after her, but Ilario had called on his runia. Eyden had barely been able to hear a few words before their connection was cut off. Something about an attack. And when Eyden had turned to inform Elyssa, his sister had been gone. Caelo knew what Elyssa was getting herself into all on her own. But Oscar and Maja were at the palace, utterly vulnerable. Elyssa, at least, knew how to defend herself.

"Should we really go in?" Ian stopped, his eyes locked on the silver gates in the distance.

Eyden didn't slow down. "You can stay here. I don't give a damn."

Tugging at his dirty grass-stained shirt, Ian followed after him. The blinding silver of the gates sparkled in the sun as Eyden broke through the trees surrounding the palace. The words he'd said to Ian felt stuck in his throat as he spotted guards sprawled on the ground, dead. Maybe the boy should have stayed back.

Drawing his dagger, Eyden observed the area, but it was silent. Until Ian spoke. "What's really going on here?"

"Nothing good."

Ian hugged himself, and Eyden realised he must be freezing with no jacket. Maybe he was better off somewhere else, but Eyden had no time to waste. His people were inside.

"I'm going." Eyden sprinted forward. He heard Ian hurrying to catch up with him.

The front doors to the palace were wide open, dead guards lying out front. Eyden slowed as he started to hear screaming from inside. He grabbed a bloody sword from a dead guard and handed it to Ian. Then he snagged another sword, putting his dagger in its sheath for later.

At a nod from Eyden, Ian hurried to his side and they ran into utter chaos. Turosian guards fought other fae in the entry hall of the palace. Eyden couldn't place the enemies' faces. He needed to find Oscar, Maja, and Ilario.

Just then, a voice drew his attention back to the door he'd come through.

"What happened?" Amira hurried inside. A fae headed their way, sword raised, and Amira used air to force him backwards against a second fae.

"I have no idea," Eyden said. "I have to find everyone and—"

Amira turned her head. "Where's Elyssa?"

Ian filled her in quickly.

Amira's lips parted. More fae came rushing at them, and Eyden drew his sword.

Eyden gritted his teeth. "She's going to get herself in trouble but..." He was torn. He didn't trust Elyssa was thinking clearly right now and his skin crawled at the thought of her out there on a solo revenge path. But the palace was in complete mayhem.

"Find the others." Amira raised her arms to throw the attackers backwards, buying them time. "I'll go after El."

"Are you sure?" Eyden's gaze drifted between her and the hallway. *Where the hell was everyone?*

"Go," Amira said, her tone serious.

"Raven's Nest. It's by the woods, follow the dirt road. Take a horse." There was a desperate urgency in Eyden's tone and Amira seemed to catch his drift. Putting two fingers behind her ear, the princess turned and sprinted outside, her cloak trailing behind her in the wind.

Eyden focused on the fae approaching. He sidestepped, avoiding a sword, and made his way down the hall. From the corner of his eye, he kept track of Ian, who followed behind as if he had nowhere else to go. When a fae tried to grab the boy, Eyden lashed out, forcing the attacker to drop her arm and step back. Ian's eyes were wide yet he gripped his sword tighter.

A burst of gunshots came from upstairs, and Eyden sprinted the rest of the way through the hall. He took the stairs at the end up to the next floor, where he spotted Maja standing protectively in front of Oscar, a gun aimed at a fae who already had multiple bullet holes in his chest. The fae was about to strike with his dagger. Eyden prepared to drift to them when a sword flew through the air and struck the back of the fae's head.

Maja's hand shook as she watched the fae crumple. Oscar went white in the face.

Eyden walked forward as Damir came towards them, pulling the sword from the fae's head with a sickening crunch. He kicked the fae until he was on his back, then gripped his sword with both hands and drove it down hard, detaching his head.

Looking up at Maja and Oscar, Damir said, "You're welcome."

Maja shook her head then straightened herself. "First of all, I totally had him. Second of all, what the actual fuck is wrong with you?"

"That's a head," Oscar whispered.

"You didn't have shit." Damir turned away, his gaze meeting Eyden.

"What the fuck happened?" Eyden asked, sprinting the rest of the way to them. "Are you okay?" Maja nodded, her eyes dim. Oscar stood by quietly, shaking. "Why aren't you in the protected wing?" Amira had spelled it to make sure they were safe there.

"The spell stopped working." Maja lowered her gun but her grip was fierce, her knuckles white.

Cursing, Eyden peered down the hallway. "Where's Ilario?"

"Fucking hell." Damir turned, but Eyden grabbed his shoulder. Damir's gaze burned a hole into Eyden's hand until he dropped it.

Damir tilted his head, then laughed. "You think this was me? This is on *you*, Kellen. I told you they wouldn't take getting dismissed from the palace well. We should have killed them when we had the chance." A scream echoed through the hall from downstairs. "I guess there's no time like the present." Sword raised, he ran off.

Eyden drew a hand down his face. "Fuck." Lora had been gone barely a day and all hell had broken loose. He hadn't expected the dismissed guards to retaliate that way. Sparing them had backfired. He needed to rectify the situation and find Ilario, but he couldn't do that with Oscar and Maja here. "Okay, here's what we're gonna do," he said to them. "I'm drifting you to my apartment, then I'm coming back here."

"No." Maja crossed her arms. "Amira's spell—we don't know how often you can drift until—"

"I know. But I also know Lora would want me to get you out of here. She'd want me to take that risk." He had to respect what she'd choose in this situation. Lora could handle herself. She'd want her little brother safe.

"I can help," Maja argued, clutching her gun.

"You'll help by looking after the two of you." Eyden's gaze swung to Ian, who stood behind him, the grip on his sword weak. "Or three."

"Who the hell is he?" Maja whispered.

"Just keep an eye on him, okay?" Eyden gestured for Ian to get closer. "We're going. I have to find Ilario."

He prayed he would still have the energy to get to Lora if she called for him.

As he drifted back to the palace hall after dropping the three of them back at his flat, with quite a bit more argument from Maja, Eyden barely dodged a sword being swung at his head. The blade grazed his chin as he leaned out of its path. Ignoring the faint sting, he kicked out, catching the fae in his shin. Before his opponent could raise his sword again, Eyden struck with his fists, hitting the fae's cheek with enough force to make him drop to the ground. Eyden lifted his sword, blade pointed at the fae's heart. If he didn't kill him now, would he come after them again? In his head, Lora's voice told him to have mercy. But she also knew when killing was unavoidable.

Before Eyden could pull back, the fae drove an almandine knife into his foot. Cursing, Eyden kicked him away and ripped the blade out, feeling his power wavering. It had gone straight through his boot. The fae had used the distraction to scramble back but Eyden was faster, striking true, this time with no hesitation.

Further off, Eyden spotted some of the guards who had remained and sworn fealty to Lora fighting off their attackers. He tried to mentally add up how many of their guards lay dead in the hall and by the front door. Too damn many.

"Watch your left!" a voice yelled, and Eyden spun in a wide arc, sword ready. He took the fae out in mere seconds. But another one was coming right at him. Blood sprayed his face as he lifted his sword to block the fae's. Eyden pushed the blade forward until it cut the fae's face. The attacker screamed in rage, dropping her sword as her hands went to her bleeding face. Eyden pulled back his weapon, ready for the killing blow, when a long blade pierced the fae's chest from behind. The fae dropped dead, revealing Damir behind her.

Damir grinned, his blood-streaked face savage. "Now that's what I'm talking about."

Eyden had to resist the urge to cut the sick smile from his face. He had no time to react as more fae attacked from all sides. There hadn't been that many guards on Damir's list of fae who Karwyn had commanded to help with his twisted games. Had they convinced others to storm the palace?

Against his instinct, Eyden ended up back to back with Damir again. They found a weird rhythm, taking out fae after fae. The floor grew sticky with blood, slowing Eyden's movements. He could feel blood welling inside his boot from the stab wound. Each step burned. Looking up, he spotted a dagger flying through the air towards him.

"Duck," he yelled as he elbowed Damir and dropped to a crouch. Damir barely avoided the blade and it left a scratch on his left cheek.

Dabbing at his wound, Damir's eyes light up with a mix of anger and...*joy?* Turning back around, he pushed his sword through the neck of a fae heading his way, then moved the dead fae in front of him as another one struck. In his movement, Damir had dropped his sword, but he didn't seem to need it as he pushed the dead fae into the new attacker. He fell and Damir stepped on the hand holding the sword with so much force Eyden could hear the fae's wrist breaking. With frightening ease, Damir picked up the sword and pushed it through the dead fae lying on top of the other one until both their life sources faded.

Bodies piled up around them, but Eyden could still hear the clash of weapons further off in the throne room.

"Not bad, Kellen." Damir picked up a fallen sword and cleaned it off on one of the bodies as if they were nothing but piles of clothes for him to use. "But your aim could use some work."

Clenching his teeth, Eyden imagined Damir among the dead. At the sound of footsteps, he raised his weapon again, his bones tired as he fought the instinct to punch Damir's face.

Ilario sprinted towards them, multiple cuts on his body. His left sleeve was ripped and bloodied and his right leg was bleeding too. "There you are," he said before his gaze landed on the bodies around them. "By Caelo."

"How many are left?" Eyden asked.

"There's too many to count. We have to stop it before the whole court is dead. It's a bloodbath."

Striding forward, Damir claimed, "I can take them."

Ilario grabbed his arm as Damir brushed past him. Damir froze, staring straight ahead.

"You can, but not in the way you're thinking," Ilario argued. "I need you to shift into Karwyn."

Damir shrugged off Ilario's hold. "And then what?"

Forcing Damir to look at him, Ilario stepped in front of him. "You know him better than any of us." His tone was piercing. Their past was as present in the room as the blood on the ground. "Are you telling me those fae wouldn't listen to him? Tell them to call it off."

Damir's lip twitched, but he didn't say anything. Briefly nodding, he turned to the stairs. "Meet me in the throne room."

Eyden racked his brain for another solution but feared Ilario was right. They wouldn't listen to anyone else. This could end up weakening Lora's hold over the Turosian throne, but what other choice did they have?

Ilario looked as if he was about to pass out, his emerald eyes dilated, his skin ashen.

"Let's go," Eyden said, laying a hand on his shoulder.

They walked towards the throne room, flattening themselves on either side of the double doors. Eyden could hear the screams of pain inside. He could feel the energy of anger reaching fury, finding nothing but blood.

With a tilt of his head, Eyden ran inside, Ilario next to him. He struck a fae in the back who was attacking one of their guards. *Their guards.* Those words sounded insane in his head.

He had no time to dwell as he lost himself in the battle until the doors closed loudly behind them and the chaos in the room began to still as fae spotted Karwyn, dressed in fine silver clothes, by the door. His hands were clasped behind his back. If he didn't know better, Eyden would have never guessed it was Damir.

A slow grin stretched across Karwyn's face and Eyden curled his hand into a fist.

"Well, this is a pleasant surprise," Damir said with Karwyn's voice. "I see you have chosen to rebel against my cousin's pathetic claim to the throne. I chose the perfect time to make my reappearance."

Guards froze midswing, looking at each other in confusion. The former guards turned enemies glanced at each other too, their weapons still at the ready.

Karwyn/Damir clapped his hands. "Very well, then. Everyone on my side, follow me. Everyone else will have to await their trial here. And if you are one of Loraine's guards, do not even attempt to follow me. You have lost your chance."

The guards seemed too shocked to act, torn between what Nouis must have promised them and seeing Karwyn, their late king, back from the dead. As Karwyn/Damir spun around, hands on the double doors, the former guards—now attackers—started to walk forward, first a few, then a whole crowd of them.

Eyden could only see Karwyn/Damir's back as the doors opened. Then Damir dropped to the ground. Eyden's hand went to his dagger in alarm until he realised Damir hadn't been hit. Arrows rained down on the group of fae gathered behind Karwyn/Damir from the hall beyond. They were struck down so fast, only a few were able to duck. The remaining guards, the ones on Lora's side, snapped back into action and took care of Karwyn's followers quickly.

As Karwyn's soldiers dropped dead one after the other, the arrows stopped, and Eyden glimpsed a group of Lora's guards on the other side of the double doors, their bows still drawn. Damir—having shifted back into himself—rose from the ground with a half-grin on his face, and Eyden realised this had been his plan all along: end one bloodbath with another.

Dusting himself off, Damir walked towards Eyden and Ilario, whose face had lost all colour. A fae twitched on the ground, and Damir took the time to pierce his heart before stopping in front of them.

"I took care of it my way," Damir said, the gash on his face from earlier flickering in and out of sight as his power dwindled.

"What do you want, a thank you?" Ilario asked, his shoulders sagging. "No one should want *this*." He gestured at all the bodies. So fucking many.

"*This*," Damir bit out, "was the only way. We don't all live in your happy world, Marsyn." He slammed past Ilario's shoulder as he walked away, stepping over the corpses in his path.

They'd won. Yet, as Eyden took in the dead bodies surrounding him, he felt they'd lost something else in the process. Something that couldn't be reclaimed. Something Damir didn't seem to have ever possessed in the first place.

CHAPTER 40

RHAY

"Wryen, sit down," Kaylanthea hissed between her teeth. Wryen had pushed back his chair, the wooden legs screeching against the shiny floor. Just as Tarnan had commanded them, the royals' guards stormed forward as soon as Wryen rose to his feet, the knife still impaled in his thigh. Their swords were drawn, ready to attack their own kings and queens. Rhay almost jumped to his feet but stopped himself from intervening. Wryen and King Quintin of Obliveryn tried to escape the room, but all the doors were either locked or blocked by compelled guards.

As the guards lashed out against their own sovereigns, the kings and queens were left with no choice but to defend themselves. King Mayrick of Emerlane slashed at one of his guards with a sword, trying to put some distance between them, while his advisor used his power to lower the guard's aggression. Kaylanthea fought alongside her husband, using her water power to push away the guards creeping close to Kaede and her.

Rhay felt two sets of eyes on him. His father's, clearly disapproving of his son's lack of action as he fought off a guard aiming at Kaede by throwing a china plate at his face. The second set of eyes were Saydren's, carefully taking in Rhay's reaction, ready for him to slip up. So instead of helping, Rhay sat back in his chair, unease filling his heart. His focus stayed on his father. Tarnan had promised to spare him.

Screams echoed through the room when one of the guards slashed at Yasir, Kaylanthea's husband, cutting him across the chest with an almandine sword and forcing him to the ground. It took all Rhay's willpower to not run to him. When the guard lifted his sword, the blade pointed at his victim's heart, Rhay gripped the arms of his chair, his vision strangely blurry.

To hell with his cover. He couldn't let him die. Rhay was about to stand when a voice drifted into the dining hall, pounding against Rhay's skull.

"*Enough,*" Tarnan yelled. All the guards went limp, zapped out of their trance.

Rhay met Lora's gaze. She had rushed in before Tarnan, anger and disappointment swirling in her stormy turquoise eyes. Unlike everyone else, Rhay was still in perfect condition, his clothes free of blood stains. What must she think of him?

"I wanted to have a nice and peaceful contest dinner, but you all seem set on twisting my hand. Now that you have all seen what I am capable of, would you please enjoy the dinner my cooks have spent hours preparing?"

In silence, everyone who wasn't injured went back to their seats, except Kaylanthea, who rushed to her husband's side, pressing on his wound with her shawl. Tarnan walked up to them as Yasir wallowed in pain, his breathing erratic.

"Saydren, please take care of Yasir. I wouldn't want him to miss the contest."

With an obedient bow, Saydren stood up and gestured to two Carnylen guards to carry the Quarnian king out the room.

"Do not touch him," Kaylanthea yelled at Tarnan.

Tarnan put his hand on Kaylanthea's shaking shoulder. "Saydren will heal him. He shall be back on his feet in no time."

As much as Tarnan tried to infuse his words with warmth, Rhay could only hear the ice slithering underneath. Kaylanthea shrugged off his hand, while her own went to the dagger strapped to her side. In one swift motion, the dagger was at Tarnan's throat. "I said let go of my husband. We'll never join you."

Rhay's grip on the armchair tightened, thinking of Amira's link to Tarnan. He sprang to his feet, his head spinning. He hadn't even had one sip of alcohol today.

"If you wish." Tarnan gestured to the guards to let go of Yasir's body. Kaylanthea released her hold on Tarnan to drop down next to her husband. She put her hand on his damp forehead.

"I wouldn't want him to suffer." Tarnan turned to a Quarnian guard. *"Finish him."*

Instantly, Kaylanthea threw water at the guard, pushing him away from her husband. The floor flooded with her anger.

"Don't move," Tarnan ordered her.

Kaylanthea's forehead creased like she was trying to fight off the compulsion. But it was too strong. She was unable to move while a guard plunged his sword into Yasir's heart before anyone could intervene. The light left his eyes fast and Kaylanthea could only watch. Lora rushed forward, but a guard grabbed her arm.

Kaede stormed towards Tarnan, her dagger raised. She got side-tracked by a Carnylen guard. Whispers spread amongst the other kings, and Wryen once again attempted to flee. As the compulsion lifted, Kaylanthea clutched her husband's body against hers, a burning anger in her eyes. The water flooding the floor rose with each furious breath, but one of Tarnan's guards threw an almandine dagger straight through Kaylanthea's hand. The water slowed as Kaylanthea bit back a yelp, eyes focused on her husband.

"I see you have learned nothing. Then so be it. *Guards, attack your own court. Make sure Lora, Kaylanthea, and Nouis live."* Tarnan's voice chilled Rhay to the bone, his mouth dry. Rhay locked eyes on Lora, who was fighting against a Turosian guard with a burning dagger. He wanted nothing more than to fight alongside her. But could he truly blow his cover when he hadn't accomplished anything?

Aware of a presence by his side, Rhay raised his sword, ready to fight off a guard, but he was met with his father's disappointed gaze.

"How come I'm protected by Tarnan? I haven't betrayed my kingdom like you." His father's words dug deep into his aching heart.

"Karwyn is gone. Haven't you taught me to be the advisor of the future high king? Isn't that why you switched from Kaede to Harten back in the day?" Around them, the fight kept going, but Rhay was focused on his father, his head buzzing.

"That had nothing to do with it, you know very well why we moved to Turosian."

"If Tarnan was to offer you a position as head advisor right now, wouldn't you take it?"

Nouis huffed. "Stop it, Rhay. First you can barely manage to be an advisor and then you go and side with the king who murdered *your* king. You never fail to disappoint me."

Rhay took a deep breath, fighting back the tears gathering in his burning eyes. Karwyn was alive, the thought should lighten his heart. *But I did betray him.*

Rhay couldn't count how many times his father had told him he was useless, a disappointment. He met his father's gaze. "You've never given me any reason to care what you think. Be honest, you probably wish I was never born. Then you wouldn't have to deal with me."

His father froze, a vein on his forehead pulsating. Lora's scream saved him from replying. Four guards dragged her towards Tarnan, who had a scroll of paper in his hand. Rhay and his father exchanged one long look before rushing to Lora's side, his father falling behind.

"What's going on?" Rhay asked, his tone forcefully light. He put a hand to his own scorching forehead, swaying on his feet. His head was spinning.

"Lora and I are about to enter an agreement. She will bring me the amulet Eyden stole from me." Tarnan pricked his finger and signed the contract.

Lora thrashed against the guards holding her.

"I gave you a chance to make a deal, you should have taken it." Tarnan held out the pen. "Think of the consequences."

Lora's desperate gaze met Rhay's as she tried to escape the guards' hold. She was running out of time. Rhay had to think fast; he couldn't let Lora reveal she was immune to Tarnan's power.

Tarnan pinned her with his blood-red eyes. "*Lora—*"

Rhay grabbed the contract from Tarnan's hand and tore it in half.

Tarnan narrowed his eyes at Rhay.

"You chose to break your promise, Rhay. So I shall break mine as well." He pointed at the one person Rhay thought was safe. "*Kill your father.*"

Rhay almost laughed in Tarnan's face. He wouldn't succumb to his compulsion. Yet, he felt himself raise his almandine sword as if his arm was no longer his to command. His head was fuzzy. His throat was as dry as a desert. His head pounded as he tried to shake the command taking over his whole body. Why wasn't he able to fight it? Meeting his father's gaze, his eyes widened as they both came to the same realisation.

Faster than Rhay could fight off the compulsion twisting his insides, he plunged his sword into his father's heart. Blood sprayed Rhay as he pulled out the sword, coming back to himself. His father's eyes, ocean blue like Rhay's, went dark as he fell to his knees.

Rhay didn't recognise the look in his father's eyes, not disappointment or annoyance. It reminded Rhay of how his father had been before Rhay's mother had passed. The lingering dissatisfaction disappeared and was replaced by *regret*. Rhay could see all the time they had missed out on since his mother's passing. So many arguments, so much disdain. It all seemed pointless now.

A scream escaped Rhay's mouth as he fully realised what he'd done. Rhay dropped to his knees at his father's side. He was only half aware of Lora using the commotion to stun the guards. She pushed Tarnan back with her fire, trapping him in smoke so he couldn't see where to direct his orders. Tarnan tried to cross the fire, burning his arm in the process.

Cupping his father's face, Rhay saw the light dwindle in his eyes. "Father, please, hold on. I'm sorry, I'm so sorry."

His father stroked his cheek. "You look so much like her," Nouis whispered faintly, blood running from the corner of his mouth, staining his teeth. "You have my eyes, but everything else is her. I...I will be with her. You are...my biggest regret. I wish....I had been there..." His eyelids fluttered.

"Please don't go." Clutching his father's hand, Rhay tried to take his pain as he'd done with Karwyn. No matter how broken his relationship with his father was, Rhay couldn't lose him. He was the last family he had left. This was his fault. It was *always* his fault. His father had died by his own hand. How could he live with that?

His father closed his eyes as his lifeless hand slipped from Rhay's cheek. His breathing stopped and so did Rhay's. The room spun around him. Everything turned hazy. *This couldn't be happening.* How cruel that the words he had longed for his father to say all his life were now his final words?

A hand gently touched his shoulder, calling him back to the chaos happening around him. Screams and the clashing of swords infiltrated his ears.

"We have to go. Eyden will come get us," Lora said, removing a piece of paper from her pocket and setting it aflame.

"We?" Rhay repeated, barely processing the word. Could it be that she didn't hate him completely?

"Don't make me regret this. We have to go before Tarnan forces me into an agreement."

"I can't leave him," Rhay pleaded, an ever-growing knot in his throat. He knew he couldn't stay a minute longer with Tarnan.

"We'll take him with us." Lora set her jaw as she took in his father's lifeless body. They waited for a minute, Lora maintaining the fire around Tarnan. But nothing happened.

Lora turned her terrified gaze to Rhay. He struggled to piece things together in his mind. She had sent a fire message, but Eyden wasn't coming. Had something happened to him? Were they stuck here?

"*Lora,*" Tarnan's commanding voice rippled through the room, preparing another compulsion as the fire died down around him. "*Stab Rhay.*"

Rhay couldn't tear his gaze away from Tarnan's blood-red eyes.

No rescue was coming to save him from his latest mistakes. He had betrayed him, and now the king was out for his blood.

CHAPTER 41

AMIRA

Anger and fear battled in Amira's heart as she slipped off her horse and tied it to a tree. She sneaked towards the edge of the woods quietly, and when she reached Raven's Nest, it was fear that won. The dim light of dusk shone down on Elyssa, locked in combat against four armed fae. A dead fae lay next to her on the grass. What kind of trouble had Elyssa gotten herself into?

When she drew closer, Amira almost didn't recognise Elyssa. Blood smeared her cheeks. Her left arm was bleeding heavily, and her hands and face were all scraped up. Yet Elyssa smiled through blood-stained teeth, gesturing for the fae nearest to her to come at her. She didn't seem the least bit bothered that she had run out of arrows. She dodged a fae woman's sword while throwing her leg out to trip another attacker. A third fae, his brow split, kicked Elyssa in the stomach, but her sick smile didn't falter as she punched him in the face. The scarred fae yelled and it only seemed to increase whatever mad rage Elyssa was lost in.

Amira threw a violent gust of air at the fae woman threatening Elyssa. Elyssa finally hesitated, glancing over her shoulder, and Amira locked eyes with her. The rage she saw in her lover's eyes took her aback. Amira almost tripped over her feet before running forward.

She used her power to throw a heavy stone against a scarily tall fae, knocking him out. Elyssa rushed forward, striking a platinum-blond fae with an almandine dagger she'd stolen from one of the fallen

311

attackers. She managed to drive it into his heart, but the blond landed a blow to her as well, plunging his long knife into her already bleeding arm. She didn't even flinch at the concerning amount of blood soaking her sleeve.

The fae woman stumbled back on her feet and tried to run away, but she didn't get far. Elyssa's throwing star impaled itself in the back of her head and the woman fell face-first to the ground. Amira took care of the last fae standing, throwing him against a tree to knock him unconscious.

"El, let's go," Amira pleaded. But Elyssa's gaze was locked on the fae woman who was attempting to crawl away. Elyssa walked up to her and pulled her head back by her hair, taking the throwing star that was still embedded in her skull.

Running towards Elyssa, Amira, yelled, "Elyssa, stop, we have to go."

Elyssa turned her head, a vengeful look in her eyes that chilled Amira's bones. "She has to be stopped or she'll hurt the others. I can't make the same mistake again." Her voice was strangled, like she was barely able to keep it from rising.

The fae woman's eyes bulged out of her head. "Please, let me go." She tried to stand up, but Elyssa pushed her head down into the grass.

"It's too late." Before Amira could stop her, Elyssa cut the woman's throat, blood spraying them both. Unbothered by the fresh blood on her cheeks and neck, Elyssa let go of the woman. Elyssa twirled her dagger in her hand and plunged it into the fae's heart.

A commotion nearby made Amira whirl around. More fae rushed out of the inn, witnessing the bloodbath. Amira grabbed Elyssa's less damaged arm and forced her up. Turning her head in the direction of the inn, Elyssa's deadly gaze locked on the swarm of fae heading their way. It had to be at least ten more. She took a step towards them, her fist clenched, blood running down her arm and staining the grass red.

"We have to go," Amira whisper-yelled, anger building in her chest.

"They could be traffickers," Elyssa argued through her teeth, ready to get herself killed.

All of a sudden, a sharp pain burned Amira's arm. Hissing, she stumbled as she clutched her arm. Elyssa's gaze snapped to hers, her fiery rage subdued with concern as she seemed to come out of a trance.

"Did they hurt you?" Elyssa asked, taking her hand.

Pushing up her sleeve, Amira revealed blistered skin, hot to the touch. The sickening smell of burnt flesh infiltrated her nose, bringing tears to her eyes.

"Tarnan," she gasped. There was no other explanation. Had Lora been forced to fight him? One of the fae from the inn was almost upon them, his hand on his sword handle. "We have to go. We're injured and outnumbered."

Before they had time to run, the fae threw his dagger at her. She lifted her arm to deflect but her burn wound stung harshly, the pain so sudden it threw her magic off. The dagger embedded itself in her thigh. Pain shot through her leg and she swayed on her feet. Elyssa caught her before she could fall.

A dark light ignited in Elyssa's eyes and Amira knew in that moment that Elyssa would lose herself in this fight. With a painful yell, Amira focused her leftover energy and pushed the fae back. More of them stormed forward, helping him up, throwing murderous glances their way.

Elyssa took a step forward, ready to continue the fight. Plucking the dagger from her thigh, hissing between her teeth, Amira grabbed Elyssa more forcefully. "Let's go, *now*."

Elyssa let herself be pulled away. Amira's chest constricted, each breath a dagger to her heart. They ran into the forest, fae yelling behind them.

It was only when no footsteps echoed behind them and they reached the safety of the woods—the spot where Amira had tied her horse—that Amira let her fury rain on Elyssa, her wounds forgotten. "What in Liraen were you thinking? It was five against one! And who knows how many more would have come after us?"

Elyssa shrugged, glancing over her shoulder at the path they'd taken as if considering going back. "We won, didn't we?" How could Elyssa be so cold, so detached from the violence she had just unleashed? "Those sick fucks captured humans. I had to help. Why are you arguing with me? We should be going back."

"You could have gotten yourself killed!" Amira's voice shook. "You're barely standing now." This was exactly what Amira had been afraid of. She had failed Farren, had failed Elyssa. She was going to lose Elyssa too and she would be partly at fault.

Elyssa twirled her dagger. "I'm still here, aren't I, sunshine?"

Amira barely contained the anger in her voice. "Where were the humans? I didn't even see them."

Elyssa's eyes flashed. "They ran away. I didn't see Jaspen. I bet he's hiding. But I'll find him. If it's the last fucking thing I do—"

"Do you even hear yourself?" Amira cut in. "You're recklessly risking your life. I could have lost you!" The thought of losing her stole her breath.

Elyssa took a step towards her. "I *had to* fight, I had to stop them from hurting more people. You've always known I'm reckless."

Amira looked at her, at the blood and grime on her, at her arm that looked almost split in two. "I've known you to be recklessly brave." She tilted her chin to where they'd come from. "That wasn't brave. That was a *suicide mission.*" Tears built in her eyes but Amira forced them back, swallowing the feeling of soot sticking to her throat. "No, what you *had to* do was go with me to Allamyst. I needed you with me. I promised you I'd wait for you and I did. *You* didn't show. My mother could already be dead by the time we reach her."

Amira's voice cracked. She didn't even know who she was mad at more, herself for leading Elyssa down this path or Elyssa for choosing revenge over helping Amira. Would they make it in time, or would Amira fail to save another person she loved?

"I..." Elyssa hesitated. "I couldn't let Jaspen get away. He betrayed us to fucking Saydren, and Tarnan is one step ahead of us—like he is every fucking time!" Her voice broke, and she clenched her teeth so hard Amira heard them grind together. "First Farren, now the camp. If I don't stop them, then what is the point? Why the fuck am I here if not to fight with everything I got so his death is somehow worth something?"

Her words were a punch to Amira's gut. Her worry had overshadowed Ian's quick recap of the camp's destruction. Once again, Tarnan had chosen to hurt the one she cared about. Amira could only imagine the horrors he would put the humans through.

Amira moved forward, taking Elyssa's bloodied hand in hers. Her heart broke at Elyssa's words. If only Amira could have saved Farren, could have saved Elyssa from this endless pain. She could imagine how hurt Elyssa must have been after finding the rebel camp in shambles. Letting her tears flow, she squeezed Elyssa's hand. "It's not just the people who have been ripped away from us who need you, El. The people who are still here—I—need you. If you die, that's not vengeance. Farren wouldn't want that. We save each other, remember?"

Amira's words finally seemed to make their way into Elyssa's heart. The blazing fury in her eyes subdued, replaced by pure sadness. "I feel like I'm running toward a cliff." Elyssa took their joined hands and pressed them against her heart. "I always thought that maybe, maybe if I run fast enough, I'll *fly*. But I was always headed for a steep fall." She inched closer, trapping their hands between them. "Unless I let someone catch me."

"I'll always catch you, El." Amira pulled Elyssa in a tight embrace, fighting against her anger, against the dread that she could be too late to save her mother. But she had to save Elyssa, and all hope wasn't lost yet. They had to make it in time. She inhaled the sweet pine scent coming from Elyssa's hair, beneath the metallic smell of blood.

"I'm sorry. I should've been there for you," Elyssa whispered, holding her tighter. "And Eyden is probably furious—"

"We have to hurry back; the palace had gone to hell when I left." Amira pulled back and watched Elyssa's face fall, an ember of that rage rekindling, but not enough to burn all her common sense away.

Elyssa tilted her head at the horse. "Let's go."

This time, Amira saw no trace of the coldness that had animated

Elyssa earlier. She was her Elyssa again, fierce and furious but rooted in nothing but good intentions.

CHAPTER 42

LORA

Lora whirled around, her gaze connecting with Rhay. If she didn't stab him, her ability to block Tarnan's compulsion would be outed. Rhay's gaze was utterly hollow as he subtly tilted his head as if granting her permission. He really had been playing double agent, hadn't he? It didn't matter now—they needed to survive.

Gritting her teeth, Lora rushed at him, dagger aimed at his shoulder. Rhay stumbled backwards against the window as the dagger sank into his skin.

Refusing to dwell on it, Lora turned back to the guards heading their way. There were too many guards cramped in the room and everyone was compelled to attack. Aiming at the guards, Lora commanded her flames to grow again, drawing a fiery path to close her and Rhay off from them. Tarnan stared at her through the fire, not at all fazed. He knew she'd burn out eventually and she was trapped. His next command would only be worse.

"We're not done here, Lora," Tarnan yelled. His voice cut out as Lora raised her fire, the crackling flames mixing with the clashing of weapons.

He wouldn't stop until he got her to agree to bring the amulet.

Rhay met her panicked gaze as he pressed on his blood-drenched shoulder. His gaze swung to the high window behind them. "Let's jump." His voice was pained, his stance uneven.

Lora's lips parted, her focus almost slipping as she forced her fire on. She leaned closer to the window. They were on the third floor. There was nothing but hard stone awaiting them below.

"We can make it. You can use air to soften the blow. I've seen Karwyn do it once." Rhay looked over her shoulder where a guard was now stepping through the fire, patting at his uniform to smother the flames. Rhay ducked to avoid the swing of his sword, then weakly kicked at the guard's legs. Lora commanded her fire to take him, increasing the flames, and the guard screamed. Sweat coated her skin. If she kept this up, she would use up too much power that she might need later.

"Trust me, it'll work." Rhay's face was ashen as he waited for Lora's signal.

She didn't trust him, but she did need to get away. Her gaze drifted to Nouis' body on the ground. "We can't take him."

Rhay's face fell, but he grabbed a lamp next to them and Lora barely had a second to shield her face before Rhay shattered the window. Glass sprayed everywhere. A few pieces rained down on Nouis' body as if burying him.

"He would understand. For the crown," Rhay said. Still, he stared at his father's body as if he couldn't survive parting with him.

"*Lora!*" Tarnan's voice drifted to her as the noise around them calmed down. "*I command you—*"

Grabbing Rhay's bloody hand, Lora turned and jumped through the shattered window. Shouts chased them into the air, but all she could focus on was the chilly wind blowing her hair out of her face as the ground came towards them at lightning speed.

Fuck. They were going to break all their bones unless she stopped it.

Her yell drowned out by the wind, Lora imagined air coming at them from the hard stone ground. Just before she hit the ground, her legs lifted as the air enveloped them. She stopped in mid-air, her body stiff as a board, hovering horizontally barely two inches from the ground. Her nose almost grazed the sandy-brown stone beneath them. She lifted her hands to drop to the ground gently. Rhay grunted next to her, not fast enough to break his fall.

Sitting up, Rhay clutched his nose. It was bleeding, probably broken. A yell drew her attention back to the broken window. Guards pointed at them from above. They were at the back of the palace. Further off, Lora could spy a beautiful garden, but here there was just stone, the area almost empty.

Lora sprang to her feet, looking every which way. Horses. A carriage. She needed something. Her gaze landed on a hot air balloon—a skyaelo, as fae called it—not far from them around the corner. It sported green and bronze stripes, the colours of the Emerlane kingdom. Lora had never ridden one, but she had air magic.

"Come on," Lora shouted at Rhay, who followed her gaze, his eyes wide. Then he shrugged as if to say 'why not.'

Lora almost slipped on the smooth stone under her feet as she looked back at the palace. Guards stormed out a back door.

As they reached the skyaelo, Lora gripped the edge and pulled herself into the basket. Rhay followed, his bloody hand leaving a handprint on the side. He detached the weights holding it down, then pointed above them. "Light it up, love."

A flame flared in Lora's palm and she aimed at the burner. The balloon started rising. She willed the air to lift them higher. Rhay held onto the railing as the skyaelo dipped dangerously to the left.

Lora glanced over the edge. Below, the guards looked like ants. They were getting away. She let out a slow breath and the skyaelo dropped a bit. Her palms grew sweaty as she focused on keeping it straight.

"That way." Rhay pointed in the direction of Turosian. His hair was wind-blown, dried blood on his nose and upper lip. He looked like a mess. He *was* a mess.

"Lora," Rhay started, and she detailed his face. His lips pressed together as he ran a hand through his dark hair, making it stick up in all directions, stiff with drying blood. He gripped his shoulder in a hiss of pain. "I just wanted to say—"

"No." Lora held up her hand. She wanted to slap him for what he had done, but he looked so utterly lost. He was already doing a good job of punishing himself all on his own. And Nouis... "I can't do this right now, Rhay. I'm sorry for your loss, I really am, and I want you to know you're not to blame for his death. But I can't forgive you for handing over the agreement right now. I don't know if I ever will."

His ocean eyes dimmed as he dropped his head. "I know you hate me right now, but can I at least explain myself?" A tear escaped his eye and Rhay quickly swept it away.

Lora's grip on the railing tightened painfully. She'd given Rhay so many chances. She'd wanted for him to find himself. And he had thanked her by going behind her back. "Nothing you can say will make it okay."

Rhay's tone turned pleading. "Can I try? *Please.*"

Sighing, Lora crossed her arms. "It's not like I can go anywhere."

Rhay straightened the collar of his shirt. "I did it because Tarnan would've figured out too quickly that the contract was fake. This way, I could actually be useful—"

"What exactly is it that you helped with? Besides risking all of our secrets."

Rhay looked like she'd slapped him. "I didn't reveal anything. And I...I found out Saydren has a drug that can turn humans into fae. It's how Karwyn survived, apparently."

Lora shivered. A drug like that could only stem from dark magic.

Shaking her head, Lora stepped back, avoiding Rhay's pained eyes. "That's not worth the risk you took. You endangered every human's life —innocents who shouldn't be caught up in this war."

"*We* shouldn't be caught up in this either," Rhay muttered. "But we are. And I chose to do something about it this time. Doesn't that count for something?"

"It's not about doing *something*, it's about doing the *right* thing. Breaking your word is not right. Taking a risk no one asked for is not right. It's selfish. You wanted to prove yourself no matter the cost." She turned her back to him. They stayed silent for a moment. She wondered if she had misjudged him completely. Could he ever be the version of himself that she had hoped he would choose to be?

"I..." Rhay said, and Lora spun around, holding up a hand. He looked broken, beaten down. She felt for him, for his loss, but none of it changed what he'd done. None of it made it right.

"I have to focus." She turned away from him.

CHAPTER 43

EYDEN

Getting Lora's signal and not being able to get her had torn at Eyden for hours. He'd used his supercharged powers to drift Maja, Oscar, and Ian to safety and then he'd used up even more energy in the fight. Drifting as far as Carnylen or Rubien was out of the question.

He'd lost too many people. Lora couldn't be one of them. He'd been ready to get on a horse when his palm had burned and he had read Lora's second message saying she'd be back in a few hours and he shouldn't worry.

In the meantime, he, Ilario, Elyssa, and Amira had tried their best to do damage control. The palace floors were painted in blood. They had burned the bodies, but the stench of death lingered in the halls. Eyden had wanted to talk with his sister, but there had been no time. Damir had said the former guards must have been able to break in because the protection spell around the palace didn't apply to them and they hadn't fixed that issue beforehand. Amira had since rectified that mistake, placing a new protective ward over the palace walls.

"Any sign?" Ilario asked as he walked up to Eyden outside the palace by the once again locked gates.

Eyden turned his head to the pathway leading to the gate, but he could only see the shadows of the trees lining the road in the night. The icy wind whipped a lock of hair across his forehead. At least it wasn't as cold here as it had been back on Earth.

"Nothing yet." Eyden shifted his feet on the grass. "Are you sure you got this?"

Ilario hesitated. "Yes."

"We could wait and go to Rubien tomorrow."

"No," Ilario replied, more sure this time. "You need to go now before Tarnan thinks of going after Lozlan himself. I can handle the palace. And I'll ask Halie to check on Maja and Oscar. They can stay at yours until you're back, just in case."

"Keep an eye on Damir."

Ilario huffed. "I can't believe he's so..."

"Violent?"

"*Different.*" He turned his head to the starry sky. Some ashes from their mass cremation still drifted through the air—tragedy mixing with the beautiful, peaceful night sky. "When I look at him, I see nothing of the person I used to know."

"You'll find someone better. Someone kind. Not Rhay—"

"Look," Ilario interrupted.

"I mean it. Rhay is gonna end up just like Damir. You—"

"No, I mean, look up." Ilario pointed upwards.

"Is that a skyaelo?" Elyssa asked as she and Amira joined them at the gate. They'd cleaned up. Elyssa's arm was bandaged, as was Amira's. His sister had multiple cuts on her face, but they didn't seem to faze her. He wanted to know what in Liraen happened, but he could guess most of it. She hadn't found Jaspen, but she'd been itching for a fight and that was what she'd gotten. He was glad Amira had been there to pull her back from the ledge. He would have never forgiven himself if Elyssa had gotten herself badly hurt—or worse.

Eyden turned his head up. It did look like a skyaelo, a shadow against the sky with a spark of fire at its centre. Was Tarnan coming to attack? Eyden reached for his dagger when a voice called down.

"Don't shoot," Lora yelled, her words barely audible over the wind.

The skyaelo drifted down not so gracefully. He glimpsed Lora leaning over the railing, her dark blonde hair illuminated by the burner in the centre of the balloon.

"How in Liraen?" Ilario muttered next to him, squinting as he looked up.

Then Rhay appeared next to Lora, looking over the railing. His gaze zeroed in on Ilario, who took a startled breath.

"Come down," Eyden yelled up at her. It felt like he could breathe again after hearing her voice.

The skyaelo went back and forth in a zig-zag. "Actually, can you come up here? I'm not sure I won't break this thing if I try to land, and what's a quicker way to Rubien than this?" She turned to Rhay, her words lost to the wind. Then she yelled, "Drift Rhay down. He's going to Allamyst."

Elyssa shook her head wildly. "No fucking way."

Amira looked torn.

Eyden turned back to Elyssa, who gestured for him to go. They'd have to talk later. He trusted Elyssa to remember where the line was. He knew she had Amira to remind her should her anger blind her again.

Focusing on Lora, Eyden willed the air to carry him through the space between them. He swam in nothingness for a second before his feet hit the tilting ground and he tripped. The balloon tipped sideways and Lora cursed. She threw out her hand and a gust of wind straightened them.

Leaning up on his elbows, Eyden grinned at her. "This might be your craziest idea yet."

Lora held out her hand, pulling him to his feet. The balloon fell a step and they got knocked into each other, Eyden's hand going around her waist to pull her to his chest.

She tipped her chin up, looking right at him. "Hi. Are you okay? I'm guessing you can't drift us to Rubien?"

Eyden tilted his head. "Sort of and yes, you guessed right."

A wide smile stretched across her face. "You like my ride?"

"Oh, I do. Very impressive using your air magic like that."

"The burner thing does most of the job, thankfully," Lora explained, tilting her chin at the burning flame creating hot air. "We might crash in the middle of Rubien. You in?"

Heading into the cursed kingdom in a skyaelo—it was insane. She was insane. And he loved her for it. Eyden laughed.

Rhay coughed, reminding them of his presence, but Eyden ignored him. "When you're involved, always." Eyden drew closer, gently kissing her as his hand caressed her face. The flame of the burner danced in her eyes as he pulled back, the wicked light warming his heart and promising this wouldn't be the last crazy idea they'd pull off together.

The Void wasn't far now. Hours later, after drifting Rhay down before heading towards Rubien, the morning sun peeked through the grey clouds. Once Eyden had filled Lora in on the attack at the palace and the rebel camp, Lora had told him about the dinner. Lora hadn't seen any humans at the Carnylen palace, but knowing the agreement had been broken, they were both sure Tarnan must have them.

Eyden fought a yawn as he put a hand up to cover his mouth. They hadn't slept, fearing the skyaelo would fall. Yet, there was a buzzing in his veins as he thought of the Void, an urge to take it all down. But that wasn't the goal. He knew Lora was dreading it, but they had to find her father.

"How close should we get?" Lora asked, shielding her eyes from the sun.

A sharp sound cut through his reply. Then it came again, and this time Eyden caught sight of an arrow piercing the balloon.

Lurching towards the edge, Eyden peeked over the railing and noticed a group of fae pointing arrows up at them. Eyden ducked just in time as one flew at his head. He pulled at Lora's leg and she dropped to her knees as more arrows came their way.

"Who the hell is that?" Lora whispered even though no one would hear them up here.

"Probably traders thinking we're transporting goods they can steal."

The skyaelo was hit again, and they dropped so fast Eyden's heart felt like it was pushed to his lungs. Lora raised her hand with gritted teeth and it steadied. Eyden took in the balloon, tiny holes covering its fabric. Exhaustion was written all over Lora's face. If she kept this up, she would use up all her energy before they even entered the Void. But had Eyden recharged enough to drift them both?

Another arrow zipped through the air and the balloon dropped a few inches, tipping sharply to the left. Eyden willed his feet to stay planted on the tilting floor as he grabbed the bannister. A scream made him turn his head.

Lora slid across the floor to the tipped-over side, her body slipping over the bannister. Her hands grabbed the bannister, knuckles white.

"Hold on!" Eyden shouted, his voice desperate. He held on to the bannister as he made his way to Lora, downhill. An arrow almost hit his shoulder but he leaned out of the way, the skyaleo tipping with him.

"I can't hold on!" Lora screamed, her head barely visible over the bannister, her body in free air. A finger loosened, then another. Eyden slid towards her faster, afraid any movement could rattle Lora's weak hold.

He had almost reached her when an arrow shot towards them, scratching Lora's hand. Time slowed as Lora's hand slipped and she with it. Her wide eyes met his as she fell and Eyden rushed forward that same instant, reaching for her hand as he threw himself over the bannister with her.

There was only the wind—in his ears, tearing his clothes, pushing against his skin—as he fell. For a second he thought he'd lost her. But then his hand grazed Lora's and Eyden drew on his newly recharged power, pulling Lora with him. Lora's scream was cut off as the air around them changed and the free fall turned into wind pushing them the other way.

His back hit sand and he grunted, pain lacing his body. Lora fell on top of him and she scrambled back, bracing herself on the ground. They stayed motionless, trying to catch their breath. Eyden turned his head to make sure no one was in sight. He could spot the entrance to the Void further down the hill.

"Not your best landing, I must say," Lora joked as she sat back next to him, her breaths coming in quick, her body shaking.

Trying to distract her, Eyden said, "But the drifting out of free fall was impressive, admit it."

Lora grinned, the hot sun highlighting her blonde hair. "Maybe. But I jumped out of a window earlier and braced myself with air. So really, who's winning here?"

Eyden laughed, pulling himself up and brushing off sand. Taking Lora's hand, he helped her up. In this setting, her turquoise dress would not be the best for blending in, but at least even with a few dirt stains and a rip on the hem, it looked rich enough. They could pretend to be buyers while they searched for Lozlan.

"You still have your dagger?"

Lora's hand drifted to her thigh. "Ready whenever." Her gaze went to the Void and her easy smile evaporated. Lora took a deep breath, straightening her messy hair.

Keeping close to her, Eyden walked down the hill. The sun had turned scorching already but he kept his jacket on, a couple of knives hidden within its sleeves.

With feigned ease, they headed into the market. Traders were setting up for the day, placing items onto their tables, writing the deals of the day on chalkboards.

He felt Lora tense as they spotted a table with glass jars full of silver-red pills. *Fortae.* The trader behind the booth stared at them a second too long for his comfort. Taking the same path as last time, through the market towards a less busy alley, he hoped they would find Lozlan there. But the more they walked, the more eyes Eyden felt on them. Every trader seemed too interested in them, their eyes lingering on them with each step. Was it the dress? Or did they recognise Lora as the queen or princess?

As he scanned the market, his eyes set on posters plastered all over a wall. Wanted posters with "dead or alive" scrawled across the top, offering a big reward for any information about the fae's whereabouts.

Not anyone's. *Theirs.* Eyden and Lora's faces stared back at him.

Lora spotted the posters at the same time as he did. She went rigid next to him. She pulled at his sleeve, and Eyden turned from the posters to the trader behind the booth whispering with the fae next to him. They had recognised them.

Lora pulled at his jacket again. "Eyden..."

Dread was written all over her face. He turned his head to where she was staring.

An elegantly dressed fae in a suit almost as white as his hair stared back at them, coming out of an alley, a group of fae hurrying to match his determined stride.

"Eyden Kellen." The fae came to stand opposite him. "It's been a long time."

Rahmur Piers twirled a knife in his hand. Eyden had hoped never to see his face again. He had tricked Eyden into a game once, a gamble Eyden had lost. As a result he'd had to work for Rahmur, the fortae trader. The name drop had come in handy when Lora and Eyden had come here a few months ago to free Farren and some other humans who had been captured. But now it would bite them in the ass. In order to appear respectable, Eyden had lied and said he was there in Rahmur Piers' name. Kelvion, the blood trafficker they had run into, had realised they had lied and had attacked them.

"Not long enough." Eyden stepped in front of Lora. Out of the corner of his eye, he noticed every trader around watching them. They were surrounded. Should he drift them out? If he revealed his power, he would be hunted. Or would no one care now with Karwyn gone?

"Ah, all that contempt," Rahmur said, sighing. "And yet it was *my* name you used the last time you were here to sneak a deal. Bad for my reputation, I must say." He spun his knife with ease. "And Kelvion, such a shame, really; he was one of my best providers."

Rahmur took a step forward, his light green eyes setting on Lora, who had come to stand next to Eyden. "Although I heard it was *you* who took out Kelvion, my dear. I'm sure you understand my issue here. Nothing personal, but lines have to be drawn." He smiled cruelly at Eyden. "I let you go once, Kellen; you should have appreciated my kindness. It has run out now. Such a waste of talent, too."

"We can pay you," Lora offered, but Eyden knew Rahmur wasn't after silver. An eye for an eye. And in this case, only their deaths would do.

Rahmur chuckled as he straightened his jacket. "Sorry, dear. It's the principle." He tilted his chin at them. "Get the girl. Kellen's my kill."

CHAPTER 44

🔥

AMIRA

It felt unreal to be heading back to Allamyst. Not even four months had passed since Amira had left her home kingdom and yet it felt like a lifetime ago.

Elyssa stared down Rhay across from her in the small carriage. "We should have thrown him out."

He had kept silent for most of the day-long journey. They had all needed sleep, and now the first rays of the morning sun streamed in through the window. Rhay had explained himself briefly, telling them there shouldn't have been a way to break the slave agreement. But there had been. He couldn't have known Karwyn was still alive and he'd thought he could gather intel.

"I bet Tarnan has already forced everyone at the rebel camp into a contract by now," Elyssa growled.

Rhay breathed in sharply. "I thought the camp was hidden?"

"Not anymore," she bit out. "And if you hadn't gone on your solo mission, Farren might still be alive."

Amira looked between them. Even though she was furious at Rhay too, there was something off about him that made her more worried than angry. No matter how much he had messed up, she couldn't help but care about him.

"We both know Farren wasn't his fault," Amira reasoned as her own guilt crushed her heart. Part of her wished Elyssa was somewhere safe instead of here with her. Anywhere away from her would be safer, wouldn't it?

Elyssa's leg bounced as she turned to Rhay. "There's plenty else to blame him for."

Sighing, Amira leaned back in her seat. "It's too late now, anyway. Rhay is here so he might as well help. And you're injured, El. There is strength in numbers."

Elyssa's arm had been bandaged up. The cuts and bruises on her face and neck were still fresh. Sahalie had given Amira a paste for her burn wound, which was itching underneath the bandage. Thankfully, the wound on her thigh wasn't too deep.

Elyssa pointed at Rhay. "He's also injured."

Rhay sank back, lightly touching his broken nose that was already healing. They hadn't had time to bandage his shoulder, but Amira had handed him a scarf to wrap around the stab wound.

"It's nothing, not like..." He choked back a sob. "I can help negotiate. I was at the contest dinner with Wryen. He knows who Tarnan is now." A shadow passed in his eyes. Amira had no idea what exactly had happened during the contest dinner. "And I'm sorry about Farren. I had no idea he was..." Rhay broke off when he met Elyssa's dark gaze. His hand shook as he pushed back his bloodied hair.

Amira sighed. "At the very least you will be a helpful distraction."

Elyssa rolled her eyes while Rhay hung his head, turning away.

As the carriage moved across the charming streets of Amryne, the capital city of Allamyst, Amira took in the sights of the colourful houses in the morning light, each one more beautiful than the last. The Allamyst fae took great pride in their stunning houses. They were a mix of different aesthetics, but they all combined pleasantly to the eye. Some had pretty ivy-wrapped pillars supporting high balconies with flowers cascading down the railings. Another house was built with stunning stained-glass windows and pastel-coloured wood panels. When she used to visit the city in disguise with her father, Amira would stop for hours to marvel at the houses.

Shifting on the bench next to her, Elyssa opened the window, letting the sound of the bustling city enter the carriage. Her brows furrowed as she tried to make out the distant sound. "Is there music playing?"

"Most of the people in Allamyst know how to play an instrument. There is always music playing in the streets."

"That's beautiful." Elyssa planted a soft kiss on Amira's lips that Amira didn't have the strength to dodge.

She was relieved to see Elyssa more like herself again. But a lingering feeling wrapped around her heart, making it hard to breathe. How long would it last until doom would fall upon them once more? Wasn't she destined to ruin any happiness she had? Amira pulled herself away from Elyssa, who frowned.

Rhay cleared his throat, turning to the window. "I think we're here."

The carriage stopped abruptly. Amira took a deep breath. Elyssa reached out, grabbing her hand. Amira knew her brother must already be back, as he most likely travelled by skyaelo. Their original plan had been to sneak in while he was away at the contest dinner, but Elyssa's fight and the uprising at the palace had slowed them down. And the chaos at the contest must have sped up Wryen's departure.

As they got out of the carriage, a guard approached them. "Princess Amira, welcome home." He bowed deeply and signaled for the other guards to open the gate.

The Amrync palace was the most impressive building in all the kingdoms. The burgundy tiled roofs were embellished with gold accents, the stone walls ornamented with colourful sculpted flowers. Two high towers framed the entrance and every window was lined with gold. Each stained-glass window was its own unique design.

Rhay barely glanced at the palace as he headed inside, but Elyssa stood still, taking it in, a strange light in her now golden eyes. They had decided it would be safer for Elyssa to wear spelled contact lenses again. Eyden had found some and Amira had managed to spell them on the way here with the help of Farren's spellbooks. When she wasn't sleeping, Amira had spent the carriage ride studying magic.

Once inside, Amira had to force herself to not stop and stare at what Wryen had done to the place. In her father's time, the Amryne palace had been filled with the most incredible pieces of art, commissioned from a wide array of artists. Now, every painting and sculpture showed Wryen in all his "glory."

Amira felt Elyssa's hand on her shoulder. "Come on, sunshine. He'll get what he deserves soon enough."

Amira led Elyssa and Rhay to the throne room. Sure enough, her brother was there, lounging on the throne, being fed a peach by a servant. He straightened when they entered the room, juice from the peach dripping from his chin onto his indigo velvet shirt.

"Excuse us," Wryen told the servant and guards present. He threw his dirty handkerchief at the servant, who barely managed to catch it before they left. Wryen sat up straight, a grin on his face. "Dear sister, I was anticipating your visit earlier. Then again, I also expected you to come with me instead of choosing to stay with Tarnan. I suppose even you have grown tired of your mother." He turned to Elyssa and Rhay, a cruel smile parting his lips. "And I see you've brought your bitch of a maid. You've always had a thing for the help. And Rhay? That's a surprise. After Karwyn and Tarnan, you've picked my little sister as your new master? You really know how to pick them."

Amira ground her teeth. "We're not here to listen to you spit your venom. Where is my mother?"

Wryen lit up his hand, watching the fire with glee. "Don't worry, little sister, I'm taking great care of her."

Power rose within her, ready to strike. "I'm only going to ask one more time. Where is she?"

Wryen laughed. "What makes you think I would ever tell you? I'm glad you're here. I won't have to go through the trouble of getting you back myself. I've added a few more locks to your bedroom door, so you'll feel right at home."

"You're not gonna tell us?" Elyssa asked, a deadly glint in her eyes.

Wryen didn't flinch from Elyssa's gaze. *His mistake.* "I won't spare you this time."

Rhay stepped forward. "Wryen, let's not escalate this. We're on the same side now, against Tarnan. You've seen what he is capable of. You need us to defeat him."

"It's *King* Wryen to you," Wryen snapped back. "And why should I trust you are against Tarnan? The last time I saw you, you stood by his side. Now, surrender or I'll have you and Elyssa executed."

An almandine throwing star struck Wryen's shoulder, taking him by surprise. "Next one goes in your eye," Elyssa threatened.

"Is that all you got?" Wryen sneered while removing the throwing star. Fire spread from his fingertips. "You have no leverage. You think the three of you will be enough to kill all of my guards? To take me on?" He turned to Amira, his fire growing. "My dearest sister, am I supposed to believe you are going to kill me when you've never been able to hurt a fly? And your poor mother..." He shook his head. "If I'm gone, she won't live much longer. A shame I wouldn't be able to watch her burn."

Amira's hands balled around the fabric of her loose trousers. Her power simmered under her skin. "Tell me what you've done to her."

"You can't force me. You can't do anything, little sister." Wryen's smile was sadistic, and Amira hated that the threat brought tears to her eyes. "You've always been useless. You couldn't even marry Karwyn, the one task you were fit for. Father would be so disappointed."

Rage boiling in her heart, Amira let her power out. The ground underneath Wryen shook, and he clutched his golden throne. "Shut up, Wryen!" He had undermined her for years, making her doubt her strength, her worth. *Not anymore.* "You underestimate how far I'd go for my mother, probably because you would never do the same for any-one but yourself. But I, *I* would ruin myself before I let you harm her. Unfortunately for you, I would ruin *you* right along with me."

Wryen narrowed his eyes. "What are you getting at?"

"How would you feel if I showed everyone who I truly am?" The high stained-glass windows rattled, and Wryen turned his head, his sly grin slipping. "What would they say about the king whose sister is a witch?"

"Never say that word again. I should've given you another beating!" He stood up from his throne, his lit-up hand pointed at Amira. She swallowed hard at the sight of the fire, remembering all the times he had used it to hurt her. Rhay and Elyssa moved at the same time, placing themselves in front of her. Elyssa threw an annoyed glance at Rhay.

"Too bad you'll never get the chance again, asshole," Elyssa said, meeting his gaze that had lost its cockiness.

"If I can't save my mother, I have nothing left here in Allamyst." Amira stepped to the front. His fire made her skin crawl, but she was no longer scared of him. "And if you're thinking of taking me out before I could reveal the truth, you should know Lora knows we're here. She'll happily ruin you if you touch any one of us."

Wryen grunted, his brows drawn together as if this was the biggest inconvenience of his life. Yet there was a hint of fear hidden in his gaze. He dropped his fire. "Fine. What do I care? Take your whore of a mother and leave Allamyst. She's in Rosleine."

"Where in Rosleine and why?" It was the town next to Amryne, but Amira had only visited it once with her father, the town too small to warrant frequent visits.

"I have another prison there. I don't like to advertise all my unruly people."

Elyssa lunged forward and grabbed Wryen's arm, twisting it behind his back. She put her throwing star against his neck, limiting his power with the almandine blade. Rhay raised his sword in a weak grip and pointed it at Wryen's chest to keep him from escaping Elyssa's hold.

"Tell us everything," Elyssa hissed in his ear. "And if you're lying, you'll be known as the ruined, *dead* king. Amira might not kill you, but I have no such qualms. The day you attacked us, I made a promise to myself that you would fucking regret that I ever entered your life." She pressed the blade closer, and a drop of blood appeared on Wryen's olive skin. Amira smiled at the impossible sight: her brother defeated, for once. "That day is today."

CHAPTER 45

LORA

"Can you drift us out of here?" Lora whispered, her lips barely moving as she scooted closer to Eyden. The group of fae behind Rahmur drew their weapons and headed their way. The traders walked around their booths to lock them into a circle.

Eyden's hand brushed hers. "I—"

An almandine dagger flew through the air, cutting off Eyden's words as he raised his hand just in time to stop the blade from hitting his head. It cut through the palm of his hand. The sharp edge glinted red in the sun. Eyden yanked at the blade. Ignoring the blood spilling from the wound, he reached for Lora again, but a fae was on him before he could. The fae aimed for his stomach and Eyden jumped back, his own dagger in his hand.

More fae stormed forward and Eyden engaged two of them. She could see in his gaze that he was about to drift to her, even if it revealed his power, when an arrow lodged itself in his back. He tried to grab it to get the almandine out of his skin, but he couldn't reach it. Lora wanted to run to him to help but a fae stepped in her path. Behind them, a sword cut through the air. Eyden stopped his effort to remove the arrow and ducked to the side. Raising his dagger, he dodged another arrow at the same time.

Lora unsheathed her dagger and it lit on fire. Dodging a fae's strike to the head, she cut his arm as he raised his fist. The fae snarled. As her blade clashed against his, someone else kicked her in the back and she staggered forward, tripping over her own feet.

Rolling quickly, she got up before anyone could pin her down. Two fae glared at her, sick smiles on their faces. She reached deep within to that part of herself she was starting to call her own. As the two fae charged, Lora swung her arms out and the wind forced them back, slamming them into the ground.

She turned her head to find Eyden surrounded, but only Rahmur interacted with him. His white suit had a blood stain on his thigh. Eyden's hand was bleeding and his shirt was ripped. The arrow still stuck out from his back, blood seeping through his shirt around the shaft.

More fae came her way, blocking her off from Eyden, and Lora stared at the burning dagger in her hand. It wouldn't be enough. She had to do more. She had to use it *all*.

Focusing on the faint buzzing in her veins, she threw her exhaustion to the side, balling her hands into fists before throwing her hand up, all her anger focused on Rahmur. The fae shot upwards and stayed suspended in the air.

Fae stared at her with a glimmer of fear and respect.

"Don't come closer or I'll drop your boss with such force there will be nothing left of him," Lora bluffed. She forced her hand to remain steady. She had been using her power so much today. Technically, it was a new day already as the morning sun stood high in the sky.

Walking forward slowly, she headed for Eyden, keeping an eye on everyone around them. Her chest heaved as she drew on her power, willing to keep it up. "Tell everyone to step back and let us go," she demanded.

Rahmur swung his hands in the air but stayed put. "I don't think so, dear."

Ignoring the dull ache in her veins, Lora forced his arms to his sides. "I won't ask again. Tell—"

A knife struck her arm and she lost her focus. Rahmur slammed to the ground, but not nearly hard enough to knock him out. He scrambled to his feet, dusting off his suit. Lora removed the knife from her skin, but she didn't duck fast enough as a fist came her way, catching her jaw. Someone twisted her arm as she saw stars and her dagger dropped. She kicked out furiously, hitting someone's stomach. Too many hands pulled her arms behind her back. The fae from before punched her stomach so hard she forgot how to breathe.

"Stop," Rahmur commanded, and Lora turned her gaze to him, wiggling in the fae's grip on her, but she could barely move. Eyden was detained as well, an almandine blade against his throat as three fae held him. "Let her watch him die."

Taking out a handkerchief, Rahmur cleaned his dagger. He stepped towards Eyden, the blade pointing at his heart. Lora struggled harder and her arms were pulled back so hard her shoulder popped. She tried to call on her power, but an almandine blade was pressed against her arm and her shoulder screamed in pain. Clenching her jaw, she bit back a yelp.

"This is how you'll kill me," Eyden said, his tone calm, "while your lackeys hold me down? You're a fucking coward."

Rahmur chuckled deeply. "You can't taunt me, Kellen. I'm a man of convenience. I know how to win and nothing is off limits. Do you know how I got you under my grip?"

Eyden didn't flinch, but even from this distance, Lora could tell he was tense. How would they get out of this one? She twisted her arms but the fae didn't budge. White hot pain spread across her left shoulder, forcing her to still. Every breath, every movement, was like tiny blades digging into her skin.

Eyden spoke slowly as if trying to come up with a plan. "You beat me in a poker game."

Rahmur glanced at the blade against Eyden's shirt, cutting a thin slash across his chest. As blood swelled, Eyden bit his lip.

"Yes, by making sure I couldn't lose."

"You cheated?" Eyden ground out, his tone genuinely surprised.

"Cheating is such an ugly word. I did what I had to do to succeed." Dragging the blade back to Eyden's heart, Rahmur pushed the edge into his flesh.

"No!" Lora screamed, trying to push past the burning flash of pain in her shoulder as she thrashed against the hands holding her back. "Don't. Please don't!"

Eyden's head turned her way. His eyes had never looked so dim, the striking pale blue nothing but a sea of misery. He couldn't drift with the almandine arrow in his back. The blade dug deeper, blood running down his chest. He shook his head at her as if to apologise, mouthing something she didn't understand. She saw "I love you" written in his eyes.

This couldn't be it. Eyden turned from her, and something heavy pulled her heart down until it sank to the pit of a black hole that only knew fear.

"Let her go. This is between you and me," Eyden gritted out, his lips pressed together as the dagger dug into his flesh. "I'll come work for you. I'll sign a blood contract. *Anything.*"

Rahmur paused.

"*No.* No, I'll give you silver. I can get you a fortune," Lora yelled. "I'm the q—"

"*Don't!*" Eyden shouted.

Rahmur laughed again. "Such enticing offers." He tilted his head at Eyden. "But really, I think this will be more satisfying."

Lora kicked and twisted, throwing her head back until it connected with someone's skull. She barely felt the sting and kept going, fighting with everything she had. Fear so primal took over and something shattered in her chest.

Rahmur struck, the blade digging deeper into Eyden's chest, and Lora felt everything around her slow down. A gut-wrenching scream left her lungs. Lava flooded her veins, her fear burning so bright within that something ripped open inside of her, and she couldn't—didn't want to—rein it in.

She moved her hands and found that she was free. She lifted her good arm to find it on fire as electricity shot through her system. She didn't feel her body, only fire.

Fire was all she saw.

Fire was all she was.

She was a living flame.

And she didn't hesitate.

Throwing out her arm, she aimed at Rahmur. Fire mixed with harsh wind hit him so hard he met the ground, his whole body swallowed by flames. The fae holding Eyden were next, going up in flames with a flick of her wrist. Eyden dropped to his knees, a hand on his chest as he stared at her with wonder in his eyes.

She headed his way, burning herself a path. When she was in front of him, she spotted her own eyes reflected back in his. They were glowing like a star, fire flickering within the brightest turquoise.

Someone came up behind her, but Lora threw her hand up and a circle of flames went around her and Eyden. The fire grew higher and higher, smoke engulfing them.

"We need to get out of here," Eyden said, but his voice felt so far away. She felt she couldn't respond, all her energy sucked away by the flames, tugging at her life source. As long as they burned, she would burn.

Eyden hissed as he got to his feet, his hand pressed to his chest wound. "Did you hear me? We have to go!"

Lora glanced at her fire. She wanted it to go higher. She wanted it *all* to burn. Every last stall. Every fortae pill. Every one of Rahmur's men. The whole market until it was nothing but an actual void. Nothing but ashes. Even if it burned her to ashes too.

The smoke around them increased, and out of the corner of her eye, Eyden covered his mouth with his sleeve, coughing.

"*Lora, please!*" Eyden touched her right shoulder, hissing in pain. "We have to get out now!"

Flames flickered in front of her. Smoke clung to her burning skin. What else was she supposed to do but burn? *Burn until there is nothing left.* The mantra repeated in her head over and over as the flames grew and spread out. She felt weightless. There was nothing and no one but her fire. A fire she controlled. Or did it control her? A sense of deja-vu hit her.

A weight struck her body and she was thrown through her fire wall.

She hit the ground hard, her left shoulder burning in a different sense as the flames died on her skin. Slowly, Lora came back to herself as she took in the flames clawing at the market, fae running away screaming, the fire having grown out of control. Burned corpses lay close by, the smell sickening.

Seeking Eyden, Lora turned her head, fear gripping her. He rolled on the ground, a flame dying on the back of his jacket. The arrow was gone—Lora didn't know when he had gotten it out. Coughing, he got to his feet, soot sticking to his skin, his jacket singed from the fire.

"We have to go," Eyden repeated.

Lora tried to stand but her legs wouldn't comply. As the adrenaline left her, the pain resurfaced, her left shoulder burning even without flames. It was torture. "I...I can't." Her body felt hollow, like ashes in the wind. She could feel her life source slipping away from her. If she had kept going...

Eyden cursed, his gaze drifting to the blood dripping down his chest. Gripping Lora's arm, he forced her up, but she stumbled. In his weakened state, he went to the ground with her. Staring up at the sky, Lora only saw smoke and flames, vibrant red mixing with dull grey. It had saved them, and now it would kill them both.

"I'm sorry," she whispered, turning her head to him. Her eyes drifted shut. Her body was a stone on the bottom of the ocean. She couldn't float to the surface. Her shoulder felt like it was trying to escape her body, stealing her breath.

"This isn't the end. You hear me?"

She forced her eyes open. Eyden pushed himself to a sitting position, his forehead wrinkling as he grunted in pain. If he could fight, so could she.

Forcing her limp muscles to move, Lora compelled herself upright, but her legs gave out. Eyden scooped her up, one hand on her good shoulder, one under her knees. She couldn't bite back the scream as her dislocated shoulder jostled from the movement.

"Stay with me, special one." He turned his head every which way, fire surrounding them. Everywhere she looked buildings were burning, fae rushing about before fire dragged them down. Broken glass crunched under Eyden's feet. If only he could drift. But he had to be injured too badly.

"This way!" someone shouted, and they turned to find the last person Lora expected. *Lozlan.*

He stood by an alley, waving.

Limping, Eyden carried Lora towards him. She felt his muscles tense as he forced himself to keep going. Reaching him, Lozlan stepped closer as Eyden stumbled and Lora almost fell to the ground. Lozlan swung an arm around her waist to keep her upright.

"Why are you helping us?" Lora asked, her voice weak. Did he know who she was? She stared at his side profile, trying to spot the resemblance. His hair was a lighter blond, soot stuck to the ends.

"I remember you two. Danger. Red door. Danger no more." Lozlan's voice sounded shrill. He stuttered as he added, "Anyone taking down the Void deserves help." They limped forward until a carriage came into view. "There."

"We're in no condition to steer it," Eyden reasoned, out of breath.

"I can take you but not far. Never far. Shackles. They bind."

Lora pushed herself away, leaning against the carriage. She swallowed, meeting Eyden's eyes. There was no other way forward now.

"You can leave Rubien." Lora forced herself to meet Lozlan's gaze. His eyes looked so much like hers but dazed. Was he drunk?

"I cannot, but—"

"I'm Lora Adelway," she blurted.

Lozlan went silent, his eyes truly taking her in as flames rose behind them, swallowing the market.

"You're...are you Karla's daughter?" His tone wasn't relieved, but panicked.

Lora bit back her anger. "Yes."

"You're my..."

"Biologically speaking, yes." An explosion went off behind them. Lora threw up her right hand as embers flew towards them. "You can drive, so drive." She climbed into the carriage, all but falling onto the bench.

Eyden mumbled something she couldn't make out. He sat down next to her in the carriage and Lozlan closed the door behind him, meeting her gaze for a brief second before he hurried on.

The carriage moved shortly after and her dislocated shoulder hit the wall. But it didn't sting as much as the disappointment in Lozlan's eyes. She barely felt the tear slipping down her cheek as her surroundings turned blurry and the last of her strength left her until Lozlan's turquoise eyes went up in flames in her mind and darkness prevailed.

The carriage took a sharp left and Lora's shoulder screamed, waking her up. She was on the floor, her head propped up on a jacket. Eyden's, she realised, as her gaze drifted to him slumped over on the bench, his chest bare except for his ripped shirt. The bleeding on his chest seemed to have stopped. The skin on his arms was reddened from the fire.

The wheels stopped and Lora sat up straighter. Glancing out the window, she noticed they were in the middle of the woods. The sun was slowly setting. How long had they been out?

A knock sounded on the door, and Lora hissed as she got up and opened it with her good arm. Lozlan stood before her. "We're at the border. You need to go on without me."

So that was it? He hadn't asked her one question. All he had to say was that he wanted them to leave?

"No." Lora stepped outside, forcing Lozlan to move back. She cupped her elbow to stop her arm from moving too much. "You don't get to leave. We came to get you, so you're coming with us."

"You came..." He drifted off, his eyes wide. "You don't understand, I've been banished. Karwyn, your cousin, would never lift it."

Lora leaned against the carriage, her bones tired, her skin hurting everywhere. Yet, she laughed. It was ridiculous, wasn't it? As if she didn't know. She knew. She fucking knew too much.

Lora laughed until tears stung her eyes. "You can't even imagine what I *understand*, what I've been through." She leaned closer. "Karwyn has no say anymore. I lifted your bloody banishment. You can leave and you will. I'm not asking."

"You sound so much like your mother," Lozlan replied. "I see it now." A small smile played on his lips but then it vanished. "How could you have lifted the banishment?"

Lora took a breath that almost got stuck in her throat, the leftover smoke burning her insides. "I'm the queen of Turosian."

Lozlan shook his head wildly. "No. No, that can't be. You're not even supposed to be in Liraen! We should head to the border, we're close. Get you back."

"I can't. People here are relying on me. My family is counting on me."

"Your family is on Earth!"

She flinched. He wasn't her family. She knew that, but the words hurt nonetheless.

"*My family* won't be safe unless I stay. And my brother is here."

"Your brother?"

"Half-brother," she clarified. "You only have one unwanted child, don't worry."

Lozlan shook his head. "He's human? How is he here?"

"Well, if you paid a little more attention to what's going on out-side the Void instead of getting drunk, you might have heard that the border spell has fallen."

He drew back as if he'd been slapped. "I'm not drunk."

"You were rambling before and you looked..." He sounded clearer now, but he seemed on something before. She hoped it wasn't fortae.

"If your brother needs you, we should get going," Lozlan interrupted, turning from her, but then he halted, looking over his shoulder. "I'll take you wherever you want, but I can't for the life of me imagine why you sought me out. I have nothing to offer you."

Lora pressed her lips together tightly, forcing back tears. When she was a child, she used to imagine what her father would say if he ever met her. None of her imaginary meetings had ended like this.

"I didn't want to seek you out," Lora bit out. "At least we have that in common." She gripped the door, turning to step back inside the carriage. "We're going to the palace. I'm sure you remember the way."

CHAPTER 46

ELYSSA

The sun grew warmer as Elyssa, Amira, and Rhay headed into the woods behind the Allamyst palace, traveling to the nearby town, Rosleine. Elyssa wished she could have shown Wryen how much she truly despised him, but Amira's mother was their priority. They'd been forced to leave Wryen behind. Elyssa hated the thought of allying with him. Yet it wouldn't be her decision to make. It was Amira's.

A weight settled in her chest as Elyssa thought of how she had run off when Amira had been waiting for her to come here with her. Elyssa couldn't quite explain the intense wave of rage that had overcome her. But Amira had been right. Elyssa had to fight for the living *and* the dead. She had no intention of dying, of leaving Amira and her friends behind. So from now on, she would force herself to weigh her options before crossing the line between brave and stupidly reckless. That was the only reason she was swallowing her anger at Rhay instead of throwing him to the ground. If Rhay had acted differently, Farren might still be alive.

Elyssa almost ran into Amira's back as the princess halted abruptly. Glancing past her, Elyssa caught sight of what looked like an abandoned shed deep in the woods, the green of the leaves brighter than back in Turosian.

Amira surveyed the space, a haunted look crossing her eyes.

"What is it?" Elyssa asked, taking her hand. Her arm stung from the movement. Blood seeped through the bandage on her arm but she ignored it the best she could, not letting on that it still hurt like hell.

"I used to go here with...when I wanted to get away." Amira twisted the fabric of her trousers. Rhay scratched his neck as he stared at the ground.

Elyssa sensed there was more to that story but she didn't want to push. Instead, she squeezed Amira's hand. If she could make the ghosts of Amira's past disappear, she would. But she could only work on their future. She hoped Amira knew how sorry she was.

Elyssa pushed a lock of hair behind Amira's ear. "Let's keep going." Amira nodded, walking forward even as her gaze stayed locked on the shed. "Wryen is so goddamn wrong, you know," Elyssa added to distract her. "Even now, he doesn't see how easily you could overthrow him."

Amira's eyes widened. "You mean challenge him for the throne? I couldn't. I was baiting him back there. If people found out I'm a witch... Besides, I have no idea how to be queen. I never—"

"Slow down, sunshine." Tugging her closer, Elyssa hoped to calm her nerves, but Amira stiffened. "I'm not saying you have to take over. That's your choice to make, and yes, it would be pretty complicated. What I'm saying is you have *power*. Not just the power to ruin his reputation." Elyssa smiled wide. "But *his reign*. You have fire too. More than him."

"I..."

The mention of fire always made her tense up. Elyssa ran a finger over the back of Amira's hand. "Believe me when I say, you can handle anything you put your mind to."

Rhay, a few steps behind them, cleared his throat. "I agree. If we want Wryen on our side instead of Tarnan's, threatening his reign is the way to go."

"No one asked you." Elyssa's free hand curled into a fist.

"I've already apologised," Rhay replied stiffly.

"It'll take more than an apology," Elyssa shot back. He had been wrong and stupidly reckless, more than Elyssa had ever been, even though she was aware it was slightly hypocritical after the stunt she'd pulled.

Rhay sighed. "I'm here, aren't I? Willing to help in any way I can."

Elyssa gave him a deadly grin. "Can I use you as a shield? That might help. A tiny bit."

Rhay's mouth opened but Amira beat him to it. "Let's focus on the mission." She tilted her chin forward. "We're here."

Elyssa turned from Rhay to where the trees parted in front of them, revealing a small town at the bottom of the hill they were on. *Rosleine.* The building on the outskirts Wryen had told them about was made of white stone. A mix of colourful, blooming flowers hung down the walls. It was beautiful, not giving away what lurked inside. A large fountain stood proudly behind the front gates. Elyssa couldn't hear the water but she craved to touch it to refresh her mind.

"Let's go." Sneaking down the hill, she kept behind trees as much as she could.

Amira halted her as they reached the front gate. A fence made out of iron bars surrounded the whole premise, at odds with the beauty of the building beyond. Two guards approached them from inside.

"What brings you here?" one of them asked through the grey metal bars of the gate, hand on the sheath of his sword.

Amira stepped forward. "My brother, King Wryen Rosston, has sent us for one of your prisoners, Edaline Ryven."

"We have no such order."

The second guard detailed Amira. "I'm sorry to disappoint you, Princess Amira. But no one is allowed in here. Go back to the palace where it's safe."

Elyssa craned her neck to see the entrance beyond the fence. Four more guards were stationed there.

"I can't—" Amira started.

Elyssa cut her off. "We'll be on our way, then."

Forcing a smile, she pulled Amira back and Rhay followed.

Out of sight, Amira asked, "What's the plan?"

"Back entrance. There has to be one. I'm being smart, princess." Elyssa winked at her.

They walked around the back and, sure enough, she spotted the back door. Only one guard stood behind the gate.

"Let me." Rhay walked up to the fence and yelled, "Hey, you there."

The guard drew her sword as she walked closer. Before she could utter a word, Rhay added, "You can trust us. You want to let us in." His tone almost reminded her of Tarnan. Rhay was playing with the guard's emotions. Goosebumps travelled over Elyssa's skin even though the warm air made her shirt stick to her.

"There is no way inside other than the front gate," the guard replied, puzzled.

Walking up to the fence, Elyssa put her hands together and crouched, looking back at Amira. "I'll boost you up."

Amira carefully stepped into her clasped hands and let Elyssa push her upwards. Elyssa bit back a yelp as her arm stung, needles pricking her skin. The princess grabbed the top of the gate, pulling herself up and over, then fell inelegantly to the ground on the other side. She fell onto her back in the grass, breathing heavily.

"You okay?" Elyssa whispered, grabbing the warm metal of the fence and fighting the urge to hiss at the pain from moving her arm.

Amira huffed. "I just need to lie down for a minute while you get in here."

"It won't take me a minute, princess." Elyssa climbed up, swinging her body over the top and dropping down next to Amira. Landing in a crouch, a faint sting shot up her legs.

Amira lifted herself up on her elbows. "Show-off." A smile graced her lips, and with the sun hitting her face, she looked radiant even with the bags under her eyes.

Holding out her hand, Elyssa pulled Amira up. Rhay struggled to climb over the fence with his bad shoulder. It took him quite a while, and if the guard wasn't allowing it she for sure would have detained Rhay before he could reach the other side. He fell even less gracefully than Amira, landing on his good shoulder.

Jumping to his feet, Rhay brushed the grass off his trousers and cursed under his breath. He tilted his chin at the back door. "Open the door, my friend. You really want to help us, remember?"

The guard stood frozen as if unsure what to do. Impatient, Elyssa rushed forward and slammed the hilt of her dagger against her head. Rhay pushed her against the wall and met her half-eyes closed. "You're feeling very sleepy." The fae slumped to the ground.

On silent feet, they crept towards the back door. No one else was within sight. The windows were covered by wooden shutters. Elyssa pulled at the door handle, but of course it was locked. She was about to raise her dagger to break the lock when Amira reached forward.

"Let me try." She grabbed the white crystal in her pocket, shutting her eyes as a thin line of sweat coated her skin. Then she pushed open the door.

"Who's showing off now?" Elyssa teased before stepping into the space. Amira's answering grin faded as she got a look inside.

Gone were the bright colours and flowery scent from outside. It was almost pitch black, and a musty smell filled the air. The corridors were a dull grey, a few torches throwing light on tasteless, undecorated walls. Elyssa couldn't see anything beyond the hallway.

"Let's go right," Amira muttered.

Keeping close to the wall, they sneaked inside. The corridor seemed endless, the atmosphere eerie. As they rounded the corner, they found rows of prison cells lining either side of the room.

Elyssa's hand clenched around the hilt of her dagger as they walked ahead. Prisoners stirred, some glared at them. Rhay removed a dagger from his coat.

"Hey!" one of the prisoners screamed, grabbing the bars in front of her face. "Get me out of here!"

Amira tensed next to her, her eyes wide in horror. The prisoner looked half-starved, her collarbones protruding too much under her skin. Her hair was greasy and matted.

"Me too!" someone else screamed, rattling the bars.

"Calm down," Elyssa whisper-yelled, throwing up her hands. "If guards storm in, it'll help no one." The hall turned quiet again. "We're here for Edaline Ryven. Help us and we'll help you."

Looking at the dirty faces of the prisoners, Elyssa meant it. Whatever reason Wryen had to imprison them here, if he thought it would harm his reputation, it was most likely undeserved.

The prisoners seemed to calm, and Elyssa spotted a drop of sweat running down Rhay's neck. He was probably influencing them.

"She's over there," someone shouted, and Amira headed that way.

"Why should we believe you?" another prisoner yelled. "I recognise her." She pointed her chin towards Amira, who stopped in her tracks. "She's the king's sister!"

Shouts filled the hall, prisoners yelling over each other. Elyssa couldn't track who was saying what. Loud clinking drowned out their words as prisoners rattled the bars to their cages.

Before Elyssa could tell them to shut up, her gaze landed on a guard rounding the corner from another hallway at the end of the rows of cells. She turned back the way they'd come, and three more guards appeared. They were trapped. *Goddammit.* Yet, the challenge ignited her heart. Here, her anger could find an outlet for the right reasons.

The nearest guard stormed forward and Elyssa ducked as his sword swung at her. She slashed at his lower legs, ignoring the pain shooting down her arm, before springing up again and hitting his face with her brass knuckles. The guard cursed under his breath as he clutched his bleeding nose. Elyssa removed a throwing star, spun around, and hit the next guard approaching her.

Rhay fought another guard, his dagger slashing at the fae's shoulder.

"Go find her!" Elyssa yelled at Amira, who glanced between her and the cells.

The words cost her a split second and someone grabbed her wrist. Clenching her teeth, Elyssa let her weapon drop as she turned to the bloodthirsty guard. With all her strength, she pushed against his chest. His body slammed into the bars. He reached for her throat but then his arm dropped. Bony, dirt-stained hands reached through the bars, circling his neck to cut off his air.

The guard scratched at the hands and Elyssa took the spare second to pick up her dagger. She plunged it into his heart and he ceased to struggle. The hands around his neck loosened as he dropped to the floor. Elyssa met the gaze of the prisoner who had helped her through the bars, but she couldn't even thank the fae woman as another guard headed towards Amira.

He aimed an arrow straight at Amira's head, who stood frozen in front of a cell, her back to the guard.

"Amira!" Elyssa warned, removing a throwing star from her boot. But she knew she would be too late. The almandine arrow was already shooting through the air.

CHAPTER 47

AMIRA

Amira's gaze collided with the tearful pale blue eyes of the woman she hadn't seen in months. A sob caught in her throat. Amira had dreamt of this moment for so long. Taking her in, Amira's heart jumped out of her chest. With the dirty clothes hanging loosely on her body and greasy hair, she looked different than Amira remembered, but she was alive.

"Mother," Amira croaked out, her eyes burning, just as Elyssa screamed her name.

Hastily turning, Amira spotted the almandine arrow coming at her. Instinct kicked in and Amira threw a gust of wind, deviating its course. She winced in pain, her arm still hurting from the burn. The arrow punctured the guard's shoulder.

With a curse, the fae pulled the almandine arrow from his skin. Amira briefly glanced at Elyssa, but she was taking care of another guard. One already lay dead on the floor. And the last guard was locked in a fight with Rhay, whose stance wavered. Amira would deal with this one on her own. She recognised him from the front gate. He seemed to know her, too, but that didn't stop him from raising his sword. It didn't stop Amira either. No one would come in between Amira and her mother ever again.

Channeling her magic, Amira threw a violent gust of wind at the guard, slamming him against a cell. Training with Saydren for a week had increased her control immensely. The memory pained her, reminding her that Farren was supposed to be by her side. The guard tried to scramble back to his feet, but Amira was faster. Using a moonstone like Farren had shown her, she pressed it against the guard's forehead. His eyes rolled back as he fell. Elyssa took out the final guard with a well-aimed dagger strike.

"Good job, sunshine." Elyssa wiped the blood from her face as she turned her way. The wound on her arm had reopened, seeping through her white bandage.

The buzz from the fight came crashing down on Amira and she whirled around. Her mother's eyes were wide, her face even paler than before. Had she known her daughter was a witch? Amira's relief was twisted by ice-cold fear. "Mother, I—"

"Here you go, love." Rhay tossed Amira a set of keys taken from a fallen guard.

Elyssa began freeing the prisoners on the opposite row with another key. Hurrying to open her mother's cell, Amira dropped the keys on the ground, the sound rattling her heart. She lowered herself to pick them up, refusing to meet her mother's gaze. Would she only read disgust and fear?

"Mira, honey, take a deep breath." Her mother's warm voice warmed her heart, fighting off the ice slithering under her skin. Even with the heartbreaking cracks in her voice, it sounded like home. The fear she had read in her mother's eyes was replaced by tenderness.

Finally opening the door, Amira threw herself into her mother's arms. Her mother kissed her cheeks, her forehead, her nose, the top of her head. "My Mira, my sweet girl. I'm so glad you're safe."

Amira felt like a little girl again. If she squeezed her eyes shut tight enough, she could almost pretend she was fourteen, wrapped up in her mother's arms. Before her father had passed. Before Wryen had torn them apart and burned all happiness from her life. She let tears streak her cheeks.

"I thought Wryen would kill you before I'd have the chance to save you." And feeling her mother's bones while she hugged her, Amira knew that her mother was near death. "I'm here now. I won't let you go this time."

A choked sound escaped her mother's lips.

"Princess, we should go before backup arrives," Elyssa said from behind them. Rhay was freeing the last prisoner. The rest had already run off.

Amira didn't want to let go of her mother, fearing she would disappear as soon as she did. Nothing good ever lasted. But she knew Elyssa was right.

As they exited the prison, rushing out the now-unguarded front gate, Amira held hands with her mother, unable to stray too far from her. They kept silent at first. How could they ever say everything they had longed to say to each other over these last months? Elyssa walked ahead of them, keeping her distance from Rhay, whose hand often strayed to his pocket where she knew he kept his flask, an old habit that refused to die. She knew the battle all too well.

As they made their way through the forest, the trees shielding them from the relentless sun, it was her mother who broke their silence first. "I saw you fight."

Amira's heart tightened in her chest.

"Fae won't accept it. They fear your kind, have done so for centuries," her mother whispered in her ear. Amira couldn't help the tears from falling. She had thought her mother would understand. But maybe it was too soon.

Amira stopped in her tracks. "I can defend myself now, Mother. You've witnessed it."

Her mother tucked a strand of hair behind her ear. "It was one guard, honey. What will you do if a whole village, a whole kingdom comes after you?"

"My friends will help me." Amira tried to push back the fear her mother was instilling in her heart. She looked at Elyssa and Rhay ahead of them. They had been there for her today. She knew her mother meant well, but she was only stirring up her recently tamed anxiety.

"Maybe they will. But this world is a dangerous place. I don't want you to get hurt. You know I would do anything, *anything*, to protect you."

"Is there a problem?" Elyssa asked, having noticed they had slowed down.

Amira forced a smile on her lips. She didn't want Elyssa to think badly of her mother when concern was guiding her words. And who could blame her after having been locked up for weeks? "Everything's fine. Let's go give Wryen a piece of our mind." No matter how much she despised her brother, it was better to have him on their side than on Tarnan's.

Elyssa furrowed her brows, clearly not buying Amira's attempt at minimising her pain. But still, she strode ahead, Rhay fast on her heels, while Amira and her mother followed more slowly, in silence again.

When the shed in the woods came into view, Amira couldn't help but remember the afternoons she used to spend there with Quynn, ditching her tutor with the young maid. Despite her father's death, those had been the last days of happiness for her. Before Wryen had decided to lock her up and remove everyone she had ever cared about from her life—some more permanently than others.

"You fucking liar," Elyssa said, storming the throne room once again. Amira would have started the conversation with Wryen in a gentler manner, but she had to admit, she enjoyed Elyssa's style.

Lounging on the throne, Wryen took a sip of wine, the lilac colour matching his eyes. He smiled at the bloodied, dishevelled state of Amira, Elyssa, and Rhay. Amira's mother stayed back, fear shining in her eyes.

"My dear sister is reunited with her mother. What more do you want?"

Amira approached him, Elyssa at her side. "To not have to fight, as you assured us we wouldn't have to."

"You have to fight for what you want in life, Amira." He raised his glass. "I'd offer you some lavender wine to celebrate, but I've heard you've gone sober. Maybe Rhay would like to join me?" Rhay shook his head, his lips set in a straight line. "What about you, Edaline? Don't tell me our fun is over."

Amira's blood burned her veins. How dare he threaten her mother again? Before Amira could react, Elyssa walked up the steps to Wryen and punched him in the face. His head snapped back against the back of the throne and he howled, spilling his wine to clutch at his broken brow bone.

Elyssa laughed, stepping back and shaking out her hand. "Damn, that felt good."

"You bitch, you'll be the first to taste my fire," Wryen snarled, his words thick with the blood gushing from his nose. He lit up his hand.

Channeling her powers, Amira lit her hand on fire too. "Two can play at that game, Wryen."

She heard her mother gasp, while Elyssa nodded in approval. But what truly mattered was Wryen's pissed-off gaze. He knew she could be his ruin, she read it in his eyes and she enjoyed the fear.

"I want you to join us against Tarnan," Amira stated.

Wryen scoffed. "Why would I do that? You think your ragtag team of rebels will win against the Dark King's son? I'll stay neutral, thank you very much. You can all kill each other off for all I care."

"You have seen what Tarnan is capable of, you can't stay neutral," Rhay interceded. "He will come for you once he's won the contest."

"Do you really think he'll let you keep your throne after what you did to me?" Amira twisted her hand, pretending to admire the flames. It took everything in her not to wince seeing the fire dance in front of her eyes. She forced away any thoughts of Quynn. Instead, she pictured Elyssa's fiery hair, her gaze proud. "You said it yourself, Tarnan has a fondness for me."

"You may have fire, but you don't have the guts to use it." Wryen threw a fireball over Amira's mother's head, barely avoiding her hair.

Amira clenched her jaw. "Try me."

When Wryen threw fire at her, she didn't move. Instead, with a flick of her wrist, she extinguished his fireball with water. "Is that enough proof for you, brother?"

Wryen narrowed his eyes, but kept silent. Smiling, Amira lit up Wryen's burgundy shirt. A scream escaped his lips as he patted himself, trying to smother the fire.

"What should I burn next? Maybe your crown?" Amira made sure the flames did not touch his skin. Yet.

"Fine," Wryen yelled, his lilac eyes furious. "Call back your fire and maybe we can come to an agreement."

With a satisfied grin, Amira recoiled her fire. She even threw a splash of water on Wryen to smother the remaining flames. His half-burned and soaked shirt almost made her laugh. Elyssa snorted. Wryen's glared daggers at them.

"Enough with your childish giggles, or I won't hold back next time." He ignored Amira's raised brow. "We both know you're playing pretend here. You won't go through with your threats."

"Remember, Amira can destroy your reputation very easily," Rhay threw in. "And Elyssa is itching to take you out. You should consider your words carefully."

Wryen straightened his wet shirt. "Here's my offer. I won't hurt you or your mother. Or even your human friend. I will even side with you against Tarnan. But only if you sign away your right to challenge me for the throne."

Amira turned to Elyssa, asking for her opinion with one look. Elyssa shrugged. It was better to have Wryen on their side even if she wished nothing more than to punch his face again. "Temporary," Elyssa mouthed to Amira.

"I can accept that," Amira replied. She wouldn't want to be queen, anyway.

"I'm not finished. Since the Rosston reputation has taken a hit with you failing to marry Karwyn and your stay at Tarnan's, I want you to stay in Allamyst until the annual Bellrasae's Feast. Show a united front," Wryen said coldly, clearly unhappy about the idea of spending more time with her. He only wanted to show everyone that he still had

Amira under his control. And Bellrasae's Feast, the celebration of the patron of Allamyst, was the perfect occasion for it.

"Bullshit." There was a deadly glint in Elyssa's eyes. "We'll take our leave, thanks."

Amira appreciated her defence, but it was worth it if it meant Wryen would finally stop harassing her and her mother.

"I agree to your terms," she said coolly.

Elyssa cursed under her breath while Rhay sighed. Amira glanced at her mother. Her expression was blank but strained, and her skin had gone even more pale.

Amira was doing this for them, so they would finally get their freedom.

Wryen despised anything witch related, so the contract they signed was not a blood contract. After signing, he had quickly given word that Amira, her mother, and her friends were expected to stay at the palace for a week. He had ordered the servants to prepare Amira's old quarters. But Amira had refused to go back to her former golden cage. She instead requested the amethyst rooms in the south wing of the palace, as far away from her old quarters as possible.

Rhay said he would take any room available. He seemed completely out of it by the time they parted ways. A deep sorrow pulled at him— Amira could see it. She had thought about following him, but he had left so quickly she assumed he needed space.

Now, she was in her old bedroom, the past calling to her as Elyssa followed. Her mother had been taken to a healer to help her regain her strength after weeks spent in that prison. Amira had stayed with her until her mother had fallen asleep, exhausted by what she had been through. Knowing her mother was safe should have calmed her worries, but Amira still felt on edge.

Taking in her old bedroom, Amira realised how much she had changed since leaving. The lilac walls reminded her too much of Wryen's eyes, as if he was constantly watching her. The wardrobe was filled with all the impractical dresses Wryen had forced her to wear on the rare occasions he had let her out of her cage. She detailed all the little treasures she had gathered during her escapades in the city when her father had still been alive: beautiful feathers fallen from exotic birds at the menagerie, small jewels bought from shops filled with endless treasures, paintings created by talented street artists.

Elyssa sat down on Amira's bed, taking in her old bedroom like Amira had done in the tent Elyssa used to live in.

"Our room will be better," Elyssa said after a moment of silence, apparently reading right through her.

"Which room?" Amira sat next to Elyssa.

"Our bedroom in the place we'll get after all this shit is over," Elyssa replied before landing a sweet kiss on Amira's lips.

Their place. Amira liked the sound of that. But she was too afraid to picture it. Too many times she'd thought she'd finally reached happiness only to have the ground beneath her feet swept away.

Silently, Amira let her head rest on Elyssa's shoulder, listening to the calm breathing of the woman she'd do anything for. She didn't deserve her, yet Amira couldn't force herself to pull away. She hadn't been able to stay away from Quynn either. Was history going to repeat itself?

"You know the shed we passed?"

Elyssa nodded, letting Amira continue.

"I used to go there after my father's death...with Quynn." She could see Quynn smiling at her, showing the cute gap in her teeth, as they were dancing in their secret spot.

"Were you in love with her?" Elyssa softly asked.

"Yes. But she was a maid and, worst of all, a woman. Wryen couldn't let scandal taint his precious bloodline. He couldn't let me be happy. So he put her on trial under a false claim that she had tried to assassinate him. The punishment for attempted regicide is death."

Amira choked on tears but kept going. She needed to say it. She wanted Elyssa to know every part of her. "I watched Quynn burn at the stake by Wryen's hand. That's what triggered my powers for the first time. Wryen beat me so badly I repressed them for years, forgetting all about it until Rhay triggered them again in Turosian."

Without saying a word, Elyssa pulled Amira into a tight embrace. The pressure of Elyssa's body against her, broke whatever barrier Amira had left. Tears rolled down her cheeks too fast to stop them. Amira didn't want to stop them, anyway. She let it all out, crying in Elyssa's arms for what seemed like hours.

Elyssa pulled back to stare into her eyes. "I'm here for you, sunshine. Forever and always. And I promise you, one day, Wryen will pay."

Amira sighed, wiping away tears. Wryen might pay, but somehow, Amira always paid the higher price.

Elyssa tilted Amira's chin up with one finger. "Quynn's death is not your fault. Neither was Farren's. You know that, right?"

In some way, Amira knew she wasn't to blame. She would have done anything to save them. But her heart said otherwise, reminding her of how much *more* she could have done. Wanting to erase her thoughts, Amira planted a fiery kiss on Elyssa's lips. She longed for her touch to erase the pain she had endured for years. To forget about her cursed destiny. To forget that she couldn't keep Elyssa forever if she wanted her safe.

Elyssa pulled away. "Are you sure this is what you want right now?" Concern radiated in her eyes.

Amira was done with sadness for today. She needed a distraction from her thoughts, from her past and the uncertain future. She needed to stop *thinking*. "We did it in your room, why not mine?"

Elyssa nibbled at Amira's ear. "Let's create some happy memories, then."

Elyssa's gaze drifted to her lips and then they were kissing and Amira couldn't feel anything but Elyssa's warm skin beneath her touch, her lips on hers.

Amira straddled Elyssa on the bed. As Elyssa's fingers unbuttoned her blouse, Amira turned her head to the window, and with a flick of her wrist, the curtain closed.

"You're getting good at that," Elyssa remarked while pulling the blouse off Amira's shoulders.

Amira laughed, her fingers playing with the hem of Elyssa's over-sized sweater. "Magic or...*this?*" Her hand shook slightly as she pulled at Elyssa's clothes.

Elyssa removed her sweater in one pull. Bruises covered her arms, her collarbone, her face, but it didn't matter—it only made her more stunning. Through it all, Elyssa prevailed, and even though Amira wasn't sure she deserved the happiness she felt right now, she was going to steal this moment for herself anyway.

"You can't be bad at this, sunshine," Elyssa teased, kissing her neck as her hand cupped her breast through her bralette. Her back arched into Elyssa's touch. "Anything you do—any touch, any kiss"—she looked up at her hooded eyes—"has me undone."

Amira's heart sped in her chest. The words made their way to her very core, igniting her. She let a devious smile play on her lips as she slid her hand under Elyssa's undershirt. Her thumb stroked the underside of her breast before circling her nipple. Elyssa arched her back as a sigh slipped through her lips. She went to the button on Amira's trousers, but Amira pulled her hand from underneath her shirt and halted her.

"I want to do what you did to me before." Amira's voice didn't waver as she added, "And I want this off." She tugged at Elyssa's shirt.

Chuckling, Elyssa lifted her shirt over her head. Amira couldn't help but marvel at Elyssa's body, all sleek muscles. Blood rushed to her cheeks. She wanted nothing more than to make Elyssa *happy.*

Amira's free hand pulled at Elyssa's trousers, slipping her hand inside. She gently stroked her over her underwear, unsure how to replicate what Elyssa had done to her before.

Pulling her closer, Elyssa's lips brushed hers before sliding her tongue over her bottom lip. It lowered Amira's inhibition and she pushed Elyssa's underwear to the side, stroking her. Elyssa dropped her forehead against hers as her breathing grew faster, a moan slipping from her lips.

Learning her body, Amira shifted, touching her more deeply,

switching the rhythm until Elyssa seemed to forget how to breathe altogether. She moved her hips in sync with Amira. Clutching Amira's waist, Elyssa fell back on the bed, taking Amira with her. Amira kept going as her lips moved to Elyssa's neck, kissing her until Elyssa was writhing beneath her. Her free hand cupped Elyssa's breast, and Elyssa cursed under her breath as her hands tangled in Amira's hair.

"Is this good?" Amira asked, trailing kisses from her neck to her chest, banishing all her fear if only for a moment.

"Yes," Elyssa moaned. "It's fucking everything, sunshine."

She closed her eyes and Amira felt Elyssa tighten around her fingers, a delicious sensation sending electricity through her as Elyssa came undone. Slumping on the bed, Amira's hand slowed.

Elyssa grinned at her. "Good isn't even close to goddamn accurate."

Pulling her in for another kiss, Elyssa's fingers slipped underneath the band of Amira's trousers. Against her lips, she whispered, "Let me show you just how good it was."

CHAPTER 48

🔥

LORA

Lora paced outside Lozlan's room as she had done a few times since they'd gotten back from Rubien over a day ago. She'd slept most of their first day back, but when she was awake her thoughts kept running back to him.

Her hand was raised to knock but then she dropped it. Why should she seek him out when he hadn't done it for her? Yet, Lora couldn't help herself. She had thought to send Nouis to check on him before realising she could no longer summon the advisor. She had never particularly liked him, yet she still felt his absence in the palace.

Instead, Lora had asked Ilario to check on Lozlan. He had said Lozlan's behavior seemed erratic and off. So when Eyden had suggested sending Sahalie to examine him, Lora had found herself agreeing. Now she was waiting for the verdict.

He had an alcohol or drug problem—that had to explain his disinterest in her. Yet she knew that wasn't it. It was the fact that she was a half-fae child from a one-night stand.

The door opened and Sahalie entered the hall. Lora hadn't talked to her since that time months ago when Eyden had introduced them. The fae looked her up and down, but the obvious hatred from back then was gone.

"Thanks for coming here," Lora started, testing the waters.

"I figured if Eyden asked me, it must be important."

"It is," Lora replied. "I'm sorry if—"

Sahalie waved her off. "Look, I'm glad Eyden is happy but, frankly, I don't see what he sees in you and I don't have to. Do you want to know about your father?"

Lora unclenched her jaw. "Go ahead."

"He's amped up on power. He hasn't used it in years."

"I don't understand."

Sahalie clicked her tongue. "Of course you don't. You have no idea about anything, do you? Well, simply put, when a fae doesn't use their power for a prolonged time, it drives them a little crazy."

Lora played with the crystal on her necklace as she thought it over. "Why would he not use them? Because of the banishment? It's lifted now."

Sahalie shrugged. "Beats me. He wouldn't say. You should try asking him instead of pacing outside his door." She gave her a knowing look, then walked off.

Drawing on her courage, Lora shrugged off her irritation at Sahalie and walked to Lozlan's door once more. Before she could overthink it, she knocked. Nothing happened. She raised her hand again, then sighed, turning around just as the door opened.

"Lora." Lozlan's blond hair was a mess and there were shadows under his eyes.

She wanted to scream at him but bit her lip. "Why aren't you using your powers?"

"It's complicated."

"That's not an answer. We're on the brink of war here and you're not helping."

"I told you, I'm of no help. I can't even think straight most days."

Lora got right in his face. His eyes, so much like hers, ripped at her heart. "Because you're not bloody trying! If you don't care about me, fine." She swallowed as he pulled back, a muscle ticking in his jaw. "But at some point you must have cared about my mum at least a tiny bit. She'd want you to help me. I have no idea what I'm doing. I'm supposed to be running this place"—she threw up her hands—"and I have no fucking clue."

Lozlan shook his head. "You're...doing better than I ever could."

"That's all you have to say?" She tilted her chin up, fighting tears. "I used to imagine why you never sought me out, never wrote back to Mum. Now I know." She met his gaze. "You're a fucking coward." Turning her back, she fled.

Tears burned her eyes so much that she almost ran into Maja.

"Jesus, where are you rushing off to?" Maja straightened her glasses. "What happened? Need me to beat someone up?"

Lora laughed darkly. "It's my so-called father. He's an ass. And no help whatsoever."

"Sorry." Maja pulled her into a quick hug. "We don't need him. We'll come up with a plan without that asshole, like we always have."

They only had a few weeks left and Lora had been hoping Lozlan could give them an ace up their sleeve. She shouldn't have had hope. Even with Oscar's invention working, alerting the guards of any crossings, Lora was still worried what Tarnan would do to get that amulet. She had checked up on her brother right after getting back from Rubien.

Her mother, Karwyn...she hated the uncertainty. Eyden had told her it was Jaspen who had sold her out to Saydren. Everything led back to Tarnan.

"Adelway," Damir called out, rounding the corner.

"Ugh, him again," Maja muttered.

"I heard that, killer." He halted before them, one hand resting atop his sword. "You'll be happy to know I come bearing good news for once."

Maja crossed her arms, her gun sticking out of her jeans. "Really? Did you kill a bunch of people? That's your idea of fun, isn't it?"

Damir's lips lifted slightly. "Don't tempt me with a good time."

Maja huffed. Lora shook her head. "What's happening?"

"Queen Kaede and Queen Kaylanthea are in the throne room."

Lora's mood lifted instantly. They wouldn't have come all this way if they hadn't reconsidered working with Lora, would they? "And they sent you to tell me?" Lora asked, wondering who had led them into the palace.

Damir remained expressionless. "I might have insisted they come alone and left their guards knocked out at the gates."

"You didn't." Lora gasped.

Maja snorted. "Oh, I bet he did."

Fuck. Giving Damir a death stare, Lora hurried towards the throne room. Over her shoulder, she told Maja, "Tell Eyden and Ilario to meet me there."

Ilario had been focused on keeping the peace at the palace. In the last two days, he had made friends with most guards and servants. He now knew how the place was running better than Lora ever would. In some ways, he was almost like her stand-in. She couldn't help but think Nouis would approve if he was still here. But he wasn't. She hadn't said as much, but if anyone deserved the title of head advisor, it was Ilario.

She couldn't help but wonder what Rhay was up to in Allamyst. She was worried about him and how his father's death was affecting him. Yet would she ever be able to forgive him? Would she ever be able to trust him and let him into her court? When this was all over, if they survived it, she couldn't imagine Rhay would even want to stay. With Karwyn gone, he could do anything. And Lora could do nothing but be the queen.

The guards opened the silver doors to the throne room as Lora neared them. She steeled herself for what was to come but was immediately overwhelmed by Kaylanthea's withering stare.

The queen crossed her arms over her chest. "I don't appreciate being locked in here."

"We come in peace." Kaede clasped her hands in front of her.

"We *did*," Kaylanthea threw in. "Now I'm not so sure."

Breathing in deeply, Lora walked up to them. "I'm sorry for the precautions. It wasn't my call."

Kaylanthea sighed. "So you have no control over your own palace?"

Lora felt a shiver of unease run down her spine. Her voice came out sharper than intended. "It was never my intention to take over the crown. But you're not here to judge my ruling. You saw what Tarnan can do. I'm truly sorry for your loss." Kaylanthea clenched her jaw. "You see now that we have to work together?"

"He's a threat to us all," Kaede agreed, putting an arm on Kaylanthea's shoulder. "What he did to Yasir...Tarnan let us leave with his body to give him a proper funeral as if he was the most generous king. We know what he is capable of now."

Lora met Kaylanthea's hard gaze. She could read the loss in her pale pink eyes even as anger took over. Lora softened her tone. "I know you think I'm after the high queen title, but believe me, I don't even want the queen's title. But what I want even less is Tarnan on the throne. He's taken from me too. From my court. We've lost friends and allies."

Kaylanthea studied her closely. Before she could reply, the doors were thrown open behind them, the sound echoing loudly. Ilario and Eyden strode in.

"And you are?" Kaylanthea asked, frowning.

"Members of my court, Eyden and Ilario," Lora said, gesturing at them. "They know Turosian better than I do, and we need as many people on our side as we can. Tarnan had years, *decades*, to plan his ascension. He won't slip up unless *we* make it so."

"The only way to win this is if we combine our strength and pull on all the allies we have," Ilario added. "Tarnan is powerful, but after the dinner he will be hated, and we can use that to our advantage."

"What good is it if Tarnan can compel us to not lift a finger?" Kaylanthea asked.

"I have ideas on how to avoid that." Kaylanthea raised a dark eyebrow at Lora. "Witchcraft. And humans can't be compelled. We can use that to our advantage."

"Humans and witches? You want to involve them in this? Why would they help us?" Kaede ran a shaking hand over the satin fabric of her sapphire dress.

"Because we have a common enemy, Tarnan." Lora peered between Kaede and Kaylanthea. "And I want to promise them a better future. One where we live in harmony—fae, humans, witches, *all* of us."

Kaede gasped. Kaylanthea squinted at her, her lips forming a straight line.

"That's not an easy task to achieve," Kaylanthea said.

"Are you against the idea?" Lora asked, refusing to drop her gaze.

Kaylanthea assessed her quietly. "No, I believe in equality, and Liraen hasn't been fair in a long time."

Lora let a half-smile lift the corner of her mouth. "Good. Because I want *you* to lead a new Liraen. Not the kind Tarnan envisions, but one formed by all of us. But you have to trust me. We know Tarnan's plan better than any of you. I need to know you'll accept everyone in my court in Liraen. Humans, witches...*everyone*. Do we have an agreement, Kaylanthea?"

Kaede still looked shell-shocked, yet she seemed to admire her courage. Eyden and Ilario looked tense, their eyes darting between the queens.

Taking a step forward, Kaylanthea offered her hand. It was a human gesture and Lora was unsure what was going through the queen's head.

"I agree to your terms, Lora. And I'll see if I can get the other kings on our side. I don't trust easily, but something tells me you don't either. I can see you have a noble goal, and so do I. I want to fight for a better Liraen." Lora reached out and shook her hand, holding back a sigh of relief. Kaylanthea squeezed her hand, a feisty grin on her face. "But when it comes to Tarnan, there will be nothing noble about his death." An understanding passed between them. They shared the same unrelenting want for justice, for revenge. "Call me Thea. Us queens have to stick together."

A half-smile lifted Lora's lips just as Damir stormed into the throne room, forcing her face to sour.

"We've got a small problem, Adelway." He tilted his head as if to tell her to follow.

Glancing at the two queens, Lora figured honesty went a long way. "What is it?"

Damir's gaze shifted between her and their guests. "Tarnan left you...a message."

Frowning, Lora excused herself and followed him. She felt Eyden next to her, his hand brushing hers. As they neared the gate outside, she noticed guards had gathered. A weight pressed down on her chest as she gestured for the guards to make room.

When they parted, the breath was knocked out of her. Outside the gate, three heads were staked on wooden pikes. Blood dripped onto the grass from where they'd been detached from their bodies. The shock made Lora's vision blurry as she covered her mouth to stifle a scream. She forced herself to swallow, wiping her eyes, and only then did she realise who she was looking at.

Her neighbors. A mother and father who had been friends with her parents and their son who had been Oscar's age. Her family had fled Bournchester, but Tarnan must have found other victims before they'd been able to secure the border with Oscar's device.

"Is that Thomas?" a strangled voice next to her said. Lora turned to her brother whose body shook as he clasped her arm before sinking to the ground.

Tears streaming down her cheeks, Lora knelt next to him, blocking his view. "Don't look, Oscar. Don't look." She grabbed his cheeks, willing him to look at her instead. Oscar buried his head in her shoulder, his tears drenching her shirt.

A hand landed on her shoulder and Lora looked up at Eyden. Behind him, Ilario, Maja, Kaede, and Thea had gathered.

"He left a note," Damir said as he appeared next to Eyden. A bloodied paper was in his hands. A *small* problem, Damir had said.

"Read it," Lora ordered, glaring at him, clenching her teeth.

Damir unfolded the note, no emotion on his face.

Dear Lora,

I'd hoped it wouldn't come to this, but you rushed off before we could come to an agreement. Give me the amulet or more surprises might follow. Your mother will be last. I give you one week as a gesture of my goodwill.

With kind intention,
Tarnan Sartoya Ellevarn

Rising on shaking legs, Lora forced bile down her throat. *One week.* What was she going to do?

Thea walked up to her, a pain they both knew too well reflected in her pale pink eyes. "We'll take him down. Let's get started."

CHAPTER 49

WRYEN

The presence of his half-sister in the palace made Wryen want to burn everything around him to the ground. Fire sparking from his fingertips, the amethyst rings he wore heated, scorching his skin as he walked by a life-sized painting of himself in the bright hallway. He used to handle it better, this rage at the sight of Amira. He'd found a way to take care of her, as their father had asked him to before his death.

She'd always needed him to show her how to behave. No matter how hard he had tried to teach her common sense, she had fought back, too blind to see what had to be done. What Wryen had done *for* her. Worst of all, she was parading around the palace with that disgusting human *friend* of hers. How could someone as perfect as him be the half-brother of such a deviant thing?

He had never understood his father's fondness for Amira. She was nothing more than a bastard. How he wished Zain Rosston was alive today to see who his beloved daughter had become.

One day had passed since he and Amira had come to an agreement. This week, he'd parade her around Amryne as the picture of the perfect, dutiful sister. Once again, he had to force her to act right. It was a dreadful duty.

As Wryen made his way to his room after holding a quick court meeting, he noticed that the door to his father's old quarters was open. He always kept his father's room locked, ensuring no one would disturb it.

Voices drifted towards him through the cracked door. Wryen drew his dagger and slammed the door open, ready to punish whoever had dared enter.

"Wryen," Amira squealed, dropping the journal she held in her hand.

Of course, it was his wretched half-sister. And her special *friend* was with her, her dirty hands all over his father's sword.

"You have no place here." Wryen tried to contain his fire, fighting against his instinct, as he had promised not to hurt them directly. It was the one thing keeping him from burning them to ashes. They should be grateful he was letting them live.

"I have every right to be here," Amira replied, more sure of herself than Wryen could stand. A muscle ticked in his jaw. Sparks filled his veins, his fire always ready to attack. She wasn't deserving of the Rosston name, yet she didn't even see what a privilege it was to have it.

"Are you trying to steal from *me*?" Wryen glared at Amira's *friend*. "Let go of that sword."

"Amira gave it to me," Elyssa said with a shit-eating grin. She raised the sword in front of her, the tip of it coming close to Wryen's throat. Wryen imagined turning that sword around, puncturing the girl's neck. He wouldn't kill her. No, he would let her bleed, then drag her to the pyre, letting Amira watch another one of her *friends* go up in flames. Maybe he would pin her to the stake with her throwing stars. Poetic justice.

Amira's smile was too big as she picked up the fallen journal. "I was just reading Father's old journals. I've found a passage I think you'll enjoy."

What had she found to further her delusion that their father wouldn't have cast her out? Wryen had done her the biggest favour of her life by getting her to block her powers instead of killing her.

Amira glared at him. "He knew. It's his bloodline."

"What is?" Wryen bit out, refusing to consider what she was saying. It could only be lies.

"Father knew that I was a witch. He—"

"*Lies.*" Wryen ripped the paper from her hands. He saw Amira's confidence falter, filling him with glee. Amira was delusional, thinking she could threaten him and their prestigious family name. But he recognised his father's handwriting.

Today, Amira made her doll fly. It exhausted her so much that she passed out in front of me. I knew immediately what she was and that I had to protect her secret. I know her gift will be seen as a curse by others. I always hoped none of my children would inherit my great-grandmother's abilities. Wryen doesn't have the gene but it's better he doesn't know about his sister. There is a jealousy in him that sometimes scares—

His heart was pushed to his lungs, cutting off his air. *It couldn't be.* Amira's mother had to be the one with the cursed blood. Wryen wasn't anything like Amira; he wasn't tainted. He was *pure.*

Lighting his hand up, Wryen watched the journal burn. Amira tried to reach for it but was too late. The ashes fell to the ground.

"He was right, you've always been jealous," she spit out.

"*My* father would never say such things." He got right up in Amira's face and she flinched, much to his joy. "Someone must have forged his handwriting. Probably you, since your only goal is to make a mockery of our family," Wryen spat out. "Does it help you sleep at night, inventing such outrageous lies? Pretending that you're not less than me?" He chuckled, letting the sound attack Amira when his fists couldn't.

Yet Amira let out a cold laugh, taking a step forward to bring them even closer. Wryen had the impulse to reach out and burn her hair, to remind her where her place was, to remind her *she* was the cursed one, not him. It could never be him.

"*You're* the one who has made a mockery of our family. Father would be ashamed of the way you're ruling his kingdom."

Wryen gritted his teeth, his hand catching on fire. Amira stepped back. "*I* have done *everything* for our family. *I* have done everything to protect you from yourself. You've always been ungrateful."

Amira's nostrils flared. "You keep pretending you did all of this for me, to save me from myself. You didn't do me any favours. You didn't protect anyone but *yourself*. You're scared. You've always been nothing but scared. And you should be."

Wryen laughed, shaking his head. "Scared? What would I need to be scared of?"

"You're afraid to lose the one thing you have going for you, your title. What a sad life, *dear* brother. Don't mess with me or Elyssa. You have everything to lose now."

"I'm the *king*, Amira. My word is law." He had *everything*. She should kneel before him, kiss his feet for even allowing her to stay in the palace.

"Maybe the people are tired of their king and his *moods*. You've heard what happened to Karwyn. Aren't you scared you'll be next? Aren't you scared I'll reveal *our* secret?" A dangerous light moved in her eyes.

Sighing, Wryen stroked her cheek, taking her by surprise. She tried to recoil, but he grabbed her by the back of her neck, delighted by her disgusted shudder. Elyssa raised her sword. "I'm not weak like Karwyn. I'd burn the whole world with me before I let you take my crown. You should thank Caelo it won't come to that since you've signed our agreement. You came here because you need me. Remember that, Amira. Remember that you'll *always* need me."

Without letting her reply, he strode out of the room, slamming the door behind him. He knew his words would linger with her, and a smile pulled at his lips, pushing back any thoughts about Amira's *lies*.

As he was about to go back to his room, Wryen picked up on hushed voices coming from another nearby room, the door left ajar. Who was conspiring in his palace?

The door opened and Wryen ducked behind the corner. A fae Wryen didn't recognise hurried out the door and down the corridor. Right behind him, to his delight, was Amira's mother.

All Wryen needed was a good excuse to take her out. Perhaps an accident. She went against his guards and they had to defend them-selves—sadly, Amira's mother accidentally got sliced into a hundred pieces. He could picture Amira's face, the grief pulling her back to him, to her role as his sister—pretty to look at but no threat. A shell for him to use.

He was the fucking King of Allamyst. He would get Amira back in his grasp. If they ever came for his crown, they would have to pry it from his dead hands.

CHAPTER 50

RHAY

Having stayed hidden in his room the last few days, Rhay had skipped lunch but was now starving. It's not that he and Amira were avoiding each other, but Wryen had made sure Amira's days were full. And when the princess had any free time, she would spend it with her mother or Elyssa. Long gone were the days when Rhay was Amira's only friend.

Then again, maybe *he* was avoiding her. He had more than one reason to. After all, he had given Tarnan the agreement. Elyssa had every reason to blame him for the death of her friend. And his comment about Elyssa's camp might have given Tarnan the idea to storm it. Rhay tried hard not to let it drown him.

Thinking about what he'd done, thinking about his father's death, all Rhay wanted was his trusted flask, but he knew it would only make things worse. It was easier to not see anyone, to not see their anger and disappointment when he could still picture his father's surprised eyes as he pushed the blade into his chest. How had Tarnan compelled him? How had Rhay failed so miserably?

When Rhay entered the kitchen he thought it was empty, but to his surprise, Amira was on a stool, eating a roll of warm bread smothered in butter. He didn't know if he should feel relieved to see her or turn right back around.

"Do you want some?" Amira asked, offering a piece of her bread. She slid the plate over on the white marble kitchen counter. Rhay gladly took it. He felt strangely at ease here. It reminded him of the kitchen in the Turosian palace, a place he had often taken refuge in.

Standing next to her, he pushed back his hair—as dark as the death staining every fibre of him. "You didn't have lunch?"

"I did, but I barely ate. Once again, Wryen ruined my appetite." She attacked her bread as if it was her insufferable brother.

"You seem to have gotten it back," Rhay joked in an attempt to lighten the mood even though he couldn't even get himself to smile.

A small grin played on Amira's lips anyway. "The cooks here make the best bread."

Rhay took a bite. It was heavenly. The outer shell was perfectly crispy while the crumbs melted in his mouth. "Do you remember when I tried to cook for you in Turosian? I wish I could have made you something as good as this bread."

Amira let out a rich laugh, warming Rhay's heart. "Worst meal I've ever had. I hope you're not still thinking about becoming a cook."

Playing with his piece of bread, Rhay picked it apart. "I don't think I'd be a much better advisor. I always mess everything up. I gave Tarnan the agreement thinking he wouldn't be able to break it. I ripped Lora's contract to avoid Tarnan finding out about her power. Yet I..." Against his will, tears flooded his eyes. He tilted his head to push them back, putting on a fake smile. He hadn't said it out loud yet. If he didn't then it wasn't real, right? But as much as Rhay had tried to avoid thinking about his father, he couldn't. Maybe a drink would have relieved him, but he couldn't help but think his father would look down on him disapprovingly from the Sky. If he was able to join Caelo. Would Tarnan burn his body?

Amira put a gentle hand on his shoulder. "What happened at the contest dinner?"

He didn't look at her. Instead he stared at his hands, invisible blood staining his skin. "I doomed my father."

Amira inhaled sharply. "Is he..."

"Dead?" Rhay turned to her, a fake smile on his face as tears escaped him. "Yes. Tarnan compelled me to kill him. If I'd never tried to play double agent, he'd still be alive."

Amira's expression broke and she pulled him into a hug. For a second, Rhay lost himself in the embrace, the pit in his stomach lifting just a smidge. Then he pushed her back. "You should be yelling at me, not trying to comfort me."

Amira sighed. "I am mad at you, but I know you didn't expect Tarnan to break the agreement. And I know the pain you're feeling, the guilt. I tried to play double agent myself and it didn't go so well either."

"I thought I would be strong enough to resist his compulsion. But I couldn't. My head was buzzing and I had this dry taste in my mouth, like I was craving something. But I hadn't drunk a sip of alcohol that day."

Amira's gaze turned somber. "That reminds me of fortae."

"I didn't take any, I swear." Rhay had had his fair share of addictions, but never that cursed drug.

Amira squinted at him. "I wouldn't put it past Tarnan to drug you. He must have known you'd be able to resist his compulsion otherwise."

His stomach twisted painfully. It all made sense. Tarnan had never trusted him. He must have slipped him fortae to be able to use Rhay at his whim. No wonder he had felt so off at the dinner. Yet the realisation didn't soothe his damaged soul. Another confession slipped from his tongue. "I think I might have given Tarnan the idea to attack Elyssa's camp."

Amira's eyes widened but then she shook her head. "Tarnan probably had the idea ever since Elyssa dared to attack him. And who knows how long Jaspen has been working with Saydren? That one isn't on you. I doomed many people. Mylner, Sydna, Nalani, Farren..."

"What do we do with it? This guilt? I tried drinking and losing myself in parties, but it didn't work. Guilt latches onto you and whispers in your ear until all you can think about is *what if.* What if I had done things differently? Could I have spared everyone the pain? Could I have saved them?"

Amira opened her eyes and gave him a sad smile. "I don't know if it ever leaves. I can't seem to let it go either. But you didn't kill your father, Tarnan did."

"All I want is to forget." Rhay clutched the kitchen counter. His gaze drifted to the shelf stacked with wine bottles.

Amira followed his gaze, her eyes turning sympathetic. "I know it's hard to quit. Without help, I wouldn't have been able to. If the craving ever gets too strong, reach out to me first, okay?"

Rhay gave her a half-smile. He knew he didn't deserve Amira's kindness, but he couldn't help but feel comforted by it. "It's not even the alcohol I crave, it's the...numbness."

"It's all linked to the guilt and despair." Amira cut herself a fresh slice of bread and bit into it. "Even if giving him the agreement turned out to be the wrong move, I know your intention wasn't bad. Just misguided. Learn from it."

Rhay ran a hand through his messy hair. He hadn't bothered to style it. "I didn't learn anything valuable there except that Tarnan has a daughter, which you apparently already knew."

"How's Saige?"

"Oblivious to the fact that her father is a monster." Rhay couldn't help but think back on his last conversation with Saige. He had abandoned her after promising to go to Rubien with her. Another person he'd let down.

"Maybe we can help her once we've defeated Tarnan. No matter who her father is, I don't think we should give up on her."

"It's funny, I kinda saw you in her."

Amira's smile was rueful. "I had the same thought."

"But you've changed so much. You're no longer the terrified young princess that I met in Turosian. I'm sorry for how I treated you after you revealed your powers. I thought it would be better for you to be far from me, but you were right, it was easier for me. I was selfish. I tried so hard to not have to choose between you and Karwyn and in the end, I've hurt you both."

Amira moved the plate with the last slice of bread closer to him on the counter. "I know saving me and hurting Karwyn in the process wasn't easy. I never thanked you for saving my life. I'm sorry that it had to come to that."

He moved the plate back to her. "You never have to thank me for that, love. I'm glad I didn't... I'm glad Karwyn didn't die in the end, but even if I did, I would always save you. I've messed up so many times, but I know now *that* was the right call."

Amira picked up the bread, broke it in two, and handed Rhay one half. He took it gratefully, a smile on his lips that felt true. "It was hard to lose you, but I'm glad we've found our way back to each other. You've changed as well, Rhay. I don't want you to go back to your old ways. You've helped me negotiate with my brother, and I thank you for that. But you're hiding again. Don't you think they'd need your help in Turosian more?"

"No one wants me there." Yet Amira's words made him think. He'd told Karwyn he wouldn't run. That he needed to figure out what the *right* thing to do was. He realised now that he wasn't taking his own advice. He might not be drinking anymore, but he was still avoiding his problems.

"I don't think that's true," Amira said. "They'll forgive you, Rhay, if you give them the chance to do so. If you put in the effort."

Rhay thought of Rio, his warm smile, his vibrant green eyes, his good heart. They hadn't had time to talk things through since their fight in the forest on Earth. Would Rio let him explain himself?

"Do you have some spelled paper?" Rhay asked, guessing Amira would have brought some to communicate with the others in Turosian.

Amira took out a piece of paper from her jacket pocket. "Who are you going to write to?"

Rhay quickly finished his half of the bread. "Someone I should apologise to."

"That doesn't narrow it down." Amira's laughter followed Rhay out of the kitchen. She was right; he had a lot of people to apologise to. But he wanted to start with Rio who always seemed to want to understand him even when Rhay couldn't understand himself. But he wouldn't stop there.

Rhay hurried back to his room. He had a letter to write and a bag to pack.

CHAPTER 51

EYDEN

"Try using your air magic to rip the dagger from my hands next time." Eyden pointed his blade at Lora's heart with enough distance to not draw blood.

Both of them were breathing heavily, sweat coating their bodies. In the last three days, when they weren't locked in the council room with Thea and Kaede, running through scenarios on how to best Tarnan and what to do about the king's threat, they were training. Elyssa regularly sent him fire messages. She would be back soon with Amira and probably Rhay, the traitor.

Lora took a step back, reaching up to fasten the hair tie keeping her dark-blonde strands out of her face. "I thought no powers this round?" A teasing smile graced her lips. "Otherwise I'd have you beat."

Eyden dropped his arm with the dagger, twirling the weapon in his hand. "I said no fire. You have other powers to fall back on." Picking up her fallen dagger, he placed it in her hand. "Come on, special one. Show me what you've got." She had improved so much since he'd first met her. The only power she was squeamish to train without Rhay to guide her was mind reading.

Her smile turned devious and the air around them seemed to heat. "I think I've shown you more than once already." Her shirt clung to her skin and Eyden found himself taking in her curves.

"Trying to distract me, are you?"

Lora shrugged innocently. "You said use what I got."

A smile tugged at his lips and before Lora could react, he rushed forward, dagger raised. She hastily took a step back, leaning back to avoid his blade. He struck again, going faster each time. Panting, she went backwards to avoid his strikes. Her back hit the wall and she ducked to the side as Eyden aimed at her.

He faked a move to the left, but Lora caught on and kneed him in the stomach hard enough to hurt. Catching her dagger with his, he smiled as they stared at each other, only their weapons between them. Then he winked and kicked her legs out from under her.

She went sideways, but at the last second, she threw out her hand and the air righted her. Eyden went to strike again when Lora curled her free hand into a fist and his dagger went flying out of his hand.

With a satisfied smirk, Lora pushed his chest lightly. The air followed her command and he was thrown backwards, sliding on the wooden floor. With quick steps, Lora was in front of him, straddling him and pointing her blade at his chest.

"Got you," she breathed, grinning so wide Eyden's brain short-circuited for a moment.

His hands went to her hips, shifting her position into just the right place, and her eyes glazed over. "I think you've earned a break."

Biting her lip, she let the dagger fall next to them before leaning forward, one hand on the floor to steady herself while using the other to run a finger along his jaw. His hands slipped under her shirt, skating over her bare skin, stirring up heat that took over his whole being.

Her lips captured his, gently and then feverish, as her hand went to his chest, fisting his shirt. Her hips moved and he cursed silently, wishing there were no layers of clothes between them. Eagerly, his hand drifted up her back under her shirt. She leaned forward until their chests touched.

The door creaked open. A strangled laugh escaped Ilario. "I didn't realise I needed to knock before entering the training room."

Eyden turned his head as Lora scrambled off of him. Ilario waited in the doorway, a folded piece of paper sticking out of his pocket.

Sighing, Eyden got up, following Lora to meet him.

"What's that?" She tilted her chin at the paper. Her cheeks were red, and Eyden bit back a laugh.

Ilario cleared his throat. "A fire message from Rhay. He's coming back today. But that's not why I'm here."

Eyden held back a sigh. He knew Lora was still furious too, but she was much kinder than him. She'd forgive Rhay eventually. The guilt Rhay must be feeling after being compelled to kill his own father must be immense. Being in the palace, Eyden's own father crossed his mind often.

"There's been some unrest in Parae and Chrysa," Ilario added. "People are unsure about your intentions as queen." The Turosian guards were aware it had been Damir and not Karwyn the day of the attack on the palace, so they'd stayed loyal to the remaining Adelway, but there were still more fae out there who wanted Lora off the throne.

Lora frowned. "I don't think throwing useless events to up my image is the best use of anyone's time right now. Can it wait until after the contest? We're less than two weeks away."

He could hear the desperate edge to her voice. There was something Eyden had been thinking over ever since they'd moved into the palace. "I might have an idea."

Lora raised a brow. "Go on."

"I think it's time we gave people the answers they've been looking for." He turned to Ilario. "It might not be the one they'd wished— hoped—for, but everyone deserves closure."

"You want to distribute the list of Karwyn's victims?" Ilario asked, his eyes wide but agreeable.

"Isn't it time we show the people we know what they have been through, that we suffered too, and we won't let it happen again?" His gaze went from Ilario, who seemed trapped in the past, to Lora, who smiled at him proudly.

Three years ago when Eyden had started his habit of drawing those lost, making sure they wouldn't be forgotten, he couldn't have imagined he would ever make it this far. Not just taking down Karwyn, but taking over the palace. For the first time, he truly realised that this was the start of the revolution Elyssa had always spoken about. Fae and humans had more than one reason to rebel. And Eyden wanted to show them the future they all deserved.

Eyden felt Ilario's nerves as they left the palace to head into Chrysa late in the afternoon. They both knew how monumental this could be not just for them but for all the people who had lost someone to Karwyn's sick experiments. It would be a day of mourning as well as of new beginnings. At least he hoped the second part was true. It was a gamble, and not all of those had worked out for Eyden in the past.

Lora stayed behind to train with Kaede and Thea, who would be heading home tomorrow. They had their own kingdoms to run but would be returning before the contest took place. That left Eyden and Ilario to deal with the Turosian people. It felt right; they'd both been working towards this for years.

Just as they headed through the gates of the palace, a carriage came into view and Rhay stepped out. Ilario halted. Rhay dropped his bag onto the stone path leading to the palace doors.

"Rio," Rhay said, his tone holding more meaning than Eyden was privy to.

"We're on our way out. You should head inside. The queens are here." Ilario brushed past Rhay, whose gaze followed him.

Eyden gave Rhay a glare as he slowed next to him. "I'll let Lora decide what to do with you, but if you betray us in any way, I will not be listening to Lora or Ilario defend you ever again."

Rhay nodded, swallowing loudly enough that Eyden could hear his throat working. Without another word, Eyden rushed to catch up to Ilario.

Ilario only slowed when River's Point came into view, their first stop. They'd decided to start small before going to the capital Parae.

And it made sense, as most of Karwyn's victims must have come from Chrysa, the neighbouring, less important town.

"Are you okay?" Eyden asked Ilario as he stopped and stared at the place where Damir had been taken over three years ago.

Ilario swallowed. "Closure hurts."

Eyden didn't think he'd ever feel closure about his father's death. Ilario turned to him, his hand playing with the sleeve of his dark green jacket. "But at least I don't have this never-ending question in my head anymore."

Eyden nodded silently and they entered the bar. It was packed. No one paid them much attention. Heading to the centre of the room, Eyden stole an empty glass and a spoon from a fae and climbed onto a table. He put the spoon to the glass with so much pressure he thought it might break. Thankfully, it didn't. Ilario stood on the floor in front of him.

The room quieted as heads turned to him. "I know you're all here to have a good time, and I apologise for interrupting, but I have an important announcement from the palace."

The crowd whispered amongst themselves.

"I know you are all aware that our town—all of Turosian—has not been the safest place to live in for a long time. Our former king, Karwyn Adelway, as well as his father before him, have kept secrets. Dark secrets that I'm sure most of you have wondered about. People have gone missing, never to be heard from again, and we all know the king has ignored this fact. Some of you may have lost people. Some of you may have even talked to me about their disappearance."

Some fae listened intently, sorrow taking over their gazes. Others glared at him, but Eyden kept going. "Some of you may have heard the claim that was made on Caelo Night that these fae were experimented on by Karwyn's hand. I'm here in the name of Queen Loraine Adelway *Whitner* to assure you all that the dark legacy Karwyn left behind will not be continued. I'm here to confirm the truth. It is a truth that is hard to face, but it is the past. And if nothing else, I hope it will bring you closure."

At the curious and confused glances of the crowd, Eyden removed a notebook from his pocket. His father's name stood out to him and he had to force his hand to stay still. "This is a list Karwyn kept of everyone he experimented on in the hopes of stealing their power."

The crowd erupted, shouting over each other. Questions were thrown at him faster than Eyden could track.

"Did any survive?"

"Off with the Adelway line!"

Eyden cleared his throat, but suddenly Ilario climbed onto the table next to him.

"I'm sorry," he shouted, taking the crowd by surprise. "I understand your pain, your anger. But don't let it lead you down a path of destruction. Turosian has been doomed for the longest time. We've all felt the effects. We've all lost so much." Ilario peered from one face to another. "I know how you feel because I feel it too. The sorrow, the not knowing, has eaten at me every second of every day. We can't undo the past. But we can give you closure. We can work together to forge a new Turosian where no one has to be afraid to use their high-level powers. Where no guards will steal you away and drag you off to be experimented on." Ilario's voice was more assured and assertive than Eyden had ever heard. "Our queen has given much to overthrow Karwyn, and what she needs now is your support to ensure a better future for all of us."

The crowd was silent, stunned. Ilario's lips parted as if he hadn't even realised he'd spoken.

"How do we know we are truly safe?" a fae woman shouted from the back.

"We're not," Eyden said, speaking honestly. "There is danger ahead of us. Tarnan Sartoya threatens us all. But—" Yells of shock and panic cut him off, but Ilario raised his hands.

"We need to stand together to overthrow those who will threaten us," Ilario shouted.

"You have nothing to fear from our queen," Eyden added. Catching the fae woman's eyes across the crowd, Eyden knew what he had to do. Every fibre of his being screamed at him not to; a fear that had been instilled in him when he was just a child warned him not to do it. But times had changed. And so had Eyden.

He pulled on his life source and let the wind carry him forward. The fae gasped as Eyden appeared in front of her.

"You can drift," the woman whispered.

"I can," Eyden said, thinking of his father who had had the same ability and was killed for it. "And I've always been afraid to reveal it. To end up as another experiment in the palace. But no more."

The woman's eyes warmed. She reached out to touch his shoulder. "May Falea be on your side. On *our* side." The crowd spoke over one another, but Eyden caught no yells of protest.

Clutching the notebook, Eyden drifted back onto the table in the centre of River's Point. "These are the names of the fallen. May they join Caelo in the Sky."

The crowd repeated his last words and Ilario gave him an encouraging smile. As Eyden began reading, the room filled with sorrow. But beyond the pain, he felt a glimpse of hope. Hope that, as a united front, they would defeat Tarnan. Hope that all their pain and anger would serve a greater purpose.

CHAPTER 52

RHAY

Watching Rio leave with Eyden, Rhay felt utterly out of place. He hadn't expected to be welcomed back with open arms, but it still stung. Telling himself to suck it up, he headed towards the entrance, where guards blocked his way.

"Come on now, let me in." He walked forward but the guards didn't move. How far had he fallen that he couldn't even enter what used to be his home?

The guards looked at each other before one of them turned to rush inside. "You're not on the list, Messler," one of the remaining guards said.

"I don't need to be on the list," Rhay muttered.

A few minutes passed. The wind biting into his bones, Rhay almost considered decking the guards.

Lora appeared at the door. "Rhay." She bit her lip, studying him.

"I know I messed up and I'm ready to apologise again. I'm here to help, give me a chance." He hoped his smile told her how much he meant it.

Lora averted her gaze. "Let him pass," she ordered, stepping back inside. Moving away from the guards, out of earshot, Lora turned back to him. Anger and something like sympathy fought in her gaze. "I'm not ready to forgive you. And I'm not ready to trust you." Rhay opened his mouth, but Lora held up her hand. "You can stay here for now. Just...don't mess anything up and we'll see. Okay?"

Rhay shut his mouth and forced himself to nod. He was here to atone, not force forgiveness. He didn't want to be selfish anymore.

Lora headed down the hall to whatever business she had to attend. Rio had mentioned the queens were here. He could help, but Lora clearly didn't want him to.

Raking a hand through his ink-black hair, Rhay took the stairs to his room. As he passed by the high windows in the hallway, he caught his reflection. Long gone was the extravagantly dressed, party-loving Rhay he used to be. Now his hair was as dull as his new reality.

As he turned from his reflection, he almost ran into Maja.

"Oh," she said, taking him in. "You're really back."

"In the flesh. Did you come looking for me, love?" Rhay asked, leaning against the window.

Maja crossed her arms. "In your dreams."

Rhay squinted at her. "Why so cold?"

"Do I really need to answer that after what you did to my people? Besides, I'm all team Ilario."

"Team Ilario..."

Maja scoffed. "You hurt him. I'm his friend. Naturally, I'm not happy with you."

Rhay stepped away from the window. "You're right. I did fuck up, and I'm sorry." Maja's glasses slipped down her nose as her brows drew up. "But," Rhay continued, a grin on his face that belonged to the old Rhay, "I think you should side with the person who gave you an orga—"

Maja jabbed a finger in his face as she rushed towards him. "Don't finish that sentence if you're not keen on getting kicked in the junk so badly that word won't even exist in your vocabulary anymore. Got it?"

"How I missed our deep conversations." Rhay chuckled. He held up his hands, then mimicked sewing his lips shut. "How's Rio?"

Maja crossed her arms, a sigh on her lips. "He's...fine. He doesn't need you to toy with him."

"That was never my intention." Rhay turned towards the window, catching his sad reflection. "I don't know what to do. The one thing I know is that I'm so fucking sorry. For what I did with the agreement. For hurting Lora, you, *everyone*. For being an asshole to Rio when he deserves...everything."

Maja watched him closely, her brows drawn up. "Have you told him that?"

"No—well, yes," Rhay corrected himself. "I wrote him a letter, but he didn't respond."

Maja huffed. "Damn you, Rhay. I'm supposed to be mad at you, not helping you. But Ilario has been miserable. He's all business now, so focused on keeping Turosian running. It's impressive, but he needs more." She looked him up and down. "And you need this too. I mean, look at you."

Rhay feigned shock. "I look ravishing as always." Maja cocked her head. "All right, perhaps I've had better days."

"Where's the Rhay with the colourful hair who knew how to lighten everyone's mood? I've only *heard of* that Rhay."

From Rio or Lora? Rhay wondered.

"I'd like to meet *that* Rhay."

Rhay glanced back at his reflection, catching the sun setting far in the sky. He pulled at a strand of his hair, looking at the dull colour. "Me too. A better version of that Rhay."

Maja's reflection appeared next to him in the window. "I have an idea. It's not going to magically make it all right, but it might just be the push you need to get some of that joy back." A faint grin spread her lips. "Let's do something about that hair."

Rhay had been waiting at Rio's door for hours by the time he finally showed up. He didn't notice Rhay right away. His gaze was on the floor. His eyes were tired, his steps weak, as if he couldn't wait to fall into bed. Yet, when Rio spotted Rhay sitting on the ground, leaning against his closed door, his face lit up. Only for a second.

Rio stopped in front of him. "What are you doing here?" His gaze lingered on Rhay's newly dyed hair. Emerald green, his father's favourite colour, with golden brown highlights. An homage to his father, who would have surely told him the colour was absurd.

Rhay brushed off his trousers as he stood up. "You like my hair?"

Rio met his gaze, his eyes almost the same deep emerald as Rhay's hair. *Purely coincidental.* "Were you waiting here to get my opinion on that? It could've waited until the morning. I'm exhausted."

Rio moved to open his door but froze when Rhay put his hand on his arm. "That's not why I'm here. I wondered if you've read my letter."

Looking at his feet, Rio exhaled loudly. Rhay could almost hear every word he'd written lingering between them. He remembered the letter word for word.

Dear Rio,

I know it might be cowardly to write this instead of telling you to your face. I'm coming back tomorrow, but I can't wait any longer. I can't bear the thought of you hating me. I can't bear the thought of you thinking I've betrayed you. You are the first person who saw something in me when I was nothing but a shadow, going through the motions to survive at the palace. Going from party to party. From drink to drink. Part of me wishes you had never met the real me. Part of me wishes you only ever knew me as Nix and his easy smile. But I know now you've always seen right through me. I know you did. It has always scared me. It still does. Because the last thing I ever want is to ruin you.

So know that each time I've hurt you with my words, I've hurt myself more in the process. I'm sorry for everything I've put you through. I know I don't deserve you. I doubt I ever will. Still, the selfish part of me can't lose you.

I hope you know I care about you more than I'll ever be able to show. I hope you know that every time I pull back, I'm only punishing myself and saving you.

Yours in more ways than one,
Rhay

Rio's eyes glazed over, his breath hitching. "I've read it," he admitted, swallowing hard. "I've wondered every second since then if you truly meant it."

Rhay pulled himself together as his skin heated. His feet wanted him to move—towards Rio or fleeing the scene, he wasn't sure. His finger stroked Rio's arm as if it wasn't his to command. "I meant every fucking word."

Watching him, Rio whispered, "But you won't act on it." The hidden subtext drifted between them like the air brushing his skin, like a kiss that only ever existed in his dreams.

"Do you still hate me?" Rhay asked, dreading the answer he knew he deserved. He wasn't offering Rio anything, he knew that. All he had to give was an apology and words thick with feelings he could never say out loud, he could never act on.

Only kiss me if you truly mean it, Rio had said. Rhay couldn't promise anything when he barely knew who he was or what he was supposed to do; when he didn't know if he wouldn't end up hurting Rio one way or another.

Rio's eyes warmed. "I could never hate you. I know you care. I know why you pull away." Rio took a tiny step forward. Rhay got lost in a sea of rich emerald, filled with so much kindness, so much *care* that he could hardly breathe. "But I still hope that one day you won't."

CHAPTER 53

🔥

ELYSSA

Elyssa had never felt more out of her depth. Wryen had gone all out on the big event Amira was supposed to attend to appease rumours. This day was dedicated to Bellrasae, the God of Beauty and patron of Allamyst. To honour Bellrasae, everything had to be the most beautiful, which apparently meant the most batshit crazy outfits Elyssa had ever seen.

The long sleeves of Amira's dress reached the floor, embroidered with hundreds of gold metal feathers that had to be cutting into her arms. The bodice showed all the colours of the morning sky. Amira had convinced Elyssa to wear trousers embroidered with amethyst crystals and a silk blouse printed with an iridescent geometric pattern. Instead of her brass knuckles, Amira had suggested rings, the sharp black crystals capable of inflicting some damage too.

Standing inside the temple of Bellrasae, Elyssa took in the crowd.

"Look at this one, she looks like a pumpkin," Elyssa whispered in Amira's ear as a woman with a round bright orange skirt entered between the stone pillars of the temple. Each pillar was painted with an array of colours. Elyssa had never seen so many colours in one space. It was bright with a touch of eccentricity, the colours blending together in perfect harmony. The flowers wrapped around the pillars and strung across the high ceiling were absolutely beautiful.

Amira hid her laugh behind her hand. She seemed lost in time as she glanced at the paintings on the walls showing Bellrasae supporting all different types of art.

Elyssa was about to comment when Wryen appeared at their side. "Sister," he started, the dark gold and amethyst crown glistening on his head, "*behave*."

Amira flinched and Elyssa took her hand, hidden behind the voluminous skirt of the princess' dress. For a second, Amira squeezed her hand before dropping it, pulling Elyssa's mood down with it. Ever since Elyssa's goddamn solo mission, it felt as if Amira wasn't fully there with her. Like she was holding back when all Elyssa wanted was to move forward. She wished Amira would look her way, but the princess was too focused on her surroundings.

As Amira had told her, Bellrasae's Feast was the start of the day-long celebration. Every cook in the kingdom had been invited to present their best dish. At the end of the feast, the king would select the most fabulous dish and the fae who had made it would become the new head cook of the palace.

Wryen grabbed Amira's hand, leading her to the long marble table that had been set up in the centre of the temple. Elyssa had to fight the urge to pummel Wryen to the ground. Soon, Amira would be free from interacting with her brother. And once Tarnan was taken out, Elyssa could make good on her promise and make Wryen regret everything he'd done to Amira. Maybe then Amira would forgive her.

Amira took a seat between her mother and Wryen while Elyssa dropped into the seat opposite her. Promptly, the first dish was served. It was beef wrapped in a fancy-looking pastry shaped like a crown. In the centre of the crown, the sauce was so shiny that Elyssa could see her face reflected in it.

Wryen's personal taster tried the second bite, the first one being placed in front of the statue of Bellrasae as an offering. The taster waited a minute before giving a nod. Wryen dug in and then the rest of the court followed. Amira gave Elyssa a sorry smile, aware she wouldn't eat the meat.

Elyssa raised her shoulders.

The next course looked like a bouquet of flowers, but it was made from different vegetables. A smile graced Amira's lips that Elyssa wanted to drink in. Digging in, Elyssa savoured the rich flavour on her tongue. At the camp, they hadn't had the privilege of being picky with food.

Amira's smile slipped as she turned to her mother's plate, which was still full. She hadn't even touched the first course. Leaning closer, Amira whispered something to her mother that Elyssa couldn't catch, but she sensed her worry. Amira's mother caressed her cheek when, at once, they both turned their heads fast.

Elyssa followed their gaze to the taster coughing, clutching his throat. Everyone tensed. They had already started eating the second dish. The taster collapsed on the ground, shaking, his mouth foaming. Wryen immediately spat out his food. Elyssa pushed her finger down her throat, leaning down to throw up. She gestured for Amira to do the same. The princess watched the room with terror in her eyes.

Fae collapsed on the ground while others tried to follow Elyssa's example. Mass panic spread through the room. There was too much noise. People were shouting over each other, retching, some screaming in fear of dying. Elyssa bent to grab a throwing star stashed in the boot she had insisted on wearing.

Screaming for the guards, Wryen straightened his lilac blouse. "Find me the cook and call for the healers!"

Guards sprinted out of the temple. As everyone was scrambling to help the fae who were shaking on the ground, a figure grabbed Amira's arm, pulling her off her chair.

Elyssa sprang onto the table, knocking aside plates and glasses full of wine, drenching her boots. But she was only focused on Amira being dragged away. The fae pressed a handkerchief against Amira's nose just as Elyssa jumped off the table, tackling them to the ground. A strange scent like strong alcohol filled her nose.

Rolling to the side, Elyssa rose to her feet and kicked at the fae, ripping him off of Amira who turned on her back, her eyes unfocused. Amira tried to raise herself on her elbows and then crumpled to the ground. Elyssa aimed her throwing star at the fae on the ground, but a violent gust of wind threw her backwards.

Her back hit the sharp edge of the long table, knocking the wind out of her. Plates shattered beneath her weight and her recent stab wound strained from the impact. Elyssa ground her teeth. Fae close to her screamed and ran off. She spotted the fae from before back on his feet, dragging Amira towards the back door.

Elyssa threw her throwing star, but at the same time another fae came at her, pulling at her arm. A grunt of pain escaped her as the fae pressed on her wound, burning pain rushing through her. Her aim was off, hitting the fae's shoulder, and he barely slowed as he pushed Amira —who looked completely out of it—forward.

Pushing past the pain and ignoring the blood on her arm, Elyssa spun around and punched the fae who'd grabbed her, striking his nose. Her rings dug into his flesh, his scream satisfying but barely audible over the shouts all around them.

Elyssa grabbed another throwing star but when she turned, the fae and Amira were gone, the back door falling shut. *Shit.* The fae next to her tried to throw a punch at Elyssa's jaw, but she ducked and aimed her own instead, her rings splitting his skin open.

Not waiting to take him out, Elyssa rushed for the door, jumping over fallen fae. The air was thick with the sweet, pungent smell of food and vomit, turning her stomach. She searched the panicked crowd in the temple for Wryen, but he had disappeared. A knot of terror wound its way into her roiling gut.

Was he behind this? Maybe he wanted an excuse to have her killed. She couldn't spot Amira's mother either; hopefully she was hiding.

As Elyssa dove out the back door, she spotted the fae who had taken Amira at the head of a carriage, pulling at the reins. Kicking up dirt, Elyssa sprinted after them, willing her feet to move faster than the galloping horses. She couldn't lose Amira. Not again.

CHAPTER 54

KARWYN

Lying in bed in the Cinnite palace, slowly dying, Karwyn had had a lot of time to dwell on his past. It was not something he enjoyed doing. His past was a stormy wave crashing against his already fragile mind.

He had replayed his last encounter with Rhay more times than he would ever admit. Heartless, cruel—was that all Rhay could see now? With his health worsening, Karwyn feared he would never get the answer.

He had tried so hard to give Rhay anything he wanted. He had tolerated his parties and drinking to keep him by his side. When that did not work anymore, he had switched to threats—all to make Rhay see where he belonged. That the two of them were meant to be in each other's lives. Who else could ever understand how big of a burden it was to grow up with your mother's death following you like a shadow? To have your father's disappointment in front of you every day? He might have used that against Rhay at some point, but only to make him see that it was Karwyn who he needed. Yet he had only succeeded in pushing Rhay away. Now he was all alone on his deathbed. He did not desire to die here, in his enemy's palace.

Had his mother felt this lonely when she had taken her own life? Was Karwyn destined to die by himself, surrounded by enemies, or had his own actions led him here?

Like clockwork, Karwyn's door opened on Tarnan. The king seemed to be taking great pleasure in visiting him. *To check on his health,* Tarnan had said, but Karwyn knew it was to taunt him. He would have done the same but much more efficiently.

"How are we feeling today?" Tarnan said, his carnelian and ruby crown glistening in the afternoon sun streaming in from the tiny round window next to his bed, too small to escape through.

"Very well," Karwyn lied through his teeth, refusing to give Tarnan the satisfaction of his suffering. Every inch of his body screamed in pain. His intestines were rotting away.

Tarnan gave him a chilling smile that Karwyn saw right through. Karwyn would not give him a reaction.

"I'm glad to hear that. I wouldn't want you to miss seeing me take over Liraen."

Karwyn repressed a cough. His throat burned and he longed for a glass of water. "Are you not worried my cousin and her friends will throw a wrench in your plan?"

They had been rather persistent, throwing Karwyn off course too. Yet, strangely, in a way it had lifted a weight off his chest. He had been pushed down so far death crept up on him. For the first time in Karwyn's life, he felt no expectations, no craving for power to prove himself. He had lost, he knew that. He had no future to plan. All that was left was messing with the people who had betrayed him until he left this world forever.

"I do like a challenge. But in the end I know I shall prevail. In a way I should thank you, you're the reason I managed to break the spell holding my power captive." Following Karwyn's eyes darting to the jug of water placed on a bedside table, just out of reach, Tarnan walked up to it and poured a glass.

Bringing the glass up to Karwyn's lips, he waited for Karwyn to drink. Instead, Karwyn turned his head. He would die, but he wouldn't be humiliated.

"You don't want it?" Tarnan asked.

Karwyn glared daggers at him. How he wished he could throw a gust of wind at Tarnan, knocking his head against the wall hard enough to leave a permanent imprint.

"Fine." Tarnan downed the glass of water. Karwyn felt his parched throat close up as water dripped from Tarnan's chin.

"If I were you, I would not be so sure about your victory." Karwyn infused each word with spite. "You are alone, even with Rhay on your side. And even if you do succeed, your power will drive you mad like your father."

Tarnan leaned in. "Soon, I'll have both amulets and—" He stopped speaking and readjusted the crown on his head. "Rhay has made the unfortunate decision to leave my side. Maybe you'll live long enough to witness his death."

Karwyn gritted his teeth, refusing to let Tarnan see the fear gripping his heart. "He chose my cousin over you, how shocking. I am familiar with Rhay's ever-changing allegiances. I could not care less about his fate. But I see your plans are not going accordingly."

Tarnan chuckled, the sound like gritting sand in Karwyn's ears. "You're forgetting something, Karwyn. I'm always one step ahead. Everything that led us to this moment, *I* have planned. Including your father's death."

Karwyn bristled. "My father died of old age. Your ploys have lost their believability."

Tarnan's smile was the picture of fake sorrow, something Karwyn had always tried to imitate too. "But there were no warning signs, were there? He could have lived another few years at least, that was Saydren's opinion. But I was tired of waiting. Saydren knew how to poison the king without drawing any unwanted attention. I knew the High King Contest would make you go to extreme lengths to secure power. You're quite predictable."

His heart sped up, his veins boiling. "You bastard!" Karwyn threw his hands forward, trying to grab Tarnan by the neck. Tarnan pulled away fast, Karwyn's attempt leaving a small scratch on Tarnan's cheek. He envisioned that scratch growing, splitting Tarnan's neck, spraying blood all over. What a glorious sight that would be.

"I'll leave you to rest," Tarnan said with an obviously pleased smile. He closed the door behind him, leaving Karwyn once again alone with his thoughts.

Karwyn could not stay in Cinnite a minute longer. He would not give Tarnan the satisfaction of seeing him slowly die, toying with him whenever he felt like it. He had dreamt of escaping for weeks now; it was time to set a plan in motion.

He needed someone to break him out of this prison. *Rhay.* Rhay might think he was free of Karwyn, but he knew Rhay too well. With the right motivation, Rhay would come running. And then he would not be alone.

Karwyn remembered what his father had told him about the Dark King. He had used an ancient artefact, the combined amulets—the ones later used to spell the border between Liraen and Earth—to feed on a fae's life source in order to sustain the toll his dark power had taken on him and to refill his power. Karwyn had tried to get his hand on the amulets, to get other fae's power. One had been hidden in the human world and the other had been at the temple in Parae, right under his nose. But he had never managed to get it from its spell-trapped spot. From what Tarnan had let slip, he did not have both amulets. Did Rhay know what the combined amulets meant to Tarnan?

The door opened, startling Karwyn. Instead of Tarnan, it was a young fae with long strawberry blonde hair who peeked inside.

She furrowed her brows. "You're not Rhay."

She was about to close the door but Karwyn saw an opportunity, holding back a sly grin. "No, but I know where he is."

The young fae sneaked back inside the room. "You do? I thought he would be here. I saw the king leave this room. Where is Rhay? He promised to come to Rubien with me."

"What is your name?" Karwyn asked, forcing himself to smile warmly at the young fae. He wished he could read her mind. It had made it so much easier to control people.

"I'm Saige." She fidgeted with her long sleeve, reminding him of Amira. "Are you all right? You look unwell."

"I am much better now. Rhay has told me about you. I know he misses you." The young fae's eyes lit up. *By Caelo, she is easy to use.*

"I know he would be delighted to hear from us," Karwyn continued. "Are you familiar with spelled paper?" Saige nodded. "Very well. If you bring me a piece and a candle, I will write Rhay a letter, and I can assure you, he will come visit us very soon. But it has to be a secret between us. The king cannot know."

"Is it a surprise?" Saige bounced on her feet.

Karwyn almost laughed. Rhay still left the same impression on people. They either despised or adored him. And fortunately for Karwyn, Saige was absolutely smitten with him.

CHAPTER 55

EYDEN

"I would estimate about two thirds of our people in Parae and the neighbouring towns are on our side. Some are willing to fight as well," Ilario said, leaning forward on the oak table in the council room. In the last four days they had gone to as many local spots around the area as they could. Turosian was the biggest kingdom in Liraen, so they weren't able to go everywhere in such a short amount of time, even with Eyden's ability quickening the travel time.

Sometimes, they had each gone on their own to cover more ground. Or Eyden had gone by himself while Ilario had brought Rhay with him. It seemed like an attempt to give Rhay something to do while no one was yet convinced to trust him.

Lora smiled at Ilario gratefully. The bags under her eyes showed just how much she'd been pushing herself to train her powers. Even mind-reading, her most unpredictable power. Although she had avoided Rhay whenever she could, she wasn't above asking him for advice to master her mind-reading ability. To Eyden's surprise, Rhay hadn't even brought up how Oscar had ransacked his room for human tech devices.

Maja, sitting next to Eyden, had a similar grin plastered on her face as she glanced at Ilario. Oscar and Ian were probably in one of their rooms, having grown closer as they both had nowhere else to go at present.

"That's great," Lora said. Then her smile slipped. "But we still have the same issue we've always had. With Tarnan's power, we can't win with numbers. And we have to give him an answer today about the amulet or he'll be delivering more...heads." She shuddered. Oscar's alarm system was working, but they had no idea if Tarnan had snatched anyone else from Lora's world before they had installed it. They still had no idea why he wanted the amulet so badly if he had no witch. What was he planning to do with both artefacts?

The double doors hit the wall loudly as Rhay threw them open and stormed into the room. His emerald hair was dishevelled as if he'd just rolled out of bed. Everyone turned to him and he slowed his steps as the doors fell shut behind him.

Taking a crumpled piece of paper out of his jacket, Rhay stopped at the end of the long table across from Lora. He slapped the piece of paper onto the wooden surface. "This is from Karwyn."

"Are you sure?" Lora pushed back her chair. Eyden rose too, heading towards Rhay.

"Quite sure." Rhay handed her the piece of paper. His gaze briefly flickered to Ilario. Maja looked over Lora's shoulder to read with her.

Unfolding the paper, Lora read out loud, "'The amulets used to create the border spell can be combined. Tarnan craves it to strengthen his power and feed on life source as Variel Sartoya has done before him. Combined they can syphon power from any source. I will not live much longer. Take this knowledge as my dying gift to you—Karwyn.'"

"That's how Cirny broke the border spell, isn't it?" Lora asked, but the question seemed directed at herself. "But the amulets weren't combined at that time." The fire message crumbled into ashes on the table.

"Maybe Tarnan didn't want to risk combining it when Amira was holding one of the amulets," Eyden stated, remembering how furious Tarnan had seemed when Amira had thrown the amulet to Eyden before he'd drifted away that day. "He wouldn't have wanted Amira to have it."

Ilario nodded. "So that's why he wants it now. Power. With the amulets, even Lora doesn't stand a chance against him. Not if he sucks away her power to fuel his."

"Afraid so," Rhay agreed.

Eyden turned to Lora who had tensed, fists on the table. Karwyn's message fully sank in then.

"If Karwyn dies..." Eyden started, and Lora looked at him, biting her lip. "He can't. We'll get him and make him break Lora's agreement."

Rhay took a step back, his eyes wide. "He must be in the Rubien palace now. Tarnan wouldn't let him out of his sight."

"What about the amulet, would it be in Rubien too?" Lora asked Rhay.

Rhay ran a hand through his messy hair. "I don't know where, but yes, I would assume the amulet is with Tarnan and Saydren in Cinnite."

Lora crossed her arms. "If he is telling the truth, then we need to get Karwyn here. If we have Karwyn, Tarnan can't threaten my mum anymore. We need that amulet. We can't hand over the one thing that makes him stronger. I don't know what to do about Tarnan's threat..." She bit her lip.

If they got Karwyn away from him, her mother would be fine, but there was no guarantee Tarnan didn't have other people in his grasp. It was an impossible choice. If they gave into Tarnans threats, more people would die once he was high king.

"We'll have to call his bluff," Eyden decided. Lora's lip trembled but she didn't disagree.

"So we need a distraction to get the other amulet?" Ilario said, exchanging a knowing look with Lora.

"You want to be the distraction," Eyden stated, a cold feeling spreading through his heart.

Lora shrugged as if it wasn't her life on the line. "He wanted to bargain for the amulet before. If I ask for a meeting on neutral ground as my response, I don't think he'd refuse. We need to get him away from the palace."

"And then what? You have nothing to offer him."

"I'll pretend to bargain for Amira's freedom in exchange for the amulet. He'll refuse and I'll make a run for it." Not even Lora herself sounded convinced.

"You need back-up. I'll go with you."

Lora shook her head. "I need you to get the amulet. Besides, Tarnan could use you against me. He knows I wouldn't risk any of you."

Ilario turned to Eyden. "We'll get the amulet then."

"No," Lora interjected. "I need someone to hold the position here and I don't trust anyone to do that except you."

Ilario's eyes widened as if shocked by her trust, but Eyden had seen how Ilario had handled himself in their court meetings, how he'd calmly spoken to the queens, how he interacted with the town folk. It came naturally to him.

Lora sighed. "And Damir needs to go too." And she'd rather Ilario didn't have to deal with him. Yet, that left Eyden to handle him. Ever since the massacre of the former guards, Eyden had watched Damir even closer than before but had spoken as little as possible with him.

"You want him to shift into someone?" Eyden asked, following her plan.

Lora met his gaze, her eyes every bit as fierce as the fire running through her veins. "Tarnan. They'll let him into the palace. But I don't trust Damir to go by himself."

"I don't trust Damir with anything." Eyden chuckled. "I still don't like the thought of you going alone."

Lora rolled her shoulder as if preparing for a fight. "Tarnan won't kill me. He wants me in the contest. I'll have to try my best not to reveal my power."

Maybe so, but at what cost? Eyden thought. A bigger distraction that didn't fully depend on Lora was what they needed, and he had only one other idea.

"I'll talk to Damir," Eyden said, already coming up with his own plan. But he wasn't sure yet if the person in question would agree.

Lora turned to Ilario. "Let's send a message to Tarnan."

Ilario nodded grimly.

"I should go to Rubien," Rhay said, catching everyone off guard. "I know what you're thinking, but I won't go off plan, and you need me. I can help clear the guards and get Karwyn to come with us without much hassle." He looked straight at Eyden. "And between Damir and myself, am I not the more trustworthy one?"

Eyden ground his teeth. He felt Lora's hand on his arm as if trying to calm him.

"Okay then." Eyden frowned at Rhay. "But I'm leaving your ass in Rubien if you get any ideas."

Knocking twice, Eyden waited behind Lozlan's door. He knew Lora would never ask Lozlan for anything after how their conversation had ended last week. Ilario had asked in her place for Lozlan to sign away his claim to the throne to ensure no one would demand Lora to step down. He'd seen the disappointment in Lora's eyes when Ilario had told her Lozlan had signed. She didn't want this and it wasn't fucking fair that she had to be the one taking all these risks when Lozlan could make it easier.

The door opened, and Lozlan took a surprised step back when he spotted Eyden. "I didn't expect you."

Eyden brushed past him into the room. "Who did you expect? Lora?"

"No. I don't..." he stuttered, his hands shaking. "...don't reckon she wants to hear from me."

Eyden's blood boiled. "You have no fucking idea, do you? She *wants* to hear from you. Do you even realise what's happening?"

Lozlan pushed his matted hair behind his ear. "She wants my help running Turosian. I don't want...she shouldn't be here. Gone. She should be gone. Back home. She can't fix the border spell herself. She should be with her mother...instead of trying to clean up the mess Karwyn and my brother left behind."

"You don't even know half the story." Eyden stepped forward, trapping him with a piercing look. It was time he knew. If the roles were reversed, Eyden would want Lora to intervene.

"Lora isn't here because she wants to be the queen. She only came here to save her mother, who is still in critical condition. And she's cleaning up this mess because no one else can. Someone has to rule. Someone has to step up." He looked Lozlan up and down, not hiding his animosity. "If there wasn't so much at stake, Lora wouldn't even think about taking part in the contest, but she's so determined—frustratingly so. Even when you knock her down, even when you force her to ashes, she'll keep fighting." Eyden shifted his feet, letting his words sink in. "Even when her opponent is the Dark King's son."

Lozlan went white in the face. "I...no. My mind's..."

"Not the sharpest, but it's the truth. Tarnan Ellevarn is a Sartoya and he's meeting with Lora soon. Alone, as a distraction. But it won't be enough." Eyden took in Lozlan's reaction—his sweaty palms, his twitching eyes. He was a mess, but he would catch Tarnan off guard.

"You want me to go with her?" Lozlan's stutter was gone for once. "I can't fight like I used to."

"You can't or you *won't?* There's a stark difference. And even so, fighting is what we're trying to avoid. This is about stalling."

Lozlan's eyes brightened as he exhaled slowly. Eyden knew with how long Lozlan had kept his fire inside, there must be a massive wave of power slumbering inside that craved to be let out. They had no time to wait for it.

"Lora would never ask, but she needs you," Eyden said, daring Lozlan to disagree. He hadn't tried at all when all Lora was doing was *trying.* She tried so fucking hard he feared it would get her killed.

"I'll do it." His tone sounded less broken and more determined, reminding Eyden of Lora. Eyden hoped there was a will, a fire, hidden within Lozlan that he would finally let out. Not for his sake, but for hers.

CHAPTER 56

AMIRA

The carriage tipped sideways, and in her dazed state, Amira felt herself flying before crashing hard against the wooden wall. *What is happening?* Her mind was utterly blank. She took in the carriage lying on its side, forcing her against the wall. Pain shot down her back, but her legs were numb. Trying to stand, Amira noticed her impractical dress. *Right, Bellrasae Feast.* Her body felt too heavy to move. A bitter taste in her mouth made her sick to her stomach.

She had been taken against her will, but by who? Wryen? Amira's vision blurred as she pulled herself up, clutching the door handle of the side that was now facing the sky. She was still under the effect of whatever drug they had used on her. It wasn't fortae, but she hated how weak it made her feel. Hated how familiar it felt to have her powers buried.

Scrambling to open the door, Amira climbed out of the broken carriage, the seam of her dress tearing. Blinking against the bright sunlight, she spotted a familiar figure locked in a fight with one of the fae who had kidnapped her. *Elyssa.*

With a sharp yell, Elyssa plunged her dagger into the fae's heart. Another fae lay on the ground, bleeding from his skull. Blood was smeared on Elyssa's blouse and her arm was bleeding again, yet she smiled when she spotted Amira.

A wave of relief washed over Amira. "El." Leaning forward, she fell from the carriage onto the dirt road. Pain sliced through her weakened body. If she had been on fortae, she wouldn't have felt the sting.

Elyssa rushed to her side. "Are you okay, princess?"

"Wryen has to be behind this." Amira let Elyssa pull her to her feet. Her head spun and Elyssa appeared double in front of her. She tried to focus, but then Elyssa was thrown to the side and Amira went right with her. The fae with the head wound was back on his feet, a curse on his lips as he leaned over them.

Another carriage stopped next to them, coming out of a hidden path in the woods. Amira's breath caught as her mother peeked out of the carriage. "Stop this!" She waved at the fae who had attacked them and he *listened*.

"I don't understand. Did Wryen..." Amira muttered as Elyssa helped her to her feet. She brushed dirt and leaves from her ruined dress.

Her mother's gaze, soft yet guilty, turned to Amira. "Wryen isn't behind this. He has no idea where you are and I intend to keep it that way."

"It was you?" Cold dread spread over her skin. Her mother nodded as she left the carriage, another man on her heels. "You had me *abducted?*"

It couldn't be true. Her mother would never cause her harm like this. Would she?

The fae with the head wound walked over to her mother, who folded her hands in front of her. "It had to look real so your brother wouldn't suspect you had any part in it."

"I *have* no part in it. Why? Why would you do this?" Amira hobbled towards her mother with Elyssa's help.

Her mother twisted her hands, her gaze apologetic. "I had to save you, take you away from Wryen, from court. They're only going to cause you harm." Her mother grimaced as she glanced from Elyssa to Amira. How could her mother have betrayed her like that? How could she have made such a decision without asking her? Didn't she realise what it meant to have her choice taken from her *again*?

Elyssa stepped in front of Amira. "Do you understand what

you've done? Drugging your own daughter after everything she's been through?"

As she read the truth on Amira's face, her mother stumbled back. "I...I didn't know. Tarnan told me it was the only way to protect you. With him, we'll be safe from Wryen, from anyone."

Amira's chest caved in. Her head pounded as she fought to accept her mother's betrayal. "You're working with Tarnan? He's the enemy!"

"It's not your fight, Mira. We have suffered enough, it's time for us to think about ourselves. Tarnan cares about you. He was a friend to your father and he always treated me kindly." Her mother grabbed her hands, squeezing them.

Amira pulled her hands back. "He manipulated you like he manipulated me. He can't be trusted, Mother. And you shouldn't keep me away from the fight I need to face. I can't run away, not anymore. Otherwise there will truly be no future for us." A sob got caught in Amira's throat. Pain flashed in her mother's eyes. She knew she was breaking her heart, but her mother had broken hers first. Amira had chosen to fight long ago, to the end if necessary.

Her mother pulled her into a tight embrace. "Please, come with me. I can't lose you again, my Mira."

Amira took a deep breath, inhaling her mother's sweet and comforting rose perfume. No matter how betrayed Amira felt, it didn't erase all the love she felt for her.

Tearing herself away from the suffocating embrace, Amira wiped the tears from her mother's eyes. "We have to go and you have to hide. Tarnan won't be happy you didn't come through." Amira tried to keep her voice from shaking but failed.

The fae who had been in the carriage with her mother grabbed Amira's wrist forcefully. "I don't think so."

"Let go of her at once! I'll make sure you'll still get your silver," Amira's mother pleaded while Elyssa drew her dagger.

A dark smile spread the fae's lips. "I don't follow your orders, lady."

Amira tried to shake off the fae's hold but she was still exhausted. Elyssa pierced his arm with her dagger, forcing him to let go of Amira.

The fae pressed on his wound, frowning at Elyssa before turning to Amira. "Get in the carriage without a fuss or I'll have to take care of your mother and your friend."

A third fae climbed down from the carriage, a sword in his hand. He launched himself at Elyssa while the other one grabbed Amira and swung her over his shoulder. Amira hit him with her hands and feet. The fae with the head wound circled Elyssa as well, two against one.

Amira's mother stepped in front of them. "I said let go of her. I'll pay you anything you want."

The fae stared her up and down. "I don't believe you have more silver than a king."

Before her mother could take another step forward, the fae pushed her hard. She fell on her back, her head hitting the ground. She didn't get up.

"Mother!" Amira yelled as cold fear battled against red-hot anger in her heart. Her chest caved in and Amira felt the drug's hold lift. Air seemed to flow through her lungs more freely. Her mind cleared as if the cobwebs disintegrated. Pressing her hands against the fae's back, she sent an electric wave straight to his heart. The fae collapsed, still holding Amira. His weight crushed her, the air leaving her lungs.

She stumbled to her feet just as Elyssa pushed her dagger through a fae's eyes, her arm bleeding heavily once again. The fae with the head wound was still standing, stalking towards Elyssa with a bloodthirsty smile. Amira rushed to her mother's side.

"My Mira," her mother faintly said as her eyes fluttered open and she got to her feet. Her hand pressed on the wound on her head. "I'm sorry. I didn't think...we can still flee. I know someone in the countryside in Emerlane. We can hide. *Together.*"

Amira stared at her until a yell drew her attention back to Elyssa, who was trapped by one fae's arms, another punching her stomach. She attempted to call on her power again but her bones felt heavy and her skin paper thin. Nothing came.

Amira couldn't run. Not again. Picking up a stone, she curled her fist as she headed towards them with a newfound fire. Her mother called out to her, but Amira kept going. The fae holding Elyssa didn't even glance her way before she jumped on his back, bashing the stone against his already bleeding skull. He let go of Elyssa and she ducked the other fae's attack, kicking him away.

Amira pulled at the fae's hair as he whirled around, trying to shake her off his back. She dug her heels into his stomach, her head turning fuzzy as he spun around wildly. Then he fell backwards, a move Amira didn't anticipate. The breath left her lungs as his weight crushed her. She blinked away tears, the stone falling from her numb hand.

"Not so brave now, are you?" the fae snarled above her, his foot lifting to kick at her. Her hands shot up to cover her face just as the fae grunted in pain. Peeking from behind her fingers, Amira spotted Elyssa next to the fae, a sword in her hand, the blade cutting through the fae's neck. Pulling the weapon free, Elyssa plunged it into his heart. He dropped to the ground next to the one-eyed fae.

"Thanks," Amira breathed as Elyssa took her hand to pull her up on shaky legs. Her whole body felt as bruised as her spirit.

"No, thank *you*, princess. Pretty kickass moves."

"Amira." Her mother stopped in front of them, a hand on her chest. Tears flooded her mother's cheeks, but Amira knew what she had to do.

"Take the horse." Amira tilted her head to the carriage. "I don't run. Come find me when Tarnan is dealt with if you wish." She turned away, Elyssa by her side.

Amira held herself together until she heard the horse take off behind them. Then she thought of her mother's devastated face and Amira broke down in Elyssa's arms.

Amira stared out the window at the beautiful city in the distance, half her face in shadows, the other half brightened by the sun streaming in. Even when she heard Elyssa come out of the bathroom, Amira didn't turn to face her. She wrapped her arms tightly around herself, still fixated on her mother's betrayal and almost losing her life in the process.

A day had passed and the drug was fully out of her system, but Amira could still smell the strong odour of it. The image of her mother appearing on the road had plagued her ever since.

When Elyssa leaned against the other side of the window, Amira glanced her way.

"Are you okay? You know, with the drug? It must have been triggering."

"I'm fine, I don't crave it. But I'll be careful." Amira shuddered at the thought of the drug infiltrating her system.

"We can go home today." Elyssa gave her a small smile. "Freaking finally."

Amira uncrossed her arms and smoothed her wide, dark purple trousers. *Home*, what a strange word. "I don't even know where home is anymore. This palace isn't. Anywhere Wryen is is not my home. The Turosian palace has never been my home."

"I don't think home is a place." Elyssa leaned forward to take Amira's hand. "It's a feeling. I feel it when I'm with my brother even when he goddamn drives me mad." Amira couldn't help but laugh, a lock of her hair falling into her face. "I feel it right now. Every time I look into your eyes."

Amira's lips parted, her eyes flitting over Elyssa's face. She felt undeserving of Elyssa's affection, the pit in her stomach fighting off butterflies. How long until it would run its course? Until Amira would ruin it, would condemn Elyssa like she had done to Quynn?

"Did I say too much?" Elyssa asked, grinning. "I kind of like this speechless look on your face."

"I can speak," Amira replied. But then she kept quiet again, her thoughts going into overdrive.

Elyssa chuckled even as a shadow passed in her eyes. "It's okay, princess. All I wanted to say is the Turosian palace might not be our home, but the people there are. I'll be your carry-with-me home. Anywhere. Always. I'm here to stay, remember."

Would she stay until Amira doomed her? Amira drew closer, her thumb brushing over the back of Elyssa's hand. She was selfish; she couldn't resist Elyssa. "The way you look at me, like you can see beneath it all, like you want to see it all, good and bad. It...scares me."

Elyssa put her hand over Amira's. "It doesn't have to. I promise I won't disappear on you again. I'll prove it." She moved Amira's hand to her heart. "I love you, sunshine. In case there was any doubt."

Her heart sped up. Her lungs felt strangled, cutting off Amira's attempt to form words. She was silent, the past plaguing her. Quynn's soft face disappearing in flames. Farren's lifeless body. All the people who had trusted her and whom she had failed.

Squeezing Elyssa's hand, Amira whispered, "I don't want to drown in the past when I can break through the surface in the present with you."

Amira traced Elyssa's bottom lip before her striking hazel eyes met hers. Kissing her, Elyssa's arms went around Amira's neck to pull her closer. Amira's back hit the window bank. Elyssa deepened the kiss, tracing Amira's lip until she sighed.

Pulling back just enough to break their kiss, Elyssa grinned. Amira couldn't help but smile. Elyssa was her home too. But could she keep that home when it meant risking Elyssa? Amira kissed her again, willing the dark thoughts away, wanting to stay in this moment.

Amira shuddered as Elyssa's lips trailed down her neck. Elyssa chuckled. "As much as I would love to continue this, I think there's something else we should do on our last day here."

"What's that? Avoid Wryen? Because we can ignore him just fine from here," Amira said, pulling Elyssa in by her waist. Wryen's guards were still looking for the fae responsible for the attack. Hopefully he would never figure it out.

"I want to see the Amryne you used to love, the city you once described as beautiful, vibrant. I know it's overshadowed by darkness now, but that's Wryen's fault, not the city's. Don't let him take your childhood home away from you."

Nostalgia pulled at Amira's heart as she turned to the window that overlooked the city from afar. Despite Wryen, Amira was happy to be back in her kingdom. She wondered if Allamyst could ever return to what it had been when her father had ruled. A place where people didn't have to fear their ruler. If she could, she would want to bring a new open-minded way of thinking here.

Her recent discovery came to her mind. Her father had known who she was all along—the witch gene came from his side of the family. If the people of Allamyst knew, would they accept her as her father had done?

But Amira had no claim to the throne anymore, and she'd never been taught how to be a queen anyway.

Breathing out deeply, she tilted her head towards Elyssa. "Let's go then. I have much to show you."

CHAPTER 57

✦ ELYSSA

Elyssa had seen glimpses of the city before, but never through Amira's eyes. Wryen's presence had always dampened the experience. She didn't want Amira to leave her former home with nothing but bad memories. If she could, Elyssa would erase them all. But she could only add new ones, good memories full of fiery kisses and whispered words of affection to make up for her own mistakes. She had told Amira she loved her and the princess hadn't echoed her feelings. Elyssa tried hard not to let it get to her, tried to give Amira time. Amira had every reason to still be upset with her.

Now it was just the two of them, cloaks over their heads to shield them from the burning sun and any curious fae. The bright colours of the buildings, the beautiful murals along the stone walls, and the shiny stained-glass windows of the shops all brought a sparkle to Amira's eyes. It made Elyssa's heart lighter despite the lingering guilt.

Pointing to a flower shop ahead of them, Amira said, "My father used to take me there. He said flowers are like his kingdom. Beautiful, but if not properly addressed and watered, they wither quickly."

Amira's face soured, probably thinking of how Wryen would rather crush flowers than nurture them. "Sometimes," she continued, the sun reflecting in her glossy hair sticking out of her hood, "he would come to my room dressed as a commoner and ask me to go on an adventure. With a cloak and simple clothing, no one recognised us."

"Let's see then," Elyssa replied, taking her hand and pulling her into the shop.

A mix of flowery scents immediately hit her—too strong for her taste, but Amira seemed delighted. Rows and rows of flowers graced the sky blue walls of the shop. Vines were strung across the ceiling, small flower-shaped lanterns throwing light to the already bright room.

"Which one is your favourite?" Elyssa asked.

Amira seemed drawn to a red one, delicate flowers growing on a stem. It sat in a beautiful lilac vase with silver lines running across it.

"That one is a symbol of courage and strength," a fae woman said, coming out from behind a curtain made out of bright feathers. "A red orchid."

Amira's finger traced the flower. "Fitting," she said as her eyes met Elyssa's.

Fighting a grin, Elyssa turned to the trader. "How much?"

"Five silver."

Elyssa pulled out coins from her pocket, feeling Amira's eyes on her. She probably wondered where she'd gotten the silver from. Elyssa had learned a thing or two from Eyden. Pickpocketing from rich, unsuspecting fae was almost too easy.

She handed the coins to the woman. Elyssa removed one of the flowers from its stem. She pushed Amira's cloak back to put the orchid behind her ear.

"Fitting indeed," Elyssa said, and Amira's eyes brightened. Elyssa had never seen the usefulness of flowers, but seeing the smile on Amira's lips, she finally understood.

"Your Highness," a voice behind them said, and Amira turned to the shopkeeper. The fae bowed. "I didn't recognise you right away. Apologies."

Amira's gaze drifted to the door as Elyssa's hand subtly shifted to the dagger hidden under her jacket.

Seemingly oblivious to their reactions, the shopkeeper walked closer. "It's been years since you've been here. I always loved watching your face light up when the king brought you to my shop. The late king, that is." Her smile slipped.

Amira raised her brows. "You knew who we were?"

"Of course. We all used to joke about how the king and his daughter walked the streets as if no one would recognise them." The shopkeeper's smile was warm. "I knew he simply wanted to be a father when he came here. He deserved that peace. He was a kind king. And he always graciously tipped me." The fae winked, but then her smile sobered. "I wondered what happened to you."

"I..." Amira stuttered, clasping her hands in front of her.

"It's a long story," Elyssa interrupted. "We should go, but thank you." She pulled Amira's cloak back over her head, giving her a smile to ease her worry.

Elyssa drew her out of the shop. "I'm surprised she remembers me," Amira said.

"You underestimate yourself. Who could ever forget you?"

Amira smiled shyly, bumping Elyssa's shoulder.

"So was that your favourite place?"

Amira shook her head. "No. My favourite is the natural pool. I always felt the most free in the water."

The thought of a free Amira enjoying the water made Elyssa smile until another thought took over her mind. Amira in the pool, her skin glistening as droplets ran down her body.

"What are you thinking?" A curious glint sparkled in Amira's eyes.

Elyssa smirked. "I'm thinking I want to try that pool."

Amira exhaled sharply. "Yes." Elyssa grinned at her. "I mean yes, I'll show you. It's in the palace."

She turned to an alleyway and Elyssa followed. Fae around them paid them little attention as they went along with their day. Children ran past them, laughing, flowers in their hair. Shopkeepers advertised their goods and Elyssa was tempted to buy some cinnamon buns, but the thought of the pool, of chasing some happiness with Amira, kept her focused.

They went back to the palace faster than they'd left. Taking a side entrance, they avoided most guards, and Amira grabbed her hand as she ran through a corridor to a part of the palace Elyssa hadn't seen yet.

The air grew warmer and then Amira pushed open a door into what almost looked like a cave. Water ran down a stone wall and into a pool that seemed deep enough to dive in. Steam rose from the water and Elyssa's skin heated as her shirt stuck to her skin.

The one downside was that the waterfall was so loud it was hard for Elyssa to hear anything else. She only realised Amira was locking the door when she turned her head, the sound lost to her.

"When I used to go here, I had swimming clothes." Amira stopped before her.

"No such luck this time, princess," Elyssa teased. She shrugged off her jacket, setting her dagger at the edge of the pool. Amira didn't move so Elyssa continued, stripping off her shirt and undershirt. She noticed Amira's eyes darkening as she took in her bare chest. The air was so hot, yet it felt pleasant against her bare skin.

Smirking, Elyssa took off her shoes before unbuttoning her dark trousers. "Enjoying the view, sunshine?"

Amira swallowed hard. She seemed to have trouble keeping eye contact as she began unbuttoning her own blouse. The princess' fingers slipped on the buttons. Her nerves were charming, but Elyssa didn't want to make it harder for her, so she took the rest of her clothes off quickly before jumping in the pool.

She thought she heard Amira shriek but she couldn't be sure as she dove under water. The warmth of the water felt heavenly.

When she resurfaced, she saw that Amira had kicked off her trousers. She turned her back to her, taking in the waterfall. Distantly in her mind, Elyssa knew they had matters to discuss. Their future. The upcoming battle. But right now, Elyssa didn't want answers. She didn't want to hear Amira tell her she was disappointed in Elyssa's actions.

The water rippled as Amira entered the pool and Elyssa turned to face her. The pool was deep enough that she couldn't touch the bottom.

Amira inclined her head to the stone wall by the waterfall. "The water is more shallow there."

She swam forward, more graceful than Elyssa could ever be when she wasn't fighting. Reaching the stone edge, Amira leaned against it. Standing, the water barely covered her chest, and Elyssa wished she could see more clearly in the dimly lit cave.

Stopping with some distance between them, Elyssa asked, "Have you ever done anything else here? Besides swimming?"

Amira's gaze dipped as she bit her lip. Elyssa was ultra-focused on a drop of water running down Amira's neck.

"No." The drop of water slid to her chest until it joined the hot water.

Elyssa stepped closer, her hands on either side of Amira's head on the stone wall behind her. "You've never used the opportunity to...unwind here?"

Amira's chest rose rapidly. Elyssa expected her to say no but then she said, "Maybe I have."

A smirk plastered Elyssa's lips. "Do elaborate."

Amira's laugh was husky, drowned out by the water around them. "Can't you imagine?"

"Trust me, I have," Elyssa said, and Amira's laughter died as heat glazed over her eyes. "But I'd rather see it with my own eyes."

Amira took Elyssa's right hand and put it to her chest, over her heart. Her skin felt softer than usual, the water heating both of them. "I would start here," Amira said, her voice barely recognisable. She moved Elyssa's hand over her chest under the water. Amira seemed to swallow a sigh as Elyssa's hand grazed her nipple and then went lower.

Amira guided Elyssa's hand down further, over her stomach and then finally between her legs. "And I would end up here," Amira whispered, not backing down from Elyssa's stare.

With a wicked grin, Elyssa stroked her like she'd learned Amira's body responded to. "Like this?" Elyssa picked up tempo and Amira's eyes closed as she dropped her head against the wall.

"Not like this," Amira breathed, a cry leaving her lips as Elyssa moved forward until their chests touched. Sparks danced on her skin wherever she touched Amira. "It's never been like this, until you."

"Fuck," Elyssa cursed, desire swirling in her belly.

Amira laughed, but it was cut off when Elyssa pushed a finger into her. Her hips moved frantically in sync with Elyssa's movement.

One hand on Elyssa's shoulder, Amira drew her closer, sighing into her mouth before her lips met hers. Her tongue ran along the seam of her mouth until Elyssa opened eagerly. Amira's free hand went to her waist, pulling her closer. Amira parted Elyssa's legs with her thigh, rubbing just the right spot. Eyes falling shut, warmth shot through her— her body moving to create friction where she ached the most while stroking Amira.

They were both out of breath when their kiss broke, foreheads touching as they watched the other's reaction, stupid grins plastered on their faces.

Steam gathered around them, throwing them into their own little paradise—their own self-made home that was just the two of them wrapped up in a moment where nothing mattered but *this*, them together. When Amira fell apart, Elyssa followed right after, sharp pleasure ringing through her body, tension leaving her soul until only relief prevailed.

When Elyssa looked into Amira's eyes as they caught their breath, she saw her future written in them. A home she'd never leave. A home she'd never give up fighting for.

CHAPTER 58

RHAY

With fake almandine shackles around Rhay's wrists, Damir—who had shifted into Tarnan—dragged him towards the newly rebuilt palace in Rubien. Eyden was hiding outside by their horses, waiting for Rhay's signal. It had taken them half a day to travel here, taking the fastest horses in the palace's stables. The impressive stone structure surrounded by ruins glistened in the midday sun. Rhay had only seen drawings of the Rubien palace, but in person it looked even more grand.

Tarnan had it rebuilt exactly as it had been in the Dark King's time. Towers of dark stone rose to the sky with sharp pointed roofs as if cutting through any barrier separating them from Caelo. The archway leading to the palace was embedded with tiny rubies, red roses crowning it. The palace looked lethal and beautiful at the same time.

As guards rushed towards them, Rhay snapped back to the mission at hand.

"My king," one of the guards said, drawing his sword as he spied Rhay.

"It was an ambush." Damir/Tarnan pushed Rhay to the guard, then straightened his singed ruby-red blouse. He wore Rubien colours in hopes of fooling everyone. His blouse was bloody, muddy, and ripped to complete his story.

The guard dragged Rhay towards the entrance. Damir strode forward as if he had every right. Rhay was almost impressed by how much he looked like Tarnan, even his strangely content smile.

"Shall we take him to the dungeons, Your Majesty?" the guard holding Rhay asked as they stepped into the palace. Another guard joined her.

"Take him to Karwyn," Damir replied. When the guards didn't move, his tone turned sharper. "Do I need to compel you?"

The guards were about to turn to the staircase with Rhay when Saydren rounded the corner, his grey eyes taking them in with surprise.

"Your Majesty. What happened?"

"An ambush. Let's walk." Damir waved at the guards to take Rhay away before gesturing for Saydren to head the opposite direction.

Saydren hesitated a second, then followed. Damir gave Rhay a brief glance before the guards pushed him towards the staircase. It was working. Rhay would free Karwyn and Damir would get the amulet. Once Rhay had Karwyn in his sight, he'd call Eyden to drift them out. Lora had given Rhay her necklace that allowed Eyden to track her whereabouts. He had seen how hard it was for Eyden to watch Lora hand over the beacon, but he hadn't argued.

Just as Damir followed Saydren, the latter turned back around.

"Where's your crown?" Saydren asked. Rhay went up the stairs, craning his neck to catch their conversation.

Damir huffed. "I will have to send guards to fetch it. I lost it in the fight."

Saydren's gaze was piercing. "How did you lose that fight?"

"I didn't *lose* anything," Damir hissed. "I chose to retreat. Don't question my ways."

"It's my job to question your decisions." Saydren moved closer to Damir. "They took out all twenty guards?"

Damir stared at him, holding eye contact. It felt like a trick question and they both seemed to know it. *Shit.* Rhay looked from the top of the stairs to Damir and Saydren below. The guard pushed him along the golden railing and Rhay dragged his feet.

Damir held Saydren's gaze as he shrugged. "We should've brought more."

Saydren nodded, pleased. "We should have." His expression changed, turning furious. "Guards! He is not your king. Seize him!"

One of the guards holding Rhay ran down the stairs.

Fast as lightning, Damir took out a dagger from his boot and threw it at Saydren. The healer moved out of the way just in time and the blade impaled his upper arm instead of his chest.

Saydren pulled the dagger out. A couple of guards came running from the other hallway, their swords raised. "This fae is an impostor, kill him." Saydren pointed at Tarnan.

The guards seemed to hesitate.

"My healer has lost his mind, I am your king and you will obey solely me. Take out Saydren," Damir ordered.

Rhay and the only remaining guard holding him had stopped to watch the spectacle from above.

Looking between Tarnan and Saydren, the guards remained unmoving. "If you really are the king, use your power," Saydren dared Tarnan.

Damir tilted his head up to face Rhay. "Plan B, Messler." Damir winked before launching himself at the closest guard, another dagger in his hand. *Plan B?* They'd never discussed a fucking plan B.

Rhay only took a second to react. With a flick of his wrist, the shackles pinning his hands fell away, startling the guard. The fae reached for her sword but Rhay was faster, slamming into her and pushing her over the railing. She landed on the stone ground below with a sickening thump.

Damir took care of the guards below with ease, slashing one's throat while kicking the other one into the sword of the third. As he turned, he saw the guard having fallen from above and quickly stabbed her heart. Blood painted the ground, but Damir seemed to be having the time of his life.

Saydren had taken advantage of the chaos, running off. Rhay unsheathed his hidden dagger and aimed at Saydren's calf from above. The healer stumbled and Damir rushed forward, pulling Saydren's head back and putting his blade against his neck.

"Take us to Karwyn."

Clenching his teeth, Saydren said, "As you wish."

Together, the blade at Saydren's skin, they joined Rhay and then went up two more sets of stairs. There was a door at the end of the hall. Two guards stood in front of it.

Ducking behind the corner, Damir hissed, "Tell them—"

His words were cut off as yells from downstairs reached them. Someone must have come across the carnage below. Footsteps echoed through the staircase.

"I'll stall," Damir whispered to Rhay. "Get Karwyn."

With no time to think, Rhay rushed into the open. The guards in front of Karwyn's door turned to him and Rhay raised his hands. "Gentlemen," Rhay said, pushing calming emotions onto them. "How about a nap?" His power had come in handy lately. Before Amira had suggested Rhay use his powers to get past the guards all those months ago, he'd never used his powers to do anything but charm people.

The guards yawned and Rhay rushed at them, knocking his elbow into one guard's nose while catching the other in the stomach. Taking the sword out of one of their sheaths, Rhay used the hilt to knock one guard out. He kicked the other against the wall hard enough for him to drop as he pushed fatigue into their system.

The clashing of weapons made Rhay turn his head to Damir, no longer in disguise, heading into the hallway, fighting two guards at once. Saydren had dropped to the ground.

Wiping the sweat from his forehead, Rhay kicked open the door, ripping it off its hinges. Karwyn sprang up on his bed. His face was completely drained of colour. Black and purple shadows marked his eyes. His skin seemed paper-thin as his sharp cheekbones peeked out.

Yet, a satisfied smile creeped onto Karwyn's face. "I knew you would come."

Rhay had no time to speak as a guard rushed into the room. He barely stepped back in time to avoid getting sliced in two. Swinging the stolen sword, Rhay caught the guard's shins and he yelled in pain, bending over. Rhay knocked the hilt against his head, then fumbled for the spelled paper in his pocket. As quickly as possible, he used his matches to set it aflame, signalling Eyden.

Turning back to Karwyn, the former king rose to his feet, his legs wobbly as he gripped the frame of the bed. He looked nothing like the king Rhay had known, like the friend he used to have—except for that smirk. That smirk that said Karwyn had gotten exactly what he wanted and Rhay had fallen for it yet again.

Rhay was about to open his mouth when footsteps echoed behind him. Turning just in time, he avoided the strike to his back, but the blade went into his shoulder instead. *Always that fucking shoulder.*

Grey eyes met his as Rhay cursed. He tried to lift his sword but his shoulder screamed, blood leaving him fast.

"You're not leaving here alive. Not again," Saydren said, swinging his sword stained with Rhay's blood.

CHAPTER 59

🔥

EYDEN

Keeping watch close to the palace gates, Eyden took note of a guard reaching for his runia. He rushed off, leaving the other fae standing guard alone. Something was wrong. Just as the thought left him, his hand burned and Rhay's signal reached him.

Eyden slipped a knife from his long sleeve before zeroing in on Rhay's location, ignoring the fear in his heart that he had no idea how Lora was doing and had no way to easily reach her should anything happen to her. He let the wind carry him, into the palace, up the stairs.

In mere seconds, Eyden was in front of Rhay, who clutched his shoulder. Before Saydren could even yell, Eyden struck the fae's arm and kicked his shins with enough force to make him drop to his knees. He knocked the sword from Saydren's grip. His grey eyes held nothing but hatred. A guard yelled at him through the door to the hallway, but Eyden let one of his knives fly to silence him, hitting the guard's throat. He craned his neck to see more guards approaching down the hall. Damir was close by, slashing out in wide arcs, blood splattered on his clothes.

Looking over his shoulder, Eyden's gaze landed on Karwyn, his chin raised high even as he could barely stand upright. Eyden flexed his fist.

"I don't know where the amulet is," Rhay said, blood staining his fingers as he kept pressure on his wound.

Gaze drifting back to Saydren, Eyden grabbed the healer's collar and drifted away with him. Saydren's back hit the window in the big foyer outside the room with such force the glass broke. The noise must have drawn attention, but Eyden was focused on pushing Saydren over the edge, half his body hanging outside the window.

"Looks like a steep fall," Eyden bit out, reaching for a knife and pointing it at Saydren's neck. He was aware of the fight happening behind him, keeping his ears open for any approaching footsteps.

"What do you want?" Saydren sneered, trying to take a hold of the window frame. Eyden pushed him out farther.

"The amulet. Where is it?"

Saydren snickered. "What makes you think I know where Tarnan keeps it?"

Eyden pulled him towards him, the knife cutting Saydren's throat before he pushed his upper body outside the window again. "I'm thinking a slit throat and fall out this window must hurt like a bitch. Don't toy with me, Saydren."

A yell drew Eyden's attention and he half turned to the big hallway, the knife leaving Saydren's throat as Eyden threw it at the guard approaching down the corridor—hitting him in the eye. His attention was split between Saydren and another guard heading towards them.

A sword struck the guard's back, and Rhay appeared in Eyden's field of vision. Rhay stepped forward, staring at Saydren whose face constricted painfully.

"Stop it," Saydren bit out.

"Don't you feel in a mood to share?" Rhay's voice was smooth like glass.

Eyden pushed against Saydren's chest. "You should be scared to death." Saydren started shaking, his eyes wide with fear.

"Fine," Saydren shrieked. Eyden knocked him back further and Saydren desperately tried to clutch at him to not fall. "I said fine! You can have it."

"Where is it?"

Saydren huffed, defeated. "I have it."

With one hand, Eyden pulled Saydren's collar down until he spotted the golden chain. Recognising it for the amulet Cirny had in her grasp after the ritual, Eyden snapped it from his neck.

"Thanks." Eyden smiled, giving him a final push. A scream pierced the air as Saydren fell out the window, onto the hard stone ground in the courtyard.

Turning to a grinning Rhay, Eyden said, "This doesn't excuse what you've done."

Rhay didn't get a chance to reply as a dagger flew through the air and Eyden pushed him aside just in time. More guards stormed in. Eyden spotted Damir with his bloody sword in his hand, his shoulders low as if tired of the fight, but he raised his weapon nonetheless. They had to get out of here. He had to drift Karwyn out first.

A guard raised his sword at him and Eyden drifted behind him, taking him out from behind. As he kicked at the guard, someone else struck him from his left, hitting his arm and forcing him to drop the amulet. Eyden tracked it as it slid across the sleek black marble floor.

He meant to drift to it when an almandine blade was put to his neck from behind. Eyden bit the hand around his throat hard enough to draw blood before throwing his skull back, hitting the fae behind him. A yell filled his ears and Eyden spun around, facing the guard and twisting his arm with the dagger until the blade stabbed the guard.

As the fae dropped, Eyden looked for the amulet, but it was gone. He searched the room. Only a couple of guards were on their feet anymore. Rhay took care of one of them while Damir slashed the other one's throat—in Damir's bloody hand was the amulet.

"Get Karwyn," Damir said as he rushed out the room. Eyden instinctively followed but Rhay stopped him, tilting his head at Karwyn's room.

Eyden glanced at where Damir had disappeared, but he wouldn't have been able to drift all four of them at once anyway. Eyden ran across the long hall, stepping over bodies, back to Karwyn's room. The door was broken and on the floor. Clutching the headboard, Karwyn stared at him.

"Are we leaving now?" Karwyn asked with too much arrogance.

Yet in his eyes, Eyden saw nothing of that power he used to exude. It didn't diminish Eyden's rage. Before Karwyn could speak, Eyden strode forward and punched his nose. Karwyn spat blood and lost consciousness.

Eyden grabbed his arm when a dagger impaled itself in his thigh. He dropped Karwyn. Cursing, Eyden turned to a guard storming through the door. Rhay stepped in front of him, swinging at the guard with a stolen sword while Eyden pulled the dagger from skin. Blood drenched his trousers, but his focus was on Karwyn. Bending, Eyden dragged a half-awake Karwyn up. Rhay kicked at the guard's stomach and he tripped backwards out the door.

"Rhay!" Eyden yelled, and Rhay caught his drift, running back to them before the guard could get back up.

Rhay rushed forward and put his hand on Eyden's shoulder. He threw the three of them into air and mist just as another horde of guards came barging into the room.

His feet hit sand and a cloud of dust flew into the air as Karwyn landed on dry ground. As Eyden turned to the tree where they'd left their carriage, his stomach twisted. There was no one there. The carriage stood all alone, their two horses gone.

Eyden turned around frantically until he spotted Damir further off on their horse, the other horse next to him as he held its reins.

"Tell Ilario...I wish things could have been different," Damir yelled at them, the amulet around his neck.

Eyden fished for his remaining dagger, but before he could drift closer Damir pulled back his arm and threw something shaped like a can. It exploded before it reached them and the blast threw Eyden backwards. As smoke gathered around them, he cleared his throat, trying to spot Damir in the fog. He couldn't see which direction he had gone. Even so, Eyden drifted some distance into the woods, straight forward. Then he drifted to the right. Then to the left. He kept going, but he couldn't spot Damir.

Fuck. He damn well knew this would happen. He'd lost Damir. He'd lost the amulet. His skin prickled with rage. As Eyden drifted back, the smoke had cleared, revealing Rhay leaning over an unconscious Karwyn. He'd come here for a way to beat Tarnan and now all Eyden had to show for it was two fae who didn't deserve to be saved.

CHAPTER 60

LORA

Lora's eyes locked onto Tarnan's golden crown adorned with a mix of tiny ruby and carnelian crystals. She had to suppress a shudder as she neared him just outside the woods along the border of Rubien. Images of her neighbours' heads on pikes flashed through her mind, making her sick to her stomach.

Beside her, Lozlan turned her way, his expression blank. Unable to read him, Lora shuffled her feet to steal more time.

"Let me do the talking," she whispered.

Lozlan's face was shielded by the shadows cast by clouds hiding the midday sun. When Eyden had suggested taking him with her as a distraction, she'd refused at first. But she saw Eyden's reasoning. Distract. Stall. And pray Tarnan wouldn't retaliate. That was their mission. They had no other choice but to risk it.

Facing Tarnan, Lora glanced between his guards, two on either side. Shivers danced across her skin. "So much for meeting me alone," Lora said. She noticed the exact moment Tarnan recognized Lozlan, surprise colouring his otherwise calm exterior.

Tarnan cleared his throat. "Well, it seems you have brought your own surprise guest. Long time no see, Lozlan. Forgive my rudeness, but I thought you were dead."

"Death would have been too kind."

Lora's gaze snapped to him, her blood running cold. Was meeting his daughter worth nothing to him?

Returning his attention to Lora, Tarnan asked, "You've requested this meeting, Lora. Have you reconsidered my offer? I'd hate to have to send more threats when I've made myself very clear."

Ice slithered against her skin. Lozlan's gaze burned her back, but she kept her focus on Tarnan. "I have considered it. But I have a second condition. Free Amira too."

Tarnan sighed. His gaze was calculating, and Lora heard Eyden's voice in her head telling her to keep up the pretence. "You know better than to demand something so idiotic. Is that really why you asked me here?"

"Tell me again, why do you want the amulet?" She knew she was playing with fire but she couldn't help herself as she tried to reach for his mind, subtly.

Tarnan's gaze narrowed. "It holds value."

"That's a cop-out answer." She tried with a bit more force, remembering what Rhay had taught her. Yet, unless she could touch Tarnan, her mind reading powers were useless.

"Is that all you have to say? I thought you were smarter than that. Instead you brought someone else I can compel."

Lora's face fell. She'd feared this might happen and scrambled for some distraction when Lozlan said, "I thought you were a man of honour? I'm willing to bargain."

Irritated at Lozlan for speaking out of turn, Lora bit her lip. What was he doing? Stalling? She couldn't read him. He was nothing but a stranger who shared her eyes.

Tarnan's lips curled into an amused smile. "Give it a try, then. Let's see if your offer is better than your daughter's."

Lozlan took a step forward, breathing hard. "The amulet for..." He cleared his throat. "For freeing Lora and her mother and...I'm taking Lora's spot in the contest. You'll leave her and her family alone on Earth."

Her head swung to him so fast she pulled a muscle in her neck. He chose *now* to act like he cared what her future held?

Tarnan scratched his chin. "Interesting offer. But alas, I'm looking forward to going up against the true ruler of Turosian." He addressed Lora. "We shall meet again soon."

Lora frantically thought of something, *anything*, to say. They needed more time.

As Tarnan was about to turn, Lozlan rushed forward, his arm outstretched as if to grab him, but Tarnan's guards stepped forward, halting him. "You're underestimating me. I'm an Adelway. If I'm no threat, why do you think my brother banished me?"

Tarnan's forehead creased and Lora followed his gaze to where Lozlan's jacket was pushed up, revealing part of Lozlan's forearm. Fire simmered beneath his skin, visible enough that it must be burning him up from the inside.

Tarnan narrowed his eyes. "Prove it then. Show me what you've got."

His smile was too kind, a warning bell ringing in Lora's head. "*Let it out.*" He looked at Lora. "*Direct it at Lora.*"

Lozlan swallowed hard, his eyes going wide. His arm trembled. "You want her in the contest." Lora was surprised he could hold off Tarnan's compulsion, but his forehead started sweating.

"I didn't tell you to kill her. She'll just burn a little. Doesn't matter if you're taking over anyway, does it?" Tarnan asked.

"You're sick," Lora said as she watched Lozlan's hands ball into fists, the fire underneath his veins travelling to his fingertips. He wouldn't be able to go against Tarnan's compulsion for much longer. Should she run? Had they bought Eyden and Rhay enough time to get the amulet?

"I like to think of myself as resourceful and creative. Important traits of a high king. *Do it*," Tarnan urged Lozlan, whose face had lost all colour.

"Please...take it...take it back," Lozlan croaked out, his whole body shuddering.

Tarnan moved closer to him. "I'm simply being fair. You asked for a chance. Don't be ungrateful."

Lozlan's fists went up in flames so suddenly the light blinded her. Looking over his shoulder at her, Lozlan's eyes widened. "*Run.*"

The word echoed through her head. *Run.* She didn't want to, but when his eyes glazed over and flames danced behind his eyes, Lora took a rushed step back. She didn't notice the vines wrapping around her ankles in time as one of the guards moved his hand, using earth magic. She tripped, her hands catching in the dirt.

She stared up at Lozlan. His eyes were pure flames, his skin glowing, his hands like fire balls. She was fucked. He drew back his hands, gathering more of his power, his body vibrating as if barely holding back. Lora could feel the heat on her skin. She could imagine how it would feel to have someone else's flames tear at her as she'd done to others. This couldn't be happening. It *wouldn't.*

Lozlan threw his hands forward and fire exploded towards her. Lora raised her hands in front of her face, willing the fire away, drawing on the wind to push it back. An invisible shield made of air stretched over her, blocking his fire, reflecting it backwards. Sparks of fire rained down all around them, catching on the surrounding trees. She faintly heard Tarnan and the guards yell as flames reached them too. But Lora was only looking at her hand, at her power deflecting Lozlan's. Fire streamed out of him, exploding all around them like a tap that had been opened and now had to be drained. Her vision was filled with red. Smoke clung to her skin, to her lungs. She couldn't help but remember the last time she'd been trapped in smoke—the day her home burned to the ground.

And then it all stopped. Lozlan's eyes shifted back to normal, his skin ashen, soot sticking to his blond hair. He fell to his knees, exhaustion written on his face. With the fire surrounding him, flames clawing at the trees, the ashes drifting in the air around him, he looked more like her father than any other time.

She didn't even realise the vines were all burned, no longer holding her, until she patted at an ember drifting onto her trousers. The motion snapped her back into the present, and Lora scrambled to her feet. The air was heavy with smoke, making it hard to see anything. She pulled her sleeve to her mouth, coughing. A tree cracked and crashed down beside her, taken down by the flames. She walked forward until she spotted Tarnan coughing as he knelt on the ground, soot smeared on his face.

Leaning over him, she put her hand on his shoulder. "Why do you *not* want us to have the amulet?" she screamed, shaking his shoulder. "Why?"

He wiped at his eyes; the soot must burn. She used her opening and dove into his mind, imagining a blade splitting his head.

"Combined they could use it...Amira's contract...any..."

Tarnan shoved her away and she lost her focus, her head pounding. His eyes were furious as he reached into his jacket for his dagger. Tarnan opened his mouth, but Lora was faster, throwing air at him until his back hit the burned ground.

Before he could get back up or the guards could spot her through the heavy smoke, Lora ran back to Lozlan.

She pulled at his arm. "Now it's time to run."

He stared up at her, his eyes so confused, so...hurt. She pulled again and he rose to his feet unsteadily. Holding him up, Lora rushed forward, tugging Lozlan with her while dodging the burning trees. Together they fled the scene.

Looking over her shoulder, Lora almost stopped breathing as she took in the extent of the fire. It was as if the sky itself was burning as the flames reached the top of the highest trees. Maybe it was. Maybe it had to.

She'd burned down the Void. Lozlan had burned down the border to Rubien. Next up, Tarnan himself once they broke that bloody contract.

CHAPTER 61

EYDEN

The carriage hit a rock and Rhay grunted next to him on the bench. Eyden was steering and Rhay had insisted on sitting next to him instead of inside where they'd dropped Karwyn. Stealing one of Tarnan's carriages had been the only solution Eyden had come up with to take Karwyn with them.

Eyden had no idea where Damir had run off to, but he guessed back to Turosian. Did he intend to sell the amulet? It seemed as if silver was the shifter's main motivation. The only way to know was a locator spell, and he needed Amira's help for that. Elyssa had sent a fire message this morning announcing their return tonight. They had to get back as quickly as possible and regroup. Eyden had to wait for Amira's return anyway, so he decided to save his strength. That way he would be able to drift wherever Damir had gone.

Eyden hoped Lora was all right. He hated that she'd put her life in danger just so he could go and lose the amulet. What would Tarnan do once he found out about their attack? Would more heads appear at their gate?

If he ever saw Damir again, Eyden would kill him. Even Eyden's runia had been missing from the carriage—Damir had thought this through. And now there was no way for Eyden to check on Lora or warn any of them about what Damir had fucking done. Eyden didn't have any more spelled paper on him.

Rhay shifted next to him, putting a hand to his arm that was bleeding and using the other to shield his eyes from the burning sun. Eyden forced himself to breathe out evenly, commanding the horses to gallop faster. He wanted to get away from Rhay—throw him off of the carriage.

"You hate this," Rhay observed.

Eyden clenched his teeth. "Don't read my emotions."

Rhay turned to him, but Eyden stared straight ahead. "Then don't be so obvious."

"If I were obvious, I'd have hit you in the face." Eyden squinted at him. "It's not too late."

"Don't blame me for Damir running off with the amulet."

"I have plenty else to blame you for," Eyden bit out, staring ahead at the dirt path to Chrysa. Trees surrounded them but still, the sun beat down on them harshly.

"I helped you get the amulet and Karwyn. I'm *trying* here."

"If you're waiting for a thank you, it's not coming. The only reason you made it out of there was me." And the only reason Eyden had given Rhay a chance at all was Lora.

"You do realise I was playing on your team the entire time, right?" Rhay argued, but his tone was weak. "I already apologised for going against the plan. Repeatedly. And I paid the price."

Eyden huffed. "You were playing on your own team, making decisions that no one else agreed with. Going against what we agreed on, *purposely*."

"You don't like me very much." Rhay huffed, straightening his torn jacket. His hand went to his pocket, but then he set it on his leg that bounced up and down.

"I just gave you reason enough not to, didn't I?" Eyden swept his hand over his forehead as sweat glistened on his skin.

"Even before that." Rhay sighed. "You think I'm good for nothing. You're not the first person to think that. Shit, everyone probably does. I was trying to prove I can be."

"And there lies your problem."

"Well, go ahead then, enlighten me, please." Rhay leaned back, putting his feet up on the railing. "Tell me all that's wrong with me. I'm sure it's nothing I haven't heard already."

Eyden shook his head, laughing under his breath. "You don't want to hear it."

"We've got an hour to go and I'm no fan of silence."

He could feel Rhay's eyes on him as he tightened his hold on the reins. "Okay then. You're a selfish, arrogant, entitled prick. You tried to prove something by going against one of the only people who still believes you're worth something. You did that for yourself, not for anyone else. You always pick the option that fits you best, which most of the time seems to be turning a blind eye."

Rhay gulped. "Well, don't go easy on me now."

"You could've stopped Karwyn if you'd really tried. You could have intervened or tried to, at least." Maybe Rhay would have been too young to save Eyden's father, but there were many others afterwards that fell prey to Harten and Karwyn.

"How do you know I didn't try?"

Eyden gave him a look, brows raised. "While I was trying to warn fae, to keep them from being taken, you were sitting in your fancy room in the palace with your expensive clothes, drinking the night away."

"And you were accomplishing what, exactly? Nothing from what I can see. I was looking the other way, but to think I could've stopped Karwyn...no one could have. Not until now."

But he could have tried. "Intention matters," Eyden muttered sternly. "I've made mistakes. I've done things for the wrong fucking reasons, but there was always some good intention behind it. I can't say the same about you."

"Have you maybe considered that my life is not as easy as you think it is?"

Eyden's nostrils flared. "It must truly be so difficult having everything handed to you."

Rhay moved his feet from the railing to turn to him. "I was *trapped.*

I didn't choose to move to the Turosian palace. I didn't choose to train to be Karwyn's advisor."

Eyden turned his head to the road in front of them. "I didn't choose to live on the streets, but hey, I feel your pain."

"I didn't choose to grow up with a father who hates me."

"I didn't choose to grow up without a father after the Adelways took him from me."

Rhay turned his head to him, his lips parted. "I didn't choose to grow up without a mother."

Eyden didn't back away from his stare. "I didn't choose that either."

Rhay was quiet for a moment. Then a laugh burst out of him. "What is this? A contest of who's most screwed up?"

Eyden's lip twitched, but he fought it off. "You'd lose."

Rhay chuckled darkly. "I killed my own father. I win."

Eyden turned his head to him, no remark on his lips.

Nodding his head, Rhay bit back a laugh that almost sounded like a sob. "You can't argue with that."

"No," Eyden said after a moment. "I can't." Even though Eyden could relate to Rhay's pain, it didn't erase his betrayal. Yet he found himself saying, "As much as I dislike you, I know your father's blood is on Tarnan's hands, not yours."

Rhay breathed out deeply as he studied him. "I grew up with no one to look up to but my father, the other advisors, and Saydren. What chance did I have to end up good?"

"I've lived on my own since I was sixteen. I had nothing to my name, no one to guide me."

"You had Elyssa. I had Karwyn." Rhay grimaced.

Eyden let out a heavy breath. "I took care of El when I could barely take care of myself, while you were letting Karwyn buy your friendship."

Rhay's grin slipped. "It wasn't like that. He wasn't always a monster. But once I realised, subconsciously at least, I had *no one*. Everyone I got too close to, deep down I knew Karwyn would take them from me."

Eyden almost pitied him, but it was his past, not an excuse for the present. "You have people now. That's what's most frustrating. You have Lora and Amira...and Ilario. And all you do is let them down or play with their feelings."

Rhay sat up straighter. "I'm not playing with anyone's feelings. I just...don't have much to give."

"Finally something we can agree on." Eyden chuckled.

"Was that a laugh?" Rhay asked, his voice warmer. "Are we friends now? Should I start making friendship bracelets?"

Eyden's laughter died. "Don't you dare."

Rhay shrugged. "You'll come around eventually. I'm fun. You'll see."

"We're at war right now. Fun is not what we need."

"Actually, I think that's exactly what we need to keep going."

Eyden turned to the path in front of them, wishing they were back in Turosian already. "What we need is that damn amulet."

Rhay leaned forward, gaze trained on the approaching woods. "What's the plan for that, anyway?"

"I'm sure Amira can do a locator spell."

"Right. They're coming back today." Rhay's hand went to his pocket and he took out a crumpled piece of paper and a pen. "I should warn Rio."

Eyden gaped at the spelled paper. He had thought there was none left. "You had that with you the entire time?"

Giving him an innocent smile, Rhay said, "You never said you wanted to send a message. And this is my last paper."

"Send it. Tell him about Damir."

"You got it. Friend." Rhay winked, a sparkle in his eyes.

"We're not friends."

Waving one hand, Rhay removed a set of matches from his pocket and sent the fire message off to Ilario.

Without that amulet, there would be no fun in their future. Only misery.

Just as the thought left him, Eyden noticed thick smoke above the trees ahead of them—at the border to Turosian where Lora had met

Tarnan. Some of the trees were on fire, sparking bright in the late afternoon gloom. What the fuck had happened?

Eyden clenched his fists around the reins, feeling the leather creak beneath his knuckles. He urged the horses to gallop faster, hoping Lora was all right. What kind of misery had she gone through this time?

CHAPTER 62

LORA

After a shower to clean off the ashes stuck to her skin and an involuntary nap, Lora sat on her bed with a heavy heart. She and Lozlan had run back to their horses and had rushed back to the palace, fearing Tarnan would follow them, but he hadn't. She hoped Eyden had had enough time to get the amulet. He hadn't responded on his runia. The silence was unnerving.

A knock on the door startled her. Rushing across her quarters, Lora hoped it was Eyden. But when she threw it open, she faced Lozlan. He'd showered, soot no longer darkening his hair.

"What are you doing here?" Lora asked, gripping the door tightly.

"I wanted to make sure you were okay." His voice was firm, unlike she'd ever heard it before.

"I'm fine," she replied with more bite than intended. "In the great scheme of things, this was nothing."

"Do you mind if I come in?"

Lora didn't move, blocking the entry. "Now you want to talk? Why? Because you could have burned me? I told you, I'm fine. You're free to go." When she closed the door, he blocked it with his foot.

"*Please.*" His tone was desperate.

Reluctantly, she drew back. "Fine."

She shut the door behind him. His eyes travelled around the room. "It's different now."

Crossing her arms, Lora fought against the headache making her dizzy. "What do you mean?"

He turned to her, his gaze shadowed by something so immense, Lora couldn't put the emotion into words. "I used to live here."

Lora took in the space and almost laughed. Of course Nouis had given her *this* room.

Keeping her emotions at bay, Lora said, "The others should be back soon, so if you want to say something, do it now."

"I owe you an explanation."

Lora stared him down. "You think?"

Shaking his head, Lozlan laughed.

"What?"

"You're so much like your mother."

Lora turned her back to him. "You barely know her. And you don't know me."

He sighed behind her. "Do you want to hear my story? I can go if you'd rather not. I understand it's not fair of me to show up when you've tried to talk more than once. I thought it would be better if I shut you out. Easier. I meant it when I said I had nothing to offer. The only thing I can offer now is an explanation."

Meeting his gaze, Lora sat down on the edge of the bed. She'd been waiting for an explanation her whole life. But she had the burning feeling she'd regret asking for one.

Lozlan shifted uncomfortably. "I had a family." Lora squinted at him. "Before the Dark King was overthrown. I promise this is relevant." When Lora remained quiet he continued. "I had a wife. A son." His voice broke at the end.

"And Variel Sartoya killed them?" Lora asked, watching her tone this time. She could imagine such a loss. She'd been—*was*—close to losing her family too.

"No." Lozlan let out a dark chuckle that almost turned into a sob. "Harten did."

His own brother? Her hands turned clammy and she put them on her knees.

"It took me years to confront him; I was scared I might be mistaken and of the consequences of voicing such a huge allegation. But deep down I knew I was not mistaken. He denied it at first but then he finally admitted it. I had a plan to overthrow him. But it backfired. He twisted everything and banished me. He was the king. His word mattered more than mine."

He took a deep breath, coming to sit beside her on the bed. The look in his eyes squeezed her throat shut tight.

"I stopped replying because I had this sinking suspicion that if Harten found out, he would come and find you both. He was paranoid about anyone coming for his throne. I didn't want to see it at the time, but that's why he killed my son. Because he was strong. Powerful. Good. He was..." He cleared his throat as a tear gathered in his eye. "When I read Karla's letter, all I felt was fear. So I destroyed it. If Harten never knew about you, you'd be safe. You wouldn't meet the same fate."

He twisted his hands. "That's the truth. When I was banished, I fought at first, but then I saw it as my punishment for failing at every single fucking thing in my life. I failed my family. I failed to see who my brother was before it was too late. I failed to save Karwyn from becoming like his father."

He looked up at her, his gaze utter torment, and Lora thought she might break in two. "I knew I would fail you and your mother too. Then you showed up and I realised I somehow did anyway. And in the mess of my mind I thought if I stayed out of it, I wouldn't make matters worse. But I fucked that up too. All I wanted was for you to be safe on Earth with your mother."

Lora let his words sink in, but they were so heavy that the weight crushed her heart. Forcing a deep breath, she said, "Karwyn found out about my existence anyway. I needed a cure for a virus for my mum, so I crossed over."

"You knew about the loophole?"

"My mum did. She'd heard you talking about Karwyn once. Except, I didn't know it was about him back then."

The ghost of a smile graced his lips. "I always wondered how much she'd overheard. But there's a cure now, isn't there?"

"Yes but..." She couldn't say it all, her mum's life was still at stake. "Just know that my mum is alive, but barely."

His brows drew together. "If Karwyn is alive and Eyden is bringing him back here, wouldn't he claim his throne back?"

"He's powerless now. And we'll make sure no one sees him."

Lozlan breathed in sharply. "You have them. That's how you stopped my fire."

Lora shrugged. "A lot has happened since I crossed over. At first, I didn't even use my fire. I wanted to be normal and it...scared me. It still does, but in a different sense now. It's hard not to burn out. Why didn't you use yours all that time in Rubien?" The question had bothered her for a while now. He could have done more, he could have fought against the blood trafficking.

"I think as a punishment for myself," Lozlan replied, rubbing his forehead. "The more you don't use them, the riskier it gets when you do let it out. I'm sorry I almost blasted you. I trained to fight off mind powers from a young age, but I'm not immune."

"For that, you don't have to apologise." She was still angry, but not all of it was directed at Lozlan anymore. More so at Harten.

"I have a lot to make up for. I still have this nagging feeling that all I'll do is fail you, but if you want my help, I'll stay. I can show you how to not burn out. I would rather you go back home and be safe, but if you're staying to put this shit show of a world back together, then so will I."

"Nowhere is safe anymore. Not unless we make it so."

"All right." He watched her then moved closer as if to hug her. She pulled back. "Sorry." He held out his hand instead, the gesture so human it almost made it all feel normal. Taking his hand, for a moment, it seemed as if the world had righted itself.

"Can I ask you something else?" she said, a stone pushing her heart down.

"Anything."

"Did you love her?"

Lozlan sighed. "I won't lie to you. I didn't know your mother long enough to call it love. But I did care for her. Deeply."

"She never talked about you. I think it hurt too much."

"I never talked about her either. But I often pictured her with you, happy. Free of the Adelways, of the shadow my bloodline has cast over Turosian. I saved her letters. Except the one where she told me she was pregnant. I wished I could have been there with her."

"Where are the letters now?"

He got up, going to the fireplace and loosening a marble stone beside it. He fished out pieces of paper. The fire reflected in his eyes as he turned to her but now it looked fitting, warm. "I'm glad no one found them."

Getting up, Lora reached for a letter, her heart tight. This was a part of her mum's history, of *her* history. It was a chance to see into the past. Her eyes stung as her finger stroked the old paper.

"You can read them," Lozlan said as she looked up at him.

With her heart in her throat, Lora unfolded the letter, but she almost dropped it as someone knocked on her door.

It swung open, revealing Oscar, who rushed in but stopped short as he spotted them. "Sorry, I didn't..."

"What's happening?" Lora asked, refolding the letter.

The corner of Oscar's mouth pulled upwards. "It's El and Amira. They're back."

Lora looked at the letter in her hand, her history, then glanced at her brother, who was her present. She was still angry with Lozlan for all the ways he had failed her, but maybe after everything that had happened, he could be part of her future.

Even so, she had her own family here, waiting for her now.

She handed Lozlan the letter and headed for the door, following Oscar. The past wasn't going anywhere. It could wait.

CHAPTER 63

ELYSSA

Entering the Turosian palace, Elyssa couldn't pinpoint her emotions. In a way it was a homecoming, but also not. The palace still gave her the shivers as if Karwyn's essence was haunting the place even from afar. Yet she knew that taking over the palace had been the right move. They were turning things around. And they would goddamn defeat Tarnan. Elyssa knew something must have been going on with Tarnan as Amira had felt fire touch her skin that hadn't been there. She hoped he got some of his own medicine as payment for manipulating Amira's mother.

Clasping Amira's hand tightly, Elyssa glanced at the princess, her home. She would fight for their future until Amira could see it too. Amira gave her a smile that washed away the cold feeling radiating off the stone walls.

"You're back!" a voice yelled, and Elyssa turned to see Lora sprinting down the stairs. She pulled Elyssa into a hug. Over her shoulder, Elyssa spotted Oscar approaching them more hesitantly.

Elyssa returned the hug, relieved to see Lora well. "I hope you didn't get into too much trouble without me."

Lora laughed lightly, then turned to Amira. The two stood there awkwardly.

"Hugging won't kill either of you," Elyssa joked, stifling a laugh.

Lora hugged Amira quickly.

Oscar stood a bit to the side as if unsure what to do with himself.

Elyssa grinned at him, pulling him into a hug. "Little Whitner, how's life in the palace been treating you?"

Oscar shrugged. "Could be better, could be worse. My alarm system is working. Ian has been teaching me some self-defence."

"Nice. Keep it up and you might be somewhat of a challenge for me," Elyssa joked. "So, where's my brother off to?"

Lora's smile dimmed. "He's with Rhay and Damir getting the second amulet. I haven't heard from them, but they should be back any minute." Her eyes brightened as she whirled to Amira. "I read Tarnan's mind. If both amulets are combined, it's not just a tool for Tarnan to suck on a fae's life source; combined they can suck the magic from *anything*. We can break any contract. If you can combine them."

Amira's eyes widened. "That's why Tarnan was so upset when I threw mine to Eyden. He wanted both. And he knows it's my only way out of this." Fidgeting with her dress, Amira paced a few steps. "I'll have to see if there's anything in Cirny's books about how to combine them."

Lora nodded, but the worry didn't leave her eyes. "What about you two?" She looked behind them. "You didn't bring your mother?"

Pulling at the fabric of her dress, Amira lowered her gaze. "She's safe for now. And Wryen won't be an issue. We've come to an agreement."

"That's good." Determination sparked in her eyes. She seemed to understand not to push Amira further. "The queens are working on getting the other kings on our side. And with the amulets, we'll be back on top. We can make this work."

She didn't sound convinced, but Elyssa had enough conviction to share. Letting a devilish grin live on her lips, Elyssa stated, "We *will*."

"Not without the amulets," Ilario said, running down the stairs.

"Did you hear from Eyden?" Lora turned to him.

He rushed towards them with a defeated look in his eyes. "Damir took it. Rhay sent me a message. I just checked and the amulet we had here in the palace is gone too." He turned his head as if ashamed on Damir's behalf.

A loud crash made all of them turn. Elyssa thought she might be imagining things, but seeing Amira's shocked face, she knew she wasn't.

Her blood ran hot as she took in Karwyn on the floor, Eyden getting to his feet beside him. Rhay, appearing behind them, looked like he had gotten the worst of the fight, the entire right side of his shoulder and arm drenched in blood.

When no one moved, Rhay clapped. "Well, that's not quite the welcome I imagined. Where's the parade?"

Elyssa balled her hand into a fist but restrained herself. They'd lost the amulets, meaning Tarnan could get his hands on them. Had Rhay really tried everything to keep Damir from getting it? She knew it wasn't fair to blame anyone besides Tarnan for Farren's death. But she had every right to blame Rhay for handing over the human-fae agreement, and that still made her distrust his every move.

Karwyn turned on the floor, lying on his back. Coughing, he raised a frail hand to his mouth and it came back bloody. His gaze drifted over Amira and Lora. Both appeared frozen, their bodies stiff. Elyssa envisioned her fist in his face.

Eyden took off his coat and threw it on Karwyn's face. "Cover your face if you don't want me to beat you up again."

Karwyn let out a yelp, trying to shrug the coat off him. Eyden kicked his head, holding back his full strength, and Karwyn went still. Rhay tensed beside him.

Elyssa reached for the throwing star hidden in her sleeve. "What the actual fuck?"

"Who is that?" Oscar asked, looking at Lora with worry in his dark eyes.

"Karwyn. The king. *Former* king."

Oscar's mouth dropped open. He stepped back, reaching for Lora's hand to pull her with him.

"Why. Is. He. Here?" Elyssa bit out.

Lora sighed. "We couldn't leave him with Tarnan. If he dies before..."

She didn't have to say it. If he died before breaking her contract then her mother might die too.

Eyden's sharp gaze scanned over everyone, looking for injuries. He put two fingers behind his ear and Elyssa returned the gesture. Walking up to Lora, he pulled her into a quick hug. He nodded his head at Oscar and he returned the gesture.

Elyssa could feel Amira fidgeting with her dress so she took her hand to calm her.

"I..." Lora started before she seemed to remember what Ilario had told them. "Did Damir really take the amulet?"

Eyden shifted his feet. "He did. We need to do a locator spell as soon as possible and track him down before he hands it over to Tarnan—if that's his plan."

Lora's eyes flashed red. "Bloody hell...I shouldn't have let him stay."

Karwyn grunted, then sat up, shrugging the jacket off him. "Did you expect anything else from my former spy? You do not know how to handle him. Pity."

Next to Elyssa, Amira almost jumped out of her skin.

Lora gave her a quick tilt of her head, probably feeling as unsettled as Amira was, before turning to Rhay. "Get him to an empty room before any of the guards see him," Lora whisper-yelled. "We can't deal with him now. We need to find Damir."

"I can do a locator spell with the right ingredients," Amira offered. The princess had spent much of her time studying every spell Farren had written down in his notes.

Ilario nodded. "Give me a list. Halie should have everything we might need." He handed her a pen and a piece of paper and Amira started scribbling down ingredients.

Lora took a step towards him. "We'll get them back. He won't get away." Ilario's gaze hardened. He headed for the exit with Amira's list.

Rhay reluctantly turned, grabbing Karwyn's shoulder. He hissed something Elyssa couldn't catch. As Karwyn seemed to barely be able to stand, Eyden walked to them and they disappeared into thin air.

That left Lora, Amira, Oscar, and Elyssa.

Taking a deep breath, Lora brushed a strand of hair from her face. "The spellbooks are in your room?" she asked Amira.

The princess wrung her hands. "They're in the carriage, I'll go grab them."

Eyden reappeared, startling Amira. Watching him, Lora said to Amira, "I'll come help you. Oscar?"

Oscar, a lost look in his eyes, turned to follow her. Amira threw Elyssa a quick smile that failed to reach her eyes before heading outside.

"And then there were two." Elyssa sat on the cold stone stairs. Eyden lowered himself beside her, pulling at the bloodied collar of his sweater. "You need a shower."

Eyden chuckled. "I need a moment to just sit and make sure you're all right."

Elyssa cocked her head at him. "All freaking right. Go ahead."

Eyden lifted a dark brow.

Rolling her eyes, Elyssa nudged his shoulder. "Come on, I know you're dying to tell me off. I know this time *I* crossed the line." Eyden remained quiet. "No comment? No *'you shouldn't have run off on me?'*"

"I know why you did it. Part of me wishes you had found Jaspen and made him pay. One day, we will." His gaze held a promise, and Elyssa knew Eyden would do anything to keep it. "Just let me be there to pull you back if you ever go too far again. We need to hold each other accountable, remember?"

A smile pulled at her lips. She did remember. She also remembered how angry she'd been at Eyden when she'd found out he'd been tangled up with fortae. It felt like another lifetime ago now. They had both made mistakes, they'd both gone through loss after loss. But they still had each other, and Elyssa realised she sometimes failed to appreciate how much that meant.

"But..." Eyden said just as the thought left her, "you *shouldn't* have run off."

Elyssa chuckled. "Got that out of your system?"

Eyden rubbed his chin. "I had a whole speech, but for your sake, I'll save it."

"You won't need it," she said and meant it.

A grin made its way across Eyden's lips. "Good, it was a shit speech anyways."

Laughing, Elyssa's shoulder brushed Eyden's. Her laughter faded as a memory flashed in her mind. "Farren would have been mad at me for going rogue, but he would have never said so. He was..."

"Endlessly patient?"

Elyssa snickered softly. "Too damn good for this world. I wish he could see us take Tarnan down. I know in my blood it'll goddamn happen. We'll get those amulets back and then it's game on." She hadn't realised her hands formed fists until Eyden uncurled one of them.

"Fucking Damir," Eyden muttered.

Elyssa sighed. "Fucking Damir, indeed. What else did I miss?"

"Ilario and I have been going around, filling people in on what Karwyn has done, what Tarnan plans to do. I know it's not the kind of revolution you were imagining, but we're getting there."

It was more than Elyssa had imagined since the rebel camp had been taken. If fae could be persuaded to their side, maybe they would learn to live with humans. They would have to once Kaylanthea ruled. She knew the humans would fight for their rights, would fight in this revolution as soon as they were free from Tarnan's binding contracts.

CHAPTER 64

❧

RHAY

Once again, Rhay was alone in a room with Karwyn. But this time, Karwyn wasn't Tarnan's prisoner, he was *theirs*.

Rhay was cleaning up the cut on Karwyn's head with a damp towel he had fetched from the adjacent bathroom. They had kept silent for what felt like an eternity, unsaid words simmering between them.

Karwyn was the first one to break the silence. "I expected better treatment from you." He traced the bruises Eyden had left on his face.

"You played me," Rhay said, stepping back as irritation ran through his body like a shiver. "You knew Lora would want to get you if you were about to die."

"I *am* dying. Just not right this instant." Karwyn slipped under the bed covers.

Rhay tried to stay focused. "The thing about the amulet, it's true?"

"As far as I know. Now, you see, I am not that heartless." Karwyn tried to make it sound like a joke, but Rhay sensed true pain in his words. They had said harsh things to one another. Would there ever be a way to repair what had been broken into a thousand pieces? Did Rhay even care to fix things after everything? He wanted to be a new Rhay, but he sensed he never would be with Karwyn in his life.

"Do you want to know why I did it?" Karwyn leaned up on the bed.

Rhay stopped himself from moving closer. "I know why. To control me. To take advantage of the situation."

Karwyn's gaze was as sharp as ice. "I wanted to die in Turosian, with you by my side." Rhay couldn't look at him. Was it the truth or another attempt at manipulation?

"Karwyn, I—" Rhay stopped himself when he heard voices on the other side of the door. Maja was talking with Rio. Amira had completed the locator spell and they were all heading out with Rio to find Damir. Rhay turned to the door.

"Stay, Rhay. We are not done here. If you go against Tarnan, you will die."

Rhay looked back at Karwyn. He saw sadness hiding behind pride in his old friend's eyes. Maybe it wasn't too late... Rhay heard footsteps down the hall.

Or maybe it was time to let him go once and for all.

"I have to go." Rhay dropped the bloody towel on the bed and walked away before Karwyn could respond. There was a point when something that had been broken too many times wasn't worth fixing anymore.

Eyden drifted Rhay and Rio first. They landed in a dark alley-way. With a quick glance at Rio, Eyden drifted away again. They were supposed to wait for the rest of the group before storming the building Amira had located. Yet Rio headed straight towards it.

"Rio, wait up," Rhay called out.

"I didn't ask you to come."

Rhay followed him nonetheless. "I really think we should wait for the others."

Rio sighed but didn't reply. Slowing down, they reached a two-storey building that had seen better days. Rio brushed away a spider web as they entered. The hallway was as dirty as the outside. The door to the only apartment on the ground floor was bricked in and completely abandoned. They took in the sprawling old staircase.

"I need to go on my own. Maybe he'll listen to me." Rio didn't meet Rhay's gaze.

"You'll need backup."

"I'm not planning on fighting him. He *owes* me this. I'll shout if I need you." Before Rhay could stop him, Rio headed upstairs.

Rhay debated going after him. This was a terrible plan and he couldn't stand the thought of Rio getting hurt. But how many more times would Rio forgive him for acting against him?

He slumped down onto the first step, his thoughts drifting back to Karwyn. He wondered what would happen to him once Amira broke Lora's contract.

At that moment, Eyden entered the building, his eyes furious. "Why in Liraen didn't you wait for us?"

Elyssa, Amira, and Lora appeared behind him. Elyssa raised her dagger while Lora glanced up the staircase, brows knitted. "Where is Ilario?" Lora asked.

"He insisted on going alone," Rhay said, standing up.

"And you didn't tell him that his plan goddamn sucks?" Elyssa interjected, getting right in his face.

"I don't hear anything. Do you think Ilario is okay?" Lora asked, her neck craned to look upstairs.

"Rio is not himself around Damir and the amulets are too important to risk losing them again," Eyden agreed, heading towards the stairs.

Rhay raised his hand. "Let me check on him first. You can split up, surround the building. Damir won't get away, but Rio deserves to try. We've been through too many fights already."

Lora sighed but nodded. Amira twisted her hands but didn't interject.

"Okay then," Eyden said. "But Ilario better be okay, or you'll regret leaving him alone." He would regret it. The thought made Rhay all but run up the stairs. His heart pounded in his chest as he reached the first floor. Picking up voices coming from behind a cracked door, he sneaked a peek inside. Rio's arms were crossed over his chest. Damir leaned against the wall of an almost barren room with a beat-up sofa as the only furniture.

"...all of it for what, some quick silver? Was I really that blind when we were together that I couldn't see your lies?" Rio's voice cracked.

"I never lied. You chose to only see the good in me and there isn't much of it," Damir replied, his tone hard but with an edge of regret.

"Never lied?" Rio let out a dry laugh. "By Caelo, why do I always fall for the wrong ones?" he muttered under his breath.

"I *withheld.* I know I did. I'm selfish, I won't deny it. But you'd never understand. You with your happy family and friends..." Damir's voice lost its harshness. He straightened himself. "You should go. Go and forget all about me."

Rio stepped forward and tapped on Damir's chest. "*No.* You had me believe you were dead!" His voice was shrill, out of control. "You owe me this. You owe for every *non-lie.* For every minute you let me believe you were rotting somewhere in the palace. You say I won't understand, yet you never gave me a damn chance!"

Damir leaned forward. "You don't really want to know. You condemned me the moment you knew what I'd done." Rio flinched as if hit. "We're not alike, Ilario. We never were. Life made it easy for you to be good and necessary for me to be the opposite. An explanation won't make you judge me any less and I don't fucking owe you one anyway."

Rio shook his head. "Fine, keep your secrets. But if you *ever* cared about me, prove it now. We *need* those amulets."

Damir gently pushed him back. "I need them too. I'm not doing this lightly."

"*Why?*" Rio shot back. Rhay could feel the tension through the door. The floorboard creaked as Rio stepped closer. "Why do you need them so badly? How can you be so heartless? If you don't care about me, fine, but all of Liraen, including you, will be doomed if Tarnan wins."

Damir hesitated. Rhay could sense a mix of emotions fighting in Damir. Guilt, anger, even a hint of fear.

"I won't leave here without the amulets. I'll fight you if I have to, and you're surrounded."

"I don't want to fight you," Damir said between gritted teeth. "And you couldn't stop me if you tried. You don't think I know you're all exhausted? And I've been watching everyone. I know your weaknesses."

Rio didn't let up, his nostrils flaring. "So that's what you've been doing at the palace? Tracking our weak spots? You'll have to kill me to stop me from chasing you until the end of Liraen." Damir's eyes flashed. "You know I won't stop. When you were gone, I didn't give up hope. I did whatever I could to find you because I hoped you were still alive. Because the Damir I knew and loved deserved to be saved. But I guess that Damir never existed." Rio choked on the last sentence.

Damir seemed stunned for a moment. Faster than expected, Rio punched Damir in the nose—hard enough for blood to spill.

For a minute neither one spoke. Rio stared at his hand. Damir wiped at his nose. "Did that make you feel better?" Damir finally asked, his tone emotionless.

Rio curled his fingers into a fist. "No. But now you know I mean it. I'll fight you if I have to."

Silence lingered between them and Rhay sneaked forward, ready to back Rio up.

But then, Damir removed the two amulets from around his neck. He stared at them for a moment, hesitating. "Sometimes I wish the Damir you thought existed was real." Taking Rio's hand, Damir dropped the two amulets into his palm. "Now we're even, Marsyn. Don't say I never did anything for you. Don't say I owe you shit." Damir turned his back to Rio, a clear dismissal.

"This isn't for me," Rio yelled at him. "It's for all of Liraen. It's the *right* thing to do."

Damir cocked his head, refusing to turn back around. "The right thing for *you*, not me. Go before I change my mind. You got what you wanted and I'll end up regretting it."

Lingering, Rio's gaze anchored on the back of Damir's head, as if waiting for him to finally apologise, to go with him. But Damir didn't budge.

Walking up to the door, Rio put the two amulets in his pocket.

Rhay moved away from the door, but he wasn't swift enough for Rio not to notice.

Rio all but ran down the stairs and out the building, moving past the rest of their group, who watched Rio in bewilderment. Only when Rio entered the alleyway did he say to Rhay, "I told you to wait downstairs." He swallowed back tears. The shadows of the night framed his face, making his hair as black as the sky.

Seeing Rio with his shoulders sunk low and tears in his eyes, Rhay knew he had to do better than Damir.

"Rio," Rhay started softly.

Rio held back a sob. "We have what we came for, let's go. There's nothing else to say."

Rio started forward, but Rhay took his arm. "I just...I want you to know that whatever may happen, I'll never abandon you."

Straightening himself, Rio took him in as if to try and catch the lie. But there was none. "I know," Rio replied. It was only two words, but the trust behind them made Rhay's heart skip a beat.

For a moment, they stared at each other, unsaid words and unspoken feelings drifting between them, filling every part of him. Then Rio turned and headed back to the palace, leaving Rhay with more than one scrambled thought.

CHAPTER 65

ﾟ

LORA

Eyden led Lora to one of the unoccupied rooms. She'd suspected he would put Karwyn somewhere close by to keep an eye on him and make sure no one saw him to avoid confusion, or an uprising. It was something Nouis might have done as well. Or maybe he would have chosen to kick Lora off the throne. She couldn't help but think of Rhay, who surprisingly hadn't followed them to Karwyn's door. Now that the amulets were back in her grasp, she could breathe a little easier. Ilario was securing them in the palace now with Amira's help.

They stopped in front of Karwyn's door. "I hate this," Eyden whispered against her hair as he pulled her into a hug. "I hate what he did to you and that I can't make him pay for it."

Lora drew back, her fingers brushing the back of his neck. "From what I saw downstairs, he's paying for it. Can't say I feel sorry for him."

Eyden cocked his head, his gaze hard. "He finally looks as rotten as he is on the inside."

Lora bit her cheek before replying, "I really hope Amira can combine the amulets."

Eyden took her hand in his. Her gaze drifted to the closed door. "You don't have to talk to him. I can do it."

She wished she didn't, but she felt in her veins that she had to. She'd never had the chance to talk with Karwyn without fearing the consequences. "I can do it."

"I know you can, special one." Eyden leaned his forehead against hers. "Doesn't mean you have to do it all."

She brushed her lips against his, savouring his warmth. "This one I need to deal with myself. But you can come with me."

Eyden grinned, leaning in for another kiss, but then he turned his head to the hall. Lozlan rounded the corner.

"I heard Oscar say something about the king being back." Lozlan stopped before them. Lora pulled back from Eyden to fully look at him. "It can't be true, can it?" As Lora glanced at the door, Lozlan's lips parted. "Is he here so you can break your contract? I'll make him dissolve it." He went to the door, but Eyden blocked his path.

Lora pulled Eyden aside gently. He seemed to realise her relationship to Lozlan had shifted for the better. At least she hoped so. She couldn't erase the hurt she'd felt her entire life, his absence a dagger in her heart for as long as she could remember.

"We need some information from him," Lora explained. "You can go in, but I'm taking the lead."

Lozlan nodded, a faint smile on his lips.

Lora felt her breath freeze in her lungs as she walked into the room, her gaze set on the double bed taking up most of the space in the small room. Karwyn lay on his back, hands clasped on his stomach.

For a second she thought he was dead but then his eyes snapped open, catching her gaze before travelling over her shoulder to Lozlan. Clearing his throat, Karwyn shuffled back on the bed so he was half sitting up. His sullen eyes made her skin run cold.

"The family reunion I never asked for." Karwyn's gaze was pointed at Lozlan, sharp and twisted like barbed wire. "I suppose that means you are the queen now, little cousin."

Lora was reminded of everything he had done to her. The virus. The contract. The countless threats. How he'd doomed them all. Yet, lying on the bed in this fragile state, Lora saw him for what he really was. A failure.

"I can't say I'm happy you're alive, but it has turned to my advantage," Lora said, drawing closer.

Karwyn chuckled darkly. "It is your mother, is it not? She is somehow still alive, too." His lips turned up in a satisfied grin. "I thought as much."

Lora's brows drew up. If he had guessed as much, that meant...

"You're not dying, are you?" Eyden asked, his tone grave. He'd wanted them to bring him here. And they had delivered.

"Oh, I am dying." Karwyn stared at Lora, freezing her blood. "Just not as quickly as I might have made you believe. So gracious of you to bring me here. Where is your dear mother? Rotting away by herself?"

Lora clenched her hand into a fist. Eyden stepped forward, but she put a hand on his chest to hold him back. "She is safe."

Karwyn's gaze unsettled every fibre of her. "I know you want me to break our contract, but there is nothing I can do without your mother's blood. Unless you can combine the amulets, but I would not be betting on Amira."

Lora breathed in sharply. She hadn't considered that they would not only need Karwyn's blood but also her mother's.

Karwyn's smile was cruel. "You are doubting it too, are you not?"

Lozlan strode forward, leaning over Karwyn until he was mere inches from his face. "Watch your mouth, Karwyn."

"Why play concerned uncle now?" Karwyn chuckled, but it turned into a cough. "It is much too late for that."

"I tried. I wish I could've stayed and tried harder."

Karwyn twisted his pale hands. "You never cared about me. Do not lie now."

"I did care. You were just a kid once. It was Harten who turned you into this. If your mother was still alive—"

"Do not bring her into this," Karwyn hissed. "She was nothing but weak. If you think she would have saved me from my father, you are wrong. She had no interest in me. She did not even care to save herself."

Lozlan sighed, a deep sadness radiating off him. Lora kept silent, wanting to know more about Karwyn's mother who must have been human. How had she died?

"Your father never told you, did he?" Lozlan asked, and Karwyn's strangely silver-lined eyes darkened. "Your mother...she wasn't in her right mind towards the end. She loved you. She really did. But she couldn't...go on. I warned Harten. He wouldn't listen. In the end, I failed her too."

Karwyn shook his head. "She was a weak human who left me with nothing."

"Your father saw it as a weakness too. He told me she wanted to change...to be strong, to truly be worthy of our royal line. The more I think back on it, the angrier I am at myself for believing it at the time."

"What in Liraen are you saying?" Karwyn asked, his tone as icy as frostbite. For once, Lora agreed with him, the same question on her mind.

Lozlan sat down on the edge of the bed and Karwyn scooted back. "Harten and Saydren were trying to find a way to turn your mother fae. They thought they succeeded, but all it did was turn your mother into a shell of herself. It did something to her mind. Something irreversible. And when she couldn't handle it anymore..."

"She threw herself into the border," Karwyn finished, his breathing laboured. Lora held back a gasp. Eyden shifted his feet.

"And you followed her." Lozlan lowered his head.

A puzzle piece clicked into place in Lora's mind.

"A stupid move," Karwyn bit out.

"An understandable reaction for a little boy who wanted to save his mother."

Karwyn turned his head. "I could not save her from herself."

"No one could." Lozlan's hand twitched as if considering taking Karwyn's. "Whatever they did to her...it was dark magic. She was lost to it. All to make her our equal when she was already better than any of us."

Karwyn's face was a mask, his lips forming a straight line. Then he laughed until a drop of blood dripped from the corner of his mouth. He wiped it with his sleeve, laughing harder.

"How fitting," Karwyn said, barely catching his breath, "that I am dying at the hand of Saydren's experiments as well."

"What happened to you?" Lora asked. Her cousin's eyes met hers slowly as if he'd forgotten she was there.

Karwyn huffed. "A drug that turns humans into fae. Saydren secretly drugged me when I was still *half-fae*"—he spat the word—"so it back-fired. Now I am practically human and dying. I am sure you are pleased to know my powers are gone."

So Rhay had been right. Lora couldn't help the mocking smile. "I am sure you are pleased to know that your powers aren't gone for good. *I* have them."

He sat up as if to lunge for her, but Eyden blocked his way. "You have no right to my powers!"

Lora leaned in closer. "Then maybe you should've thought twice about that ritual. Face it, Karwyn, your time is over. Why else did you tell Rhay about the amulets? Is it your last attempt at screwing with us, bringing you here, or are you trying to do at least one good thing in your life?"

His lips were pressed shut, and Lora lost her seal on her anger. She grabbed his arm and focused all her energy on getting into his head. Karwyn gasped as he tried to pull back, but Lora was stronger now. She felt him build a wall, but with one breath, it crumbled. She was getting better at this.

"*She cannot read me,*" Karwyn mumbled in his mind. Lora dug deeper. "*The amulets...if Tarnan ever gets his hands on them, everyone will be doomed. It will be chaos. They will pay.*" She heard Karwyn yelp in pain but Lora pressed on. "*Combined they can remove any spell, but they can also syphon away a fae's life source.*" Karwyn struggled against her hold. She could feel his hand sweating. "*Rhay...Rhay must know. I owe him...I owe him so much. There is no one else—*"

Lora took a startled step back, releasing her hold on him. When she turned, she saw Lozlan next to her, a hand on her shoulder.

"Don't stoop to his level," he said. Eyden watched them, frowning. But Lozlan had a point, his thoughts about Rhay were not important.

Karwyn stared at her with so much anger as she said, "So it's true then, Tarnan can use the combined amulets to strengthen himself?"

Karwyn remained silent.

"I can force it out of you or you can talk. Your choice."

Nostrils flaring, Karwyn cleared his throat. "When the Dark King used dark magic to bless, or curse, himself with mind-control powers, he had to pay a price. He needed to feed on other fae's life source and he used the amulets to do so."

"Did you ever try to find them to turn yourself fully fae?"

Karwyn turned his head away. "I could never get to them. Only you."

"Lucky me." She'd gotten what she needed, yet she couldn't make herself move. Something else lingered in her mind even though she wished it didn't. "Was there ever any thought, any thought at all, of wanting a family? Of wanting to find me, not to kill me, but to have someone of your blood by your side?"

Karwyn's eyes were pools of turquoise overrun by liquid silver. It made Lora's breath hitch. Before she could even blink, a veil fell over his eyes. She might as well have been staring into a black hole.

"No," he said. "You were only ever a pawn."

Lora nodded, biting her lip to hold back the anger simmering inside her as she turned to the door. His words hurt, yet she had a suspicion it wasn't fully true. Behind the layers of cruelty and evil schemes, Karwyn had always been afraid. Behind it all was a scared child who had never known anything but hate.

Karwyn couldn't be redeemed in her eyes, hadn't even tried to. But for the first time, she understood how he had ended up the person he was today.

Lying on her back on the bed, Lora listened to the shower running in the adjoining bathroom. Eyden was washing off the blood and grime sticking to his skin. Though Lora was exhausted, part of her mind sought a distraction to take her mind off waiting for Amira to study how to combine the amulets. Too much hinged on it. They had gone against Tarnan's threat. It couldn't be for nothing. Lora expected Damir to storm in any second, announcing Tarnan had left another *message.*

Damir wouldn't show up but the threat was still present and it would be her fault, just like her neighbours' deaths had been.

A knock on the door made her sit up. Sighing, she got up on tired feet and walked to the door. Expecting Oscar, she was prepared to tell him she was fine after her conversation with Karwyn. But instead she found Rhay in front of her door.

He'd changed, no longer wearing the blood-soaked brown sweater. Now he wore a silver blouse and royal blue shiny trousers. His emerald green hair was towel-dry as if he'd just stepped out of the shower. He lingered in the doorway.

Overcome with relief about the amulets, Lora didn't think and hugged him. Tears stung her eyes. Without those amulets her mother, Amira...none of them would have had a chance. Somehow, they still stood a chance, and Lora hoped against all odds that they would all make it through.

Rhay startled but then his arms went around her waist. Pulling back, Rhay grinned at her. "Does that mean you forgive me?"

She'd given Rhay so many chances. She'd wanted for him to find himself. And he had thanked her by going behind her back. But she could feel the end was drawing close. The contest was six days away. They didn't know what awaited them and they needed each other more than ever now.

Sighing, Lora stepped aside, letting him in. The door fell shut behind them. Turning to him, she said, "I don't know, but I'm ready to listen."

"You were right," Rhay said as he straightened the collar of his shirt. "I shouldn't have gone rogue. It was selfish of me. I wanted to prove myself. It wasn't as calculated a move as I told myself. I guess I'm still too good at deflecting." He hung his head, swiping away strands of golden and green hair. She had missed his colourful hair.

"It's not you," she said without thinking, but she felt it was true. Rhay tilted his head at her. "This persona you tried to play, the double agent who goes above everyone's vote and doesn't care what others think. When I said you need to figure out who you want to be, I didn't mean pick a persona. I didn't mean change your personality, change your hair." She gestured at his head. "You're not blue, Rhay. You're not a lost cause. You can choose the best version of yourself. The one who looks at the truth and fights for the people he cares about. The one who jokes to make people feel better, not to trick them."

"I don't know if that Rhay ever existed." His voice was uncharacteristically quiet.

Lora gave him a half smile. "If he didn't then how would I have met him? I've seen him resurface this past week. And I'm not just talking about the hair change."

Rhay chuckled. "You still have faith in me even after I messed up so badly?"

It was a good question, one Lora had trouble answering. "If I give you another chance and you waste it, then that's it, Rhay. Do you understand? I hate to play the queen card, but when in need..."

Rhay's smile was sombre as he nodded, but then his eyes sparked. "I guess I can't call you little Adelway anymore. Shall I call you Queen Adelway now?" Lora rolled her eyes. "No? You prefer Queen Lora?" He laughed. "Or how about my *most precious queen?*"

She snorted. "Don't make me regret this."

Putting a hand to his heart, Rhay said, "I promise you won't."

Before Lora could reply, the word promise echoing through her heart, the bathroom door opened on a shirtless Eyden. He was drying his hair with a towel as he entered the bedroom, steam from the shower following him.

Eyden halted when he spotted Rhay. "Didn't know we had company." He threw the towel on the bed and went to the wardrobe, picking up a shirt.

Lora couldn't help but watch him as a few drops of water clung to his bare chest.

As he shrugged on a shirt, Rhay said, "No need to dress for me, friend."

She turned to Rhay, who held up his hands as if to say, *Don't blame me your boyfriend is hot.*

"We're not friends," Eyden said as he turned to them, now dressed.

Rhay smirked at Lora. "He's in denial. We'll be friends for life."

Lora bit her lip to stifle her laughter as Eyden squinted at them. But then Eyden's gaze on her turned warmer, heating her skin.

"Okay, time to go," Lora told Rhay, pointing to the door. She was exhausted and all she wanted was to lie down next to Eyden and forget the battle ahead of them for just a moment.

Rhay chuckled and headed out the door.

Eyden's hands landed on her waist, spinning her around to face him. "Are you okay?"

"I'm better now." Her heart was freer, lighter. "We have the amulets. Now we just have to put them to use."

Her chest tightened as another thought crept back into her mind, Rhay's new nickname echoing through her head. Even if they came up with a plan and succeeded, could Lora find a way to accept the life that she'd never wanted but had claimed anyway?

CHAPTER 66

EYDEN

After twisting and turning all night, Eyden glanced at Lora asleep next to him. The first rays of sun flickered in through the slit between the turquoise curtains, throwing a strip of light across the sheets. His thoughts kept travelling back to his father. Eyden knew he was long gone, but seeing Karwyn had raised questions Eyden couldn't shake. If only he could let his anger out—but even now, it would doom Lora. He thought back on when he'd beaten Karwyn so badly he could have killed him if he hadn't stopped in time. The universe was cruel, keeping vengeance from him. Eyden couldn't let it go.

Knowing it was a bad idea, Eyden quietly got out of bed. No one stood guard in front of Karwyn's door, but they'd secured it with multiple locks. Fishing for the key in his pocket, Eyden unlocked it and let it fall shut behind him.

Karwyn stirred on the bed, blinking up at him in confusion. "Can a dying person not be left alone?"

He sat up, hissing as his joints cracked.

Stalking forward, Eyden squeezed the bedpost, the wood creaking loudly. How Eyden wished he could beat Karwyn bloody. "You don't know who I am, do you? You don't even know what you've done to me."

"Let me guess, I harmed the love of your life?" Karwyn laughed, the sound poison to Eyden's ears. "Yet Loraine is the queen now, so why are you making a fuss?"

"I'm not talking about Lora." Eyden leaned forward, expecting Karwyn to flinch back, but he didn't. "Your family killed my father, Adelio Kelstrel. He was on your list."

They locked eyes, the room eerily quiet. "What is it you are seeking?" Karwyn finally asked. "I may have killed your father, or maybe my father did, but did you really come here expecting me to remember one name out of the long list of...*sacrifices?*"

Eyden's hand was around Karwyn's throat before he even noticed the movement. "You should be rotting in hell for all eternity." Karwyn's face went white as he clutched at Eyden's wrist weakly, trying to get him to ease up. A tear left the corner of Karwyn's eye. His breathing became shallow.

Eyden could kill him. He could end it. Maybe Eyden's pain would finally end then too.

But as he stared into Karwyn's silver-lined turquoise eyes, he saw Lora's gaze. Lora, who would suffer because of Eyden's choice. Karwyn's death wouldn't fix anything. Letting up, Eyden moved back until his back hit the wall. Karwyn coughed, his hand going to his reddened neck.

"You are in luck," Karwyn hissed, his voice strained. "I will be gone soon enough. I will join my father wherever he has gone, that will be punishment enough."

He would be gone and then there would be no one left who might have the answer to the question that haunted Eyden. "What did you do with the bodies?"

Karwyn swallowed, a grunt of pain leaving his lips. "If I tell you, will you leave me alone?"

"There's nothing else I'd ever want from you except to see you take your last breath." Karwyn chuckled. "What's so funny?"

"You think my death will somehow make it right, but we both know it will not." Eyden flexed his fists. Karwyn turned his head to the small window. "I buried them right under everyone's noses. One of the tunnels leads directly to Chrysa, to an abandoned building right by the woods, close to the black market." He said it proudly yet with a twinge of regret.

Eyden didn't wait for Karwyn to turn back to him, instead he walked out, locking the door and rushing through the cold halls until he was back in his room. Closing the door, Eyden leaned his head against the wood, letting his eyes fall shut as his whole body shook. The realisation of his father's fate came crashing down on him like a riptide taking him from the shore that was his last hope.

"Eyden?" Lora's voice was thick with sleep. Eyden forced his eyes open, taking in Lora sitting up on their bed. When Eyden didn't move, trembling, Lora got up. One hand stroked his cheek. "Are you okay? What happened?"

He put his hand over hers, concentrating on her warmth, on the present instead of the bleak past. "I talked to Karwyn. I had to know."

Lora frowned. "About your father? I thought..."

"He is. The name meant nothing to Karwyn. To him, it's *nothing*."

Lora brushed a tear away from under his eye. "Karwyn is no one we have to worry about any longer. He'll never hurt anyone again. I'm sorry you can't find the closure you need."

Eyden sighed. "I thought I did when I read his name on Karwyn's list, but I was fooling myself."

"I know you want revenge and it must kill you not to go through with it." Lora's gaze dropped as if it was her fault when it wasn't.

He intertwined their hands. "I do want it, and I'll have it, even if it's different from what I pictured. But even then..."

"The pain remains," Lora finished, nodding.

"He died because he had the same power as me. Yet I'm still alive. Because of him." His father had gone with the guards willingly, convincing them Eyden hadn't shown any powers yet. He could have put up more of a fight—drifted away before they managed to put almandine shackles on him. Yet his father had chosen to protect Eyden instead.

"If it had been Elyssa, wouldn't you have done the same for her?" Lora asked, pulling him out of the dark memory that had shaped his childhood.

"In a heartbeat."

Lora gave him a sad smile. "I'm sure if he knew what fate awaited him he would have still made the same choice."

Eyden pulled her into a hug, dropping his head to her shoulder. "I know we can't change the past, but I wish my father had a different ending."

Lora curled her fingers into his hair in a comforting gesture. "Was there a funeral?" Eyden went stiff. "You don't have to, but maybe that will give you a sliver of closure."

Eyden pulled back to look into her eyes. "Karwyn told me where he buried the bodies."

Lora held out her hand. "If you want to go, I'll be by your side the entire time."

Feeling his throat close up, Eyden took her hand and thought of the building Karwyn had spoken of. He had come across it before. He knew every inch of Chrysa.

Cold air wrapped around them as his feet landed on dry earth. Glancing around him, he found the building as it was in his memory. Half of it was destroyed, offering a look inside the broken facade.

Shifting his feet on the hard ground, Eyden tried to spot the grave, but by now it would be impossible to see. Lora squeezed his hand and pulled him forward. A single flower grew from the icy ground, rich violet petals turned towards them.

"I think this is a good spot," Lora said. "Do you want to say something?" Eyden opened his mouth, then closed it. Lora wrapped her arm around his. "Here lies Adelio Kelstrel. Beloved father. Fierce protector. Kind soul. May he rest in peace."

Feeling tears sting in his eyes, Eyden stared at the flower, imagining his father's smile, his encouraging words and endless love. "May he join Caelo in the Sky. Finally," Eyden concluded, his voice wavering.

He nodded at Lora and fire rose behind the flower. Flames stretched in all directions, lighting up the lilac morning sky. Wherever Karwyn had buried them, the bodies would finally burn, returning to the Sky.

As Eyden imagined his father finding peace, looking down at him, a weight he'd carried for as long as he could remember lifted off his chest.

CHAPTER 67

AMIRA

A good night of sleep hadn't eased Amira's worries about combining the amulets and breaking Lora's contract. So much rested on her shoulders. She hadn't even been able to keep up the spell protecting Oscar and Maja in their rooms. She had miscalculated how long it would last and had put them at risk during the attack on the palace. Yet, Amira was expected to combine the two most powerful artefacts in Liraen? Even with Saydren's extensive training, Farren's notebooks, and Cirny's decades of research, it seemed like an impossible feat.

But there was more on her mind. Three little words that Amira couldn't shake, the eight letters seeping into her veins and taking root in her heart. *I love you.* Elyssa's confession made her heart constrict with worry. Amira hadn't been able to say it back.

Those words were a promise that Amira wished she could make, but one day Elyssa would see that Amira wasn't good for her. Amira had been naive in the past, thinking she could have happiness, thinking she could protect the people she loved. It was a hopeless thought.

Sneaking away to study before her attempt at combining the amulets, Amira rose from the bed she shared with Elyssa.

Amira grabbed some of Cirny's spellbooks from her vast collection and left the room, deciding to study them in the sitting room across the hall. Reading through Cirny's notes, Amira couldn't help the knot in her throat from growing. Cirny had been the first to fall victim to

Tarnan's power of compulsion. If only she had trusted Lora, then Cirny would still be alive. As much as she felt repulsed by Cirny's actions, Amira knew that the witch had been forced. If things had gone differently, Amira could have met the same fate.

Shivering, Amira forced herself to focus on the scrawled notes. She spent hours studying what Cirny had written. She mentioned the two amulets multiple times. Combined they were the most powerful, but even split up they retained power. The artefacts had been created centuries ago, sculpted from powerful amplifiers and fused into magical amulets that would ensure their amplifying power would hold for a long time. Yet, it hadn't been enough for the Dark King, so he had chosen to combine them with the help of powerful witches, using them for dark magic.

A knock on the door made her lose her focus. She looked up and met Elyssa's gaze. "They're ready for you in the council room, sunshine."

She hadn't realised how much time had passed. When had morning come? With a deep breath, Amira closed the book and stood up. Elyssa grabbed her hand. "Remember, you're unstoppable."

If there wasn't an invisible rope wrapped around her heart, squeezing too tight at all times, Amira would've smiled at that.

When they entered the council room, everyone was already waiting for them. Lora's gaze snapped to Amira's. She could read all the hope in it, cutting off the air in her lungs. She couldn't fail Lora after all she had been through. Oscar, looking as stressed as his sister, and Eyden, his forehead wrinkled, stood next to Lora.

In the corner of the room, looking unsure about his place, Lozlan twisted his hands. Ilario and Rhay chatted with Sahalie. Maja was analysing the two amulets and the black tourmaline crystals Amira would use to protect herself during the spell.

"Since we're all here, we should discuss the plan for the contest before Kaede and Thea arrive tomorrow." Lora's eyes lingered on the amulets on the table.

"We need to break Amira's contract and the humans'—that's the most important step. Tarnan must have forced them into signing blood contracts now that the human-fae agreement has been broken," Elyssa said, taking Amira's hand in hers. The touch grounded Amira to the present, preventing her mind from running wild.

"I don't think Tarnan would risk bringing them to the contest," Ilario suggested.

"He'll probably keep them at the palace. I wish we would've had time to find them, but our ruse didn't last long." Rhay sighed. "I can look for them."

"I'll go with you." Ilario tilted his head at Rhay. Eyden and Lora exchanged a knowing look.

"You need to be fast. We'll try to stall the contest as long as possible," Lora added.

"I'll prepare some healing items for you," Sahalie offered.

Everyone had their part to play. Yet Amira couldn't help but think if she hadn't been stupid enough to sign the contract, they wouldn't be in this mess.

Elyssa pressed her hand. "We'll have to make damn sure Tarnan doesn't get his hands on the amulet because otherwise everyone except us humans will be screwed." Tarnan could use the combined amulets to draw on the life sources of fae and gain more power. But humans had no magical life source to draw from.

Amira gave Elyssa a warm smile before she turned to Lora. "Let's combine the amulets. Do you have the contract?"

Lora took out the contract from her pocket. Amira placed it on the table next to the amulets, the black tourmaline crystals, and mix of herbs Cirny had described.

Taking a deep breath, Amira stood in front of the amulets. She lifted her hands and they rose in the air, above her head. Closing her eyes, she felt the two amulets shake under her control, as if they were trying to whisper something to her. They told her all the wrong and twisted ways they had been used when they had been united. Amira channelled her power to try to push them together. She envisioned the two stones fusing into one. The amulets sparked in the air, pulsing as if listening. She pulled on the crystals to strengthen herself.

The amulets fought back, wanting nothing more than to be apart. Sweat drenched Amira's forehead. The muscles in her arms tensed, being pulled apart by the strength of the amulets. Amira gritted her teeth, digging deep into her core to not let the amulets win. The protective power of the black tourmalines saved her from being ripped apart. Yet her insides twisted and a chill ran through her bones.

Something wet ran from her nose onto the floor. She was bleeding. The amulets resisted with all their power. Amira pushed her hands together, willing the amulets to do the same. The bones in Amira's hands cracked loudly, breaking in multiple places. Amira couldn't suppress her yell of pain. She heard someone calling her name but she could only focus on her blood buzzing in her ears.

Amira pleaded with the amulets to let them know she had no evil intention, to tell them she simply wanted to reunite a mother with her children. She *had to* save Lora's mother. As her strength left her, her body close to collapsing, the amulets finally listened.

Amira opened her eyes. Inching together, the two amulets almost touched. Amira's breathing quickened as she drew on her power one last time. It felt like her hands were engulfed in flames. When the amulets finally met, light exploded and a surge of energy pushed her back. She hit the ground hard, disoriented. She only saw white.

"Amira, are you all right?" she heard someone call. The light vanished and Amira blinked, now seeing the brightness of the sun shining through the high windows. Elyssa appeared by her side, pulling her head into her lap.

"I'm fine," Amira croaked out.

"Did it work?" Anxiety laced Lora's words.

Looking up from the ground, Amira saw the two amulets fused together as if they had always been one, the turquoise stone and the ruby blending into one another in a dark purple hue.

Standing up with the help of Elyssa, Amira tried to pick up the amulet, eyeing the contract on the table as she swayed on her feet. Her hands burned where her bones had broken and she was unable to grasp it.

"Are you sure you're okay?" Elyssa whispered in her ear urgently.

"I'll do it." Lora lowered herself to grab the newly fused amulet while Amira leaned heavily on Elyssa, wiping the blood from her nose. The movement hurt. Two of her fingers were broken on each hand.

Lora took the contract in her hand and put the amulet above the two signatures: Karwyn's and Lora's, written in her mother's blood. For a second, Amira had the sinking feeling that nothing would happen, but then the contract glowed brightly, the signatures disappearing as if Lora had never sealed her fate.

"It worked, right?" Oscar asked, with so much hope in his voice.

"I think it did." Amira's voice almost gave out.

"You need rest," Elyssa said. Amira's head spun. Her eyes were so heavy she thought she might drift into darkness any second.

"I think I felt the contract lift," Lora whispered.

Sahalie went up to Amira and Elyssa. "I'll go with you. Amira could use some healing herbs."

Before Amira could leave the room, Oscar stopped her. To her surprise, he hugged her, careful of her weakened state. Tears filled his eyes. "Thank you."

Overwhelmed by the boy's emotion, Amira met Lora's gaze and read the same gratitude there.

"No one should lose their mother," Amira said, relieved to finally be able to save someone. She wanted to smile, but darkness finally caught up with her and her eyes drifted shut on their own accord.

CHAPTER 68

LORA

Back in her room, Lora went to her desk where she'd stashed the new phone and WiFi cube Eyden had found at the run-down black market. She hoped Amira would recover quickly. The kind of energy she must have drawn on... Thankfully, Sahalie would look after her. Lora would check up on her later.

Turning on the devices, Lora sat on the edge of her bed. Eyden, Maja, Oscar, and Lozlan were all with her, staring at her with a mix of hope and hesitation. She thought back on this morning when she'd gone with Eyden to say goodbye to his father. With her stomach in knots, she hoped there would be no more funerals from now on.

Oscar came to sit beside her.

"Are we sure this is safe?" Lora asked, clutching the phone in her hands. She hadn't wanted to risk any communication in case Tarnan or the human government had found some way to track it to her family. After what had happened to her neighbours, she was glad she'd taken the precaution. With Oscar's device working, their guards were aware of anyone crossing, and so far Tarnan hadn't brought anyone else over to Liraen. Still, a cold dread filled her.

"It's a new phone and you're calling a—" Eyden started, looking at Maja for help.

"A burner." Maja moved to sit on Lora's other side. "My dad has a few, and this one is for emergencies only."

"We have to try," Oscar said. "Please."

His dark eyes were so hopeful. Lora had to fight the instinct to tell him to be careful. Hope could burn your soul. Yet, she had to admit, when she had felt the coldness of the contract lift from under her skin, a spark of hope had taken root in her heart.

Eyden gave her a smile, his gaze telling her it was her decision. Lozlan seemed unsure how to act, his smile awkward and strained. He would never really be her father, but perhaps he could be a friend.

Squeezing Oscar's hand, Lora handed the phone to Maja, who knew Marcel's emergency number by heart. After typing in the number, Maja handed it back to Lora, who pressed call and put it on speaker. It rang, the sound like drum rolls before the big reveal. Her heart beat faster. Oscar's hand tightened almost painfully around hers.

And then the call ended as if disconnected. Lora's skin froze, the spark of hope in her heart turning to ashes. Her gaze went up to the photo of her family she had taken from her house before it burned down. She had stuck it on the wall above her desk, reminding herself who she was fighting for.

"Try again," Maja urged, but Lora felt unable to move. Maja took the phone from her hand and dialled. The same ringing, then nothing. "Fuck."

"It could mean anything, couldn't it?" Oscar asked, and Lora turned her head to his. "They could've lost the phone or maybe hidden it some-where. Maybe they'll call back. Right?"

She could see the exact moment the light dimmed in his eyes when she didn't respond. "It's possible."

"But you don't think so?"

"I don't know what to believe anymore. It's been weeks since we saw Dad. But I do know he'd do anything to keep Mum safe." Lora tried to pull on the last ember of hope she still had. "Maybe that means no contact at all."

Oscar nodded, leaning his head against her shoulder. Lora tried to imagine what her life would be now if she'd never been pulled into the fae land. If Karwyn had never learned of her existence. It was late December now, so Lora would be—

"Bloody hell." Realisation hit her and she sat up straighter. "We forgot Christmas." If she was home now, the holidays would have just passed. She glanced at the phone screen for confirmation—it was December 26th. She had only focused on what the 31st of December meant: The contest.

Oscar wrung his hands while Maja bit her lip.

"You knew?" Lora asked, reading the room.

"I didn't want to stress you out more than you already are," Oscar said sheepishly as Maja shrugged. "And it wouldn't have been the same here anyway. Without Mum and Dad. We can celebrate once all of this is over."

"It'll be a victory/Christmas party for the ages." Maja winked at her.

Lora nodded, but in her head another idea took hold. Tomorrow, Kaede and Thea would arrive at the palace so they could finalise their plans. It would be nonstop planning and training until the contest in four days. But today, after all the uncertainty that still tainted her heart and Oscar's, it was time to focus on the good.

Stringing fairy lights across the ballroom, Lora cursed as one end loosened and dropped from the wall. She stretched her arm, trying to stick it back in place.

Lounging on a velvet chair with a cup of caftee in his hand, Rhay glanced at the high ceiling, then at Lora. Boxes of decorations were thrown open in front of him. "You know, this would be easier if you used your air power." He held out one of the garlands.

Lifting her hands, Lora commanded the air to lift the garland from Rhay's hand, stringing it around the chandelier. Rhay's grin was radiant as he signalled for Lora to sit too. His sparkly magenta blouse glittered in the sunlight shining through the high windows. While leaning back in the comfortable chair, Lora filled the room with stars and leaves, taking Rhay's directions. He looked unburdened for the first time in as long as Lora could remember.

"So this is how it's done now," Maja said as she strode into the room. Lora turned to the door. Eyden and Ilario followed behind her. "I gotta say, pretty cool."

"Cool? It's incredible." Rhay took a sip of his caftee, the sweet scent drifting towards her. His eyes searched Ilario's, but the trader was glancing around the ballroom instead, a soft smile on his lips.

"It's stunning," Ilario agreed, meeting Rhay's gaze, and his grin widened a bit. Rhay smiled in return, and she could tell he was relieved. Had they talked things out?

Eyden crossed his arms, his eyes sparkling as he took in her grin. She had been glad to see the relief on his face when they'd returned to the palace earlier this morning.

"The one thing missing is the tree," Lora said, getting up. "And maybe some candles."

Rhay pointed at Eyden. "My dear friend, what do you say? Can you drift us a tree here?"

She could see Eyden biting back a comment about him being Rhay's friend. "A tree? You want me to get an axe, chop down a tree, and drift it here?"

Rhay glanced at Lora. "If you can't do it for your bestest friend, perhaps you can for our precious queen?"

Lora went to hit him but Rhay dodged her, half falling out of his chair. "Our *violent* queen."

"I told you not to call me that," Lora said, but she couldn't help but grin. Somehow, this felt normal. Eyden smiled too. Maja laughed, holding her stomach as she looked at Rhay half on the floor. Ilario hid his grin behind his hand.

"I'll go." Eyden's pointed gaze was on Rhay. "For Lora."

As he disappeared, drifting away, Rhay said, "What a wonderful friendship we have."

Lora shook her head, keeping her grin at bay.

"You know Eyden will take time to come around, right? Jokes won't win him over," Ilario said.

Rhay waved his hand. "Nonsense, my jokes charm everyone."

"Not everyone," Ilario said.

"They charmed you."

Ilario squinted at him. Rhay shut his mouth, his smile slipping slightly. Something Lora couldn't quite read drifted between them.

Swallowing hard, Rhay turned back to the box filled with decorations.

"Maja, you want to help me get more candles?" Lora asked, going to stand beside her.

Ilario threw her a look as if to say *very subtle*.

"Yes, let's leave them to their relationship drama," Maja said. On their way out, Maja looked at Rhay over her shoulder. "You better behave, or no jokes will save you from us."

She winked at Ilario. With all the time Lora had spent training or on missions, she hadn't realised how close the two had grown. It made her smile. If nothing else, at least their dire situations had created bonds that Lora was sure would last longer than Rhay's jokes.

Lora was almost unfamiliar with the giddy feeling taking over her as she took Oscar's hand and ran down the hall until they were both breathless. The sun had finally set and she was dressed in an emerald gown with a heart-shaped neckline. She had made Oscar dress up too before pulling him out of his room. She recalled Christmas back when they were children and she would take Oscar's hand as they went down the stairs to see the tree and presents on Christmas Day.

Approaching the ballroom, Lora threw open the double silver doors. Her eyes were focused on Oscar. The fairy lights sparkled in his eyes that widened at the view. His breath hitched as a wide grin stretched his lips.

The ballroom was spectacular, filled with lights strung from the ceiling, candles placed all around, and leaves cascading down the walls. A huge pine tree stood in the middle, vibrant lights making it stand out. All her friends and Lozlan stood around the tree, enjoying themselves with drinks in hand.

"You did all this?" Oscar asked, looking at her.

She squeezed his hand twice. "Mum wouldn't want us to skip Christmas. I'll always be here for you. You know that now, don't you?"

Oscar's eyes turned glassy. "I do."

She smiled and Oscar laughed as music filled the room. Rhay had brought a radio and it was playing *Last Christmas*. Pulling Oscar into the room, Lora made him twirl and then they were dancing as if they were back home, with no worries, just having fun.

She pulled Ian in too and Oscar showed him his robot move that always made Lora laugh. She felt two hands on her waist from behind and turned to curl her arms around Eyden's neck, swaying to the music with him.

Dancing with him threw her into another memory. Eyden and her on Falea Night when she'd been too afraid to let him kiss her. Eyden and her at the masquerade ball when she'd thrown caution to hell and pulled him into a study to have her way with him. She didn't have to be careful now. She didn't have to be afraid.

Capturing his lips, she traced her tongue along his bottom lip until he sighed against her parted mouth. His hands tightened on her waist. The heat radiating off him made her lose her breath.

When she broke the kiss, the look in his eyes reminded her that everything that had happened between them had led them to this moment. This moment where Lora knew with certainty that she loved him and he felt the same and there were no more lies. No ruin. She once thought she was nothing but ashes, but with Eyden and her friends beside her, they were unstoppable embers that would never cease.

As the party died down and she was drunk on wine and smiles, Lora pulled Eyden down the hall, away from the music. Laughing, she almost tripped, and Eyden wound his arm around her before spinning until her back hit the stone wall.

The smirk on his face was devastating. Pushing off the wall, she kissed him fiercely, her tongue dancing with his. Her hands pulled at his black suit jacket. His hands clasped her dress, almost tearing the material.

He drew back enough to whisper, "We should head back to our room before we lose all modesty."

Lora laughed against his lips. "We can't leave yet. It's not over."

"Then why did you pull me away, special one?" His eyes sparked with intrigue. His hands roamed from her shoulders to her waist and she couldn't help but crave more.

Her gaze flickered down the hall. "Maybe I wanted you to myself."

"To do what?" he asked, all innocent even as his eyes undressed her.

"I have some ideas." She tilted her head. "I'll show you."

She headed down the hall, knowing he'd follow as he always would. Throwing open the door, she went inside the drawing room. Eyden pulled up a chair to block the door. He went to her but she pulled back, walking backwards until she hit the sturdy wooden desk.

"So what are those ideas?" he asked as he followed her. His hands landed on the desk behind her, caging her in. Her skin tingled. "Because I have some brilliant ones of my own."

She grinned up at him and silenced him with her lips. Eyden kissed her back until she could hardly stand anymore, her legs wobbly as her skin burned waiting for his touch. Her fingers tangled in his hair as his hands went to her backside, pulling her up until she sat on the desk. With skilled hands, he bunched up her dress. She wound her legs around his waist to pull him closer, gasping as their bodies connected even with layers of clothes between them.

He kissed her neck as his hands went under her dress and she lifted her hips, letting him drag her underwear down.

"Is this my idea or yours?" Eyden whispered in her ear, his voice husky, drawing shivers over her scorching skin.

She unbuckled his belt, then pulled at his trousers, stroking him. He gasped, his lips travelling to the nook of her neck.

"Does it matter?" Lora replied before his hand inched up her inner thigh and she couldn't help but cry out.

He chuckled, the sound vibrating through her body. "We'll call it even."

Her heart beat fast with anticipation as she felt him line himself up. He kept still, catching her gaze, waiting for permission, before pushing in. The notion of consent made him all the more sexy.

Her legs tightened around his torso as he moaned against her skin, going slow. She dug her nails into his back, urging him on. Her hips lifted, meeting his wild thrusts. Lora leaned her head back, giving Eyden better access as he trailed kisses down her neck. The room drowned in their sighs of pleasure.

Lora clutched at his shoulders, holding on to him, to the moment, to them. She let herself fall, her power encouraging her on, every part of her on fire as Eyden's hand went up and down her leg. He came with her, leaning his forehead against hers as he caught his breath.

Lora grinned as he pulled back, catching his gaze. "Just so you know, that was only one of my ideas." She scooted off the table on weak legs, retrieving her underwear. "But the rest will have to wait for another day."

A smirk graced her lips and Eyden's eyes darkened as he grinned back.

They had time. That was what Lora wished for the most. *Time.* Time to be with Eyden. Time to reunite with her family. Time to see that sparkle in Oscar's eyes more often. Time to bring this doomed kingdom into the light even if she wished it wasn't her place to do so.

CHAPTER 69

ELYSSA

The flames of dozens of candles mixed with the fairy lights streaming across the ceiling as Elyssa twirled in a circle, her curls loose and wild for once. She felt Amira close to her, dancing much more gracefully. Amira's long dark hair and light pink dress were a blur in her vision.

She stumbled forward, drawing Amira in by her waist until the princess' gaze met hers, the amethyst in her eyes sparkling.

"Your dancing is still every bit as breathtaking." Elyssa tracked the blush creeping into Amira's cheeks.

Amira tilted her head down, moving closer as she took Elyssa's hands, but then a throat cleared next to them. Reluctantly, Elyssa turned to Rhay, who brushed back his newly coloured emerald green hair.

"Can I cut in?" Rhay held out his hand to Amira. Elyssa held in a sigh, but she knew Amira still cared about him, still wanted to save him.

Amira glanced at Elyssa and she gave her a smile, moving back. Taking her hand, Rhay spun her in a circle. Behind them, Elyssa spied Eyden and Lora sneaking back into the party, their hair and clothes dishevelled.

Maja appeared next to her. "They're not always stealthy, are they?"

Laughing, Elyssa spun to face her. "Love makes you a bit reckless. But we could all use some recklessness. Well, except for me, I already have a goddamn load of it."

"I wouldn't know." Maja's voice was almost too low for Elyssa to catch if she couldn't read her lips. Before Elyssa could respond, Maja walked off, joining Ilario at the drink table and picking up a glass of indigo wine.

As she watched Lora join the two, Elyssa headed to Eyden at the Christmas tree, hands in his pockets. The colourful lights strung around the tree danced in his eyes.

Elyssa halted next to him. "I hear you brought the tree."

"I have to be useful somehow," Eyden joked, but his brows drew together as his gaze turned more serious. "Do you ever think about what your life could have been like if you had grown up on Earth?"

"Don't," Elyssa cut in. "You know I don't see the damn point in imagining what ifs. This is the life we've been given and I think we made the most of it so far." She looked towards Lora chatting with Maja and Ilario, then to Amira laughing with Rhay. "It all led us here. Right now, it feels right."

Eyden's lips formed a half smile. "It does."

"Bit ironic considering we're in our enemy's palace, drinking his wine." Elyssa chuckled to herself. "I guess it's the least he owes us."

Eyden tilted his chin down. "Part of me wants to take him out so badly. But he'll get what he deserves."

She hated the thought of Karwyn in the same place as them, but it was better than letting him plot against them with Tarnan. "He's living his worst nightmare. That's a damn good start."

"But if you could, you'd rather break his face too, wouldn't you?"

She let a savage grin stretch her lips. "This is why I can never imagine a reality where you're not my brother."

Eyden's smile turned soft, then a twinge of sadness spilled into his grin. Elyssa punched his shoulder.

"What was that for?" Eyden asked, his hand moving to his shoulder, the smile brighter now.

Elyssa shrugged. "I don't need a reason."

"If I could change anything"—Eyden started, and he held up a hand as Elyssa was about to interrupt him—"I wish your parents could see you now. Your uncle. Farren."

Her smile dropped at Farren's name, the wound still fresh. "They would be fighting with us. Your parents too." That much she was sure of. And since they could fight no longer, she would do it for them while keeping her own life in mind. For Liraen, for her family, and for herself. With all her strength, all her anger.

Eyden's gaze turned thoughtful. "They would be."

"We can't lose anyone else," Elyssa whispered, her eyes trained on Amira. "We've already lost too damn much."

"No more loss," he agreed, though his tone suggested he wasn't fully convinced either.

"No more loss." If she said it enough times, it had to come true.

Elyssa fell face-first onto the huge bed, the mattress making her body jump upward before she sank into the soft sheets.

"This bed is heavenly," Elyssa muttered, turning her head to Amira by the foot of the bed. The princess laughed, a hand raised to detangle a lock of hair.

"You just realised that now?" Amira asked, coming to sit on the bed. "How much wine did you have?"

Elyssa sat up, scooting closer to her. "Not enough to keep me from doing this." Rising up on her knees, she angled her head, capturing Amira's lips. The kiss was sweet, barely a brush, but it zapped through Elyssa like adrenaline, awakening all her senses.

Amira smiled at her as she pulled back. "Are you sure? I wouldn't want to take advantage of you."

A chuckle bubbled out of her throat. "Sunshine, you could never take advantage of me. Unless you count making me fall in love with you. Then I'm completely at your mercy, wine or no wine."

Amira was quiet for a moment, the words *I love you* floating through the room like a ghost haunting them. The princess traced her jawline with one finger, her touch mesmerising. Sighing, Amira leaned closer as if she couldn't help herself. "Then we're at each other's mercy."

She kissed her, drowning out any response as her tongue slipped in and every thought evaporated from Elyssa's mind.

Elyssa pulled closer, her hands on Amira's waist, clinging to her until their bodies were flush against each other. She caught the little gasp coming from Amira's lips as she broke the kiss. Biting her lip, Amira reached for the pink strap on her shoulder, pushing it down to reveal her olive skin. Elyssa's hand went to her other shoulder, pushing that strap down too. She itched to have it all gone.

"Turn around," Elyssa said, and the way Amira's eyes darkened made every part of her heat up.

Amira turned, pulling her hair over her shoulder so Elyssa could see the buttons on the back of her long dress. The anticipation made her less precise than usual and Elyssa's finger slipped. A curse left her lips.

"Just rip it," Amira said, her body almost shaking as if she too couldn't survive waiting one more second.

Elyssa bent forward to kiss her shoulder, then her ear. Amira's breathing quickened under her touch. Against the shell of her ear, she whispered, "Not very princess-like."

Amira half turned, the grin on her face both daring and a touch shy. "Being a princess is overrated."

Elyssa laughed but followed Amira's command, clutching the expensive fabric of her dress in the back and pulling it until it ripped. Amira shifted to turn back around but Elyssa stopped her, kissing a path down her spine that had Amira writhing under her touch. When she came back up, Amira turned around fast, standing up and letting the dress fall down her legs until she was only in her underwear.

She knelt on the bed, pushing Elyssa backwards on the mattress. Her hands undid Elyssa's blouse quickly. Amira's eyes drank her in greedily when she pushed the fabric aside to reveal her bare breasts. Leaning forward, Amira's lips went to her neck, then down her throat, her tongue finally swirling around her nipple until Elyssa couldn't see anything but sparks.

She fumbled for the button holding Amira's bralette in place and undid it. One hand went to the swell of her breast as the other dipped into Amira's underwear. The princess cried out, her head tilted to the ceiling.

Before she could find her release, Elyssa removed her hand and pushed Amira off her so she could move on top. She kissed her once, invisible flames stretching between them, then slid down her body. Elyssa stopped between her legs, knowing they'd never done this before.

"Can I?" Elyssa asked, licking her lips, and Amira nodded. Grinning like the devil, Elyssa turned Amira's leg, planting kisses up her inner thigh. Amira was panting before Elyssa even pushed down her underwear. Elyssa lowered her head, flicking her tongue to see what Amira enjoyed. As she cried out, Elyssa put a hand on Amira's stomach to keep her still while her hips moved with Elyssa.

Elyssa kept up the pace until Amira's shattered cries filled the room, her body responding to Elyssa's touch as if they were perfectly in tune. Slowly backing away, Elyssa sat up, and Amira's lazy smile made her want to do it all over again. She moved up her body, kissing Amira, twisting her fingers in her hair.

With a wicked grin that made heat flow from Elyssa's tingling lips to her stomach and lower, Amira's hand moved to her trousers. She pushed them down and Elyssa pulled back enough to shrug them off and her underwear with it.

"I want to do the same..." Amira started, her hand shaking on Elyssa's waist. She traced the scar on Elyssa's arm, kissing it gently. "I'm not sure how."

Elyssa put a finger under Amira's chin, lifting her head to hers and melding their lips before replying, "You don't have to, but anything you do, I'll enjoy."

Amira's smile widened and she gently pushed against her until Elyssa laid down on her back. Amira hovered over her, capturing her lips as her hand went between her legs. Elyssa deepened the kiss until she could barely breathe.

Kissing her cheek, her jawline, her neck, Amira moved down and Elyssa let her knees fall apart—an invitation as desire pooled in her lower stomach. Trailing her inner thigh, Elyssa watched Amira as she worked her way up. She thought her skin might set aflame as Amira's tongue claimed her.

With whispered commands, Elyssa told her what she liked, what she needed. Amira followed, staring up at her with a look in her eye that said she knew exactly what she was doing to Elyssa. That look pushed her over the edge, the confidence and vulnerability so damn irresistible.

Elyssa turned her head on the pillow, moans leaving her lips as her body fell apart and her hand found Amira's on the mattress. She held her hand as the aftershocks went through her. She couldn't think of a more perfect end to the night.

Amira laid next to her, squeezing her hand, kissing her gently. Her grin was wide yet sleepy.

"I never want to lose you," Amira said, not meeting her gaze. "Sometimes that's all I can think about."

Elyssa drew closer, her hand stroking Amira's back. Was Amira holding back not because of what Elyssa had done but out of fear? "I love you," Elyssa whispered.

Amira swallowed, her hand leaving Elyssa's to cup her cheek. She didn't say it back, but Elyssa heard it in every touch, in every kiss. One day, Amira would be ready to accept all the happiness in her life. One day, there would be no fear, only love. Elyssa would wait for that day however long it took.

"Are you feeling a bit better now that you've combined the amulets?" Elyssa asked, leaning into Amira's touch.

"Yes and no. It all hinges on Rhay and Ilario getting the contracts in time. And if they don't..." Sighing, Amira rolled onto her back, staring at the ceiling as if it held the answers.

"They will," Elyssa replied. They goddamn had to. The alternative was unacceptable.

Amira tilted her head towards her, their noses almost brushing. Taking Elyssa's hand, Amira's gaze turned haunted yet determined. "I hope it won't come to it, but..."

"No." Elyssa shook her head. "I *won't* lose you either. You're here to stay." She raised Amira's hand, planting a kiss on her knuckles.

Nodding, Amira took a deep breath. "I need you to promise me something. You won't want to, but we have no plan B and we need one. After everything, I think we both know we have to let each other take risks if necessary. You trust me, right?"

"Always," Elyssa said with no hesitation even as a cold shiver ran down her back. She'd be there for Amira, *always*, even if she wished she could keep Amira far from any danger.

Amira's lips curved into a bittersweet smile. And then she told Elyssa her plan. Staring at the ceiling, Elyssa waited for another answer but came up empty. With everything she had, all the anger, all the sadness, she hoped they would never have to fall back on Amira's back-up plan.

Yet she turned to Amira and agreed, swallowing the lump in her throat.

CHAPTER 70

❦

LORA

Lora twisted her hands in her lap, the afternoon sun streaming through the thin curtains blocking her view out the carriage window. Tarnan had decided the contest would be held at the newly rebuilt Rubien temple, which was close to the border to Turosian.

It was strange to think that, not long ago, she'd been sitting in a carriage with Rhay on the way to the plaza on Caelo Night. A similar doom had hung over her then. She'd been so sure she would die that day. Today, on the other hand, was still full of possibilities. Squeezing the tracking crystal around her neck, Lora tried to hold on to the smidge of hope she still had. She was relieved to have her necklace back after briefly lending it to Rhay.

Next to her, Amira drew back the turquoise curtain. Through the trees ahead of them, Lora spied a clearing and a building made of stone. Four high towers with flat rooftops surrounded what looked to be an oval-shaped structure. It reminded Lora of a colosseum. Open archways let the sun into the building, lighting it up as if it would be anything but the setting of a battle. She could spot the trees Lozlan had burned down the last time they'd been here in the distance.

If Karwyn was in her place, would he feel as if nerves were eating him alive too? Lora hadn't spoken to him since she'd tried to read his mind. She hoped for everyone's sake that Karwyn would die soon once

Lora was able to get in contact with her family. Knowing he was in the palace had Lora twisting and turning all night.

Taking a deep breath, she turned to Amira. "Are you ready?"

Amira's hand went to the combined amulet hidden under her blouse. It would give her strength for what was to come—hopefully enough of it.

"Are you?"

Lora stared back out the window to see other courts had already gathered. She wouldn't spot Eyden, Maja, or Elyssa. They had their own mission, as did Rhay and Ilario.

"No," Lora said, catching Amira's gaze again. "But let's do this."

Amira nodded, her fingers curling around the loose fabric of her olive green trousers. "As Elyssa always says, no holding back."

Lora smiled at that. If she had to face ruin, she wouldn't want to do it with anyone else but the friends she'd made here. She was glad Oscar was safe in Eyden's flat. He'd wanted to join them when Ian had insisted he needed to help, but Eyden had convinced Oscar that he would only distract her.

The carriage came to a stop and Lora climbed out, taking in the Rubien temple from up close. The towers were riddled with vines. The bright stone structures were polished in a way that made the sun reflect off of them, making light patterns on the grass.

She turned her head to spot Lozlan and a few Turosian guards coming from another carriage to join her and Amira. Up ahead was a large open doorway, blood-red roses and vines adorning the archway.

Together, they entered the temple, their few Turosian guards trailing after them. The pathway was marked by statues of the gods and goddesses, including Adeartas, the God of Justice—the patron of Rubien who had supposedly abandoned all fae after the Dark King's twisted acts. Though Lora wasn't religious, she hoped that today the god was present. Justice had to be served.

Straight ahead, she found other royals already seated, facing the wooden platform in the centre where Tarnan stood, talking with Saydren. Guards were stationed around the platform, dressed in Rubien uniforms. Rows of benches surrounded the stage in a half circle, starting from the ground and rising with each row.

The guard closest to Tarnan looked fae, but she recognised some of the humans from the camp dressed up in guard's uniforms next to the other royals by the benches, their expressions stern yet fearful. The humans didn't want to be here but they had no choice. As Lora had expected, Tarnan had brought the humans from the rebel camp, knowing she and her friends wouldn't want to kill them, even if the humans were forced to attack.

As Lora reached the end of the pathway with Amira by her side, Tarnan looked their way, raising a hand in polite greeting. Lora focused on the other kings and queens sitting close to the stage, talking amongst themselves tensely—except for Thea, who looked fierce as always. She had taken a seat right up front. Lora joined her in the first row after throwing Amira and Lozlan a quick nod. They took the stairs to an upper row. Hushed whispers filled the air as the other rulers took note of Lozlan.

Lora straightened her silver jacket as Thea craned her neck to glance at Kaede a few rows behind them with her husband.

Sitting up straight, head tilted forward, Thea said, "Good to see you again, Loraine."

Lora gave her a slight nod. "And you, Kaylanthea."

In Thea's pale pink eyes, Lora could read the subtext. She knew as much as Lora did that *everything* was at stake. And everything was what they would do to beat Tarnan.

"Welcome!" Tarnan's voice filled the space, drawing everyone's attention. Lora's hands started sweating. "I'm so pleased you could all make it." He walked to the edge of the platform and Saydren retreated to a corner. "Today marks true change for all of Liraen, a fresh chapter for us all. We all know it is by Caelo's will that our true leader will be chosen. And all of you here are witnesses to today's contest. I know that most of you may be on the fence about my true heritage, but as I assured you at the contest dinner, I plan to play fair as long as my opponents grant me the same courtesy."

A calm smile lifted the corners of his mouth and Lora fought back a shiver. He stared right at her, his eyes a mix of red and orange, like bleeding honey.

"Without further ado," Tarnan said, "I ask my first opponent, Queen Kaylanthea Zhengassi, to join me."

Lora relaxed slightly but forced herself to keep a neutral expression, her hands clasped in front of her. The dagger under her jacket helped calm her nerves. She and Thea would be going against Tarnan in the contest and they had planned for Thea to go first.

Thea rose to her feet, walking onto the stage without an ounce of fear radiating off her. When she joined Tarnan, they stood opposite each other. Tarnan appeared the picture of calmness, but so did Thea in a less unsettling way. Lora wished to see a crack in Tarnan's exterior but there was none.

Saydren walked to the centre of the stage. "The rules are the same as they've always been. The contestants shall not be helped by others, only Caelo's will shall intervene. It will go on until either one falls unconscious, dies, or surrenders. The winner will move on to compete against the ruler of Turosian."

He looked at Tarnan, who gave him a grin that made Lora shiver, then at Thea, whose lips formed a tight line when she nodded. Raising his arms, he stepped to the back of the stage. "On three, the High King Contest shall commence."

Tarnan tilted his head as if stretching his neck. His eyes were laser focused on Thea who stood straight, shoulders back and chin raised high. Lora could read the pain in her eyes. Tarnan had taken so much from her. Thea knew she wouldn't beat Tarnan, but she would draw out the fight as long as possible. Lora sent a silent prayer to Rhay and Ilario, hoping they'd already stormed the Rubien palace by now.

Saydren counted down, his voice resonating across the arena. "Three, two..."

Lora balled her hands into fists, feeling the fire in her wake, but it would have to wait.

"One!"

Thea lifted her arm, hand pointed at Tarnan as a wave of water hit him, drenching him. His smile slipped but only for a second. Thea raised her hand again but this time Tarnan shouted, "*Aim at yourself.*"

Thea's hand shook as she struggled against Tarnan's command. Her level five magic was strong, stronger than usual, but Tarnan's mind control was another league. Her own water threw her backwards. As she fell, she aimed at Tarnan again—right at his throat so he had no choice but to swallow it, his voice silenced.

Thea rose, water clinging to her leather trousers and jacket. The black liner under her eyes ran down in streaks like war paint.

With outstretched arms, she squeezed her hands, commanding the water to stay in his lungs. Tarnan grabbed at his throat, trying to spit out the water. His eyes showed a twinge of anger. His gaze went from Thea to the audience and Lora followed his line of sight to Amira, whose hand covered her mouth as she tried to catch her breath but couldn't.

That bloody contract. Thea couldn't kill Tarnan, but that wasn't the plan anyway. Weakening him was, and Lora felt she could breathe a little easier knowing it was working.

Tarnan turned to Lora and she gave him a smile. Did he know that if Amira hadn't supercharged Thea's powers beforehand, she wouldn't have been able to get to him as she was now?

Spitting water, Tarnan managed to shake off Thea's power. Thea aimed at him again but Tarnan yelled, "*No more. Drown yourself.*" He turned back to Lora, his small smile almost as polite as it was cruel. Thea was shaking but her gaze was still every bit as fierce. Tarnan stepped closer to Thea, her shaking hand in front of her face as if to deflect his command. "*Do it!*"

Thea coughed up water, her hands going to her throat in obvious panic. Turning pale, she dropped to her knees, clutching at her neck, her mouth open, but the water wouldn't come out. She was drowning in front of them.

She should surrender now. As if hearing her, Thea raised her hands.

Saydren strode forward. "Queen Kaylanthea surrenders. King Tarnan is the winner!"

Tarnan didn't drop his focus. Thea pounded at the ground. Her fists turned bloody.

"Stop it!" Lora yelled, getting to her feet. "It's my turn, let her go."

Half turning to her, Tarnan clicked his tongue. *"You're free, Kaylanthea."*

Thea coughed up water, her hands on her knees. She threw Tarnan a murderous glare before walking off on wobbly legs. Kaede met her halfway, helping her to the bench.

Lora felt Tarnan analysing her. She let him believe they'd put all their hope on Thea. She let him think she was defeated, burned to less than ashes. But he wouldn't defeat her. She'd stall for as long as she had to. Without compulsion, she could draw out the fight.

Saydren stepped up next to Tarnan, clearing his throat. "I call forth the next contestant, the true ruler of Turosian."

Lora grabbed the fire message she had prepared to signal Eyden in her pocket and discreetly set it aflame. She was about to walk towards the platform, willing her heart to stay calm, when Tarnan's gaze chilled her bones.

"I call forth King Karwyn Adelway," Tarnan announced, his voice echoing through the temple and shattering their plan.

CHAPTER 71

RHAY

There was an eerie silence in Cinnite. The streets were empty and the half-finished stone buildings made it look like the city had been abandoned yet again. In the late afternoon sun, the palace glistened in front of them, stone towers piercing the sky like dark omens.

Rhay, Rio, and around thirty Turosian fae who had decided to accompany them to storm the palace moved as stealthily as possible between the empty buildings, following Rio's silent commands. For now, the coast appeared clear. Rhay and Rio's mission to get the contracts relied heavily on most of the guards being at the temple where the contest took place.

From the outside, the palace seemed quiet, but Rhay was sure Tarnan wouldn't have left it unguarded. With Amira's locator spell, they knew the contracts were in the palace, they just needed a guard to show them where. She hadn't been able to narrow it down more than that. Locating people was easier than items.

Rio gestured for the Turosian fae to follow them and they closed the distance between the alley and the back entrance Rhay had noticed when fleeing last time. Only two guards blocked the door. They didn't have time to react before the Turosian fae threw themselves at them, armed with almandine daggers and swords taken from the Turosian palace.

"Keep one alive," Rhay whisper-yelled, taken aback by the fury of the Turosian fae. He hadn't realised how much anger boiled inside the Turosian people. Harten and then Karwyn's reign had left bitterness in their citizens' hearts.

One of the Rubien guards was impaled by a sword and Rio and Rhay had to intervene to stop the other from being killed.

Rio turned to the Rubien guard, dressed in bloodthirsty red. He looked terrified, his round face making him look like a child.

Focusing on the guard's fear, Rhay used his power to increase it. "Show us where Tarnan keeps his blood contracts."

"I have no idea." The guard panicked, trying to avoid Rhay's gaze as he glanced at the red roses adorning the back door. The sun beat down on them, and Rhay wasn't sure if it was the heat or his fear that made the guard sleek with sweat.

Rhay pushed further. "Lead me to where Tarnan keeps his most valuable possessions." The guard nodded his head fast, terror haunting his dark grey eyes.

Keeping his almandine dagger against the guard's neck, Rio let the guard lead the way, Rhay and the Turosian fae following.

When they entered the palace grounds, Rhay joined Rio's side and pushed the guard forward, aware of the time they were losing. As long as Amira's contract was still standing, she would get hurt every time Tarnan's was hurt—and worse, she would die with him if he was killed. The same applied to the humans under contract. They would die with Tarnan too. Rhay couldn't help the knot in his stomach when he thought of the part he had played.

A chill ran through his body as they wandered through the Cinnite palace. It was quiet—too quiet. The signs of the fight for the amulet were long gone. The dark marble stairs were polished with no hint of bloodstains. The chandelier sparkled above them. He could see his own reflection on the shiny dark floor.

The captured guard's eyes darted around, but they encountered no one as he led them to a dark corridor. They took the stairs, ending up in a larger corridor downstairs that Rhay had never been to. And then, just as they turned the corner, the guard yelled, "We're under attack!"

"Fuck," Rhay muttered as Rio dragged his dagger across the guard's throat. But it was too late. Ten guards rushed towards them from the end of the corridor, drawing their swords. Rhay glanced at Rio to signal him to keep going. The others should be able to deal with the guards.

As soon as the thought crossed his mind, Rhay heard footsteps coming from behind them. He turned as twenty more guards stormed in from upstairs. They were trapped in between the two groups of guards. *Would have been too fucking easy.*

Rhay's hand went to the sword strapped to his side. Before he could intervene, Rio raised his hands and cracks appeared on the stone floor. From it emerged vines which twisted themselves around the guards' ankles, tripping them.

Rhay sprung into action, taking advantage of the guards' confusion. In one swift motion, he slashed at someone's arms with his sword, cutting deep and making him drop his sword. He focused on the guards closest to him, pushing fatigue into their systems, slowing their movements. Rhay was getting more used to using his powers in battles. The narrow hallway echoed with the metallic sounds of clashing swords and grunts of pain.

Rhay struck at one of the guards who scrambled up on his feet and drew a dagger strapped to his hip. He was ready to strike again, this time to kill, when Rio's yell distracted him. A guard slammed Rio against the wall with her air power. He put his hand to the back of his head as he slid to the ground, and his fingers came away covered in blood.

With a yell, Rhay threw his dagger at the guard, but she diverted it with her air power and the dagger plunged into Rio's arm. *Shit.* Another guard launched himself at Rhay. Twirling the sword in his hand, Rhay pierced the guard's heart. Then he turned to the guard who was now lifting Rio into the air with her power. Throwing his hand forward, Rio tried to use his own power to counterattack. But the guard yanked him to the left and dodged the cracks appearing in the ground.

Rhay dashed forward, taking advantage of her momentary distraction, and cut her throat. She collapsed, blood spraying from her wound, coating Rhay's face and clothes. But Rhay was already moving. Running fast, he managed to catch Rio before he dropped on the floor. Rhay crashed to the ground under Rio's weight.

"Hello there," Rhay said with a mischievous smile, looking up at Rio on top of him. Their faces were so close Rhay could taste Rio's breath on his lips.

"Watch out!" Rio yelled as he threw his hands forward. Rhay turned his head around swiftly. Rio's vines sprouted from the cracked floor, wrapping tightly around a guard's arm, stopping him from dealing a deadly blow. A burly Turosian fae stabbed the guard from behind, killing him.

Rio helped Rhay up. Taking a moment to breathe, Rhay noticed that the ten guards that had rushed them from up ahead had abandoned their post at the end of the corridor. No longer blocked by guards, an iron door secured by a series of locks called to him. It had to be the treasure room. Rhay gestured for Rio to follow him and they scrambled forward on weak legs.

They made a run for the door but a wall of fire appeared in front of them, stopping them in their tracks. Rhay turned to a guard further up the corridor, his hands stretched in front of him. Focusing on him, Rhay tried to lower his hostility. But the guard only smiled as he pushed his fire towards Rhay and Rio.

Using his power to splinter the stone floor, Rio picked up a mass of stones and threw them at the guard. He dodged it, springing up and doing a somersault before landing back on his feet.

A Turosian fae noticed their struggle and slashed at the guard's back, taking him by surprise. "Thank you," Rhay said. The dark-haired woman tilted her chin, then turned to another guard fast approaching.

Bodies littered the blood-stained ground. Most were guards, but a dozen were Turosian fae. Rhay's heart tightened in his chest. They had given their life to help them.

Hearing a clicking noise, Rhay glanced at Rio, who was already busy twisting vines inside the locks on the door to make them expand until they cracked.

Rhay ran to Rio's side as he threw open the door. The small round room was filled to the brim with gold, precious jewels, and stunning art pieces.

Rhay's heart pounded in his chest. "I don't see the contracts." Had they lost all this time for nothing?

"They could be hidden," Rio said, his tone unable to mask his stress.

They turned over every object in the room. Rhay rattled an elegant golden rug with floral patterns. Rio cut up paintings of Tarnan and the Ellevarn family. They tapped on the stone walls, listening for hollow spots. They searched the ground for an underground passage.

But there was nothing. The contracts weren't there.

CHAPTER 72

EYDEN

Eyden watched Elyssa pace back and forth between the two wagons—used to transport large groups of people—they'd brought to the edge of the border in the woods. The Rubien temple was close enough that Eyden could see the tops of the high towers but far enough that they wouldn't attract attention. Was Lora already going against Tarnan or was Thea still stalling?

Maja leaned against a tree, her fingers drumming a pattern on her leg. They were all on edge. Ian kept himself busy petting the horses they'd used to get here. Eyden hadn't wanted to bring the boy, but Elyssa had said if Ian needed to do this to let go of some of his guilt, then they should let him.

Eyden knew that kind of guilt. He still carried it with him, but his past, the gambling, Rahmur Piers, it all felt much smaller than it used to. It no longer threatened to swallow him. Now it was merely a reminder to never fall so low again. He would do better.

His hand burned and Eyden opened his palm to see Lora's signal. It was time. Elyssa had stopped next to him, a rope already in her hands. Maja pushed off the tree to come closer.

"Go get them," Elyssa told Eyden before turning to Ian. "Open the carriages."

Eyden didn't waste a second and drifted to the temple. The warm wind pushed him forward and his feet hit the stone ground as he appeared on the top of one of the towers. It gave him the perfect view of the events going on beneath. Shielding his eyes from the sun, he spotted Lora. But she wasn't on the stage as planned.

Saydren, standing on the edge of the stage, gestured at the guards behind him and they dragged someone out from under the stage. The fae's head hung low as they held him by each arm, forcing him forward onto the platform. When he tilted his chin, a gasp went through the temple. The kings and queens tensed, visibly shocked by this turn of events, but no one dared to intervene.

Eyden thought he must be seeing things, but the audience's reaction told him he wasn't. It was Karwyn. His eyes were depleted of all light. His body looked frail, as if his bones could break all on their own. They'd left him in the palace but somehow Tarnan had stolen him right back. It must have been Saydren. Karwyn's former royal healer had to be aware of every secret passage and loophole into the palace and Karwyn was too weak to fight against him. They had stationed guards at Karwyn's door but not enough, it seemed. They should've checked on Karwyn before they left for the temple which was only two hours away. Saydren might have used a skyaelo, cutting down the journey time.

Tarnan grinned at Lora, who stood by the benches, her fists curled tight. The other kings and queens seemed unsure how to proceed. Amira's gaze was locked on Tarnan, her hand wandering to the amulet around her neck.

Eyden took in the guards spread across the temple. He had a mission. Even if Lora and Amira's had been derailed, he had to keep going. Judging from Karwyn's stance, he wouldn't last long.

Spotting a guard close to Kaede, Eyden drifted down, Amira's supercharge quickening his powers. Before the guard could react, Eyden grabbed the shoulder of the familiar human. He met Kaede's gaze for a split second before they drifted away.

Landing in the woods, Eyden threw the guard to the ground.

"Wylliam," Elyssa said as she rushed forward, aiming her foot at his head, but he was fast. Wylliam grabbed her ankle, twisting until Elyssa fell on the ground. She curled up, rolling to the side and springing to her feet. Wylliam rushed at her but Elyssa kicked him between the legs. As he doubled over, she used the back of her dagger to knock him out.

"Go," she told Eyden. Elyssa signalled for Ian and he rushed to her, helping her tie Wylliam up. As he was bound to Tarnan by a blood contract like the other human rebels, he couldn't go against Tarnan. They didn't want to hurt the humans, but they were a liability in the fight until Rhay and Ilario found their contracts.

Maja held the carriage door open as Elyssa and Ian dragged Wylliam forward to lock him up.

Drifting again, Eyden repeated the same pattern. He watched from above, pinpointed who could be human, watching for familiar faces, then drifted to the woods. He fought against the instinct to drift to Lora's side, not wanting to attract Tarnan's attention.

Soon the carriages filled up. The humans sat next to each other on the wooden benches with their hands tied behind their backs.

"I think that's all of them," Eyden said as he twisted the hands of an older man behind his back. Ian headed to him and bound the man's hands. He pulled the man up and helped him into one of the carriages. Elyssa locked the door behind him, keeping the key in her pocket. She now wore one of the blood-red uniforms to blend in. So did Maja.

"Are you sure you want to go with us?" Eyden asked Maja. Lora had suggested she stay with Oscar.

Pulling the gun out of the waistband of her burgundy trousers, Maja cocked her head. "I'm not going to sit out the epic conclusion to Lora's tale."

"I second that," Elyssa said, laughing. She went up to Eyden, strapping her bow and arrows to her back as she walked. She looked like a living flame with her red curls and Rubien uniform. "How is it going back there?"

"I think it's about to explode. Tarnan brought Karwyn."

"*Fucker*. Rhay and Ilario better hurry up," Elyssa muttered. She gave Ian a stern look. "Make sure they stay here."

"I will." Ian leaned against one of the carriages. It rattled behind him. The humans were waking up and they weren't happy about being caged in.

Maja stepped forward, her left shoulder weighed down by a duffle bag. Her gun was in her right hand. "Let's get going."

They started toward the temple, gleaming bright in the near distance through the trees. He was saving his power for the fight after already using much of it drifting the humans to safety. The only sounds disturbing the peaceful forest were birds singing and their footsteps. Until a scream echoed behind them. Eyden froze, turning around.

"What was that?" Elyssa asked, taking in his expression.

"Sounded like a scream," Maja said. "Ian?"

"I'll check it out." Eyden gave his sister a nod before drifting back to the carriages.

He'd been hoping it was a false alarm, but as his feet hit the grass, he spotted Jaspen holding a knife to Ian's throat.

"I said unlock it!" Jaspen screamed at the boy.

Ian struggled against Jaspen's hold, but as the blade nicked his throat, he froze. "Why are you doing this? Why did you sell us out?"

"Good question," Eyden said, and Jaspen's head twisted in his direction.

"Don't come any closer," Jaspen commanded. Ian whimpered as the blade drew a drop of blood from his neck.

Eyden raised his hands. "All the trouble you gave me and it ended up being you who betrayed the camp. Why are you here, Jaspen? Are you Tarnan's lackey now?"

Jaspen gritted his teeth. "I'm no one's lackey. I did this for the future of all humans. Some sacrifices have to be made."

An arrow shot through the air so fast Eyden could barely track it as it struck Jaspen's hand. Yelling, Jaspen dropped his arm and Ian scrambled away, his hand going to his injured throat.

Elyssa, appearing next to him, nocked another arrow. Maja followed after Elyssa, both hands on her gun.

"*Some sacrifices?*" Elyssa yelled at Jaspen. "You call selling out the whole camp a necessary sacrifice? You're a fucking traitor." She stalked closer, the arrow so close to him, Jaspen flinched. "You sold out Lora too. For what?" She kicked out, her foot hitting Jaspen in the stomach, and he fell backwards.

Ian watched everything with a pained expression, leaning against one of the carriages. As Jaspen got back up, Eyden drifted to him, throwing him against the side of the carriage. His hands were buried in Jaspen's jacket, pulling him forward and then shoving him back against the carriage with so much force the humans inside yelped.

"You owe us a fucking explanation," Eyden bit out.

Jaspen stared at him, his dark eyes calculating. Then he laughed, his chuckle sending a wave of irritation through Eyden. He thought he might snap Jaspen's neck right then.

"Stop fucking around," Elyssa yelled next to them. She pointed an arrow at Jaspen's head. "Give me one reason why I shouldn't shoot you right now."

"You're not a murderer," Jaspen spat out, squinting to the side at Elyssa.

Elyssa pulled her arrow back farther. "Not good enough. Try again."

"I'm playing the long game here. You think I want to do Tarnan's or Saydren's bidding? They're fae. They're fucking *scum*." Eyden tightened his hold on the man's collar. "You and I," he continued, looking straight at Elyssa, "we're at a disadvantage. Sometimes you have to be the bad guy to even out the playing field. The camp...it is a shame it had to come to that. But if that's the way to get to a future where humans finally gain the upper hand, isn't it worth it?"

Elyssa huffed. "You're fucking sick."

Jaspen's mouth turned up in a snarl. "Don't pretend you really care about any of them. I always saw right through you. You like that they need you but really, you only care about Eyden. So what's it to you if this camp got raided? Be glad it's not like the last time. Your *family* is safe."

The way Jaspen spoke as if he knew something they didn't scratched at Eyden's memory. In a flash he saw the first camp destroyed when Elyssa's uncle had gotten killed. He saw everyone's faces when Eyden had been blamed for it. He had seen Jaspen's expression back then, saddened by the loss of his own family. But not just sad, he realised now. *Guilty.*

"It was you then too," Eyden said, pulling Jaspen forward until he met his gaze. "Wasn't it?"

His dark eyes shifted between Eyden and Elyssa. The past stared back at him, reflecting in Elyssa and Jaspen's gaze. No one had believed Eyden back then. No one but Elyssa and her parents. They'd kicked him out at sixteen with nothing to his name.

"*You're* the reason the first camp got discovered," Eyden forced out. He could hear Elyssa gasp but his focus was on Jaspen who didn't flinch from his stare.

"My parents died there," Jaspen gritted out. "Why would you think that?"

"I can spot guilt a mile away. And you're looking guilty as hell."

Jaspen was silent. The birds seemed to have stopped singing as if they too were waiting for the bomb to drop.

Eyden hit him square across the face. Jaspen spit out blood, cursing loudly. Before he could recover, Eyden hit him again, breaking his nose.

Jaspen's eyes were half closed as he tried to catch his breath. Huffing, Jaspen clicked his tongue, blood streaming from his nose. "All right. I stand by it. My only regret is my parents. They shouldn't have been there. I told them to go, but they stupidly didn't listen."

Eyden threw him back against the carriage, the loud crack of the wood echoing through the trees. "You fucking bastard. Only a coward would blame a sixteen-year-old for his deeds."

He had jump started it all. Eyden being kicked out. Eyden living on the streets. Elyssa's parents wanting to cross over. How could Jaspen betray his own people *twice*?

"Why?" Elyssa asked, her voice uncharacteristically quiet. "They god-damn trusted you. You used the camp's destruction to become the next leader and then you used that power to betray them *again*. How can you justify any of that?"

"I thought everything you did was to protect us," Ian added quietly.

The sadness in his eyes made him look younger, reminding Eyden of himself when he was around that age.

"I'm protecting humankind," Jaspen spat out. "It's a heavy cross to bear, but someone has to."

Eyden tilted his head at Elyssa, catching the glassy look in her eyes that quickly turned to red-hot rage. With a deep sigh that held so much fury—the trauma of their past—Elyssa let her arrow fly.

Jaspen twisted to the side just in time, the arrow landing less than an inch from his face. Eyden had let himself be distracted and he didn't catch on to Jaspen's move until he'd already pulled back his hand. Eyden's gaze landed on a round device ticking furiously.

He distantly heard Maja shout *duck* and he stepped back fast, intending to drift just as Jaspen threw the bomb onto the carriage roof.

CHAPTER 73

LORA

Lora fought to find her voice. *"I'm the Queen of Turosian,"* she shouted, nearing the stage as she held Tarnan's gaze. "I was crowned."

Karwyn's sudden appearance had completely thrown her. Tarnan grinned at her as if he knew it. "You were crowned when the current ruler, Karwyn Adelway, hadn't abdicated or died. Your reign is *void*. And fortunately, Saydren got Karwyn here just in time."

Lora stood at the edge of the stage, her gaze locked on Tarnan, who seemed to dare her to look away. Had he known all along that Lora could withstand his compulsion? Was that why he had gotten himself an opponent who didn't stand a chance against him? He must have fucking known. She hadn't been worried anymore about Karwyn replacing her, not when she had all his power. But no one would dare oppose Tarnan.

Swallowing her rage, Lora gave Tarnan one more glare before turning to Karwyn. Her cousin's strange silver-lined eyes met hers. He seemed utterly depleted of strength, yet there was a stubbornness that won out. It seemed she and Karwyn had a common enemy now.

"Shall we begin?" Tarnan asked the crowd who all stared at Karwyn as if looking at a ghost. Then shouts of protest erupted around her—disbelief mixed with disagreement.

Thea sprang up next to her. "It's Lora's place to fight. She has earned the right!"

Waving her away, Tarnan added, "I suggest you sit down. Karwyn has been chosen. It's the law, Caelo's will."

Karwyn wouldn't be able to stall Tarnan. He could barely stand. Biting her lip, Lora turned around. What other choice did she have? With a heavy heart, Lora took her seat next to Thea, who bent over again, wiping water from her lips. Lora reached into her jacket and handed her a handkerchief.

"Let's begin," Saydren shouted. The guards let go of Karwyn and he almost fell to his knees. Karwyn craned his neck, taking in the audience. Lora knew who he was looking for but he wouldn't find Rhay in the crowd.

"Three, two..." Saydren said, retreating to the back, "one...go!"

Tarnan stalked forward until Karwyn and him could almost share the same breath.

"Have at it then," Karwyn gritted out.

Tarnan's gaze hardened. "This was always meant to happen. Your father took out mine and now I shall triumph over you." The smile on Tarnan's face made Lora grip the wooden bench she sat on. "Get on your knees and surrender, then you shall live. For a little while longer, at least."

Karwyn stared at him, calculating, then he laughed, the sound broken as he ended up spitting blood. He inched closer to Tarnan. "You want the high king title? Then you will have to kill me for it. I will *never* surrender."

For a long second, Tarnan remained silent. Then he chuckled. "Too bad." He took out a dagger, throwing it at Karwyn's feet. "Let's make it interesting then, show everyone who Caelo truly chooses, whose destiny it is to rule." Tarnan removed another blade from his jacket.

Karwyn carefully eyed the dagger on the ground. Quicker than Lora would have expected, Karwyn grabbed the weapon then moved back, pointing the blade at Tarnan. His hand was unsteady, the weight of the dagger too much for him.

"Last chance to go out easy." Tarnan twirled his dagger. "Surrender to the Sartoya name."

"Never," Karwyn repeated.

He rushed at Tarnan, but his steps were uneven and his strike clumsy. Tarnan dodged it easily, stepping back with a laugh. Karwyn glared at him, swinging out again but only cutting air.

Tarnan let him try a few more times, each of Karwyn's attempts weaker than the last. Even from her position, Lora could tell Karwyn was breathless; sweat glistened on his skin, making his blouse stick to his back.

As Karwyn tried again, Tarnan finally countered his attack, his blade hitting Karwyn's dagger with such force Karwyn flinched. Gripping Karwyn's wrist, Tarnan twisted it and Lora heard the sickening crunch of bones breaking. A yell of pain left Karwyn's lips as the dagger fell from his limp hand. He barely looked up in time to avoid a slash to his face. Kicking out, Tarnan caught him in the stomach and Karwyn fell like a rag doll.

Karwyn turned his head, coughing up blood. He tried to stand up but Tarnan pushed his boot down on his chest, forcing him back.

"Surrender," Tarnan demanded, leaning over Karwyn.

Karwyn spat blood at him. "*No.*" His teeth were stained red.

Wiping bloody spit from his face, Tarnan drew back his foot. "So be it."

He kicked Karwyn's face hard enough to leave an imprint. Karwyn covered his face with his hands, but it did nothing against Tarnan's vicious attacks. After kicking him in the ribs, then his back, Tarnan leaned down and clutched Karwyn's blouse, hitting him square in the face over and over again. Karwyn's body went limp, his swollen, bruised eyes barely open as Tarnan let out his rage.

When Tarnan dropped his hold on him, Karwyn's head hit the ground with a loud thump. He didn't move, his eyes closed. Lora squinted to get a closer glimpse. There it was, a faint flutter of Karwyn's chest. He was alive but unconscious.

Saydren rushed towards them, kneeling next to Karwyn and nudging him. He didn't move.

"We have a winner." Saydren rose to his feet and bowed to Tarnan, who removed a sunset orange handkerchief from his pocket to clean his bloody knuckles. "High King Tarnan Sartoya Ellevarn."

The name made Lora's heart speed up, a deep panic nestling in her chest. She turned her head to Amira, whose gaze held the same fear. They hadn't wanted it to come to this, for Tarnan to win the contest. But it didn't matter. He wouldn't leave here alive. He had to go through each one of them first.

"The time has come to choose a side," Tarnan said, walking to the edge of the stage. He took in the queens and kings present, their advisors and significant others. "Anyone not swearing fealty to me, recognising me as the chosen High King of Liraen, will not leave here today. Choose wisely. Lora isn't even the true queen of Turosian, but *I* am the high king."

For a sickening second that felt endless, Lora expected another betrayal, but no one moved, not even Wryen. Lora curled her hands into fists, wishing her stare could slice right through Tarnan.

"Now!" Amira screamed behind her, and Lora sprang to her feet, pushing aside all her panic and locking it up tight.

Faster than Tarnan could track, all the queens and kings got up, aiming their power at his guards, his army. Wryen aimed his fire. King Quintin of Obliveryn threw air. One of King Mayrick of Emerlane's guards commanded the vines wrapped around the towers to move. Kaede looked deep in thought, trying to get through to his guards, to turn them against him.

"*Cease your power!*" Tarnan shouted. But they didn't listen. Tarnan tripped as he sidestepped Wryen's fire and a vine swirled around his leg. His gaze went to Amira, her hand clasped around the amulet. Magic simmered in the air as she trapped the royals and their guards in an invisible bubble, safe from manipulation. Amira had practised every waking moment for this spell to work.

"*Kill them all, except Amira!*" Tarnan shouted. His guards stormed forward, weapons drawn, their magic ready to aim.

Lora faced him, calling on her fire, her air, all her power.

Tarnan rose to his feet, dusting off his shirt. "I'll never surrender the title I've *earned*, that Caelo has bestowed upon me. If that's your goal, I won't do it. And you can't kill me."

Because of Amira. All the kings and queens were aware of it. But all they needed to do was stall a little longer.

CHAPTER 74

❧

ELYSSA

The explosion Jaspen had set off was so loud Elyssa instinctively covered her ears, letting go of her bow. The ground shook and she almost lost her balance. Dust and splinters of wood filled her vision. Her gaze travelled from Eyden standing next to her—having drifted there—to Ian covering his ears, to Maja cleaning her glasses, and finally to Jaspen, who had thrown himself to the ground with his arms over his head.

What the fuck has he done?

Storming forward, Elyssa pummelled into Jaspen, throwing him on his back as her fist caught his nose. More blood ran down his already badly bruised face. Not enough. He had so much fucking blood on his hands.

Jaspen lifted his hands to protect his face when Elyssa raised her arm for another hit. But her focus was drawn to the carriage behind him.

The roof had exploded and some of the walls had crumbled. Through the dust in the air, she spotted people bleeding on the benches inside what was left of the bombed carriage. Those who weren't badly hurt scrambled out of the carriage, running back towards the temple. Elyssa was torn between running after them and punching Jaspen until he felt a smidge of the pain he'd inflicted on them.

"El!" Eyden yelled, and Elyssa turned every which way until she spotted him. "You got this?" He pointed his chin at Jaspen, who was breathing heavily under her. *Divide and conquer.*

She nodded and Eyden rushed off, throwing a small knife at someone's ankle, tripping them. Ian tried to rebind someone's hands. Maja fired a warning shot.

Elyssa returned her attention to Jaspen. She hit his cheek twice until he spat blood. She felt a splash of it hit her cheek and a deep repulsion coursed through her. Fishing out a throwing star, she pointed one sharp end at Jaspen's throat. "What did Saydren promise you?"

Jaspen laughed, more blood spilling from the corner of his mouth. He looked half insane, his smile mockingly cruel. "Why would I tell you? You don't deserve it. You'll never see the truth. What must be done." He turned his gaze to where Ian struggled to hold back a woman half his size. "I thought Ian would see it, understand it. But he's just a stupid, lost boy."

Elyssa kneed him in the stomach. "Cut the crap, Jaspen." Something he'd said before about gaining the upper hand pulled at her memory, connecting dots until an icy shiver spread through her.

"Is this about dark magic?" she asked, tracking his reaction. His laughter stopped. His eyes crinkled. "I heard a rumour." A rumour that Karwyn had pretty much revealed to be true.

"We're never going to take over without some...help."

"But you hate all fae. How is using dark magic to become like them the goddamn solution?"

"I'll never be like them." Jaspen lifted his head, pulling closer. "I'll be *better*. Human but with an unstoppable edge."

She shook her head. "You're deranged. Dark magic...it's unpredictable. There's always a price. And whatever Saydren promised you, he clearly didn't deliver. You're as weak as always."

Jaspen breathed out sharply, his eyes flaring. "I'm close. You could still join me."

Elyssa snorted. "Yeah, right. Dream on."

A loud crash made her turn her head, unsure where it was coming from. She spotted Maja and Ian binding people to trees outside the destroyed carriage. But the noise came from the carriage that was still intact. One of the freed humans, Wylliam, had dented the door with a knife, trying to get it open.

The distraction cost her, and Jaspen slapped her hand away. She fell off him, her shoulder hitting the ground hard. She swallowed a grunt as she rolled to the side, springing to her feet. Jaspen stood opposite her, a dagger in his hand.

She still had her throwing star but she aimed above Jaspen's head, at Wylliam. The man must have cursed as it struck his hand, forcing the knife from his grip. Ian tracked it and ran forward, pulling Wylliam back.

Elyssa turned to Jaspen, weaponless. But she could goddamn take him anyway.

Raising her fists, she mocked him. "Give it your best shot, Jaspen. It's time this ends."

He ran at her, dagger raised to slash her face. She ducked, kicking out with a wide arc, her leg hitting his shin. He managed to keep upright, swinging out again, the dagger barely missing her shoulder. She grabbed the wrist holding the dagger. He gritted his teeth, trying to move his arm, but her hold was fierce.

Grinning, Elyssa pulled at his arm with both her hands until she heard his shoulder pop and a hiss slithered from his lips. She kicked out again, cracking his kneecap. He swayed until she hit him once more— fist to the stomach. Cradling his arm, he dropped the dagger and Elyssa caught it mid-air.

Spinning to gain momentum, she kicked his stomach, throwing him backwards.

Elyssa dropped to the ground, one knee on either side of him. With both hands she clutched the dagger, pointing at his heart.

"You won't do it," Jaspen rasped, out of breath.

She thought of all the deaths she had witnessed because of him— this fucking traitor. Memories flooded her. Her uncle telling her to hide and then being killed right in front of her. Eyden's pained face as he had left the camp, her mother crying into her father's shoulder. Lora being dragged away to the palace because of Jaspen's intel. She pictured the last camp, what had been left of it after Jaspen had led Tarnan there. So much death that could have been avoided. And all for what?

She had to overcome so much guilt—for surviving, for not saving her parents, her uncle, Farren, Iris...the list went on and on. And yet Jaspen should be the one drowning in guilt. He should be fucking crippled with it.

Elyssa was no executioner, but she knew there was only one way to end the cycle of suffering Jaspen had created not just for her, but for the whole camp.

"You're wrong." Elyssa met his startled eyes. "You're always so god-damn wrong."

She sank the blade into his chest. His arms slacked at his sides. Blood dripped from his mouth. She checked his pulse. It was over. She didn't feel guilty for his death. Instead, a weird sense of peace settled over her, as if an open, aching wound finally closed.

Pulling the dagger free, Elyssa wiped it on the grass before pocketing it. She got to her feet and her gaze collided with Eyden as he reappeared with one of the humans.

"That should be everyone," he said, pushing the unconscious human to a tree where Ian got to work, binding him up. When Eyden spot-ted Jaspen, he put two fingers behind his ear and Elyssa returned the gesture.

"What's the plan?" Maja brushed grass off her burgundy trousers. "Are we going now?"

"You should drift," Elyssa said to Eyden. "We've lost too much time. And with Karwyn there... Go. Maja and I will catch up."

Eyden quickly tilted his head, then he was gone.

Breathing out slowly, Elyssa turned to Maja. "You good?"

Maja swung the duffle bag back over her shoulder. "Let's burn some shit up."

Elyssa smirked, determination sparking in her veins. She went to pick up her bow and arrows, then tilted her chin to the temple.

Looking over her shoulder, she saw Ian watching them as they ran forward, through the trees. Jaspen's death must be difficult for him to process but there was no time for that now. Gaze forward, Elyssa increased her speed. The wind blew loudly in her ears but she noticed Maja breathing heavily beside her. Elyssa's legs burned but she drowned it out. Amira and Lora were waiting for her. She hoped they weren't too late.

Reaching the temple, Maja dropped the duffle bag and pulled out two canisters of gasoline mixed with herbs. They each took one and headed inside the temple.

Chaos greeted them. Swords clashing, blood drawn, indistinguishable curses drifting in the air. Elyssa spotted Amira deep in focus, watching the royals fight against Tarnan's army. Lora fought off the guards Tarnan had sicced on her, raising her fiery dagger.

Exchanging a quick nod with Maja, Elyssa split off to the right. Heading in opposite directions, they drew a circle of gasoline around the stage, trying to stay out of Tarnan's view in the madness. Once completed, they met at the back of the platform.

Maja swiped at her fringe, messy from sweat. "Let's light it up."

Elyssa nodded, removing matches from her pocket. She was about to light them when Maja's eyes widened and her lips formed a warning. Spinning around, Elyssa ducked as a sword swung at her head. A guard was on her and she dropped the matches as she spun around, aiming at his crotch.

The guard stepped back, his sword almost grazing her side. Grabbing her throwing star, Elyssa aimed at the guard's arm. She kicked the sword from his grip and it clattered to the ground. As the guard clutched his bleeding arm, Elyssa punched his nose, her brass knuckles cutting into his flesh. Spinning around and kneeling down, she picked the sword up and punched it blindly behind her. She met flesh. Springing to her feet, she drew the sword back and swiftly aimed at his heart, taking the guard out for good.

Brushing a loose curl behind her ear, Elyssa turned to Maja, leaning the tip of her sword on the ground.

"Impressive," Maja said. Her gaze darkened as it moved over Elyssa's shoulder. "Can you do that like fifty more times?"

Elyssa turned. More guards stormed out of a door not far from them, coming from the underground. Tarnan had brought goddamn backup. A guard aimed his bow straight at Maja and Elyssa grabbed her arm to draw her back just as another fae in a Rubien uniform struck his sword through the guard's chest. One of Tarnan's guards, switching sides? He vanished from her field of vision, trapped in between other guards.

Maja's hand shook slightly as she retrieved the gun jammed into the back of her trousers. She was supposed to head back to Ian, but with the guards approaching, she wouldn't get out. Elyssa turned her head, trying to spy over the stage, but she could only see Tarnan's lower half. She couldn't spot Lora or Amira. And she couldn't find the goddamn matches to light up the firewall to block Tarnan off.

"Fifty or however many it takes," Elyssa said, and Maja nodded next to her, her hands on her gun steadying. Elyssa dropped the sword and pulled back an arrow.

"Bring on the epic conclusion." Maja's voice no longer showed a hint of fear.

CHAPTER 75

RHAY

"What do we do now?" Rio asked Rhay, desperation taking hold of his voice.

Rhay pushed his hair away from his face, walking back and forth in the treasure room. For all they knew, the others could already be hanging on by a thread—or worse, dead.

Sighing, Rhay stilled. "If Tarnan doesn't keep the contracts here, then where? And who would know about it?"

"Besides Tarnan, possibly Saydren? He's the closest person to Tarnan and he had the amulet on him. But he must be with Tarnan now," Rio added.

"Great, so basically the two fae who would never help us and are not even in the palace." Rhay took a deep breath, the sound of the fight outside the room dying down. The one task he had been entrusted with, and he couldn't even manage it.

"Let's interrogate some of the guards, they might know something."

"I'm sure he took the guards he trusts the most with him. He wouldn't leave them here to protect an empty—" Something clicked in Rhay's mind. "Rio, you're a genius!" Rhay grabbed Rio's hands.

"What did I do?" Rio's eyes zeroed in on Rhay's hands.

"You gave me an idea and—" Rhay stopped himself, his gaze lost in Rio's vibrant emerald eyes. *God, he was beautiful.* What if one of them didn't make it out alive today? There was something he would always regret not doing.

With his bloodied hand, Rhay cupped Rio's cheek. Their eyes met—Rio's questioning, Rhay's promising. Rhay's lips melted against Rio's, burning everything inside him. Hands winding around the back of Rhay's head, Rio pulled closer, opening up to him. Rhay took the invitation, his tongue running along Rio's bottom lip softly, teasing.

As he deepened the kiss, Rio's fingers got lost in Rhay's hair. Rhay pushed forward, their chests touching. He caught Rio's sharp exhale, drinking it in, saving it to memory. He'd never heard anything sweeter.

Rhay couldn't believe he had waited this long, denied himself this feeling. Everything around him disappeared, Rio was the only thing that mattered. He wanted to keep going forever, but he knew he couldn't.

Forcing himself to break the kiss, Rhay breathed out heavily. "We need to go. Follow me."

Wide-eyed, Rio touched his own lips. Rhay raced to the door, trying to shake off the lingering taste. He heard Rio following him.

At that moment, more guards stormed the corridor. "Hold them back," Rio told the remaining Turosian fae. They nodded, launching themselves at the guards. Rhay and Rio used the distraction to sneak through the chaos.

Rhay grabbed a guard who was staring at the bodies on the floor, his gaze shocked. Pushing his sword against the guard's throat, Rhay whispered in his ear, "Lead us to Saige's room." He fed the guard's fear, coaxing him into agreement. Walking ahead, Rhay and Rio followed the guard. The palace was huge, it would take too long to search it all. But maybe Saige could help them narrow down the location of the contracts. Rhay knew Tarnan would never risk bringing her to the fight, for fear of getting her hurt or found out.

Running through the corridors, Rhay, Rio, and the guard finally stopped once they reached the right spot. Four guards stood in front of a door, looking uneasy. Glancing at the guard who had led them here, Rhay convinced him he was so tired he could no longer stand upright. Slumping to the ground, the guard closed his eyes.

"Let's tie this one up and then knock the other guards unconscious to not disturb Saige," Rhay whispered to Rio. Amira had told their group about Saige back in Turosian, but they had never properly discussed what to do about her. That was a problem for future Rhay to solve.

Rio nodded in agreement and, still hidden by the corner of the corridor, Rhay locked his gaze on the four guards while Rio tied the passed-out guard up with his vines. Rhay was already exhausted, a headache taking over. Even though the blood had dried on the back of his head, Rio had been hit pretty badly. Rhay could feel him shaking next to him.

Focusing his power on the first guard, the tallest of the bunch, Rhay envisioned him so tired he could fall asleep standing up. Clenching his teeth, Rhay pushed back against the guard's mental shield. The guard collapsed to the ground. Surprised, the other guards looked him over.

Not wanting to lose his momentum, Rhay quickly focused on another guard, who soon joined the first guard in deep slumber. Rhay stumbled on his feet. Seeing his state, Rio sprouted vines from the ground, wrapping them around the two remaining guards, muffling their yells.

The guards fought back against the vines, trying to slash at them with their swords, but Rio kept sprouting more until they completely tangled around the guards, dragging them to the ground. When the two guards were stuck, Rio and Rhay ran out of their hiding spot and knocked them out with the hilts of their daggers.

"I'll tie them up, go get her," Rio told Rhay.

Rhay entered the bedroom, startling Saige awake on her bed. "Rhay, you're back! Your friend was right." She stood up, rubbing sleep from her eyes. Noticing the blood on Rhay's clothes, her mouth dropped open.

"I don't have time to explain everything, but if you don't help me, Amira will die and it will be the end of Liraen." Rhay stumbled over his words, knowing that each passing second brought them closer to ruin.

"Amira will die?" Saige twisted her hands in front of her, her breathing quickening.

"Yes, come with me, please."

Saige's eyes were wide with panic. "But the king told me to stay hidden in my room. There are bad people who could hurt me."

Rhay joined her in two long strides, grabbing her hands. "Listen to me. I promise I will always protect you, okay? No matter what, I'll be there to help you. But right now, it's your time to help. There are a lot of people's lives on the line, people I care about. Has the king ever told you where he hides his most valuable possessions?"

Saige nodded. "In the treasure room."

"Not the treasure room." Rhay squeezed Saige's hands, startling her. "Think, Saige, *think*. Has he ever mentioned contracts to you? Or showed you scrolls of papers?"

Saige shook her head, tears building in her eyes. Rhay focused on lowering her fear, pushing back his exhaustion. It didn't seem to work well.

"I don't know. *I don't know*." Sitting on her bed, she put her head in her hands. "What does that have to do with Amira?"

Rio entered the room. "Did you find them?"

Saige looked up, fear etched in her eyes. "Who is he?"

"I'm Rio, a friend of Rhay and Amira." His tone was warm, reassuring. When Rio turned his questioning gaze to Rhay, he shook his head.

Rio lowered himself to be on Saige's level, kneeling beside the bed. "Saige, what did the king say before leaving? I know you must be confused, but we need your help to save our friends."

"He said I shouldn't be afraid because he left guards to protect me," Saige replied, her voice thin and close to tears.

"Did he do anything special?" Rhay insisted.

Saige blinked. "He looked at my books. He likes looking at my collection. He's been doing it more recently."

Rhay and Rio exchanged a knowing glance before sprinting to the bookcase. All the books from Saige's room in Pyria had been brought here. It had to be over two thousand. It would take them forever to search them all.

Rhay got an idea. "Saige, do you notice any new books in your selection?"

Saige stood up from the bed and joined them in front of the book-case. She furrowed her brows, staring intently. "This one!" She pointed at a large book with a ruby red binding on the top shelf.

Climbing up the book ladder, Rhay excitedly grabbed it. Inside, bound together as a book, were the humans' contracts and, best of all, Amira's. He handed it to Rio, who stashed it in their duffel bag.

Rhay planted a kiss on Saige's forehead. "You're amazing, love!" Looking at them dumbfounded, she took a seat on her bed.

Taking out the runia he had strapped against his thigh, Rhay called Amira, hoping he wasn't too late.

"Rhay!" Hearing Amira's voice, no matter how desperate she sounded, was music to his ears. "We're running out of time." Her voice sounded hollow.

"Hang on. We'll get it to you in no time, I promise," Rhay assured her as Rio pulled up the duffel bag.

A crackling noise came from the runia. The call was disconnected. Would they get there in time? He wished Eyden could get them, but he needed his power for his own mission, and Amira would have used much of her energy supercharging Thea as well as Eyden and protecting them from Tarnan's compulsion by now.

As they made their way out of the room, Saige rushed forward on unsteady legs. "Wait, I'm coming with you. I don't want Amira to die."

Rhay stopped in his tracks. "Saige, love, you'll be safer here."

Saige pushed her shoulders back. "You said I'd be safe with you. You *promised*. I want to help—*please*."

Rio and Rhay exchanged a glance. They seemed to come to the same conclusion. Who were they to deny someone the chance to help?

CHAPTER 76

AMIRA

The runia fell out of Amira's hand as a guard smashed into her. It hit the bench, then rolled down another row to the ground floor, breaking into pieces. Distracted, the guard drew his sword and Amira pointed her hand at him, intending to throw him backwards. But he didn't hit the ground. Instead, he swung his sword at her. She barely dodged the sharp blade, a thin line of blood swelling on her collarbone. Keeping the royals from Tarnan's compulsion was depleting her energy much too fast. The amulet burned her chest under her blouse but she could hardly feel the sting as her every sense was in overload with the fight surrounding her.

Throwing both hands out, she forced the guard back. He stumbled but kept upright. Sweat made her hair stick to her neck. They were losing. The few advisors and guards each royal had brought with them to the contest were under merciless attack from Tarnan's guards down by the stage. Just when Amira had thought they could take on Tarnan's army, more had poured out from the underground like rats.

Amira had no idea where Elyssa was. She was supposed to light up a firewall to block Tarnan's view around the stage so he would be unable to shout specific commands. But he was still eyeing them with a content grin, as if this madness was exactly what he had anticipated and he wasn't worried one bit. Karwyn's unconscious body, not far from

530

Tarnan on the wooden platform, made the image even more eerie. He hadn't moved since his fight with Tarnan. Was he still alive?

The guard came at her again but before he could reach her, Eyden appeared in his path, slicing his chest with one strike. Giving her a quick nod, Eyden moved behind her to where Lora was trapped between a mass of guards. Amira tried to catch her gaze but there were too many people between them.

A presence by her side made Amira swirl around. Close to her, as if he wanted to be the most protected, Wryen threw his fire at any guard who tried to get to him.

Kaede slashed viciously at a guard's arm to Amira's left. Relentlessly, he came at Kaede, leaving a deep gash in her shoulder. Thea rushed to her friend's side, throwing a wave of water at the guard with enough strength to make him hit the ground.

Amira was surrounded by screams, smoke from Wryen's fire, and weapons striking against each other. It was disorienting and her head felt fuzzy, yet she forced her mind to stay sharp. Shaking badly, she felt her protection circle wavering. She couldn't let it go now, it would be even more of a bloodbath.

"Amira, you know I don't want to hurt you." Tarnan stopped at the edge of the stage. "You can't keep this up forever and I have all day. We can still rebuild a better Liraen together if you stop this nonsense now." His voice was laced with fake tenderness.

"I trusted you, I put so much faith in you. And you used me just like everyone has always done." Amira turned her gaze to Wryen, who pretended not to have heard her. Scoffing, she returned her attention to Tarnan. "I won't ever let it happen again. I have all day too." Her skin was hot to the touch but she ignored the way her muscles constricted with effort, forcing herself to keep the spell up. She grabbed the amulet around her neck so tight it pricked her skin.

Tarnan let out a curt, dark laugh. "I care about you, Amira, I really do. But not enough to turn my back on what is rightfully mine. Give me the amulet—I knew you'd manage to combine them—or I'll have to take it from you." He took out a dagger from his side.

Fearing he was going to aim it at her, Amira ducked while Lora fought her way towards her. But Tarnan didn't need to touch her to hurt her. Grasping the dagger, Tarnan cut the palm of his right hand, the hand Amira was using to hold on to the amulet.

Pain shot through her, blood dripping onto her blouse. She let go of the amulet as Tarnan sliced from his upper arm to his elbow. Red-hot pain took over and Amira lost her focus.

"Are you all right? Is the shield still on?" Lora whispered in her ear, rushing to her side. Her blonde hair was tangled and she had multiple cuts on her body.

Tarnan seemed to have the same idea. "*Kaylanthea,*" he started, and Thea swung her head to him, already under his influence. Amira gripped the amulet with both hands, blood smearing everywhere, yet her attempt was weak. "*Attack Kaede!*" Tarnan finished.

Thea seemed to withstand it for a second, but then her sword lifted as she shook her head at Kaede. "*Run,*" she told her friend, and Kaede jumped from the bench.

Tarnan smiled, catching the royals' attention. "No matter how powerful that amulet is, Amira can't protect you all. If you don't submit now, every kingdom will have to find a new king or queen." His sick smile grew as he wiped his bloody hand on his shirt, barely affected by the blood dripping from his upper arm all the way to his fingertips.

Wryen shifted next to her, withdrawing his fire. His lilac gaze was calculating as he glanced at the mess they were in and then to Tarnan.

Amira shook her head, reading his intention. "Don't you dare—"

He gripped her wrist. She yelped, her skin blistering from his touch.

Fire zipped past her head as Lora aimed at Wryen, but he deflected with his own flames and then guards were upon Lora from all sides, pushing Amira and Wryen to the side.

Digging his nails into Amira's arm, Wryen dragged her towards the stage. She tried to kick at him but her bones were heavy and his grip was unrelenting. An advisor from Emerlane threw himself at Tarnan, knocking him down. Yet Wryen continued to push Amira forward.

Turning her head, Amira caught Lora's gaze as she burned through a guard's armour. Amira drew on her energy and kicked at Wryen's shin hard enough that he yelped, glancing at his leg. Swiftly, Amira threw the amulet towards Lora, who used her air power to catch it. Before anyone noticed, Amira turned back to Wryen. Tarnan pushed away the Emerlane advisor, yelling a command she couldn't catch. The advisor turned his blade on himself, hitting his own heart. Tarnan scrambled back to his feet.

"You're making a mistake," she bit out as Wryen dragged her off further. "Tarnan won't spare you."

Wryen increased his binding flames, shackling both her hands. The fire bit into her skin, a familiar torture. "I tried it your way, but I should've known it was the losing side."

They left the benches, nearing the stage. Embers drifted from where Wryen held on to her to the ground. Fear shot through her. She dragged her feet, pulling back with all her strength.

"Stop fighting it," Wryen sneered in her ear. "Tarnan won't kill you. You always were such a pretty card in my game."

Amira rooted her feet into the dry ground, staring at the glowing embers at their feet. "No, Wryen, you don't understand—"

He clamped a hand over her mouth. Her eyes were wide as their feet moved towards the invisible line Elyssa and Maja were supposed to have drawn along the stage. At the last moment, she bit down on Wryen's hand. He cursed, giving her a violent push forward, and Amira braced herself against the wooden stage, trying to catch her breath. She whirled around, about to warn Wryen when a gut-wrenching scream tore through him.

Heat exploded in her face as a wall of flames circled around the stage, mere inches from her. Wryen's whole body was on fire, the wall stretching twice his height. The spell had worked. Amira had magically enhanced the gasoline Elyssa and Maja had distributed to block Tarnan off. But now, it had done much more than she had planned. In shocked silence, she watched the flames claw at Wryen's body, blackening his skin. A sickening smell wafted towards her as he fell to his knees, the flesh melting from his bones. He lost his voice as his whole body was swallowed by fire.

His wild lilac eyes met hers through the flames. She had tried to warn him. She had seen the embers of his fire flickering to the ground. Yet even now, there was only hatred in Wryen's gaze. Blame. Fury. She didn't deserve any of it. He had never shown her an inkling of love. He had abused her for years, making her hopeless about ever finding happiness. By Caelo, he had even tried to kill her on multiple occasions.

But he was her brother—*had been*—she realised as a dull shock zapped through her. Arms grabbed her from behind, dragging her onto the platform, away from Wryen's burning corpse. Amira fell on her back, pain rattling her bones.

Tarnan leaned over her, a sigh on his lips. "Wryen has always been an inconvenience. You would make a much better ruler. Give me the amulet and I'll let you have Allamyst."

"No," Amira spat at him.

He grabbed her shoulders, drawing her up. "Then I'll take it." His hand brushed back the top of her blouse but there was nothing around her neck.

Amira chuckled, her mind in shambles, burning flesh flashing through her head. "I don't have it."

His smile slipped as he gritted his teeth. "*Who has it?*"

The compulsion wrapped itself around Amira's entire being. She clenched her teeth, fighting against it, sharp ice scratching the inside of her head.

Tarnan's gaze slipped to the firewall around them. "*Where is it?*"

Holding her breath, she forced her mouth shut, but her insides felt as if they were on fire. Against every shred of resolve she had left, she gasped, "Lora has it."

CHAPTER 77

LORA

Lora pushed the amulet further into her pocket as she struck the guard in front of her, dealing a killing blow. Fire lit up the temple, heat flowing through the air. Eyden was by her side, a sword in his hand as he attacked two guards at once. She spotted Elyssa and Maja further off, coming towards them from the back of the temple. Lozlan stood a few rows below her, fighting two guards, his power seemingly close to depleted, much like her own.

Through the flames surrounding the stage, Lora couldn't find Amira. How long until Tarnan realised she no longer had the amulet?

Her question seemed to be answered as a few of Tarnan's guards aimed their water magic at the firewall, tearing it down.

"I think it's time you cease," Tarnan yelled at Lora, appearing at the edge of the stage behind the smoke lingering in the air. Amira stood next to him, hunched over.

Sweat coated her back as Lora met Tarnan's blood-red gaze. "I won't."

Tarnan's smile didn't falter. He looked from Amira to Lora, a sigh on his lips. "I've reached the end of my patience. I gave you every chance to cease before I start taking out one after the other."

"If you really think you wouldn't have tried to take us out whether we stop or not, then you're lying to yourself."

"You think you're so righteous, but all you are is another power-hungry king," Amira added, and Lora swore Tarnan flinched.

"We'll never know, will we?" Tarnan's gaze turned sinister. "I'm done playing nice. *Eyden—*" Eyden drifted away from Lora's side, halting his attack on the guards, before Tarnan could finish his command. "*Everyone,*" Tarnan corrected, looking at the remaining royals and their advisors gathered in front of the benches, "*please take care of Elyssa.*" He looked pleased with himself when Amira shuddered, turning to find Elyssa in the crowd at the back of the stage. The royals and advisors headed towards where Elyssa and Maja were taking care of the remaining guards. Eyden appeared by Elyssa's side, a short knife in his hand.

Lora tried to call on her power, but it was like drawing on an empty well.

"Saydren," Tarnan said, and the healer stepped out of the shadows. "It's time." The fae nodded and Lora glanced at Amira, who seemed as anxious as she was. *Time for what?* Tarnan hadn't even tried to compel Lora, making it clear he knew it wouldn't have any effect.

Lora was racking her brain on how to keep stalling, but all thoughts exited her brain when she spotted Saydren opening a hatch on the ground and pulling someone out by their hair. Long dark hair shielded the person's dark chocolate eyes that were so familiar to Lora even though she hadn't seen them in so long.

Her mother's gaze met Lora's as Saydren threw her onto the wooden platform. Her hands were bound behind her back. Dirty hair hung into her face, her mouth gagged. Her jeans had a bloody rip in them and her shirt was torn on one sleeve.

"Mum," Lora whispered, her voice choked, her breathing stuttering. Everything seemed distant to her now. The fight. Tarnan's cruel words. All she saw was her mother, bloodied on the ground, but *alive.* A sob got caught in her throat. Tears burned her eyes. *This is real. She's alive.*

The words kept repeating in her head until Lora knew she wasn't seeing things. A joy filled her heart that she couldn't describe. It was like coming up for air after swimming a marathon in the pitch dark.

Tarnan's voice cut through Lora's brief relief. "I warned you, Lora. Your neighbours were just the appetiser. I had your family in my grasp before I even promised you I would stay away from the border—my assurance that once Amira combined the amulets, I would get my hands on it. I know how much you've done to save your mother. You wouldn't let her die now, would you? Because I will kill her if you don't hand me that amulet." Tarnan had played them again. He'd *let* them keep the amulets, knowing Lora wouldn't let her mother die.

Saydren pushed another person next to her mother, his green eyes taking her in. It was her father. He had been gagged and tied up as well. Tarnan must have found them weeks ago before Oscar's alarm was installed by the border.

Tarnan unhooked a knife from his belt and pulled her mother's head back by her hair, holding the blade to her exposed neck.

"Don't!" Lora yelled, the scream so guttural it drew everyone's attention. The royals were still compelled to attack Elyssa. Maja and Eyden stood on either side of her, fighting them off. Lora tried to run forward but two guards took a hold of each of her arms. Amira attempted to run forward, but guards stepped onto the stage to keep her contained.

"The amulet?" Tarnan asked again. She could see tears glistening in her mother's eyes. Her father struggled against his binds, and Saydren kicked him in the side until he fell over.

"I..." Lora started, at a loss. The blade nicked her mum's skin, drawing blood. Her dark eyes were filled with fear. Lora had come so far, risked so much, she couldn't give up now. But her mother's life was on the line. "Fine," she yelled, pushing against the guards with no result. "You can have it."

Tarnan tilted his chin and the guards let go of her. When she hesitated, Tarnan increased the pressure of the blade. A tear ran down her mother's cheek.

"I said fine!" Lora screamed, fishing the amulet out of her pocket and holding it up. She felt everyone's eyes on her and knew she was their doom. She knew she was about to regret this. *But her mother...*

Tarnan held out his hand, the other still gripping the knife. She threw the amulet towards him and it landed at his feet. Bending, he picked it up.

Tarnan drew back his knife, his smile so bright, like a child getting candy. "Finally." He took a step back, looking at Saydren. "You can take them out." He tilted his head at her parents.

"*What?*" Lora stepped forward, but the guards were immediately upon her. She thrashed against the guards' hold. "I did what you asked!"

"And *I'm* not killing her," Tarnan said, his smile schooling as if she was a misbehaved child. "Look at the chaos you created. Lessons have to be learned."

"Don't you dare, Tarnan."

Saydren aimed his knife just as Eyden appeared out of thin air, tackling the healer to the ground.

Tarnan opened his mouth right before a knife flew at his head. He barely dodged it, the blade nicking his cheek. He wiped at the spot, his smile dimming. Lozlan came onto the stage, hands curled into fists.

"*Lozlan, kill—*" Tarnan started, and Eyden teleported to him, letting go of Saydren. He grabbed Lozlan's shoulder, but nothing happened. Eyden froze for a second as he seemed to realise his power had been exhausted.

The second cost them both. Saydren struggled to his feet and a dagger flew from his hand. At the same time, Tarnan finished his sentence, "*Kill Lora's mother.*"

The dagger hit Eyden's shoulder as he stepped to the side. He pulled the almandine blade from his skin, his gaze locked on Lozlan whose turquoise eyes were nothing but pain.

Lozlan's body shook. "Don't let me kill her."

Eyden's gaze dipped to the dagger in his hand then up to Lozlan, shaking his head. He turned to Lora. She didn't know what to say.

"Save them both," her lips mouthed, but she had a gut feeling he couldn't. The fighting around the stage was nothing but white noise to her.

Lozlan stormed forward, but before he could reach her mum, Eyden attacked. Dagger raised, he swung at him. Lozlan leaned back with grace. As he dodged Eyden's attempt, Lora could see who Lozlan used to be. Skilled. Deadly.

Eyden seemed to realise it too, his attacks growing more brutal as he kicked out, but Lozlan grabbed his leg. Eyden lost his balance. Lozlan stomped down, almost hitting Eyden, who rolled to the side and sprang up. Pretending to go left then hitting right, the blade nicked Lozlan's arm.

Eyden pulled back his arm but then his whole body froze. Looking down, a blade stuck out of his stomach. Lora thought she was screaming but everything turned quiet around her, a shockwave zapping through her. She met Eyden's panicked face as Saydren pulled the blade out of Eyden's back. Turning around, Eyden twisted Saydren's arm until the blade struck him in the stomach. They both fell hard, their blood mixing on the wooden stage.

Tarnan watched the events unfold with a satisfied smirk, in no hurry to intervene when he was getting right what he wanted: making them suffer. Making *her* suffer.

Lozlan ran towards her mother as if possessed, his steps fast then slow as if he fought with everything he had. He lowered himself to the ground, taking her mother's head in his arms. The muscles in his arms strained. He was going to break her neck.

"Stop!" Lora yelled until her voice was raw. "*Please!*"

Eyden clutched his stomach with one hand, crawling forward with the other, trying to save her. His free hand was wrapped around Saydren's dagger as he shifted his body forward on the sun-bathed ground.

Lozlan closed his eyes, his blond hair tangled from sweat. He was going to do it.

"*No!*" Lora yelled with the last of her voice. She called on all her strength, digging so deep within herself her head felt dizzy, but a flicker ignited, a barely existing ember that hadn't given up hope yet. She willed it to spread, ignoring the pain it caused, the exhaustion deep in her bones. She could feel blood running from her nose but she didn't care.

Throwing her hands out, her grip burned the guards holding her, barely, but enough to stun them. That was all she needed. Lora kicked one in the crotch and then ducked as the other one went for her. Slipping under his arm, she ran off.

Lora willed her feet to go faster as she ran to the stage. Lozlan's hands seemed to move in slow motion. Her mother's eyes were locked on his, then slowly closed as if accepting her death.

And then Lozlan's arms slumped. His eyes went wide and Lora almost stumbled, not seeing the full picture until she spotted the dagger in Lozlan's back, her step-father's bound hands clutched around the hilt. Eyden's hand was empty, the dagger no longer with him but with her step-father instead.

Lozlan knocked his head back against her step-father's, splitting open his lips. Her step-father fell backwards, hitting his head hard on the ground, his eyes falling shut. Grabbing the hilt on his back, Lozlan freed the blade just as Lora reached them. Blood drenched the back of his shirt.

She threw her weight against him, tackling Lozlan to the ground. Rolling on top of him, she ripped the dagger from his hands and pointed it at his chest. He gripped her wrists with enough strength that she yelped, fearing her bones might break. The dagger twisted to point at her.

"Don't let me kill you," Lozlan gritted out. "Please, walk away."

"I can't," Lora replied, fighting against his hold. If only she could knock him out, bind his hands and feet, get him away from here.

Movement caught her eye. Her mother shuffled towards them, a dangerous urgency in her gaze. "Stay back," Lora shrieked.

Lozlan's arms shook, his gaze flashing between pain and forced determination.

"I'm sorry, midnight girl," he said to her mother, who stopped moving but watched them from a distance. A tear escaped his eye. "I was never there." He locked eyes with Lora and she sensed a new determination taking over his mind. She couldn't follow his intention until he whispered, "But your mother always will be."

Lora's brows pinched together as Lozlan grunted in pain, fighting an invisible battle as he twisted the dagger. Before Lora could react, he drove the blade into his own chest, her hands still on the hilt. It sank into his skin, right to his heart.

"No, no," Lora pleaded, snatching her hands free, letting the dagger clatter to the ground. She moved her shaking, bloodied hand to his cheek. "Open your eyes." She tapped at his cheek, her vision turned blurry.

Blinking, tears reflected in his turquoise eyes that were a mirror of her own. She'd barely gotten to know him.

He couldn't go.

He couldn't leave her yet again.

But she knew he'd chosen this. He'd chosen her mother over himself. For her. He'd seen the chance to be there for her and he'd taken it.

"It's all right," he murmured, his voice barely audible. Blood spilled down his chin as life left his eyes, his light dimming irrevocably. "You'll be all right." His tone was strangely light as if that was all that mattered.

"*Dad.*" Lora touched his cheek, wanting him to stay with her. To be there. To make up for all the years they'd lost. Lozlan smiled at her ruefully and it tore at her heart. As Lora watched Lozlan—her father—take his last breath, she was anything but all right and she wasn't sure she ever would be again.

CHAPTER 78

AMIRA

Seeing Lora cling to her biological father's body while her mother and step-father watched, beaten up and desperate, broke something in Amira.

Tarnan observed the scene peacefully, one hand curled around the amulet. Twisting, she tried to throw off the guards holding her but they wouldn't budge. They needed to take Tarnan out, to make this blood-bath end. Warm blood ran down her arm, but she could do nothing with the guards' grip on her.

Amira spotted Eyden getting to his feet, still bleeding heavily. Thea and Kaede were locked in a fight. Kaede tried hard not to kill her friend who was compelled to not show the same mercy.

Off to the side, Elyssa fought two advisors, kicking instead of slashing with the knife in her hand. Maja jumped on King Mayrick's back, trying to hold him off.

A grunt to her left drew Amira's attention back to the scene in front of her. Saydren stood up with difficulty, his hand pressed against his stomach wound.

"I think we've reached the end." Tarnan turned from Lora, who glared murder at him, to Amira. Guards surrounded the stage but waited to attack.

"It's not over," Amira yelled. But she knew it was a lie. Eyden couldn't drift anymore. They were all beaten up while Tarnan was still standing with guards to spare.

Where in Liraen is Rhay?

Tarnan smiled at her, glancing at the amulet in his hand. It caught the sun, almost blinding Amira. Squinting, she tracked Tarnan's gaze to Kaede and Thea further off. *"Kaylanthea, you can stop,"* Tarnan commanded. *"Kaede, come here."*

As if she was a puppet, Kaede dropped her sword and marched through the crowd of dead bodies, guards, and advisors. With a deep cut from her brow to her nose, blood staining the ground beneath her feet, and the exhaustion written on her face it looked like Kaede was marching to a battle already lost.

As she stepped onto the stage, Tarnan grabbed her arm forcefully. His smile turned wide when Kaede screamed in pain, dropping to her knees as she put a hand to her chest. The amulet glowed in Tarnan's hand. He gripped it so fiercely that a fresh drop of blood appeared on the palm of Amira's hand.

The queen's face turned ashen. Tears streamed down her cheeks and her breathing quickened. Tarnan closed his eyes, breathing in deeply as he rolled his shoulders. He was syphoning the life out of her.

Amira thrashed against the guards holding her. Lora looked torn, holding back a guard from coming at her family. Eyden had reached her side. Elyssa and Maja had drawn closer too, surrounding Lora's family.

Energised and laughing with glee, Tarnan let go of Kaede's arm. With her eyes wide open in shock, she fell backwards, unmoving. Her face looked hollow. Her skin had lost all its shine.

Thea screamed in the distance, the sound utterly broken. Amira couldn't process the sheer joy on Tarnan's face as he straightened.

"Who's next?" Tarnan asked, glancing at each of them. His smile mocked her, his voice scratched at her battered heart, anger and sadness filling her up.

Everything around her seemed to slow. She barely registered anything around her anymore—metal clashing against metal, fists pounding against flesh, the feeling of the wind brushing against her bruised and torn skin. Amira knew the moment had come. Rhay and Ilario weren't going to make it in time. Tarnan would take out each and everyone one of them, growing more powerful with each death. And all because of her. Because they wouldn't kill her.

But *she* would. Amira would die to save them all.

Meeting Elyssa's gaze on the opposite side of the stage, Amira gave her a nod. A signal. Elyssa seemed to swallow a knot in her throat but she tilted her chin and pushed back a guard to head her way.

They had discussed this. If everything went wrong, this was the only way. If she died, the contract would most likely die with her. She had faith Elyssa could bring her back, reanimate her heart. But even if she couldn't, then it was Amira's fate. Saving Elyssa, her friends—Amira couldn't imagine a more fortunate way to go. She thought of Farren, his choice. She was willing to do the same.

Amira took a deep breath, willing her power to turn on herself, to zap through her body right to her heart—forcing it to stop beating for a moment. She distantly heard the guards yelp on either side of her, dropping their hands. Her vision turned dark as her legs shook. Her foot slipped as she stumbled to the side, not realising how close to the edge of the stage she'd been. For a brief moment, Amira felt weightless, free. Then her heart seized as she fell, painfully constricting her breathing until she saw nothing, felt nothing.

She was nothing.

CHAPTER 79

🔥

ELYSSA

Elyssa jumped off the stage just as Amira fell. Rushing to her side, she lowered herself to the ground. Her heart felt like it had stopped beating too as Elyssa touched Amira's cold cheek. A deep despair clawed at her but she threw it all aside. She had to bring Amira back as she'd promised. The princess' plan had been to stop her own heart for just a minute, so Elyssa could revive it.

Putting one hand over the other, Elyssa pressed on Amira's chest like she'd learned when she was younger. Nothing existed except Amira. She didn't even pay attention to whatever Tarnan was up to. Her sole focus was on bringing life back into Amira's motionless body.

Ten compressions. She kept going. Twenty.

Nothing.

Elyssa swore. Cursed Tarnan. Cursed Amira's plan B. Cursed the whole fucking world. Amira's lips were parted but no breath escaped her mouth. Her eyes were closed. Her hands were completely still at her sides.

A loud shot made Elyssa's head turn. Eyden, gripping Maja's gun, aimed at Tarnan who was bleeding from his shoulder. Whirling back around, Elyssa spotted no new wounds on Amira's body. Amira had done it. She'd been right. Her death had broken the goddamn contract. She threw Eyden a quick nod.

Another five compressions. Elyssa's hands grew stiff but she didn't care. She had to keep going. *Don't leave me, sunshine. You did it, now come back.*

Eyden, following Elyssa's signal, shot Tarnan again. The royals and advisors seemed to regain their minds as Tarnan was distracted. Instead of attacking their people, they turned on Tarnan's guards. Thea was at the forefront, anger blazing in her eyes. Amira had turned the game around, played the joker.

Someone tapped her shoulder and Elyssa met green eyes—Lora's stepfather. Further off, she spotted Maja tending to Lora's mother. Their people held back the guards rushing at Lora's family.

"Let me," Lora's father said, and at Lora's look of encouragement, Elyssa moved aside.

He moved his hands to Amira's chest, similar as she'd done but with more force. He stopped only to tilt her chin up, breathing into her mouth twice before resuming compressions. He repeated the same pattern a few times. When nothing happened, Elyssa caught the look he gave Lora.

"No," Elyssa told him. "Keep going. She *will* come back from this." Anything else was fucking unacceptable. Amira had told her to bring her back. And Elyssa would do so. She didn't care what she had to do, who she had to beg, what she had to give. She'd force the goddamn universe to do her bidding if she had to.

Lora's eyes widened and Elyssa followed her gaze to find Rhay and Ilario running towards them, a duffle bag around Ilario's shoulder and a rolled-up paper in Rhay's hand. A third person followed them but a cloak hid most of their face. Elyssa only glimpsed long strawberry-blonde hair.

"We're here." Rhay threw himself to the ground next to them. "What happened? Is she hurt? I have the contract." He unrolled the paper and Elyssa looked over his shoulder to the space where Amira and Tarnan's signatures used to be. It was now blank. A void contract.

"What the fuck?" Rhay exclaimed, his hand on the paper shaking. He watched as Lora's father tried to bring her back to life. "No. No, I can't be too late."

Lora's father kept going, a frown on his face. "I'll keep trying but the odds are..."

"Fuck the odds." Elyssa rose on her knees.

The odds had never been in their favour. This world was cruel and unfair and tragic. Amira's life had been riddled with pain. She'd just begun to truly live, to see her worth. This wasn't how her life would end. This wasn't the end of their story. She knew Amira was still in there. She knew Amira wanted to live, wanted to explore all that life had to offer beyond all the doom and suffering they'd been forced into.

"Go inside her head." Elyssa turned to Lora. "She has no mental shields now. If she's still there, read her, try to project into her head." They had to help her fight her way back to herself.

Lora exhaled loudly. "I don't know if it'll work."

A yell sounded somewhere close to them, drawing Lora's attention. The fight was still ongoing, but Elyssa couldn't care less.

"I'll go help Eyden. You stay," Ilario said before running off. Elyssa spotted Eyden fighting five guards in his wounded state. Tarnan was blocked from her view by more guards and the other royals.

"Try with everything you've got," Elyssa said, her tone determined yet on the edge of broken. Lora nodded, wiping away a tear.

Leaning down, Lora touched Amira's shoulder. Lora's father moved back, his gaze unsure.

"You got this, love," Rhay whispered, loud enough for Elyssa to catch over the noise of swords clashing close by. "Remember, don't let fear hold you captive."

Lora closed her eyes, her forehead wrinkling as she focused.

"I think...I think she's there." Lora squeezed her eyes shut tight. "I'm trying but I can't make sense of it."

Elyssa grabbed Lora's hand, a desperate thought sparking in her mind. "Bring me into her head."

Lora's eyes flew open. "I've never done that."

"Doesn't mean you can't," Rhay said with encouraging warmth. "Picture it. You can do anything you set your mind to, love. Let your walls down. As we practised."

Reaching down, Lora touched Amira's cheek. Elyssa took Lora's free hand and with her other, she grabbed Amira's lifeless hand. Closing her eyes, Elyssa tried to imagine her mind was blank, letting Lora in. Lora's grip on her tightened, her arm shaking.

Elyssa's mind was as dark as a night sky without stars. She was falling into a pit, her breath hitching. Somehow, Elyssa landed on her feet, bright colours around her bleeding into each other, blinding her. Her body was weightless. She was standing yet couldn't feel the ground beneath her. There was only endless darkness below her feet, threatening to swallow her whole.

"Do you see that?" Lora asked, and Elyssa turned her head to her. Her body seemed transparent, glitching in and out of existence.

"See what?" Elyssa blinked to see beyond the mess of colours until the picture in front of her became clear. It wasn't mere colours. They were memories, flashing around her almost too fast to track.

There was Wryen, a twisted grin on his face as he pointed down a balcony to a blonde girl burning alive. *Quynn.* Screams surrounded her, overlapping with those of different memories. Wryen holding strands of singed hair, his words lost to Elyssa in the mess of noise around her.

There was Karwyn choking Amira, her body pressed against the railing of a balcony. Karwyn laughing at her. Karwyn smiling, his gaze focused on an execution as a fae woman's eyes met Amira's just before she met her end.

There was Amira's mother in a memory Elyssa knew as she tried to force Amira to flee with her.

There was Saydren taking Lora from the tavern in Chrysa, and Amira rushing back to the palace with urgency.

There was Cirny on the floor, a sheet twisted in her hand that revealed a body on a table.

There was Rhay staring at her with contempt and a mocking grin on his face, a fae sitting in his lap.

There was Amira taking fortae, Elyssa's eyes judging her.

And there was Tarnan at a funeral, handing Amira a handkerchief, taking her hand to console her. Tarnan helping her to her room with

Rhay in the Turosian palace. Tarnan handing her the key to his library. Tarnan clinking his glass with hers. Tarnan telling Wryen to stop that day in Pyria when he had attacked them both.

And then Tarnan taking Varsha's life. Tarnan locking Amira in as Wryen had once done. Tarnan threatening her at every turn. Farren getting struck outside the Carnylen palace. Tarnan today—standing on the stage, his grin so sure of himself.

It was all the people who had failed her or whom Amira thought she had failed. It was a mix of pain and guilt playing on a loop around her, trapping her, weighing her down into darkness. The pain was so loud, it struck Elyssa like blades digging into her skin over and over.

The noise was too much, blending together like the soundtrack of an endless nightmare. Elyssa could hear Amira scream. She could hear Karwyn's dark laughter. She could hear Tarnan telling Amira to join her. Putting her hands over her ears, Elyssa forced her gaze away. And then she saw her.

Amira, standing in the middle of it all, her head tilted up. Her eyes were blank as she took it all in, colours flashing across her ashen face.

"She's trapped," Lora shouted next to her, echoing Elyssa's thoughts.

Elyssa walked forward, shielding her eyes as if she could shake off the memories. At the end of the day, everyone would turn into a memory, forever engraved in their loved one's head. And there had been many people Amira cared about but just as many who loved her, who would want her to go on.

Amira hadn't failed anyone. It was others who had failed her. Guilt was a powerful emotion. It festered. It grew. It carved into one's heart so deep you'd think you'd never get it out of your system. And it was poisoning Amira now. Holding her here.

Elyssa thought of Farren and of all the people she had lost. She'd carried guilt around since she was ten years old, like an anchor keeping her from ever truly coming up for air. But being with Amira, it was like she didn't need to let it all go. She was holding her up, giving her strength to breathe, to *live*, despite the weight of her past. It was Elyssa's turn to do the same for her.

Reaching Amira, Elyssa waved her hand in front of her face. She didn't even blink.

"We need to change the memories," Elyssa shouted. Lora held out her hand and Elyssa took it. Staring at Amira's memories, she thought of the first time she had ever seen her.

Lora's hand squeezed hers hard enough to bruise, but Elyssa held on. And then Amira's memory flickered. Wryen's cruel smile turned into Elyssa's easy smirk as she took in Amira's ripped dress that day they had first met after running away from River's Point. Elyssa remembered the day she had helped Amira fix her window in the Carnylen palace. The day Amira had made her first arrow fly. The day she'd decided to never take fortae again.

Lora hissed next to her and Elyssa lost her grip—or perhaps Lora had. Panic shot back into her like red-hot lava under her skin, but when Elyssa glanced around her the memories were changing on their own. The noise and whispers around her were no longer those of pain and suffering.

There was a glimpse of Amira's mother, younger, brushing Amira's hair.

There was an older man who must be Amira's father, bouncing a young Amira on his leg.

There was Quynn, long blonde hair and bright green eyes taking Amira in. A gap in her teeth was visible as she grinned at Amira and threw open the door to the shed Elyssa had seen before.

There was Farren taking Amira's hand, trying to dissolve her worry.

There was Varsha grinning at her from behind an easel, paint on her cheek.

There was Rhay dancing with her, twirling her in a circle.

There was Lora, her eyes kind and understanding.

There was Eyden apologising to her.

There was a fae in a servant's uniform, Nalani, handing Amira a tray of food, warmth radiating from her.

And there was so much of Elyssa. Her wicked smile as she aimed an arrow. Her hair tousled, lying in bed. Kissing Amira in over a dozen different memories. Her hand pulling Amira with her through the streets of Pyria. Holding on to her as Amira was bleeding from Karwyn's attack, whispering in her ear to stay awake. Amira's hand searching for hers when she'd freed Elyssa the day they'd gotten one of the amulets.

Over and over again, Amira sought out Elyssa's gaze, her smile, her hand, her love.

"Take my hand," Elyssa offered, reaching for Amira's in her mind. She tried to touch her but her hand went right through as if Amira was nothing but mist. "You're still here. Don't let guilt hold you back. Remember what you told me—they'd want you to live. *I* want you to live." Elyssa stepped in front of Amira. "*You* want to live."

Amira's brows drew together. Her red lips opened and closed.

"I do," Amira said, her voice hoarse. She glanced down at Elyssa's outstretched hand, her lips turning up into a smile. "I want to live." Her fingers wrapped around Elyssa's, their bodies solidifying as the memories around them turned into smoke, leaving the pain and guilt in ashes.

Elyssa felt herself come back into her body, into the present. A grin made its way to her lips. "Then live, sunshine."

CHAPTER 80

RHAY

A loud gasp echoed in his bones as if someone who had been underwater for too long finally took a deep breath. Rhay's head jerked to Amira propping herself on her elbows, living, breathing. She had done it. She had managed to break the contract and survive.

Elyssa, coming back to herself too, threw her arms around Amira, pulling her head to her chest, whispering words of relief.

"Amira, I'm glad you're okay," Saige rasped, her face still half-hidden by her cloak. Amira looked between her and Rhay, a question in her tired eyes. They weren't supposed to bring anyone to the temple. The Turosian fae who had survived had stayed back at the Rubien palace, waiting for any of Tarnan's guards who might try to claim it back.

Rhay grabbed the book filled with about thirty contracts, opening it. The humans were still bound to Tarnan. If he died, they would too. "Let's break—"

Lora yelled out, a hand to her heart. She wrenched her head to the stage where Tarnan lingered. And in his hand, the amulet. Rhay's face dropped. Tarnan had to be syphoning Lora's life source.

Lora threw her free hand forward but nothing came of it as her face constricted in pain.

Reaching for his dagger, Rhay got to his feet. Tarnan cocked his head at them. "You're volunteering next? Are you keen on joining your father in the Sky? I burned his body, I might be convinced to give you the same respect if you cease now," he said to Rhay, his smile big as he squeezed the amulet in his hand. Lora screamed.

All of a sudden, a shadow came up from behind Tarnan, throwing himself at him. Rhay almost didn't recognise the person, his blond hair dirty and tangled. His clothes were torn and bloodied. Was he imagining Karwyn?

But then his turquoise eyes met Rhay's before Tarnan fell sideways, taking Karwyn with him as they toppled off the stage and out of sight.

"Karwyn," Rhay whispered.

He hadn't meant it as a question, but Lora, out of breath, explained, "Tarnan brought him."

Rhay didn't think. He ran forward, dodging guards. Someone yelled his name but he could barely hear it.

As he rounded the stage, he spotted Karwyn on the ground, blood pooling by his head. An image of Karwyn dying after the merge flashed through Rhay's head. This was all too familiar. Yet there was a faint flutter as Karwyn's chest rose. Tarnan lay next to him. Before he could get up, Rhay plunged his almandine dagger into Tarnan's chest, purposely missing his heart as his life was still linked to the humans he had forced into blood contracts.

Footsteps stomped behind him and Rhay turned to see Elyssa and Lora running to him. Ripping the amulet from Tarnan's hand, Rhay threw it to Elyssa, who caught it. She spun around, no doubt heading back to those contracts. Like they had done to Lora's contract, they could use the amulet to nullify the humans' contracts.

Distracted, Rhay didn't anticipate being kicked. He lost his grip on the dagger as Tarnan removed it, rising to his feet, his smile still on. How was he still standing?

"*Rhay...*" Tarnan started, but Rhay fought against the compulsion, no fortae affecting his powers this time.

"You're out of luck, Tarnan." Lora appeared at Rhay's side. "Your compulsion won't work on either of us."

Tarnan brushed off the dirt staining his burgundy trousers, then retrieved a knife from his pocket. "*Guards!*" A few jumped off the stage to join them.

Lora picked up the fallen dagger and aimed at the first guard who came rushing at her, shielding Tarnan from her. Rhay grabbed the closest guard's arm, twisting and kicking him as he stole the sword from his grip.

"Rhay..." a shallow voice said. Rhay turned to Karwyn coughing up blood on the ground.

Lora pushed Rhay aside and a sword almost grazed his skin. Looking at Karwyn, something like pity shone in Lora's eyes. "Go," she told Rhay. Spinning, she slashed at a guard's arm. A faint flicker of a flame engulfed her dagger. Glancing over her shoulder, Lora tilted her chin to Karwyn. "Say your goodbyes, I got this."

In her eyes, he could read everything she didn't say. *Sorry it has come to this once again. This is the end, but it's for the best.*

Rhay tried to find Tarnan but he was nowhere in sight, guards blocking his view. Rushing, he fell to his knees next to Karwyn, taking out a guard on the way with a clean jab to the heart.

"Rhay, I—" A coughing fit interrupted him. Karwyn clenched Rhay's hand as if it was his lifeline. There was too much blood. Blood on his lips. Blood on the back of his head. One of his wrists was bent in a strange angle. His eyes were almost completely swollen shut, bruises covering his entire face. Seeing the light dwindle in Karwyn's eyes, Rhay felt like he was reliving Caelo Night.

But this time there would be no coming back. They both knew it.

"Karwyn," Rhay whispered, at a loss for words. No matter how messy their relationship had turned out to be in the end, the only thing Rhay could see now was the child who had befriended him when he was all alone. A child as lost as him, longing for someone to care. "I'm sorry." What for, he didn't know. That he was dying? That Rhay was able to accept it this time? That Rhay knew he would be better off without him?

Karwyn drew in a shallow breath. "No. I see it now, Rhay."

"See what?"

"You said you wanted to learn to do the right thing, and all I ever learned was the opposite. I had a choice and I always chose wrong. But I did this one last thing for you, Rhay. I did it all for you. At least now I will be dying by your side." Karwyn smiled. It was the smile of a man who had made his peace with death.

Rhay pressed his forehead against Karwyn's, refusing to let go of him just yet. As much as Karwyn had darkened his heart, he was still a part of him, deeply rooted in everything Rhay was.

"Promise me one thing." Karwyn's voice faded as his breathing slowed down. "Promise to never let anyone like me on the throne. You were meant to be an advisor, Rhay. Do not let my actions keep you from your destiny. You were...you *are* the only person I ever..." Rhay could almost hear the unspoken word, could feel it wrap around his heart. Karwyn squeezed his eyes shut.

Rhay nodded, a tear running down his cheek. "I promise," he said even though he barely had time to think it through, the word *love* dragging through his skull like scratching nails. He knew that was what Karwyn was feeling in that twisted heart of his.

"Do you think...I will see my mother again?" Karwyn murmured, staring up at the sky as his eyes fluttered slowly. His chest barely rose now.

Would Karwyn join Caelo in the Sky, in heaven? Would his sins be forgiven?

Rhay leaned down and cupped Karwyn's cheek. "I will make sure to burn your body and your ashes will drift to the sky where your mother will be waiting." It was a fantasy Rhay couldn't be sure of, but if Karwyn could admit he'd been wrong, wasn't that the first step?

"Thank you for lying," Karwyn whispered, his voice barely audible as his eyes fell shut forever. His head turned to the side, his last breath leaving his chest.

Rhay drew his hand back from Karwyn's cheek. With his eyes closed and faint smile, Karwyn looked peaceful, no longer the mad king he had turned into. Maybe Rhay hadn't been lying. Maybe Karwyn would find closure. Maybe this had been his second chance at life and he had used it to stand up against Tarnan. He had done the right thing. Once was better than never. Rhay looked up at the sky, clouds hiding the afternoon sun, and for a moment, he felt at peace too.

Then a yell cut through the air. Rhay became aware of the world again as though swimming slowly up to the surface from the depths of the ocean. Glancing around, he realised Lora was gone and so were the guards. Rio appeared at the edge of the stage. Rhay sprang to his feet.

"He's going after Amira," Rio said, out of breath, fresh blood staining his cheek and neck.

Giving Karwyn one last look, Rhay took Rio's hand and let him pull him onto the stage, back into the fight—away from his past and into the future they were fighting for.

CHAPTER 81

AMIRA

Amira was barely able to stand, still catching her breath after almost dying. Thea, weak from multiple attacks, lowered her sword next to her. Saige lingered close by, shrinking into herself. The remaining guards seemed to have rushed to the side of the stage where Lora, Rhay, Ilario, and Elyssa had gone, running after Tarnan. Standing protectively by Lora's family, Eyden and Maja got rid of any stray guards. King Mayrick Palendro and King Quintin Nylwood were still standing too. In possession of healing powers, King Mayrick rushed to heal Eyden as the latter was heavily bleeding from Saydren's stab wound. The healer was unconscious on the stage nearby.

Lozlan's dead body lay on the ground close to them. Wryen's burned corpse was not far off. So was Kaede's lifeless body. Amira fought back tears. She was still here. She had survived so much and she wanted to live in the world they would create once Tarnan was gone. She wanted to see Elyssa's smile again, every day for the rest of their lives. If they survived this, she swore to herself she would finally fully open her heart to Elyssa. She would leave all the pain and suffering of her past behind, let it die while she *lived*.

"Amira!" Elyssa yelled, and Amira turned her head. In Elyssa's hand was the amulet. Relief spread through her and Amira bent to grab the book filled with the humans' blood contracts.

Reaching her side, Elyssa handed her the amulet and Amira got to it, pressing the amulet to each page until the signatures disappeared, the magic binding them lifting. They had more than two dozen contracts to get through.

"Hurry," Thea whispered, drawing her sword again. Tears streaked her face, yet she remained fierce.

Looking up but not slowing down, Amira spotted Tarnan coming towards them. Blood stained his shirt but he seemed more angry than bothered by the wound. Even without the amulet, everyone was depleted. Would Amira stand a chance against him one on one?

Still, everyone around her drew their weapons, ready to keep stalling until all the human contracts were void.

Tarnan cleared his throat, drawing everyone's attention. He looked at each of her friends and allies, ready to fight till the death if need be. *"Amira, stop. Kill yourself if anyone attacks me."*

Amira's heart constricted in her chest, a painful echo to her near death just moments ago. Tarnan had always protected her in a strange, twisted way. Never telling his guards to kill her, never compelling her into hurting herself. He had always insisted he *loved* her like a daughter. Turned out that too was a lie.

"You fucking coward, are you ever going to fight for yourself?" Elyssa yelled, balling her fists next to Amira. Lora appeared from behind the stage, slowing down as she caught Tarnan's words.

Amira's mind was screaming at her to fight back, to use her power against Tarnan, to wipe the carefree smile from his face. But her body moved against her will. Inside, she banged against an ice wall, screaming silently to break the barrier that kept her out of her own body. She dropped her hand and Elyssa rushed to take over, breaking more contracts. Only a few were left to nullify.

"Let's finish this." Tarnan gestured to the few remaining guards and pointed at the amulet. *"Take the—"*

Rhay, jumping onto the stage, threw himself at Tarnan, who dodged his attack, a chuckle carrying in the wind. Ilario followed behind Rhay, a knife in his hand.

Amira tried to fight back, but Tarnan's command had been clear: if he was attacked, she had to kill herself.

Slumped on the ground, Tarnan raised himself on his elbows, spitting blood. "Foolish, Rhay. You just cost Amira her life." He turned to Ilario. "*Attack Rhay.*"

Rhay's gaze was full of confusion before he sprang to his feet, Ilario coming at him with a knife. Holding up his hand, Rhay tried to reason with Ilario, but his mind was lost.

Against her will, Amira grabbed a dead guard's bloody dagger from the warm stone ground. "Amira, you have to fight back," Elyssa begged her, backing away from the void contracts, the amulet still clutched in her hand. Reaching forward, Elyssa made a grab for the dagger, but Amira held firm. Tears flooded her eyes as she pushed Elyssa away.

"Fa—my king," Saige said in a small voice, drawing back the hood of her cloak.

For the first time, Tarnan seemed surprised, his smile faltering. "Saige? Why are you here? You must go. Guards"—he pointed at a couple—"take her away."

Saige's hands were steady as she shook her head. "Why are you hurting them? It's *Amira*. You said she was our friend."

"It's too complicated for you to understand," Tarnan replied, his tone unsure. "Get back to safety. Amira, *hand over the amulet, then kill yourself.*"

Elyssa pulled back, taking the amulet with her. Amira felt her body move without her command, aiming for Elyssa now instead of her own heart. She'd let go of so much guilt, but she would never forgive herself if she hurt Elyssa.

"*No!*" Saige screamed. She looked so young, so innocent in the middle of this battlefield. But her gaze was clear, determined. She anchored her eyes in Amira's.

Slowly, Amira felt Tarnan's claws being yanked from her mind one by one like vines snapping free from her skin. And this time, they didn't grow back. Amira imagined a tainted glass shielding her mind as she had learned from Rhay, throwing Tarnan out of her head completely like she had done to Karwyn in the past.

Glancing between Tarnan's bloodthirsty eyes and the amulet clutched in Elyssa's hand, Amira came to one conclusion. As long as the amulet existed, there would always be the risk of misuse. A phrase she had read in Cirny's book came to her mind. The amulets had been created from amplifiers.

"Trust me," Amira whispered to Elyssa, who narrowed her eyes. Taking her hand, Amira removed the amulet from Elyssa's palm. Tarnan's smile increased as Amira threw it into the air.

But not to him.

Channelling the inkling of magic she had left, Amira sent a wave of electricity, pure magic, right at the ancient artefact. As Tarnan's gaze darkened and Amira's smile grew, the crystal of the amulet shattered into pieces.

CHAPTER 82

LORA

Reaching out, Lora caught a piece of the crystal drifting in the wind. The broken piece shimmered both ruby red and a striking turquoise when she turned it over in the palm of her hand. Clasping her fingers around it, Lora felt a surge of energy rush through her. Her whole body was so tired, but it wasn't over yet.

Elyssa steadied Amira, who clutched the last piece of the amulet in her hand. Eyden, Rhay, and Ilario had the other pieces. Tarnan backed away from the stage, running off, apparently aware his power must be close to giving out. Saige, gripped by guards, was pushed towards Tarnan, who grabbed her hand. Tarnan dragged her away to the back entrance.

No way in hell. This had to end. Today. *Now.*

Lora was about to head towards him when her mum's strained voice reached her. "Lora! Come with us."

Her mum's eyes searched Lora's across the space. Maja was leading her parents away from the battlefield. *Good.*

But Lora wouldn't be going anywhere until she finally got her revenge. *Her justice.* She'd made a promise to herself that Tarnan would pay. She intended to keep that promise no matter the cost.

Shaking her head, Lora yelled, "Go!" She turned from her mum's panicked, confused eyes to her father. "Maja will take you to Oscar."

Her father nodded, taking her mum's hand, her expression a mix of bewilderment and hurt.

Maja ushered them towards the exit, her gun raised and ready to fire. But a guard sprinted towards her out of nowhere, hitting Maja across her face. He knocked the gun out of her hand. Wiping her nose, Maja's hand came away bloody.

With no hesitation, Lora threw fire at the guard, flames clawing at him until he fell screaming to the ground. Maja scrambled to grab her gun then moved forward, giving Lora a brief nod. But when Maja moved past Lora's mother, she didn't follow. Her mother's gaze was locked on Lora, her hand covering her mouth. Had she seen Lora use her powers before in the mess of the fight? Had she seen her use her powers to kill?

Lora thought she'd feel shame. She'd imagined this moment for such a long time, the time when her mother would realise Lora was embracing her fae side. That she *was* fae. A fact she no longer wished to change. But in all her imaginations, this had never been one of them, and Lora had no time to apologise, to make excuses. She didn't bloody want to anyway.

Taking her mother's hand, her father pulled her back. Lora turned away first, seeking Tarnan, her priority now that her family was safe. He reached the back entrance. Lora started sprinting when Eyden appeared in front of her, having teleported.

"Let's get him." He offered her his hand, seemingly also recharged through his piece of the amulet.

A tired smile graced her lips as she took his hand and then wind engulfed them, pushing them forward. Eyden steadied her when her feet hit the ground again.

Tarnan came to a halt as they blocked his path. Saige whimpered when Tarnan squeezed her arm, pulling her close to him—as a shield or to protect her, Lora wasn't sure.

"It's over, Tarnan." Staring him down, Lora wished she still had her dagger.

As Eyden took a step forward, Tarnan snarled, "*Stay back!*"

Eyden hesitated but only for a moment. Tarnan's power was depleted now without the amulet to fuel him. He must have used his last energy to compel Amira. And he knew it too, his calm expression slipping as sweat glistened on his forehead.

"Saige, tell them to stay back," Tarnan told his daughter, who looked torn. Her long hair had come partly undone from her braid, blowing in the light wind. Her eyes were shell-shocked. She looked so young. Lora felt for her. How could she let her father die even if he deserved it?

When Saige hesitated, Tarnan tore at her arm.

"Father, please," Saige whimpered, "you're hurting me."

"Tell them to stay back. They'll kill us both if you don't stop them."

Saige turned from him to Lora and Eyden. Goosebumps travelled over Lora's skin.

"I..." Saige started just as a knife flew through the air, impaling Tarnan's shoulder.

Tarnan stumbled a step back, letting go of Saige as he clasped the knife stuck in his skin, blood further drenching his ruby shirt.

"As you like to say," Elyssa said as she approached them, holding Amira up with one arm, "we've reached the freaking end."

Tarnan pulled the knife from his shoulder. "We could've been unstoppable," he told Amira, who shook her head.

Amira stood up straight beside Elyssa. "We may both want to re-make Liraen, but our intentions are the opposite. Yours is power, some act of revenge for your family and a need to be recognised. Mine is peace, acceptance."

Tarnan let out a curt laugh. "Don't pretend you're above revenge, Amira." He looked at each of them and Lora felt a shiver in her flaming heart. "You're all after revenge, but you wouldn't have had to be if you had played by my rules. We could have all worked together. We could have built a Liraen like it's never been before."

Amira sighed. "We still can. Without you," she stated, her voice calm.

Tarnan's gaze narrowed at her, and then quicker than anyone could track, he pulled Saige in front of him, setting the knife from his shoulder to her throat.

"Father," Saige whimpered.

Tarnan's gaze softened slightly. "Tell them to turn on each other. Help me, *us*, get away."

Saige observed Amira with obvious regret. Was she going to do it?

Amira stepped forward but halted when Tarnan bit out, "If you don't let me go, I'll kill her." When he drew a drop of blood, Saige cried out.

Amira held up her hands. "You'd kill me, and now you'd kill your own daughter? Don't you see how wrong you've gone? You're no better than your father."

Tarnan gritted his teeth as tears ran down Saige's cheeks. "I did everything I could to protect Saige and now she can't return the favour. She has disappointed me just like you did."

Eyden shifted his feet. Amira held up her hand as if to hold them back. Could they risk Saige to take out Tarnan? Could they live with themselves?

"Saige," Rhay said, coming up to them, Ilario following him. Behind them was a wasteland of dead bodies—guards, advisors, royals. Lora had lost count of how many had died today. "You'll never be free unless you stand up for yourself. He never protected you, he kept the *world* from you."

"Don't feed her lies," Tarnan hissed.

"He doesn't need to," Amira said. "You're proving his point. Saige, remember the story you told me about? No princess should be locked in. She should live freely, she should make her own choices. If you had followed that story, you would have never chosen to be here. You would have never had the chance to save Liraen."

Saige's gaze softened, turning pleading.

Tarnan glanced between all of them. Sweat glistened on his forehead. "So be it." Amira screamed as Tarnan moved his hand, the knife digging into Saige's throat.

Just then, Saige yelled, "*Stop!*" Lora looked around but it wasn't directed at them, it was directed at Tarnan. "*Drop the knife.*"

Tarnan's arm shook, his eyes crazed with fury. "Saige—"

"I said drop it!" A thin line of blood dripped from her throat under the neckline of her yellow dress.

Lora turned to Eyden, chin tilted at the knife. Tarnan cursed as the knife clattered to the ground. As soon as the blade hit the floor, everyone jumped into action. Eyden teleported, taking Saige and dropping her off into Rhay's arms faster than Lora had ever seen him move.

Lora threw fire at Tarnan just as he bent to pick the knife back up. Flames encircled him, blocking him off from the weapon. Her fire dwindled fast, and when Lora stared at the crystal in her hand, its light dimmed. She cursed under her breath, so tired of it all. All she wanted was the end.

Amira appeared next to her, taking her hand, and she felt her power grow again, fresh air in her lungs. She turned to Amira, a grateful smile on her face.

"Let's end this," Amira said, her dark locks blowing in the wind, the sun setting behind her as if announcing the end. They shared so much of the same pain, the same suffering that had been inflicted on them by Karwyn and then Tarnan. But together, they shined brighter than any doom threatening to smother the spark inside them.

The fire grew, halting Tarnan in place as he tried to run off again. Eyden reappeared in front of him.

"Eyden!" Elyssa yelled, and he turned to her. At the same moment Elyssa, who had gotten a hold of the knife, threw the blade to Eyden.

He caught it easily and Lora willed the flames to shift, giving Eyden access to Tarnan trapped within. Eyden aimed true, hitting Tarnan in the chest. Tarnan grabbed Eyden's arm before the blade could dig too deep and strike his heart. Eyden's muscles strained.

"Stop!" Tarnan tried to compel Eyden to give up, the knife barely piercing his flesh.

Squeezing Lora's hand, Amira turned to her.

"Air?" Lora asked, and Amira nodded fiercely. Elyssa, standing on Amira's other side, gave them a determined smirk.

Lora focused on the power she had once thought she'd stolen. A power that didn't belong to her but would now be her tool of vengeance, of justice. Karwyn was gone, but in a weird twist of fate, his power lived on in her.

Drawing on the last of her strength, Lora willed the knife to dig deeper. She felt Amira doing the same, using the wind around them. Her hair blew in her face as she caught Tarnan's stricken expression. Terror filled his blood-red eyes as the knife finally sank into his heart.

Slowly, his eyes turned a warm orange as his power dwindled. Eyden stepped back, watching as Tarnan's hand went to his chest. His gaze, full of betrayal that he had no right to feel, turned to Amira, and she moved her hand, twisting the knife in his chest.

He fell to his knees, his hand—bloody as if painted red—on his heart. Lora heard screaming behind her, probably Saige. Amira kept going until Tarnan sank fully to the ground, his eyes drifting shut as he stared at the sky as if Caelo had forsaken him. Without an ounce of regret, Lora set his body on fire, dooming him to ashes, a fate he'd summoned himself.

Only then did she pull her power back, and Amira's hand slipped from hers.

Staring at Tarnan's ashes blowing in the wind, Lora felt peace and sorrow fighting in her heart. It had gotten darker. The ground was scorched everywhere, bloodied by death all around them. Lora knew they'd won but also lost.

She glanced at the sky, at the bright stars peeking through the clouds as if highlighting their glory. No one had ever told her that justice came at such a price.

Sinking to her knees, sorrow won. Eyden's arm wrapped around her shoulders. Lora could barely see through the tears blinding her. They said nothing, just stared at the sky, their bruises—physical and mental —fresh in their battered hearts.

Tarnan was gone, but he had been right about one thing. This would be a new Liraen now, with so many dead. Lora didn't know what would come next, but she had made it through this day. She'd gotten her justice even though it had come at a price that Lora knew she wouldn't be able to shake.

She was broken, exhausted, hollow with grief. Yet, she would face anything coming her way. She would see that every sacrifice, every death, led to a new Liraen—one they could be proud of.

CHAPTER 83

EYDEN

The sun was already high in the sky when Eyden opened his eyes and turned to the curtain that was half drawn shut. Two days had passed since the contest, yet it felt like mere hours ago after sleeping away most of it.

A finger traced a circle on his back. He felt Lora's warm touch through the thin fabric of his white shirt. Rolling over, he faced her on the bed. The shadows underneath her bright turquoise eyes had lightened, the exhaustion having worn off, but there was a sadness in her gaze that he felt too.

"I wish I could make it better." Sorry wasn't enough, wouldn't change anything.

Lora sighed, reaching out to tangle her hand with his. He put his other hand on her back, sliding underneath her shirt and pulling her closer.

"This does make me feel better," Lora whispered, her eyes half-closed. "Mornings are hard. For a split second when I wake up, I forget. I forget that Lozlan is dead. I forget the image of my mum with a knife to her throat. I forget Kaede's expression when Tarnan killed her." She squeezed his hand. "Does that ever happen to you?"

"Yes." Even after he'd finally found some closure, it didn't mean his father, all those lost, didn't cross his mind. "When my father was taken, for the first few months, I would wake up each morning thinking today would be the day he'd come back. And when he didn't, I'd curse the universe. Then, I slowly started to get into a routine without him and I'd wake up forgetting that he was never coming back. But it would only last a few seconds before it all came back. The anger. The pain." He pulled her hand to his lips, kissing it gently. "It does get easier. But it will always hurt."

A tear filled the corner of her eye. "Can you..." Lora swallowed, fresh tears escaping her. "Can you draw him? Later. I...I don't want him to be forgotten. I have so little to remember him by, but what he did for me, for my mum, he deserves to be remembered."

"Anything," he promised.

"I wish we could stay here forever. In this room, it feels like the world stopped turning. Like time froze and I can finally catch my breath. But I know we have to go out there." She bit her lip as the corner of her mouth dropped. "I have to make sure the border is secure. Without the amulets, we have no way to reinstall the border spell. Ilario said there's enough guards stationed there and we have Oscar's security system, but it could all turn to utter chaos. And Thea...I have to reach out to her."

When they'd left the battlefield, Lora had offered Thea a place in the palace to heal, but she'd chosen to go home. He could understand why. She needed time and her loved ones around her to heal. But there was the matter of the high queen title.

"This is the first time since the Dark King that there's no high king or queen appointed. Not even an interim high king or queen," Eyden said. Tarnan had technically won the contest, so with his death the interim title would go to his next of kin until a new contest would take place. But no one except their inner court knew about Saige's existence. The other kings and queens had seen Saige at the contest but didn't know her identity. The young fae currently resided at the Turosian palace.

"You're thinking about Saige, aren't you?" Lora's legs tangled in between his.

"She's a Sartoya." She was a risk.

"She's a seventeen-year-old who was raised by a monster yet still chose to save Amira."

Eyden breathed out deeply. "You're right. But if people knew her identity, she'd be hunted either to be killed or worshipped by however many of Tarnan's followers are still out there."

They didn't know what had happened to Saydren. He had been gone when they'd left the temple. If Eyden ever saw him again, he'd take him out for good.

"No one needs to know who she is," Lora said. "But she should have a say in what happens to her, where she'll go. There's too much to figure out. The only thing I know is that if there has to be some kind of new contest, I'll give Thea the high queen title without a fight."

"What about Turosian? Have you changed your mind about staying queen?"

Lora turned on her back, staring at the ceiling. "I do want to make an impact. I want to help shape Liraen into the version it could be. I want to make sure Earth is safe even without the border spell in place. I want to help establish a new agreement between fae and humans."

"Big goals, special one." Eyden grinned at her. "But if anyone can pull it off, it's you."

A small smile played on her lips. "I want to do all that...but not as queen." She sighed. "I don't know what I want."

"An ambassador." Eyden had thought about this often. He expected Lora wouldn't be able to completely excuse herself from politics. She cared too much and she was so far in it now, one foot in each world.

"An ambassador. From Earth. I'd like that." The light in her eyes dimmed. "I'm not sure the government back home would agree. I'm on their wanted list, after all."

"They'd be fools to not see your potential. Without you, Earth would be fucked."

Lora smiled. "What about you? What do you want to do?"

"I'm a trader, I'm used to talking people into things. I'd like to think that can be applied to politics. And I always wanted to travel. I just never wanted to leave El on her own before." He laughed softly. "Then she left. To Carnylen, I mean. She might leave again with Amira. And she should, if she wants to. The camp doesn't exist anymore. There is nothing tying her here."

"She'll always come back." Her grip on his hand tightened. "Where would you want to go?"

Eyden brushed his lips against hers in a ghost of a kiss. "Is it too cheesy if I say wherever you go?"

Lora hit his shoulder lightly. "Yes. I'm serious. *Anywhere.*"

He hadn't really been anywhere other than Turosian and those brief trips to Rubien. "Honestly, any place. There's so much to see. If I can, I would want to go anywhere and everywhere."

"Even Earth?" Lora bit her lip. "I have to go back. I keep checking in with Maja and Oscar but it's not enough. I have to see it for myself. And I have to talk to my mum." Her lips quivered.

"Are you asking me to go with you?" He raised a brow at her.

"Would you?" Lora countered, and the uncertainty in her eyes didn't sit well with him.

He put an arm around her waist, pulling her against him. "Special one, when I said *anywhere,* I meant it."

Grinning, Lora brushed her fingers through his curls. "I love you. I don't say it enough."

"You have time to say it over and over again because I'm not going anywhere."

It was strange to think how much had changed since he'd met Lora. Eyden could never have imagined crossing the border. He could never have imagined using his power so freely around people. He could never have imagined trusting anyone as much as he trusted Lora. Not in his wildest dreams could he have predicted he'd ever find someone like her, love and trust her, and have that love be returned. It was a rare gift and he would never hold back again, never go back to keeping to the shadows.

Closing the distance between them, Eyden brushed his lips against Lora's. He fell into the kiss and Lora pressed herself against him, her hand going to his back as she rocked her hips against his. When her hand brushed over the wound on his lower back, he hissed at the sting.

Pulling back, Lora asked, "It still hurts?"

Eyden shook his head, the pain barely noticeable when all he could think of was kissing Lora, losing himself in her touch. "It's fine. Good enough to do this." Smirking, he went to kiss her again, but she tilted her chin.

"Mind if I see for myself?" Playing with the hem of his shirt, a wicked grin spread on her lips. The sunlight streaming in from the window lightened her hair. Her eyes sparked as the light drifted over her beautiful face. "Hopefully after today, we can retire the tradition of either one of us with a stab wound in bed."

A grin took over his lips and his stomach flipped. He could hardly think straight when she gave him that smile. "Are you trying to get me to take my shirt off?"

Lora tapped her chin. "Maybe."

Grinning, Eyden captured her lips before nudging her onto her back. Lora let out a surprised yelp when his hips pinned her to the mattress. With heated eyes, she took him in as her hands went under his shirt, over his abs, before lingering on the waistband of his trousers.

Pulling back, Eyden lifted his shirt over his head and Lora hummed in agreement, her hands going to her own shirt and raising it, but her head got stuck in the collar. Laughing, Eyden leaned down to help her, tearing the shirt off her.

Lora brushed her hair with her fingers as she grinned up at him sheepishly. "That was supposed to be sexy."

Looking over her bare skin, her tousled hair, the slight blush to her cheeks, he was convinced there was nothing more attractive. "I love you," he said, tracing her lip with one finger.

Her grin was radiant, like endless starlight he wished he could bottle up. "I love you too." She pulled his head closer, moulding their lips together. Her nails lightly scratched his back as she pushed their bodies together. Eyden rocked his hips against hers, chasing her sigh of pleasure.

"I love you," she whispered again, but it was drowned out by a soft moan leaving her lips.

He kissed her neck. His hand travelled to her breast, teasing her until she arched her back for more.

I love you—the thought so loud in his head he was sure Lora would pick up on it. Her eyes were glazed as she looked at him, a smile curving her lips. *I'll show you just how much.*

The thought must have registered as Lora cocked a brow, waiting for him to make good on his promise. He always did. Every promise he ever made her, he would do anything to keep them. He would fight any battle with her and then take her mind off the pain. Until however long they had together, he would be there and he had no doubt that Lora would be too.

Kissing her neck, her collarbone, her breasts, Eyden went lower, his hand splaying on her stomach to keep her still. Quickly, he pulled her trousers and underwear down her legs. He teased her, his finger stroking her inner thigh until her fingers tangled in his hair, wanting to keep him where she needed him.

Patience, special one.

She huffed but the sound was overtaken as she cried out when his tongue claimed her. With one hand, he pressed her to the mattress as the other skimmed up her thigh, joining his tongue as her whole body shook, her legs trembling under his touch.

Her grip on his hair loosened as her body tensed, a cry leaving her lips. She fell apart under him, her skin hot to the touch.

Slowly, Eyden drew back, shifting forward to kiss her mouth. Her arms wrapped around his neck as her legs tightened around his waist, and even without reading her mind he knew she wanted more. Her smile was wicked, filled with a list of brilliant ideas they'd only just started on.

What do you want, special one? His lip curved upwards while his hand squeezed her hip.

"Everything," she whispered, her voice husky and laced with heat. Lora's grin widened and it ruined him. Ruined him in the best way, as it had always done since the first time they'd met. He'd been scared of it back then. Now he knew that this kind of ruin—love—was worth the pain, the risk, *everything*.

CHAPTER 84

ELYSSA

"You're awake," Elyssa said as she walked out of the bathroom, finding Amira at her desk in the adjacent room. Elyssa had rested too much these last two days. Staying inside made her restless. The battle had ended and they'd goddamn won, but everything felt far from over.

Amira turned in her chair. A lavender robe was wrapped around her and a letter was laid out in front of her. Elyssa could spy the purple Allamyst sigil on the envelope.

"A servant came by with this. The remaining court in Allamyst has asked for my return as I'm next in line for the throne." She clasped her hands in front of her, her arms shaking.

Elyssa walked closer, putting a hand on Amira's shoulder as she peeked at the letter. "When?"

Amira sighed. "Soon. The earlier the better, according to them. Wryen probably left a mess behind. His last *gift* to me." She chuckled darkly.

Elyssa came to stand in front of her, catching her gaze. "He made his own bed, you know that, right? You tried to warn him but he wouldn't listen. In a way it's fitting that his own damn stupidity caused his death."

Amira's knuckles turned white from her fierce grip. "I'm not exactly sad he's dead. And that fact alone makes me feel guilty. Even with all the abuse, he's still my brother, my flesh and blood. I should feel sad, shouldn't I? Watching him die, I felt this deep...*relief*. What does that say about me?"

Elyssa knelt in front of her, taking her hands. "It means you're strong and kind. You still tried to save him, which is something I could have never done. It's your goddamn right to feel relief. There's no shame in that."

She turned Amira's hand over, tracing a pattern on her skin. "I felt relief when I killed Jaspen. Maybe I should feel guilty about that, but I don't. He deserved it." Just thinking about Jaspen made her blood curdle. "If anything, I feel guilty that I didn't take him out sooner. I knew he was an asshole but I always thought he'd protect the camp at all costs, in his close-minded way. I was so freaking wrong." How was everyone from the camp now? They'd given them shelter at the palace, but even with their bond to Tarnan gone, it must be hard to put behind them.

Amira leaned forward, dropping her forehead against Elyssa's. "I'm sorry he destroyed the camp. Will you build another one? I'm sure Lora and Thea will implement a new law that forbids fae and humans from attacking each other."

"It'll take time for that to work." But they would make it happen. Patience wasn't her strong suit, but they were closer to that future now than they'd ever been. "I don't know if they'd want me involved." Without Elyssa, the camp never would have been roped into Tarnan's web. She had been the one to convince them to help take care of Karwyn and then Tarnan had forced her friends at the camp into blood contracts.

Amira pulled back to look at her. "They chose to fight. It was their decision as much as it was yours to risk yourself."

Elyssa knew that, but a part of her couldn't help but be afraid they wouldn't accept her anymore. "Guilt cuts deep, doesn't it?"

Amira swallowed visibly.

"I saw how deep your guilt runs. I hope by choosing to come back, you can leave it behind." *I hope you can run into the future with me.* Elyssa scooted closer to her. "And I hope you can forgive me for running off the way I did."

Squeezing her hand, Amira gave her a brilliant smile. "There's nothing to forgive. I'm not scared you'll run off. I'm scared because...a few months ago, I would have thought someone was playing tricks on me because I couldn't possibly be so lucky." Her voice almost broke. "I never thought I could have this. That I could feel this...happy. Even now it's hard to accept that I deserve happiness. That it won't be snatched away from me."

Glancing at their joined hands, Elyssa smiled at her. "Happiness is so goddamn hard to come by. No one who loves us would want us to throw it away. We can be brave together. We can make it last." As she looked up at the princess, a heavy silence filled the space between them, unsaid words still lingering between them. But Elyssa wouldn't push. She had all the time in the world now. She knew how Amira felt, the love so loud in every smile, every look.

Clearing her throat, Elyssa broke the tension. "I don't think it's my place to lead the rebel camp. I want to seek out all the humans who are in hiding and offer them a safe place to stay. There's more people out there. They all deserve a home."

"You mean outside of Chrysa?"

Elyssa grinned at her. "I mean outside of Turosian. You didn't think I'd go back on my word, did you? My kind must be everywhere. So why not start with Allamyst? I'll have a talk with Wylliam, maybe he can figure out the situation here. And I'll go back and forth if they'll have me, of course, but I'll be with you."

Amira's eyes turned glassy. "I don't even know if I can rule. What if they find out I'm a witch? And they'll never approve of our relationship there. It will be difficult. It'll be one obstacle after another."

"Do you want to keep us a secret?" Elyssa asked, her brows pinched together. She didn't. They'd goddamn make them approve. It might take time, it might get bloody, but she'd take it all on.

Amira shook her head. "No, but it will mean more battles to fight."

Elyssa's lips turned into a half-smile. "When have I ever backed down from a fight? Turosian had its revolution, now it's Allamyst's turn. And who better to reign in a new era than you, sunshine? I couldn't imagine anyone with a bigger heart than yours. People will oppose, they might riot. But no revolution comes easy. No risk is too goddamn crazy."

A stunning grin stretched Amira's lips as she kissed her knuckles. "For you, for a better world, every risk is worth it."

Amira's lips melted against hers and her hands tangled in Elyssa's hair. Elyssa pulled her to the floor with her. A chuckle carried through the air as Amira fell half on top of her. Elyssa brushed a lock of hair behind Amira's ear before her gaze dipped to her robe that had fallen open.

The laughter died on her lips as her stomach flipped, her skin heating up. As her hand travelled to the edges of Amira's robe, barely brushing bare skin, and she heard Amira's sharp inhale, Elyssa knew that as long as they had each other, as long as they could still enjoy moments like this even with everything that had happened, they could face anything.

The sun was starting to set when Elyssa hurried down the dim corridor to the kitchen. As they'd spent so much time sleeping, they'd skipped meals, and they needed food to recover. Leaving Amira resting in bed, Elyssa decided to fetch them something.

As she rounded the corner to the kitchen she almost ran into Eyden who was leaving the kitchen with bread in one hand and two bowls of some kind of broth in the other.

"I see we had the same idea," Elyssa remarked. "For Lora?"

Eyden nodded. "There's more than enough." Eyden hesitated before tilting his chin to the small table at the kitchen entrance. "Do you want to sit for a minute?"

Elyssa grinned at him as she took a seat and Eyden put the food on the table.

"So, what's up? You all rested up?" Elyssa stole a slice of bread.

"Well enough," he said. But he was acting strangely quiet—too quiet.

"Spit it out," Elyssa said, chucking a piece of bread at him.

Eyden ducked his head. "Your aim has been better."

Elyssa let out an outraged sigh. "Take that back or you'll see my wrath." She squinted at him, tearing off a fresh piece of bread.

Eyden chuckled, raising his hands. "I surrender." His smile slipped as he crossed his arms on the table. "When are you leaving?"

Leaving. She would go, but in her head it hadn't sounded like leaving. But he was right, eventually she would leave even if she would be going back and forth.

"I don't know yet," Elyssa replied. "What about you? Are you staying here, in the palace?"

Eyden nodded. "For now. But first, I'm going back to Earth with Lora to see her family."

"Life's funny, isn't it?" Elyssa leaned back on the wooden chair, her gaze travelling over the vast kitchen. "Who would have thought we'd end up here? You, with the Queen of Turosian in the freaking palace. Me, going off to another kingdom with a princess, soon-to-be queen. We've really moved up in the world, haven't we?"

Eyden's laugh sounded like a snort. "Fate is unpredictable."

"I don't know if I believe in fate. I believe in choices. And each one, good or bad, has led us here. All the pain, all the loss we've gone through, it all led us here. Now we have to make the most of the time we've been given."

"If your parents could see you now, they would be smiling," Eyden said.

She pictured her parents and knew it was true. "Yours too."

"You know that no matter where you are, one word and I'll be there."

Leaning forward, Elyssa gave him her brightest smile. "I know. And it goes both ways. I might make fun of you if you get yourself in a pickle, but I'll be there to help no matter what."

Eyden laughed. "I wouldn't have it any other way." His expression sobered. "How's Amira?"

"She'll be okay. We'll all be okay. Have you checked on Ian or anyone else?"

"No."

"The whole Jaspen thing can't be easy for him. I should see how he's holding up." She should visit them all, but the thought made her heart race and not in a good way.

"That reminds me," Eyden started, uncrossing his arms, "I stopped by where Jaspen died."

"And?" A shiver ran down her spine.

"His body was gone."

She frowned, thinking back to that day. "He was dead. He *is* dead. Maybe some wild animals took care of him." She shrugged. "I guess he doesn't deserve to be burned, anyway. Iris never got that courtesy."

"You're probably right," Eyden said, but his bright eyes didn't look fully convinced.

"I was wondering where you were," Lora interrupted as she halted in the doorway to the kitchen, her arms wrapped around herself. Her stomach rumbled loudly, causing laughter.

Elyssa stood up, pulling back her chair. "It's all yours. I promised Amira some food and she's probably starving now too."

As Lora took a seat with a sheepish grin, Elyssa grabbed some food, but when she turned back around, Amira was in the doorway.

"Hey," Lora said, her hand in front of her mouth as she choked down some bread.

"Hi." Amira's gaze moved to Elyssa.

"I was about to head back up," Elyssa said, her arms full of food.

Eyeing the empty chairs, Amira tilted her head to the side. "Let's eat here."

Eyden pulled back a chair and Amira sat down with a smile.

Putting more food on the table, Elyssa went to get some glasses and filled them with water. When she almost dropped one of them, the glass lifted in the air and drifted to the table on its own. Turning to Lora, who had raised her finger, Elyssa smirked at her, glad to see Lora in control, so casually using her power.

"So," Elyssa said as she sat down and took a sip of water, "when are you heading to Bournchester?"

Lora looked at Eyden. "Tomorrow?" He nodded, handing her another piece of bread. "I'll try to reach Thea today to inform her of my plans and see what needs to be done for her to officially take over as high queen. And I should talk to Ilario too to make sure he is here while we're gone."

"What about Rhay?" Amira asked, dunking a piece of bread into the broth. "Have you talked to him about what he plans to do now? And Saige..."

"We'll figure it out," Lora replied. "Rhay needs to decide for himself. I'll talk to him." She turned to Eyden, a small smile playing on her lips. "You should come with me. As his best friend, I'm sure Rhay values your opinion."

Eyden wiped his mouth with a napkin, clearly holding back a laugh. "Out of everything, that is the strangest outcome."

"So you're admitting it then?" Elyssa asked. "He grew on you? Can't really say the same, but I guess he did do his part during the contest." She couldn't really blame him for his timing. She knew he had tried to get there as fast as possible. But she still blamed him for handing over the agreement in the first place. Farren's death was Tarnan's fault and his fault alone, but that didn't mean that Rhay didn't goddamn irritate her to no end.

"Rhay has a way of sneaking into your heart," Amira said, and Elyssa lifted her brows teasingly, remembering that he'd kissed her once. A fact Amira had shared with her recently. "Not in that way." Amira's cheeks turned pink.

Eyden looked around the table. "What am I missing here?"

Lora bit her lip, looking away, but Elyssa caught her. "You know. How do you know?"

"Rhay told me back at the cabin. I didn't think mentioning it would help de-escalate the situation."

Eyden tapped on the table. "I'm still lost."

Elyssa tilted her head at him, smiling innocently. "You don't like secrets now? Not so fun being on the other side?"

Eyden shook his head. "Okay, okay, I get it. I learned my lesson."

"Good," Lora joked, smiling at him around the rim of her glass.

"It's nothing," Amira said, a flush creeping up her neck. "He kissed me once. It's water under the bridge now."

Eyden was quiet for a second. Then he laughed, the sound carrying through the spacious kitchen. Elyssa couldn't help but join in and when she reached under the table to take Amira's hand, the princess laughed too, leaving the past behind her.

It had been a rocky journey, but looking at the faces around the kitchen table, Elyssa felt at ease. She'd always felt antsy sitting still, enjoying the moment instead of planning her next move. But now she knew not to take these quiet moments for granted. They wouldn't last forever and she goddamn deserved to enjoy them for however long they did last.

And whenever the moment broke, she'd fight with everything she got to get it back each and every time.

Not wanting to put it off any longer, Elyssa strode along the dark corridor to the wing that had been temporarily assigned to the humans. The sun had set and starlight drifted in through the high windows lining the corridor. She'd been dreading this. It was so easy for her to jump into danger, yet moments like these truly frightened her. Would they turn her away, blame her?

Rounding the corridor, she almost ran into Wylliam.

"Standing guard?" Elyssa asked as he straightened himself and rubbed the sleep from his eyes.

"Wouldn't you do the same?" A smile graced his lips. It was tired yet genuine, and the knot around her heart untwisted slowly.

"How's everyone?" She tilted her head at the door behind him, to the camp's quarters.

"Healing, some more slowly than others."

"I wish I could've done more."

Wylliam rushed forward, taking her arm gently. "You did everything, El. You gave us the fight, the revolution we've been waiting for."

She swallowed the frog in her throat. "Not everyone made it here."

Wylliam sighed. "No, they didn't. But all those lost, they knew what they were getting themselves into. They died proudly for the cause. There's no regret here, only gratitude for those who have given their lives. And to you."

"I don't want gratitude." She shook her head, her fist curling at her side as if she could fight off this feeling in her chest that painted her heart black. For the longest time their future had looked bleak, colourless. "I only want to help. I want everyone to be free, to see the fruits of this revolution we've all goddamn bled for."

Wylliam's smile widened. "I believe with your help, we can be. See for yourself." He gestured to the door and Elyssa forced her feet to move.

Gathering her courage, she pulled the door open. The spacious room was filled with beds, people sitting on most of them, chatting with each other, bandages covering various body parts. Medical equipment littered the floor, yet the smell of fresh bread drifted through the air. Food and drinks were placed on a big table in the middle of the room. At Elyssa's entrance, the voices turned hushed. A shiver danced over her skin.

Then Ian appeared in front of her, his face less grim than the last time she'd seen him.

"He's dead, right?" he asked, and everyone moved closer, listening in.

Elyssa clenched her jaw. "Jaspen won't betray you again."

"*Us*," Sera, a woman from the camp, said as she stopped in front of them. "He won't betray any of us ever again. We'll rebuild. Better than ever." People around them nodded, their eyes filled with the pain of their past, yet the light of their future shone through.

Wylliam came closer, swinging an arm around Sera. "We will. Together we can finally ignite the change we've all been waiting for." As he smiled at Elyssa, the rest of the camp joining in, a sense of peace washed over her.

There had been too much death. Too much suffering. It was time for change. It was time for them to truly live in this world that had tried so hard to get rid of them. Elyssa had always dreamed of a revolution, of winning. But what truly mattered was what came afterward, what they would achieve now with a new high queen, a new law. Glancing at the faces staring back at her—bruised but smiling—she knew they would take this chance and fill their future with the most breathtaking colours.

CHAPTER 85

RHAY

Every time Rhay closed his eyes he relived the events of the contest: Amira almost dying because he was too late. Tarnan trying to syphon Lora's life source. Karwyn choosing to help and dying in the process. At least Karwyn had looked at peace when—

A knock on his door interrupted his train of thoughts. He wondered who was on the other side. Rhay had mostly kept to himself the last two days, staying holed up in his room. He didn't really know if everyone had forgiven him completely. Now that Liraen was safe, would they cast him away?

He secretly hoped it was Rio. Thinking back on their kiss, Rhay touched his lips. What would Rio say to him now? Did he regret it?

"Come in." Rhay took a deep breath, fearing the confrontation ahead.

But Lora smiled when she entered the room, followed by a more serious Eyden. Traces of the fight were still visible on their bodies—a bruise on Lora's cheek, a cut on Eyden's brow.

"What gives me the honour of a visit from the Queen of Turosian and my bestest friend?" Rhay forced the excitement in his voice.

Eyden sighed, but Rhay knew it was just for show. Or he would hope until it was the truth.

"I told you not to call me that," Lora started.

Rhay gestured for them to take a seat on the stylish armchairs in his bedroom. "You'll get used to it."

Lora's smile slipped a smidge. "I hope I won't. But I can't leave Liraen now, I'm part of it."

"I'm glad you've accepted that." Turning to Eyden, Rhay added, "I noticed you didn't correct me when I said *best friend*." Rhay winked at Eyden, who rolled his eyes.

"Let's start with *not-my-enemy*," Eyden replied with a tone warmer than usual when it came to Rhay.

Lora let out a giggle and Eyden looked at her like she was the most precious thing in the world. Rhay wondered if he would ever experience a closeness like that with anyone, a perfect connection of body and mind.

"I've come to ask you something, Rhay." Lora's tone grew more serious and Rhay braced himself. "There's still a lot to be done. It won't be easy and I'll need all the help I can get. Have you decided who you want to be?"

All of his life, he had done what was expected of him, what he thought people wanted him to do. His father and Karwyn, they had a vision of who Rhay should be. But now, Karwyn was gone and so was his father. His first thought was to lose himself in senseless parties, travel the world, work in taverns and be paid in drinks. That was what the old Rhay would have wanted.

But now, it didn't sound that appealing. He wanted to do more, to *be* more. His encounters with Amira, Lora, and Rio, joining the fight against Tarnan, had changed him. He could see that now. There was a part of him that wanted to party, enjoy life, not think about any consequences. But that part had been overshadowed. He had enjoyed helping out, doing things that mattered. Taking action like a real advisor would instead of following Karwyn and Tarnan's twisted rules. Even if it had cost him.

"I want to stay, to be an advisor. If you would have me." Rhay lowered his head, expecting Lora to take it all back. He had spent so much time refusing to be an advisor and now he realised there was nothing he would rather be doing now that Turosian had a good-hearted ruler.

Lora stood up from her chair and went to hug him, her smile big. "I always knew there was something behind all that booze and deflection. Keep proving me right."

Rhay broke away from their hug to look at Lora. "Thank you for getting me to step up. For seeing who I could be."

"The potential for good was always in you, Rhay. You just needed to see it." Lora squeezed his shoulder. "I'm going to call Maja to let her know I'm coming soon. I'll see you later."

Lora left the room, but to Rhay's surprise, Eyden didn't follow her.

"Can't leave me, huh? I wasn't expecting our friendship to grow that fast," Rhay teased.

Eyden crossed his arms against his chest. "Careful, you're almost making me wish you weren't staying, and I have an in with the queen."

Rhay waved his hand as he laughed.

"On a serious note," Eyden continued, his tone sombre. "Are you sure about being an advisor? Even if Lora won't stay queen forever, she needs to be able to count on you."

"I'll be there." This time, Rhay meant it full-heartedly and he didn't doubt himself. "If she isn't going to stay queen, who might be her successor?"

Eyden sighed as he stood up. "That's a problem for another day. You should go check on Saige. Figure out what to do with her."

Heading for the door, Eyden left, cutting off Rhay's chance to reply. But their conversation left him feeling lighter than he had in weeks—in years, maybe. If he could earn Eyden's trust, he could earn anyone's. He would be the kind of advisor who would make his father proud if he could see him now.

Following Eyden's advice, Rhay went to see Saige later that day. She was living in the palace under a false identity. Like him, Saige seemed to have kept to her room for the last two days. The young fae was lying in bed, her back turned to the door when he entered. She didn't even move when he closed the door loudly. Was she asleep?

"Hey, Saige," he started softly. Silence answered him. He made a move to retreat when Saige spoke.

"Do you think I'm a monster?" Her voice was raw, like she had spent the last two days crying.

Rhay sat at the edge of her bed. "Of course not, love."

She turned to face him. Her eyes were red and puffy, her hair all messed up from staying in bed all day. "But I killed my own father. And I have this power, this power that can make others do terrible things."

Rhay gently smoothed her hair. He had struggled with the same feeling not that long ago. "You didn't kill your father, we did. And you used your power to save people, not hurt them."

"Then why do I feel like a monster?" Tears filled the young fae's honey-coloured eyes.

"You were confronted with a choice no one should have to make. You're not responsible for your father's decisions. He chose violence and revenge, you chose redemption. But it's okay to feel sad. You're grieving, it takes time. Truth be told, you never truly get over the death of a loved one, you just learn to live with it. I don't think I've even started grieving my father."

Rhay gave her a warm smile, wiping her tears tenderly. His own eyes welled up as he thought back on his father's death. It was still fresh in his mind, the guilt refusing to leave him even though he knew Tarnan was to blame. There was consolation in knowing that Tarnan had burned his father's body, letting him join Caelo in the Sky. Rhay hoped that one day, he'd be reunited with his family. After a long life of doing right by them.

And then there was Karwyn. Rhay had known Karwyn was living on borrowed time. But losing him a second time, no matter how badly things had turned out between them, it had broken his heart nonetheless. They had taken Karwyn's body back to Turosian. Rhay and Rio had been the only ones at the funeral. As he had watched his ashes drift into the starry night, Rio holding his hand, Rhay had thought that the stars looked brighter than usual. Maybe Karwyn would join his mother after all.

"So it will get better?" Saige asked, her voice low.

"One day, it will get better. And I'll be here to help you every step of the way. You can stay here as long as you want, Saige. We won't turn you away."

A sad smile graced her lips and Rhay pulled her into a hug. He had let down so many people in his life. He wouldn't turn on Saige. He would be the person that he wished he'd had when his mother had passed.

As Rhay left Saige's room, he ran smack into Rio. They both blushed, heavy questions lingering in the air.

Rio took a step back, barely so. "I've heard you're staying in Turosian."

"You'll have to keep putting up with me," Rhay joked, trying to defuse the tension between them.

"I'm used to people leaving," Rio said, a sad smile on his lips.

"You haven't heard from Damir?" Rhay hoped Rio would say no, then told himself off. It was a selfish thought—he'd learned to recognise them as such.

"No, and I don't think I ever will." Pain shone in his emerald eyes. "I've accepted that the Damir I was in love with isn't the real Damir. It was the version I wanted to see or that he made me see. I'm sure he's somewhere chasing fortune, breaking hearts on his way." Rio shook his head, leaning against the corridor wall. "He'll never change and I now know he was never right for me."

Rhay tried to meet his gaze. "I hope you know *I* care about you."

Rio raised his head. Moving away from the wall, he closed the gap between them. Rhay's heart flipped. Rio was so close he could almost feel the press of his lips on his. "The kiss...do you remember what I told you?"

Only kiss me if you truly mean it. It had been ingrained in Rhay's head. Had he meant it? Was he capable of it? Rhay blinked, shedding fresh tears. He dropped his forehead against Rio's. His mouth almost graced his. His breath scattered on his lips. If he leaned in a tiny bit more...

Rhay wrenched his head away. He wouldn't ruin this—whatever it was that was brewing between them. He couldn't survive ruining this. He had to focus on himself, on staying the Rhay he wanted to be and do the right thing. If Rio was going to stay the head advisor, he deserved the best from Rhay.

"I didn't *not* mean it," Rhay whispered, and Rio nodded as if he understood the war waging in his mind. "I'm glad we're both staying."

"I don't really know what I'm doing," Rio admitted, biting his lip. "Now that the dust has settled, the real work begins."

He knew Rio would do amazing things, had seen how much he'd given of himself to help Lora, to help everyone, including Rhay. "You don't have to figure it all out now. Your story has just begun."

Rio put his hands on Rhay's shoulders, his touch the most comforting thing Rhay had ever felt. "Yours too, Nix. This is a new beginning. Your past doesn't define you. Your future does. And I know you'll do great."

"Thank you." Rhay's voice almost gave out. Just weeks ago, that statement would have seemed impossible. Rio's hands tightened on his shoulders, and even though there was still so much left unsaid between them, Rhay knew this wasn't the end of their story either.

He would give everything to do right by Lora, by Amira, by Rio, by Liraen. That was what he aspired to do now: make the right choice, help people instead of turning a blind eye.

For the first time, Rhay felt like he was no longer some lost, wounded fae, acting on impulse, chasing senseless pleasure with no care for who he was hurting on the way. Now, he felt like someone worth a fresh start, even though he had much to repent for. He would honour the second chance he got and never fail to act again.

CHAPTER 86

AMIRA

Sitting in the indoor garden of the Turosian palace, Amira took in the blooming flowers and the pleasant smell of lavender drifting in the air. It looked untouched by the battle and grief they had all gone through. It had been months since she had discovered this garden for the first time—back when her only wish had been to escape her brother. In a way, coming to Turosian had been the first step in gaining her freedom. It just hadn't happened the way she thought it would.

Soon, she would be leaving for Allamyst to become the queen, a fate she had never dared envision for herself. It was a daunting task, one Amira wasn't completely sure she was ready for. But she knew her father would have believed in her as Elyssa did now. For the first time, Amira felt as if she'd truly freed herself of the demons of her past.

While Elyssa had gone to talk to Wylliam about the new human camp, Amira had decided to find some peace and quiet in the garden. Her moment of reflection was interrupted by the sound of footsteps. Amira turned her head, almost expecting Rhay like all those months ago. But her eyes met Lora's.

Lora sat next to her on the stone bench. "Rhay told me I might find you here."

"I heard he wants to be an advisor. I'm glad he's found his purpose." Amira picked a nearby rose, its scent sweet. It reminded her of her mother's perfume. Amira shook her head, refusing to let sadness overtake her. Her mother would tell her to run instead of taking on the toll of remaking Allamyst. Yet Amira couldn't help but miss her.

Sensing her trouble, Lora put a hand over Amira's. "I think we all found purpose, gained perspective. I don't think I would have ever accepted myself, my fae side, if I hadn't come here."

Amira smiled brightly. "If it wasn't for El, I don't think I would have accepted my powers either. I tried so hard to erase them, to change who I was because I was afraid of how others would treat me."

"My mother, she must have been so afraid. And she instilled that fear in me. I thought I would have to keep it inside forever." Lora's breath hitched. "I still don't know if she'll ever accept me."

Amira pressed Lora's hand. "By Caelo, it feels good to let it all out."

"It does. I feel like I am truly myself now. Even with Karwyn's powers, I'm starting to get used to it all."

Amira paused, a question crossing her mind. "Do you think he would have changed if he had survived the contest?"

"I don't know. He could have done nothing and he chose to help as his final gesture. I'm trying to let go of all the resentment."

Amira nodded. She thought of her brother, who had been despicable until the very end. Yet, feeling angry, guilty, or anything else towards him was merely wasted energy. "It's better than my brother's final gesture. He tried to use me again, and paid the price."

Lora let out a dry laugh. "Karma is a bitch, as we say on Earth."

"It's all over now."

"Or maybe it's just the beginning. It's a new year, after all. We still have to rebuild Liraen, make it a better place for everyone—fae, witches, humans."

"We will." Hope filled Amira's heart. They had been through hell and back. If anyone could change Liraen, it was them.

Smiling, Lora pressed her hand before standing up. "I should go, I have to get ready to go see my family. Brace myself for another confrontation."

Amira waved goodbye as jealousy pinched her heart. Her father was gone, and so was Wryen now. With her mother's betrayal, Amira felt like an island, cut off from her family roots. She hadn't told Elyssa how hurt she was that her mother hadn't written her to apologise. It was the least she could have done.

Standing up, Amira placed the flower she had picked in her hair. The scent drifted through the air, pulling at her heartstrings. She made her way out of the garden when a voice halted her.

"I see you still enjoy the garden; I haven't ruined it for you." Rhay came up behind her, an easy smile on his face. For the first time since she had met him, Amira could sense there was no darkness lingering behind his smile.

"It is the most beautiful place in this palace."

"And you've always had an eye for beauty." He winked at her. "That's why you chose to be my friend."

Amira let out a carefree laugh, forgetting her heartache for a moment. "You didn't give me much of a choice. No matter how many times you screw up, I've always known you're a good person."

Rhay took her hand and pressed it to his heart. "It's an honour to be your friend. But I feel like I've been neglecting our friendship. So I have a little gift for you."

Amira raised an eyebrow. "Another scandalous book?"

Laughing, he shook his head. "No, but I think you'll enjoy it even more." He turned towards the flower-covered entrance he had come through. "You can come out." Patting Amira's shoulder, a wide smile stretched his lips. "I'll leave you two to it." As he walked off, Amira wrinkled her forehead, but then her lips parted in an exhale when her mother entered the garden.

"My Mira," her mother said.

Amira refused to believe her mother was truly here. She must have wished so hard for her mother to come back that she had hallucinated her. But no, she was here, in front of her. Her face was fuller and healthier than when she had left her.

"Mother," was all Amira could say.

"I've heard you're coming back to Allamyst to rule," her mother started. Amira's heart dropped, anticipating another argument. "You will make a great queen, I see that now. Your father would be very proud of you." Amira's mother's voice hitched. "*I'm* very proud of you."

"Thank you." Amira felt incapable of completely erasing the coldness from her voice.

"My Mira, I'm so sorry for what I put you through. I was trying to protect you, but I went about it the wrong way." Her mother twisted her hands. "I'm so glad Rhay tracked me down. He said you needed me. I *want* to be there for you."

Amira took a deep breath. "I trusted you. After all Wryen put me through—taking away my freedom, my choice—how did you think kidnapping me would make me feel?"

Her mother stepped closer, her voice wavering. "I acted out of fear. I was afraid he would take you away from me once more."

"Was that the only reason?"

Her mother lowered her head. "I didn't want you to fight. Not because I thought you weren't capable. But because I knew your heart is too kind. You would risk yourself."

She wasn't wrong. Amira had stopped her own heart to break her contract with Tarnan. "My friends risked just as much for me," Amira said, thinking about Elyssa bringing her back to life.

"I have lost your trust, but I'll work hard on rebuilding what I have broken. Please tell me I'm not too late." Her mother's eyes were filled with tears, her tone pleading.

Amira couldn't stay still, hearing the words she had hoped to hear for over a week. They had a long way to go, but Amira wasn't one to give up anymore. She wrapped her arms around her mother, taking comfort in her as she had longed to do for so many months.

"It's not too late."

"I have brought you some buns from the market," Elyssa said as she entered their bedroom. Amira sat up on the bed, having taken a quick nap after talking with her mother for hours. She was truly grateful Rhay had made the effort to find her.

"I hope the seller wasn't cute," Amira teased.

"I only have eyes for one." Elyssa stole a kiss from her as she threw herself on the bed.

"You taste like warm bread," Amira mumbled against Elyssa's lips.

"I already had one on the way." She nuzzled her head in Amira's neck.

"Always a rebel." Amira laughed.

"For you, I'd rebel against a whole kingdom." Elyssa gently pushed her shoulder and Amira fell back on the bed, Elyssa with her. As Elyssa leaned over her, the bread was long forgotten. She was a vision in the late afternoon sun, her red hair glowing like a bonfire.

Amira had let fear and guilt rule her heart for too long. But her brother was gone, and so were Tarnan and Karwyn. Amira had won. There had been some immense losses: Farren, Varsha, Kaede, Lozlan. Amira had felt responsible for some. She had carried so much guilt and let it rule over her. Amira knew the guilt wouldn't leave completely, but she wouldn't let it win. Happiness seemed strangely easy now, like she couldn't understand why she'd ever chosen to let fear win. She felt the shadows in her heart lift, and she wouldn't allow them entrance again.

"By Caelo, I love you." The words escaped her, but she didn't regret them one bit.

Amira loved Elyssa. It was that simple. She had always loved her, but was finally able to let herself admit it now. It was a peacefulness mixed with a desire to be in Elyssa's presence constantly. Rhay had been wrong all those months ago when they'd talked about love. Love wasn't either a burning flame or a slow storm. The best kind of love was both. It was lightning hitting her heart but also a connection that kept building, strengthening. And she couldn't wait to see what the future held for them.

"I love you too, sunshine," Elyssa said, her smile more radiant than ever. Inching forward, Elyssa's lips brushed hers, the sparks between them brighter and bigger than any pain.

Amira's hand cupped Elyssa's cheek, deepening the kiss. Elyssa's lips left hers as she whispered, "God, you smell delicious. Are you sure you haven't tried the bread?"

Amira laughed while Elyssa kissed her all over her face: her nose, her cheeks, her forehead. Amira's hands tangled in Elyssa's soft hair.

"I'm hungry for something else." Amira surprised herself with her boldness.

Elyssa grinned and let herself be pushed against the mattress. Amira traced a line of fiery kisses from Elyssa's mouth to her collarbone. Her hands lifted Elyssa's shirt, revealing her freckled skin. At the view, Amira felt a fire burning deep in her core. She kissed a trail towards Elyssa's belly, feeling the warmth of her soft skin.

Elyssa shimmied out of her trousers, letting Amira continue her trail of kisses. With one hand, Amira caressed the swell of Elyssa's breasts, teasing her before her hand travelled south.

Gripping Elyssa's thigh, Amira's tongue flicked over Elyssa's bundle of nerves, and she drowned in the sound of Elyssa's moans. She increased her speed at Elyssa's encouragement, flicking her tongue until Elyssa came completely undone, her hips lifting in rhythm with Amira's strokes.

Amira joined Elyssa's side, the taste of her still in her mouth. "That was better than bread."

Kissing her, Elyssa smiled against her lips, laughter ringing in the room. Then, with a sinful grin, Elyssa pushed her back and straddled Amira's hips faster than she could track. "My turn, sunshine." Leaning down, Elyssa melded their lips together as her hand slipped under Amira's shirt, stealing all her thoughts, blocking out the bad memories she was leaving in the dust.

Losing herself in the kiss, Amira felt like her heart was about to explode. Against all odds, she was living and loving more deeply than she had ever thought possible.

CHAPTER 87

LORA

They went through the underground market to cross over in the cover of nightfall.

Pulling her black hat down her forehead, Lora hurried through the little corner shop where the door from the underground market led. The shop was utterly abandoned; groceries lying on the ground, dust covering the ransacked shelves. Eyden walked beside her. Following behind them was Ian, who Lora had suggested to bring with them since she knew Oscar and Ian had become friends.

As Lora opened the glass door of the shop—sporting multiple cracks —she took in the snow-covered street in her hometown. Breathing in the fresh air, Lora calmed her nerves. It was good to be back, yet also the strangest sensation. A homecoming, yet at the same time she was leaving another home behind. And she couldn't go back to her house— the thought still strangled her heart. Her father had informed her that a part of it had survived but it would take time to rebuild.

Lora had ordered guards to watch the entrance to the black market on the fae side and they had Oscar's device to help secure it. But as Maja had warned her, the police hadn't blocked off the entrance on Earth's side. They might not even know it was here. Although her father had told her that they'd spent the last days answering police questions and that Lora was no longer wanted by the law as she was now known as the Queen of Turosian who'd fought for Earth, she knew crossing over visibly on the beach would lead to quite a fuss. The police would try to hold her for questioning.

It had to wait until the treaty meeting she planned to arrange. She was in contact with Thea about setting up a treaty meeting with Earth to discuss the border now that there would be no spell since the amulets had been destroyed and the pieces had lost their magic. As none of the remaining kings had any issue with Thea becoming high queen and Lora had given Thea her own blessing in writing, Thea was now officially the high queen of Liraen. She had much to do with Lora's help, but that was tomorrow's problem.

As Lora spotted a car parked down the dark street, its headlights blinked twice.

"Come on," Lora said to Eyden and Ian as she hurried down the street before anyone noticed them.

Opening the passenger door, she was met with Maja's grin.

"Fancy seeing you here," Maja joked, looking over her shoulder as Eyden and Ian got into the car. Lora smiled at her as she closed the door and Maja hit the gas fast, forcing Lora back into her seat. She steadied herself against the glove compartment.

"How's everything?" Lora asked, a bit breathless. *How's my mum?* Her mother was the only one Lora hadn't talked to or even sent a message to since the battle. She knew her mum was all right because of her father and Oscar, but she'd gotten so used to fearing for her life that it was hard to accept that her mother was truly safe.

"Well, I had to endure multiple lectures from my dad about running off to Liraen. My mum barely seems to care though, so that's great." Maja glanced at the rearview mirror to the backseat and cleared her throat. "But enough about me, how is it going at the palace without my sparkling presence?"

Sensing Maja's discomfort, Lora joked, "Dreadful. I've spent most of the time resting and not accomplishing much."

"You needed that rest," Eyden threw in.

"Yeah, you deserve a break," Maja agreed. "And three days is hardly enough. I'm sure you and Mister Broody here were very *busy*."

Lora's mouth dropped open as she stared at her. "You're crude."

"You love it." Maja smirked, and Lora couldn't help but laugh. She heard Eyden chuckling behind her while Ian stared out the window, ignoring them.

They pulled up to her mum's diner overlooking the beach. The border shimmered in the distance. As her home was uninhabitable, her family had been staying with Marcel, Maja's father. Yet her father had told Lora to meet at the diner. Apparently, they were trying to get things ready to reopen soon.

When the car stopped, Lora glanced over her shoulder. "Do you mind going in without me?"

Eyden leaned forward, squeezing her shoulder briefly before gesturing for Ian to get out of the car. As she watched the two of them head to the diner's door, Lora felt an overwhelming wave of anxiety ice her veins.

"Hey," Maja softly said, and Lora turned to her. "Are you really doing okay?"

Lora sighed. "Are you?"

Shutting off the engine, Maja leaned back in her seat. "No. I guess no one is. But your mum will understand; I have a good feeling about it."

Lora wasn't convinced. How could she understand when her mum's number one priority had always been to hide Lora's secret? Instilling in her that her powers can never be seen, should never be used?

"I have to get it over with, don't I?" Lora huffed, glancing at her necklace and remembering the almandine heart-shaped one she used to wear that her mum had gifted her. "And your mum?"

Shrugging, Maja brushed her fringe from her face that had grown too long. "Same as always. My dad was pissed, but at least he seemed to get it."

"Get it how?"

Her warm brown eyes met Lora's. "That it changed me. That I don't want the same things I used to."

That Lora could understand perfectly.

"I'm sorry I dragged you into this." She reached out to take her friend's hand.

"I'm not," Maja said fiercely. "I can't imagine not being part of this. I don't want to *not* be part of this."

"Are you saying you want to come back with me?"

Maja might be adventurous, but politics could be quite dry too. At least Lora hoped there would be no more great battles in their future.

Maja's smile said she was sure of her decision. "Yes. I don't know in what way exactly, but I want to remain in your court as long as you're in charge. I want to see this through. Ilario is staying too?"

Lora nodded, smiling. Having Maja with her was like having a part of her hometown with her. "So is Rhay."

"Great." Maja winced. "I love that I made that awkward."

"What's a court without scandal?"

Maja chuckled, shaking her head. "I knew you needed me around."

With Maja following after her, Lora entered her mum's rustic diner. The last time she was here she'd been trying to convince Maja to help her cross the border. It felt like a lifetime ago. Though the diner looked the same, the brown leather booths appeared dusty, the floor not as shiny. The windows overlooking the beach and the Ferris wheel were blocked off by thick black curtains that hadn't been there before.

Eyden and her father sat at the bar, chatting casually in a way that warmed her heart. "Lora!" Oscar yelled as he leaned his head into the room from the kitchen. Ian followed after him, a bowl of fries in his hand. Walking up to her, Oscar hugged her tightly. When Lora held on for too long, Oscar said, "I missed you too, but I need to breathe."

Laughing under her breath, Lora pulled back and looked up at Oscar's face. He appeared less burdened and more like his old self. It made her smile. "You look good."

Oscar tilted his head but her father replied first as he walked up to them from the bar, Eyden following. "As opposed to usually when he looks bloody awful?" Ian hid his grin as he turned away, setting the bowl on the counter and taking a seat at the bar. Picking up a fry, he savoured the taste.

Oscar rolled his eyes as her father came around and tousled Oscar's dark hair, making it stick up every which way. "There, much better. Hi, Maja. Thanks for picking them up," her father added as Maja came to stand next to her.

"I agree," Lora said, biting her lip to keep from laughing.

"I hate you both," Oscar said, but Lora knew he meant the opposite.

Lingering close, Eyden crossed his arms. "I'm on your side, Oscar." Her brother narrowed his eyes. "It looks goddamn awful."

Oscar flipped him off and the casual conversation made Lora laugh despite the weight pulling her heart under water.

Before Lora could ask where her mum was, the front door opened again and Marcel strode in, stamping his feet on the entrance mat to shake the snow off his boots.

"I see my timing is impeccable," Marcel said, pulling Maja into a half hug and whispering something in her ear before he walked up to Lora. "Glad you're back. I was afraid Karla would kill me for helping you cross, but I told her she can hardly kill me if she's dead. Good thing you're both all right. I had a feeling you'd pull this off, kid." He embraced her in a quick hug.

"I'm glad you were right," Lora joked as he pulled back, grinning at her.

Eyden appeared next to them, holding out his hand. *Very human of him,* she thought. "Eyden Kelstrel, it's a pleasure to finally meet you."

Marcel glanced at his hand, then grinned, pulling Eyden into a side-hug. "I have to admit, I was less sure about trusting you, but I see that has paid off too." He winked at her. "What do you think about rebuilding the black market or establishing a new trading area?" Marcel asked Eyden, and Lora stepped to the side to let them talk.

Oscar tapped her shoulder. "Mum is in the back office. I can come with you if you want."

Her heart warmed at his offer, at how far their relationship had

602 - JENNIFER BECKER, ALICE KARPIEL

come these last weeks. She tried to force a smile on her face. "Thanks, but I'll be all right."

"I can always tell when you fake it. But I get it. If you need me, I'll be at the bar eating fries with Ian. He doesn't know what he's been missing all his life."

Giving her a real smile, Oscar headed back to Ian. Her father joined Marcel and Eyden's discussion. Eyden caught her gaze and put two fingers behind his ear. Returning the gesture, Lora spun around to glance at Maja, who went to join Oscar and Ian, stealing a fry.

Staring at the door to the office, Lora braced herself. There was nothing holding her back. It was time she faced her last fear. Her feet felt like they were made out of stone as Lora headed to the back. With a heavy heart she went to the closed office door. Lora took a deep breath and raised her hand to knock when the door flew open.

Her mum stared at her. Bruises covered her face but she looked healthier than Lora had seen her in a long time. She had been so pale when she'd been in that coma and before then, when she'd caught the virus. Now her tan skin was glowing and her cheeks had a slight flush to them.

"Lora," her mum said, and a knot formed around her heart, squeezing tightly. "I thought I heard voices. I was just about to come out."

"You were?" Lora almost choked on her words.

Her mum's eyes saddened but then she composed herself and stepped to the side. "Come in, I want to talk to you."

Walking in, Lora took in the familiar space. On her mum's big desk, her laptop and two screens were turned on. Four shelves lined the wall, filled with folders. Two worn-down armchairs faced the window. Lora sat on the window bank looking out the back alley. It was pitch black outside but the warm light from the room highlighted the snow covering the edges of the glass on the other side. It felt cold against her back, almost as cold as the dread filling her.

Her mum went to sit on the chair opposite her. The silence was deafening, making Lora's skin itch. She didn't know where to start or how to explain. She didn't want to break her mum's heart but she also couldn't lie or pretend any longer—couldn't deny her fae side and everything she'd experienced these past three and a half months.

"I'm so glad—" her mum said as Lora blurted, "I'm sorry."

"Sorry?" her mum asked, leaning forward to catch her gaze as the corners of her mouth dropped. "You have nothing to be sorry for, honey." She scooted off the chair and sat next to Lora on the window bank. Raising a hand to cup Lora's cheek, she looked in her eyes that shined so bright, so utterly fae. Lora forced herself not to turn away.

"It's me who should apologise. You did so much to save me, to save our family, to save the whole *world*. I can't even imagine what you've gone through and I wasn't there for any of it. I couldn't help you. Worst of all, you probably thought I'd be disappointed because I never gave you any reason to think otherwise." Lora pressed her lips together, a well of emotions travelling up her throat.

A tear ran down her mum's cheek. Her voice turned quiet and tortured. "I never knew how you felt about hiding your fae side. That it felt like you were only half alive." Lora frowned, her mum's words too familiar. "Maja showed me the video you sent her. The goodbye—" Her voice broke off as tears glistened in her dark eyes. "I had no idea how wrong I'd been. That I made you feel ashamed. It breaks my heart. I *never* wanted you to feel that way. I only ever wanted to protect you, and giving you that almandine necklace was the only way I knew how to."

Her mum's gaze drifted to her collarbone where a new necklace rested, the one Eyden had given her.

Lora put her hand over her mum's on her cheek. "I know it would've been so much easier if I was just human. Sometimes I liked pretending that I was. Before, all I wanted was to be normal."

Her mum smiled at her, tears shining on her cheeks. "You were never normal." Lora cringed, turning her head, but her mum's hand tightened on her cheek. "You were and will always be *extraordinary*. And that's something I should have praised, I should have let you explore—even if in secret to protect you."

The knot wrapped around Lora's heart slowly untwisted. A lightness settled over her entire body even as her gaze turned blurry from unshed tears. "You're not disappointed that I crossed and used my powers?"

She took a deep breath, her hand moving from Lora's cheek to clasp her hand on her lap. "A big part of me wishes you'd never crossed over." Lora thought as much, her hand shaking, but her mum hastily added, "Not because you're half-fae, but because of all you had to endure. I wish it would have been me. I wish *I* could have taken it all on. The burden you must have felt, still feel, as the queen—how crazy is that?"

Lora laughed through her tears.

"You're stronger than I ever knew, than I ever could be. And I'm so proud of you."

Lora couldn't stop her tears now, nor did she want to. Her mother wrapped her arms around her and Lora cried into her sweater, letting her stroke her hair as if she was a child again—as if everything bad that had happened could be erased with just one hug. It couldn't, but it did make it better.

Squeezing her eyes shut, Lora shuddered when she remembered what they had both lost. "I'm so sorry about the house," Lora whispered.

Her mum stroked her hair again. "It's not your fault. We'll rebuild. As long as we're all safe, we'll be fine." As Lora pulled back, her mum wiped the tears on Lora's cheeks. "I can't believe how much has changed these past three months. I want you to know that I'll support you no matter what you intend to do next. You want to stay in Liraen and rule? I'll cheer you on. You want to leave it behind and stay here but never hide your powers again, no matter what people say? I'll fight with you to make that happen. Whatever you need, I promise."

Lora gave her a tired smile. "I want to do both. I want to make a change for the sake of Liraen *and* Earth. I want to live in both worlds and be accepted. It's a lot to ask for and it won't happen overnight, but it's no longer impossible."

Her mum gave her an encouraging smile. "Then that's what I wish for you. And whenever you need me, I'll come running." She squeezed Lora's hand.

Lora looked down at their joined hands. "There is something...Lozlan's funeral." She bit her lip as fresh tears burned her eyes. "He deserves a proper one. I want to do it soon. Tomorrow. I know he would want you there."

Her mum frowned, stunned. "I'll forever be grateful to him for saving me, but I think he did that because he thought he owed us something. I'm sorry, honey. But if *you* want me there, I'll be there."

Lora shook her head. "It's not what you think. He didn't stop replying to you because he didn't care. He stopped because he cared so much. His brother, Harten Adelway, killed Lozlan's family. His wife and son." Lora had to force the words out as bile rose in her throat.

Her mum put a hand to her heart, her lips parted in shock. "That's...unimaginable. Back then, I remember Lan mentioned that he feared his brother had done something. I never imagined *this*."

"He was scared the same thing would happen to us, so he stopped replying. He burned the letter in which you told him about, well, me. But the rest, he saved them, kept them for all these years."

Her mum stared at her in disbelief, a fresh tear sliding down her cheek. "I...I can't believe I spent all these years holding such hatred for him. And his kind."

"Me too."

The loss still felt like a fresh wound that hadn't yet scabbed over. She knew with time it would, but there would always be a scar on her heart where he should've been. Just like the gaping wound that she'd been carrying around since crossing over—her mother's disappointment—had now finally healed over, only a faint whisper of it echoing in her heart.

Her mum stood up, walking to her shelves. Digging through boxes, she turned back to Lora with a letter in her hand.

"I only kept the first letter he sent me. I stored it here so no one would find it," her mum said. She sat back down, holding the paper out to Lora.

With shaking hands, Lora took the letter. "Can I read it? I wasn't sure if you wanted me to read the ones you sent to him. They're at the palace."

"I think," her mum said, biting her lip, "I would like to read them first. But you can read this one."

Glancing at the letter, Lora slowly unfolded it.

Dear Midnight Girl,
I broke my promise. I know. I couldn't help it. These past weeks, all I could think about...

Breathing in deeply, Lora fought a sob. Her mum's hand covered hers and Lora turned from the paper mid-sentence to face her.

"I'm glad I was wrong," her mum said, her tone bittersweet. "About Lan, about fae in general. My experience with fae wasn't great, to say the least, when I was at the treaty meeting twenty-five years ago. But it seems you have found fae who really care."

"I found fae, witches, other humans," Lora replied, a chuckle leaving her lips, "you name it." They more than cared, they had fought—*bled*—for their future.

"Your father mentioned there was someone special in particular..."

Special. Eyden was more than that. Even *especially special* didn't come close to it.

Lora wiped away a stray tear and sat up straight, feeling more confident and comfortable than she ever thought possible in the presence of her mum. She finally felt like she could tell her anything and would never be judged, never be anything but loved.

So Lora said, "There is. Would you like to meet him?"

CHAPTER 88

ᕽ

AMIRA
Epilogue

They stayed almost two weeks in Turosian. As happy as Amira was that Elyssa had agreed to come with her to Allamyst, she couldn't help but worry. Amira wanted to do right by her people. After years under her brother's reign, they deserved a good ruler.

Sitting on the bed next to her, Elyssa pressed her forehead against Amira's, drawing her away from her thoughts. "I've packed all my things, not that I had much to pack anyway. It's all in the carriage."

Amira stole a kiss from her, grounding herself with the taste of Elyssa's lips. "How much of it was weapons?"

"Oh, not much. Just enough to scare away anyone who would dare mess with us," Elyssa replied with a grin as she stood up from the bed.

"I hope we won't have to use them at all." Amira wrapped her arms around herself. When she had gone to Amryne, she had seen that some people there still cared about her. But were they ready for the *real* her, or merely the image they had of her?

"If need be, we'll be ready for anything. Come on, everyone is waiting for us downstairs." Elyssa extended her hand, a brilliant smile on her lips. Amira knew then that as long as Elyssa was by her side, she would be okay. They had chosen each other and neither one of them would leave the other behind out of fear ever again.

She took Elyssa's hand and let herself be led downstairs. Passing through the Turosian corridors, Amira couldn't help but think back on her first time here. It had been almost four months ago, but so much had happened that it felt like ten years.

By the front gate, everyone was waiting for them. It was so different from when Amira had left for Carnylen, all alone except for her brother and Nouis. Now they were both gone. Instead, Amira was welcomed by friendly faces in the warm afternoon sun: Lora, Rhay, Eyden, Ilario, Maja, Sahalie, and Saige.

Lora was the first to step forward, embracing Amira in a tight hug.

"It's funny that I feared you initially," Amira started. "And now I couldn't be more grateful to have met you. You ignited the change Liraen needed, the spark that started it all."

"I wouldn't have made it if it wasn't for you and everyone else. We won together. I know you'll make an amazing queen," Lora said after breaking from their embrace. "And we'll always be here for you if you need anything."

A proud smile graced Amira's lip. "I'll write to you when I'm in Allamyst. Politics will always tie us together. And we're kind of sisters-in-law now." They both laughed, drawing the attention of Eyden and Elyssa who were saying goodbye next to them.

"What's so funny?" Elyssa asked, her hand on her brother's shoulder.

"I was just saying the four of us are sort of family now," Amira replied, beaming at Elyssa's visible happiness.

"I like that. This way I'm not the only one who has to deal with Eyden being his moody self." Elyssa playfully punched Eyden's shoulder.

"And here I thought you had your fill of violence for at least a few months." Eyden rubbed his shoulder, exaggerating his pain. His eyes shone with laughter.

"Never!" Elyssa laughed before her face turned serious and she grabbed her brother in a tight embrace. "I'm going to miss you. You better write often."

"I'll do even better, I'll visit. To see the human community you'll build." Sadness and joy swirled in Eyden and Elyssa's eyes. It would be difficult for them to be apart, but they'd always have each other.

Eyden and Elyssa broke away from one another and Amira turned to Eyden. They hadn't had the time to grow close, but Amira was sure that they would become fast friends now that impending doom was no longer on the horizon.

"Take care of my sister," Eyden told her.

"I can goddamn take care of myself," Elyssa protested.

"She sure can. But I will take care of her." Amira took Elyssa's hand and kissed it. Elyssa immediately softened, that violent spark turning warm.

Amira exchanged a quick goodbye with Ilario, Maja, and Sahalie. She knew the Turosian kingdom was in good hands with them. Saige stood a bit away from the group, still not used to all the company, and Amira joined her while Elyssa said goodbye to Lora.

"Hey," Amira started. "I'm sorry I haven't visited you often. I had a lot to plan with my return to Allamyst." Saige had eventually started to join them for breakfast, lunch, and dinner, convinced by Rhay. But it was difficult for her to get used to her new life. Amira had barely spent time with her because she was busy but mostly because she didn't know what to say to her. She regretted it now that she was leaving.

"It's all right, I have Rhay." She paused. "Everything is...strange now. But I don't feel alone anymore. In Carnylen, I never had any friends, just my father. I loved him so much...but I only had him."

Amira took Saige's hands and pressed them. "I'll be there for you when you need me."

"Rhay has given me options about my future. He said that I can choose how my story continues. Father never..." Saige broke off, and Amira squeezed her hand. "I'm going to Earth, it will be safer there. I can start over, a new book. Lora's family has agreed to take me in. They're so kind." Saige's eyes lit up for the first time. Getting used to life on Earth might be tricky but Saige was right, no one would suspect who she truly was there. There would be no fae royals around to question who she was, and since Saige was half-fae—as Saige had confirmed herself—she could pass as human.

After Amira detached herself from Saige, Rhay was the only one left who she hadn't parted with.

"I was the first to welcome you back then and now I'm the last to say goodbye," Rhay said, giving Saige a smile before coming closer to Amira.

"You made my time in Turosian bearable."

Rhay lowered his head. "Until I ruined everything with that stupid kiss."

Amira furrowed her brows. "I don't think it ruined anything, actually. It revealed things to me—who I truly was, who I wanted to be. In a way, I should thank you."

Rhay grinned at her. "But you won't?"

Amira laughed. "No, that kiss was really misguided. And you've made some mistakes since then, but you did come through in the end." She hugged Rhay, the tight embrace making her travel through time to when Rhay was the only beacon of hope in her life. "Thank you for bringing my mother back. I'm proud of you for deciding to stay."

"Thank you," Rhay said, his voice choked.

They broke away from each other, knowing that from a terrible situation a true friendship had blossomed.

"Ready, sunshine?" Elyssa asked, a smile on her face. She held the carriage door open with one hand.

Amira took one last look at the Turosian palace and everyone gathered in front of it, letting the hopeful smiles of her friends warm her heart. Four months ago, she had left Allamyst a broken girl, with no one in her corner and her fate set in stone. Now, she was returning with a new destiny and a love she never dreamed possible. After all she had been through, Amira was ready for anything. She would never let happiness leave her sight, never give up hope ever again.

"I'm ready," Amira said, turning towards the carriage and the promise of a bright future.

CHAPTER 89

LORA
Epilogue

As Amira and Elyssa's carriage disappeared through the silver gates, Lora reached for Eyden's hand, intertwining their fingers. His ice-blue eyes shone bright, yet a sadness radiated off them. She shared the same feeling. She was happy for Amira and Elyssa and she knew she'd see them again, but it felt strangely final. The end of an era. Or the beginning of a new one.

Eyden tugged at her hand when the carriage fully vanished from their sight, down the sunlit path into the woods. "Let's go," he said, pushing past the evident sadness as he gave her a small smile.

Nodding, Lora headed inside. As her friends—her court—went up the stairs to the council room, she couldn't help but picture herself the first time she'd walked down the cold stone corridor when Rhay had insisted she'd go to his party after Karwyn had tasked Rhay with training her. She had felt so doomed then. She could have never imagined that it would lead her here, entering the council room as the Queen of Turosian.

She took a seat at the head of the table, Eyden on one side of her, Ilario on the other. Maja, Rhay, and Sahalie, who Lora had appointed as the new royal healer, took their seats too. Saige had probably gone back to her room.

Lora hadn't decided yet whether she needed to extend the Turosian court. It was all a matter of how long she'd remain queen. Back when they'd first come back to the palace, Nouis had told her she should consider reinstating some of the old advisors, but anyone who had agreed with Karwyn's politics could never be part of Lora's reign. Nouis might have been the exception, his absence strangely present in the palace.

"What's the first order of business, boss?" Rhay asked, leaning back in his chair. He'd taken his role as advisor more seriously than Lora had first imagined.

Glancing at the expectant faces around the table, Lora cleared her throat. "As we all know, yesterday Thea officially announced that from now on, witches, humans, and fae alike all have the same rights in all of Liraen. The remaining kings, the new queen of Sapharos—Kaede's niece—and myself all agreed."

No one ruled over Carnylen yet, but there were talks of appointing a new king or queen, someone beyond Tarnan's reach of influence. Rubien, on the other hand, would be left alone as the majority of the royals still saw the land as cursed. Any banishments to Rubien were to be trialled anew by Thea. Who knew why Karwyn, or Harten before him, had banished them? It could very well be unjustified.

Lora tugged at her necklace. "Guards have already reported the first signs of push-back. We need to get ahead of it, make the people see it's for the best."

Maja leaned forward, her glasses slipping down her nose. "Wylliam wants to keep the new human camp hidden at least until the situation has calmed down and fae have gotten more used to the idea. I think it's for the best."

Elyssa and Wylliam had worked hard these last two weeks to build a new camp and gather up any humans in the area who had been fending for themselves. With Amira's help, they'd spelled it as Farren had done to the old camp, keeping it out of sight.

"These fae from the protests," Ilario started, leaning forward on the oak table, "can we invite them to the palace to hear their concerns? To let them know everyone will be heard?"

Maja huffed. "Even the ignorant ones."

"There will always be some people who need their eyes opened,"

Rhay threw in. Winking at Lora, he added, "Thankfully, Lora is good at that."

Eyden leaned back in his chair, glancing between them. "So we'll hear their complaints."

"And then we'll change their minds." Rhay put his elbows on the table as he gave Eyden a grin. "With my charming personality."

"Oh dear," Sahalie said, straightening in her chair, "Caelo save us if that's our only hope."

Rhay squinted at her, dark green glitter lining his eyes. "I don't know you very well yet, but I like you."

Sahalie raised her dark brows as she assessed him. "I haven't made up my mind about you."

"In Halie's words, that's a compliment." Ilario hid a smile.

Rhay grinned, his ocean eyes sparkling, putting a smile on Lora's face too.

"Okay, so first step, invite them here, reason with them," Maja said. "Second step if that fails is...?"

"We'll have to put guards on them." Rhay's smile sobered. "Make sure they don't hurt anyone and abide by the new law. They should be discreet. We don't want them to feel watched either, that'll escalate the situation."

"We have to highlight the benefits," Ilario said. "Fae already know how purposeful spells are. And the better we treat humans, the easier our trade with Earth will be. When is the treaty meeting? Has the human government confirmed a date?"

"At the end of the month," Lora replied, feeling a rush of anxiety. She'd been in contact with the UK government to discuss the treaty meeting. She'd assured them Thea came in peace and they would both benefit from an agreement. Hopefully they would agree with her and Thea's vision for the border. And there was also the matter of the human-fae agreement. They had to find a way to prevent fae again from forcing humans into blood contracts.

They both knew there had to be restrictions, but Lora didn't want to completely close off any access, and not just for her sake. With the right system in place they could manage people crossing over to either side. Anyone crossing would have to give a reason beforehand and be thoroughly vetted to avoid any bloodshed.

Eyden and Marcel had also been working on plans for a new market, a place where people from either side could go without going through a lengthy vetting process purely for the sake of trading. Eyden had pointed out there would be a lot of interest and Marcel had whole-heartedly agreed.

"In two weeks," Ilario observed. "That's good."

Rolling her shoulders, Lora said, "There is also the matter of me being the ambassador for Earth, if they let me. Thea has argued that I can't be both an ambassador and the queen in the long run. The human government won't stand for it and it's too many responsibilities for one person."

Eyden brushed his leg against hers underneath the table. He knew she'd been anxious about this. She wanted to be the ambassador but she had a responsibility here, as the queen.

Huffing, Sahalie sank back in her chair. "What are you suggesting we do? I have to admit you do seem to be good at this; it seems risky to change that."

Lora startled at the compliment hidden in the harsh words. Sahalie was a hard one to warm up to, but she valued her straightforwardness.

"If you're stepping down and handing over the crown, it has to be to someone we can trust." Rhay exchanged a secretive look with Maja that had Lora frowning. Sitting up straight, Rhay announced, "I nominate Rio."

Ilario whirled around, looking at Rhay with big eyes. He opened his mouth then closed it again.

"I second that." Maja raised her hand as if they were in school. She dropped it when Rhay tilted his head at her, a mocking light in his eyes.

"I can agree with that suggestion," Sahalie said calmly. If she was surprised, she didn't show it.

Eyden glanced around, his eyes calculating. "I agree too."

Rhay turned to Lora, his emerald hair showing a golden glint when the light from the chandelier hit it. "It's your vote, love."

Lora shook her head. "No, it's not. I wouldn't force this upon anyone. I didn't mean someone here had to take it upon themselves."

"We can't trust anyone else," Rhay said, and Lora realised he was right. She couldn't give this kind of power to anyone other than her trusted circle. But she would also never force Ilario or anyone else to take over, even if she could picture it now. Ilario would rule with care and kindness, just like—or even more so—than she would have done.

"It's entirely Ilario's decision," Lora said, seeking his gaze. "You can say no and I wouldn't fault you one bit."

"I..." Ilario stuttered, twisting his hands on the table. "I wouldn't have nominated myself. I don't know if I can handle that kind of power."

"You did," Rhay said. "You've already been Lora's stand-in whenever she couldn't be present. You're the most loyal, kind person I've ever known, and the fact that you're not jumping at the chance to take over means you're exactly the kind of person who should be on the throne. Someone who is not after power but instead focused on making things right."

Ilario's emerald eyes glistened. Lora sensed Rhay had been thinking about this for quite a while, and when she turned to Maja, she knew the two had discussed this.

"You really have thought about this, haven't you?" Ilario asked Rhay, his tone holding surprised wonder.

"I have." A light smile played on Rhay's lips. "The question is, what do you want to do with your life, Rio?"

Ilario took in each and every one of them, Lora following his gaze. Sahalie's lips turned up into a savage smile. Maja gave him two thumbs up. Eyden tilted his head subtly. And when Ilario turned to Lora again, she found herself smiling too. She felt it now—the last missing piece clicking into place. This was what was meant to happen. This was their fate.

Ilario seemed to mirror her thoughts, his eyes widening as he let out a shaky breath that led to a laugh.

"Well, in that case, I accept. On one condition." Ilario tapped his fingers on the oak table, his eyes certain yet scared. Scared wasn't a bad thing. Lora would be worried if he wasn't. "We'll wait until things have calmed down for Lora to step down. And then we let the people vote whether to appoint me. Everyone should have a say, and appointing a non-royal without a vote would cause an uprising. It still might."

Lora nodded. "I agree."

Rhay sprang to his feet, hitting the table in the process. The sound echoed through the room, making Lora's heart jolt as joy spread through the room. "This calls for a party. I might be an advisor for real now, but I'm versatile." He winked at Ilario, and the soon-to-be-king broke into laughter, everyone joining in. "Someone get a bottle of wine and some non-alcoholic cider."

Lora glanced at Rhay, who seemed so certain of himself now, of his role, not at all scared anymore to decide, to act. He tilted his head at her, emerald hair falling into his eye. "What is it, love?" he asked while chatter broke out around them.

"Nothing." She didn't fight the smile pulling at her lips. "I'm glad you stayed."

Rhay's grin widened as he set his hand on her shoulder. "Me too."

Hours later, Lora watched the sun set as she lounged on the window bank in the council room. Bottles of iridos and empty glasses covered the table. Rhay had brought his stereo and was blasting music, taking Ilario's hand as he urged him to dance with him. Maja and Sahalie sat in a corner, glasses in their hands, laughing at something. It was a sight Lora wouldn't have imagined in her wildest dreams.

Eyden appeared next to her, sitting down. He put his glass filled with shimmering iridos behind him on the window bank. "Are you feeling okay?"

Turning to the sky, Lora watched the stars appear out of nowhere as if they were always there to count on even when she couldn't see them.

Like a promise, not tangible yet still present in the darkest of times. Eyden had always done everything in his power to keep his promises and so had she. The only promise left now was one she'd made to herself. To never hide again. To never fail to accept every part of her—both her worlds.

"I'm both okay and not. Does that make sense?" Lora brushed back her hair as she caught her faint reflection in the window. "I think this is our fate. We're where we're supposed to be and that makes me think that one day, I'll be okay."

Eyden's hand went to her knee, the gesture calming any worries she couldn't quite shut off. He was about to reply when a shooting star flashed across the sky, so bright it was almost blinding.

Eyden lifted his brow but Lora shrugged, laughing softly as she remembered the Turosian superstition.

The beginning of ruin. She could still hear Eyden's whispered words on Falea Night when he'd told her about it on the floor of Ilario's family home.

"In my world, a shooting star means luck." Lora took Eyden's hand, squeezing it tight. "I choose to believe that." She no longer thought she was doomed, that any of them were. They had turned fate to their side even though it had cost them. She liked to think those lost watched over them, invisible like stars during daylight but still present evermore.

"You're right, we're lucky. I have hope. More than I ever did." The sparkle in Eyden's eyes was startling, making her stomach flip as it always did. His lips pulled into a half-grin.

Leaning in, his mouth almost brushed hers and Lora felt at ease, at home. His voice turned into a whisper, caressing her lips. "We create our own fate out of the ashes of our pain. Some risks are ruin. Some are embers waiting to be ignited."

Lora grinned at him, the fire flowing through her veins pulsing as if in agreement. The feeling was as familiar, as freeing, as breathing now. "We blew it all up, created a blank slate. I have hope too. For the first time, it doesn't feel like it could ever drown me."

It was lifting her up, igniting her, raising her from the ashes of her pain. The future was a blank slate and Lora would light it up so brilliantly no shooting star threatening ruin would ever dare touch her fate.

Thank you for reading the conclusion to *Through Fire & Ruin!*

If you enjoyed *Beyond Ember & Hope* and the previous two books, we would be so immensely grateful if you could leave a review on Amazon, Goodreads, The StoryGraph, and any other booksite. Recommendations go a long way, especially for us indie authors.

We're so grateful for every review—even if it's just a sentence or two! It truly means so much and makes our day <3

Sign up for our newsletter on **authorsjbandak.com** to stay up to date with our writing projects. The *Through Fire & Ruin* series was only the beginning! As a thank you for signing up, you get the prequel novella *The Promise of Midnight* for free—available for a limited time only!

Turn the page for a sneak peek...

THE PROMISE OF MIDNIGHT

CHAPTER 1

Twenty-five years before the events
of *Through Fire & Ruin*

"Are you aware of the risks, Miss Costales?" the young police officer asked, sitting across from Karla on the faded lavender sofa. He had calmly detailed what the government expected from her if she agreed to be their eyes and ears. It sounded simple: Soak up any information, act normal, get the fae to trust her. All in the name of security. Humans and fae may have a treaty of peace going, but their history of enslavement would never be forgotten.

Turning her head to the rain softly hitting the window, Karla replied, "I'm aware." She straightened in her chair, and it creaked loudly, reminding her of just how run-down her flat was. The tiny space Karla shared with her flatmate felt cramped. The furniture was old and close to breaking, which in turn reminded her of *why* she was considering taking these risks in the first place. *Money.* Her own security.

"I'm required to list them anyway." Officer Ratcliff sought out her gaze. His eyes were almost as dark as his short black hair. "Although police will be present during the five-day event and we are forced to assume it's in the fae's best interest to keep the peace between our species, the fae remain an unpredictable threat. Which is precisely why we want all of our crew to be on high alert and willing to learn as much as they can."

Karla already knew as much. There was nothing humanity wanted from the fae, but they had agreed to a treaty meeting, so they would be forced to attend. They took place every quarter century, and this would only be the second one. Karla had never imagined herself volunteering to take any kind of part in it. She had no interest in meeting fae, no hidden fascination—unlike others. But she was desperate and had little to lose. There was no one left in her life who would tell her to stay safe and decline Officer Ratcliff's offer. Not anymore.

"I didn't hear a list in there," Karla replied, trying to force herself to stay on track as she pushed a dark lock of hair behind her ear. This was yet another thing she had to do to stay afloat. If there was one thing Karla knew how to do, it was adapt and make do; it came with the territory of growing up as a foster kid.

Officer Ratcliff leaned forward, a smile tugging at his lips. His skin looked pale in the gloomy light streaming in from the rain-kissed window. "I'll be straight with you...Karla is your name, right?"

She nodded, bouncing her leg.

"Fae are powerful. They have magical abilities we cannot begin to comprehend. They are stronger than us. They live longer. They had us trapped once before. Even though they have signed the agreement to never enslave humans again, history is telling us that they're not beneath hurting us in other ways."

Doubt was creeping into Karla's mind. This wasn't like pulling double shifts or working two jobs at the same time to get herself through university. This could lead to more danger than exhausting herself.

"Are you ready to take that risk?" the officer asked, looking her over. "There is no shame in turning back." But what they were offering wasn't like anything she'd ever been offered before.

Clearing her throat to ease the tension, Karla asked, "If I agree, you mentioned there's a bonus for any piece of useful information?"

Officer Ratcliff's grin widened. "Yes. On top of the flat fee for joining the kitchen crew and gathering information, if you can bring us details that *matter*, you will be additionally compensated." He paused. "In secret, of course. This is a sensitive matter, as I'm sure you're aware."

Karla glanced around the small living room. The furniture was falling apart, the stains on the old carpet made her stomach turn, and the ceiling was leaking from the heavy rain in the English seaside town she now lived in. When she had moved here after graduating from culinary school a few months ago, Karla had hoped for a better life, a better job.

So when her flatmate Ava had come to her with this job opening at the treaty meeting, saying this could be their chance to get out of this dump, Karla hadn't disagreed. Because really, would an opportunity this valuable come knocking again? Karla had had to deal with more set-backs in life than she could count on two hands. Surely, she could handle dealing with fae for five days.

"All right," Karla said to the officer, putting her hands on her knees. "Count me in."

It was a spectacle. There were no other words to describe what was happening in Bournchester the first day of the treaty meeting. Cold snow fell down on Karla as she watched the mob of people that had formed around the perimeter of the portal. The door that would lead to the treaty spot was a shimmering turquoise, not giving away what lurked on the other side. It was otherworldly. The border leading directly to Liraen, the fae land, was always there, but this door that was now before her, only appeared for the purpose of the treaty. The thought made Karla shudder.

Some people were screaming excitedly as they watched the portal while others held up signs, protesting against fraternising with the enemy. Police had blocked off the perimeter, but it didn't quiet their chants.

"No more fae!"

"Stop engaging with our slavers!"

"We don't need that scum!"

Karla stood frozen in place, watching the madness from the bus stop, a duffle bag thrown over her shoulder. She wondered if some of the protesters were part of the activist group LFH—Liberty For Humans. They had been the ones to graffiti the entrance of the police station in protest when their demands that the government not attend the treaty meeting had failed. She'd also heard they'd been involved in a recent stabbing. Apparently, they had been targeting people who were rumoured to be making illegal trading deals with fae. Karla couldn't imagine it to be true, at least not the trading part.

Her breathing stuttered as she struggled to grasp the fact that she was headed right into the storm. Karla's gaze flickered from the door that only appeared every twenty-five years on New Year's Eve to the bigger, constant portal further away. From her position, she could only catch a glimpse of the indigo tear in their universe that stretched across town to further down the beach. Before witches of Liraen had placed a spell on the border to make it impossible for humans or fae to cross without dying, the portal had been something every human feared.

Now, it was more of a spectacle. In Karla's mind, there were three types of people who lived in the so-called "border town." There were those whose families had lived here long before fae had invaded Earth and were loyal to their home. There were those who were fascinated by fae and magic; they got a thrill from living here or from protesting against it. And then there were those like herself, the ones who had heard it was a cheap place to live since most people had been sane enough to move far away.

"You're not chickening out, are you?" Ava asked, bringing Karla back into the moment. Her flatmate was walking towards her, having driven here after saying goodbye to her family. Ava was part of the first category of people; this was her home, and although Karla had only known her for a few months, she knew Ava could never imagine leaving. Whereas leaving was all Karla had ever known, moving from one family, one town, to the next for most of her life.

"No, I stick to my word." Sighing, Karla pushed her long hair out of her face, but the strong icy wind messed it up again. There was no sign of the sun on this early, gloomy Monday morning.

Ava gave her a bright smile, her shoulder-length bleached hair trailing in the wind. Even in the dull light, her brown skin still glowed—and so did her personality. "Good, let's get going, then. Nothing like taking part in history to start the New Year." Tilting her chin towards the crowd of people, Ava headed into the storm. Karla followed after her, throwing her uncertainty to the chilly wind.

The police checked their ID before leading them through the barricades. They stopped close to the portal amongst others who Karla assumed were all part of the staff. To the side, surrounded by police, was the prime minister and a few politicians from other countries. Karla craned her neck to see more of them, but there were too many bodies blocking her view.

She tried her best to tune out the angry crowd. Although they were getting on her nerves, Karla couldn't quite blame them. If she had any say, she wouldn't have chosen to let this treaty meeting happen. When people wronged you, you cut them out of your life. That was how it worked. You didn't give them a second chance to screw you over again. And the fae had dragged humanity through hell.

Heart pounding in her chest as she fully realised what she was about to do, where she was about to go, Karla wrapped a lock of hair around her finger. The cold bit into her skin and bones, worsening her anxiety.

Ava's shoulder brushed against hers, and Karla locked onto her dark eyes. Karla wasn't heading there alone. She hadn't known Ava for long, but living together in such close quarters had made them grow close. Besides Ava, Karla didn't really know anyone in town. She'd never had much interest in big friend groups; all of her relationships ended eventually, so Karla only put in the energy to keep up the ones she had to.

"Remember, besides spying, you might also get to cook," Ava whispered, apparently sensing her discomfort.

Karla's dark brows drew together. "I wish. We may be part of the kitchen staff, but I doubt they'll let me cook anything. They have chefs for that." She didn't have any illusions about this job. It wouldn't make her dream of becoming a chef come true. But it could give her the money to push forward.

"If they had tasted your food, *you* would be the chef," Ava insisted.

"They didn't bother. It's fine. All I'm expecting from this experience is to get paid. A lot." Karla watched as the first group of people headed into the portal that would lead them to a space neither on Earth nor Liraen, a magical space existing only for the purpose of the treaty meeting. Only humans could take the door back to Earth once the event was over, and only fae could take the path back to Liraen.

Bumping her shoulder with her own, Ava grinned. "Their loss. But if we get paid enough, we can get a place with an actual kitchen, and then you can cook me all the delicious meals you always talk about."

Karla was about to reply when an officer addressed their group. "Please move forward in an orderly fashion. The portal might upset your stomach and make you feel disoriented. Be sure to stick with your group."

Pressing her cold lips together, Karla stepped into the line leading to the portal, Ava in front of her. One by one, they walked through. When it was Ava's turn, she glanced over her shoulder, throwing her a smirk before she disappeared from her view.

The portal was a shimmer of turquoise and grey up close, distorting the ongoings on the other side. This was her last chance to back out. But as much as the thought of encountering fae made her skin crawl, Karla was anything but a quitter. So, with her eyes squeezed shut, Karla stepped forward.

The day had been long and exhausting. Karla had spent the whole day helping out in the kitchen. She had soon realised they were severely understaffed for this event. A voice in her head told her it was because most people viewed this job as too dangerous. Yet today, she hadn't even glimpsed a fae. The most danger Karla had encountered was almost burning herself with soup when a waiter tripped over his feet and spilled hot liquid over her.

Turning in her narrow bed in the room she shared with Ava, Karla couldn't sleep. The room was dark and eerie. There were no windows anywhere in this place since it basically didn't exist. Vents circulated the air through the old stone structure of what seemed to be a huge building. The thought of floating in some kind of magical void made her stomach drop.

From what Karla had seen, this place was like an old castle. The walls were all stone, the floors a dark wood. The corridors were dimly lit and long, giving Karla the impression she had only seen a small part of the castle.

But the part she *had* seen fully was the massive kitchen. It had made her culinary heart sing even though she had been given basic tasks all day. She'd kill to have a kitchen like that.

A thought struck her: It was late. No one was using the kitchen. Why not take advantage of the hand she'd been dealt?

Knowing sleep wouldn't take her, Karla threw her covers back and stumbled towards her duffle bag in the dark. She pulled the first sweater she found over the thin shirt she wore, tied her shoes, and then headed for the door.

Peeking out the door, she saw Officer Ratcliff glance her way. "Karla, headed for a little midnight stroll?" he asked, a half smile on his thin lips.

"I forgot something in the kitchen," she lied even though she clearly didn't have to.

His brows drew up, amusement sparking in his dark eyes. "Right. Well, have a good start to the new year and good luck."

She kept forgetting that it was almost the new year. Usually, she liked the idea of a new year—she could erase all her disappointments from the past year and start on a blank page. But this year, Karla's head was elsewhere. She wasn't at culinary school anymore. This was real life, and she didn't want to fail.

Chewing her lip, Karla moved past Officer Ratcliff, taking the stairs to the kitchen. Her room wasn't far.

Opening the kitchen door, Karla switched the light on—which she realised must be spelled with magic as there was no electricity here—and marvelled at the empty kitchen with its fancy marble counters and huge stove. She sprang into action, gathering ingredients and turning the stove on. Soon, she was fully in her element. Cooking never failed to relax her as her mind focused on the task at hand and nothing else.

So much so that she must not have heard the door open behind her before a low voice said, "Midnight craving?"

Karla's hand stopped moving, hovering over the handle of the pan she meant to move from the stove. The voice was deep, and there was a foreignness to his dialect that made her freeze all over.

"Don't stop on my account. Whatever you're making smells amazing."

Gathering her wits, Karla turned around, facing the person standing across from her, closer than she had expected. His hair was a dirty blond, curling around the edges. He was pale but not in a sickly way, his skin glowing in the kitchen light. And his eyes were the most striking turquoise she had ever seen, confirming her suspicion. This man was *fae*.

An alarm bell in her head told her to run before clarity seeped back into her. Why run when she was here to gather intel? This kitchen she loved so much could one day be hers if she could just get a leg up. If she could have the means—

"Are you all right?" the fae asked, staring at her. His lips quirked up, and she glanced down at herself to realise she must look like a mess. She was wearing grey sweatpants and an oversized emerald sweater. Her long wavy hair was all over the place. "Are all humans as chatty as you are?"

Getting a grip, Karla squinted at him. "Depends."

"On what?"

"If what is being said is worth a reply."

The stupid grin on his face increased, and damn her if it wasn't cute. She scratched the thought from her mind.

"So asking if you're all right is not appreciated," he teased. "Noted. I will try my best to be less considerate. Shall I yell at you for being here after hours instead? Is that what gets you going?"

Her stomach flipped. "You're twisting my words. And what gives you the right to yell at me?"

He shrugged. "I'm a guard."

She looked him up and down. His dark trousers and light blue sweater didn't scream guard. "You're not wearing a uniform." And she didn't see any weapons on him either, thankfully. She couldn't help but think she liked what she saw.

"Because it's *after hours*." His tone was condescending but in a joking matter, yet it still made her blood run hot.

"Tell me, what exactly is a *fae* guard doing in the part of the castle that is assigned to us humans?"

The joking light in his eyes dimmed. "Fae is not a dirty word, you know."

"What?"

"The way you said *fae*," he explained, moving closer to her, "I don't like it."

She laughed nervously, his presence overwhelming as he invaded her space. "And I should care why?"

He tilted his head at her, seemingly perplexed. "I suppose you have no reason to care." The words surprised her. She only now realised her comment hadn't been smart. For one, fae could be dangerous. And secondly, if she wanted information from him, she should be friendly. She cringed inwardly.

His nose crinkled. "Is your food burning?"

A burned smell drifted through the air, and Karla whirled back around to the stove. Her signature blueberry pancakes had blackened. She switched off the stove and dumped the burned dish into the bin. "Dammit," she muttered.

"Indeed. I really wanted to try that."

Looking at him, Karla raised her brows.

"I admit, I was a bit curious about human food. I couldn't sleep, so I snuck in here. I would have raided the fridge, but whatever you were making definitely piqued my interest. Can you make it again? I promise not to distract you this time."

For a second, Karla was stunned. Then she laughed. The fae's lip curled into a confused half smile. "I'm *not* your personal chef," Karla said. His gaze raked over her and she felt her skin heat up.

"I take it that's a no?"

Karla tilted her chin up. "Yeah, that's a no."

"I can't change your mind? What do you want in exchange?" His smile grew devilish, and she felt a shiver run down her spine. This fae was getting under her skin, and she didn't like it. She should call it a night.

A door slamming in the distance drew their attention to the kitchen door, but it remained closed. Karla wasn't at all sure if she was allowed to be here at this hour. Officer Ratcliff seemed to think so, but it couldn't be safe.

"I have to go," she said, walking past the fae to the door.

"Just think about it."

Pausing, Karla looked over her shoulder. "About what?"

"Cooking for me. There must be *something* I can give you in return." At her silence, he added, "I'll be here again tomorrow. Same time. Think on it...I didn't catch your name."

"I didn't tell you my name."

He bounced on his feet. "Well, here's your chance."

"No, thank you."

He laughed, the sound rich, diving right under her skin in an unsettling way. She couldn't shake how her skin tingled from his gaze. "All right, midnight girl. I'll see you tomorrow. Happy New Year." He brushed past her, heading out of the kitchen before her.

"You won't!" she called after him, not returning the sentiment.

He shook his head but didn't turn around again as he disappeared down the stone corridor.

She shouldn't meet with him, a fae, *alone*. Except maybe this was her chance to get information. Maybe this was the risk she needed to take. It was serious business, a strategic move, nothing more.

Karla had no reason to smile, yet she found herself fighting off a grin as she headed back towards her room.

Thank you for reading this sneak peek of *The Promise of Midnight!*

Sign up for our newsletter on **authorsjbandak.com** to get the full prequel novella for free—available for a limited time only.

The e-book of *The Promise of Midnight* is also available on Amazon!

If you enjoyed Karla's story, please leave a review on **Amazon** and **Goodreads**.

Thank you so much for following the *Through Fire & Ruin* series <3

Acknowledgments - Jennifer Becker

I can't believe that I'm writing the acknowledgements to the third and final book in this trilogy. I don't think I can properly put into words how much these books mean to me. I've always loved stories, but the thought of writing and publishing my own seemed impossible. If anything, this experience has shown me that we often limit ourselves. It was far from easy, but Alice and I did it! We wrote all the words, edited and proofread endlessly, figured out self-publishing and marketing (sort of) and I'd do it all over again in a heartbeat. These characters are a part of us and if anyone can relate to them and find joy in this story, then that's all that matters.

As I always say, this novel wouldn't have been the same without the encouragement of my friends and family. Thank you, Kris and Anna, for being the first ones to read book 3 and for giving us honest feedback for every book we wrote with the same excitement each time. Thank you, Jana, for your endless support throughout the years. My mum's excitement for my writing as well as my dad's makes me so incredibly happy. Thank you to Philipp for always reminding me what an achievement this is and for picking up my novel—your commentary while reading books 1+2 made me all the more excited about book 3.

Thank you to all our beta readers for taking the time to read our novel and sharing your thoughts—your comments made me giddy with excitement. Thank you, thank you, thank you!! Charlotte, Victoria, Anakha, Mich, Chloe, Sandi, Hailey, and Amanda—you are all the absolute best. A HUGE thank you to our amazing Hype Team for all their support—couldn't have done it without you! Thank you to our development editor Elise—your feedback remains invaluable and I've loved working with you. I also want to thank our copy editor RaeAnne for going through our massive manuscript and polishing it up.

I'm immensely grateful to Rena for creating our beautiful cover (this one might be my fave!) and Emily for making our title design spot on once again. To all the writers I've met online—I'm so grateful to have met you all and I appreciate your support so much.

Most of all, I want to thank my co-author Alice without whom I don't think I would've ever tried to publish a book, which is wild considering I now want to keep doing that forever. I'm so glad we decided to write a book together on a random day during lockdown. I don't think either one of us expected we would end up writing and self-publishing a whole trilogy. I will always treasure our book babies <3

Last but not least, thank you to everyone who finished our trilogy! It really means more to me than I could ever put into words and I hope you continue to follow me on my writing journey. I hope *Beyond Ember & Hope* gave you the ending you've longed for and that—just like Lora and Amira—you can create your own fate and turn your pain to ashes.

Jennifer Becker

Acknowledgments - Alice Karpiel

The time has finally come to write the acknowledgments for the final book in a trilogy I started writing with my dear friend Jenni in March 2020. It's been an uphill battle, but from the first video call we did, where the first elements of the story came to life to now, to the release of our third book, I couldn't be more happy to have joined Jenni on this adventure. I can't believe how far we've come. It's been an incredible journey and I learned so much along the way thanks to many amazing people.

First, my friends and family who have been supporting me since the very beginning of my writing journey and who have helped me believe in myself when I was doubting. Thank you to my parents and sisters for being there, always, and for your constant and reassuring love. Thank you to Jana for supporting us all through the years and for always being willing to lend a helping hand. I want to especially thank Kris and Anna, the first to read book three. You gave us such precious feedback and it was so nice to see that you have grown as attached to the book series as we did.

This book wouldn't have been the same without the help of some amazing people, who, without knowing us or our book in the first place, decided to embark on this journey alongside us. So thank you to our incredible beta readers: Charlotte, Victoria, Anakha, Mich, Chloe, Sandi, Hailey, and Amanda. It's always such an exciting time to read over your comments, as they are both helpful and confidence boosting. I loved seeing your reactions to our characters' respective endings and all the funny comments you sent us, it always makes our day. Thank you also to our development editor Elise, who didn't run away as our books got longer and longer! Your feedback is always incisive and thought provoking. It has been a pleasure to work with you. Another big thank you to our copy editor, RaeAnne who polished our book with our tight deadline.

Of course, I want to thank Rena for creating this fabulous book cover and Emily for designing our book title with both efficiency and quality. Finally I'm so grateful for the community of writers I met online. I felt incredibly supported whenever I had a question, no matter how dumb!

But I wouldn't be here, today, writing this acknowledgement, if it wasn't for my co-author Jenni. Look at us now! From meeting on the first day of uni to being the proud parents of three book babies. Our journey together has been a rollercoaster, but ultimately so fun and rewarding. So thank you Jenni for saying yes to writing this book with me and thank you for deciding to go study in the UK in 2018. My life wouldn't be the same without you in it <3

Finally, I want to thank YOU, the reader, for reading our whole trilogy! It means so much that you decided to pick up this book, a book written by two young, first-time authors and give it a chance. I hope you've enjoyed *Beyond Ember & Hope* and that the ending of this trilogy was everything you hoped for (or even better!).

Alice Karpiel

Printed in the USA
CPSIA information can be obtained
at www.ICGtesting.com
CBHW031946220824
13587CB00017BA/114/J